Eye of the Storm

Eye of the Storm

Melissa Good

YellowRoseBooks
a Division of
RENAISSANCE ALLIANCE PUBLISHING, INC.
Nederland, Texas

ISBN 1-930928-74-2

First Printing 2001

9 8 7 6 5 4 3 2 1

Cover design by Mary D. Brooks

Published by:

Renaissance Alliance Publishing, Inc.
PMB 238, 8691 9th Avenue
Port Arthur, TX 77642

Find us on the World Wide Web at
http://www.rapbooks.com

Printed in the United States of America

I'd like to dedicate *Eye of the Storm* to Gabrielle the Labrador, my wildly happy and sock stealing Retriever. She keeps waiting for me to bring her literary alter ego, Chino, home for her to play with.

— Melissa Good

Chapter
1

The air was thick with nervous dread, even though the plain, if neatly furnished conference room provided a relatively relaxed appearance. Six people were seated around the nicked, wooden table, all eyeing each other with looks of trepidation. It was mid afternoon, and several beams of warm sunlight entered through a high set of windows, painting the opposite wall in lurid stripes.

"So," a short, dark haired woman shuffled the papers in front of her, "never thought I'd see this happen."

A taller, equally dark haired man across from her leaned back and folded his arms. "C'mon, Ann. We were sitting targets. Six new contracts, and two of them directly competing?" He sighed in disgust. "Just a matter of time." He glanced at his watch. "Speaking of...when's this piece of bad news going to get here?"

Ann Delaney stood and paced to the window, barely tall enough to peer out. "Beats me. Maybe the plane was late. You know these people. They'll come when they're good and ready, and I hear this one's a tough customer."

A stocky, balding man stood up, went to the coffee pot, and poured himself a cup. "What else is new? They don't send nice guys to do this sort of thing. I've told accounting to be on their toes, God knows what they'll ask for."

Footsteps sounded on the carpet outside, the door latch worked, and then the wooden door pushed open. A thin, pale haired man walked in followed by a stranger. "Good morning, folks. Please be seated."

"Morning, Charlie," Ann murmured, resuming her seat and watching their visitor as the woman walked around to the front of the conference table and set her briefcase down.

Charles Efton took a seat and folded his hands. "Well, here we all

are, just like you asked." He turned his attention to the silent figure waiting at the head of the table. "I guess we can start."

Cool eyes regarded them. "Thank you." The voice was calm, yet
vibrant. "I have a list of things I'm going to need for us to start this process." Strong, powerful hands opened the briefcase and removed a sheaf
of papers, which were slid down the table. "I don't think there's anything
unusual there. Once I have this information, we can proceed."

Ann took the top sheet and passed the stack down, then looked at it.
A list of reports topped the requests. Some were expected, others...
"Dependents?" She looked up sharply, meeting intelligent eyes looking
evenly back at her. "Is that necessary?"

"You'd be surprised what I find necessary," the woman answered
briskly. "I'd like to drop my things off at the hotel. That should give you
about two hours to gather everything. You shouldn't need more than that."
She paused. "Right?"

Ann shuffled the papers and arranged them with small, precise
motions. "Right."

"Good." The sound of a briefcase being zipped was suddenly loud.

Charlie stood up hastily and moved forward, joined by the tall, dark
haired man. "Ah, yeah, that'll give us time...um, Sam, sorry...I should
have introduced you but we—"

The woman turned and held out a hand. "Sam Gershwin, right?
You're the comptroller."

Sharp brown eyes regarded her carefully, before her grip was
returned. "Right...and, sorry...we didn't catch your name?"

The pale eyes warmed briefly. "Kerry Stuart." A smile appeared,
breaking through the business facade easily, then disappearing. "Good to
meet you. I'm sure we can make this a smooth transition."

"I'm sure," Sam murmured as he watched the slim, blond woman
shoulder her case. "You need a ride out?" The intense green eyes flicked
to his face, then dropped.

"No, thanks." Kerry gave him a brief smile. "It's the Courtyard, right
down the road. See you all shortly." She stepped around the table and
went to the door, aware of the eyes at her back, which were cut off as she
closed the door behind her, and hearing the voices already rising.

With a sigh, she stepped out into the pleasant sunlight, taking in a
breath of the pine scented air. "Maybe three hours," she decided, heading
for her rental car across a gravel strewn lot.

❖ ⌘ ❖ ⌘ ❖ ⌘ ❖

The soft shuffle of booted feet against the padded deck broke the
silence, and the ring of watchers shifted to watch as two opponents circled
each other. The taller of the two stepped backwards and twisted to avoid a

kick from the shorter, and then caught the extended leg under the knee and turned, bringing the other body down and over an outstretched thigh to the mat.

"Shit." The shorter figure rolled to its feet and circled again. This time diving right into an attack and grappling with powerful hands. He managed a solid hold but it was broken moments later when his opponent dropped to one knee and delivered a blow to his ribcage. "Oof."

"Sorry," the low voice drawled as they separated and then went at it again. This time kicks and blows were traded in a rapid exchange that finally ended with the taller of the two taking them both through the air with a rolling attack and landing with a thump to toss the shorter outside the fight area.

He stayed there.

Dar got to her feet and flexed her hands inside their padded covering as she walked over. "You okay, Ken?" She extended an arm down to help him up. "Didn't mean to toss you quite that far."

"Sure, sure." Ken Yamamura took the hand good-naturedly and allowed himself to be hauled upright. "Nah. I'm fine, Dar. Just needed to catch my breath. We've been at it for a while."

"That's true," the tall, dark haired woman agreed mildly, looking around as the crowd broke up, giving her lingering, appreciative glances. "I think I'm finally getting used to being part of the freak show."

"Phew." Ken dusted his body off, covered in a neat fabric outfit matching Dar's, and tightened his black belt. "They love watching me get my butt kicked, is what it is, Dar. Believe me, there's a bunch of those kids who are loving every minute of this." He gave his opponent a smile to take the sting out of the words.

Dar bit off a smile and riffled her fingers through her sweat damp-ened hair. "Well, you're the one who haggled me into entering that meet. You can only blame yourself."

"Ugh. Don't remind me." Ken winced as he rubbed his shoulder. "They're not going to know what hit them." He paused. "Literally." His voice held warm admiration though. "Seriously, Dar. You've really been working hard. I'm totally impressed."

They walked towards the changing rooms. "Thanks." Dar exhaled. "It's come back faster than I thought it would, frankly. I had half con-vinced myself I was being an idiot. Trying to recapture lost youth or something stupid like that."

Ken paused, peering up at the strong, angular face with a puzzled look. "Lost? Did you lose that somewhere? Why Dar, you should have told me. I'd have put up a wanted poster."

Blue eyes fastened on him with a dryly amused expression. "Very funny." But the compliment pleased her and she clapped the younger man on the shoulder as she headed in to change clothes. "Thanks, Ken. See you tomorrow?"

"Oh yeah." Ken grinned wryly. "Same splat time, same splat channel. See ya, Dar."

Chuckling, Dar entered the locker room and found her locker, then untied her belt and slung it over the door before she changed clothes. Light beach shorts replaced her long cotton pants, with a tank top tucked into them. She stuffed her gear into the small gym bag and closed the locker door, then shouldered the bag's strap and headed for the door.

❖ ⌘ ❖ ⌘ ❖ ⌘ ❖

The hotel room was quiet. The soft sound of rustling leaves coming in through the window acted as a counterpoint to the soft clicking of keys and the occasional shuffle of papers. Kerry rested her chin on one fist briefly and reviewed her laptop screen, which contained the beginnings of a status report.

"Okay." She sighed. "Maybe this won't be too bad, but they're not going to be happy giving up those perks." Kerry reviewed the report again, then dropped her eyes to the pages of reports and leafed through them for the tenth time. "I wonder if they realize how lucky they are to be so remote. We don't have an office within three hundred miles of here."

She stood and stretched, wincing as her back protested from being seated in one place for far too long. Then she trudged over to the window and leaned on the sill to gaze out at the forest her snug little room was nestled in.

It was the silence, she realized, that was so significant. There was no traffic, or very little up here in this part of Vermont, and the entire pace of life seemed slower than she was used to. The hotel was a collection of small cabins, each tucked into pockets of trees and underbrush, with unobstructed views of the wilderness around them. It gave the illusion of complete privacy, and Kerry remained gazing out at it for a long moment before she turned and padded across the wooden floor, to throw herself down on the large, quilt covered bed.

It was nice, she considered, to be able to see different places. She rolled over and reached for the TV remote, clicked it on and sorted through the available cable channels. A familiar scene caught her eye and she paused, then put the remote down, and rested her chin on her forearm as she watched the travel channel focus on a skyline she knew.

Home.

A wistful smile tugged at her lips as she checked her watch. She'd been on the road for two very long weeks, though that was coming to an end after she wrapped up this assignment.

Good thing, too. Kerry pulled a pillow out from under the quilt and wrapped her arms around it, exhaling softly and turning her mind to figuring out where she could rustle up some dinner. Being apart from Dar had been tougher than she'd anticipated and as the days counted themselves down, she found her thoughts turning more and more eagerly to their reunion.

They talked on the phone to each other every day, of course, and exchanged email, but it wasn't the same. Kerry gazed at the nondescript walls and sighed. Nights were the worst. During the day she was either working or traveling, but alone in her hotel room at night she had to force herself to find something to do other than think about...

Well, think about what Dar was doing, actually. Or wonder if she was being missed in return, while her previously solitary partner went back to her lone pursuits.

Or if maybe Dar was enjoying that.

Scowling a little at her own insecurity, Kerry got up and walked back over to her laptop. She paused for a moment, gazing at the report, then clicked over to her mail program and started up a new message.

❖ ⌘ ❖ ⌘ ❖ ⌘ ❖

"Hey girl." Dar managed to get inside the door to the condo without allowing the frantic Labrador to escape. "Hey. Take it easy. Take it easy. I know it's late."

Chino bucked around in a circle and whined, grabbing hold of the edge of Dar's shorts in her teeth and tugging fiercely.

"Okay, okay." The tall woman tossed her gym bag down and surrendered, sitting down on the cold tile floor and hugging the dog. "Yeah. Okay. I missed you too." She closed her eyes as the Labrador licked her face thoroughly and climbed up her chest, her half grown paws scrabbling for a good hold. "Easy...easy..."

Finally, Chino calmed down and curled up inside the circle of Dar's arms, panting. "Good girl." Dar leaned back against the door and rubbed the dog's ears idly. In reflex, she looked up towards the kitchen, half expecting Kerry to appear from the doorway, then sighed as the emptiness of the condo settled around her. "You know something, Chino?"

Brown eyes looked up at her in question.

"It's too damn quiet in here."

The dog barked at her.

"You think Kerry misses us as much as we miss her?"

"Growf."

Dar smiled and gave her a final hug, then stood up and retrieved her bag, crossed the large living room and entered the kitchen. It was almost painfully clean, and Dar averted her eyes as she ducked into the laundry room. She tugged her outfit from the bag and dumped it into the washing machine, along with her towel and underwear, and set the device running.

Then she re-entered the kitchen and went to the cupboard, opened it and removed a tall glass, which she filled with milk from the refrigerator.

"Mail."

"Dar Roberts, six messages, none urgent. Kerry Stuart, twelve messages, three urgent," the console answered, bringing a faint smile to Dar's face.

"Display mail, Dar Roberts." She scanned the headers, then produced a real smile. "Read two."

> Hey Boss.
> Vermont is nice.

"Eh. If you like trees," Dar commented aloud, a habit of hers when reading Kerry's mails.

> It would be a lot nicer if you were in it, though...it's really quiet up here in the woods. I keep thinking some raccoon is going to hop up on my windowsill and start talking to me.

"Trapped in a Disney movie. Very scary, Ker."

> Oh well. The account is going all right—I have all the information, and a copy of the plan is attached to this mail for you to check out. They were kind of upset when I first got here, but I think I made them relax a little, and maybe they realize I'm not here to turn everything upside down for them.

"I'm sure they warmed right up to you."

> Only some things, I guess. They've got some very strange acquisition flowcharts...I wasn't sure what they were doing, Dar, so I scanned those in and attached them too. If you could take a minute and look them over, it'd be great.

"Sure," Dar murmured softly, taking a sip of her milk. "No problem."

> It's been a really long two weeks.

"Yeah. No kidding."

> I think it really hit me today, when I
> was driving to the hotel, just how much I
> miss you.

Dar bit down on the rim of her glass, rereading the words in silence.
A tiny grin formed on her lips.

> It was really strange. I dreamt about
> you last night, and when I woke up and you
> weren't here, I felt awful. I know a busi-
> ness email isn't the place to say that,
> but...I just wanted you to know.
> Anyway, I'm going to go see if I can
> find something around here for dinner. I
> noticed an advertisement at the front desk
> for maple ice cream. It sounded interest-
> ing. Call you later.
> Ker

"Mmm." Dar leaned a hip against the counter and permitted herself a
few moments of idle daydreaming, then she sighed as the computer
beeped.

"Incoming video conference request, Alastair M."

"Go."

A square opened, revealing the familiar features of her boss, a round
faced man in his fifties, with a perennially cheerful expression. "Evening,
Dar."

"Hi," the dark haired woman drawled. "Little late for you, isn't it?"

"Who me? Nah." Alastair waved a hand at her. "Listen. I need a
favor."

Uh oh. "And that would be..."

"I've got a little problem here. Well, " Alastair looked uncharacteris-
tically troubled, "more than a little. You know David Ankow?"

"Mmm. The new board member. Yeah." Dar grimaced. An outsider.
He'd been voted onto the board by the stockholders two months prior, as a
sort of watchdog, and had been challenging Alastair ever since. The timing was bad since they were right in the middle of a huge network rede-
sign project, which Dar was heading up, and that meant large
expenditures without an immediate return to account for them.

"He's called an emergency board meeting tomorrow morning to
debate the new network. I've got the answers he's looking for, but just to
be sure, I could use your support."

That, Dar realized, was as close to a scream for help as she'd ever hear from her boss. "Hang on." She pulled the seldom used pointing device out from the console and clicked to a browser screen, then entered an address. Moments later, she reviewed the results of a query and approved them. Then she clicked back to Alastair's window. "Okay."

"Listen, I know it's short notice, but you know I don't really ask that often and I—okay what?" His brow creased.

"Okay, I'll be there tomorrow morning," Dar replied. "Anything else you need?"

Alastair merely gazed at her for a long moment. "Well," he propped his chin up on one hand, "yeah, in fact. What's Kerry's favorite kind of flowers?"

Dar blinked in startlement. "What?"

"C'mon. Roses? Tulips? What?" Alastair pursued. "I want to send her something, because I honestly appreciate just how much of a human being she's made you into in the last few months."

Dar stared at him, shocked.

"I'll make it roses. That's safe. Later, Dar. See ya tomorrow." Alastair's face disappeared, leaving a company logo behind in the box.

"T...b...you...hold on there you son of a..." Her voice rose in outrage and she stopped, realizing that yelling at a blank computer screen was less than useful. *What in the hell had that been about anyway?* "I certainly haven't changed that much."

Chino wagged her tail.

"Have I?" Dar almost jumped when the phone rang, then she set her glass down and answered it, feeling a little rattled. "Yeah?"

"Um...hi?" Kerry's voice came back at her.

"Oh. Hi." Dar picked up her milk and wandered into the living room, dropped down onto the leather love seat and slung one leg over the arm of it. "Sorry. Alastair just called. I've got to go out there tomorrow."

"Oh? What's up?"

"Some meeting. That damn new board member. What's up with you?" Dar swallowed a mouthful of milk. "Did you get your maple ice cream?"

A soft chuckle trickled down the line. "Oh yeah. I was bad," Kerry admitted. "I'd bring you home some, but I think it'd melt." She paused a moment. "Got my mail, I guess, huh?"

"Yeah," her lover responded. "I'll take a look at your paperwork. But I'm sure it's fine. You've got a knack for that."

"Mmm."

"And I miss you too."

"Ah." The smile was very evident through the phone line. "How long are you going to be in Texas?"

"Just an up and back. Probably fly back tomorrow night." Dar sighed. "Sounds like he's getting a lot of crap from that new guy...and it's about the network, so..."

"Ew."

"Yeah." Dar relaxed and closed her eyes. "He's a pinhead. I'm going to have to come up with Sesame Street words to describe a global Intranet to him tomorrow. Wish me luck." The project was hers, really. Something she'd been able to do because Kerry had really stepped up to the plate in the last few months and taken most of the day to day headaches off her shoulders. It would triple productivity and almost quadruple the amount of bandwidth they had to offer, and Dar was quietly proud of herself in the design.

It had been damn nice to have the time to sit back and really think about it, working with a hand picked engineering team and laying out a new design that replaced circuits in some places twenty years old. But it was obscenely expensive, and Dar knew that's what the newbie had picked up on, as a way to make a name for himself with the stockholders, since they wouldn't see any benefit from the new system for at least two quarters, maybe more.

Pinhead.

"Hey, Dar?"

"Hmm? Sorry. I was just thinking."

"I love you."

Dar smiled at the ceiling. "I love you, too."

"What were you thinking about?"

"When?" came the puzzled response.

Kerry laughed. "Never mind. Listen, my flight's due in at nine on Friday, assuming I finish up by then. Can I get a ride?"

Dar snorted. "You have to ask? What kind of dumb question is that? You bet your ass I'm going to be at that gate, my friend, And you tell those people in Vermont their butts better be done by then, or they're going to have a lot bigger problem than a consolidation to worry about."

"Like you?"

"Like me," Dar growled. "Live and in color, and wanting to know why they're monopolizing a very, very valuable company resource."

Kerry giggled. "Oh my god. You have no idea how cute you sound."

"Cute?" Dar affected a wounded tone. "That's the second time tonight. Alastair accused me of turning into a mushball, too."

"Did he?" Her lover laughed. "Well, he didn't hear you with those network carriers before I left, I guess. They could have heard you in Atlanta without the phone." She'd been privately thinking that she'd detected some changes in Dar recently and had wondered if anyone else had noticed.

Apparently they had.

"How'd practice go tonight?" Kerry asked.

"Pretty good," Dar allowed. "I think it's possible I won't embarrass myself totally at that damn meet."

"Great. I have my little flag and T-shirt all ready," Kerry teased gently.

"Ermph." Dar rolled her eyes. "I hope I don't regret this." She stretched her legs out, feeling the strong pull of newly redefined thigh muscles. "Me and a bunch of kids."

"Ooo. Listen to old grandma there. Want me to send you a nice frilly cap for your cane?" Kerry retorted. "C'mon, Dar. Don't start that. You bounce Ken all over the place and leave most of those other people in the gym standing slack jawed."

It was true, Dar acknowledged silently. *But what do I say, that most isn't good enough? That I'm not happy unless I beat them all? Do I tell her coming close ain't gonna cut it?* "We'll see," she finally compromised. "Anyway, let me let you get some sleep. It'll be a long day tomorrow."

"You're right." Kerry sighed. "Have a safe flight and say hi to Alastair for me, okay?"

"Mmm. I will. He's...um," Dar shifted a little, "sending you flowers."

Dead silence.

"Huh?" Kerry finally spluttered. "For what?"

"Apparently he, ah, thinks you're a good influence on me," her lover replied. "He appreciates that." She could imagine the stunned look on Kerry's face. "I think he may be right."

A long, in-drawn breath was clearly heard. "Oh," Kerry murmured. "Well, it's mutual, you know. I couldn't do half of this stuff if you hadn't shown me the way." She paused a moment. "God, I so want to hug you right now."

Dar smiled wistfully at the phone. "Yeah. That'd be nice," she responded. "Anyway, have a good night, Ker. I'll be in touch tomorrow."

"G'night." Kerry sighed, then closed the phone, and rested her chin on it thoughtfully. "Be careful," she murmured softly. "Give 'em heck."

Chapter
2

A cold, wet nose poked her in the eyeball. Dar jerked her head back in startlement, then blinked and looked around dazedly. "What th—" Chino was curled up against her chest, the puppy's tail thumping against Dar's leg. The condo was lit warmly with dawn light and the TV displayed an infomercial for a revolutionary new pooper scooper.

"Damn it." Dar hitched herself up on one elbow and rubbed her face. "Gotta stop doing that," she muttered to Chino, who was apparently getting used to her falling asleep on the couch. Not that the leather surface was uncomfortable, but it threw off her internal alarm clock and made her have to scramble in the mornings.

Like now, for instance, especially since she had a damn plane to catch. Groggily, she sat up, then got to her feet, eyeing the cute abalone clock Kerry had insisted on getting, deciding they didn't have one piece of tacky South Florida stuff in their living room. "Oh, hell." Her flight was at eight, and here it was almost seven. "Chino, I'll tell ya. They're not getting a wool suit."

"Woof."

Dar ambled over and opened the back door for the puppy, then she ducked into the kitchen and grabbed a container of grape juice, which she popped open and sucked at as she headed for the shower.

Ten minutes later she was toweling off and rummaging through her clean clothes, wondering if her presence was worth the scandal she'd cause by showing up casual. Then Alastair's comments of the previous night poked her and she grinned. "Guess we'll find out." She tugged out a pair of faded jeans and neatly ironed cotton shirt.

She pulled the shirt on and brushed a few errant Chino hairs off the sleeves, then slid into the jeans and buttoned them, eyeing the mirror to check the results. A tanned and lean figure was reflected back, showing the effect of three hard months of martial arts training and a multitude of weekends spent diving in the sunny waters offshore. "Oh yeah." A twinkle entered the pale blue eyes gazing back at her as she added a belt, then clipped her pager and phone on. "Nice, huh? I'll give you nice." She pulled a jacket from the closet and slung it over her arm, then shouldered her briefcase and headed for the door. "Think you've forgotten just how much trouble I can be when I put my mind to it, Alastair."

Then she stopped. "Whoa." She put her things down, jogged to the back door, and whistled for Chino, who came bounding up the steps. "C'mon, girl. I gotta go." The puppy put paws up on her leg and whined, and she gave her a quick hug. "Don't worry. I'll be back tonight." She glanced around then gave the dog a kiss on the head. "And don't you tell anyone I did that, okay?"

"Grrrr." Chino chewed on her belt loop.

"Okay. Be good." Dar stood up and checked to make sure the puppy had water and biscuits, then she grabbed her case and headed out the door.

It was close. Fortunately, the causeway she lived off of angled right across the city, and onto the one leading to the airport. She dropped her keys in the valet's hand and jogged through the terminal, arriving at the gate just as the plane was boarding. Moments later, she was sprawled in a comfortable leather seat at the front of the plane, being offered her choice of beverage. "Chocolate milk," she responded, sending the stewardess off to rummage.

It was a pretty day, Dar reflected, as she gazed out her window and watched the ground crew finish their routine. The sun came in the small portal and she closed her eyes against its brightness, finding a comfortable spot to rest her head as she let the world fade out a little.

"Wonder what Kerry's up to?" She allowed an image of her lover to form against the inside of her eyelids.

❖ ⌘ ❖ ⌘ ❖ ⌘ ❖

Kerry sighed gently as the first light trickled into her window. She hadn't slept much, her thoughts keeping her tossing and turning until she'd finally dropped off well after midnight. Now here she was awake before dawn.

Oh well. She sat up and dangled her feet over the bed, rubbing her bare arms and yawning. It would give her a chance to get a run in, at any rate, something she'd had only sporadic success at while she was out on the road. At least it would be pretty scenery.

Kerry stood and trudged into the rustic bathroom, turned on the water, and splashed a handful of it on her face before she realized the temperature difference between Vermont and Miami. "Yow!" Her green eyes popped wide open and she hastily adjusted the warm water faucet a little to cut the chill. "That's one way to wake up."

She investigated the little courtesy refrigerator in the room and found tiny crocks of cold apple cider and some little coffee cakes. "Mmm." She took one of each, dropped into the curved wooden desk chair, and hit the key to retrieve her mail while she nibbled on her breakfast.

The laptop connected and she logged in with two fingers, then sat back as her mail downloaded. "Oo." She clicked on one mail from Dar and smiled as a small, dancing raccoon shimmied across the screen, singing "Dixie." Kerry muffled a laugh, almost sending a spray of crumbs all over her keyboard. "Where in the hell did she find *that*?" She watched the cartoon for a moment more, then shook her head and checked the rest of the mails, leaving the three urgent ones open and waiting for attention.

Her juice finished, she got into a pair of shorts and a T-shirt. She tied her hair back into a tail and put on her running shoes before slipping out the door to the cabin and into the early morning air. It was cool and dry, very different from the late June heat she faced in Miami, and Kerry drew in an appreciative breath as she chose a path and started up it at a walk.

She let her leg muscles stretch out a little before she broke into a jog, not wanting to push herself too hard after being relatively inactive for a few weeks. Between flights, hotels, and the four accounts she'd consolidated on her trip, she'd hardly had time to figure out what state she was in, much less where the nearest gym was.

So, she asked herself, *why drag yourself out here today, hmm?* Kerry picked up her pace a little, feeling her body settle into the activity. *Couldn't possibly be because you're going home in two days, could it? And you're going to have to keep up with Dar after two weeks of being a lazy bum, or risk a first class teasing?* She laughed at herself, acknowledging the eager thrill that danced over her skin at the thought of seeing her lover again.

The little path meandered upward, and she welcomed the effort, enjoying the pretty trees as she lengthened her stride. It had been an interesting couple of months, really. Both she and Dar had settled down and gotten used to being with each other, and now that they'd worked out timing, and schedules, it was really becoming a lot of fun. She'd half expected there to be large areas of contention between them since they were so different, but the condo allowed them both their space and they'd started off by setting a few ground rules.

Like no talking work at home. That was a biggie, since they were both so involved with the same subjects it was hard not to. After a while, though, Kerry had noticed a distinct change in Dar's attitude when she was home—the taller woman seemed to shed her tough and often impatient shell when she walked through the door, displaying a warmer and gentler side that Kerry was becoming very addicted to.

What a sweetie she was—not that she'd ever admit to it, though. As they'd grown closer, she'd been able to get Dar to open up a little and share some of her inner demons, just as Kerry had slowly started to unburden herself from her own.

Kerry's path took her up and over a small ridge and down parallel to a stream that trickled through the wooded area. She slowed her steps as she reached a wooden bridge, crossed it, and ambled to a halt, finding a log nearby and sitting down on it, just to watch the water go by her.

Ducks floated past, nibbling at the reeds, and making the occasional foray under the water. Kerry looked up from watching them as soft footsteps approached her. From the path opposite the way she'd come, a tall, burly man in corduroy pants and a flannel shirt came into view, with a carved walking stick he was using to disguise a faint limp.

Seeing her, he stopped in surprise. "Why, hello there."

Kerry smiled in reflex, finding nothing to dislike in his broad, open face with its light covering of beard. "Hello."

"You're a strange bit of a thing to be sitting out here on a log, now aren't you?" The man ambled closer and cocked his head, studying her. "Without your clothes on and all."

Kerry stood up. "I was just out for a run." She pointed towards the bridge. "Where does that go?"

"Just down by the old mill," the man answered. "You don't want to go down there. Ground's very rocky and there're snakes."

"Ah." Kerry glanced around her. "You're right. That wouldn't be a good idea. Oh well." She circled him and regained the path. "Time to get to work anyway."

He moved suddenly and blocked her. "Hey, hey. So what kind of work do you do?" His hands stroked his cane. "Pretty little thing like you?"

Oh boy. Kerry drew in a breath, then expelled it. "I'm a network analyst." She forced a smile. "But thanks for the compliment. Now, I do have to be going." The cane snaked out and caught her upper arm, and her heart started pounding. "Sir, you don't want to do that."

"Now, I just want to talk. Take it easy, little girl." The man laughed. "Not often I get to see someone as nice looking as you up here. Surely not half naked." He tugged her closer.

Kerry almost panicked, but just as she was about to scream she could almost hear Dar's calm words in the back of her mind. *Don't lose your mind. Stay calm. Hit hard.* She grabbed the stick with one hand and jerked hard, then spun and swept a leg out, pulling his feet from under him and dumping him on the ground.

The stick came free into her hands and she backed off, spreading her grip across the length of it with a feeling of weird familiarity.

It was strange. Her body shifted, coming over her center of balance as her knees unlocked, and her shoulders tensed in readiness. "Like I said, you really don't want to do that," she said quietly.

"Son of a bitch." Oddly, the man didn't seem upset. He laughed. "Joke's on me, then, I guess. Sorry about that, young lady. I really did think you were just out to tease an old goat like me."

Kerry eyed him uncertainly, but she relaxed a little. She stepped back, but kept the cane between herself and the prone man. Her thumbs slid out to balance her grip and she was aware of how comforting it felt to have the thing in her hands. "That's a pretty disgusting thing to think."

"Well," he got to his knees, then heaved himself up onto his feet, "if I'd a known you were some kind of a ninja, I surely would have kept my thoughts a deal more pure." He held up his hands. "I am sorry, ma'am."

Slowly, she let the stick's end drop, then extended it towards him. "It's all right. Sorry I threw you that hard." She felt a faint pang of regret in releasing the cane, but she put that down to her natural caution and focused on keeping her knees from shaking in pure reaction. "Are you all right?"

"Surely." The man brushed his pants off then wrapped his hands around the walking stick. "I am sorry, Ms. ..."

"Stuart." Kerry offered her hand. "Kerry Stuart. And you are?"

"Jess Walters." He gingerly returned her grip. "You new around here, Ms. Stuart?" He gestured towards the path. "I don't want to keep you."

Kerry started walking back the way she'd come, and he fell into step next to her, his limp hardly keeping him from matching her stride. "No. I'm just visiting. My company sent me here for a few days."

"Ah." Jess nodded. "I live up past the hill top there. I'm a web designer."

Kerry gave him a startled look. "Really?"

"Ayup." He nodded. "Last job was with Tungsten Aerospace. Just finished their web site last week."

"I work for ILS."

Now it was his turn to stare. "No. Really?"

"Mmm. They just bought Allison Consulting. That's what I'm here for." Kerry felt the shakiness fade as she continued walking and decided Mr. Walters was probably harmless for now.

"Ah." The tall, burly man chewed his lower lip. "Well, since I put a scare in you, let me try and make amends. You be careful of those people, Ms. Stuart. They're not nice folks."

Kerry turned her head. "Really? They seemed all right. What do you mean?"

"I can't really say." His jaw firmed and he looked off into the distance. "Just you be careful, all right? Nice talking to you, Ms. Stuart. And sorry about the misunderstanding." Abruptly, he chose an offshoot of the path and was gone before Kerry could answer, his tall form disappearing into the brush with startling speed.

Kerry put her hands on her hips and stared at the spot for a moment in deep puzzlement. "What in the heck was that?" She shook her head, then resumed her jogging towards the cabin, now wondering what in the world she'd gotten into.

She was still wondering after a hot shower had removed the sweat from her body and she stood in the middle of her room deciding what to wear. "Hmm." She eyed her possible choices. The staff at Allison had been wearing business dress, so her maroon suit wouldn't be out of place, however...

Dar had this theory about power trips, and it went something like, "Find out what they think is important, then turn it around and show them how unimportant you think it is." So. They thought appearances were important.

Kerry smiled, and tugged her oldest, most comfortable jeans out of her bag and added a brightly colored shirt to it, along with her hiking boots. "Let's shake 'em up a little."

❖ ⌘ ❖ ⌘ ❖ ⌘ ❖

The Houston airport was busy, and Dar had to dodge around a multitude of moving bodies on her way to the car rental desks. She managed to arrive just after a handful of businessmen in suits and took her place in line with a feeling of mild irritation. The single clerk made her wonder if it was early lunchtime, then she noticed two others in a small office in the back, apparently working on a problem.

Dar turned her attention to watching people go by, playing her usual mental game of trying to guess the person's occupation. She'd picked out three geeks, two accountants, and a TV star before a loud voice drew her eyes back to the desk.

One of the businessmen was at the counter arguing, slapping his hand down on the Formica countertop. The clerk behind the desk simply shrugged and held her hands out and pointed at the clock. The man grabbed his briefcase and stormed off towards an airport limo desk.

"What's up?" Dar asked her neighbor in line.

"They're out of cars." The man grunted. "Figures. They got some damn convention up here going on. And they're all empty, even the luxury models."

"Convention?" Dar mused.

"Yeah. Southern Baptists, or something like that." The man pointed at a group of travelers heading towards a large tour bus.

Dar followed them with her eyes, then considered her options. She could, of course, take a cab to the office, but she hated cabs. Her eyes went to the limo desk. There was that possibility. But she wasn't sure she wanted to send that kind of message.

Then her eyes drifted back over to a small kiosk near the door, where a young man in denims and a cowboy hat sat, evidently bored.

Fun Rentals. Dar studied the pictures of RV's, Skidoos, and...

A smile appeared on her face. "Excuse me." She stepped past the men in line and ambled over to the kiosk. She leaned on the desk and waited for the cowboy to look up. "Hi."

His eyes widened and he sat up, blinking at her. "Um, sorry, ma'am. Can I help you?"

Dar pointed. "One of those, please."

He looked. "Uh, sure." He scrabbled around his desk for paperwork. "Um, sorry. Not many...ah, we usually have folks taking out the RV's first and I...oh, here we go." He retrieved two forms and slid one across the desk to Dar. "Could you fill that out for me? And I'll need to see your driver's license."

"Uh huh." Dar pulled her wallet out, removed the license, and handed it over. She took a pen out and started writing. "Here." She also handed over her credit card.

"Okay. Um, I have to call in your license. Do you have any outstanding tickets, ma'am?"

"No." Dar continued writing. She ignored his low voice as he called in the license, then straightened as he hung up. "Got what you need?"

"Yes, ma'am." The boy scribbled something on her form, then pulled a set of keys from a small board near his left hip. "Would you come with me, please?"

Dar followed him out the door into a blast of bright sunlight. She pulled her sunglasses out of her jacket pocket and shoved them into place, then stood back as the boy opened a door to one side of the parking area.

"Gotcha a nice one. Have you ever driven one of these, ma'am?" The boy looked up, tipping his hat back a little. "They can be a little tricky."

"I've ridden one." Dar took the helmet off the handlebars and removed the keys from the attendant's hand. "Thanks." She checked the motorcycle over, biting off a grin. "Harley, eh? Nice."

"Yeah." The boy backed off, then waved. "Have a great day."

"Oh, I will." Dar seated herself, and started the motorcycle up, adjusted the throttle and slid the helmet over her head. "I definitely will."

❖ ⌘ ❖ ⌘ ❖ ⌘ ❖

Kerry was aware of the eyes fastened on her as she entered Allison's offices and she returned the looks with pleasant smiles as she made her way to the conference room. She walked by the startled occupants and put her briefcase down, then unzipped it and pulled out a thick manila envelope. "All right. This is what the plan is."

She took out several packets and passed them around. "We have certain criteria your systems need to meet before we permit the connection up to the Intranet. I'll need your server specifications before the end of today."

"That's a lot of machines," Ann objected coolly. "We'd have to pull resources for that." She ran her pencil over her lips in thought. "Our clients are already calling, asking what the impact of the merger is going to be on their services."

"Well," Kerry leaned on the table, meeting her eyes, "once their traffic's on our backbone, it'll double their throughput. I bet they can't wait." She smiled. "Isn't it nice to have great news for them?"

An awkward silence fell. "Ann, that's a minor detail, just put some people on it," Sam drawled. "What else?"

Kerry lifted a sheet of paper. "It's mostly procedural at this point. Our personnel people will be in contact with you to transition staff. But I want you to know in advance everyone will be subject to background checks and screening."

A low murmur rose. Ann leaned close to Sam, as she watched the slim blond woman review her papers. "That could be an issue."

The comptroller grunted.

"Is that really necessary? We've had most of these people on board for years," Charlie objected. "I'd hate to have them think we think they're criminals or something."

The cool green eyes fastened on him. "Nothing personal," Kerry replied, smiling for no apparent reason. "It really isn't. Everyone has to go through it because of all of our government contracts and the fact that you all will have access to our Intranet." She paused. "Is there a problem with that? Sometimes it's easier if we know in advance."

They exchanged glances. "Oh. No, no. No problem." Charlie waved a hand at her. "I was just asking. Seemed like a waste of money to me, and we all know how important that is."

"Mmm." Kerry put her paper down and slid her hands into her jeans pockets. "Well, we've found that in the long run it's worth it. One security breach can cost us a lot." Her fingers touched a small, unfamiliar object and her brow creased, but she merely closed her hand around it inside her pocket. "Okay. I'll need a current print of your payables and receivables, preferably in soft copy, then we can get started."

Sam stood up and stretched. "All right. I'll get that going. Charlie? Want to coordinate these things with me? We don't want to keep Ms. Stuart waiting." The two men left, closing the conference room door behind them.

Ann leaned back in her chair and slid her pencil between her fingers. "Anything else I can do?" she asked, politely.

Kerry picked up her paper. "My boss had some questions."

The petite woman smiled. "Would that be the infamous Dar Roberts?" she inquired. "I've heard some very impressive things about her. In fact, it's one of the things I was most intrigued about after I heard we were being bought out."

"Yes, it would be." Kerry sat down and folded her hands. "She definitely lives up to her reputation. And as a matter of fact, one of her questions was regarding the bidding process. She found it really...interesting that your company always got the bid on the day of last refusal."

A guarded look slipped over Ann's face. "Oh, really? Well, that's a coincidence. I don't think I ever noticed that."

Kerry watched her expression and body language, something Dar had been coaching her in. Ms. Ann was nervous all right and hiding something. "Yeah. She was going to give the account reps at those companies a call. Just to check out how the deals went through." The pencil moved faster, and she could almost sense the other woman's tension rising.

"Well, I'm sure she'll find out it was just a coincidence...and some sharp bidding." Ann stood up abruptly. "Excuse me. I need to use the restroom. Ah...there's coffee down the hall if you're interested." She took her papers and left quickly, her heels making a staccato tattoo on the tile floor.

"Hmmm." Kerry pulled a mug from her briefcase and retrieved a teabag from a side pocket, then she strolled to the door and slipped through it, her curiosity fully aroused.

Chapter
3

The company headquarters complex was, in a word, huge. Dar was on the perimeter road under a hot sun, but the wind provided by her nice shiny Harley more than compensated. She accelerated, enjoying the feel of the large engine under her and the sensation of being exposed to nature, in a way she never got while driving in Miami.

Maybe she'd get a cycle back home. Dar waggled an eyebrow, glancing aside to watch a herd of buffalo thunder past, raising a cloud of dust and sending the scent of warm wool to her nose. *Wonder if Kerry would like this?* She imagined her lover behind her, holding on as they raced around, and a grin split her face. *I bet she would.*

The road curved around towards the entrance, and Dar throttled down the cycle, slowing the machine to a rumbling crawl as she came up to the gates. The guard darted out and another joined him as she pulled to a halt and fished in her jacket pocket for her ID badge.

"Hold on." The man held up a warning hand. His partner stood off and put a hand on his holstered gun.

Dar almost laughed as she unhooked her helmet and pulled it off, shaking her hair loose. "Here," she handed him the badge, "I'm not a terrorist."

The man came forward and took the card, giving her a suspicious look before he glanced down at it. Then his attitude changed so fast it was a wonder, Dar thought, that his tie didn't spin around his head and choke him. He stiffened up and ducked his head at her. "Ma'am," a hand waved off his partner urgently, "I think they're expecting you."

Dar gave him a whole hearted, sexy grin. "I bet they aren't." She took her badge back and waited while the gate opened, then gunned the engine cheerfully and swept on by, thoroughly enjoying herself. She pulled up into a spot near the front door and left the helmet perched on the handlebars.

Four steps up, then a small waterfall filled pool, another six steps, then a weird sculpture, another four steps, and she was at the front doors, massive glass portals so perfectly balanced they opened at a touch of her fingertips. She walked in, her boots sounding loud on the marble tile, and let the door whisper shut behind her. The lobby was very quiet, only a small fountain in the corner breaking the stillness, and Dar spent a moment merely standing and absorbing it all.

"Hasn't changed a bit." Dar shook her head in mild disgust and headed for the elevators, perched behind an imposing guard desk. "Pretentious piece of..."

"Can I help you, ma'am?" The guard's voice stopped her. "Are you looking for someone?"

Dar walked over and leaned on the counter. "Yeah." She pulled off her sunglasses and chewed on an earpiece. "Alastair McLean."

The cool hazel eyes studied her, before scanning a list behind the desk. "Is he expecting you, ma'am?" His voice was pointed on the title.

"Yep." Dar flipped her badge onto the counter.

Reluctantly, the man took it and put it on the desk, then started typing in something, glancing at the badge as he did so. His hands stopped, and he leaned closer, then looked up at her in evident shock.

Dar smiled. "Not what you expected?"

He slowly handed her the badge back. "No, ma'am, Ms. Roberts, not exactly." Now the voice was respectful. "You can go on up. You know the way, I guess."

The dark haired woman smiled, then moved past him to the bank of glass and marble lined elevators, one of which was resting on ground level in all its brassy splendor. Dar entered it and punched the twenty-third floor, then leaned against the wall as the doors slid shut and the car moved upward.

It stopped on fifteen and two men got on, arguing over a Y2K upgrade on a legacy program Dar remembered writing seven or eight years prior. She listened in amusement as they debated, ignoring the glances they kept giving her.

"If they'd have left that original code in place, Dave, we'd be fine."

"You tell them that. I tried to tell them that two years ago, but no. No. They had their heads stuck too far up their butts to go and ask the original coder." The shorter man shook his head in disgust. "Pansy asses."

"Well," the taller man chuckled, as they got out on the twentieth floor, "I don't know. I'm not sure I'd have the balls to go tell Dar Roberts I'd messed up her code either."

The doors slid shut and Dar snickered, then eyed her reflection, flicking her dark hair into a semblance of order as the elevator reached its destination and the doors opened.

It was, if anything, even quieter up here than in the lobby. There was soundproofing weave on all the walls and the floors had plush, padded carpeting on them. Dar walked silently through the entryway, lit by sunlight that poured in through the vaulted glass ceilings, and turned down the largest corridor, which had plaques all down its length.

The soft sounds of business could be heard through the wooden doors she passed and she exchanged nods with two other women who passed her. Finally she was at the last set of doors and she grabbed the ornate brass handles and pulled them open.

Inside was a large, airy antechamber, roughly circular, with three doors leading off it. In the center was a small fountain and to one side, a huge, laminated wood circular desk presided, with a tall, austere woman seated precisely in the center, her attention focused on a paper.

"Hello, Beatrice." Dar's voice broke the quiet.

Startled, the woman glanced up. "Oh I..." Then she turned her head fully. "Well, my God, Paladar Roberts. It's been forever." Beatrice laughed and stood up. "Or at least, what...five years?"

"At least," Dar allowed, walking over and folding her arms over her chest. "You know I hate this place."

Alastair's long time assistant cocked her head and smiled, pulling down her half glasses a little. "You show up like that just to tweak him?" she asked gently. "Bad timing, if it was. Ankow's really giving it to him in there."

"I know. That's why he asked me to show up," Dar replied. "They still in session?"

"Mmm." Beatrice nodded her neatly coifed gray head. "He's trouble, Dar. He wants to get Alastair out." The older woman folded her hands and sighed. "Have you met him?"

"No."

"Well, I can't say I like him much. He's in his early forties, good looking, sporty type," Beatrice told her. "Thinks anyone who can remember World War II should be gone and buried. He doesn't have much patience with what he regards as the old ways."

"Really." Dar considered the door to the conference room. "Change for the sake of change gets no one anything but trouble, Beatrice. You know that."

"Mmm. Well, he's on a campaign to get the board restructured and remove Alastair. He thinks he has the leverage. You know last quarter's results weren't that great."

"We're trying to fix that," Dar replied quietly. "You can't sell facilities you don't have."

"I know that, and you know that. Maybe you should tell Mr. Ankow that." Beatrice's dark eyes twinkled. "He took one look at your sixteen year tenure and he wants you out, too." She gazed at Dar. "You look great for such an old-timer, Paladar."

A look of wry amusement crossed Dar's tanned features. "Thanks." She walked over and put her hands on the door latches into the conference room. "See ya."

"Good luck." Beatrice waved.

Dar paused, hearing the raised voices inside, and took a breath, rousting her more aggressive, darker side up before she worked the handles and pulled the doors open.

❖ ⌘ ❖ ⌘ ❖ ⌘ ❖

Kerry entered the break room, winding her way around several employees seated at the small tables, most of whom ignored her. She went to the hot water dispenser and ran the steaming liquid over her teabag, focusing her ears on the conversations behind her.

"Think they'll fire us?"

"Nah. They can't. Sam'll get them locked up. Just give it a chance."

"I dunno, Rex. This ain't no little two bit graphics company coming in here."

"I heard they just got rid of the last three companies they bought out. You came in and they handed you a box with your stuff in it."

Kerry rolled her eyes and dunked her teabag. *Not quite.* Though she had needed to make some hard decisions on the first of them, where the departments pretty much mirrored the business unit that was acquiring them.

It had been a very lonely moment, that night in a strange hotel room in a tiny corner of North Carolina. She'd sat up for hours, locked in a fierce debate with herself as she tried to come up with some way–any way–to justify not screwing up those people's lives.

And she couldn't.

At four a.m., she'd given up and, feeling small and foolish, called Dar. "How can I make decisions like this?" she'd asked her lover.

"Don't," Dar had answered, apparently wide awake. "I'll do it."

It had been so tempting, Kerry sighed. She'd been exhausted and emotionally drained and every instinct she had was begging her to give in and let Dar take the weight off her shoulders.

But she'd said no. And she'd collected herself, gotten a few hours sleep, and went into the place the next morning to give them their limited options.

"Well," the company's director had said, "we thought we were all out. That's good news." And he'd smiled at her. "Thanks, Ms. Stuart. It's sure been a pleasure working with you."

Kerry put some sweetener in her cup and stirred it.

"Yeah, well they'd better take care of us or I'll have something to say about it," a tall, younger man in the corner spoke up in an irritated voice. "We held up our end of things."

"You'd better shut up, Alvin," a woman answered. "Or you'll end up like Mary."

An odd silence fell, and Kerry experienced a sudden prickly feeling up and down her spine. Casually, she turned, to find everyone looking at her. She took a sip of her tea. "I didn't bring any boxes with me, so you can relax."

It got ten degrees cooler immediately. "You're from the new company?" someone muttered from the back of the room.

Kerry nodded. "Yep." She took another sip, feeling the waves of hostility beating against her. "It's really not that bad."

"Not from your perspective," the woman who had last spoken retorted.

"Well, I was in your shoes a couple months ago," Kerry answered evenly. "So you never know. I got a promotion out of it." She went out the door and down the hall, but not fast enough to escape the comment that floated after her.

"Yeah? Wonder who she slept with."

Kerry sighed. "And you know, I can't even really get mad at that," she remarked to the empty hallway. "I hate living a cliché sometimes."

She slipped back into the conference room and stopped, finding Sam waiting for her. "Oh, I took you up on the offer of coffee." She lifted her cup and circled the table to the opposite side.

"Great," the comptroller replied, with a friendly smile. "We've got the reports you asked for running. But it'll take a couple of hours. Listen, you up for an early lunch? There's a nice spot near here we all go to."

A tiny, faint warning bell rang in Kerry's mind's ear. "Sure." She pulled out her cell phone. "Let me just check in with the office." She dialed a number, then waited. "Hey, María."

"Kerrisita." María's warm tones came through the phone at her. "I am glad to hear your voice."

"Thanks." Kerry smiled in reflex. "Listen, did the boss call in yet?"

"No. She is in a meeting in Texas," María told her. "Beatrice tells me it is not a good one."

"Mmm." Kerry sighed. "She was afraid of that...yeah...well, things are in process here, but I'm going to step out for lunch so if anyone's looking for me, have them use my pager, or the cell."

There was a little silence, then María cleared her throat. "*Sí*, I will do that, Kerrisita."

"I shouldn't be more than an hour or two."

"*Sí*."

"Thanks, María." Kerry hung up and clipped her phone to her belt. "Okay. Let's go." She glanced up at the tall accountant and found his

interesting hazel eyes gazing back at her. His face was nicely propor-
tioned and he had a straight nose and thin, but well formed lips. *Not a bad
face to have to sit across a lunch table at,* she decided.

"Right this way." Sam gestured towards the door and followed her
out, making small talk as they exited the building, and he guided her
towards a four door sedan parked nearby. "So, have you been to Vermont
before, Ms. Stuart?"

Kerry settled into the passenger seat and buckled the seat belt. "No.
I'm from Michigan, originally, and I've spent some time around the northeast."

"Really?" Sam got behind the wheel and started the car, locking the
doors as he pulled out of the parking lot. "Michigan. Hmm. I had a friend
that went to school up there. Don't think I've ever been, though. I'm from
Oregon, but I moved here when I was just a kid."

"Do you like it here?" Kerry gazed out the window at the beautiful,
stately trees. "It's lovely country. Must be nice when the leaves change."

"It's gorgeous," Sam told her, with an easy smile. "Do you miss that
in Florida?"

"Sometimes."

Kerry watched the road idly, marking the streets until the car turned
into a driveway, continued down a crunching gravel path and through a
line of neatly trimmed hedges before it pulled up next to a small inn. She
released the safety belt and waited until the doors unlocked, then got out
of the car.

She was fairly sure there was more to this than lunch and, as she felt
Sam's speculative eyes examining her as they walked towards the inn, she
found herself wondering just exactly what that something more was.

❖ ⌘ ❖ ⌘ ❖ ⌘ ❖

"This isn't a debate, Alastair." The tall, dark haired man leaned back
in his chair and threw his arms up. "You can't argue with numbers, and
that's what the shareholders are concerned with."

Alastair folded his hands on the table and kept a patient smile on his
face. "Now, David, you've seen the plans for next quarter. I agree the last
one wasn't what we'd want, but projections on towards the end of the year
are excellent."

"That's right," Stuart Kissington, the chief financial officer agreed,
his low, gruff voice a counterpoint to Alastair's polished tones. Kissington had been on the board of directors for as many years as Alastair and
was a formidable bulwark to the CEO's left, a burly, bearded man with
white hair and a grizzled beard. "Damn shame we had to take that charge
last quarter, but it couldn't be helped. Weather."

"Not good enough." Ankow shook his head. "Gentlemen, we're

rounding the corner to the twenty-first century and, frankly, this company's not ready for it." He stood up and paced the room, an annoying habit of his. "Our shareholders expect us to be cutting edge and that's not just on technology. We have to be ready to provide all the services our clients need into the next century." He turned and spread his arms. "We can't be stuck in the past and I think that's exactly where we are right now. I don't see any indication that this company is up to the challenge."

Alastair propped his chin up on one hand. "David, I don't get why you're so against the new network, then. That's all the new technology you've been bab–I mean, referring to in the last five minutes."

He ticked off his fingers. "It's overpriced. It's under designed. I can't think of one reason why this company should invest in a lot of wires and cables that won't get us squat in the marketplace."

"I can."

David's voice had covered the sound of doors opening and now a low, vibrant drawl overrode his speech and echoed across the conference room.

Ankow turned, startled to see a tall, dark haired young woman in jeans and a faded crimson shirt standing in the doorway, sunglasses perched on her nose, and both hands planted firmly on her hips.

One hand lifted and a long, narrow finger raised. "It's all fiber technology. It's state of the art. It triples our available public bandwidth." The tall form stalked towards him. "The one problem this company has is our lack of infrastructure. You can't goddamn well sell what you don't have. And if, Mr. Ankow, if you can't see that," Dar pulled off her sunglasses and treated him to an ice blue stare, "get your eyes checked." She held her ground for a moment as he stared at her in shock, then she turned and walked to the conference table, picked a chair and stripped her leather jacket off as she dropped down into it. She tossed her sunglasses on the polished wood surface and glanced down its length. "Hello, Alastair."

Her boss beamed at her. "Hi, Dar. It's so nice to see you." He turned the beatific smile on the now furious David Ankow. "David? I don't think you've ever met Dar, have you? Sorry. This is Dar Roberts, our CIO."

Dar rolled her head around and peered at her target. "Hi."

Alastair cleared his throat and stood up. "Well, now that we're all here. David, why don't you sit down? I believe Dar is prepared to give us a briefing on the new network."

Ankow visibly wrestled with his temper, then allowed a smile to cross his face. "I'd like that." He took a seat opposite Dar. "Go ahead. I've got lots of questions."

❖ ⌘ ❖ ⌘ ❖ ⌘ ❖

"Hope you like stick-to-your-ribs type foods, Ms. Stuart. That's their specialty here," Sam remarked, as he opened the menu. "We're not big on salads."

Kerry eyed the selections and bit back a wry grin, deciding Dar would be in heaven here. "I'll be fine, thanks," she answered politely, making her choices and putting the folded linen panel down. Though, she reflected while Sam examined his options, Dar had been getting better about that lately, and she'd done her darndest to nudge her lover towards a healthier diet.

Of course, during these two weeks, the woman was probably living on cheeseburgers and fries, but... Kerry sighed and folded her arms, looking around. The restaurant was a cozy one, with about two dozen tables and a wooden interior liberally sprinkled with gingham and crafts-work. Roughly half the tables were filled, despite the early hour, and that at least boded well for the quality of the food.

A waitress came over, taking a pencil from behind one ear. She was an older woman, with a cheerful face and a sturdy body. "Hello there, Sam. How are you doing today?"

The accountant looked up and smiled. "Hi, Sadie. I'm doing fine, thanks. How's the husband?"

"Cantankerous as always." The woman laughed. "What'll you have, the usual?"

"That'll be fine...and a mug of coffee." Sam glanced across the table. "Ms. Stuart?"

The waitress blinked, then turned her head. "Sorry, hon. You're so quiet there. What can I get for you?" She paused, evaluating her subject. "We've got some poached fish for the special."

"No. I'll take the pot roast, thanks," Kerry replied mildly.

The waitress looked surprised. "All righty. That comes with mashed potatoes but we can put steamed vegetables on if you like."

"Nope. Potatoes are just fine," the blond woman reassured her. "And a chocolate milkshake, please."

The writing stopped, then started again. "Coming right up." Sadie took both menus and trundled off, after a long look at Kerry.

Keep them off balance. Dar had told her. *Figure out what they expect you to do, then do something else. Don't let them get comfortable thinking they know you.* "So," Kerry leaned back in her chair and regarded her table mate, "what is it you want to talk about, Mr. Gershwin?"

The dark haired man looked honestly nonplussed for a long moment. Finally, he leaned on his elbows and laced his fingers together as he studied her face. "You do keep surprising me, Ms. Stuart. I'll give you that." A faint smile flickered on and off his face. "I'm not sure what to think about you."

Kerry merely waited.

"Ann tells me you were interested in our bidding methods," Sam finally drawled. "She seemed to think you wanted more information."

Hmm. Kerry's nostrils flared a little, smelling trouble. She carefully considered her answer. "On reviewing them we just thought it was interesting that you won the bid on last call," she remarked casually. "After not really being a contender in the preliminary stages."

"We?"

"My boss and I, yes."

"Ah." Sam pressed his fingertips against his lips. "That would be Ms. Roberts, correct?"

Kerry nodded. "Yes."

"I hadn't thought Dar Roberts would argue with success. And certainly not that she'd quibble with tactics to get there," Sam tilted his head, "not with her reputation."

"I didn't say she was arguing," Kerry replied mildly. "Just that she was interested...and curious. Dar's like that. She likes to know what the real story is." She paused. "So. Are you going to tell me the real story, Mr. Gershwin? Because sooner or later, she'll find out anyway."

The waitress came, breaking the tension and delivering their food. They were quiet for a few minutes and Kerry took the opportunity to concentrate on eating, finding the pot roast delicious. "This is very good," she commented, as she put her fork down and took a sip of her milkshake.

"Glad you approve," Sam replied. "As for our bidding strategy. Well, I'm afraid your boss is going to be disappointed. It just comes down to really getting to know your customer, shall we say?" He smiled at Kerry. "And being local...let's just say we had a definite advantage in that."

"Really?" Kerry digested the information. "Well, that's great. She'll be glad to hear it." Green eyes flicked up and caught him staring at her. "We're hoping to continue your streak. This is a new market for us."

He settled back in his chair and laced his hands over his stomach. "I bet you are." He picked up his coffee cup and took a sip. "We've put a lot of effort into building a team here. That's part of our success. You come in and break it up...well, I can't guarantee anything."

Ah. Now that motive, Kerry understood only too well. "We're running everyone through the checks, Mr. Gershwin. I don't see any reason to make wholesale changes." She put a reassuring tone in her voice. "That's not part of the current plan."

He started to answer, then stopped as Kerry's cell phone rang. "Ever in demand, eh?"

Kerry unhooked it and opened the phone. "Hello?"

"Hi."

It took a lot of effort to not smile. "How are things going?"

"We're on a break. It's not pretty." Dar's voice sounded slightly hoarse. "How about you?"

"Same," Kerry replied.

"You all right? María said you sounded upset." The concern almost leaked through the phone at her, giving Kerry a warm feeling.

"Yeah. I'm just clarifying some of the plans here. I should have something for you later this afternoon."

"Caught you in front of them, huh?"

"Yes, ma'am."

A soft, gentle chuckle traveled over the connection. "All right. Call me later."

"I will," Kerry promised, as the line disconnected. She folded the phone back up and tucked it into her belt. "Sorry. What were you saying?"

"Just was going to say I'm glad to hear that," Sam replied, a smile lurking around his lips. "Though some of our people found your...security...very intrusive." He paused. "Almost communistic." He bit down on a French fry. "They were very upset."

Kerry considered that. "I'm sorry if they were," she told him, sincerely. "If it's any consolation, everyone goes through it." She shrugged. "I did. We just hate surprises."

"Mmm." Sam paused. "I suppose it comes down to privacy. Everyone's got something in their life they'd like to keep secret, don't you agree?"

Kerry felt a chill. "I never thought about it."

He smiled. "C'mon, Ms. Stuart. You're telling me you've got no closed doors in your life?"

A tiny, wry smile tugged at Kerry's lips. "Mr. Gershwin, you'd be surprised at just how open a book my life really is."

He studied her intently, then laughed. "Maybe I would be."

Kerry sucked on her milkshake, unsure of what, exactly, to answer to that.

Chapter
4

Dar took a sip of water, rolling it around in her mouth before she swallowed it. Her throat hurt from talking and she really wanted nothing more than to find a quiet place with hot tea in it.

Beatrice looked up from her computer and gave Dar a sympathetic look. "Long day?"

"You know it." The dark haired woman sighed. "I must have explained the concept of burst bottlenecking a dozen times, if I did it once. God. He's got the comprehension of a Dead Sea snail."

Beatrice snickered and covered her mouth. "You know, Paladar. We could use more of you around here. I'd forgotten just how colorful you can be when you put your mind to it."

"No thanks." Dar shook her head. "Not if this is a sample of what it's like. He's had Alastair in there listening to him whine for over an hour. How does he stand it?"

"That's his job." The older woman turned and leaned on her elbows, regarding Dar thoughtfully. "And he knows he has someone who can make things happen for him. So it makes it a little easier to take." Her face grew serious. "I don't think you realize just how much he depends on you, Dar. When you resigned, I thought he was going to go insane. I walked into his office and he was almost crying."

Dar blinked, truly surprised. "I just do what he pays me to do, Beatrice."

A door slammed and David Ankow walked swiftly by, not giving either of them so much as a glance. He exited the reception area and slammed that door too, making Dar jump a little. She turned her head and gave Beatrice an inquiring look. The secretary shook her head.

"Well," Alastair appeared from his office, loosening his tie, "glad that's over with."

Dar gazed at him. "How'd we do?"

The CEO sighed. "He's not happy. He's not happy with me, with the board, with the company...and boy, oh boy, oh boy, Paladar, he's really not happy with you."

Dar shrugged.

"Fortunately, however, you nearly bludgeoned him to death with some very pointed logic and a very impressive set of statistics, by the way, and he had to back off."

Dar smirked.

"For now." Alastair shook his head. "He'll be back, though. He's not nearly done." He held a hand out. "C'mon inside, Dar. Let's chat a bit. I know you must be ready to get going."

Dar stood up, sorry to leave the comfortable couch, and followed her boss into his office, closing the door behind them. It was quiet, and Dar glanced around as she crossed the soft carpet, remembering the last time she'd been in the place. "Hasn't changed."

Alastair circled his fine mahogany desk and sat down, letting his hands drop onto his knees. "Not a whole lot, no." He watched his CIO as she sauntered over, dropped into one of his visitor's chairs and gazed at him with those incredibly blue eyes. "You're looking good, Dar. You losing weight?"

"A couple of pounds, yeah," Dar replied, with a shrug. "I started working out a little more...been pretty busy."

Alastair nodded. "How's Kerrison?"

Dar's face relaxed briefly into a smile. "She's fine. In Vermont, as a matter of fact, consolidating Allison Consulting." She paused, fingering her sunglasses. "This jerk's going to be real trouble, isn't he?"

"Yeap." Her boss pursed his lips. "If he gets enough support, he can force a stockholder vote and overturn the board. But you know that."

"Yeah."

Alastair shifted, looking a little uncomfortable. "Dar. The new network's about ready isn't it?"

Dar nodded. "First components start coming online next week."

He sighed. "It'll be six months before we see results. It's going to be a very long, very tough six months." Alastair leaned back in his leather chair and crossed a pinstriped leg over one knee. "Especially since the stockholders' meeting is next month."

"Yeah."

"Dar," Alastair looked down at his hands, "he's going to be looking for any bit of ammunition he can get, and he's the type to get personal."

Dar went very still. "What do you mean?"

Her boss looked uneasy. "I mean, he's going to go after anything that will make any of us look bad and..." He sighed and finally looked up. "He's not going to ignore the things that I do."

Dar drew in a quiet breath. "Oh."

"It's pretty common knowledge, Dar." Alastair cleared his throat. "Not so much here, but certainly in Miami."

It hit hard. Somehow Dar had managed to make herself forget just how out of bounds her relationship with Kerry was. She'd actually broken company rules by simply dating her assistant; now that they lived together... "Yeah. We don't bring our personal lives to the office, but," Dar sighed, "it's no secret, no."

"And it's in Personnel," Alastair responded simply. "Autonomics flagged it when it discovered two employees in the direct chain with the same address." He paused. "I overrode it."

They were silent for a long while. Dar lifted her head finally and looked him in the eye. "Do you want me to resign from the board?" she asked quietly. "Because if it's a choice between the company and Kerry, you have no chance."

Alastair rested his chin in his hands and gazed fondly at her. "If you think I'm so cowpoke dumb as to not know that, I might have to be insulted." Then he exhaled. "No. I just want you to be aware of what might happen and make Kerry aware. This could get nasty." He drummed his fingers on his cheek. "I have a mandate to do the best I can for this company, and losing two of my very top employees runs counter to that mandate."

Dar nodded unhappily. "All right." She paused. "Does that mean I can expect to see his ugly puss around my neck of the swamp?"

Alastair nodded. "He mentioned tonight he was planning a trip over the Gulf. Probably next week or so." He made a face. "Maybe he won't find out, Dar. He's not likely to hang out in the lunch room collecting gossip and you two must be relatively old news by now."

"True," Dar acknowledged. "And it's not like we...ahm..."

"Make out on your desk?" Her boss finally smiled, as he watched his normally icy CIO turn a deep crimson. "My god, Dar Roberts blushing. Where's my damn digital camera?" He laughed in genuine delight.

Dar rubbed her face and tried to get her rebellious body back under control. "Glad you're amused," she muttered, standing up and putting on her jacket. "I gotta get out of here."

Alastair let his chuckles run down. "All right. Have a good flight, Dar...and thanks." He stood and held out a hand. "You really made the difference today."

"Glad I could help." Dar returned his grip. "See ya."

"See ya, Dar." Alastair lifted a hand towards her. "Good luck."

Yeah. Dar shoved her sunglasses on as she headed back through the reception area. "Nice seeing you, Beatrice."

"Same to you, Dar." The secretary smiled at her. "Safe flight."

Dar closed the door behind her and headed for the elevator.

The airport had just passed its evening rush, and Dar only had to dodge several dozen hurrying businessmen as she made her way through the concourse to her assigned gate. She sat down and leaned back, her mind still churning over Alastair's warning.

And it was, she knew, very clearly a warning.

Damn. Dar folded her arms over her chest and exhaled. *Just when things were settling down and really starting to work out. Kerry had been in her position long enough to really make an impact and they'd started to achieve a real balance at home too.*

A fact that had slammed itself into her conscious awareness over the past two weeks, when she found herself missing Kerry more than she could have possibly imagined. This was by far the longest they'd been apart since they'd met and when she wasn't careful her mind had chewed over the question of whether things would be different when Kerry got back.

Dar had no reason to think it would, but... She sighed and allowed herself the moment of insecurity. Things had been going along so well, it almost seemed logical to wonder when the other shoe was going to drop.

She didn't want anything to change. Dar gazed sullenly out from behind her glasses. She really didn't want anything to change because of an uptight pinhead who couldn't find his butt with both hands and a flashlight.

Her stomach rumbled, reminding her that she hadn't eaten anything since breakfast on the plane. She glanced around and spotted a small food court nearby. *Ah.* She perked up a little. *Ice cream.* Dar got up, walked over, and studied her choices with only a twinge of guilt at deciding on dessert before dinner. "Double scoop of chocolate mousse fudge, please."

She accepted the cone and nibbled a little off the top as she handed over a five dollar bill. Then she turned and wandered back towards her gate, stopping to lean against the post outside it and watch the sun slowly sinking to the west. Three college age women crossed in front of her, clad in flannel shirts and carrying backpacks. Her eyes idly followed them as they moved into the waiting area of the next gate.

Her eyes flicked up to the destination.

❖ ⌘ ❖ ⌘ ❖ ⌘ ❖

Kerry shoved the hotel room door open and trudged inside letting it close behind her. She dropped her briefcase by the small desk and sat down on the desk chair, as her head fell with a small groan into her hands.

What a mess.

She rubbed her eyes tiredly. *That was the trouble when you suspected something was going on–you started looking. When you started looking, very often, you found, not necessarily what you were looking for, but things that got out of place very fast.*

They'd run those reports. She'd taken the soft copies and dumped them into the twelve gigabyte storage of her laptop. But then she'd scanned the printed versions, and to her statistics trained mind, numbers jumped out at her, making her look deeper and deeper into the deceptively docile black and white printouts.

Questions. Lots of them, and the answers were either a little too pat, or a little too vague. Yet they'd passed due diligence. Kerry shook her head. *How? Something wasn't right.* She hadn't had time, really, to analyze it. That would be up to Duk's auditors, who would be getting her files tomorrow and, armed with her preliminary report, would start hunting.

She wondered if Allison's staff suspected. She'd tried to be noncommittal, but the fact that she'd kept them there until after nine at night should have told them something. The atmosphere had grown steadily more hostile as the day went on, and Kerry had to force her body not to hunch up defensively as she brought yet another question to the table.

It had made her sort of nervous and she'd had trouble not watching the lights behind her as she drove to the hotel, half convinced she was being followed. That was the kind of paranoia, she realized, that could easily make you nuts pretty fast.

And yet. Kerry eyed the window speculatively, conscious of the silence around the small cabin and just how dark it was outside, and the fact that the hotel was isolated by the woods around it for some distance around.

Her heartbeat picked up a little. Did she hear footsteps outside? She concentrated, and the soft crunching of boots on gravel came to her again. The sound moved closer, then stopped and Kerry's eyes widened as she stood up.

A soft knock came at the door and her pulse shot up, a chill running up and down her spine. She stared at the door in a half panic, her mind momentarily blanking on what to do.

The knock came again, a little louder, and she exhaled, getting a hold of herself. "All right. Just relax, calm down, and answer it." She walked over on unsteady feet and put her hand on the knob, taking a deep breath. "Yes?"

"Hey."

Kerry stared at the door in total, numb shock, then yanked the handle down and pulled it back so fast she almost knocked herself down. An incoherent sound gurgled from her throat as her eyes confirmed her hearing and she drank in the tall, dark haired form leaning casually in her doorway. "Urk."

Dar's eyebrows shot up. "Interesting reaction. Can I come in?"

Kerry reached out and grabbed handfuls of Dar and pulled her inside, hardly waiting for the door to close before throwing herself at her lover,

tiny, incoherent sounds of delight coming from her throat. "Dar!" She
wrapped her arms around the taller woman's body and squeezed as hard as
she could. "Eurrgghhh!"

"That would be me, yeah." Dar leaned back against the wall, afraid
her knees were going to collapse on her as she hugged Kerry, basking in
the obvious welcoming joy the blond woman displayed.

The reaction was everything she'd hoped it would be. Dar let a
breath out slowly and rested her cheek against Kerry's soft hair, absorbing
it, and feeling like a dried sponge tossed into a pond.

Kerry buried her face into Dar's shoulder, scarcely able to believe
what her senses were telling her. But it was her lover's sturdy body she
held and she could hear Dar's heart pounding under her ear, a rapid pattern that slowed as fingertips rubbed lightly up and down her back.

She finally turned her head to one side, and reveled in the sight of
her lover's angular profile just above her. "Wow."

Dar smiled in pure reflex. "Wow?"

Kerry exhaled, and nuzzled her. "Wow. As in, wow, that was one of
the neatest surprises I've ever gotten." She squeezed Dar's ribs. "Wow, as
in wow, you have *no* idea how glad I am to see you. And wow, as in wow,
you just made a really cruddy day absolutely perfect."

Dar blushed at the effusiveness. "Hmm."

Kerry laughed in delight. "Oh, my god. It is so darn good to see you,
Dar."

The blue eyes twinkled happily. "Same here." She hugged the
smaller woman. "I was in the Houston airport, and the gate for my flight
back to Miami was right next to the gate for a plane coming here. I just
ended up on the wrong one."

"Uh uh. Right one," Kerry mumbled contentedly. "I was just about to
call you. This thing blew up on me today."

"Yeah?" Dar asked, surprised. "Thought it was pretty straightforward." Impulsively she scooped Kerry up, getting a startled squawk from
her lover, then dropped them both onto the bed. "But that's all right. I had
a pretty lousy day myself."

Kerry sprawled lazily over her and rested her chin on Dar's collarbone. "Somehow, it's really hard for me to give a raccoon's butt about that
stuff right now."

Hmm. Dar had been having the same thought, as the aggravation of
the day evaporated effortlessly. "You can fill me in tomorrow. And I
booked myself back to Miami on the same flight as you have."

"Awesome." Kerry chuckled. "They all wanted to meet my boss. Just
goes to show you, be careful what you ask for in life, huh?" She spared a
moment to indulge in the guilty pleasure of imagining walking into Allison Consulting tomorrow with the ultimate in attitude with her. "Heh."
She studied Dar. "Do you have any luggage with you, or did you just..."

"I just." Dar grinned. "So I've gotta wash this stuff out tonight and wear it again. Guess I'll have to buff it tonight." They grinned and chuckled.

Kerry plucked at her jeans button. "You went to HQ in this?"

"Yup. I woke up late this morning and I didn't have time for anything else. Figured Alastair would rather me there in this, than not there."

"Were you right?"

"Oh yeah. We managed to get the pinhead to back down, but it's gonna get ugly." Dar sighed. "He's gonna tour Miami." She combed her fingers through Kerry's pale hair. "Alastair warned me he likes to get personal." She hesitated, worried about her lover's reaction. "And that he'd make us an issue."

A blond eyebrow lifted. "My job performance stands for itself," Kerry answered proudly. "As for anything else, he can kiss my butt."

Dar grinned. "That's my girl." She half sat up, leaning closer to whisper. "And if he comes within a foot of your butt, I'm going to remove his testicles." She paused. "Got me?"

Kerry held it in for a moment, then she laughed helplessly. Dar joined in, then they let that wind down. Kerry sighed. "Is Alastair really worried?"

Dar nodded. "Yeah. But I had time to think about it on the flight up here. Unless he can prove it's affecting the company in a negative way, there's not much he can do." She paused. "I mean, yeah, we broke the rules. But it's not like it's the first time it's happened at ILS. He can make it pretty public, though, and damned uncomfortable for us."

"Everyone knows anyway, Dar. We get invitations addressed to both of us all the time," Kerry reminded her, with a smile. "And being publicly linked with you doesn't bother me." She paused. "I've had a lot of time to myself to think about that the last couple of weeks."

Dar studied the determined look on her lover's face and a sense of relief flooded through her. "Guess we'll take it as it comes, then." She traced Kerry's jaw-line with a finger. "I told Alastair if I had to choose, there wasn't any contest."

"He knew that," Kerry replied quietly. "He's not stupid."

Dar laughed. "Funny. That's exactly what he said." She lifted her body up and leaned over, finding Kerry waiting for her. Their lips touched and a shudder of pure reaction swept through her body. Fingers started exploring her, then Kerry paused and nudged her with her head. "Mmm?"

"Let's get your clothes taken care of. 'Cause you certainly can't borrow mine."

Obligingly, Dar rolled up off the bed and pulled Kerry up with her. The smaller woman immediately unbuckled her belt, then slid fingers under Dar's waistband and unbuttoned them.

Dar reciprocated by tugging Kerry's shirt free and unfastening it, unable to prevent her hands from slipping beneath the fabric and starting a teasing exploration of the familiar body pressed lightly against hers.

The cool air of the room hit her shoulders as Kerry pulled her shirt off and she reluctantly relinquished first one hand, then the other to remove it entirely, managing to do the same for her without totally tangling them both up in fabric.

"Sometimes," Kerry breathed against her skin, as she nibbled a path up her breastbone and reached around to unhook her bra, "it's very nice being shorter than you."

"Oh really?" Dar purred, working on her lover's jeans, then running light fingers over her back as Kerry kicked her pants free. "Mmm. Red hearts, huh?" she teased gently, pulling at the waistband of Kerry's underwear.

"Look who's taking." Kerry moved down and kissed her navel, then bit at the sedate, white briefs covered with a plethora of Dogberts. "Nerd."

Dar slid her arms around Kerry and picked her up, then fell sideways onto the bed, rolled over and settled her lover's bare body on top of her, welcoming the explosion in her senses as Kerry's touch claimed her.

Guess I'm wearing wet clothes tomorrow, she remembered thinking, just before a low, breathy growl in her ear made tomorrow, and clothing, and everything else...

Irrelevant.

❖⌘❖⌘❖⌘❖

Waking up naked in bed with Dar Roberts was about the nicest thing Kerry could readily conceive of, she decided, having done just that. She stretched a little under the soft quilt and snuggled closer, feeling really rested for the first time in two weeks.

They had managed to get Dar's clothes washed and hung up in the bathroom, but it had been pretty late before that happened, and she wondered if the darn things would even be half dry by now.

The sun peeked in and Kerry peeked back, then put her head down on Dar's shoulder, using her lover's body to block out the intrusive rays. A soft chime made her look up again to see her mail icon blinking.

She made a face at it. Dar had done a very quick review of her initial findings last night and, with a grim look and a shake of her head, immediately sent the files off to Duk's auditors.

Not good.

Though, watching Dar browse Allison's data files in the nude certainly had lent a piquant note to the proceedings. Or maybe surreal was the word she was looking for. At any rate, her instincts had been confirmed by her lover's experience and now that bleeping blinking icon was probably Duks having a multiple coronary over the prelims.

But she didn't want to check it. She didn't want to move one inch from where she was, or tear her ear away from the soothing sound of Dar's heartbeat, slow and steady under her.

Dear Lord, I've missed this. She hadn't really acknowledged just how much until now, after becoming used to it for the several months of their intimate relationship. She wondered if Dar felt the same way.

The laptop chimed again, this time causing Dar to stir, and Kerry looked up to see her lover open one clear blue eye to stare at the PC in irritation. "Probably from our notes."

"Grumph." Dar sighed, then rolled over and wrapped Kerry up in her arms. "To hell with them. I want a longer night."

Mmm. Guess she did feel the same way. Kerry smiled. "Me too."

The phone rang, and they both groaned, then Kerry reached over and pulled it from the cradle. "Hello?"

"Morning, Kerry."

"Hey, Mark." Kerry stifled a yawn. "What're you doing up this early?"

"The usual. Can I talk to the boss, please?"

Kerry snorted. "Excuse me? You call me at *my* hotel room in Vermont, when Dar is supposed to be in Houston, and you expect her to be here?"

"Yup."

She covered the receiver. "How does he do that?"

Dar just held out a hand. "Don't ask. You'll be a happier person for it." She took the phone and cradled it between her ear and shoulder. "Yeah?"

"Good morning, Boss."

Dar considered that. "Yeah, it is. Thanks." She gave Kerry a squeeze and smiled.

There was a momentary silence, then Mark cleared his throat. "Ah, right. Anyway. Listen, those circuit diagrams of yours finally came in over the CAD server."

"Mmm, 'bout time."

"Yeah, and the Cisco rep is busting my ass to try and convince you to upgrade the regional hubs to 7000's."

"Now?"

"Uh huh. He's one of those granola and sunshine nerds. Gets up at dawn and goes to commune with the squirrels or something."

"Good for him." Dar rested her forearm over her eyes. "All right. Have the print shop mount those diagrams on foam and get them up in my office...and tell Mr. Granola I'll think about it."

"Cool." The sound of a keyboard came through the phone. "Oh yeah. María's looking for you."

"Put me through." Dar made a face and covered the mouthpiece. "I forgot to tell her I wasn't going to be in today." She waited through a moment of the company's incredibly annoying hold music, then heard María's voice. "Morning, María."

"Ay. Dar. Where are you?" The secretary sounded worried.

"Vermont."

"Ah, good." María came right back. "This is good. Very good. Is Kerrisita there?"

Dar eyed the disheveled blond head resting on her stomach. "Yes, in fact, she is." Kerry looked up in question. "What's up?"

"Is a policeman here. He has some papers. He says she must sign for them," María responded.

"Police?" Blue and green eyes met. "A regular policeman?"

"No, no. In the plain clothing."

Dar muffled the receiver. "You're being served papers."

"Shit." Kerry mouthed, tightening her lips. "Only one thing that could be."

"María, is he a federal policeman?"

"*Sí.*"

"Ah. Okay. It's all right. Have Penny notarize your signature on them and take 'em from him." Dar sighed.

"Is not trouble?" María's voice lowered. "I could tell him she went to Cuba. He will not be back then."

Dar chuckled wanly. "No. It's...more complicated than that, María. Kerry's not in trouble, but they need to ask her some questions. She's got to testify. That kind of thing."

"Ay. Is for her *familia*?"

"Yes."

"I will take them, Dar. You will be gone all day, no?" María now sounded briskly businesslike. "I have canceled your two meetings and Mr. Draefus is pacing in little circles here waiting to talk to you."

Kerry felt a weight settle on her, as she considered the newest developments. Not that she hadn't been expecting the summons. She had. But she'd hoped the matter would take the usual government forever.

Guess not. She wondered briefly what the investigators would get into, remembering the last few she'd seen on CNN. Fortunately she'd been on her own for the last several years, without her father's support. That, at least, they couldn't dispute.

College. Well, they'd all gone, though she'd taken at least a three quarter scholastic scholarship the whole four years. Michael, though... Kerry winced. Angie had, at least, been only the Bachelors degree.

Well, she could honestly go in there and say she'd never had any idea her father was involved in the illegal acts—legally she was in the clear, and she actually couldn't give any evidence against him, as a matter of fact.

Should be a short ordeal.

Might even be a little...satisfying?...to see her father squirm.

"Okay, Dukky. Lemme know what they find. I figure they won't get anything before I've got to get out of here tonight." Dar sighed. "We'll keep them in a holding pattern. But tell Mari to push on those security checks." She paused. "Right." She pause again and looked down. "I'll tell her. Thanks. Bye."

Dar hung up the phone and exhaled. "Ho boy."

Kerry traced a bare rib. "Had to come sooner or later," she remarked. "I can't tell them much. It won't take long. Did María say when it was for?"

"Three weeks from now," Dar replied. "Duks pulled the auditing team off T and T and reassigned them to us. He says it's gonna take time to figure everything out, though." She considered. "And, it may be that some of those numbers just cross check strangely. Though I doubt it." She tapped her nose. "Something stinks."

Both blond brows shot up. "I should be insulted."

"Not here." Dar slid her hands under Kerry's arms and pulled her up until they were chin to chin. "Do you have a local lawyer to go up there with you?"

"No. Do I need one? I'm not being investigated, Dar."

"Tch. Someone as politically savvy as you saying that, Ker? You know how out of hand those things get."

"Mmm." She sighed. "I'll see what I can do."

Dar rubbed noses with her. "Okay. I guess a shower is in order. And let's see how we can play your friends at Allison." She tilted her head. "I could just go in there and kick them around a little."

Kerry thought about that, then smiled. "Nah. I've got a better idea."

❖ ⌘ ❖ ⌘ ❖ ⌘ ❖

Kerry dusted the sleeve on her silk shirt off and twitched her gray linen jacket straight before she entered the conference room, aware of the tall, silent figure that followed her. She motioned to a chair then proceeded across the room and circled it, giving the other occupants a brief smile as she did so. "Good morning."

Eyes had flicked to the casually dressed woman sprawled in the chair near the door, but now they focused back on her. The attitude was wary, but lacked the nervousness of the day before, and even held a hint of complacence.

"All right. Thank you for getting me those reports. I've reviewed them and referred the findings to our main office. Our personnel department is processing the security checks, so things are in a holding pattern until those two items are completed."

Kerry paused. "However, since the interconnectivity takes a while, we're going to get started with that. We borrowed one of our local field technicians and asked her to come in to give your IS people a hand in the network migration. I'd like to get that started as soon as possible." She stared pensively down at her briefcase, trying to ignore the mischievous face Dar was making at her. "I'm sure...um...Bunny here will get you up and rolling in short order."

Paybacks. Kerry peeked up at her lover, who was giving her one of those "I'm gonna get you later" looks. She returned it with a charming smile. "Right, Bun?"

"Aaabsolutely," Dar drawled, adding a hint of the South to her voice.

Sam swiveled in his chair, then tapped his teeth with a pencil. "Sue, can you get someone up here to show our guest the server farm? I'm sure she wants to get started." He looked pleased. "In the meantime, I thought maybe you'd like to sit in on a client briefing, Ms. Stuart. Since you're here, and all. Perhaps you'd like to see our methods firsthand."

Kerry let him wait for a few seconds, while she considered the request. "All right. I'd like that."

They all stood, and Sue brushed herself off, then walked over to Dar. "Come with me, please?" Her voice was pleasant, but held a note of condescension.

"Sure." Dar unfolded her length from the bucket shaped chair and stood, towering over the smaller woman. She was dressed in her jeans and short sleeved shirt, the rolled sleeves exposing her toned arms, and had pulled her dark hair back into a tail at the base of her neck. "Lead on." Her eyes flicked to Kerry's face, then followed Sue out, pulling the door shut behind her.

"Funny," Sam drawled. "I thought you people liked to present a much sharper image."

Kerry bit the inside of her lip to keep the retort from emerging, then cleared her throat. "Well, it's Bunny's day off. She's doing us a favor."

The accountant shook his head. "I hope she knows what she's doing. We can't afford down time today."

"Oh," the blond woman scratched her nose, "don't worry. She does."

Chapter
5

Dar followed her officious guide down a long, gray carpeted hallway, passing offices on either side full of paper covered desks. Eyes looked up as they passed, then dropped, and Dar sensed a feeling of reticence that made her spine prickle.

"Nice office," she commented.

Sue glanced at her. "Thank you." She led the way into a larger room, full of cables and other telecommunication gear. "Roger?"

A tall, lanky man in a painfully white shirt and blue pants ducked his head from under a rack. "Yes? Oh." He straightened up and ran his fingers through bushy brown hair, blinking out from behind a pair of very thick glasses. "Can I help you?"

"The new company sent a technician over to start getting us hooked up to them." Sue waved Dar forward. "All yours." She turned and walked out, leaving them regarding each other.

"Hi," Dar finally said. "So you're Roger, huh?"

He seemed to realize he was staring. "Ah...um...yeah. Hi. Roger Milken. Yeah. And um...there're a couple of others around here. Bill, and Tom and Squeeziks."

One of Dar's eyebrows lifted. "All right."

He scratched his neck under an ill-fitting collar. "Did you want to see something or...um...what's your name, anyway?"

Dar held out a hand, deciding on her middle name rather than the label Kerry had pinned on her. "Katherine." She released him. "I'd like to see your setup. W...they've got certain things they like to see before they let you connect."

"Mmph. Okay." Roger waved at her. "C'mon. I'll give you the five cent tour. Watch your step. We're redoing the patch panel."

Dar strolled along behind him, her eyes taking in the room's equipment and evaluating it as he rambled on about the hardware. An NT server farm, a chugging AS400, and a bank of routers on one side of the room, with the rack of Ethernet hubs mounted next to them. "Nice."

"Uh. Thanks. Yeah, this is the main box." He indicated the AS400. "We keep all the database stuff in there. And that's our webserver and we just got these two new Cisco 7000's..."

"Mmm." Dar stopped in front of the routers and leaned on the console that programmed them. She idly signed into one and browsed its statistics. "Send a lot of traffic out?"

"Uh, yeah. They do lots of searches. That kinda thing." Roger now sounded just a touch evasive. "You know."

"Mmm." Dar pointed. "What about those?"

"Oh, that's the SQL servers. I wrote 'em." Roger walked over and signed into one. "See? It runs concurrent copies. Saves all the stuff to the RAID arrays. They go bonkers about downtime."

Dar signed out of the router and patted it. "Firewall?"

"You bet." Roger went to the next machine. "All our access in and out is logged. Make sure no one's downloading nudie pics." He laughed lamely. "So. What is it you want so we can get hooked up?"

Dar sat down on a chair. "Got a pad?" She started listing off requirements as he scrambled for a pen.

❖ ⌘ ❖ ⌘ ❖ ⌘ ❖

Kerry caught up with the fair haired, heavyset woman as they took a break, and wandered into the coffee room. The clients had been quiet, almost passive, and she'd been curious about the attitude which seemed more cowed then anything else.

"Hi."

The woman glanced at her. "Oh, hello. I'm sorry, I didn't catch your name in there."

"Kerry." They shook hands. "I'm with ILS."

The faded hazel eyes darted around the almost empty room, then settled back on Kerry's face. "Oh."

"We...um...we bought Allison Consulting. You knew that, right?"

"Oh, yes. Yes, I did. Um...excuse me. I've just got to use the rest room." The woman edged around Kerry's slim form.

"Me too," Kerry agreed pleasantly. "C'mon. It's this way." She guided the way to the bathroom and held the door open politely. "That's a nice dress."

The woman looked a little startled. "Um, why, thank you." She walked to the sink, turned the water on, and washed her hands quietly.

Kerry waited, leaning against the door with both hands behind her.

"So, are you here just to watch?"

"Something like that. To observe. To get reports. Start putting things together, that kind of thing," Kerry replied. "Find out what they do right. What they do wrong." She watched the broad shoulders twitch. "Why they're successful."

The woman slowly straightened, wiping her hands on a paper towel. "Is that why your company bought them? Because they were successful?"

"Mmhm," Kerry agreed. "There's always a lot of questions to ask, though. We want to make sure we give their clients the service they contracted for."

Hazel eyes turned and regarded her with an emotion startlingly like wan hatred. Kerry's nape hairs prickled and she wondered what nerve she'd struck.

"And he promised it wouldn't go any further," the woman hissed, advancing on Kerry. "Now all of you know? That bastard..."

"Hold on." Kerry lifted a hand. "I'm not sure—"

"Get out of my way, you little..." The woman grabbed Kerry's arm and shoved hard, throwing her against the door. "If it's over, it's over. He's going to get what I owe him."

"Wait!" Kerry caught her balance, confused and startled. "Ms. Andrews. Please. Hold on a minute. I think there's some mistake." She took hold of the hand that reached for her again and held it, tensing muscles strengthened by months of activity. "Please don't do that again."

The woman tried to wrench her hand free, but found it held very securely. "Let me go, you bitch."

"Ms. Andrews, I am not your enemy," Kerry told her forcefully. "Now calm down, please." She kept her voice low. "Just take it easy."

They stared at each other in silence.

"Okay. Now, listen. We know something's going on here. We just don't know what it is yet."

"We?"

"My boss and I, yes," Kerry replied. "So, if you tell me what happened, maybe I can help." She released the woman's arm and straightened, just as the door opened and Ann breezed in.

"Well, well. Is this a party?" the petite executive inquired, with a smile. "Getting an early start, aren't you, Ms. Stuart?"

"I'm not one for parties." Kerry opened the door and waited for Ms. Andrews to escape out in front of her. "Excuse me."

"Funny." Ann chuckled. "That's not what I heard."

Kerry watched her enter a stall and close the door, and she backed out, pausing in the hallway to consider the words.

Wondering what they'd meant.

Suspecting it was nothing good.

❖ ⌘ ❖ ⌘ ❖ ⌘ ❖

"So." Sam leaned back in his chair. "What did you think?"

Kerry stood near his office window, gazing out. Now, she turned and leaned against the wall. "They seem very quiet."

He chuckled. "Yeah, they're nice enough folks, but not very lively."

"I was a little surprised they didn't question some of the outline, though." Kerry watched him carefully.

"Really? Why?"

She folded her arms. "Because most of it was bullshit." The words were spoken matter-of-fact. "You can't deliver the services you sold them and they're being left without any back up whatsoever."

"Now, you look—" Sam's face darkened.

"So either those clients were completely ignorant, or they were being quiet for a reason." Kerry crossed her ankles. "I think you'd better level with me, Mr. Gershwin."

Hostility bristled across the desk at her. "I don't know what you're talking about."

Kerry shrugged. "You can say that. But I need to tell you we're going to eventually find out what's going on and what it was that woman was so afraid would get out."

Sam Gershwin went very still, as he studied her in silence. "You sure you want to do that, Ms. Stuart?" he finally asked. "If I were you, I'd just leave things alone. You'll be a happier person for it, I promise you."

Kerry chewed the inside of her lip, wondering how far she should push. "I'm not sure what you mean by that."

He steepled his fingers. "Aren't you? Perception is such a fluid thing, Ms. Stuart. I'm sure your company has a perception of you as a fine, upstanding woman, a credit to their reputation, don't they?"

A chill ran up Kerry's spine. "Is that a relevant question?"

"Well," he stood up and strolled towards her, "it's your job to use your judgment, isn't it? To find a way to, oh, bring us in the fold, so to speak. They must think highly of your decision making skills, don't they?"

"Yes, they do."

Sam stopped and leaned against the wall next to her, his taller form throwing a shadow over her body. "Would it take much to change that? Say...what if they found out their fine, upstanding operations director...oh, got drunk and had to be carried out of a bar? Hmm?"

Kerry's eyebrow lifted. "The subject's not likely to come up, so I have no idea how they'd react."

"Really?" Sam smiled. "Well, I've got ten people who'll swear that's exactly what happened last night, little Ms. Kerry."

The reaction wasn't what he expected. Kerry burst into laughter.

"You're not seriously threatening me with that, are you?"

He was a little disconcerted, but retained his slightly mocking attitude. "Is it so farfetched? You're a pretty little thing and I bet you know how to have fun, don't you?" Then he picked up a folder on his desk and flipped it open. "And they say a picture's worth a thousand words."

Kerry glanced at the folder, then blinked, startled to see an image of herself, very obviously out of control in an unfamiliar setting. "Nice piece of editing," she finally stated, her voice taking on a harder edge. "What's your point?"

"Ah." He smiled. "Now we're getting somewhere. Tell you what. It's really easy, and no skin off your nose, Ms. Kerry. You just put in a nice report on us and go on your merry way, and we'll just never have had this conversation."

"And if I don't?" Kerry asked.

"Then I've got no choice but to contact your boss and put in a formal protest. I can't have my company being evaluated by someone who shows such...lapsed judgement." He lifted the picture. "What would your boss say about that, hmm?"

Kerry rubbed her jaw. "I don't know. I guess you'll have to ask her," she told him, her chin lifting in challenge as she met his gaze. "But you're putting your eggs in a flimsy basket, Mr. Gershwin."

"Am I?"

"You're assuming I was alone last night." Kerry smiled.

He laughed in delight. "Oh, that's even better. You're going to pull out some flannel shirted bum you found in a bar to defend you?" He snapped the folder shut. "If that's the way you want to play it, fine." He looked up as the door opened and a tall, dark haired form slipped in. "Excuse me, but this is a private meeting."

Dar continued across the room, with every step shedding her casual persona and taking on the dynamic fierceness that was part and parcel of who she was. "Meeting's over," she enunciated sharply. "You've got six minutes to pick up your personal effects and be out of the building."

"What?" Gershwin stared at her. "Have you lost your mind? Get the hell out of my office before I call security. Who in the hell do you think you are?"

Dar pointed a thumb at her own chest. "Me? I'm Dar Roberts." She paused for delicious moment. "And you're unemployed. Now get out." She got between the comptroller and his desk. "My people have all your accounting records and the client files and by the time they finish sifting it for chargeable offenses, you're going to be more than out of a job."

He was in shock. "You're Dar Roberts?"

Dar pulled her wallet from her back pocket, fished her Florida driver's license out, and showed it to him. "Three minutes." She poked a finger at him. "Out."

"You're out of your mind. You can't just walk in here and fire me," Gershwin rasped. "I'll slap a lawsuit on you so fast..."

Kerry picked up the folder on the desk. "Hmm, yeah. This'll make an interesting exhibit when I testify." She showed the picture to Dar. "This is where I was last night."

Dar took one look at the picture, then at Sam, putting two and two together and going from irritated rumpled executive to borderline murderous lover in the blink of an eye. "You stinking son of a..." She stepped forward and curled her hands in his lapels as she shoved him against the wall.

"Get your hands off me you..."

"Dar." Kerry put a hand on her back, taking a nervous breath.

Dar stared into his eyes, her own ice cold. "Time's up. You're out of here right now, before I do something we're both going to regret." She released him and stepped back. "Now."

He straightened his lapels, then gave her a hateful look. "You'll hear from me. This isn't the end of this, you can be sure of that."

They watched him walk to the door and go through it, brushing by Charlie Efton on the way out. "Good bye, Charlie."

The thin, bespectacled man stared after him puzzled, then looked inside the office, clearly at sea. "Ah, did I miss something? What's going on?" His eyes went to Kerry and he was clearly surprised when whom he considered a common field tech answered.

"Get your people in the conference room in five minutes," Dar growled.

Charlie stared at her in bewilderment.

"Please," Kerry added, folding her arms, "let's get this over with."

He walked out shaking his head, closing the door and leaving them alone.

Dar opened the folder and stared at the picture in disgust. "Pig."

Kerry put out a hand and rubbed her back, feeling the warm tension under her fingers. "I thought it was sort of funny, Dar. I mean it's so obviously doctored. You think this is how they got those accounts?"

"Pig." Blue eyes narrowed intently as she studied the photo. "I should have kicked him in the nuts."

"Um, Dar." Kerry laughed a bit. "Take it easy, okay? Not that I don't appreciate the noble protection of my honor, but..." She massaged Dar's back. "What brought that on? What'd you find?"

Dar sat down on the desk, rubbing her temples and sighing. "Sorry. I um...he just hit me the wrong way, I guess. I was able to get Mark in to their system and he did a complete dump for me, then started parsing records and he found this dumb bastard's damn online Filofax."

Kerry's jaw sagged. "You're telling me he put illegal stuff he was doing in his computer?"

"No. Worse. He put it up on a network server, with multiple back-ups."

"Oh, my god." Kerry covered her eyes. "That's worse than the illegal sales to China we found in that export company last month. At least they only kept those records on their Powership PC."

Dar exhaled, as her body relaxed after its unexpected call to arms. She'd been finishing up her inspection and the initial stages of conversion in the operations center when she'd gotten a cell phone call from Mark.

That had led to a guarded conference outside the office door, confirming Dar's vague suspicions and marking the largest target of wrongdoing. She was sure that was what caused the sudden knot to form in her guts and sent her to Sam's office, knowing she had to get him out of the building before he had a chance to cover any tracks.

That was what had caused it, right? The fact that the son of a bitch had been in here, threatening Kerry was just a coincidence.

Right?

"You all right?" Kerry's voice held a note of concern.

Dar looked up, and allowed herself a very brief moment of drowning in those sea green eyes. "Yeah. This is going to be ugly, Ker. I don't know who knows what right now. I think it would be better to call in a team and lock the management out of here until we get some answers."

"All right." Kerry straightened. "That's what I'll tell them."

Dar tilted her dark head. "Why don't you let me do that?"

"Because this is my job." Kerry put a fingertip on her bosses well shaped nose. "That's why. You can come and watch, though."

Dar stood. "Let's get it done, then. You and I have a plane to catch and a place to go to."

"Yeah. Home." Kerry allowed a big smile to take over her face. "I can't wait."

A hand ruffled her hair affectionately. "Me either. C'mon."

They left the office and headed down the hall, aware of the tense silence surrounding them.

❖ ⌘ ❖ ⌘ ❖ ⌘ ❖

"They just fired him?" Ann hissed in disbelief. "Charlie, how could that happen? I thought he—"

"I don't know." The company president paced up and down nervously. "He just walked out. Told Carol he'd been fired. I have no idea what's going on."

"Shit." Ann played with her pencil. "Maybe that plan of his backfired. I told him not to mess with that Stuart woman. She's a lot more than a fluffy blond cheerleader."

The short, dark haired assistant comptroller cleared his throat. "Um.

She's Roger Stuart's daughter. You knew that, right?"

They all looked at him. "Oh shit." Charlie covered his eyes. "That stupid bastard Sam. How could he miss something like that?"

"Oh, well, I figured when you saw who was with her—" the man started to answer, but the door opening silenced him.

Kerry strode in and motioned for Dar to take a seat in the back of the room, which her boss did, folding a leg under her and leaning on the arm of the chair.

"Thank you." Kerry circled the table and went to its head, stood behind the chair, and let her hands rest on it. "This is going to be a very short meeting."

"Look," Charlie interjected. "Would you mind telling us what's going on? What happened to Sam? What are you people doing?"

Kerry took a breath. Now that it had come down to it and she was looking these people in the eye, she found it hard to say the words. Not that she felt sorry for them. No, she didn't. They weren't nice people and she had a feeling the deeper they dug into the company, the worse they'd find. But they were people, and she was a person, and she held their fate in her hands for this one, timeless moment.

It was a very odd feeling and it sort of reminded her, just a little, of how she'd felt when she'd sent the damning information about her father to the press.

Sad. And relieved.

A little scared.

"The review of your systems has turned up a number of extensive irregularities," Kerry stated quietly. "Our auditing department is review-ing them. Until they complete their review, I'd like all of you to leave the building and go home."

They stared at her in utter shock.

"Are you firing us?" Ann blurted.

Kerry had a sudden flashback to a phone call and a sinking feeling. "I'm asking you to go home and wait until we contact you," she replied. "Your pay and benefits will continue until our management makes a final determination."

"You can't just—" Charlie objected angrily.

"I can," Kerry's inflexibly precise tones corrected him. "Now, please. Just go home and don't make this harder than it has to be." Kerry took a breath. "An operations team will be here Monday morning to take over."

There was a stunned silence.

"Son of a bitch." Ann got up and threw her papers down. "I'm call-ing my lawyer." She pointed at Kerry. "I don't know who you people think you are, but you've pissed off the wrong person here."

A soft scraping sound followed her words, then fabric shifting, and soft footsteps as Dar circled the table and came around to Kerry's side.

"In fact, I don't think you have the authority to do what you just did. I want to talk to your boss, right now!" Ann slammed her hand down on the desk.

Kerry tilted her head in faint amusement, then half turned and lifted her eyebrows. "Okay. Dar, she wants to talk to you."

"Oh really," the tall executive drawled, turning her eyes on the now silent woman. "I don't think you have anything more to say." Dar spoke into deafening silence. "Ladies and gentlemen, you got caught. Now go home and hope all you get is fired."

"You...are Dar Roberts?" Ann's voice held a strange hint of amusement.

Dar merely looked at her.

"Interesting." The woman picked up her folder and walked out. "Let's go, boys. I guess we know when we're beaten."

Dar and Kerry watched them file out and the door close behind them.

"That was really weird."

"Gotta agree." Dar shook her head. "What a mess. I locked their accounts out on their domain controller and forced a reset on everyone else's passwords."

"Mmm. You pull everyone except for you out of the domain admin group?"

"Uh huh."

"That'll do it then. I guess we'd better get out of here. It's almost five o'clock anyway, so I think we can just send everyone home and let the ops team take over on Monday." Kerry sighed. "This feels really strange, Dar. Like there's something here I'm not seeing."

"Well, if you're not seeing it, I'm not either," the taller woman confessed. "Maybe Mark'll find something. C'mon. We've got a chance to get a snack before we've got to get on the plane."

"Yeah." Kerry shouldered her briefcase and followed her lover out the door, still thinking.

❖ ⌘ ❖ ⌘ ❖ ⌘ ❖

The smell of pancakes woke her up. Dar lifted an eyelid, and examined the room, it's cool, blue walls lit with tiny stripes of sunlight from the blinds. She stretched and regarded the ceiling with sleepy contentment, as subtle sounds from the kitchen indicated her missing bedmate's current location.

Mmm. Kerry's home. A smile spread across her face. *I missed her.* Dar yawned and stretched again, then rolled up out of the waterbed and went into the bathroom, threw a little water on her face and brushed her teeth. "Mmm." She chewed the toothpaste curiously, having picked

Kerry's up by mistake. "Grape. How did this woman find grape tooth-paste?"

"Dar?"

"Hmm?" Dar hastily swallowed and wiped her mouth off, then pad-ded out of the bathroom and found her blond haired lover leaning in the doorway to the bedroom. "Morning. You're up early."

"Not that much." Kerry tickled her navel with a finger. "Just long enough to get breakfast started. I wanted to make sure you got something other than coffee and Frosted Flakes before you went out to win trophies."

"Speaks the woman who uses grape toothpaste," Dar responded dryly, as Kerry blushed and laughed. "Gotcha."

"Weeell. It was all they had in the airport, Dar. It was that, or that baking powder stuff, and you know I hate how gritty that is." Kerry pulled Dar's baseball shirt off the back of the loveseat and handed it to her. "It's a gorgeous day out."

"Oh yeah?" Dar slipped the garment on then curled her arms around the smaller woman, pulling her into a hug. "It's pretty nice in here, too." She released Kerry and followed her into the kitchen, where Chino was patiently waiting. "Oh, I get it. There must be food somewhere."

"Gruff."

"Mmm. Certainly was spotless in here." Kerry poked her friend with the end of her spatula. "Did you even make coffee while I was gone?"

Dar looked suitably penitent. "Um...I was out late most nights at the gym," she offered. "Just picked up something on the way home."

Kerry eyed her. "Chicken wings?"

Dar gave a faint hint of a grin. "Among other things."

"Dar." Kerry turned back to her pancakes and flipped one expertly. "I was worried about you. Though that's kind of silly, I guess. You're a grown person, who can certainly take care of herself."

Dar slid her arms around her and rested her cheek against Kerry's hair. "Yes, I can do that," she murmured. "But I'm glad I don't have to." She nipped an ear. "I'm glad you're back."

"Mmm." Kerry smiled. "Even though I make you eat vegetables?" She felt Dar's head nod against hers and she leaned back. "So what do I do for two weeks? I pig out on tacos and shrimp toasts."

Dar chuckled. "Hotel food is kinda limited."

"Don't make excuses for me. The limited menus included salads," Kerry retorted, flipping another pancake and then turning the bacon in the next pan. "You've corrupted me, Dardar."

The chuckle turned into a full laugh, rumbling down Dar's chest and making a pleasant vibration against Kerry's back.

The phone rang, and Dar released her, then wandered over to the por-table phone and lifted it up. "Hello?"

Kerry almost felt the change, and she turned her head to see a dark, still expression on her lover's face. She quickly shifted the pans off the stove, walked over, and put a hand on Dar's belly. "Hey?" she mouthed.

Dar tucked a hand behind Kerry's neck and pulled her close. "All right." She spoke quietly into the phone. "Next Friday. I'll be there." A pause. "Goodbye." She set the phone down with deliberate precision and exhaled.

"Who on earth was that?" Kerry whispered. "From your face, I thought it was my father."

"Worse," Dar answered, with a sigh. "It was my mother."

Kerry looked up at her. "Whoa. That was unexpected."

"Yeah." The blue eyes focused on something Kerry wasn't sure she wanted to be able to see.

Chapter
6

Kerry finished packing a small towel in the gym bag Dar habitually carried, then zipped the bag closed and walked to the double doors, regarding the tall, silent figure leaning against the railing.

Dar was upset and shocked. Kerry could tell. Hearing from her mother was difficult, but finding out it was due to the passing of her grandmother was even worse. After not hearing from that side of her family for such a long time, getting news like that was tough and knowing she'd have to go and face being with those people next week was eating at her.

Kerry pushed the door open and walked outside into the warm sea breeze. "You ready, champ?"

Dar turned her head and adjusted her sunglasses, pulling them down a little to regard Kerry's face. "I think my focus is off," she told her regretfully. "I wasn't expecting that. Even though I haven't seen Gran in..." Dar thought a moment. "Damn. Has it been ten years?" She exhaled. "She was a...a very tough woman."

"Mmm." Kerry put an arm around her. "I'm sorry, Dar. I don't remember my grandparents. They died when I was very young." She considered that. "I wish I had. My uncles tell some really great stories about them."

Dar leaned against her. "I never knew my father's parents. When he and my mother got married, they disowned him, sort of. The only one who spoke to him at all was Aunt May." She exhaled. "Then there was Gran and Grandpa. He and my father argued all the time, but I think they liked each other. He died in a car accident, and Gran wasn't the same after that."

Kerry pursed her lips, then forged on. "Dar. You know, um, maybe your mother...maybe she's using this as a sort of excuse to get back in touch with you."

Her lover went quite still for a few heartbeats, then straightened and pushed her sunglasses back. "I think it's too late for that," she answered briskly. "C'mon. I got myself into this contest. Let's go watch me make a fool of myself."

Kerry took the hint and dropped the subject. "I bet you don't." She followed Dar inside. "Remember, you promised me a trophy."

"Aw, Kerry."

"You promised."

❖ ⌘ ❖ ⌘ ❖ ⌘ ❖

I promised. Dar leaned against her locker, surprised at just how nervous she was. *What in the hell was I thinking? I'll be lucky to last the first damn round.* She scrubbed her face with both hands, then dropped them, shaking her arms to loosen the tight muscles brought on by the sudden stress.

Okay.

Dar closed her eyes, took a deep breath and let it out slowly as she forced calm on herself. Too many outside distractions were hitting her, and she knew if she didn't just push them out of the way, she wasn't going to be able to go out there, or worse, she would and get hurt because she lost focus.

So, okay. Forget about your mother. Forget about the asshole board member. Forget about Kerry's testifying.

Forget about Gran.

Damn. Dar's eyes opened and she gazed at the wooden surface. *Wish I'd said goodbye to her.*

"You need to find a nice boy and settle down, honey." Gran's eyes had twinkled at her, as she stood uncomfortably in Gran's small house. "Come here and sit down and tell me what you've been up to."

Dar settled her long frame awkwardly on the frilly chair next to the old woman and tried to come up with something she'd find interesting to hear. Programming? Gran had a radio, and a TV she never turned on, preferring to use it as a shelf to hold a beautiful creeping ivy. School? Gran had been self schooled. Personal stuff? Dar had just figured out she preferred girls to boys, and doubted Gran would appreciate hearing that. "Same as usual, Gran. Just stuff."

"Oh, come on now. You telling me a nice looking young girl like you just sits around all day? What do you do with yourself, Paladar?"

"Um, work with my computer, do my gym stuff. You know," Dar answered. "I go to school, I go to work. Not much to tell, really."

Gran looked at her. "Do you have a boyfriend?"

"No." That, at least, she could answer.

Her grandmother leaned much closer and lowered her voice. "Do you have a girlfriend?" she whispered with a wink.

Dar almost swallowed her tongue. "Uhh...no." Her voice rose to almost a squeak. "I um..."

"Ha. Didn't think old grumps like me know what's what, eh?" Gran poked her in the knee. "Figured you out years ago. Had a best friend when I was a girl went the same way."

She turned brick red, and endured the old woman's chuckles until she finally cleared her throat and muttered something banal.

"What'd the folks say?" Gran asked conspiratorially.

"They don't know," Dar managed to answer. "Yet."

That made Gran laugh even more. "Figures. My daughter never could see the darn forest for the trees." She patted Dar on the arm. "Don't you worry, honey. I won't say anything. You just be careful now, here? Chicken fights can be a lot nastier than cock fights, let me tell you. They'll peck your eyes right out, and you've got really pretty ones."

Dar blushed again. "Thanks, Gran," she muttered.

"Here. Stop putting your head down." Gran picked her chin up and looked at her. "You got nothing to be ashamed of, Paladar, so you keep those baby blues up just like that." She paused. "Oh. You're going to break some hearts, you are."

Dar managed a smile. "Think so?"

A wrinkled hand patted her cheek. "Keep smiling like that and I guarantee it."

Dar found herself smiling again in reflex memory and she wished briefly that her mother hadn't gone to live with Gran. That, more than anything, had kept her from calling and certainly from visiting.

And that hadn't really been fair to either of them.

"Hey, Dar?"

She turned to find Kerry slipping through the locker room door. "Sorry. I was just loosening up."

Kerry came over and slid up against her with a barely held back smile. "Your dad's here."

"Urk." Dar's nostrils flared. "Like I needed more pressure."

"Tch." The blond woman gave her a much needed hug. "He's lurking back under the seats. I got him some pop and a candy bar."

"I think I need a candy bar or maybe some ice cream."

Green eyes twinkled. "Trade you a trophy for a cone, how about that?"

Dar turned, and put her hands on Kerry's shoulders, her face taking on a serious expression. "Listen—"

Fingertips touched her lips. "No. I was just kidding. I don't care if

you win anything at all, Dar. Just have fun and don't worry about it." She
pulled Dar's head down and kissed her. "Okay?"

"Just have fun?"

"Yes."

"Okay." Dar returned the kiss and let some of the tension roll off her.
"I think I can manage that." Her nerves settled and she considered the
contest. Without question, there'd be some fighters she could beat, and
equally, some she couldn't. That was all right. She'd just do the best she
could, that was all.

"C'mon." She put an arm around Kerry's shoulders and guided her
out of the locker room, into the main area of the gym. A wide open space
had been cleared, covered with mats, and some rows of chairs added
around it with platforms after a few rows to raise the seats up into viewing
areas.

People dressed like her were all around, warming up and chatting in
small groups, or standing alone in fierce concentration. They ranged in
age from teens to middle-aged men and women, and Dar felt a little more
comfortable, realizing she wouldn't be the oldest person in the room by
any means.

Her eyes flicked around and into corners and found a dark one, with
a shadowy form in it. She kept her gaze pinned there, and smiled, holding
it until she saw a flash of motion and a hand wave. She waved back.

"This is sort of fun," Kerry remarked. "Hey. Did you know they have
a novice class tournament too? You think maybe I could take a shot next
time?"

Hmm. Dar mulled that over. *Good question.* "I don't know. I think
you're too nice," she confessed. "You're not supposed to apologize every
time you hit someone."

Kerry grinned ruefully. "Hitting people doesn't quite come naturally
to me, I guess. But I've been getting better. I didn't scream the last time I
flipped you."

Dar rubbed her tailbone in memory. "You grunted. A definite
improvement."

They walked to the warm up area and Dar released her lover as she
joined the group of combatants already working there. "Wish me luck."

Kerry smiled and tugged her belt. "You won't need it." She backed
off. "I'm going to go sit down over there." She pointed at the bleachers.

Dar lifted a hand and watched her go, then turned her attention to the
task at hand. After about twenty minutes of light warm up, a man walked
to the center of the mats and lifted a bullhorn.

"All right ladies and gents. Let's get rrrrroollling."

The exercises paused as all eyes turned towards him.

"We'll do this the easy way. Double elimination, one ring for the
pros, one ring for the kiddies, the judges picked the matches out of a hat.

See the nice lady with the pink shirt to get your slots and stay the heck out of the way until it's your turn. Everybody got it?"

A chorus of yells.

"Good! Let's kick some ass."

Kerry found a nice bench and sat down, resting her elbows on her knees. This was definitely different. The closest she'd ever come to this kind of atmosphere was during her high school bowling days.

"Hey there, kumquat." A low, growly voice made her jump, and she looked down between the bleachers to see Andrew Roberts perched under them, peering out between the seats with interest. "Looks like a damn bathrobe convention, don't it?"

"It's...unique," Kerry agreed, as she watched some of the younger contestants run at each other screaming.

Andrew grunted, his head moving back and forth inside his hood as he observed. "My kid looks damned good, you know that?"

Kerry obligingly turned to the tall, dark haired form running through a few basic warm-up drills while she waited. "Does she? I mean, well, yeah, I think she does anyway, but..."

"Yeap." Dar's father nodded. "Lookit that kick. I couldn't get that high when I was getting paid for it."

"She's very flexible," Kerry agreed.

"Huh." Andrew chuckled, deep in his throat. "You'd know."

Kerry stared at him in puzzlement, then blushed. "Oh, god." She was saved by the bell, literally, and she turned to watch the first set of matches.

She really hoped Dar did well.

After all, she had a bet on with Andrew about that trophy.

❖ ⌘ ❖ ⌘ ❖ ⌘ ❖

Dar's first match was the third one listed. She spent a moment wishing she were somewhere else just before she had to pad onto the mat and spent another moment hoping she didn't throw up before she got there.

It was really ludicrous, goddamn it, she was an internationally known corporate CIO, who ate company managers for lunch, and here she stood, worrying about upchucking in front of a boisterous Saturday afternoon crowd at the local gym.

Shit.

Dar glared at her opponent in pure annoyance, a man slightly her junior, with a sturdy, well knit body and intelligent eyes.

Which widened a little as they met hers. Dar could only wonder what her expression looked like, before the whistle blew and they circled each other. He dodged towards her and she blocked him, feeling the nervous energy make her reactions sharp and almost edgy. He tried again, and she evaded the kick, countering with one of her own that, with help from her longer legs, connected and turned him halfway around and almost dumped him.

Okay. Dar flexed her hands, and watched him, feeling her heartbeat settle a little. She tried a little feint of her own, then realized it was going to work and followed through, neatly sweeping her opponent off his feet and taking advantage of that.

One fall down.

Hmm. Dar watched him dust himself off and face her, seeing something in his eyes that sent a shot of adrenaline right through her.

Now, intimidation...that she recognized and her aggressive instincts flared as she swept in again, this time with more assurance, letting the watching crowd fade out as she dropped him a second time.

The whistle blew a minute later and she stepped back, clearing the mat for the next match, feeling a little surprised and a lot less nauseous. She snuck a look at Kerry and found a grin waiting for her, along with a little wink.

Maybe it wouldn't be so bad after all.

"She did okay, right?" Kerry whispered.

"Damn straight." Andrew had his chin almost resting on the step her feet were on. "Knocked that silly assed punk right on his keester. That's my girl."

Kerry muffled a chuckle. "You are so cute."

One blue eye edged around the corner of his hood and pierced her. "'Scuse me there, young lady. Watch yer mouth." He growled. "I am not having no little kumquats calling me stuff like that."

"Ah. I see where she gets that, too." Kerry grinned and turned her attention back to her lover, who was getting a drink of water from the blue neoprene thermos she habitually carried.

Dar's eyes were a little brighter now, she noticed, and she seemed looser and more relaxed. She was talking with Ken, who had finished his own bout just prior to hers, and watched the action.

Kerry wondered if she realized just how many people were actually watching *her*, instead of the matches. She kinda hoped she didn't. At least until it was over.

"Who you got next?" Ken craned his neck to peer at the small piece of paper Dar had. "Oh. Nice slate." He nodded. "They're all pretty decent fighters. I got lucky with mine. The first three of 'em are strictly hacks."

"Mmm." Dar tucked the paper away and took another sip of water. She watched the match in progress, and replayed her last one with a sense of mild satisfaction.

Her next match was an easy one, then the third was a little harder, her opponent a tough, determined woman with a permanent scowl and a feisty attitude that almost made Dar want to offer her a job. The woman used her smaller size to get inside Dar's defenses, but found out, a little too late, that it was a mistake to get caught by the taller woman's powerful grip.

Dar wiped the back of her neck with her towel, clearing the sweat a little, and glanced at the board, where a perky scorekeeper was moving names around. Hers was in one of the upper tiers, and she felt a sense of satisfaction at her accomplishment so far. Six matches and she'd won half. That was not too goddamned bad for someone who'd been out of competition for as long as she had and Dar knew she had every right to be completely happy if she lost every single one of her remaining three matches.

Her name was called for her fourth match. She put her thermos down and flexed her fingers as she re-entered the circle sketched on the mats. This time, her opponent was an older man, with the hard eyes and callused hands of an instructor, and her pulse picked up as her now warmed up body scented a challenge.

He eyed her coolly, intent on intimidating, and received a dazzling smile in return, which made him blink in surprise just before he was caught in a combination move that knocked him backwards almost onto his butt.

"Son of a bitch," he blurted.

Dar patted her chest. "Nope. Wrong gender and don't you be calling my daddy names like that." She roundhouse kicked him and sent him flying out side the circle with a thud as he hit the mat. He got back up and they circled each other, trading feints and jabs.

Weeks of pushing herself and weeks of sharpening rusting skills now came to bear as Dar loosened up and tried some more advanced moves, which she hadn't bothered with in her earlier matches. Her opponent countered one, then backed off a little, apparently realizing the skill level facing him was higher than he'd expected. He tried a counter, and Dar absolutely nailed him with a block and a throw over her shoulder that made his bones audibly rattle.

The whistle blew and she stepped back, noticing the crowd slowly gathering around the mat, as the other bouts ended. Her name moved up a tier, and with a sense of shock, she realized she was positioned to come in no worse than fourth in the competition.

That was great, wasn't it? Dar was now aware of the growing crowd, most of them watching the match that just started, between a tall, aggressive redhead and a smaller, blond haired man whose quick style and fluid motion Dar admired. She concentrated on it and was surprised when a voice invaded her close presence, calling her name. She turned. "Yes?"

It was the match coordinator, in all her pink glory. "I'm sorry...you're Roberts?"

"Yeah. What's wrong?" Dar turned and faced the blond woman. "Did

I step outside the circle or something?"

"Oh. No, no." Pinky shook her head. "No. The guy you were sup-
posed to fight next just sprained his ankle." She made a mark on the sheet.
"He forfeited, so you got that one. So you've only got the one match left."
She looked up. "Whoever wins this one. So don't wander off."

"Sure." Dar gave her a look. "I was going to see if there were any
good nature trails around, but I guess I'll hold off."

Pinky looked up at her. "Hah hah." She turned and left, as Dar
merely shook her head.

"What's up?" Ken came over, having finished his day. "Hey. Third.
Not too damn bad." He slapped Dar on the back. "John over there
knocked me on my butt in the fourth round. So I guess it's between you
and him. He's gonna beat Rusty."

Dar almost snorted her water as the words penetrated. "What?"

Ken stared at her. "You didn't realize? The guy who just conked out
was in second place. Whichever one of you wins the next one, gets the
trophy." He almost laughed at Dar's expression. "C'mon Dar. Don't look
like you've been hit by a flying fish, okay? You've been kicking everyone's ass all day long. You're the talk of the match."

❖ ⌘ ❖ ⌘ ❖ ⌘ ❖

"That last one thar's trouble," Andrew commented, sucking on a
straw poking out of his soda pop.

"Yeah?" Kerry had found herself getting excited, as the energy in the
room rose, and everyone gathered around the ring for what was turning
out to be the bout to decide the winner. "Well, Dar's doing pretty good
anyway, right?"

"Sure. Sure. Worst she'll be is second. But see...I know my kid."
Andrew rested his forearm on the bench. "She don't like being anything
but first."

"Wonder where she got that from?" Kerry smiled, but knew he was
telling the truth. "Do you think she can beat that guy?"

"Depends."

"On?" Kerry rested her elbows on her knees, her back aching from
the long afternoon sitting on the hard benches.

"How bad she wants to."

Kerry drummed her fingers on the bench for a moment, then stood
up, wincing a little before she carefully stepped down the mini bleachers
and made her way through the milling crowd of sweaty, cotton clad people to Dar.

Her lover turned as she came up and gave her a smile, stepped back
from the clump of people and ducked her head a little against the noise.
"Hey there."

"Hi." Kerry glanced at the board, then gave her a little pat on the back, a grin taking over her face.

Dar cleared her throat and shrugged, then laughed sheepishly. "Not too bad, huh? I didn't expect that."

"I did." Kerry sniffed, blinking innocently as she peered around. The last bout was over, and the tall redhead, the winner, was resting before the final match started. "Your father's been giving me pointers."

"On the fighting?"

Green eyes slid up her body and twinkled. "That too." She leaned closer. "You know something? He's really proud of you." Dar merely shrugged in response, but a coral blush colored her skin. "So am I, by the way. Maybe we could all go out afterward and celebrate, huh?"

Dar looked thoughtful for a moment. "Maybe...it depends."

"On what?" Kerry asked, just before they called Dar's name to come back up to the mat.

"What it is we're celebrating." A faint smile played around Dar's lips. "And right now, that guy's between me and sharing a sundae with my dad." Her head angled a little as she eased through the crowd, giving her a slightly more predatory look.

"He's toast." Kerry put her hands behind her back and rocked on her heels. "I'll get the marmalade."

❖ ⌘ ❖ ⌘ ❖ ⌘ ❖

The bout was mostly a blur. Dar stood on the edge of the mat after the bell rang and sucked air into her lungs, trying to catch her breath. She clearly remembered going into the match, but now that it was over, the details were fading rapidly.

Her body was covered in sweat, though, and she was feeling the beginnings of bruises that were going to make waking up the next morning a little less than comfortable. She was hot and sticky and wanted little more than a cold shower and a nice, large, dripping, oozing with caramel and chocolate with maybe, maybe a cherry on top sundae.

After all, she deserved it.

She'd won the goddamned meet and this last match had been a toughie, since John, the tall redhead, was the local I-am-the-great-American-hope-pseudo-sensai that every decent sized martial arts community seemed to spawn like unwanted weasels, who terrorized the lighter belts and had more testosterone than sense.

Well. Dar caught a movement out of the corner of her eye and turned, to see the organizer heading towards her with a completely obnoxious looking trophy that she realized she was going to have to accept and carry home.

"I think you should keep it on your desk." Kerry slipped in next to her and gave her a slap on the butt. "Dar, you rock."

"Ohhh. No, no, no, no. I think you should keep it on *your* desk," her boss corrected. "Since *you* wanted one."

"Hey. Congratulations." The match organizer reached out a hand. "Haven't seen you around before. But I hope I will again. You really stirred up some excitement around here." He was maybe in his mid twenties, had cute freckles, and almost orange hair, and sported a slim, muscular body. "I'm Shaun Ryan, by the way."

Dar returned the handshake. "Thanks. It was um...fun." She accepted the trophy with her other hand. "I used to compete around ten years back, I was just sort of getting back into it."

His eyes opened wider. "Yeah? Wow. Well, you're hot, let me tell you. It was a pleasure watching. You do sports for a living, or..."

He sidled a step closer and Dar realized she was being flirted with. "No. I'm in the computer business."

"Who isn't?" Richie laughed. "Hey, listen. You got any plans? A bunch of us," he gestured towards a group of the competitors, regular cronies apparently, "are going over to Chevys. You interested?"

"No thanks." Dar gave him a brief smile. "I've got a date. But thanks for asking."

"No problem. No problem." Richie held up both hands. "Maybe next time...and hey, congratulations again, okay?"

Dar watched him rejoin the group, and by the regretful shrugs and glances in her direction, gathered she was the topic of conversation. The man she'd beaten wasn't part of the group, she noticed then, as he walked off with four or five of the others, apparently their own little clique.

"A date?" Kerry elbowed her. "He liked you."

Dar gave her a look. "Here." She thrust the huge trophy at her lover. "I believe this is yours...and stop looking at me like that."

Kerry snickered. "Like what? I don't know what you're talking about, Dar." She gave the black belt tied around the taller woman a tug.

"Yeah, yeah." Dar sighed. "All right. Let me go shower and I'll be right out. You owe me ice cream, if I recall." Her eyes went to the stands, finding an inconspicuously hidden figure in one dark corner. "Did you ask..."

"He already said yes," Kerry murmured. "Go on. We'll wait for you over there."

Dar nodded and headed into the locker room, which was mostly empty. One or two women were just finishing up their changing, and the nearest looked up and gave Dar a little wave as she came in.

"Hey. Great job." The blond woman smiled, offering a hand as Dar passed. "I'm Sheila. And you're Dar, is it?"

"Yep. Thanks." Dar briefly clasped her hand and went to her locker, opened it, and removed her towel. "You did pretty well yourself. You a regular in this bunch?"

"Eh." Sheila waggled a hand. "When I'm into it. You know how it goes. I cycle through this, triathlon, blading...I'm in the chop socky phase right now."

Dar chuckled. "Yeah. I'm just getting back into it myself." She slung her towel over her shoulder and started towards the shower.

"Hey. That your girlfriend out there with you?" Sheila called out, unexpectedly.

Dar hesitated briefly, then nodded. "Yeah, why?"

Sheila gave her a double thumbs up. "She's a babe. Nice job." Then she walked out, whistling.

Dar chewed her lip thoughtfully, then resumed her trek. "Well, thanks. I think so," she commented to the minute fungus on the wall as she turned the cold water on, waiting a moment to achieve lukewarmdom before stepping into the shower's path. Cold showers really didn't have much meaning in Florida, naturally, where the water took on the temperature of the pipes, which by necessity were near or aboveground. But this felt refreshing, and she stood for a moment, just letting it run over her body before she scrubbed the sweat off.

When she was finished, she let the water run again, as she leaned back against the wall and allowed the reality of what she'd just done seep in.

Not too damn bad, Roberts. She grinned at her reflection, seen through the water's distortion. *Not too damn bad.* Especially that last one, where for a few minutes, she'd felt herself go all out and push past her normal caution, letting loose a wild energy that had both surprised and delighted her.

With a chuckle, Dar finally shut the water off and toweled her body mostly dry, wrapping the fabric around her as she padded back out to the locker, her sweat soaked gear hung over one arm.

Funny, she mused idly as she changed. *I though this place had emptied out. Guess there were a few stragglers left after all.* Certainly, the locker room's attendance had grown, as various women busied themselves earnestly about the place. *Whatever.*

Dar folded her gear neatly and tucked it inside the gym bag, then coiled up her belt and added that, as well, before running her fingers through her damp hair and shouldering the bag's strap. As she headed towards the entrance, she saw a familiar blond head poke in, and she cocked her head at the half amused, half outraged look on her lover's face. "What's up?"

"Are you done being the center of attention?"

"Huh?" Dar looked behind her in puzzlement. "What are you talking about? C'mon. Let's go. I hear that ice cream calling my name." She put a hand on Kerry's shoulder and steered her towards the exit, where her father waited, none to patiently.

"Oh. So...you didn't hear the blond with the crew cut come out here and yell for everyone to come look. That you were naked in the shower?" Kerry inquired archly. "Wow. Gotta check for—careful there, Dar. Don't trip."

"She didn't," Dar choked out indignantly.

Kerry pulled down her sunglasses and peered over them at her lover. "You're their new poster child, Dardar."

Dar groaned. "Just get me to some ice cream, please?" She covered her eyes and allowed Kerry to lead the way.

Chapter
7

They ended up raiding the local Publix and escaping back to the island when three possible ice cream parlors turned out to be packed with people or, in one case, a huge children's birthday party.

So now they were home, and Dar was sprawled comfortably on the couch with a huge bowl of ice cream resting on her stomach. Andrew had taken over the love seat with a similar dish, and Kerry was seated on the floor next to Dar, sucking contentedly on a root beer float.

Chino, of course, roamed hopefully from human to human, the tip of her black nose already white and sticky with ice cream. The large screen TV was on, but mostly silent, with scenes of ancient Asia playing across it.

"Mmm. This is a nice way to end a really disgusting week," Kerry commented around her straw.

"Yeah?" Andrew looked up. "What'cha get into, kumquat? More of that gibberish you two are a always talking about?"

"Not really." Dar sucked on her spoon as she remembered the phone call she'd gotten the previous day. "I heard from Mom."

There was an awkward silence and stillness before Andrew went back to his ice cream. "Didja now?"

"Yeah. Um...Gran passed on. She wanted me to come up for the service." Dar exhaled softly.

"You gonna go?" her father asked.

Dar considered the question. "I-I should."

"But you don't wanta."

"Not really, no," the dark haired woman answered honestly. "I haven't seen any of them in damn near ten years. I don't know."

"Mmph." Andrew slid a little lower in the cushions. "The old lady was always partial to you, Dardar." He messed around with the ice cream a minute. "And it's a...it's not a bad thing for you t'see your mother. I'd um...I'd like to know how she's doing."

Kerry tipped her head back and let it make contact with her lover's arm in mute comfort, feeling Dar's hand come to rest on her shoulder in silent response.

"All right. I'll go." Dar took a spoon of ice cream and mouthed it, able to convince herself easily that her father wanting her to do it was reason enough. "I was surprised she called."

Andrew put his bowl down on the table and leaned forward, resting his elbows on his knees. "Dardar, I'm sorry about that," he told her softly. "It's so damn hard on everybody."

Dar shrugged it off. "Old history. I am what I am. A chip off the old block, and that's never going to change."

A faint, pained smile crossed Andrew's scarred lips. "Squirt, that's some true, but there's more of your mamma in you that neither of you realize." He exhaled audibly and changed the subject, which was making them both very uncomfortable. "That all what made it a bad week?"

Kerry cleared her throat. "No. I was at an account that went pretty badly...and I finally got subpoenaed to testify about my father."

Andrew made a face, recaptured his bowl, and resumed his aborted attack on the melting treat. "Sorry to hear that, kumquat. That means you'll be mixing with your folks soon, eh?"

"Yeah. That'll be pleasant," Kerry agreed ruefully. "My sister says I'm a persona non grata in their house. I don't get mentioned." She paused. "They took all the pictures out of albums...that sort of thing." Dar's arm moved and surrounded her suddenly, in a very welcome hug. "Fortunately, Angie got a hold of most of my stuff there. She's shipping it down."

Andrew scowled. "I thought he didn't know you spilled the beans?"

"He doesn't," Dar interjected.

"So he's just doin' that because—"

"Of us," Kerry told him. "Yeah. You know, something? That's one of the things I like most about you—it was never an issue." She smiled at Andrew.

"Wall, I like t'think I'm as liberal as the next Southern Baptist career military type," he answered with a totally straight face. "Went out and got me a rainbow sticker to fit between my NRA poster and my pitcher of Stormin' Norman the other day."

They all laughed and the tension that had been building relaxed perceptibly. "Did you really?" Kerry suddenly asked.

"Damn straight. I walked right on in to that little place up in Lauderdale. Scared the bejezus out of them two little boys kissin' behind the counter and bought me a sticker and one of these." Andrew pulled something out of his pocket and tossed it over. "Got me a nice cuppa coffee, too."

Kerry handed Dar the tiny rainbow striped keychain. "You're so outside the box sometimes I never know what to expect from you, Dad."

"Do what I do, Kerry, and what you find out is, doesn't much matter what kinda packaging people got. They all bleed the same damn color," Andrew replied with quiet meaning. "Then you stop seeing people as this kind or that kind. Just they're either a friend or they're not."

"Yeah. Well, I wish that attitude was contagious." Dar sighed. "My other bad news was a new board member that's making more trouble than he's worth. Alastair's worried he's going to start digging in the wrong places."

"Again? Damn that company's a pain in mah butt," her father complained. "You should jest cut out and start your own company that does whatever the hell it is you do. Put them all the hell out of friggin' business."

They were all quiet for a moment, then Kerry turned her head and looked at Dar speculatively. "You know..."

"It's crossed my mind." Dar spoke at the same moment.

"Would backing be a problem? I'm sure we could—" Kerry spoke up eagerly.

"No." Dar munched on a spoonful of ice cream. "All those bonuses could finally be useful. Last time I counted, which was a while ago honestly, there was about twenty million dollars in those damn accounts."

She could feel the waves of utter shock beating against her. Dar glanced up right into Kerry's astonished green eyes. "Which you, by the way, are heir to. Just thought I'd mention that. I've got some guy at Smith Barney who's been investing and reinvesting everything I've gotten from them in fifteen years. He's pretty damn good, and thanks to Aunt May, I don't really spend much."

"Jesus," Kerry whispered. "Good Lord, Dar. I knew you said you had money stashed away but..."

"Wow," Andrew muttered, for once at a loss for words. "I never done expected to be related to no millionaire, that's fer damn sure."

Dar shrugged. "Anyway, maybe after I finish this network project we'll do some research on it. Would you come work for me?" she asked Kerry.

"That's not a serious question, is it?" The blond woman laughed in delight.

"What about you, Dad?"

"Hell yes," Andrew answered immediately. "I want to get me some of those hot shot corporate executive perks I keep hearing so much about. It ain't bad working for Uncle Sam, but let me tell ya, you don't get no leather chairs."

They all laughed, then Dar put her bowl down for Chino to finish off
and stretched, easing out strained muscles. She then relaxed into the
leather's soft, inviting surface as Kerry gave Andrew a humorous run
down on Allison Consulting.

Start her own company. Would she want the headaches? *What the
hell?* She had them now, didn't she? Cutting out on her own was...a little
scary. A little intimidating, because she was, she knew, much better at
organizing and designing things than selling them.

Well, okay. So she'd hire a furking salesman for that...and maybe
Mark would come work for her. *Yeah...maybe María...*

*Aw, c'mon Dar. That's been a daydream of yours for years. Who are
you kidding? You don't want to be responsible for the entire damn thing.*

Right?

Huh.

❖ ⌘ ❖ ⌘ ❖ ⌘ ❖

María put her cup down and sighed contentedly, enjoying the peace
and quiet of the early morning. It was Monday, and she knew it would
stop being peaceful very soon, but for right now, just after sunrise, she
could sit and listen to the lack of voices, and the phone not ringing, and
think clearly.

Having Dar gone for two days had thrown a wrench into quite a few
things, and María had set aside items her boss needed to go into immediately in a bright red folder set exactly in the center of Dar's almost painfully clean desktop. They'd all expected Dar back on Friday, but her
sudden detour had been stated as both dire and necessary by Lou Draefus,
whose status email on the Allison account had gotten more and more dras-
tic as the day went on.

So it was good that Dar had gone there.

Of course, María knew perfectly well that Allison Consulting had
nothing to do with why Dar was in Vermont, but that was all right as well.
Kerry had been starting to sound very stressed in the last few days of her
first long trip, and it was a good thing that Dar wanted to make sure the
visit was a success. Kerry had been doing a fantastic job in the last few
months, getting compliments from even the sour Eleanor, and a few, very
grudging, from José as she worked their problems with her own, gentler
style. But it paid to make sure of things, and that was reason enough for
Dar to have gone.

She would be glad to have them both back, though. Things were piling up, and she'd started sorting them in colors. Blue for Dar, green for
Kerry, with little red tabs on the items that were the most urgent. Truthfully, Kerry was at a level where she could easily justify having her own
admin, but María felt a little protective of her boss's partner and had

decided the extra work was well worth the peace of mind it gave her. At least until she could find someone Kerrisita could trust.

Who would understand and not judge.

Coincidentally, her eldest daughter, Mayte was just graduating junior college and looking for a nice, respectable job. María snapped a rubber band around a package of Dar's mail. Family was always the best to trust, no? She had spoken to Mariana already, and the personnel VP had promised to earmark the position for her, dryly thanking María for solving what could become the personnel nightmare of her life for her.

It was good, yes. Mayte was a smart girl, very good with the computers, and this would get her out of the house most of the day and away from her brother's friends, who had little to do and lots of trouble to get into. Also, María smiled, it would give her eldest daughter a chance to be exposed to a new kind of person, since Kerrisita was also very smart, very strong, and not afraid of saying what she thought. She would be a good influence on her.

Besides, did Mayte not think she, María, who had a lifetime of experience, knew that the Jon Secada concert she and a few of her friends were supposed to have gone to the other week was actually a Melissa Etheridge one? Foolish girl. If she thought that she was not sure of what she wanted, better she be exposed to people like Kerrisita, and her boss, Dar, then what she would find with her friends in not so nice places.

Not that she was hoping Mayte would choose the same. María was human enough to want a home and a family and a husband for all her daughters and she felt the family tradition was strong and very important. No. She was not hoping for that. But life, ay, life tended to give to you what it wanted and not what you did, so it was best to be prepared and do the best things you could for those you loved.

Ah. The elevator.

María heard the doors open, then two sets of footsteps approached, accompanied by familiar voices. She could hear Kerry's low laugh, and she smiled as the door opened and the two of them came into the office. "Good morning, Dar. Welcome back, Kerrisita."

"Morning María." Dar picked up her blue folder and leafed through it. "How was your weekend?"

"Very nice, thank you," María answered. "Kerrisita, is that a new outfit? It is very nice. How was your trip?"

"Ugh." Kerry collected her own folder. "I didn't have time to get anything cleaned. So I ended up at the mall yesterday." She plucked at the neat cotton shirt, which was tucked into pressed pleated pants. "I'm glad we went to business casual for the summer." She removed the long, legal sized envelope tucked into her folder. "This the papers?"

"*Sí.*" María gave her a sympathetic look. "Is not nice, but the policeman was very sweet, who brought them."

Kerry sighed and put the envelope back. "Other than the last few days, the trip was great. I don't know what we're going to do with Allison though. Did the security team make it out there?"

"Yes. Brady called in one half hour ago and said he had things taken care of," María responded. "I passed him through to Mark."

"Great. I'll check on that, Dar, and let you know what the deal is. Are you going to that meeting at ten?"

Dar had been perusing her folder. "Yeah...and we need a team meeting after lunch, because Mark bullied facilities into finishing the two hub sites. We're ahead of schedule." She glanced up. "María, cancel anything I've got late Friday afternoon. I've got to fly up to Connecticut."

"*Sí.*" María took notes. "Do you want me to book you?"

The tall executive nodded. "After lunch flight going up." She paused, considering. "See if they have a really late flight coming back that night. Otherwise, early next morning return."

Kerry looked up. "Don't you want to maybe stay around there a day or so?"

Blue eyes met hers. "No." Dar closed her folder and headed into her inner office.

María put down the pencil she had picked up to make notes and inclined her head inquisitively at Kerry.

"Mmm. Dar's grandmother passed on," the blond woman explained. "She hasn't seen that part of her family in a while. They don't get on well."

"Ahh. That is too bad." María clucked softly. "A funeral is always so hard."

They fell introspectively silent, then spoke at once.

"María, what does my schedule show for Friday?"

"You know, your schedule is clear for that day, Kerrisita."

They both chuckled.

"Do you want me to book you for that as well?" María asked.

Kerry considered. "Yeah. But book me separately, okay? I haven't talked to her about it. And María. Book those tickets on my credit card this time." She shook a finger at the secretary. "Dar doesn't need any help in that department from you. She spoils me more than enough on her own."

María smiled and held up a hand. "Ay, Kerrisita, the two of you are just like my children, sometimes. You'd better go check your office. I am thinking that my boss has missed you just a little being gone."

"My office?" Kerry queried. "What did she do in my office?"

No answer, just a smile.

"Oh, my god." Kerry exhaled, and headed for the door. "I should have brought that darn trophy in."

❖ ⌘ ❖ ⌘ ❖ ⌘ ❖

Dar was halfway through the red folder, one hand propping up her head as she studied the paper in front of her. She reached over and took a swig of apple juice, then put her bottle down and turned the page. "No." She picked up the sheet and tossed it into her out bin. "No." She tossed the next one after it. "You've got to be kidding." A third went wafting.

She picked up a pen and scribbled her signature over the next, then turned it over. A soft chime made her look up and she watched her mailbox fill with dark lines. Then she turned her head and went peacefully back to her papers.

A buzz. "Dar. Mr. Alastair on line *número uno.*"

Dar hit the button. "Morning, Alastair."

"Good morning, Dar. Hear we had some trouble with the Allison account."

Right to the point. Dar liked that. "Yeah. I've got a team up there and Duks has the auditors working on their books. Looks like someone bought off someone at Ernst and Young."

Alastair made a soft clucking noise. "You're kidding?"

"Nope. Unless the analysis comes up weird we managed to retrieve records that show they were buying their contracts. I can't think of how they passed due diligence otherwise." Dar signed a page, then flipped it over. "I fired their comptroller."

"I heard," Alastair murmured. "His uncle's the president of Intercorp."

Dar put her papers down and folded her hands. "And?"

"I got a call from him."

"And?" Dar asked again, her eyes narrowing.

"He's not happy."

"I wasn't happy on Friday. The idiot was stupid enough to keep records of what he was doing in his goddamned corporate server, Alastair. If they couldn't find an angle to force the bid, they manufactured one. We're talking major league slimeballs, here."

She could hear the sigh. "He's threatening to pull the French deal."

Dar felt nauseous. "Did you tell him what we found?"

"He doesn't much care," Alastair told her, bluntly. "This kid's a protégé of his, and it's a lot of not nice smelling stuff on his face if he gets tossed on his rear."

A silence lengthened. "Are you suggesting we rehire him?" Dar asked carefully.

"I'm suggesting you give me a reason not to," her boss replied. "Something that would make him ineligible to be employed by ILS."

"How about filing criminal charges?" Dar snorted. "Jesus, Alastair, I can't believe we're having this conversation. Tell you what. Give me this guy's phone number."

"Who?"

"The uncle. I'll call him." Dar pulled a pad and her pencil over. "I don't give a damn if he's got egg on his face. He should have taught the little bastard better or at least made sure he had the sense to cover his ass."

"Um no, Dar, I don't think that's a good idea," Alastair told her, delicately. "He's got a hot temper."

"And I don't?"

"That was my point," her boss remarked dryly. "Listen. Just get me something on him, so I can go back to the uncle with something other than lame excuses, huh?"

Dar glowered at the phone. "You know what I'd tell him?"

"Yes, in fact, I do and we need that contract, Dar. So be a sport, hmm?"

"Grumph," the executive grunted. "All right. I'll see what I can do. But I'll tell you, Alastair. Even if we don't get something concrete, I'm not integrating that bastard." She hung up the line and scowled at the desktop before dialing another number. "Mark?"

"Hmm?" The MIS chief cleared his throat. "Yes, Boss? What's up? Welcome home."

"I need you to pull everything you can on that jerk from Allison," Dar told him. "He's got some pull somewhere, and I need to nail him down hard."

"Okay. I'll see what I can get," Mark promised. "Hey. Has Kerry seen her office yet?"

Oh shit. "She hasn't come barreling in here, so I guess not." Dar found her annoyance fading. "I'll let you know."

Mark laughed. "She's gonna have a fit. Wish I could tape it. Later, Boss."

Dar leaned back in her chair and crossed an ankle over her knee, her hand smoothing down the soft cotton of her casual slacks. She took a sip of her juice and waited, hearing familiar footsteps coming down the back hallway.

❖ ⌘ ❖ ⌘ ❖ ⌘ ❖

Kerry ducked into the kitchen before she made it to her office, going to the cabinet and retrieving one of the extra mugs she'd stashed there. As she started a cup of espresso brewing, a familiar voice came in behind her.

"Hey, Kerry. Welcome back." Mary Ann, Duk's assistant bounced in, and grabbed her own cup. "We've missed you at the gym. How'd the trip go?"

"Eh." Kerry leaned back and crossed her arms. "Great, until the last few days. I think the mess is sitting over in your office." She smiled at the tall, heavyset blond woman. "I've missed you guys, too. Finding a place to work out on the road is pretty tough."

Mary Ann poured a cup of regular coffee and added cream to it, then she glanced around and lowered her voice. "So. How'd the meet go Saturday?"

Kerry grinned fully, her nose wrinkling up. "It was great. She came in first place, after all that grumping."

"Really?" Mary Ann clapped a hand over her mouth. "Ohmigod. That's so funny. She really won it?"

"Uh huh. Got a trophy almost as tall as me." Kerry laughed. "It was really something else. I wish you guys had been there."

"You told us not to come."

"I know, I know." Kerry made a shushing motion. "Shh. She was really nervous about it, but I think the next one will be okay. But hey, can we get the class together before Wednesday? It'd be fun to do something to her before class starts."

"Ooo." Mary Ann's eyes lit. "Yeah. We could get a cake. Would she kill us?"

"Not if it was chocolate," Kerry replied, wryly. "Chocolate cake, chocolate filling, chocolate frosting. Trust me."

"Gotcha." Mary Ann grinned. "This is going to be fun. It's been such a blast watching her unbend the past few months. No one would believe it if I told them."

Kerry took her cup and poured the strong coffee into it, then added the steamed milk she'd been frothing during their conversation. "She'll make faces, but she'll like that," she said over her shoulder. "Yikes. I better get going. I've got a conference call in ten minutes." She ducked past the taller woman, headed across the hall, pushed her door handle down, and shoved the door open with one shoulder. She got inside, letting the door shut, and got halfway across the room before two things hit her.

What was on her desk, which wasn't her large screen monitor, and...

The smell of a new computer.

"Ooo." Kerry stopped and put her cup down, circling her desk and staring avidly. "Ooo. Ooo...ooo...ooo." Her eyes widened as she absorbed the sleek, twenty-six inch slim liquid crystal display that now smugly sat on the surface. "Wooowww." The screen saver swirled a brilliant morphing of shapes that disappeared as she touched the brand new ergonomic trackball. "New CRT...new mouse..."

Kerry dropped to her knees, shoved her chair aside, and squirmed under her desk to see the new, dark gray box underneath. "Ooo...I'm in geek heaven." She got up and pulled her chair back over, then cracked her knuckles and opened the machine's system information, her eyes scanning it rapidly. "Ohh...my...god. That's more RAM than the Space Shuttle could hold in its cargo bay." She sat up and did a little dance in her chair, then she got up and patted the display. "Honey, you wait right here, okay? I need to go thank my fairy godmother for you."

❖ ⌘ ❖ ⌘ ❖ ⌘ ❖

Dar pinned a serious look on her face as she watched the inner door open and Kerry appeared. It lasted all of a second before she clapped a hand over her mouth to stifle a laugh, since the blond woman was doing a little dance in the middle of her carpet.

"You know what this is, Dar?" Kerry asked her, doing her best Snoopy imitation. "This is a happy nerd dance."

Dar fell out of her chair, and hit the floor, laughing helplessly.

Kerry paused, delighted at the reaction. "Wow. That was almost as good as seeing that new 'puter." She put her hands on her hips and smiled, then walked over and extended a hand down to her boss. "Here."

Dar gripped the hand and allowed herself to be hauled upright, then dusted herself off. "Whew. Didn't expect that reaction." She chuckled wryly. "Glad you liked the new box. I told Mark to hold off on changing mine out till you saw yours."

"It's awesome," Kerry enthused. "That screen is so much clearer. My eyes thank you."

"Mmm." Dar nodded. "Yeah. That was one of its selling points for me, too." She walked over to her system and rolled the trackball, then selected a screen. "Couple weeks of reading these convinced me."

Kerry squinted at the complicated CAD drawing, recognizing the network symbols. "Yow. I see what you mean." She looked up at Dar. "Were you getting those headaches again?"

The taller woman nodded mutely.

"Definitely worth it, in that case," Kerry decided, giving Dar's nearby leg a pat. "Thanks, Boss."

Dar grinned, and dialed. "Hey Mark."

"Uh? Oh. Hi, Boss. What's up?"

"You missed a dancing nerd up here a minute ago."

"A wh— Oh, man. I thought you meant the candy for minute. I was gonna say." Mark laughed. "Hey, Kerry. Like the new box?"

"Oooooo," Kerry responded. "Very much. Thanks, Mark."

"Bring mine up." Dar chuckled. "When you get a chance."

"I love working for the head geek." Mark sighed. "Okay. Brent'll be up in a minute."

Dar hung up the line and perched on the edge of her desk, folding her arms over her chest with a satisfied expression. "So. You like it, huh?" She was pleased with her surprise, having hand picked the systems in question.

"Very much." The blond woman smiled. "Now, let me get back to my new toy and try to get some work done. Hope those reports are in."

Dar lost her good humor. "Ah. Me too. Apparently our slimy friend has relations in sticky places. Alastair's getting pressured to rehire him." Kerry's jaw drop. "I know, I know. I've got Mark checking. But you keep your eye out for solid stuff, too."

"That sucks," Kerry replied forthrightly. "He's big time trouble, Dar. I'll tell you what, I'm going to contact that woman from the account they just got. She was really upset about whatever they had over her. Maybe I can get her to talk now."

"Good." The executive looked up as the door swung open, and an audio visual cart entered, pushed by a short, stocky man in his early twenties, with a pugnacious buzz cut. "Thanks, Brent."

"No problem, ma'am," the tech stated briskly, visibly holding back from a salute. "I'll get this hooked right up."

Kerry peeked at him from around Dar's desk. "Hi, Brent."

The man visibly blushed. "Morning, ma'am."

"Did you set up my new system, too?" the blond woman inquired, a tiny, playful smile crossing her lips. "If you did, thanks."

Furtively, he looked at her. "Yeah, that was me. No problem." He messed around with some cables, then peeked up again. "If you want the cords tied back a different way, or anything let me know, okay?"

"I sure will." Kerry caught his eye and smiled, making him almost drop the keyboard he'd picked up. Brent had a well known crush on her, and she wasn't above tweaking him just a little because of it. Besides, he was cute and almost painfully shy, and Kerry liked him for his accuracy and good attitude.

"Can't plug a mouse in there, Brent." Dar's voice rumbled dryly from across the desk. "Try the round hole."

Kerry decided to leave before she caused the poor man any more trouble. "I'll get those reports to you." She waved her fingers at Dar and slipped through the back hallway door, closing it behind her.

Dar took pity on the tech. She strolled away from her desk and ended up at the window, gazing out over the water with an air of serene patience she'd rented from somewhere and kept in her drawer for special occasions. She thought of her dancing nerd, and the glass reflected back a cheerful grin as she waited for Brent to finish.

Chapter
8

"Ugh." Kerry closed her eyes and allowed Dar to steer her inside the condo, where a cold blast of refreshing air conditioning immediately dried the sweat on her forehead. "I feel like an airboat rolled over me." They'd just gotten back from the island gym, and she was fiercely regretting the two weeks of slacking off while she was traveling. It had been a really long day at work as well, and with the two combined, Kerry felt like crawling into bed right that very instant and curling up into a ball of exhausted and sore muscles, both physical and mental.

Chino wriggled in Dar's arms, and now the taller woman leaned closer, and allowed the Labrador puppy to lick Kerry's face. "C'mon. How about we share a shower, then relax? I've got my stuff all packed, so..."

Ah. Kerry forced her eyes open. *That's right. Tomorrow was Friday, and Dar's flight up to Connecticut.* She hadn't had the chance the past few days to broach the subject of joining her, so now... She sighed. Now she'd have to find a moment and just accept whatever answer Dar gave her.

It was bothering her lover badly, she knew. Dar had been very quiet the past few days, almost withdrawn, and had taken to retreating into silent reserve, obviously deep in thought. Kerry had been caught between her anxiety and the understanding that this was one area Dar kept her barriers up about. Well, maybe after they relaxed a little, she could test the waters. And speaking of waters... "Shower. Mmm."

Dar set Chino down then put their bags on the couch before she led Kerry into the bathroom. She turned the water on before she stripped the smaller woman's workout gear off.

Kerry blinked wearily, sucking in a breath before she gathered some energy and did the same for her partner. "What a day."

"Mmhmm," Dar agreed, tugging Kerry's sports bra off, then tickling her under her arm. "Got some bad news right before we left. Our friend David Ankow's supposed to be here on Monday."

"Ugh Great. Just great." Kerry stifled a yawn, then tugged Dar along with her as they entered the large octagonal stall shower, where warm water hit them. "Boy, that feels good."

Dar picked up a sponge and poured some body wash on it, then scrubbed Kerry, beginning with her shoulders, then moving down her strong back as the blond woman simply fell against her. "Yeah, it sure does," she teased.

"Mmm." Kerry nuzzled her, taking a playful nip as her hands circled Dar and ran lightly over her lover's powerful body. "Are you still mad at me for that cake?" She felt the movement as Dar laughed. "You were so cute yesterday. My god, Dar, I've never seen you blush like that before."

Dar made a gurgling noise. "I can't believe you let them do that."

"Let them?"

Her lover sighed. "It...no, it was nice. Thank you. I appreciated it, Kerry. I was just...um..."

"Surprised?"

"Yeah."

"That was the point." Kerry captured the sponge and made little soapy sculptures across Dar's belly. There were lots of little valleys and ridges there for her to explore now, and she made sure all of them were clean, hitting several ticklish spots and getting soap flying all over when Dar laughed and her abs contracted. "You've got a nice laugh. Have I ever told you that?"

Dar lathered up Kerry's hair, scratching her behind the ears where she had a sensitive spot and making her utter a little moan of pleasure. "No, you hadn't mentioned that before," she rumbled. "Have I ever told you you've got really tasty ears?" She explored one with tiny nibbles.

A mewling sound escaped the smaller woman, as the weariness of the day fell away from her, banished by a rush of energy. Her skin tingled and her touch changed from playful to seductive, getting an immediate response from Dar, as she nuzzled sensitive areas and stepped forward, pressing her body against her lover's and reveling in the skin on skin contact.

A dilemma. Kerry was losing the ability to really decide, but she wondered if the effort of getting out of the shower would be worth the greater comfort of the waterbed. Then Dar slid a knee between hers, and she was beyond caring, wanting Dar's touch with an intensity that was almost scary.

The water's pressure alternated with Dar's touch, and she forgot about the day, concentrating only on the skin under her fingertips, and the taste of Dar's lips, and the rapidly building sensations that made it hard to breathe. Then the world tilted, and she was vaguely aware of being lifted up, and the chill of the air conditioning, and the warm, slightly rough texture of the sheets as she was put gently down, and the touch became relentless.

She surrendered to it gladly.

❖ ⌘ ❖ ⌘ ❖ ⌘ ❖

Dar wasn't sleeping, Kerry realized, as she lay tangled in the sheets and her lover, contentedly somnolent in the low light. She tilted her head and confirmed her thoughts, seeing the half open eyes pensively regarding the ceiling. "Mmm."

Blue eyes opened wider, and Dar's head inclined. "Thought you were asleep."

"Almost," Kerry admitted, tracing the thin line of very fine hairs that went down the center of Dar's chest. "Why aren't you?"

"I was thinking."

Kerry nodded solemnly. "About tomorrow?"

Dar exhaled heavily. "Yeah."

"Is it going to be a big ceremony?" Kerry probed, very gently.

Long silence, and Kerry had decided Dar wasn't going to answer when she did.

"Probably. My mother has a fairly large family, five brothers and sisters." Dar paused. "Lots of cousins...friends..."

"Who you haven't seen in a while."

"Mmm."

"They going to be surprised?" Kerry whispered, getting a short, wry chuckle in return. "I bet they are."

"Last time I saw most of them was at the service for my father." Dar's voice spoke from the darkness, colored with a sad pain she usually didn't exhibit. "Going back there just rakes that whole scene up again for me. I felt very alone among all of them."

"Sounds pretty awful."

"It was. They're all pretty intelligent...sophisticated. I had always gotten the idea that they looked down on Dad, because he wasn't that kind of person. I know. My mother didn't take him to big family gatherings a lot." Dar spoke slowly and awkwardly. "God knows I was far from...I really wasn't very polished back then, let's just put it that way. I felt...pretty small, with all of them looking at me...the way I was dressed. My world was so different than theirs."

"Dar, you're not the same person you were then," Kerry murmured, hurting for her.

"I know. But that was a very bad time for me," Dar admitted. "Brings up all kinds of nasty memories."

Kerry rubbed Dar's skin with tender fingers. "I'm glad you decided

to talk about it. I was getting sort of worried. I know it's hard for you."
With her ear pressed against Dar's chest, she could hear the irregular
heartbeat and feel the increase in her lover's breathing. "Is there anything
I can to do help you?"

The heartbeat skipped, then sped up a few beats.

Kerry waited through the silence then started a soothing trace over
Dar's skin.

"No. I'll be all right."

"Dar." Kerry laid her hand flat on her lover's stomach. "You're my
best friend. If you can't ask me, who can you ask?"

"It's...juvenile," Dar muttered.

"C'mon, Dar. Cough it up. Do you want to take one of my teddy
bears?" Kerry asked, in a gently kidding tone.

"No." The blue eyes were now looking at her, glints of light in the
gloom.

"Do you want me to go along with you?" Kerry felt the movement
under her fingers stop for what seemed like a long time.

Dar shifted, as though her body wanted to escape, but was being
pinned in place by Kerry's weight and her own will. "I can't ask you to do
that...and it's too late anyway," the dark haired woman muttered. "But
thank you for offering."

"Tch tch tch." Kerry hiked herself up and kissed Dar on the lips, then
rolled over and reached into the drawer next to the bed. She pulled something out and dropped it on her lover's naked chest.

"What's that?" Dar asked, in a small voice.

"My tickets."

"When did you get those?"

"Same day you did."

Dar lifted the folder and examined it, then looked at Kerry. "Why
didn't you say anything?" she asked curiously, a look of consternation
mixed with relief on her face. "Damn, Ker. I've been trying to find a way
to ask you..."

Kerry curled her arm over Dar's shoulder and put her head down.
"Well," she exhaled thoughtfully, "you're a very private person, Dar, and
I know this is a very sensitive area for you." She ran a finger down Dar's
jaw-line. "If it's any consolation. I was trying to find a way all week to
ask you if you wanted me there." She smiled. "I'm glad you do."

Dar let out an audible sigh of relief. "No wonder María looked at me
so damn funny when I told her you were going to schedule a meeting
tomorrow afternoon." She gave her lover a wry look. "It's not going to be
pleasant, Kerry."

"That's all right. Coming to Michigan after me wasn't very pleasant
for you, was it?" Kerry inquired. "It makes me feel good to be able to give
you something back that way."

Dar hugged her suddenly, trading speech for physical contact.

Look down on Dar, would they? Kerry felt her protective instincts rising. *Intellectual snobs? Uh huh. We'll just see.*

❖ ⌘ ❖ ⌘ ❖ ⌘ ❖

The chapel had, as chapels do, an air of reserved peace about it, a hushed stillness that came as much from the natural human instinct to defer to death than anything else. There were discrete floral arrangements placed around the room and a decorous bunting of midnight blue draped around the pale wood coffin.

The chapel employees were making their final adjustments, watched in silence by a slight, thin boned woman with pale, silvered blond hair and even, delicate features. A tall, almost bald man entered, glanced around, then walked over to join the woman. "Evening, Ceci. Damn shame."

Cecilia Roberts glanced up at him and inclined her head with studied grace. "Thanks, Allan." Her voice was low, but vibrant. "She held on a long time. I'm glad she's finally at peace."

The man nodded solemnly. "She was a strong woman." His eyes flicked around the room. "They did a nice job."

A faintly sardonic smile crossed Ceci's lips. "If you say so," she drawled, watching as people filtered in, most of them known to her. Most of them giving her sympathetic looks and nods. "Nice flowers."

He grunted. "Mmm. That one there's lovely. Are those orchids?"

"I believe they are," the woman mused.

They were both comfortably silent as the room continued to fill. Allan finally inhaled. "I hear your daughter's going to show?"

A cool mask slipped down over Cecilia's face. "She said she'd be here, yes," she replied. "I gave my word to mama I'd ask her." She paused. "I did."

A short, coifed woman came over. "Ceci. I'm so sorry." She held out hands, which the slighter woman grasped briefly, then released. "It's been a long road, I know."

"Yes, it has," Cecilia answered. "I'll miss her, though, despite how much I wanted peace for her."

The short woman stepped closer. "Ceci. Andrea said...I'm sure she got this wrong, but she said your daughter was going to be here?"

Cecilia sighed inwardly. "Let's not make this a side show, Elli. Yes, mama wanted Paladar here, and I asked her to attend. She said she'd be here. Enough?"

"Mmph." Elli made a small face. "It's just been such a long time. I hardly know what to expect." She paused, delicately. "She was such an...individual person."

"I'm sure she still is," Ceci remarked dryly. "I only hope she decides not to disgrace my mother's memory by coming in blue jeans."

"I hardly think you've got to worry about that," Allan remarked, a curious tone in his voice. "If the person who just came in the door is who you're talking about."

Cecilia turned her head and found her attention drawn immediately to the tall, strikingly attractive woman framed in the doorway, dressed in an impeccably cut black suit. The pale blue eyes stood out vividly against the tanned skin as they scanned the crowd, and, at the last, met her own.

The sense of presence was almost overwhelming. Cecilia was almost slack jawed in surprise at the sheer power of her daughter's personality, which muted itself as their eyes touched and she received a single, gracious, inclination of the head.

"Goddess," she muttered, under her breath.

"Well," Elli's voice vocalized her own surprise, "she certainly has grown up, Ceci. My god, she's gorgeous."

"Yes," Ceci agreed absently, tearing her eyes away as a second woman appeared at her daughter's elbow, apparently a friend of hers, and they moved to a rear pew, a little apart from the milling crowd.

"Andrew's image," Allan mused. "Always was."

Cecilia didn't answer.

❖ ⌘ ❖ ⌘ ❖ ⌘ ❖

"Is that your mother over there?" Kerry kept her voice almost sub vocal.

"Yes." Dar folded her hands in her lap, trying to will them not to shake. She was cold and her stomach hurt, and it took an enormous amount of effort just to keep up a shell of composure around her. A very warm hand curled around hers and she drew in a breath and let it out very slowly as her nerves settled.

Okay. The hard part was over, that first eye to eye contact. She'd come out the winner in that one, at least, watching her mother's face react in surprise and shock in that first, unguarded moment. *Wasn't what you expected, was it, Mother?* "How'd you guess? Don't tell me a family resemblance."

"She's watching you," Kerry murmured, a hint of amusement in her voice. "She looks sort of stunned."

"Figures." Dar's body relaxed a little, and she glanced around. Most of the attendees hadn't noticed their entry, so she had a brief period to check things out before her family realized she was there. "Last time she saw me I...um...I was sort of still in a rebellious phase."

"And that changed—when?" Kerry inquired mildly, getting a hint of a smile on Dar's strained face. "Was I supposed to have noticed this streak of conservatism?" The fabric across her partner's shoulders shifted, then relaxed a little as Dar sat back. "You going to register as a Republican next?"

"Kerrison." The pale blue eyes flicked her way, warming with quiet affection.

"That has such a nice ring when you say it." The skin under Kerry's fingers lost its chill, and she looked around deliberately, eyeing the carved, polished wood. "This is a really pretty chapel." She hesitated, then questioned. "Is this where...um..."

Dar nodded. "The service, yes." She got lost in the memory for a moment. "Her family has a big plot here. She wanted the memorial stone close by." She sighed. "Listen. I'll be right back. I'm going to," Dar inclined her head towards the front of the chapel, "pay my respects."

"Okay." Kerry released her hand and watched as Dar rose and walked up the center aisle. The subdued lighting in the room kept her in shadows until she reached the front rail, where she entered a soft pool of illumination. She rested her hands on the polished wood and gazed into the casket, her face quiet and composed.

More interesting was the reaction of the rest of the room. Kerry watched her neighbors' eyes fasten on the tall, still figure, and a low murmur buzzed her ears. She listened to the some of the comments and her green eyes narrowed, her fingertips twitching as she fought the desire to butt in to some of the conversations going on around her.

Dar gazed down at a face her mind hardly recognized. Death did that, she knew, but she'd last seen her grandmother before her last illness and remembered her older, but not gaunt, weathered, or ravaged, as the sickness had left her.

Her eyes closed and she took in a breath. *Sorry, Gran,* she silently whispered. *I should have called you, at least.* Dar studied the quiet form. *I started to, a dozen times. But every time I did...the thought of having Mother answer stopped me. I did send cards, though. Did you get them?* Dar felt the pressure of eyes boring through her back and sighed.

A small rustling behind the curtains to her left caught her attention. *Time to go, Gran. At least you're in a nicer place now. And if you can hear me, I hope some day we can meet up. Maybe just sit down and talk for a while. I really wanted to tell you about Kerry, Gran. I finally found that one you told me was out there.* Dar's eyes dropped for a moment, then she turned and walked back down the aisle, avoiding the avidly curious stares that hit her. She resumed her seat and resisted the urge to slide down and hunch her shoulders.

There was an expectant rustle of motion. Dar glanced to her left and realized her mother had chosen to sit down in their row, taking a place right next to her. Her blood pressure skyrocketed, but she folded her arms over her chest and fastened a calm, disinterested look on her face.

"Hello, Paladar." Her mother kept her voice to a low murmur.

Dar turned her head slightly. "Mother." She knew her tone was even, but she was desperately grateful for the pressure of Kerry's hand against her side, giving her little, friendly scratches.

"Glad you could make it."

Dar merely nodded.

The minister stepped out at that moment and cleared his throat, providing a very welcome distraction. For the moment, at any rate. However with this and the reception afterward, it was, Dar realized soberly, going to be a very long night.

Chapter
9

"Thank you." Kerry accepted the two glasses and turned, pausing a moment to survey the crowd before she made her way back to Dar. Her lover was against the far wall, making polite conversation with two or three of what Kerry assumed to be uncles and aunts. Certainly, they were of her mother's generation and had a similar set of features.

"Excuse me." A voice to Kerry's right caught her ear and she turned to find the short woman with silvered chestnut hair at her elbow, smiling politely. Kerry smiled politely back at her.

"Yes?"

"I'm sorry. Forgive me for asking, but are you a friend of Paladar's?"

Kerry briefly toyed with the notion of flatly denying it, then decided she should be nice. "Yes, I am. Why?"

"It's just been so long since any of us have seen her." The woman disregarded Kerry's question. "I'm Elli. Elli Bainister. I'm a good friend of her mother's, you see. We're so glad Paladar decided to join us here."

"That's nice to hear," Kerry responded. "It's too bad it had to be such a sad occasion."

"Yes. Isn't it? We've been wondering how she's doing."

Kerry blinked mildly. "Why don't you ask her?" She glanced at her partner.

"Oh. I don't want to bother her. She's talking with her uncles. I was just wondering...are you in the computer business, too?"

Kerry caught the clue that had been wandering aimlessly around. "Yes. As a matter of fact, I am." She put down one of the drinks and held a hand out. "Kerry Stuart." She waited for the woman to return her grip hesitantly then smiled.

"Really. Well, my husband works for Ethrington Consulting. Have you heard of them?" Elli edged a little closer. "They do work for the government."

"Sure." Kerry nodded. "We've done some co bids with them, in fact, I'm the operations director of ILS."

Elli's eyes widened. "Oh. Then you work with Paladar?"

"I work for her," Kerry replied, with a kind smile. "She's my boss at ILS."

"Ahh." The woman smiled, evidently figuring out whatever it is she was fishing for. "And what part are you director of? My husband specializes in retail."

"All of it," came the prompt, amiable reply. "I'm the Executive Operations Director."

There was a long pause as the woman's head tilted to one side. "And you...work for..."

"The Chief Information Officer for ILS, mmhmm," Kerry agreed cheerfully, pointing across the room. "That's her, my boss. She's great."

Elli put a hand on her arm. "Excuse me a minute." She turned and scurried away, as Kerry lifted her hand and waggled her fingers at her retreating back.

"Bye." She scooped up the other drink and resumed her aborted trek across the room, arriving just as Dar was nodding a farewell to her latest group of questioners. "Here." She handed the taller woman her glass.

"Is there alcohol in here?"

"Yes."

Dar drank the entire thing down in a draft. She lowered the glass, then licked her lips. "Got another one around?"

Kerry handed her the glass she'd gotten for herself without a word and took the empty one from her lover. So far, at least, her mother seemed to be steering clear of them, letting the various family members come up and renew their acquaintance with what Kerry realized was their version of the black sheep of the family.

Who turned up, shockingly, with a snowy white fleece and golden hooves, and now no one knew quite what to do with her. It would have been funny, if it had been anyone other than Dar who was very obviously hating every moment of the affair. "Hey, Dar?"

Dar had been busy chewing on a piece of ice, and now she finished crunching and leaned back against her chosen wall. "Yeah?"

"This rebellious phase. Just how rebellious are we talking about?"

"Mmm. I wasn't too bad at work. But off hours," Dar chewed her lip a little, "I tended to leather and spiked collars." Her eyes darted to Kerry's face, which went slack with shock. "Yeah...and clothes with strategically placed rips." She paused. "I almost had a tattoo."

"Almost?" Kerry croaked, her mind still busy constructing a picture of her lover in leather and chains. "What stopped you?"

"Dad. He said, 'Dardar, you kin do what you want, but so kin I, and if you put any damn pictures on any part of that body of yours, I'm gonna take steel wool and scrub 'em off.'"

Kerry covered her face with one hand and stifled a giggle. "That would have stopped me," she admitted, glancing up as more people closed in on them. "Whoops. Next shift."

"Paladar. It's been so long. You look marvelous. What have you been doing with yourself?" A tall, willow thin woman with uniformly yellow hair wafted up, followed by a heavyset man that reminded Kerry of Duks.

"Hello, Aunt Seleine. Uncle Rob," Dar replied quietly. "I haven't been up to much. Um...this is my friend Kerry."

Kerry returned the greetings with a warm cordiality that made it seem like she'd been performing onerous social duties all her life. Which, of course, she had. "Shake 'em and bake 'em" had been a part of her normal existence since she'd been old enough to stand and she had a lot less problem dealing with the sea of faces than Dar did, who was used to mostly small, closed meetings and faceless conferences. A large event where everyone knew her personally and where she was the focus of some not always friendly curiosity was getting on the taller woman's nerves, and Kerry felt a pang of sympathy as she watched Dar muster her energy for yet another assault.

"Paladar." The low voice was enough like her partner's to make her jerk and Kerry turned to see Dar's mother standing at her elbow, her diminutive height inches shy of Kerry's own. "Excuse me." Her eyes flicked to Kerry's face, then away, dismissing her.

Dar hadn't noticed as she turned and backed away a little in wariness as she regarded her mother. "Yes?"

"Are you set with a place to stay tonight?"

One of Dar's dark eyebrows curved up a little. "We have a room, yes," she answered guardedly. "We have an early flight back home."

Cecilia digested that. "If you could change your plans, I'd like a few minutes with you tomorrow."

Dar slowly folded her arms over her chest. "What did you have in mind?"

"Stop by the house. Midmorning," her mother directed. "Can I expect you?"

For a long minute, Kerry thought Dar was going to turn her down flat. But she finally inclined her head slightly in assent, her face a mask.

"All right."

"Good." Cecilia turned and started to walk away almost slamming into Kerry. For a moment she was forced to look into a pair of very intense green eyes, as Kerry held her ground, then sidestepped with a polite smile.

"Sorry."

The older woman paused uncertainly. "No. It was my fault," she replied. "I should have watched where I was going." She paused again, slightly expectant, her eyes flicking up to Dar's face.

"This is Kerry Stuart," Dar supplied quietly, "my partner."

Kerry held out an obliging hand. "Pleasure to meet you." She returned Cecilia's grip with her own strong one, then released her. "That was a beautiful service."

Dar's mother nodded absently. "Thank you. It's nice to meet you, too," she remarked, then turned and threaded her way through the crowd gracefully.

Kerry turned and met the pale blue eyes peering down at her. "You know something, Dar? I didn't think I'd ever meet someone with more nerve wracking relatives than me." She reflected on that and shook her head. "Wow."

"Sorry." The taller woman sighed. "It's not exactly fun for me either." She rubbed her temple lightly. "What time is it?"

"Ten," Kerry answered.

"Let's get out of here." Dar set her glass down and straightened, running impatient fingers through her hair to settle its waves, then twitching her suit jacket straight. She turned and almost bumped into a distinguished looking man who had just come up. "Hello, Richard." It was close to a relief to see a face that wasn't family. "Kerry, this is Richard Edgerton. Something of a family lawyer."

Kerry smiled at the tall man. "Pleased to meet you, Mr. Edgerton." She extended a hand and found it clasped firmly, then released.

"Pleasure to meet you, too, Ms. Stuart," the lawyer replied courteously. "It's nice knowing someone whom Dar speaks so highly of."

Ah. Kerry's ears perked up. He was the first person that night not to call her lover by her highly disliked full name and, on top of it, he knew who she was. *Two points for him.* "Hmm." She released a gentle laugh. "I'm not sure I want to know what tales she's telling about me, but..."

The man laughed as well. "Nothing to scare the children with, Ms. Stuart, trust me." He turned to Dar. "It's unfortunate why you're here, Dar. But since you are, can I get you to take a moment out and swing by the office? I've got some forms I need you to sign. May's trust fund comes up next month and it needs to be transferred over to you."

"I'd forgotten completely about that," Dar admitted. "Yeah. I promised my mother I'd stop by her place tomorrow morning. I can make it by your office by lunch, if that's all right with you."

"Perfect. See you then." Richard gave her a friendly pat on the arm. "Good to see you, Dar. You're looking great. Ms. Stuart, a pleasure." He smiled at both of them, then sauntered off, heading in an oblique line towards the bar.

They managed to get outside the room without being stopped again and handed the valet the ticket for their rental car. They waited quietly for it to be brought around, then Dar hesitated. "Do you mind driving?"

Kerry shook her head. "No. I think I remember where the airport guy said to go. It can't be that hard." She tipped the valet, then rested a hand on the doorframe. "Excuse me. There's a Hilton near here?"

"Yes, ma'am." The boy nodded. "Get on that road there, go north for about ten minutes, it's on your right. Can't miss it."

"Thanks." Kerry got in the car and almost laughed at the distance between her and the steering wheel. She adjusted the seat forward and put the car in gear, then pulled out of the parking lot. "Well."

"Mmm." Dar had slid down in her seat and had her eyes closed.

"Glad that's over."

"Oh god, yes," her lover muttered. "That was worse than I'd imagined."

Kerry reached over and patted her knee, then left her hand there just because she could. "I know it was rough on you. Did you even get anything to eat?"

"Nu uh."

"The hotel has room service."

"Oh yeah."

"I bet they have ice cream."

"They'd better the hell and damnation have some goddamned ice cream," Dar replied testily.

Kerry peered at her, since she had to stop at a light, and noticed the lines of tension around her lover's eyes. "You okay?"

Dar rested her head against the doorframe. "Headache."

"I think I've got something for that," came the sympathetic response. "Soon as we get to the room, okay?"

Dar wrapped her fingers around Kerry's, still resting on her leg, and exhaled. "I've got something for it right here." She half opened her eyes and peered over. "Thanks."

"No problem." The blond woman smiled. "But what have you been telling your family lawyer about me?" She turned into the well marked entrance to the hotel. "Hmm?"

"I had to explain to him who this person was that I was making my heir," came the quiet reply. "When I had my will and the papers for all the accounts and stuff changed."

Kerry pulled the car up to the valet stand and turned. "You didn't have to do that."

Dar shrugged. "I wanted to make sure you were taken care of, just in case."

Kerry had perhaps a moment before the valet came. A moment in which to try and relate a truth so deeply ingrained, it came to her lips like second nature. "Dar." She took a breath. "If anything ever happened to

you, there wouldn't be enough money in the world to patch the hole it
would leave in me."

A stillness filled with only two sets of breathing lengthened, then
broke as the door was opened, and a bright eyed young girl smiled at
them. "You checking in?"

Dar got out and snagged both overnight bags from the back seat then
joined Kerry as she walked around and they headed for the steps. "You
mean that." The taller woman pulled the hotel door open and courteously
motioned her forward.

"I mean it," Kerry replied peacefully, heading for the front desk.

Dar followed her, absorbed in thought.

❖ ⌘ ❖ ⌘ ❖ ⌘ ❖

Why, Kerry wondered, *did all hotel rooms smell the same?* She
pushed the door open and held it as Dar entered, headed past her, and
dropped their overnight bags on the large king sized bed. *Was it some
weird air freshener they all used, Eau de Plastique, or something?* Dar
paused a moment to rub the back of her neck, then stripped off her jacket.
She laid it over the back of the comfortable looking chair and sighed as
she took her shoes off.

Kerry did the same, glad to shed her gray wool jacket, the silk shirt,
and the matching wool knee length skirt and hose. She tugged her favorite
Tweety Bird T-shirt from her bag and wriggled into it, enjoying the
freshly laundered scent. Dar changed next to her in silence, then stretched
out her arms, and cracked her back and shoulders, making a small sound
of discomfort as she did.

"Long day." Dar sat down on the edge of the bed and rested her
elbows on her knees.

Kerry picked up the room service menu and stretched out next to her,
pulling a pillow out as a prop. "Considering it started with an eight a.m.
meeting...yeah." She touched Dar's arm, then patted her stomach. "Want
a pillow?"

Dar accepted, laying back and resting her head on her lover and folding her hands. "Ungh. That feels good." She wriggled a little to get more
comfortable and turned her head to watch Kerry study her choices. It was
much more relaxing to do that, than to think about her evening, and she
decided to keep it that way, carefully locking the tense memories away for
later.

Much later.

One more hopefully short meeting and they were outta there. She
tried to engage her interest in the sideways written food items, but the
headache that now worked its way across her skull was so intense, it made
her sick to her stomach. She closed her eyes and recalled the last time

she'd felt this lousy.

A hand on her shoulder brought her lashes fluttering open to see Kerry's concerned green eyes watching her. "You look really washed out. How's your head?"

"Reminds me of a certain day during a certain storm." Dar managed a wry smile.

"That bad?" Kerry put the menu down. "Why didn't you say something? I've got some stuff in my bag. Hang on." She gently slid out from under Dar's head and padded over to the chair, rummaged in her bag and returned with a pill bottle. "Shoot. You've got to eat something before you take this, Dar, or you'll get sick."

"I am sick."

"Sicker." Kerry grabbed the phone and glanced at the menu. "Hello. Yes, room 322. I need a bowl of the chicken soup." A dark eyebrow lifted at her. "Two of the club sandwiches, and..." The blue eyes gazed at her sadly. Kerry sighed. "And a bowl of chocolate ice cream." She put the phone down and set the menu aside. "Have some soup and you can take this stuff. I figured that was fastest."

"Okay." Dar rolled over and rested her head on her folded arms, feeling completely drained. "Mind turning that light down?"

Kerry turned off the light closest to the bed. "Sure." She rubbed Dar's back lightly with her fingertips, eliciting an incoherent sound from her friend. "Want me to see if I can loosen those up a little?"

"Uh."

Kerry slid over and sat cross-legged in front of Dar, flexing her hands before carefully kneading the painfully tense muscles. "Ooo." She winced, touching the back of Dar's neck. "This must be driving you nuts."

It was easier just to grunt, so Dar did, curling her body up a little and trying to concentrate on not throwing up. *It was too much for one day*, she decided. Three meetings, two of them fairly adversarial, then the flight which usually gave her a headache anyway, then the funeral. Add to that the knowledge she was going to have to deal with an inquisitive Ankow next week, and what she really felt like doing was taking off to the Keys and disappearing.

She thought about that for a bit.

C'mon, Dar. You never backed down from anything. Don't go starting now, just because a few bad apples hit you on the head in the same day. A slight grin tugged at her lips at the sound of her father's voice echoing in her head and turned, letting her eyes crack open and observe the attractive kneecap inches from her face.

Experimentally, she licked it.

"Yeow!" Kerry almost levitated off the bed. "Dar! What are you trying to do, scare me to death?"

"With a single measly lick?" Dar opened one blue eye fully and raised its brow. "You flatter me."

Kerry turned an appealing shade of crimson, which made her fair hair and eyebrows stand out vividly. "You must be feeling better," she accused, leaning over to continue her work.

Dar rocked a hand back and forth. "A little." She exhaled, warming Kerry's knee. "Just the peace and quiet's helping," her finger touched Kerry's calf, "and having you here."

"Thanks."

"Mmm." Dar closed her eyes again.

"Tell me something. I mean, I've met people like your mother's family before."

"Ungh."

"How on earth did she and your father hook up? I'm trying to figure out where they could have met. Did they crash into each other on the highway or something?" Privately, Kerry had been imagining a combination sushi bar/shooting range.

"Ah. Well, that's a tale," her lover acknowledged. "I wondered, myself, after I got old enough to realize just how different they really were." She tilted her head. "Like us."

Kerry burst out laughing. "Not. Dar. We are not anywhere near that different. C'mon now."

"No, we are." The blue eye regarded her. "You grew up with a silver spoon, didncha?"

She thought about that. "I guess. Yeah. If you mean my family always had money, sure. But you're worth a heck of a lot more than I am."

"I'd firmly disagree. But in dollars, right now, okay," Dar acknowledged. "That's only been in the last few years, though. Growing up, we were living on my dad's military pay. It's why I started working so young."

"Mmm." It was Kerry's turn to be thoughtful.

"I have this," Dar's brow creased, "outer veneer of...I mean, I learned how to buy the right clothes and all that, but underneath I'm still a scruffy military brat, who's more comfortable barefoot on the beach than dressed in the boardroom." She paused. "I think that's why I'm so...why my mother's family gets to me so much. They know that and they've all got that old money thing going. I always felt..."

"Like they were looking down on you?"

Dar nodded.

"You kicked their attitude right up through their nostrils today, you do realize that, right?" Kerry pronounced, with an understanding grin. "I remember the first time I saw you, and let me tell you something, Dar, you knocked my socks off and I *am* old money. I can smell a bourgeoisie at twenty paces."

"It was the power suit," Dar mumbled, faintly embarrassed. "And the first time you saw me, I was going to fire you. That doesn't count."

A soft knock at the door caused Kerry to roll up to her feet and answer it, allowing the room service waiter to enter and put the tray down on the small table. "Thanks." She signed the bill and closed the door after him, then went to the tray and examined its contents. "I don't know, Dar. There's something very appealing about the thought of you sitting in that kazillion dollar condo munching on a bowl of Frosted Flakes and milk. I like that about you." She uncovered the soup bowl and brought it over to the bed, sitting down carefully so she wouldn't spill anything. "C'mon. Roll over."

With a sigh, Dar complied, sitting up and pulling her body closer to accept a spoonful of the broth. It was tasty and she readily took the bowl from her lover and discarded the spoon, sipping it directly from the side as Kerry shook her head and chuckled. "You got a problem with me drinking from this here utensil, young lady?" Dar produced a reasonable facsimile of her father's growly tones.

Kerry laughed.

"In a bus station." Dar glanced at her.

"Huh?"

"You asked where they met." Dar swallowed the pill Kerry now offered her, chasing it down with a little more soup. "It was in a bus station. My mother had...I don't know, I guess she was in a rebellious stage herself. She'd decided to run away from home and ended up in the local Greyhound stop."

Kerry leaned her chin on her fist. "Really?"

"Mmm. Dad had gotten caught between transports and decided to switch to the bus because it was going to take half of forever for him to get back to Atlanta otherwise." Dar smiled. "He just had enough cash for the ticket and he was sitting in there with his gear, in his uniform when she came in."

"Uh huh. Then what?" Kerry got up, retrieved the sandwiches and put the plates down on the bed.

"Depends on which one you ask," Dar responded. "Dad says 'musta been the damn uniform, all them shiny things blinded her butt.'"

Kerry giggled. "And your mother said?"

"She said she looked into those eyes and was lost." Dar's lips tightened slightly. "She asked where his ticket was for and that's where she went." She took a breath. "She never looked back."

They regarded each other quietly for a moment.

"Wow." Kerry finally sighed, gaining an unexpected understanding of someone she barely knew. "That sounds really intense."

A slow nod. "It was. Her family tried everything to get her home. Finally they just gave up."

"And accepted it?"

Dar shook her head. "They never did. He was always an outsider to them."

Kerry pulled a bit of turkey out of her sandwich and chewed it slowly and thoughtfully. Dar took a bite of her own, and they ate in silence. "Wow," the blond woman finally said, as she studied the angular face opposite her. Even given their different genders and age, and Andrew's scarring, she could see the uncanny similarities, from the dark hair, and pale eyes, even to the shape of her friend's jaw. "She must miss him a lot."

A serious nod.

What would it be like, Kerry wondered, *to have that kind of ache, and be reminded of it every time you looked into someone's eyes?* "Are you going to tell her, Dar?" The question neither of them had brought up all week surfaced unexpectedly from her lips.

The blue eyes lowered. "I gave him my word I wouldn't." She could ask the same vow of Kerry, she knew.

But she didn't.

Dar raised her head to find Kerry looking back at her with quiet intelligence. "Can I come with you tomorrow?" the blond woman asked, with just a hint of a smile. "I think I have more in common with your mother than she realizes."

"Could be," Dar agreed softly, glad of the offer. She eyed Kerry and produced a smile. "Wanna share some ice cream?"

Kerry chuckled and retrieved the bowl.

Chapter
10

The phone, when it rang, was a thin, discrete warble. It echoed gently off spotless tile floors and the eggshell walls that bore only abstract, thinly drawn art. After a moment, soft bare footfalls scuffed against the tile, and the phone was answered.

"Yes?"

"Ceci. Are you there?"

"Of course I am. Do you think this is the machine?" Cecilia sighed. "What is it, Richard? I have things I have to do this morning."

"Did you arrange to talk to Dar?"

Another sigh. "For all the good it's going to do for either of us, yes."

"C'mon, Cec. Give it a chance, will you? She's not the kid you knew," Richard Edgerton coaxed. "Do you know what she's doing now?"

"I don't want to know," the slim silver blond woman stated sharply. "Richard, we've been through this. I'm only doing this because I think I'm obligated to, and why in the world you'd think she'd confide or listen to me, I haven't clue number one on."

"You're her mother."

"I used to be her mother, Richard," came the quiet response. "And even then, it didn't work."

The lawyer sighed. "She's not a bad person, Ceci."

"I don't much care what kind of person she is, Richard. Now, if you don't have anything else to nag me about, I've got things to do."

"She's coming here after she leaves your place," Edgerton commented.

Cecilia frowned. "Then you already knew she was coming here? Richard, I don't have time for games." She hung the phone up and straightened its position, then glanced around the spacious townhouse, with its neutral toned, spare furniture and its air of almost painful neatness. "I really don't have time for this, either," she murmured, with a tiny shake of her head.

Or, at least, she told herself that. Her eyes ran over the living room one more time before she moved into the austere kitchen and picked up a glass of vegetable juice she'd just pressed and sipped it slowly to settle her stomach. She leaned against the counter and watched out the window, putting everything out of her mind. Finally, the occasional car passing by outside became one that didn't pass, but turned into the small driveway instead. A rental car, with two passengers, and Cecilia closed her eyes at that. "You always do have to find the most difficult way, don't you?"

She remained where she was as both doors opened and the two passengers emerged, then her eyes and attention focused on the taller of the two.

Richard was right about one thing.

Dar had changed.

Oh, she was recognizable, surely. The same tall, lanky frame, with its cap of dark hair, and the southern tanned skin. Those same blue eyes.

But the dynamics behind it had all changed. The sullen, somewhat gawky, truculent young adult she'd last seen had been magically replaced by this confident, self assured woman whose poised movements bespoke an athleticism she frankly thought her sometimes impatient daughter would have given up by now. Today, Dar was wearing something a little more familiar, jeans that fit snugly all down the length of her long legs and a simple cotton shirt tucked into the waistband, the short sleeves revealing powerful, toned arms.

Cecilia watched them walk up the long driveway, and finally, briefly turned her attention to her daughter's shorter companion.

So.

This was Kerrison Stuart.

Interesting.

She straightened, then set her glass down very precisely on the counter, and spared a single moment of memory for the last time she'd seen Dar. The awkward, stumbling speech she'd cut short, divining Dar's intent to go with her and fulfill what she mistakenly thought was her father's responsibilities.

Just go. She'd said it simply. *I don't want you around me.*

And Dar had went, after a single, timeless moment of silent regard, in which she'd seen a glimpse of a hurt almost as profound as her own had been.

Academically, that surprised her, but they hadn't spoken since, so she hadn't had a chance to examine what she'd caused, though in later years, she'd started to wonder just a little, what kind of person this spawn of hers had turned into.

Time to find out.

Cecilia brushed her hands off and walked into the hall, striding forward to time her hand hitting the knob of the door as the first chime disturbed the silence of the house.

❖ ⌘ ❖ ⌘ ❖ ⌘ ❖

"You all right?" Kerry asked softly, as they came up the driveway.

"Yeah," Dar replied, desperately glad her lover was there with her. She owed Kerry big on this one. "Shouldn't take long." Her eyes went to the white, neatly painted townhouse with black and gold trim. "She might ask you to leave."

Kerry's eyebrows lifted. "Is it okay for me to tell her to kiss my ass?" she inquired mildly.

Dar couldn't help smiling. "It's all right. She doesn't know you, and God knows, she might have something she wants to say in private." She paused. "Then again, probably not." They got to the door and Kerry exhaled, then rang the bell.

The door opened as it sounded, and Dar's mother stood there, dressed in a pair of soft, white cotton drawstring pants, and a silk shirt, with a delicate rose embroidery on one shoulder. She was barefoot, and even Kerry felt large next to her.

"Mother." Dar's voice was cool and even, with its best boardroom cordiality.

"Come in." Cecilia pulled the door open and stepped back. "Ms. Stuart." She inclined her head towards Kerry, who decided to kick her friendliness gene in its recalcitrant butt.

"Hello." She let the door close behind her and looked around. "Wow. What a nice apartment."

"Thank you," Dar's mother responded politely. "Please. Sit down." She led them into the living room and indicated the couch.

Kerry circled the room instead, gazing at the walls. The precisely placed art hanging there had a certain geometric appeal and she decided she liked the colors. "That's your work, isn't it?" she asked Cecilia, not missing her lover's slightly raised eyebrow.

Ceci had stopped on her way towards the other couch and regarded Kerry with a mildly surprised expression. "Yes, it is," she murmured. "Are you in the art trade, Ms. Stuart?" Her voice held a note of bemusement.

"No." Kerry returned to Dar's side and seated herself on the couch. "I've spent a lot of time in Washington. The Museum of Art is a favorite spot of mine." Dar's eyebrow lifted a notch further. "You had a mini exhibit there last year."

Cecilia felt very unsettled. "Yes, I did." She decided to move the scene along. "Well, I would love to discuss art with you, Ms. Stuart, but there's something I need to discuss with Paladar, so if you'd excuse us for a moment? There's some ice tea on the porch if you'd like." She watched the exchanged looks between the two of them, then Kerry rose.

"Not a problem," she replied. "Dar, I'm going to go check my mail."

"Check mine," Dar responded, folding her arms over her chest.

Kerry walked out and the door closed behind her, leaving them looking at each other in silence.

Dar waited, having learned patience over the years and the value in letting others speak first. She studied her mother's face, noting the new lines and the added silver in her hair, and withstood the same searching look in return.

"There's no point in my going into long preambles, Paladar." Ceci chose her words precisely. "I was asked by the family to speak with you and, for reasons I can't begin to understand, I agreed, though I certainly have no idea what good they thought it might do."

Dar chose not to answer. She merely tilted her head to one side.

"Aunt May's estate." Ceci paused. "It gets signed over to you in total today."

It was the last thing Dar expected to hear from her mother. "And?" She injected a bit of puzzlement into her voice.

"There's a concern. The estate might pass out of the family." Her mother bit the words off. "To someone who is, perhaps, taking advantage of you."

Dar blinked, going over the words two or three times. "Is that a reference to Kerry?"

"I would suppose."

Dar felt anger easing the nervous dread out of her gut. She stood and walked to the fireplace, turned and leaned back against it. "In the first place, you can tell them from me, that I can leave my net worth to a tap dancing muskrat and they've got nothing to say about it."

"Mmm."

"In the second place, unlike Uncle Mike's six bimbos, Kerry's not a passing fancy."

Dar's mother glanced at her hands and pursed her lips.

"In the third place, her damn trust fund is four million dollars."

Cecilia stood up, regretting getting involved to an enormous degree. "Well, that's the point, Paladar. It's a large amount of money, and frankly, I would have a concern regarding your involvement with that myself." She took a breath to continue when Dar did something very surprising.

She laughed.

Ceci gazed at her in surprise. "What exactly are you finding funny?"

"The idiocy of people who are too stupid to do some basic research."

Dar's amusement disappeared and she let her anger steady into a dull burn. "The incredible arrogance of you to ask me here, after not bothering to talk to me for how many years? And worry about what I'll do with a lousy inheritance, or who I share my life with."

"Paladar."

"You can kiss my ass, *Mother*, and tell the rest of the family they can do the same."

"It was a *justifiable* concern." Her mother's voice rose.

Dar flipped a card through the air, watching it hit her mother in the chest. "Not if you'd bothered to find out who I am now."

Cecilia glanced impatiently at the piece of white cardboard, then stopped and read it more carefully.

Chief Information Officer? Paladar. No. She exhaled softly. *Dar Roberts. Goddess. Richard must have known. I'll have his head for not telling me.*

She tasted the knowledge that she'd made a fairly huge mistake. Question was, should she acknowledge it, or let it pass? After all, there were just so many levels of hate Dar could feel for her, right?

Her eyes lifted to meet a cold, angry stillness looking back, but her sense of fairness won out, and she lowered her gaze, and her voice. "You're right," she finally admitted, quietly. "I'm sorry, Paladar. I should have checked before I took on the responsibility. I wouldn't have bothered to ask you to come here."

Ceci expected an sharp retort, something spiteful. Something nasty. Instead, her daughter leaned back against the mantel and crossed her arms over her chest.

"It's funny," Dar remarked. "When you called last week, Kerry speculated that maybe you were using this whole thing as an excuse to get back in touch."

Cecilia drew in a soundless breath.

"And I told her it was too late for that." She paused. "I was right." Dar pushed off the wall and headed for the door. "Goodbye, Mother."

Let her go. A voice advised her in mental echo. "Paladar."

Dar kept walking, taking the two steps up in a smooth motion.

"Dar."

Her hand on the doorknob, Dar turned and waited.

"I don't expect you to understand what I did." Cecilia put her slim hands on the back of the chair.

"Maybe that's the problem," came the soft, bitter reply. "You never thought I was capable of understanding."

Her mother came forward, anger starting to surface. "You have no idea. You can't begin to realize what I went through...what is it to lose half of yourself."

"No," Dar replied, her nostrils flaring. "But I do know what it felt like to lose the only friend I had in the world." Her voice deepened. "The only person I could talk to. Who accepted who I was." She paused, needing a breath. "Who loved me." She tried to relax the lump in her throat. "Is that good enough on your scale?"

Goddess. Cecilia suddenly felt very tired. *I don't want to deal with this. I don't want to deal with her. Just let her go and forget about all this. Let it fade out like everything else. It was so much easier that way.* "I'm sure you think so," she murmured. "I hope for your sake, Dar, that you never find out any different." She was too tired to dissemble. "It was cruel to you. I know that." Her eyes lifted and met blue eyes so hauntingly familiar she had to look away. "But it was the only way I could survive." A quiet regret settled over her and she forced herself to look back at Dar's face, seeing a serious quietude there that unexpectedly made her see past the common stamp of her features and through to the person her daughter had become.

This was not her beloved, this tall, strange creature, who smelled of sun-warmed cotton and a light, spicy scent.

Perhaps, even that echo was gone.

"I'm sorry," she finally said.

There was a long pause, as her daughter studied her. "So am I."

They were quiet then the door opened and Kerry slipped inside, blinking at the silent tableau before her. Dar reached out blindly and brought her closer by pure reflex.

"Hey." Kerry glanced from one to the other, a hand on Dar's back revealing an almost unbearable tension. "Everything okay in here?"

"Yeah," Dar answered. "Seems my...family was worried you might be sponging off me."

A blond brow lifted. "They should hear us arguing about who gets to pay the grocery bill, then," she remarked, slipping an arm around her lover and leaning against her. "I'm going to hurt you if you don't stop switching that card."

The tension relaxed a little. Cecilia sighed. "Let's...ah, please sit down."

"Sure." Kerry started towards the couch, tugging Dar along with her. They all moved down the stairs, the atmosphere uncomfortable and strained.

"So. Did you two meet at work?" Ceci fished around for something to say.

"Actually," Kerry smiled, "Dar showed up to fire me. I managed to talk her out of it and we've been friends ever since."

"Really?" the older woman murmured. "Well, I'll go get that tea." Cecilia walked quickly to the kitchen and sanctuary.

Kerry watched her go, a thoughtful look on her face.

❖ ⌘ ❖ ⌘ ❖ ⌘ ❖

She stood with her eyes closed and her hands on the counter while the tea steeped. It had been worse than she'd expected, but in a curious way, better at the same time. She'd thought to find Dar cold and remote, her feelings locked down tight away just like they'd always been since her teenage years.

Instead, she'd halfway seen a glimpse of a child she'd thought long lost. Part of her—most of her—wanted to forget that and she felt a definite urge to send Dar on her way and allow her life to return to its sterile peace.

Surely, it would be better for both of them. It wasn't like Dar was in need. She'd done well. Better, to be honest, than Ceci had ever dreamed she would. She had a good life, a nice home. She seemed happy with her companion...

Footsteps made her open her eyes and turn her head to see Kerry enter the kitchen. The blond woman paused a few feet a way and studied her.

"Can I help with that?"

Kerry's voice was, Ceci noted, gentle and cultured, with a Midwest note in the vowels. It went with her wholesome good looks and was at distinct odds with the gleam of intense intelligence glinting off the interesting green of her eyes. "All right."

Kerry took that as permission to approach and did so, setting a few blue tinted glasses on the small tray Ceci had taken out and adding the pitcher to it.

"So." The older woman went to the white refrigerator and retrieved some ice in a separate pitcher. "What makes you hang around the Capitol, Ms. Stuart?"

"My father," Kerry replied quietly. "He's a senator."

Cecilia blinked, then her brows creased. "Not Roger Stuart, surely?" Kerry nodded. "Yes."

"Interesting." Gray eyes studied Kerry's face curiously. "Does he know about you and Paladar?"

Another nod. "He does."

Ceci's lips twitched briefly. "Not his year, hmm?" She took the pitcher and walked out, leaving Kerry to follow her with the tray.

She did with an almost silent sigh, turning the corner to see her lover standing at the window, peering out, her hands clasped behind her back. Dar turned as they entered and leaned against the sill, the sunlight backlighting her tall form and throwing her face into shadow. Kerry poured two glasses and picked one up, brought it over and handed it to her.

"Thanks."

Kerry gave her belly a friendly scratch and wrinkled her nose, her back turned to Cecilia. Dar's lips tightened and she inclined her head, then pushed off from the window and returned to the couch, sitting opposite her mother. Kerry followed her, and they sat in an uncomfortable silence, the faint tinkle of ice the only sound as they drank their tea.

Then Dar put her glass down and folded her hands together. She hesitated before speaking. "I'm glad I had a chance to say goodbye to Gran."

Safer subject. "I promised her I'd ask you," Cecilia remarked softly. "She kept all your cards in a book. I know she always appreciated getting them." She considered a moment, then stood and glided over to a chest of drawers. She put her hand on the knob of one, pulled it open, removed a large manila envelope and returned to hand it to her daughter. "You never put your return address on them. I could never mail these for her back to you."

Dar held the package with uncertainty then put it down on her knees. "Richard knew where I was."

Ceci nodded. "Probably. But I figured if you wanted us to know what your address was, you'd have put it down."

"Mmm." Dar had to acknowledge the truth of that. "Well, we need to get over and take care of things with him, then catch our flight." She stood up with her envelope, taking in the sight of the slight, silver blond woman seated across from her. "Take care, Mother."

"You too," Ceci murmured, allowing a long, guarded look into the pale blue eyes, and a single brief memory that made her heart clench and was discarded immediately. She stood and accompanied them to the door, pulled it open and waited for them to go through it.

They did, and she shut it behind them, as the silence settled comfortably around her again. She watched them out the window, though, unable to take her eyes off Dar until her daughter ducked into the passenger side seat and the car pulled away.

Ceci turned around and stared at the now empty room.

It was over.

She was safe. She'd fulfilled a promise and now she never had to see Dar again, if she didn't want to.

That was good.

Wasn't it?

It was hard to stand here, with the memories so fresh in her mind, and remember a time when it hadn't been like this. A time before she had to look up to her daughter.

When a small child had sat on her lap and looked up at her trustingly with those big blue eyes as they watched fireworks over the cow fields, in air so thick and moist it seemed to flow over them.

It was faint, that echo. But she could, if she tried, remember loving her daughter.

Maybe, at some level, she still did.

Ceci looked around the emptiness and wished they were still here. Painful as Dar's presence was, there was a link there, a solid, living, breathing link, that touched her down deep in places she'd shied away from for years.

Slowly, she was drawn through the living room and into the plain bedroom, with its low, platform bed and crisp white sheets. To her right was her closet, with its seldom opened door and she stopped with her hand on the knob for a long time before her fingers turned it reluctantly, and she pulled the door open, closing her eyes as the scent hit her.

Why?

Why do this?

In that moment she hated Dar all over again.

But her feet carried her inside and she simply stood, letting the memories surround her as her fingers touched remembered wool and her eyes drank in the rich colors and remembered shapes of what was once her life.

His things. Their things. Neatly folded clothes in the blues and greens he'd preferred.

The chest with their wedding gifts, carefully packed away and saved, most from the friends they'd made in the south or his service buddies.

Dar's cradle and the baby blanket, a gift from her mother.

It smelled of wool, from his uniforms and old polish, mixed with the faint tang of oil. She ran a shaking finger down a perfectly starched sleeve, then laid her cheek against it, feeling the scratchiness of the fabric and remembering what it had felt like with a living, breathing body inside.

Her legs folded and she sat down on a box full of remnants, carefully hoarded and stored away here. She picked up the soft, cheerful quilt that had once covered their bed and pulled it around her shoulders, tears hitting her knees as she hugged it to her, burying her face in the fabric.

Chapter
11

Kerry drove in silence for a bit, casting the occasional glance at the tall, silent form slumped in the seat next to her. "Hey," she finally said, tugging a fold in the knee of Dar's jeans. "You doing okay?"

Blue eyes picked up a bit of the sun's glare from outside. "Yeah. Listen, I'm sorry you had to get in the middle of all that." Dar gave her an apologetic look.

"Well," Kerry watched the signs overhead, and changed lanes, "I know how it is with families. And I remember how I felt when I went home for Thanksgiving." A large tractor trailer whipped by, making the smaller rental car shake. "Jerk," she muttered. "I couldn't do much, but I was glad I was here."

Dar covered her hand and rubbed a thumb over her knuckles. "Me too. Glad that's over, though." She faced forward. "You'll like Richard. He's decent, even though he's a lawyer."

Kerry nibbled the inside of her lip, debating on touching still sensitive nerves. "Dar, can I say something kind of personal to you?"

Her lover lifted an eyebrow. "Um...sure."

"Okay." Kerry made a turn and merged carefully into fitful traffic. "You're going to have to give me more specific directions soon."

"That's personal," Dar remarked, with a wary smile.

Green eyes flicked very briefly to her. "What I was going to say was...I know we were talking before we left and all and, I don't know, Dar. I mean, I just met your mother, but I think I sort of figured out that I don't think she hates you."

Dar sorted through the statement, feeling it rub against her smarting defenses. She realized she really didn't want to talk about the subject, but found it hard to brush Kerry's obvious concern off. "No. I..." she fingered the envelope, still sealed, "I never really thought that."

Kerry remained quiet.

"Maybe that would have been better."

"Why?"

"Hate is a lot more powerful than indifference," Dar murmured. "I felt like, after my father was gone, she was getting rid of an unwanted problem." She paused. "Not hate. Just an indifferent dislike that made me feel pretty damn insignificant."

"So you went out and conquered the world."

Dar consider that, then reluctantly nodded. "Yeah. Maybe."

"I think she loves you, Dar."

Dar shook her head. "No. She loved my father, Kerry. I was just a part of that. Once he was gone we had nothing in common, and all we did was hurt each other."

"No," Kerry disagreed stubbornly. "I don't believe that, Dar. I think she was trying to find a way back to you."

Oh yeah. Dar remembered the exchange they'd had. "Well, I'm out of relatives I give a damn about, so I guess she had her one chance." She folded her arms over her chest and gazed out the window.

Kerry drummed her fingers on the steering wheel. "You could call her once in a while," she suggested. "Just to say hi, now that you've seen each other and all."

Dar sighed. "She doesn't want me doing that."

"How d'you know?"

"Kerry..."

"Dar. You know what? I think the problem is you guys are too much alike." Kerry turned the wheel, paying attention to her route. "I saw her watching you and I don't think she's indifferent, honey. Honestly, I don't." She straightened the car out. "You're not."

Dar stared grumpily out the window, a half dozen retorts rising to her lips, only to subside unspoken. "Can we change the subject?" she muttered testily.

Kerry glanced at her. "Okay," she agreed, as her shoulders slumped in reaction. "Sorry. I know I...I can't fix my family and I sort of really like yours."

Dar turned her head and traced Kerry's profile with contrite eyes. "I appreciate that...and maybe you're right, Ker." She plucked at the envelope, pulling the flap up. "Her birthday's next month. Maybe I'll send a card."

Ooo. Kerry refrained from smiling too widely. "We can both send one," she offered. "I think she'd like that."

"Mmm." Dar pulled the small stack of envelopes out and set them on her lap. She turned the first over curiously and examined it. "Yeah. All right."

Kerry leaned back, flexing her hands and exhaling in mild satisfaction. *One down.*

❖ ⌘ ❖ ⌘ ❖ ⌘ ❖

The study was quiet, save the soft sound of a hard drive humming and the occasional rustle as the desk chair's occupant shifted. Chino was curled up on the couch, her muzzle resting on the arm as she watched Dar work.

"Goddamn it," Dar muttered, selecting a section of text, then copying it. "That's not what I asked for." She pasted it into an email then typed furiously and sent the message with a savage keystroke. "And you'd better have that in by Tuesday, mister, or I'm going to ram that IMUX in a place even extended cables won't reach it."

"Grr," Chino agreed, yawning and poking her pink tongue out.

"Yeah." Dar leaned back and rocked her head back and forth, rubbing her neck with one hand. She'd been crouched over her email for hours, trying to catch up on things that had been building all week. Kerry had gone out to pick up a few things off the island, and she'd taken the opportunity to concentrate on her project. "Okay. Next."

She leaned forward and clicked on the next mail. "Ah." This, at least, was moderately good news. Mark's analysis of the data they'd recovered from Allison had turned up a copy of their friend's online banking account and that had been sent to not only Duks and Dar, but to the corporate legal department as well.

Dar clicked on it to forward and typed in Alastair's name. "There. You wanted a smoking gun, you got one. The bastard was billing those customer's a 'management fee' and pocketing it." She hit send with considerably more satisfaction this time.

The next mail was from Ankow's office, and she skimmed through it, making small disgusted noises. "Yeah, right. I'll provide an onsite aide and escort for you, buddy. Right out the loading dock door." With a sigh, she forwarded the mail to María. "This is a visiting board member. He thinks he's God's gift to ILS, please treat him accordingly."

A bit of warm sunset trickled in, striping her forearms as they lay on the desk. It reminded her of just how long a day it had been and she surveyed her half full mailbox, then closed the window out and let the underwater scene she currently had as her backdrop replace it.

"That's enough, Chino." Dar let her head rest against the soft leather back of the chair. "I'll do the rest of that later, okay?"

"Yawp." Chino yawned sleepily, then climbed down, ambled over, and sat down on Dar's bare foot and licking her ankle.

Dar picked the half grown puppy up and put her on her lap. She scratched her ears and smiled a little as Chino transferred her licking to the underside of Dar's chin. "Hey. That's cold." Dar hugged the puppy and kissed her nose, glancing around a little guiltily as she did so. "You want to go for a walk? I think I need a walk, Chino. Your green eyed friend stuffed me like a pig with that spicy noodle thing she made for lunch."

She stood and carried the animal into the kitchen to retrieve her leash, then put her down and opened the back door. "G'wan."

Chino happily frisked down the steps and galloped over to the gate, then waited impatiently as Dar worked the latch, and they walked out onto the path heading towards the beach.

❖ ⌘ ❖ ⌘ ❖ ⌘ ❖

Kerry tucked the bags she'd acquired under an arm and strolled towards the outside cafe at Bayside. The sun was setting and a cool breeze came off the water. She took a deep breath of the salty air and found a seat, then tucked her purchases under her and leaned back against the railing. A waiter drifted towards her and she ordered a strawberry banana smoothie, then settled back to wait.

It didn't take long. She had her drink and was sucking contentedly on it when she caught a motion out of the corner of her eye and turned to see a tall, hooded figure casually making its way towards her. *Right on time.* Briefly, Kerry wrestled with her conscience, considering what she was doing was meddling rated a twelve on a one to ten scale.

On the other hand, she reasoned, as Andrew paused and watched a seagull before he continued. *On the other hand, this is my family now, and I love them. Dar understood that, right?* "Hi, Dad."

"Hey there, kumquat." Andrew dropped into the chair across from her. "Whatcha got in the glass?"

"It's a fruit and yogurt milkshake." Kerry pushed it towards him. "Try it."

He picked it up and sniffed it suspiciously, then took a small sip. "Huh. That ain't half bad."

Kerry smiled, then leaned forward and cocked her head. "Did you get hurt?" A bandage covered half the shadowed face, almost obscuring his right eye.

"Naw." Andrew returned her glass. "Some damn crazy stuff the VA's doin'." He cleared his throat. "Gov'ment gimme pig kinda thing."

"Are they trying to fix some of the scars?" Kerry inched her chair closer. "That's where the really bad ones were." She peered curiously at him, noting the embarrassed glower that was the very image of his daughter's. "Can I see?"

"No you may not, young lady." Andrew growled at her. "So don't you be looking at me like that."

Kerry gazed compassionately at him.

"Stop that."

She gave him her best sad puppy look, the one that always worked on Dar.

"I said stop that," the tall man rasped. "Those damn green eyes ain't workin' on me, hear?"

She mentally counted to ten.

"Aw, shit." Andrew scooted his chair closer. "It ain't hardly nothing. Damn doctors were just tryin' t'fix it so it didn't smart so damn much."

Kerry lifted a hand up slowly and touched the fastener on the bandage, feeling the skin tense under her touch, as Andrew's eyes closed in reflex. She pulled the white gauze aside, and leaned closer. "Oh. I see." The two large, knotted scars that had almost covered the right side of his face had been seemingly removed, replaced by what looked like a thin layer of reddened, tacked in place skin. "Is that a graft?"

The blue eyes opened and regarded her. "Fake. Some new stuff," he muttered.

"Ohh. Artificial skin. Yeah. I saw a special on that." Kerry gently put the bandage back into place. "Cutting edge technology. In fact, um," she laughed softly, "we administer the mainframes it was developed on."

"Yeah, well, won't look any prettier, but it sure damn 'nough feels better," Andrew admitted. "Hurt to move the other way."

Kerry brushed his other cheek with her fingertips, resisting the urge to give him a hug. "I'm glad. I know Dar will be glad to hear it too."

"Mmph." Andrew leaned back and stuck his hands in the pockets of his hooded sweatshirt. This was his summer version, she realized, as it had the sleeves cut off to expose his muscular arms. "How's my kid?"

"She's all right." Kerry settled back too. "It was kind of a tough couple of days."

"You go up there with her?"

Kerry nodded.

"Good girl."

They were silent for a bit.

"She kind of knocked everyone's socks off," Kerry finally said, feeling her way very cautiously.

Andrew smiled, his eyes briefly glinting with paternal pride. "I bet." Then he fell silent again.

"I...got to meet your wife." Kerry saw the flinch. "At the service and then we stopped by where she lives this morning."

His eyes focused on something out on the horizon and he remained quiet, watching and listening.

Kerry took her time, wanting above all not to hurt him. "It's...I've been wondering all day what I was going to say to you when I saw you."

"She's doin' all right," Andrew finally rasped. "Ain't she?"

How to answer that? "No. I don't think she is." She spoke on an exhale. "She seemed really alone."

He stared at her intently, devouring everything.

"I mean she lives in a nice place but," Kerry clasped her hands to keep them from shaking, aware of how delicate a line she was treading, "everything was very...stark, very plain and functional and it was so strange. There weren't any colors."

The waiter drifted back over. "Something for you, sir?"

"Whiskey," Andrew answered in a clipped voice.

Kerry waited for the waiter to leave then put a hand on Andrew's knee. "I'll stop, if you want me to."

"No." He seemed tired. "G'wan. She wasn't...sick or nothin', was she? I mean..."

"I don't think so, no." She took a breath. "Just very alone." Kerry steeled herself. "I think she really misses you."

He was totally motionless for a long moment. "Thought she'd have started over by now," he answered in a remote voice. "S'what she said she'd do. Find her someone who wouldn't run off on her like I done."

Kerry took his hand in hers. "That's not what she did." She took a breath. "I think she lost the most important thing in her life and there was nothing that could replace that, so she didn't even try."

The waiter came and delivered Andrew's shot. "Get you folks an appetizer or something?"

"Um...a basket of Cajun shrimp," Kerry told him, just to make him go away.

The shadowed eyes regarded her in bleak shock. "Dar tell her about me?" Andrew finally asked bluntly.

"No," Kerry replied quietly. "She promised she wouldn't and I know she'd never break a promise to you." She took a folded piece of paper from her shirt pocket and put it in the palm of his hand, closing his fingers around it. "And I didn't think I had the right. Not without talking to you first. But I did write down the phone and the address." Her eyes searched his face. "If you wanted to use them."

His hand tightened around the paper and he sat very still, blue eyes shifting in intense thought. "She didn't forget about me, huh?" he asked, at last, in a mild wondering tone.

The awful tension gripping Kerry relaxed. "I don't think anyone who met you could forget you," she murmured. "You're a very special person." She leaned back, emotionally exhausted, then deliberately picked up the shot of whiskey and downed it in a single gulp. "Brr." She shuddered as the alcohol burned its way down, sending a relaxing flow through a body not accustomed to the hard stuff.

Andrew blinked at her in surprise, then drew his hand back and opened it, looking at the piece of paper before he tightened his fist and stuck it into his pocket. "Yer pretty damn special yourself, Kerry," he remarked in a gentle voice. "I can see why my kid's so stuck on you." He watched her lick her lips. "You want 'nother one?"

Kerry rubbed her nose. "Um. No. I don't usually do that. I was just a little wound up. Sorry. I'll have him get another."

Andrew snagged her smoothie glass and sucked on that instead. "Naw. This is all right." He looked up as the waiter put the basket down. "Can you get me one more of these damn things?"

"Um, sure." The man looked confused but willing, and left, after marking down something on his pad.

Dar's father leaned forward, resting his elbows on his knees. "How'd my kid handle it?"

Kerry took a shrimp, examining it. "It was rough. I think what happened really hurt her." She booted the bags next her lightly. "I got her some treats. Just to cheer her up a little."

Andrew peeked into the bag. "Lord." He managed a slight grin. "Got you enough chocolate there?"

Kerry smiled back. "Want to come help administer it?"

The answer came back surprisingly fast. "Yeap. I think I'd like to do that. Need to talk at her about a few things anyhow."

Kerry put a bill down on the table and picked up the styrofoam plate of shrimp. "C'mon." She offered him a spicy nugget. "Share?"

"I'd better take custody of them bags," came the gruff reply, as Andrew joined her and they walked down the patio into the setting sun. "No sense in risking good chocolate. You might trip or something."

"You sound just like Dar when you say that."

"Doncha mean she sounds like me?" Andrew countered, tasting a shrimp. "Jesus H. Christ in a Humvee, girl. What the hell are you eating there?" He swallowed a mouthful of the drink he'd taken along.

"Um. It's kinda spicy, huh?" Kerry smiled sheepishly. "Sorry. Shoulda warned you. I've gotten to like things a lot hotter since I've met Dar."

"Heh." Andrew chuckled.

"Hmm?" Kerry gave him a puzzled look and saw the amused twinkle in his eyes. "Ow." She realized what she'd said and groaned. "Daaaadd."

"Heh. Tips of yer ears turn pinker than a pig's butt, y'know that?"

Kerry reached her free hand up and covered her ear in reflex. "Ugh. I know, I know."

❖ ⌘ ❖ ⌘ ❖ ⌘ ❖

Dar was sprawled on the beach, her butt firmly perched on dry sand and her legs stretched out into the surf, glistening as the incoming tide washed over them. She leaned against a piece of up thrust coral rock and tossed bits of broken shell lazily into the water, watched alertly by a curled up Chino next to her.

She wiggled her toes and watched the long shadows cast by the setting sun behind her flicker, the warmth on her back and shoulders combined with the somnolent salty air coaxing her almost into sleep.

The waves moved in softly with their familiar rush and hiss, and the faint tinkle of shells being left behind for lucky hunters to find. Dar closed her eyes and enjoyed the peace, sorely needed after the past few days.

At least she had a whole day tomorrow to relax before the new week started. She ran through a list of possible activities, then decided to ask Kerry if she'd like some time underwater. A nice trip out on the boat. Maybe they'd picnic...

Dar opened her eyes and gazed out at the empty horizon. "Damn, my life has sure changed, Chino."

"Rrfh." The Labrador licked her chops and put her head back down on Dar's thigh.

"I used to work all weekend." She stroked the dog's soft ears. "Or sleep. If I'd finally worn myself out enough. I definitely never looked forward to Fridays before." Now, she not only did, but also resented when meetings or conference calls kept her late at the office, and she wondered briefly just how much that had impacted her job performance.

Probably a lot, she admitted privately. She knew she used to keep up on every minute detail, sometimes startling staff members with her sharp questions. That...just didn't happen anymore. She had let a lot of things slip, left a bunch of issues resting on her crew, and mostly on Kerry's shoulders, trusting them to do their jobs, and hoping it didn't come back to bite her in the butt.

It felt so strange.

But so far...so far, no major disasters had happened, amazingly enough. Little things, sure, but they always did anyway, and she'd come to realize lately that maybe, just maybe she'd been a touch too involved.

"Bet I drove everyone out of their cotton picking minds, Chino," she confessed. "I'm lucky they didn't toss me off the fourteenth floor balcony." She stifled a yawn and tossed a last shell into the water. "We'd better go back. See what your other mommy's been up to, hmm?" She leaned over. "Where's Kerry?"

The milky ears shot up and Chino raised her head, cocking it to one side.

"Go find Kerry," Dar urged with a grin, watching as the puppy scrambled to her feet and ambled off. She pulled herself up and dusted her shorts off, then followed, digging her toes into the warm sand with a feeling of distinct pleasure.

❖ ⌘ ❖ ⌘ ❖ ⌘ ❖

"Hmm." Kerry ducked into the kitchen. "She must have taken Chino for a walk." She put her packages down, slipped the chocolate out and set it on the counter. "She loves to run on the beach."

"My kid or the dog?" Andrew asked, leaning on the counter.

"Yes," the blond woman answered, with a smile.

"Mmph. She always wanted a dog."

"She told me," Kerry replied quietly.

The tall man pushed off the counter and went to stand by the sink, gazing out at the water. "Wasn't easy for a kid. The way we lived." He paused. "Moving round all the time. Dar didn't make too many friends."

"Moving doesn't always cause that." Kerry moved over and leaned next to him. "I lived most of my life in the same spot. I knew a lot of people, but I figured out pretty early on that most of the people who wanted to be friends with me had a motive."

Andrew nodded a couple of times.

"It wasn't that bad, really. I had a lot of fun growing up. I think it was best before I was old enough to realize what was going on with my family," she mused. "I was a pretty happy kid."

They stood in silence for bit. "Miss yer family?" Dar's father finally asked.

Kerry had to think about that. "I miss my sister...and my brother. We were close." She paused. "My aunts and uncles...we used to have big gatherings. They'd all be there, with all my cousins. We'd get pretty rowdy sometimes."

Andrew merely listened and watched, a natural state with him.

"I don't miss checking myself in the mirror six times before leaving my room." A distant look entered the green eyes. "Or never being quite good enough." Her head cocked to one side thoughtfully. "Being here on my own was such a change. I'd go back there for holidays and wonder how I ever lived like that for so long."

The outer gate clanked, audible even through the closed windows, and they peered out to see Dar entering with Chino bouncing around near her knees. A smile crossed Kerry's face in unconscious reaction at the sight, as the crimson rays turned her lover's tanned skin a burnished golden hue. She wore a very brief, cut off sleeveless sweatshirt and a pair of ragged denim shorts and there certainly was a lot showing to admire.

"Good Lord," Andrew complained. "Think she's living in the streets with them clothes." He shook his head and stomped to the door, flung it open, and put his hands on his hips. "Whatcha think ye're doing out there half naked young lady?"

Dar's dark head jerked up from where she brushed off the sand from her knees and she blinked. "Dad?"

"J'think it's the mail man talkin' t'you like that?"

His daughter straightened up and mimicked him, putting her hands on her hips, then glanced down her long frame. "Half naked? This isn't half naked." She paused, then grinned and pulled off the sweatshirt, leaving nothing but her sports bra and muscle tone. "This...is half naked." She spread her arms cheerfully. "See?"

"Lord have mercy." Andrew clapped a hand over his eyes. "Git in here." He pointed off to his right. "And you stop laughing."

Kerry was leaning over the sink, trying to catch her breath from giggling. "Oh god. I can't."

Dar trotted up the steps with Chino scrambling next to her and entered. "C'mon, Dad. It's not like you've never seen my in my underwear."

One blue eye appeared. "There was a lot less of you t'see when you were six and running round without yer clothes on, I'll tell ya that," Andrew groused. "Or when you were a tot and pulled yer diapers off all the time."

"Dad." Dar rolled her eyes.

Kerry felt a new set of giggles coming on.

"Damn good aim you had," her father went on, irrepressibly. "Used them things like a slingshot."

"Dad!" his daughter got out an outraged squawk.

"Heh. Teach you to sass me, won't it?" But the blue eyes twinkled gently. "Didn't figure back then, though, such a scrappy little thing'd grow up so damn pretty."

It caught Dar off guard. She produced the most tongue tied, bashful look Kerry had ever seen on an adult human being and she sorely wished she had the digital camera to capture it forever. "I'm not surprised." She distracted Andrew from his blushing offspring. "Look who she takes after." She winked at him, then laughed. "Oh. Neat. Now I can say I made a sailor blush."

"Sonofabiscuit," Andrew muttered.

"I'm going to go get some email sorted." Kerry slipped past them and diplomatically left the two alone. "Come get me when you feel like dinner."

Dar watched her go wistfully, then took a breath and ducked into the laundry room, retrieved a white cotton T-shirt and pulled it on. "Better?" She gave her father a wry look.

He grunted, but his mouth twitched into a grin.

"Thirsty?" Dar went to the refrigerator and retrieved a pitcher of grape juice. She could feel the unspoken emotion between them and it was making her a little nervous. "Wasn't expecting you to be by. You in the neighborhood?"

He took the glass she offered and held it. "Not really. Kerry done gave me a call. Had a few things to say."

Dar was a little surprised, but she nodded. "Want to go inside?" She led the way into the living room and staked out a corner of the couch, watching him settle into the corner of the loveseat at right angles to her. They were both, she realized, a little uncomfortable. "What's the Band-Aid about?"

He reached a hand up and touched it. "Just some stuff they're doing to make it hurt a little less."

"Mmm."

They were silent for a bit.

"Tough up there, huh?" Andrew asked, after several sips of juice.

"Wasn't the most pleasant experience I've ever had, no." Dar squared her shoulders and faced him. "But I'm glad I went."

He nodded slowly.

"Family's the same."

His lips twitched.

Dar studied the tile, tracing the grout lines intently. "Mom's doing all right. I guess. I...um..." She shook her head, "I wish you'd call her." She had to force the words out, in a quiet mutter. "It was hard as hell to see her and not say anything." She exhaled unhappily, then glanced up.

Andrew shifted uncomfortably. "Been so damn long. I don't know...can't just call..."

It would be a shock, true. "You could write," Dar suggested softly.

"Never was much good at that." He sighed, and stared at the bit of paper. "You...really think it'll be... She won't just tell me to go t'hell or something?"

Dar considered the question very seriously. The fear she understood only too well. "I think she's in a lot of pain." She almost felt her father flinch at that. "And I think you're the only fix for that, Daddy." Now, she looked up, putting all the sincerity she could into her voice and eyes. "That's what I honestly believe."

He was very still, only the pale eyes flicked around the room as he thought. Finally, he let out a tired little sigh. "I miss her." He paused. "Damn, I do."

Dar had to clamp her jaw down hard. "I know," she said, after a moment for the lump to go down.

"The whole damn thing with the family though... I don't know if I can fight that fight again, Dar." Andrew closed his eyes. "Can't ask her to give that up again. You know they won't put up with me."

Dar got up and went to her study. She returned a moment later holding an envelope and sat down again. "To hell with them," she stated softly, holding one hand out to him. "C'mere."

Hesitantly, he leaned forward. "What?" He watched as she put the envelope into one hand and curled his fingers over it. "What is that, honey?"

"Your pension."

Andrew's brows, almost obscured against his scarred skin, drew together. "What?" Puzzled, he opened the envelope and took the papers out, unfolding them, and running his eyes over their contents.

Then he stopped.

And his face went totally blank in utter shock.

"Paladar Katherine Roberts, what in the name of God is this?" he asked in a strangled whisper.

It was a very sweet moment. Dar absorbed it and tucked it away down deep. "May's trust fund came due," she answered calmly. "I signed it over to you and had Richard put it in your name."

"M..." He simply stared at her.

"I think May would have liked that." Dar smiled wistfully. "I know I did." She looked up. "You gave me so much. It felt great to give something back." A tear escaped and she wiped it away impatiently. "Don't say you won't take it, because it's too late for that."

He folded the papers up and leaned his forehead against them, too overcome to say anything at all.

"I knew if I asked you it'd be no." Dar ticked a finger off. "If I offered, you'd refuse. If I gave you a chance to turn it down, you would." Her jaw jutted out. "So I didn't."

He gazed at her.

Dar smiled and glanced up to see a pair of green eyes peeking at her from the stairwell. "Kerry, could you get Dad more juice? I think he's about to cough up a kidney on the floor here."

"Sure." The blond woman ambled down the stairs and ducked into the kitchen, then reappeared with the pitcher, pouring some in Andrew's empty glass. "You okay?" She put a hand on the silent man's shoulder.

"No, I am not okay," he managed to rasp. "Did you know about this?"

"Sure." Kerry sat down next to him on the loveseat and put an arm around him. "I thought it was the most incredibly great idea I'd ever heard."

"Did you?" Andrew seemed to still be in shock.

"Yes, I did." Kerry didn't feel any resistance to her touch, so she scratched his back between the shoulder blades, where his daughter always liked it.

He fingered the papers. "Can't think of a damn thing to say," he muttered at last.

Dar smiled and regarded her now empty, clasped hands.

That meant he wouldn't say no.

May would have definitely approved. And as for the rest of the family... Dar's eyes glinted in the dusky light.

They can most certainly kiss my ass.

Chapter
12

Of course, it rained the next day. Kerry stood for a moment, yawning and peering out the double glass sliding doors that opened to the ocean, watching the sheets of thick raindrops almost obscure the surf.

Well, she considered, *that was okay too.* It was a great morning for sleeping in—and they had—and here it was almost noon and she was just crawling out to put up some coffee. She continued on into the kitchen and flipped the light on, since the weather outside made it gloomy, and measured off the coffee before hitting the start switch.

It made a friendly, percolating sound as the water emerged, and she stepped back, stretching her arms overhead and considering what to rummage up for breakfast.

Okay, brunch.

Kerry glanced at the clock. Lunch, if they followed their usual schedule. She ran her hands through her hair and yawned again, smiling as Chino trotted into the kitchen and sat down in front of her biscuit jar, looking up at Kerry expectantly.

"Oh." She put one fist on her hip. "So. You think you've got me trained, huh?"

"Woof," Chino barked, then looked up at the jar.

"I don't think so, madam."

"Woof!"

Dar peeked inside, then slid her long body around the doorjamb and padded barefoot across the tile, going right to the jar and taking a biscuit out for the puppy, which Chino crunched contentedly.

"Dar!"

The taller woman paused, blinked, then removed a second biscuit and handed it to Kerry. "Sorry. Didn't know you liked them," she drawled. "Try some peanut butter on it."

"Hah, hah." She tossed the cookie back, as Dar caught it one handed. "You spoil her so much."

"Mmm," Dar acknowledged, a trifle sheepishly. "Seems to be a habit of mine lately." She slid an arm around Kerry, who had sidled closer, and welcomed the warmth of her body against the kitchen's air conditioned chill. "Maybe I'm coming down with a virus."

Kerry snorted into the cotton of her shirt. "You'd be more likely to write a virus than catch one. You're disgustingly healthy, Dar. Did you know that? I've had two colds and a stomach flu since I've known you and you haven't caught anything."

Dar chuckled. "My body knows how much I hate being sick and it hates putting up with me so much, if I do catch something, it pretends not to notice." She considered. "I can't even remember the last time...oh, wait, yes I can." Her eyes rolled. "I caught food poisoning from the cafeteria at some account I was...consolidating."

"Ew." Kerry winced. "I've never had it but Mike did once, and the colors he turned would have done Van Gogh proud."

"Yeah. I was so sick I didn't stop throwing up for...God, it seemed like forever," Dar acknowledged. "I finally ended up just staying in the bathroom. I was too weak to get up." She pensively paused. "Long couple of days."

Kerry's brow creased. "Why didn't you call someone to help you? God, Dar."

The blue eyes studied her. "There wasn't anyone to call," she replied, very simply. "It was in my old place in the grove. Just me and a few lizards."

It struck her, now, the realization of just how alone Dar had been before they'd met. "Wow," she touched the dark haired woman comfortingly, "well, if your body happens to forget now rest assured you'll be taken care of."

Dar's lips briefly tensed into a smile. "That might be worth getting sick for," she allowed, resting her forearms on Kerry's shoulders. "So," her eyes went to the window, "what do you feel like doing today?"

"Well, we've both got inboxes to clear...and laundry. We could get caught up on everything for a change."

"Mmm." Dar sounded very noncommittal.

"Or, we could laze around together on the couch all day and watch cartoons."

A frank, unrepentant grin flashed back at her.

"Okay. So. Now that we've got that settled, go find *Space Ghost*, and I'll bring out the coffee and whatever I find for breakfast."

Dar obediently ambled out into the living room and flipped the TV on. Grabbing the remote, she found a nice, soft spot on the couch to curl up on, wincing a bit as the cold leather took its time warming to her body.

Thunder rolled outside, and she lay down on her side, propping her head up with one hand as she surfed.

Always liked rainy days, she reflected idly, listening to the hard pattering outside. *They were good times to read, or watch old movies, or...* A grin played over her face, remembering the long summer afternoons on the base spent constructing models. Much to her mother's despair. All those intricate, tiny pieces and the scent of glue, so carefully painted and put into place.

Haven't thought about that in forever. How many hours had she lost herself in those? All the ships of the fleet, each with its proper, exact markings and then coming home from college one time, and finding them gone. Given to some shelter or other because her mother thought she'd outgrown them.

She'd rarely ever been that angry. She hadn't spoken to her mother for a month after that, until her father had sought her out and made peace. Like always, able to bridge their differences with his love for her mother and his understanding of Dar, they'd depended on him for that. Maybe that was why after he was gone...

Dar sighed, releasing the memories as Kerry entered, bearing a small tray with two steaming cups and a basket of something that smelled cinnamony and sweet. "Ooo...what have we here?" She grinned at her lover. "A nice healthy breakfast, I see."

Kerry stuck her tongue out. "We're low on bean sprouts. I had to improvise." She set the tray down with the coffee and cinnamon rolls and then took a seat on the wide couch next to Dar's sprawled form. "I didn't think you'd object." She tore a roll in half and offered it to her lover.

"Nope." Dar chewed the sweet pastry contentedly, saving a small piece for the cream colored Labrador head that magically appeared in front of her face. Then she licked her fingers off and took a sip of her coffee, put it back down, and curled an arm around Kerry to bring her closer.

"Hmm." The blond woman relaxed onto her side and pressed her back against Dar's warmth, sharing the colorful, soft throw pillow. "Oh yeah. I can deal with this all day." She yawned and snuggled closer. "I like rainy days." Idly, she picked up a few bits of mail lying on the table and sorted through them. "How did we get on a mailing list for X rated videos?"

Dar lifted her head to peer at the item. "Mmm...videos...means video recorders, which means electronics, which means high technology which means computers. Can you figure out how we got on a list for that?"

Kerry paused and thought. "Nope." She shrugged and chucked the mail, which Chino ran and retrieved for her, setting it down hopefully next to the couch. "Let's see...your Microsoft newsletter. Want that?"

"No."

"Here you go, Chino. What about the small computer book club offer?"

"Oh. Right. I need more small computer books."

"Right." Toss. "Invitation to a time share in Las Vegas?"

"Nah. They don't like me there," Dar responded. "I know too much about the systems programming."

"Okay." Kerry peered at the next envelope. "Oh. You're having a class reunion."

A brow arched.

She passed the envelope back. "Here. Oh wait. Don't move. I'll open it."

Dar hadn't stirred an inch. "Did I say I wanted to see it?" she grumbled, then sighed as Kerry opened the green and orange striped envelope and pulled out its contents. "I'm not going."

"Aw." Kerry read with interest. "Why not? It's here next weekend. It looks like fun, Dar. It's a 'come as you were' party." She showed the flyer to her lover. "C'mon."

A blue eye pinned her. "High school wasn't a time I remember all that fondly, Kerry. I think I was voted 'Girl Most Likely To Be Incarcerated.'" She chuckled self deprecatingly. "It was the start of that rebellious phase I mentioned."

"All the more reason," the blond woman responded. "Don't you want to go back there and prove otherwise? Didn't you really get a kick out of doing that with your relatives?"

Hmm. A brow lifted in thought.

"I wouldn't call it a kick," Dar murmured, then shook her head. "No. I really didn't get along with the crowd that's organizing this." She pointed at some names. "Key Clubbers. Bet they haven't changed." She gave Kerry a suspicious look. "Why are you so enthusiastic about this?"

Kerry grinned, her nose wrinkling up cheerfully. "I want to indulge my newly discovered hedonistic tendencies. I want to see you in leather."

She got a definite "look" in return. "You what?"

"And chains and the torn clothes." Green eyes sparkled. "Though," Kerry riffled through Dar's hair, "I think we can fake the spikes."

Dar started laughing. "Jesus, Kerry. You gotta be kidding. I don't have that stuff around anymore and even if I did, it'd never fit." Then she remembered the boxes still sealed in the storage area. She bit her lip. *Nah.*

A finger touched her nose. "I bet we could find something," Kerry coaxed. "C'mon, Dar. Hey. Tell you what. I'll even rent you a motorcycle or something for the night."

Dar clapped a hand over her eyes. "How d'you even know I know how to ride one?" she objected faintly. "Kerry, I can't just—"

"Sure you can. Lots of people go to their high school reunions."

Long fingers drummed on the couch's leather surface. "Okay," Dar finally responded. "On one condition."

Triumph! Kerry squirmed around and faced her, with a delighted grin. "Name it."

Now it was Dar's turn to grin. "You come with me."

A snort. "Of course. You think I'd let an opportunity like this go by? Me and the digital camera—"

"Dressed the same way," the low voice interrupted her slyly.

Kerry stopped and blinked. "Uh." Slowly a finger pointed at her own chest. "Me?" Her face scrunched up in comedic dismay, as she fingered her Tweety shirt. "Dar, I'm not very convincing in leather. Really."

Dar waited, her eyes twinkling.

Kerry sighed. "Well, okay. I'm pretty sure I'll look goofy, but if that's what it takes, that's what I'll do." She gave Dar a firm nod. "Kerry, Biker Chick, will be there."

Hmm. Dar let a chuckle escape as they snuggled together, and the thunder rolled around them. *This might even be kind of fun.*

❖ ⌘ ❖ ⌘ ❖ ⌘ ❖

It was still raining as Kerry pulled up to the office. She tugged up her rain hood before she ducked out of the Mustang and made the short dash to the front door. The security guard saw her coming and stepped on the plate, making the glass portals open and letting her inside with only a minimum drenching. "Morning, Ms. Stuart."

"Hi. Morning." Kerry pushed her hood back and shook her head, scattering a few droplets from her hair. "Wow. Lousy weather, huh?"

"Yes, ma'am." The guard peered behind her expectantly. "Ms. Roberts coming along with you?"

Kerry smiled. "No. She's got a meeting this morning." Not true. "She'll be by in a bit." Dar was, in reality, not far behind her, but they decided to take separate cars this week, since their unwelcome board member was roaming around and Kerry had been assigned to escort him. Neither of them went out of their way to hide their relationship, but there was no point in advertising it to the already antagonistic Ankow.

She was alone in the elevator and remained that way as she got out on the fourteenth floor—not surprising given the hour. María was in, though, and she smiled at the secretary as she poked her head in Dar's outer office. "Morning."

"Ah. Good morning, Kerrisita." María smiled back. "Is terrible weather, no?" Her eyes went to the barely visible hallway behind Kerry's head. "Dar is not with you?"

It occurred to Kerry that coming separately might possibly cause more comment than just arriving together would. "She took her car," she explained. "Is our visitor here yet?"

The dark head shook no. "His plane is landing at nine. We are sending Consuelo for him."

Ah, Consuelo. Not a bad idea. "Is she still moonlighting as a dancer?"

"*Sí.*" María smiled primly. "Is so cultural, no?"

Kerry bit off a grin. "Absolutely. Hey, Mariana tells me she's gotten approval for my assistant. I hear it's someone familiar." She'd been surprised at the move and astounded at the person Mariana had hired for her. They'd been putting off the addition for a while, with Kerry stating she really didn't need one, more to prevent having to deal with the awkwardness of bringing a stranger in than anything else. But now, with all the new projects, it was unfair to ask María to coordinate for both of them and Mariana had gone ahead, putting Kerry's fears to rest by hiring María's young daughter whom she and Dar already knew.

Who also knew about them and was a quiet, reserved girl not much for spreading rumors around.

María beamed. "Mayte is so excited. She spent the entire weekend choosing what clothes and how to do her hair. She cannot wait to start. She will be here at nine also to do her paperwork."

"Great." Kerry waved. "Gotta go get ready for my squiring assignment. See you later, María." She pulled her head back out and went down the hallway into the little alcove where her office door was.

There, she paused, watching the busy activity. A small room just off to one side had been used for storage and now everything was being moved out. To the left, a handsome wooden desk stood on one end, waiting to go in, and behind that an MIS cart was parked with a PC and monitor on it. She poked her head in the room as the last of the boxes left and nodded.

It wasn't huge, about twelve feet square, but it was carpeted, and the walls were clean, with soft blue soundproofing weave on them.

"Excuse me, Ms. Stuart." A polite voice made her jump and she ducked out of the way as the maintenance worker maneuvered the desk through the door and got it positioned. Then he glanced up and wiped his brow. "This all right?"

Kerry blinked. "Um." She studied the room. "Yes. Sideways to that wall would be good, I think. It's near the powerstrip."

He nodded. "I always like to ask. 'Specially with you ops people. Dear Lord knows I was in that office," he pointed towards hers, "hours getting things how Ms. Roberts wanted 'em."

It was an unexpectedly revealing moment, and Kerry smiled. "Well, you did a great job. I didn't have to move a thing." She patted the doorframe and left the man to his work, going through her door and into her office and closing it behind her. Her eyes moved around the now familiar confines. "Hours, huh? And you let me think it was just an extra office you had hanging around." She chuckled and went to her desk, flipped the switch to turn on her PC, then wandered over to the window while it booted.

It was dark and gloomy outside, with sheets of rain still falling over the drenched landscape, and fractious whitecaps lashing the shoreline just visible from her window and ruffling even the usually calm waters of Biscayne Bay, which the office overlooked. "Maybe we'll get lucky and they'll close the airport," she remarked. "Or make him land in Tampa."

Not likely. MIA was used to this weather and only ever shut down in the worst possible scenarios, such as tornado watches and hurricanes.

Her phone buzzed, and she sighed, then turned and eyed the display. *Ah.* She punched a button. "Morning, Mark."

"Hey. Where's the boss?" The MIS manager's voice was preoccupied. "She's not answering in her office."

"Probably because she's not here yet," Kerry answered dryly.

"Oh. I saw your IP come active so I figured she'd be around," Mark replied. "I'll page her. Thanks."

He hung up, and Kerry shook her head, then looked up as a knock came at the door. "What is this? Did the entire building come in early today? C'mon in!"

Maríana opened the door and entered, carrying several folders and small pot of geraniums. "Morning, Kerry. Your new administrative assistant is starting today."

"I know. I saw the movers outside."

"Right. Okay, here's her profile. We've already done the background and government screening and she came out clean."

"I'd hope so. Since she's barely twenty." Kerry took the folder and put it on her desk. "We got to meet her at her sister's quinces not too long ago. She's really nice."

Maríana nodded. "Yes, she is. She's got nice things to say about you, too." She smiled at the younger woman. "Not that people generally don't have, mind you." She took a seat in Kerry's visitor's chair. "Which reminds me."

Uh oh. Kerry sat down, and rested her arms on her desk.

"Your six month evaluation is coming up."

Ah. "I know."

The Personnel VP considered a moment, sucking on her lower lip. "Usually, the person who does that is your direct supervisor."

Kerry nodded, folding her hands. "I don't see any need to deviate from that," she told the woman calmly.

"Kerry," Maríana lowered her voice, "the purpose is to get an objective report on your professional qualifications."

"And Dar can be very objective," she responded. "She always has been. Right from the start. When I do things right, I get commended.

When I do things wrong, and I have, I get reprimanded, just like everyone else."

The older woman looked surprised. "Really?"

"Really. I've gotten called on the carpet several times and believe me, it hurts," Kerry admitted. "But it's never personal, Mari. It's all very 'you did this, you should have done that, this is what happened, don't let it happen again kind of stuff.'" She shrugged. "Just like everyone else."

"Hmm."

"The only difference is, after a day when that happens, I get to go home and get a big hug." Kerry's lips pressed into a thin smile. "And I try not to let it happen very often. So, no. I'm pretty sure I'll get an objective report, as objective as anyone else would give, at any rate." She paused. "At least I'll know she's not holding the fact that I'm sleeping with my boss against me."

Maríana winced.

"I trust her," Kerry added, very softly.

"All right." Mari held up a hand. "You've made good points. Let me go drop off the forms in her office. Mind if I use your back way?"

She sighed. "Go ahead. But she's not in yet. I don't think."

"Really? Something wrong? You guys all right?" Concerned hazel eyes studied her.

Kerry threw up her hands. "We were trying to be inconspicuous for a week while that board member's here. Instead, I think the most talked about thing in the lunchroom's going to be the fact we didn't drive in together."

Maríana stared at her, then laughed. "Oh, my god. That is so true," she admitted, lifting her hands with the geranium and all, and letting them drop. "Apologies, Kerry. It's just that you get used to a routine around here and when it changes, people notice." She held up the plant. "This, for instance. I gave it to Duks, because he was moaning that his office has no color."

"Yeah?"

"Mmm. Except he's had to explain a dozen times to people why he's suddenly showing an interest in horticulture. He gave up and made me take it back. Said he'd just go out and get a couple of beer steins instead or put a stuffed fish on the wall."

Kerry laughed.

"All right, Kerry. I'll send Mayte over when she gets done with her paperwork. Hopefully that'll be before our guest shows up." She waved her geranium and walked out, leaving behind a scent of earth, flowers, and Chanel.

Kerry sighed and shook her head, then turned and opened up her mail program, watching the inbox fill to bursting with lots of little exclamation points indicating urgent messages. "Happy Monday."

Chapter
13

"Dar."

The tall woman looked back from her worktable where she studied a new set of bandwidth reports. "Yes?" she called out, knowing the intercom would pick her voice up.

"Mr. Ankow is here."·

Yippee. "Thank you. Show him in, please." Dar allowed her voice to ooze with mock charm. She expelled a breath, and glanced at her pager noting the time. *Well, the storm had bought them a few hours, at least, and trapped Ankow in an airplane for the same length of time.*

The door opened and María came in, allowing the tall man to enter behind her and giving both him and her boss a polite smile. "Dar, they have canceled your conference call at eleven. They will reschedule for later this week."

"Thanks, María." Dar turned and faced her unwelcome guest. "Morning. Hear you had a rough flight coming in."

Ankow was dressed in an impeccable dark gray suit and expensive looking midnight blue silk tie with very thin maroon stripes. "A waste of my time. Let's stop compounding that, Roberts." He walked across the floor and sat down in one of her chairs, peering out at the rain. "Now that you've had your little fun sending Carmen Miranda after me, you can just assign me to whatever blond bimbo with the brains of a pencil you have planned and let me get on my way."

Dar finished making a note on her notepad, then took her time meandering around to her desk chair and sitting down in it. She leaned back and crossed an ankle over her knee, very aware of her comfortable cotton shirt and khakis contrast to his formal wear. "Carmen who?" She put a faint smile on her face. "You mean Consuelo?"

"The dancer you thought you'd distract me with." He smiled right back. "She's not my type."

"Ah." Dar rubbed her cheek. "Consuelo González is our top marketing strategist. She's got three bachelor's degrees, a masters in business, and she's working on her doctorate in finance and applied statistics...and all you noticed was her body?" Dar clucked. "We thought you'd want to ask her questions about how we do business. Must have been an interesting ride from the airport."

He glared at her.

Dar smiled charmingly. "We don't keep bimbos on staff." She pressed a button on her intercom and a quiet voice answered. "C'mon over."

Ankow decided to ignore her win over Consuelo. "I want access to everything."

"With the exception of the ladies room, you've got it," Dar deadpanned. "Just don't touch anything. I don't want to spend half the day reprogramming mainframes."

He gazed at her. "Enjoy the jokes while you can," he remarked mildly. "I would guess you've got about a month, until the stockholder's meeting. After that, if you're in this office, I'll be very surprised."

Dar didn't react. "You seem to think that worries me."

The inner door opened and Kerry entered giving Ankow a quick, almost invisible once over. "Morning," she greeted both of them politely.

"Morning," Dar replied. "Kerry, this is David Ankow, a member of the board of directors. He's here to review operations."

"Sir." Kerry inclined her head graciously. Certainly, she fit the blond part of Ankow's assumptions, but Kerry's well bred air and quiet intelligence should have clued him otherwise.

"This is Kerrison Stuart, our Director of Operations." Dar circled her knee with both hands and interlaced the fingers. "She'll be your contact while you're here. If you have any questions, she can answer them."

"Great." Ankow stood up. "First thing you can show me is a cup of coffee. Is that starting off simply enough for you?"

"Regular or espresso?" Kerry inquired, as she followed him to the door. "Or would you like to try *café con leche*, the local specialty?" She managed to get to the knob before he did and opened the door for him. "Out, and to your left." She spared a glance behind her for her boss, who made a sympathetic face before she closed the door.

❖ ⌘ ❖ ⌘ ❖ ⌘ ❖

"So. What is it you do here, exactly, Ms. uh...Stuart, was it?" Ankow inquired, as they left the break room. "I'm not sure what an operations director does."

"Good question," Kerry replied. "It depends, unfortunately, on what day of the week it is and what time of the month." She passed by her office and caught Mayte, installed in her new office, peeking out at her. She smiled and rolled her eyes outside of Ankow's field of vision, and the girl smiled back, then went back to checking some reports Kerry had left her.

"Oh, really."

"Really. I mostly handle day to day operational problems, like outages, customer contact issues, utilization...those areas. But I also structure and organize the consolidation of new acquisitions and make decisions on integration when we buy into companies or join with them as part of a common effort." Kerry motioned down the hall. "Our main operations center is down here."

"You do, huh?" Ankow seemed either bemused or amused, Kerry couldn't tell. "How long have you been doing this?"

"About six months," she answered, scanning her ID card through the large security door. "I was working for Associated Synergenics when they were acquired, as the manager of operations there, and when a position opened up, I applied for it and was hired."

"This position?' Ankow inquired.

"No." Kerry slid her card through a second door and opened it for him. "But then, you already know that, Mr. Ankow, since you requested my personnel file." She smiled and stood back. "This way, please. I was hired as Dar Roberts' assistant and moved into my current role when she took on the responsibilities of CIO."

"She is your boss, then." Ankow stopped and watched her face intently.

"Yes."

"Just wanted to clarify that." He smiled and walked on into the brightly light expanse and low key activity of the operations center.

❖ ⌘ ❖ ⌘ ❖ ⌘ ❖

Kerry indicated the door ahead of her, exhaling a little as they approached the cafeteria. It had been hours of pointed questions and the acceptance of her answers with an air of smugness that was frankly, getting on her nerves.

The smell of *arroz con pollo* hit her as the door opened, and she entered the line just behind her guest and debated on whether to stick to her usual chef salad or go for one of her favorites.

"Do they have anything American here?" Ankow asked, giving the dish a distasteful look.

"Well," Kerry smiled at the attendant, who looked at her expectantly, "I'll have the chicken, thanks, and some flan and a *café con leche*." She turned to Ankow. "They're Perdue chickens, if that makes you feel better."

"*Sí, señora.*" The lady behind the counter wrinkled her nose at Kerry. "*¿Señor?*" She turned her attention to Ankow.

"Give me one of those chef salads," he ordered, "and a bottled water."

They took their trays and moved to a table near the window. Kerry took a bite of her chicken and glanced around, noting the eyes watching them and glad it wasn't just her they were watching for a change.

"You were involved in the Allison Consulting fiasco, weren't you?" Ankow inquired, after spearing a forkful of lettuce.

"Yes, I was," Kerry replied. "I did the initial analysis on the data that came from them. It was very disappointing." She took a sip of her coffee.

"My question is, how did it get as far as it did? How did you allow us to be duped like that?" The acid comment surprised her. "Do you understand how much that cost?"

Keep cool. He's an asshole. Dar's words echoed gently in her mind. "I beg your pardon?" Kerry inquired. "I'm operations. I think it's acquisitions you want to discuss that with or maybe Ernst and Young, who did the due diligence they very obviously should have failed."

"Yes, but how long did it take you to figure that out?"

Kerry chewed thoughtfully. "I was suspicious the first day. I sent the data the second day. Dar came out that Thursday night and by Friday we had them locked up."

"Ah. So your...boss had to come bail you out, is that it?" Ankow now looked amused. "Well, that's understandable." He dismissed the subject and looked around. The buzz of Spanish around them was perceptible, as well as a lower hum of English, and a few tables of Creole. "Interesting place."

"I think so." Kerry scooped up the last of her rice and washed it down with some coffee. "I enjoy the different cultures. It's very different from where I grew up."

"Michigan, wasn't it?"

Kerry nodded.

"So. What's it like having a scandal in the family?"

Kerry put her silverware down and laced her fingers together. "Mr. Ankow, I've had to put up with your being deliberately antagonistic all day."

"Too bad."

"I don't have to put up with personal questions. That's not part of the job. So in answer to your question, that's not your concern." She paused. "Sir."

"All right, fair enough." David Ankow sipped his water and regarded her coolly. "I'm not here to make enemies, Ms. Stuart. And despite what everyone seems to think, I'm not here to tear down you, or anyone else."

Kerry lifted an eyebrow.

"My job." He paused for emphasis. "My job, Ms. Stuart, is to protect the investment that people...just regular people, like you and me, have made in this company. Some of those people depend on that investment to carry them through lean times. Some of them depend on it when they retire. It's my responsibility to make sure we don't betray that trust. You understand me? That means I have to come in and ask hard questions, like why an account that cost us twenty million dollars to acquire had to be scrapped. That's not your money, Ms. Stuart."

Kerry had listened to him, waiting patiently. "Part of it is," she remarked softly. "I'm a stockholder."

He was silent.

"So is Dar. So are most of the people around you." She leaned forward. "I understand about being responsible to people, Mr. Ankow. *My* job is to try and make everything run, so the company can do what it's paid to do and provide value to those very same stockholders." She studied his face. "You represent me, just as much as you do those faceless people out there who invest without being personally involved in the company."

A smile quirked the very corners of his lips. "You are Roger Stuart's kid, aren't you?" There was a touch of wry admiration in his tone. "I interned in his office for a year. I remember seeing a picture of you in his office."

It hit her so hard, Kerry almost lost her lunch on the spot, and it took everything she had to keep a politely interested look on her face.

"Hi." The interruption was doubly welcome and the voice put a covering of calm over her very jangled nerves. "Mind if I join you?"

Dar hadn't eaten lunch with her in the cafeteria for at least three months, but Kerry had never been so glad to see anyone in her life. "Sure."

The tall executive dropped down next to her and put a tray down with a meal the duplicate of Kerry's on it. "How's the tour?" she asked Ankow, drawing his attention to her. "Find any roaches?"

"Very educational." Ankow went back to sipping his water. "I owe you an apology, Roberts. My compliments on your selection of a babysitter for me." He tipped his water bottle in Kerry's direction. "I've learned a lot."

"Good to hear." Dar speared a bit of chicken and chewed it. "Considering your being here is putting a huge kink in operations with Kerry playing tour guide. How much more time are you going to need?"

"Hard to say." He leaned back. "I'll have to let you know." He took another sip. "I'd like to speak to Lou Draefus. I want reports pulled on all the account consolidations this year, so I can review them."

Dar shrugged, unconcerned. "Suit yourself. But you'll do that without Kerry." She took a swallow of coffee. "We've got an Operations staff meeting this afternoon."

"It can wait then. I'd love to sit in on your meeting." He changed his mind smoothly. "I've heard so much about your managerial style." He smiled. "I'm looking forward to seeing it in action."

Dar chuckled humorlessly. "Try coming to the board meetings sometime." She finished her coffee and picked her tray up. "See you upstairs in a few minutes." She met Kerry's eyes.

"Will do," Kerry answered briskly. "Can you have María print the minutes? I haven't had a chance to get back to my desk."

Dar nodded, then threaded her way through the crowd with a powerful stride that cleared a path before her like magic.

Kerry let her breath out slowly, grateful beyond measure for the few minutes Dar had allowed her to collect herself and regain her composure. *Cookies for that, honey, or maybe an ice cream cone, hmm?* She put her silverware on her tray. "Are you done?"

"Just starting." He smiled at her, with a slight twinkle in his eyes.

❖ ⌘ ❖ ⌘ ❖ ⌘ ❖

It had been months, Kerry reflected, *since they'd seen a full fledged, all out temper tantrum from Dar.* The tall executive had been businesslike, but fairly mellow for her. Accepting reports at their weekly meetings and doling out assignments without her usual bouts of calling people on the carpet, or picking apart a particular operational issue until whoever it was felt like curling up under the conference room table.

Today, however. Kerry sighed and kept an eye on her boss, who was seated in her usual chair, leaning forward and fiddling with a long stick pen she'd just been using to doodle. Ankow was in the seat next to her, questioning a reallocation of server resources that had taken down a fairly important client for an hour, to maintain the integrity of the network.

It had been a chancy decision, Kerry knew, since she was the one who had made it. But her options hadn't been extensive and it was that, or lose two critical financial applications for the balance of the day. "Without having a backup routing center, there wasn't much else we could do." She spoke quietly, catching his attention and drawing it from her visibly edgy lover. "It was my decision."

"Did anyone call Interspatial and tell them?" he asked her.

"I did, personally," Kerry replied. "They weren't happy."

"No, they certainly weren't," Ankow agreed. "And what's to say it won't happen again, if you don't have any backups?"

Kerry propped her chin up on one fist. "That's exactly why Dar's spending all her time designing our new network. So it won't happen again." She shifted her gaze. "Right, Boss?"

A very wry blue twinkle. "That's the theory, yes."

Ankow sat back and lifted a hand.

"Mark. What about those server farms, did we get them online?" Dar asked, making a tick mark on her agenda. *Was a time,* she reflected, *when I wouldn't have had to ask.* She'd have known.

"Bank A came online Tuesday, Bank B on Thursday," Mark answered, batting a small, red rubber ball between two pens on the table. "They're running pretty good, but A's taking three percent more utilization than they projected. I'm gonna have to monitor that." He glanced at Dar. "They've got some weird traffic going across."

"Don't we know what they're running over our network?" Ankow asked immediately.

"Not always," Dar interjected quietly.

"Why not?"

"Depends on the contract." Dar was drawing a pig. "Sometimes we're just the carrier."

"I disagree with that." David Ankow shook his head. "We should know what we're putting down those pipes. It's our responsibility."

"Talk to the people who sign the contracts," Dar shot back. "I don't make the deals."

"But you approve them."

"I approve the technology." Blue eyes took on a dangerous glint. "I make sure we can deliver what we promise. I don't judge the content."

Ankow met her eyes and returned her intent glare.

Kerry cleared her throat gently, distracting them. "Actually, we generally do know what kind of data's being carried. Just not the specifics of the packet structure, unless we're asked to analyze that to improve network performance or if there's a problem."

"Generally?" Ankow turned to her.

"Sure. Banks send banking data. Graphics companies send graphics files." Kerry smiled at him. "We don't need to know more than that. In fact, in some cases, intercepting that data is strictly against the contract, like with the airlines."

"Really."

"Of course." Mark picked up the thread. "We transmit ninety percent of the air traffic control and communications data. We could, technically, intercept an in-air mayday or a vital directional instruction if we dipped into the data stream at the wrong time."

"Yeah," Mark's assistant agreed. "We just make sure the right packets are going to the right people."

Ankow sat back and regarded them in silence.

Dar made another tick point and wished she were home. "That's it for open issues. Anything out there you want me to know about?"

"Shouldn't they be asking you that?" Ankow got a last snipe in.

Dar didn't dignify that with an answer. Normally this was where her team told her about all the goofs and mistakes they'd made, which she'd be likely to catch wind of, or have to explain. They'd tried to keep something like that from her once and she'd given them the "if it's going to come out of Alastair's mouth, I want to know about it" speech.

Today, however, everyone kept prudently quiet.

"Nothing?" Dar prodded. "Don't tell me we had a mistake free week?"

They all looked at each other, then at her.

"Ops, nothing?" She looked at Kerry, who gravely shook her head. "Facilities?" Now she glanced at tall, bookish Bill Bowers, who blinked and shook his head.

"Not this week, Boss."

"MIS?"

Mark cracked his knuckles. "Nope."

"Security?"

Mark grinned. "Sixteen attempted accesses, sixteen repulsions, resulting in four IP traces, and two hits, which I turned over to the goon squad."

Dar nodded. "All right. That's it. See you next week." She stood and gathered her papers. "I believe you had an appointment in Accounting?"

Ankow also stood. "Actually, I wanted a word with you first."

Dar sighed inwardly. "C'mon."

Mark edged around the table and ended up next to Kerry, as they watched the two leave. "Is she gonna hurt him or what?" He shook his head. "What a rhino sized butthead."

"Ugh. You don't know the worst." Kerry drank down her glass of water and exhaled. "I'm going to run down to the cafeteria and grab some coffee. Then I've got an inbox the size of Manhattan to work out."

"I'll walk you down," Mark offered. "I could use a soda myself." He followed Kerry out the door. "Besides, you'll need an extra hand to help carry her milkshake back up here."

Kerry gave him a look. "Am I that predictable?" She hit the elevator door button.

Mark grinned and rocked up and down on his heels. "No. But she is."

❖ ⌘ ❖ ⌘ ❖ ⌘ ❖

"All right." Dar dropped her notes on her desk and sat down. She gave her trackball a spin to bring her monitor to life. Another page of messages appeared, this one with a scattering of exclamation points. "What do you want?"

David Ankow crossed behind her and gazed out the window, admiring the view. "Nice."

Asshole. Dar closed her eyes against the pounding headache. Then she opened them and surveyed the screen, deciding to ignore her unwanted guest until he decided to say his piece. She clicked on her first mail and reviewed it.

"You think I'm here to bust your chops, don't you?"

"I don't much care why you're here," Dar replied, typing rapidly.

Ankow circled her and sat on her desk. "You don't like being questioned, do you, Roberts?"

Dar half turned and regarded him. "I don't like wasting my time answering questions you could have looked up in the corporate database, no." She paused. "You're wasting a company resource."

His eyebrow, so even she suspected he plucked it, lifted. "Is that how you view yourself, as a resource?" He didn't get an answer. "All right. I'm going to surprise you." He stood and walked around to the front of her desk, then sat down. "I agree. I think you are a resource." He leaned back. "Much as I hate to admit it and I do. Trust me, you're not just a resource, you're damn near the cornerstone this operation's built on."

Dar folded her hands. "And your point is what?"

"My point is...you think you've got this company over a barrel."

Dar rolled her eyes. "You know what?" She gave him a disgusted look. "You're stupider than I gave you credit for. Get the hell out of my office and go find something useful to do, will you?"

He blinked at her.

"Catch a goddamned clue, Ankow. I don't want anything from the damn company other than my bimonthly goddamned paycheck, if that's not asking too much." Dar stood and leaned forward, using her height to good advantage. "I don't ask for trouble, I don't ask for help, I don't ask for assholes to come flying in here from Texas who don't have the sense that God gave a squirrel and waste my time."

Surprisingly, he chuckled. "Now, that's the Dar Roberts I heard about. I was wondering where you were hiding."

"What," Dar let her voice lift, "do you want?"

"Me?"

"Either talk, or get out."

"And if I do neither?" Ankow seemed amused.

"Then I'll pick you up and throw you out." Dar felt her darker side waking up, as her temper flared.

"Would you?" her antagonist asked, softly. "I'd be a little careful there, Roberts. I'm not one of your Texas two steppers." He stood and advanced towards her. "I don't spend all my time around a desk."

Dar remained still, allowing only a faint smile to crease her lips. "Neither do I."

They were eye to eye now, wills clashing over the wooden surface of

Dar's desk. "So...talk, or you'll leave, one way or the other."

He let her wonder for a moment, then cocked his head and broke the tension. "All right." He sat on the edge of the desk, and crossed his arms over his chest. "I'll tell you what I want. Since you asked so nicely." He smiled. "I want the company."

Dar rolled pale blue eyes. "There's a shock," she muttered.

"I want McLean out. I want his job," Ankow continued. "And I want you to help me get it."

"Ah." Dar nodded. "Is that all?"

"You think I'm joking."

"I think you're two squid short of a seafood salad," the tall woman replied. "One, for wanting to run this place and two, for thinking I'd help you."

Ankow didn't seem to be surprised at the answer, he rose and went to the window, watching the rain fall. "Well...one, I've got my reasons and two, you'll help me all right." He turned and smiled viciously. "Or I'll make your life miserable until you do."

Dar resumed her seat and propped a knee against the edge of her desk. "You don't have the power to do that." She lifted a hand and pointed. "Now, get out."

He gazed at her. "You don't think so, hmm?"

"Nope." The blue eyes held him in hooded disdain. "To do that, I'd have to give a damn about you or this job and I don't." She pointed again. "So take your sleazy little plan and don't let the door hit you on the way out." He didn't move. "You think *I'm* joking?" Dar inquired. "Right now, this company needs me a hell of a lot more than I need it, mister. And if you think you can do this job better. G'wan. Give it a try."

"Oh, I won't bother with that." Ankow smiled. "I'll just have our lawyers file a lawsuit against you for this quarter's losses. Since you made those decisions, Roberts, and you are liable for them, you did realize that, right?"

Dar was silent for a moment. "You'd never win that," she finally responded.

"Maybe," Ankow purred. "Maybe not. You've profited nicely from this company. How would the stockholders feel about you sitting there on your little nest egg, while they have to eat losses caused by your blunders?"

"If they were mine," Dar kept her breathing even, "I wouldn't wait for you to sue me. I pay my debts."

"Well. We'll just see. Why don't you think about it, hmm? I can file suit against your friend Alastair, which I was planning on doing. Have you seen his portfolio lately? Or I can do both of you and we can make a profit this quarter." Ankow stood. "It's your move, Roberts. But I'd guess you were used to that nice lifestyle."

Dar watched him saunter out, holding the door open for Kerry as she entered. Her stomach hurt, thinking about the threat, and she exhaled slowly as the door closed and her lover stood quietly watching her. "Hi."

Kerry walked over and put a styrofoam cup down on her desk. "Hi. What happened? You're white as a sheet."

"Bastard," Dar whispered.

A glance over her shoulder showed the tightly closed door, so Kerry rounded the desk and leaned on the edge, putting a hand on Dar's arm. "Hey. What the heck did he say to you?"

Dar took a deep breath. "He wants me to help him oust Alastair."

"What?"

"Yeah. I told him forget it...but..."

Kerry closed her hand around her lover's. "But what?"

Dar was silent for a moment. "He threatened to file suit against me. To recoup the losses from this quarter."

The blond woman's jaw dropped. "Can he do that?"

"I don't think so. I mean, he can file, sure." Dar's brow creased. "But he'd have to prove criminal negligence, and frankly, there's no chance of that." She lifted her eyes to meet Kerry's. "I may have been a touch absentminded lately, but not negligent."

"You haven't been absentminded at all," Kerry replied sharply. "No one has. The entire division's been running better this quarter by stats than the past four." Her eyes glinted a bit. "I could take personal affront for him even making that statement."

Dar patted her leg. "Easy there. No, you're right. We just had a string of bad luck this quarter. God knows it would have been worse if we hadn't caught some of it and there's no doubt about it, but..." She sighed. "It's gonna raise questions. They'll drag out all my personal and financial records."

Kerry shrugged. "So? Dar, you've never even paid your phone bill a day late. What's the big deal?"

A dark brow lifted at her. "The big deal is going to be the fact that the half owner of everything I have happens to be my second in command here." She paused. "Who also lives with me and shares a bank account."

"Ah." Kerry felt like slapping herself. "Right. Yeah, I forgot that part." She thought about the problem. "That's going to look kinda bad, huh?"

Bad. Dar rubbed her temples. "It's certainly going to throw a doubt on a few things. Like my personal judgement, for instance. Not to mention the fact that a number of the board members are a little more conservative than George Patton."

"Mmm."

They looked at each other. "So. What's the plan?" Kerry finally murmured.

"I've got no idea. I want to talk to Alastair, see what he's got to say. Maybe there's a way to pay this guy off. I don't know." Dar closed her eyes and leaned back against the cool leather of her chair. "Damn."

"C'mon, Dar. What's the very worst that could happen?" Kerry stroked her knee gently.

A blue eye appeared. "If they sue me and win? They wipe me out. Wouldn't be much left but the clothes on my back and the damn car."

"Mmm." Kerry got a peculiar look. "Well, we could go on the road then," she mused, "just sort of wander from place to place. Maybe I could read poetry for a couple of quarters. You could give self defense lessons. It might be fun."

Dar cocked her head.

"Sleep under the stars. Fish for our dinner. How about it?"

Blue and green eyes met and shadows within them twinkled and danced together. "Sounds...like an adventure," Dar murmured.

Kerry smiled. "Doesn't it?"

They both chuckled and looked away. "What's that?" Dar pointed at the cup.

"Chocolate milkshake." Kerry nudged it towards her. "I figured you might need it."

"Mmm." Dar captured the cup and sucked at the straw with a look of absorbed delight, then she peeked over the rim and offered it to Kerry. "Share?"

Kerry sighed. "Yeah." She took a slurp. "What an aggravating day."

"Looking forward to the gym tonight," Dar growled, then punched a number into her phone. It rang twice, then was answered.

"Hey, Boss."

"Mark. I need a full profile on Ankow. Everything. From his birth certificate to last year's taxes."

Mark's voice was definitely smug. "Already running." They could almost hear him buffing his nails on his shirt. "Figured you'd ask. What a jerk." A clatter of keys. "Should be about four, five hours. I'll queue it to you when it's done."

Dar nodded, her eyes narrowing. "Good." A light flaring of her nostrils. "He wants trouble?" she murmured. "He's going to get it. Thanks, Mark."

"No problemo."

She hung up and took the proffered cup back, sucking on the milkshake with a thoughtful look. "Sleeping under the stars, huh? You know, I hate camping, but there's something very appealing about that thought."

"Mmm, yeah." Kerry smiled a bit. "I can almost smell the wood smoke of the campfire, can't you?"

Dar's nose twitched.

Chapter
14

It was gathering twilight as Dar packed up her briefcase and stood, stretching out shoulders stiff from hunching over her keyboard for the last few hours. Kerry had left already and she'd stayed, getting an unruly inbox cleared and finishing up some reports that had been hanging around for a couple of days.

Dar walked over to the wall and peered up. With any luck, they'd be able to start preliminary testing on the new backbones at the end of the week, and Dar got a big piece of satisfaction out of that. Three weeks ahead of schedule and she was just a touch under budget. She smiled and ran a finger over the newly printed schematic, nodding a little at the spidery trace-work of interconnections.

At the bottom, in the designer block, was the description and the engineer.

Dar Roberts.

Yeah. Dar exhaled. *This is my baby, all right.* There were so few, concrete things in her career that she could point to and make that claim for. Most of her accomplishments had been behind the scenes, making the parts run with little or no visibility other than her notoriety within the management staff.

But not this. This was right out there, in plain sight, for everyone to look at, and Dar was absolutely damned positive she was going to put out the very best product she was capable of. What have you done for us lately, Dar?

She'd point. That's what.

The door opened and she turned, surprised, then irritated to see David Ankow standing in the opening, his jacket slung over his shoulder. Not what she wanted to see at the end of a very long day, that's for sure. "You want something?"

"Thought about what I asked?"

Dar went back to her desk and picked up her briefcase. "Nope. I had real work to do this afternoon." She shouldered the case and fingered her car keys. "Anything else?"

"Oh." He stepped back to allow her to exit. "I thought I'd just take the opportunity to try and find out a little more about you, Roberts."

"You've got the time it takes to go down fourteen floors and out to the parking lot," Dar replied, heading past him and closing her door.

He followed her down the hall and through the elevator doors, waiting for them to close. "You know what I find funny?"

"Jock itch."

He smiled thinly. "You're quite the mystery woman around here, Roberts. That intrigues me."

"You're easily intrigued, then," Dar replied dryly. The elevator made a soft hissing noise as it descended and smelled strongly of the brass polish the cleaning crew had used on the rails.

"No one seems to know anything about you. Not where you live. Not what your hobbies are. I find that very strange in a place like this."

One of Dar's eyebrows lifted. "Why would they?"

"Human curiosity. Same as what I'm feeling," Ankow answered. "I tried to get your personnel file, but they stonewalled me with disclosure regs. And not one person I asked, from accounting to sales seemed to know anything about you, outside this office building."

Unexpectedly, Dar smiled, feeling a sudden, surprising affection for her coworkers, quite a few of which certainly could have divulged any number of juicy personal details to him. Things on that front had gotten a lot better since she'd quit and been rehired a few months back. Even José and Eleanor had called a truce. In fact, José was actually really excited about the new network. "They mind their own business. Maybe you should take a hint."

"That won't keep me from finding out what I want to know."

The doors opened. "All right." Dar crossed out onto the marble floor. "What do you want to know?" She waved at the security guard, who waved back and smiled. "My favorite color? It's blue."

"Where's home?"

"Miami." Dar started across the mostly empty lot.

"Live alone?"

"Why do you care? If you're looking for a night out, I'll give you directions to 79th street." Dar felt a prickly edge enter her voice. "Or the addresses to a few clubs."

He laughed. "Any hobbies?"

Dar reached her Lexus and unlocked it remotely, opened the door and tossed her briefcase in. "Time's up." She leaned on the doorframe. "I scuba dive."

"Nice." He indicated the car. "Diving's a pretty expensive hobby. Guess we paid for that too, hmm?"

Asshole. Dar got in the Lexus and started it, then turned. "What did you do with your dividend last quarter?"

Ankow was surprised at the question. He cocked his handsome head to one side and studied her, then shrugged. "Ski vacation in Aspen, as a matter of fact. Why?"

Dar smiled. "Guess I paid for that since I delivered that dividend." She closed the door and their eyes met through the tinted glass.

He stepped forward and put a hand on her mirror, then curled his finger down, indicating the window.

She briefly considered driving off, perhaps with his hand attached to her car, then decided the ton and a half of paperwork wouldn't be worth it. She rolled the window down. "Yes?"

The slightly mocking air was gone, as he leaned towards her, a predatory sparkle in his gray eyes. "You know, I spent eight years as a Ranger and we used to love to get new people in like you so we could beat the smartass out of them."

A chill went down Dar's back at the note in his voice. "Is that a threat?"

"No. Just a warning," Ankow answered. "I don't like you, Ms. Roberts. And I don't take kindly to people with smart mouths and attitudes." His expression was deadly serious. "Don't play games with me."

She felt it happen. That dark, animal part of her that so very, very seldom awakened stirred, sending a chase of warm blood to her skin and lifting her nape hairs. *Ev'rybody's got a fight or flight reflex, Dardar. You get yers from me, and it ain't inta runnin' nowhere.* "Guess we finally found something to agree on them." Dar's voice slipped in pitch, dropped deeper and took on a slightly husky tone. "Because I don't like you either, Mr. Ankow. And this is the only attitude I've got." She leaned forward, almost nose to nose with him. "Don't *you* play games with *me.*"

His eyes narrowed. "You will regret this." His answer was deceptively mild. "I promise you that."

Then he released her mirror and stepped back, watching intently as she closed the window and shifted the Lexus into gear, heading for the parking lot exit.

Dar watched his shadowy figure until it disappeared into the distance.

❖ ⌘ ❖ ⌘ ❖ ⌘ ❖

Kerry circled her neck with her towel and trotted up the back stairs, opening the door for Chino who had sprinted ahead of her. "Hey. Take it easy." She peered inside as she cleared the doorframe, then made a face.

"Where's mommy Dar, huh?"

"Argrrr!" Chino bolted for the door, then chased her tail around in a circle when she found it closed, making Kerry laugh.

"Cut that out. You're going to slip and fall." She used the edge of the towel to wipe her face off, after her hour's run along the path circling the island. "Whew. It's muggy out there, but not as wet as it was this morning, I'll tell ya, Chino."

The air conditioning felt good against her overheated skin, and she just stood for a minute, letting her body cool down. It was hot, sure, and not really comfortable to run in such humidity, but completing her laps made her happy with herself, and she stretched her arms over her head, enjoying the sensation of strength in her body.

"Okay." She exhaled. "Shower, then dinner. But first..." She walked over and picked up the portable phone, then dialed Dar's cell number. It rang a few times, then clicked and a familiar, deep voice answered. "Hey, sweetie."

She could almost imagine the smile on Dar's face, since it changed the tenor of her voice slightly.

"On my way. Just getting on the ferry."

"Oh, good. I just finished my run, and I'm going to take a shower." Kerry felt a little relieved. "Everything okay?"

"Mmm." Dar grunted softly. "Ankow just stomped all over my last nerve and FedExed it to Cleveland."

"Ooo." Kerry winced. "Well, I can offer you a massage, some stuffed salmon filets, and tiramisu. How's that sound?"

A low moan. "Sounds like heaven. What do you get out of this deal?"

"You," the blond woman answered softly.

She'd hit Dar's soft spot and she knew it, by the significant, awkward silence on the other end of the phone. Her lover never expected her to say things like that and she occasionally pulled a sappy little bit of mush out of her pocket because it was so cute to see Dar blush and go all tongue tied.

Not too often, though. It'd lose its shock value. "Dar?"

"Um. Yeah, I'm here." She cleared her throat. "G'wan. Take your shower. I'll be there in a minute."

"Okay." Kerry smiled. "See you in a few." She hung up the phone and set it down, then padded into the bathroom in their bedroom and started the water running. She then closed the door to the eight sided stall and peeled off her running gear.

Her eyes caught her reflection in the mirror and she gazed speculatively at herself, tensing her stomach muscles just to watch them move, and making a fist. "Good god. No one who knew me in high school would believe this, that's for darn sure." She shook her head and ambled into the shower, sticking her head under the spray and scrubbing it vigorously. "Uuugggggghhhh."

For a short while she just stood, letting the water pound down over her, easing the aches from her muscles. The shower made so much noise she didn't hear the door open. She looked up with a start as a cold draft blew in, preceding a pair of appreciative blue eyes, and a tall expanse of naked, tanned skin that her fingers itched to touch. "Hey."

"Well, hello there." Dar joined her under the spray and circled her with both arms. "Funny meeting you in a place like this." She pulled Kerry closer and hugged her tightly.

Ooo. That definitely felt very, very nice. Kerry abandoned herself to the mixture of warmth and chills the skin on skin contact provided. "Mmmmmm." She sighed blissfully. "What a nice end to a rotten day."

"Ugh." Dar groaned in agreement. "I swear, that guy's missing some chips in strategic places." She picked up the scrubber buffy and the liquid soap and started cleaning her lover's back. "He came back to the office tonight. I think he was just trying to goad me, but..."

"Proof positive of his stupidity." Kerry found an interesting bit of skin to nibble.

"I don't think he's stupid," Dar corrected quietly. "He just has an agenda. Wish I knew what it was. He was poking around the place looking for gossip about me today, by the way."

"Oh god." Kerry buried her face into the warm skin she'd been tasting.

"No, no." Dar chuckled softly. "For whatever reason, they all closed ranks and made me out to be the great mystery woman of Miami."

"Oh?" Kerry lifted her head and peered up in pleased surprise. "Awesome. But you know, I've kinda got the feeling that whole attitude thing has changed in the last few months." She ran her hands over Dar's sides and gave her ribs a little tickle. "It's become fashionable to admire you."

Lazy blue eyes regarded her. "It's all your fault." Dar tilted her head and claimed a kiss. "What you haven't done for my reputation..." She laced her fingers behind Kerry's neck as the smaller woman fell against her, and Kerry's hand roamed slowly down her body, tracing her curves.

"I just tell people the truth," Kerry murmured, as a powerful thigh slipped between hers and the scrubber tickled over her suddenly oversensitive skin.

"The whole truth?" Dar whispered in her ear playfully, nibbling a tasty earlobe.

"Well," Kerry laughed faintly, as the sensation shot a jolt right through her groin, "I leave out a few details."

"Ah." Dar slid a hand lower. "Like that?"

"Uhhhh. Yeah."

A nibble. "And that?"

"Oh, definitely."

Dar chuckled deep in her throat.

❖ ⌘ ❖ ⌘ ❖ ⌘ ❖

"Okay, we're set for tomorrow, right, Col?" Kerry held the phone against her ear with one shoulder while she neatly removed two fish fillets from the oven. "I'm telling you right now though that bowling is not a skill of mine."

"Who cares?" Colleen laughed. "It's disco bowling. Just the gang. They want to see you like crazy, Ker, and no one takes it seriously."

"Okay." Kerry smiled. "Sounds like fun."

"Think Dar'll be interested?"

Kerry stuck her head out around the kitchen door and regarded the tall, lanky form sprawled on the couch with a Labrador tucked between her knees. "Dar, how do you feel about bowling?"

A tan eyelid opened, revealing a slightly astonished blue eye. "Bowling?"

"Mmm. Colleen and my old gang invited me out tomorrow. It's disco bowling, you know."

The other eye appeared. "Disco bowling? No, I don't know."

"She's never heard of disco bowling, Col," Kerry announced into the receiver.

"Figures," her friend replied, with a chuckle. "It's in the dark, mostly and they put fluorescent stripes down, and there's music–"

"Okay, okay. Hold on." Kerry covered the mouthpiece. "We're going to be in the dark, throwing large, round, heavy objects and trying not to kill each other."

Both eyebrows lifted. "Oh. I wouldn't miss that for anything," Dar responded seriously. "Do they serve alcohol?"

"They have a bar there, Col?"

"Darn straight," Colleen told her cheerfully. "And a junk food snack counter."

"She's there." Kerry grinned. "Eight, right? It'll be great just to fool around after all the junk that's been happening at work and I can't wait to see the guys." She'd made it a point to get together frequently with Colleen, but had only seen the rest of the Synergenics bunch twice. "I hear Ray got a buzz cut."

"Omigod." Colleen sighed exaggeratedly. "You have no idea. He looks like someone ran his head over with a lawnmower. You have to promise not to laugh."

"I promise," Kerry replied solemnly. "See you tomorrow." She hung up the phone and put it down. "Dinner's done."

"Mmm. So I smell." Dar hauled her body up out of the couch's comfortable embrace and stood, tugging down her barely decent T-shirt and ambled over to Kerry. "Disco bowling, huh?"

Kerry sucked in a pleasant breath full of clean cotton and warm skin. "Hmm?" She looked up. "Oh. Yeah, well...it's mindless. Just something everyone can do that isn't miniature golf." She patted Dar on the side. "C'mon. I'm hungry, and I know you must be."

Dar followed her agreeably, retrieving a pair of plates from the cupboard and holding them as Kerry removed the fish from their pan and settled them on the china. "Mmm. Nice, healthy fish."

"Uh huh." Kerry gave her a wry look. "Stuffed with crabmeat and covered in Parmesan, but life's a compromise, right?"

A wicked chuckled. "Right." Dar took both plates, additionally adorned with a baked potato each into the dining room and set them on the table. Kerry followed her with a couple of glasses and a bottle of apple juice, which she poured as they settled down to eat.

Dar applied herself seriously to her potato, making very sure that every square inch of the inoffensive vegetable was covered in substances designed to disguise its taste.

"Dar, why don't you just eat spoonfuls of sour cream, bacon bits, and cheddar cheese?" Kerry wryly asked. "Wouldn't it be faster?"

"You mean it isn't healthier this way?" The blue eyes opened in mock innocence. "I could put pineapple bits on it."

"Ew." Kerry winced.

Dar grinned and handed over the handy carrier with the toppings on it. Kerry peered at it, then sighed and helped herself to them. "You are so subversive."

It had become a friendly, comfortable banter between them, with Kerry virtuously trying to insure neither of them got scurvy, and Dar persisting on finding the darndest ways to circumvent her.

Not that it didn't have an effect, the blond woman conceded, since she at least managed to keep her lover from eating cheeseburgers and fries every night. What she cooked was mostly very healthy and she'd convinced Dar to ease off on her consumption of sugar and coffee.

Of course, she wisely kept her paws off the sacred ice cream. Kerry smiled to herself as she watched her lover methodically decimate her fish, breaking off bite full's and alternating them with scoops of her potato. "Listen. Seriously, Dar—"

"Were we being serious?" Dar glanced up, inquisitively. "This is wonderful, by the way."

"Thanks. And no. But listen, don't feel you have to do the bowling thing tomorrow if you don't want to. I know you always feel a little weird around those guys." Kerry nibbled a piece of her fish.

Dar ate in silence for a minute or two, considering. "No. I..." She paused, and put her fork down, picked up her glass and took a sip of her juice. "They're fine. I had a good time the last time we went out with them," she admitted. "And if Ankow's going to be up to his tricks all day, I'll be ready for some mindless playing around."

"Mmm." Kerry nodded. "Good point."

"Too bad we can't get him to go," Dar remarked. "Dark place like that. Bowling balls can get out of control pretty easily."

"Ooo."

"He was an Army Ranger."

Kerry blinked. "How'd you find that out? Mark's stuff come back?"

"He told me." Dar exhaled. "I wasn't sure whether he was trying to impress me or scare me. Needless to say, he didn't get much satisfaction either way." She shook her head.

"Maybe you could introduce him to Dad." The green eyes took on a wicked twinkle, then sobered. "Wait. Was he threatening you, Dar?"

A half shake of the dark head. "No...well," Dar sucked on her fork, "hard to say. It was more of a..." She paused and thought hard. "It was more like he was trying to intimidate me."

"Why?"

"Part of his game, I guess." Dar shrugged. "I gave it right back to him. I don't intimidate easily, but damn, he gave me the creeps."

"Hmm." Kerry slowly broke off a bit of potato and chewed it. "Ick."

They finished dinner and retired to the living room, cuddling on the couch and sharing a piece of Kerry's tirimisu. "Mmm. Did you spike this?"

"A little." The blond woman grinned. "Do you like it?"

Dar nodded and put her arms around Kerry as she flipped channels, settling on the Discover Channel. "Oh. It's that extreme whatever show. Hey, aircraft carriers. I used to have a model of that one."

"Yeah?" Kerry fed her a spoonful of pastry.

"Yeah. Used to be a hobby." Dar sighed.

"Mmm." Kerry smiled to herself.

Chapter
15

"Tell me again, *chica*. Who had this idea?" Ray ducked, as a rubber ball went flying flew over his head, and the lights started to dance. "This a circus."

"Eh." Colleen grinned, and motioned over a skating waitress. "It's cute. There are a lot of company groups here. Look, there're the guys from FedEx."

Ray moved his head, then laughed. "In those tight blue shorts. I see them." There were four of them there, Ray and Colleen, and two others from Synergenics who had worked with Kerry before her promotion. "You want something to drink, Susan?"

The programmer nodded. "Hell, yes. A beer, please." She leaned back in her chair and put her feet up on the one next to her. "Feels good not to be in front of a screen. That last project nearly killed me." She rolled her head towards Colleen. "What time's Ker getting here? Eight?"

"Supposedly, yep." Colleen glanced up at the door, some distance away, then chuckled. "Right on time. Just like always. You can set your watch by the woman."

They watched as Kerry opened the door and slipped inside. She was alone and she paused for a moment, letting her eyes adjust before she spotted them and waved.

"Good god." Susan sat up. "I can't believe that's the same person. Would you look at her?" The programmer ran her hand through her silvered auburn hair and shook her head.

Kerry headed towards them, trotted down the short series of stairs and dodged the busy crowd. She was dressed in faded jeans and a snug fitting aqua colored tank top which exposed a good portion of her upper body to the watching eyes.

"*Mi Madre*." Ray shook his head. "I remember her all frills and lace, and being so quiet. She has changed so much." The support manager of Synergenics, who had taken Kerry's position, hadn't seen his ex-boss in over four months.

"She sure has," Colleen mused, observing the self assured figure moving towards them, seemingly oblivious to the appreciative looks from the people she brushed by.

"Hey guys." Kerry dropped into the nearest chair and let out a breath. "Just made it. We had a wild day at work." She watched the eyes flick over her shoulder and smiled. "Dar'll be here in a bit. She was just finishing up a call when I left." Her gaze turned towards her former coworkers. "So. How are you guys doing? Susan, I got your email with those jokes. I hope you know they're floating around HQ now."

The programmer chuckled. "That's okay. Things are fine by us. We just finished up remapping that IRS website program. Put them on IIS with some custom scripting. They like it."

"I know." The green eyes twinkled. "I keep track of stuff coming from you all. It's been fun watching everything come together." She looked up as the waitress rolled back up and delivered drinks. "Ooo. What's that? Draft beer? Can I have one?"

The lights dimmed and the strobes started up, throwing patterns of balls and beams around the bowling alley. Tacky music added to the atmosphere, as teams moved towards their assigned alleys. "Do they really expect you to...um...bowl...in this?" Kerry, with a wry grin, peered around.

"Nah. It's more of a gag than anything." Susan waved a hand at it. "The proceeds go to the United Way, so..." She held up a ticket. "You'd better go get a pair of ugly shoes and we'll claim our spot. They'll bring the beer over there for ya." She pointed. "Lane 32."

"Good idea." Kerry stood up and Ray joined her. "We'll meet you guys over there." She edged around the table and walked towards the control desk, with the slim Latin man right at her heels. "This is just goofy enough to be fun, Ray."

Ray laughed. "*Sí*, you got that right, *jefa*." He patted her back, a touch gingerly. "Kerry, I have to say this to you, I think you look fantastic."

Her friendly smile and warm green eyes were the same. "Thanks, Ray. You look great yourself. Is that a new haircut?" Ray's dark hair was almost shaved in back and the front wasn't much longer. She reached over and ruffled it.

"I hate to tell you what happened." He lowered his voice, as they waited their turn at the desk. "I was under the sink, you know? Fixing the pipes and I turned that little torch on."

Kerry cocked her head. "For the copper things?"

"*Sí, sí.* Only the dog, she's so cute, but she put her nose...I was not wearing..." Ray stopped, and cleared his throat. "Anyway, I jumped up, and forgot the torch, and burned my hairs off."

She clapped a hand over her mouth to keep from bursting out laughing. "I'm sorry. That's not funny."

"Oh, honey. Of course, yes, it is." Ray smiled sheepishly. "But it does not look so bad, does it?"

Kerry smiled back. "No. Not at all. You just look different." She paused. "Younger, I think."

"You too." The dark eyes flickered beneath even darker lashes. "Look at all those muscles."

She glanced down, then spread her arms a little and shrugged. "Yeah. I know. All that wall climbing, and diving, and..." Kerry exhaled. "Took me a little while to get used to it but it doesn't look too bad, huh?"

"Tch." Ray bit his lip, and given this permission, indulged in a long look. "Honey, you look gorgeous...and so happy." He leaned closer. "I am so glad for you, *jefa*. The *chupa*, she did good for you, no?"

Kerry nodded slowly. "Better than good, Ray." She turned around as they reached the desk and handed the ticket over, ordering shoes for herself and Dar and paying for them. "It's the best thing that's ever happened to me."

❖ ⌘ ❖ ⌘ ❖ ⌘ ❖

"Okay, okay, okay." Dar finally checked off the last box in the form she was filling out, carefully writing in several notes near the bottom of it. "Can we beta or not?"

An aggrieved sigh came through the speakerphone. "Dar, we have *just* gotten the routers in place. Willya give me a damn week to get them programmed and tested before you start tossing packets at them?"

"A week?" Dar protested, leaning over her work and writing a long paragraph in her strong, but confusing handwriting. "Jesus, Byron. I got twenty of the damn things programmed in one night. What do you mean, a week?"

"Dar..."

Another scribble, and a pause for thought. "Shows exceptional grasp of business cases and acts with solid responsibility," she muttered.

"Excuse me?"

"Not you, Byron." Dar chewed the end of her pen. "All right. I'm tired of arguing and I gotta go. You've got a week but when that's over, I want a clearance to bring the system up."

A grumble. "Okay. I think I can do that."

"You think?" Dar's voice dropped.

"We'll do it."

"Night, Byron. Tell Sandra I said hello."

"Tell her yourself," Byron grumbled. "She's right here laughing her ass off. She loves watching me squirm."

Dar smiled. "Hey, Sandy."

A low, melodic voice answered, full of the musical quality common in the East. "Hello, Dar, long time. I've been enjoying every minute of this." Sandra chuckled. "I keep picturing this eighteen-year-old punk sitting in the CIO's office though. It's making my brain hurt."

Sandra Weing had been Dar's first supervisor after the company had bought out the tiny programming group she'd joined as a summer job. Dar was fairly certain she'd driven the lovely, talented, patient, and serene Dr. Weing to banging her head against the wall and she was always surprised the woman remembered her fondly.

She'd also been Dar's first crush and a medium of startling revelation. Sandra had married Byron, a well thought of systems engineer, and decided to settle down at home and have kids, though, and Dar had always wondered how that'd worked out for her. "Well, I'm certainly not eighteen anymore," she remarked, filling in another line on her form. "But I'm glad you're having fun."

"No. I realized that when they posted those pictures of you online." Sandra chuckled. "Well, dinner's calling. Nice talking to you, Dar."

"Same here. Next week, Byron," Dar warned.

"Yeah, yeah." He sighed. "You'll have it."

"Night." Dar hit the phone button with her pen and finished a last entry, her real reason for staying late.

Kerry's evaluation, which would be a touch difficult to do during the chaotic day, or at home with the very tangible reminder of her lover's presence so close by. She glanced at her watch. "Only eight-thirty. Not bad." She added her recommendations for Kerry's future and signed the review, with a strong scribbling, smiling as she sat back and let the pen drop on the desk.

The sound of footsteps didn't surprise her. She'd known Ankow was still in the building, based on little security pop-ups that had been helpfully tracking him for her for the last few hours. "Well," she stood up and locked her PC, then slid Kerry's evaluation into her top desk drawer and locked that, too, "it's not going to be a repeat of last night, that's for sure."

She already had her gym bag over her shoulder as he walked in and she peered briefly and uninterestedly at him as she picked up her keys. "Just leaving." She paused. "Sorry."

He leaned against the doorframe, regarding her sourly. Maybe he doesn't like parrots. She had two of them in a snuggly pose on her left breast, embroidered into a faded blue denim shirt tucked into natural stone washed jeans.

"Slumming tonight?"

Dar moved towards the door. "Disco bowling," she answered, with strict truthfulness, as she stopped in front of him and gestured towards the outer office. "Bar's closed."

For a minute, she thought he was going to remain standing there, then he eased out ahead of her. "I'm surprised. Someone who lives out on a ritzy island spends her evenings bowling?"

Dar didn't react. "Better than spending my time digging through public records in the Dade County Courthouse."

He got to the door first and leaned against it, holding it shut and smiling at her. "But you find out such fascinating things leafing through those microfilmed titles." He paused. "I've got you, Roberts."

"With an inherited condo?" Dar glanced at her watch. "Get out of my way, I've got a lot more important things to do than this."

"With your co-owner."

Uh oh. Dar exhaled inwardly, but kept her composure. "Who? Kerry?" She managed a completely bland look. "Why? She pays her half of the taxes."

A moment's doubt shone in his eyes. "You live together." He'd obviously expected a different reaction from her.

"Yep. Sure do," Dar agreed amiably. "Best roommate I ever had. Now, is there a point to this conversation? Because otherwise, I'm leaving." She shouldered the gym bag and moved several steps closer.

Slowly, he moved away from the door and opened it, watching her face intently. "Roommate, hmm?"

Dar felt like punching him. She really, really did, and maybe he realized that, and it excited him. "Yeah." Then she smiled with feral intensity. "What'd you think? We were screwing like squirrels on the coffee table?" She almost laughed at the look on his face. "Get your head out of your groin, Ankow, and your ass out of my office." Dar brushed by him and strode towards the elevator, leaving him behind her in dangerous silence.

At the last minute as the doors opened and she stepped inside, he joined her, the elevator doors closing them both into a charged stillness.

They stared at each other in the oppressive atmosphere, the floors seeming to crawl by. At last the trip was over, and Dar escaped into the cool peace of the lobby, trying to ignore the stalking figure at her side.

He waited until they were past the doors and past the security guard, before he reached out and grabbed her arm.

Dar stopped.

And turned ice cold eyes on him. "Take your hands off me." She kept her voice down, but it rumbled with intent.

He let go of her biceps, then pointed a finger at her chest. "I'm going to find out the truth," he promised softly, "and bury you with it."

Then he turned and headed for his rental car that was parked near the front of the building.

Dar took a deep breath and turned, then almost yelped when she came close to crashing headlong into a tall, menacing figure. "Hey!"

"Easy thar, Dardar." Andrew peered over her shoulder, his eyes mere slits in the lamplight. "Whointhehell was that?"

"An asshole." Dar felt like hugging him in pathetic gratitude. "Just a real asshole, who's got it out for me." A hand patted her arm awkwardly. "What brings you here?" She nodded her head towards the Lexus. "Don't worry about him."

Andrew turned his attention from the car Ankow was driving back to his daughter. "I need yer help," he muttered, embarrassed. "Got a minute?"

"Are you kidding?" Dar unlocked the car and motioned him into the passenger side. "What is it?"

Andrew climbed in and shut the door, waiting for her to start up the engine before he blew a breath out and peered sideways at her. "Been trying to figure out...good Lord, all the clock round the past few days how I could get...get my butt in a place where I could...um..."

"Contact Mom?" Dar paused at the stoplight, then turned when it changed.

"Yeah." Her father blinked and rubbed his eyes. Dar recognized the gesture with a faint smile. "And I want to. Damn, I do. But I can't figger a way." He studied his scarred hands. "Picked up the phone a dozen hundred times, started to dial...just couldn't." He looked up at her. "What do I say? What kin I say?"

"Hello?" Dar joked faintly, as she drove. "I know what you mean, though. I remember how shocked I was. She's gonna lose it."

He remained silent, just twisting his fingers.

Dar thought, turning her mind to the puzzle as she did throughout the day on less personal, less vital matters. Her father was counting on her. Finally, she exhaled. "Let the Navy do it."

He looked up. "What?"

"Let the Navy do it. Have them contact her, say there was a mistake. You know it happens," Dar responded quietly. "It's damn close to the truth."

Andrew considered the words. "Doesn't explain the months I been here."

Dar had stopped at a red light, and now she turned. "No." She searched his face. "That's gonna be the tough part. Your tough part."

The light turned green and she drove on, trying not to hear the audible sounds as he swallowed a few times.

"Damn it," Andrew finally whispered. "I want to have the guts to just call up and do this and I don't, Dardar. That's a damn tough thing for someone's stared down death as many times as I have and not cared." He dropped his head against one hand. "Don't wanta get the Navy into it."

Dar pulled into the parking lot and turned off the Lexus, then pulled her cell phone out and checked the charge. "I understand being scared." She leaned her forearms against the wheel. "It's like being in a dark pit and there's no way out and you only go deeper into it, the longer you stay."

They looked somberly at each other.

Dar keyed in her phone's memory, and dialed a number, then held the instrument to her ear, until it was answered. "It's Dar." Hesitation, then a quiet response. "I've got someone here that wants to talk to you." She handed the phone to her father, who took it purely by reflex. "Here, say hello to Mom."

Then she opened the door and tossed him the keys, closed it, and walked towards the building, without looking back.

Crossing her fingers and hoping they both would forgive her.

❖ ⌘ ❖ ⌘ ❖ ⌘ ❖

"Okay. Ow, watch where you're swinging that, Col." Kerry ducked around the heavy blue ball Colleen was swinging. "I have no idea where—ah, there she is." She spotted her lover enter and stop, her ears visibly twitching at the assault of noise around her. Dar had a strained expression on her face, though, and Kerry set her ball down on the tray. "Uh oh. Be right back, guys."

She trotted up the stairs and dodged around moving waitresses, relieved when the roving blue eyes fell on her and softened in perceptible relief. "Hey." She got up next to Dar and tugged her into a corner. "What's the matter?"

Dar chewed her lip. "What do you want to hear about first? Ankow figuring out we live together or me calling my mother and handing the cell phone to my father?"

Kerry's jaw dropped. "Dar, I only left you alone for forty five minutes," she spluttered in protest. "Jesus...wh...bu..." She rubbed her head in shock.

The tall, dark haired woman managed a faint smile. "Everyone here? Let's...just...I um...I need a distraction." She put a hand on Kerry's back. "We can talk about it all later. The Ankow thing wasn't that big a deal. I just told him we were roommates."

"Yeah. Yeah, sure." Kerry took her arm and guided her back to the lane, where their friends were waiting, watching with interested faces. "Well, we are roommates," she replied reasonably, then stopped. "Wait. Where is Dad?"

"Outside," Dar replied quietly. "I didn't know what to do. I...he was so frustrated, and I...so I just...I..."

"Dialed her number and said 'here you go.'" Kerry winced.

"Honey..."

"Tactless, huh?"

Kerry sighed. "Well, it's direct and straightforward, and both you and your daddy are certainly that." She exhaled again and smiled as they reached the lane. "Hey guys. Sorry about that. Dar had some problems before she left the office."

"And after," her lover muttered.

"Mmm. Would you like a drink?" Kerry signaled the waitress.

"Oh, yeah." Dar ordered a Kahlua milkshake, then paused. "On second thought make that a double."

The waitress popped her bubble gum and smiled. "Shawer." Then she rolled happily off.

❖ ⌘ ❖ ⌘ ❖ ⌘ ❖

Cecelia stared at the phone, deeply puzzled. Getting called out of the blue like that from Dar was shocking enough, but who in Miami would want to talk to her? Unless Dar wasn't in Miami, of course. Impatiently, she put the phone to her ear. "Hello?"

All she could hear was the faintest sound of breathing.

For no reason she could detect, a chill passed over her. "Hello?" she asked again, softer. "Is there someone there?"

A soft rasp of in drawn air, then an almost inaudible sound came through the phone and touched her ears. "Cec?"

No. She was frozen in place, unmoving. Unbreathing. *No.* No, that voice couldn't be what she'd heard. Her chest moved, pulling in air audibly.

"Ceci?" The sound again, a little stronger.

It couldn't be. It was just another dream.

Just another nightmare. She should hang up. That's what she should do, hang up and forget about it.

Yes.

Her hand moved.

Her heart spoke. "Andy?"

"Yeah."

Her world collapsed around her, becoming a small space filled with only that voice. "Andy." She curled around the phone, cradling it with both hands.

"Ceci, it's me."

She gasped softly. "Oh."

"Cec?"

She closed her eyes. "Yes?"

The voice took on an aching sadness. "I'm sorry."

Her chest suddenly erupted in a sob. "Where are you?" She managed

to get the words out. "Andy, where are you?" She started crying helplessly, hugging the phone to her so tightly it creaked.

"Cec. There's so damn much I have to say I..."

"I don't care," Cecilia whispered. "I don't care where you've been or
what you've done. Just come here. Come home. Please." She stopped, as
the tears choked her. "Please."

He was curled up in the front seat, shaking so badly he could hardly
hold the phone. "All right," he finally choked out.

"When?" came back a barely audible whisper.

Andrew opened his fist, seeing the blood where his hand had
clenched down over the set of keys his daughter had given him.

*Cast bread up on the waters and it came back to you, didn't it? God
bless you, Dar.* "Now," he answered, hearing the almost hysterical sob on
the other end.

God bless you.

Chapter
16

"You okay?" Kerry leaned forward, resting her elbows on her knees as she sat next to a very quiet and very pensive Dar. The taller woman was sucking on her milkshake, cradling it in both hands and trying to ignore the chaotic sounds and sights around them. "Worried about your dad?"

Dar nodded slightly.

"Well." Kerry glanced up as Colleen announced they were ready to start. Everyone was furtively watching Dar, and she realized her friends knew something was wrong. "Listen. I've been thinking. Maybe it wasn't such a bad idea, you know?" She patted Dar's knee. "Sometimes, when you think about something too much, you get too scared to do it."

"Mmm. I know." Dar sucked on her straw. "Kissing you on the beach comes to mind."

Kerry felt her train of thought run right off its track and wander down Biscayne Boulevard. "Uh...what?"

"That was a major scared witless moment for me," Dar remarked.

"It was?" Kerry sounded totally amazed.

A slight cock of Dar's head. "Would have been an ugly moment if I'd have been wrong, wouldn't it?"

"Tch. You knew you weren't."

"No, I didn't," Dar replied seriously. "Sure. I was hoping, but..." She sighed. "I'd been wrong so many times before."

"Not this time."

Dar smiled and leaned against her. "No. I got it right this time."

They watched Colleen grasp her ball firmly and face the alley, flashes of disco light flicking over her sturdy form. Then she walked up to the line with a dignified air, spread her legs, and tossed the ball down the alley with a distinct crashing thump.

"Nice technique," Dar muttered.

"She got two of them," Kerry protested mildly. "I'm not much better."

"You're going to look a lot cuter with your butt up in the air."

Outraged green eyes peered at her. "Oh great. Forget it. I'll crawl up to the line."

Dar smiled.

"Can you bowl?" Kerry asked, suddenly suspicious. She never got an answer because at that very moment, her cell phone went off and scared the heck out of her. "Jesus!" She grabbed at the device, which she'd set to vibrate and was pressing against her side. She glanced at the caller ID, then hesitated, before showing Dar. "It's you."

Dar bit her lip, then took the phone very gingerly and opened it, pressing it to her ear. "Hello?"

A low, raspy voice answered, "Git out here."

Dar swallowed. "Yes, sir." She folded the phone carefully and handed it to Kerry, then stood. "Excuse me." It was like being an adolescent again, she realized. The years peeled back and she was twelve or fourteen and knowing she'd done something that rated a first class dressing down for. "Be right back."

Kerry caught the edge of her jeans and held it. "You okay? You need some backup?"

She exhaled. "No. I got myself into this. Lemme go pay my dues. It's my father, remember? The worst he's gonna do is chew my head off."

"Well, remind him I have a real fondness for your head and I like it where it is." Her lover gave the fabric a gentle tug. "Okay?"

That got a faint smile out of Dar. "Okay." She tweaked a bit of Kerry's hair, then turned and made her way through the crowd.

Kerry immediately got a pod of bodies attached to her. "What's going on?" Colleen whispered. "Are you guys okay?"

"We're fine. It's…just…complicated." Kerry tried to find a place to start.

❖ ⌘ ❖ ⌘ ❖ ⌘ ❖

The air outside was humid, and Dar could smell a distinct tang of rain on it. The door closed behind her and she headed towards the car, trying to convince her guts to stop quaking. Her father was standing outside the Lexus, leaning against its tall side, his face hidden in the shadows of his hood, and she swallowed hard more than once as she forced herself to keep walking.

Finally, she was there, finding it very hard not to hang her head and stare at her sneakers as she stopped a few paces away and waited. It wasn't a physical fear. Andrew had never so much as laid a hand on her—ever—even in times where Dar now felt he probably should have.

He hadn't had to. His disappointment in her had been enough.

"C'mere."

Hesitantly, she took a few more steps, until she was almost even with him, his height topping hers by a mere inch or two as he straightened up. "Everything okay?" she murmured, still unable to distinguish his features in the dark. She wasn't expecting the hug, and it took her a moment to throw off her shock and respond. "Dad?" she whispered, as she felt the rare pleasure of enfolding her father in her arms. He was solid, and warm, but she could feel the faint shaking as he breathed. "Daddy?"

The arms squeezed her. "Thank you."

Dar's knees almost gave out as the tension drained from her in a startling flood. She released her held breath and let her head rest on his shoulder until he released her, but didn't let go. They backed off a little and looked at each other. Dar risked a tiny smile. "So, I was right, huh?"

Her father nodded slightly.

"Sorry I did it that way." Dar hung her head, studying the ground between them. "She want you to come up there?"

A long, shaky breath. "Yeah."

Dar shifted her energy away from the intense emotion and towards the practical. "Want me to take care of getting you there?" She peeked up at him. "I think I can get you a flight out tonight, yet."

He let his grip on her go and leaned back against the car, either dazed or exhausted, it was hard for Dar to tell. "Lord, I can't believe this is happening." He raised his head with an obvious effort. "If'n that's t'only way. Yeah, I guess."

Dar took the keys of the Lexus and unlocked it, then opened the door and grasped his arm gently. "C'mere. Siddown."

"She...wanted t'come here," Andrew murmured. "Wasn't fair, case things don't work out."

"They'll work out." Dar glanced around, then realized her father had taken the cell phone, and tucked it under one arm, where he had it pressed against his body. "I need..." She looked at the building and found worried green eyes in the doorway, looking back at her. "Ah. Yeah. That's what I need."

She gave Kerry a smile, and a jerk of her head and the blond woman practically flew out of the alley and bounded across the parking lot.

"Let me borrow your cell. I've got to get some tickets to Connecticut," Dar announced, as her lover reached them.

"Really?" Kerry handed it over, then got in closer. "Awesome!" Her face lit up with a delighted grin.

Andrew lifted his head at that, and regarded her with a faint smile tugging at the very corners of his lips.

She threw her arms around him and squeezed. "Wow. I'm so glad," she whispered in his ear. "I had fingers and toes and everything else crossed for you." He returned the hug and patted her on the side. "Can you get a flight?"

"Yeah." Her lover held up a finger, the pressed the phone to her ear. "Yes. Open return. My card's on file."

Andrew stirred, but found it difficult to stand with Kerry wrapped around him. "Ah."

"Don't argue with her," Kerry advised softly, hanging on. "Just let her do her thing and get her back later."

"Yeah. That's right," Dar was saying. "E-ticket it. We're on the way over now." She paused. "Thanks. No, that's fine. Right. Bye." Dar closed the phone and nodded. "All set." Then she put a hand on her father's knee. "You got ID?"

He nodded.

"Do you have something to wear other than that?" Kerry inquired.

He shook his head.

"Okay." Kerry released him and exhaled. "I'll stop and pick something up and meet you there?"

"Right," Dar agreed. "Let's go." She glanced behind her. "What about..."

"Rain check."

"Right," Dar considered. "Men's extra large, he likes blue."

"Right," Kerry agreed, making a note on her palm pilot. "See you there." She patted Andrew's arm and trotted off.

Finally regaining a little equilibrium, Dar's father stared bemusedly after her. "You two always just take over stuff?"

"The occasional multi-billion dollar company, sure," Dar replied. "C'mon. We haven't got that much time."

"Good." He sighed. "Less time for me to chuck up my guts with."

Dar got in and started the engine, then shifted the Lexus into gear. She spared a glance sideways, catching the reflection of her father's face in the passenger side window, where silent tears made glittering tracks from scared, haunted eyes.

❖ ⌘ ❖ ⌘ ❖ ⌘ ❖

For a long while, she merely sat there, curled up on the couch, the phone cradled against her chest. Every so often she would press the caller ID button, watching the familiar name blink at her, just to prove it had really happened.

D Roberts. 305 930 1101

She traced the letters and numbers with a trembling fingertip. It was like being inside a dream, really. She didn't feel like moving, or thinking.

She just wanted to savor the simple pleasure of lying here outside the cloud of despair that had cloaked her for so very long. It hadn't really sunk in yet. Not really. She was just caught between a wild hysteria and a need to hold this feeling to her and breathe in its rare and special fragrance.

Andy. Her lips shaped the name, for so long banned from her speech. She curled around the phone again and started crying helplessly.

She had no idea how long she laid there, before the phone sent shocks through her as it rang softly again.

Cecilia's eyes went anxiously to the display, not wanting it to change.

And, as though obedient to her heart, it didn't.

She pressed the button. "He-hello?" Greedily, she wanted to hear him again.

"Cec?"

"Yes."

It was noisy, where he was. "'Bout to get on an airplane. I—"

She started counting the hours. "Which one?" She was aware, suddenly, of Dar's voice in the background and a warmer, lighter, tone answering. "I'll meet you."

There was a rustling of papers. "All right. Won't be there till damn near midnight."

"I don't care."

"Ceci. I...something I need to tell you...I'm not—"

"Andy."

He stopped speaking.

"Whatever it is can wait." Cecilia wished she could simply crawl through the phone, and out the other end. "I just want you here."

"I want to be there." His voice was rough and strained. "I gotta go on."

A fumbling sound and soft, muffled voices. Cecilia simply closed her eyes and waited. Then a lighter, richer tone came down the line.

"Mother?"

She had to breathe a few times before she could answer. "Yes."

"I have his flight number. If you..."

Oh, Of course. "He's really there?"

Dar got very quiet. "He's really here."

The hot tears spilled over her eyes again and she stifled a sob. "What flight?"

"Continental...1822," Dar murmured. "Mother, he's had a tough time. He got messed up pretty badly. There're a lot of scars."

She had to run that through her wildly scattered mind a few times before she understood what her daughter was saying. "You think I care what he looks like?" she gasped.

"No," Dar's voice came back, warm and positive, "but I think he does."

"Oh." Cecilia moaned. "No...no...I just want him here." She started crying again.

"I know." Dar sighed audibly. "Plane just pushed back from the gate." She paused. "If you need anything, let us know."

Ceci quieted a bit. "All right." She closed her eyes for a long moment, tasting the bittersweet irony. "Thank you, Dar."

There was a very lengthy silence. "You're welcome." The words finally came back to her, low and subdued.

Dar slowly closed the phone and leaned her head against the cold glass, staring out into the darkness at the retreating running lights of a Boeing 757.

Kerry leaned next to her, the blond woman's sigh fogging the glass lightly. "Boy. What a night." She turned and regarded her lover. "Are you okay?"

"Still in shock, I think," Dar murmured. "I can't believe what just happened."

Kerry rubbed her eyes and stifled a yawn. "I think your dad's in total shock. I put a blanket around him on the plane and told the steward to keep an eye on him." She smiled up at Dar. "I'm so glad for them, though."

"Yeah." Dar watched the plane disappear with a faintly wistful look.

"Wish we could be there to see them get together." Kerry sighed. "It makes me feel great thinking about Dad being happy."

Dar watched the tears well up in Kerry's eyes, to be quickly brushed away, and she reached out to capture one of the blond woman's hands. "You know he really likes you."

Kerry didn't answer, visibly holding back her emotions. Finally she cleared her throat. "You and he have taught me so much..." She had to stop, putting a hand to her mouth, then went on. "About what love is."

Dar stepped closer and pulled Kerry's head into her shoulder, sliding an arm around her back. "We taught *you* that?" she whispered in an amazed tone, as she stroked the soft hair. "C'mon. Let's go home." They started side by side down the long, almost empty concourse.

Outside, a rumble of man made thunder rolled overhead as a plane shot skyward, heading north.

❖ ⌘ ❖ ⌘ ❖ ⌘ ❖

He was twenty minutes into the flight before he remembered, way too late, that he hated flying. He clutched the soft, blue blanket around his shoulders and slowly turned his head, regarding his surroundings with some surprise.

"Sir, can I get you something to drink?" The steward smiled kindly at him across the empty first class seat next to him.

"You got any warm milk?" he muttered, surprised at how cold it was in the plane.

"Sure." The steward disappeared

Andrew peered out of the window at the darkness, then let his head fall back against the leather seat. Least there was room up here. He stretched his long legs out towards the bulkhead and tried not to think about exactly what he was doing.

"Here you go." The steward put a napkin down at his elbow, and settled a steaming cup into the holder between the seats. "We're working on a little snack right now. It'll be out shortly."

"Mhm." Andrew decided on a grunt, as he picked up the cup and sucked gingerly at the warm milk. Tucked under his knees he could feel the soft warmth of the leather bag Kerry had given him, full of God only knew what stuff the sweet little kid had picked out.

Frankly, he was scared to look.

Andrew sighed. *Hell.* He was scared, period. But like in battle, now that he was committed to the action at hand, the fear was fading, replaced by an odd mix of fatalistic acceptance and anticipation.

After all this time, in less than three hours he'd walk off this damn plane, and she'd be there. She might not like what she found, but she'd be there, and he'd get to see her and...

He sipped at his milk shakily. The voice on that phone haunted him.

Hadn't known whether to spank his kid, or kiss her for that. Andrew found a tiny smile somewhere. Based on Dar's expression when she'd come outside, she hadn't known either. *Well, better to act now, and apologize later, wasn't that what I taught her? Got that whacked up side your head this time, boy.*

Maybe it'd been the right thing. Hell, maybe that's what he'd been hoping for when he went looking for his kid, trusting her judgement more than his own.

And wouldn't it just kick her butt to know that?

"Sir, if you'd let me put this down for you?" The steward held out a piece of linen, and a tray.

Chow was not an option. Andrew started to protest, then just pulled the arm tray out, figuring it was better to let the damn thing go. He could ignore it until they got the picture and—

The smell of warm chocolate hit him.

He blinked. "What is that?"

"It's a warm brownie, with some vanilla ice cream, and hot fudge drizzled over it," the steward responded efficiently. "Here's your silverware. If you need anything, give me a buzz."

"This what you people consider a snack?" he rasped.

The man smiled. "No, sir. But it was requested by the young lady who came down the jetway with you." He glanced over his shoulder.

"Everyone else is getting pasta salad."

Why that little green eyed son of a biscuit. "Thanks." He locked his jaw as that tiny, offhand but so characteristic bit of kindness caught him by surprise, and started him off again. He picked up his spoon and tasted a bit of the fudge, then rubbed his eyes.

Damn kids.

❖ ⌘ ❖ ⌘ ❖ ⌘ ❖

The phone rang, just as she was about to leave. Cecilia hesitated, then picked it up, checking the number and frowning. "Yes?"

"Ceci. Hello. How are you darling?" Elli's voice sounded cheerful and pleasant as usual. "Don't forget our card game tonight, hmm?"

Ceci looked at her watch. "I won't be there," she replied quietly. "I've got something I need to do."

"What? But darling you promised. When did this come up? We spoke yesterday."

"I know. I'm sorry." She paused. "I got a call earlier. It's just something I have to take care of."

"But—"

"Elli, good bye." Cecilia put the phone down and picked up her keys. She smoothed the soft, blue fabric of her shirt down and gazed at herself in the mirror before she closed her eyes and went into the dark that brought exciting scents of night blooming flowers to her as she moved through the heavy air.

Strange. She'd never noticed them before.

The drive to the airport was a dream, of oncoming headlights and street lamps, until she reached the parking lot and got out, her legs already shivering and weak.

She closed the door and leaned against it, waiting for her heart to settle. Then she straightened and went to the terminal. It was quiet inside, only a few flights still waiting to come in, and most of the shops and stands were closed.

Cecilia got herself a bottle of ice tea from the one snack shop open, found the gate, and settled into a chair right next to the window. Outside, she could see a long expanse of mostly deserted tarmac, only the occasional working truck speeding past, its lights blinking as it made its way around the landing areas.

After a minute, she got up, and went to the desk. "Excuse me."

The clerk looked up. "Yes, ma'am?"

"Is this flight coming in on time?"

The clerk smiled. "Yes, ma'am. It's ten minutes early, as a matter of fact."

Ceci took in a breath, and released it. "I'm waiting for someone.

Could you possibly tell me if...if they're on the plane?"

The clerk glanced around. "Ma'am, we're not really supp—"

"It's my husband."

The terminal was almost empty. "Sure." The clerk looked around again. "What's his name?"

Her tongue felt numb. "Roberts." She managed to force the sound out. "Andrew Roberts."

A clattering of keystrokes, and the clerk scanned the monitor, the greenish reflection showing against his glasses. Then he smiled. "Yes, ma'am. He's there. Seat 2A."

Ceci held on to the counter, afraid she'd fall if she let go. "Thank you." She waited a moment, then walked back to her seat, sank down into it, and leaned her head against the window. Her eyes focused on a spot nearby, where the nose of an airplane would surely soon come.

The only thing left to do now was wait.

❖ ⌘ ❖ ⌘ ❖ ⌘ ❖

His ears popped. Andrew tore his eyes away from the passing clouds, outlined eerily against the running lights of the plane, and swallowed, recognizing the decent. Sure enough, a few minutes later the fasten seat belts light went on, and his breathing increased.

"Ladies and gentlemen, we've begun our initial decent into the greater New Haven area. We estimate being on the ground in about fifteen minutes or so and another ten minutes for taxiing, so that puts us at the gate about ten minutes early. Please fasten your seat belts and enjoy the rest of your flight."

Twenty-five minutes. Andrew closed his eyes and folded his arms across his chest. *All these damn years, and it comes down to twenty-five damn minutes.* He fastened his safety belt, and tried to take deep breaths—hard when his guts were tensing up as though he were thinking of jumping out the damn plane before it landed.

He thought it would last forever, but before he realized it, the loud grinding noise of the gear being lowered sent shivers through him, and he looked outside to see the lights of the city flashing by past the plane's long wings.

A thump, then the engines reversed, whirling up to full speed in order to slow the big plane down. Andrew stared out the window, finding the terminal lights and fastening on them.

It took minutes of a slightly bouncy motion, then the plane turned its nose towards the welcoming bays of the terminal, and selected one, where dark figures stood, guiding it in with fluorescent wands.

And then the plane stopped.

Andrew unhooked his belt, reached between his knees, and pulled the soft leather bag up and into his lap. He waited a bit for his heart to stop racing, but it didn't, so he pushed to his feet and held onto the seat back, hoping his knees wouldn't give way and send him sprawling over the carpet.

He went on automatic then, as the airplane door opened inward, allowing a gust of damp, musty smelling air to enter. The steward gave him a smile as he walked past, turned the corner and headed up the jetway, his heartbeat pounding so hard he couldn't even hear the conversations around him.

He could see the terminal ahead, through the door.

Just a few steps away.

Chapter
17

Ceci stood, as the plane bounced to a halt and the jetway extended, cupping its end around the doorway of the craft. She pressed her hands against the window and watched the airport staff get ready, then the aircraft door opened. She could see only a small square of light there, but her eyes never left that, as first uniformed bodies passed.

Then, for a split second an outline flashed through that single square of light, and her breathing stopped.

Just that one glimpse.

Just that one second.

And she knew.

Hand over hand she moved down the line of chairs until she was near the entrance, gripping a pillar just to hold herself up as she heard footsteps approaching.

And then, he was there.

Filling the doorway. A dark blue sweatshirt draping the tall, broad shouldered body, its hood framing a scarred face whose eyes flicked over the room, then found hers.

She was lost all over again. She never remembered walking those last few steps, only that his eyes never left hers, and she only stopped when her hands touched a warm, living body that had existed only in her dreams for seven long years.

A soft gasp left her lips. "Andy."

The gentle blue eyes searching hers teared up. "Hey there, pretty lady."

It was too much. Her knees buckled and he caught her, and she fell into an embrace whose feel and scent overwhelmed all of her defenses.

She was so small and so light. Andrew kept his eyes closed and just savored the feel of her against him, her heartbeat thrumming against his chest as he wrapped his arms around her and let his heart come home.

At last.

He realized, unknown moments later, that they were blocking the passage, as the other passengers had to edge around them, giving them looks ranging from amusement to annoyance. Ceci had her head buried in his chest and held onto him for dear life, her body racked with sobs, so he took the short route and simply lifted her up, cradling her as he walked over to a secluded area that was quiet and empty.

Then he sat down and dropped his head down until he could breathe in her scent. Her hands stroked his chest through the fabric and he pulled her closer, letting his sense of time drift away as he felt his face tense into a strange and unpracticed expression.

A smile.

❖ ⌘ ❖ ⌘ ❖ ⌘ ❖

Kerry was just finishing putting up some coffee in the kitchen when the phone rang. She reached over and snagged it from the worktable. "Hello?"

"Hey, Ker."

She blinked in surprise. "Hey, Angie. What's up?" She'd last spoken to her sister on the weekend and she hardly expected another call so soon.

A pensive sigh. "Nothing good."

"Yeah?" Kerry wiped her hands off and walked into the living room, which was empty since Dar was in the study working on part of her inbox. "You feeling okay? It's not the baby, is it?" She turned the volume down on the television and sat down on the loveseat, leaning back and propping one leg up against the side of the couch.

"No. It's more about the hearings."

Oh. Kerry leaned her head against her fist. "Yeah. I'm not looking forward to that."

There was an awkward pause. "No. I...listen, Ker? You're my sister and I love you. You know that, right?"

She took a breath. "Yeah. Same here."

"Right. Well, Dad put the word out... He doesn't want anyone talking to you during the whole thing." Angie hesitated. "And Richard came down on me pretty hard about it. I—"

"So you'll be going along with it," Kerry finished quietly, swallowing a lump in her throat.

"Kerry, you don't have to live here with him." Her sister sighed unhappily. "It's just...like for show. It's not like I mean it. You know me better than that."

"Yeah, sure."

"Kerry..."

She rubbed her eyes. *Too much stress tonight.* "Sorry, Angie. It's really all right. I understand." She exhaled. "We just have a lot going on here. I'm a little strung."

A short silence. "Are you okay?"

"Yeah, yeah. I'm fine. We just...um..." Kerry shifted the phone a little and patted Chino, who had jumped up next to her and laid down. "You remember I told you about Dar's parents?"

"Mmm. Yeah, yeah. I do. That was really sad and kind of awful."

"Uh huh. Well, we got them back together tonight."

"Really?" Angie's voice perked up. "My god, Ker. That's wonderful. Wow." A muffled sound came through the receiver and Angie sighed. "Gotta go. I just wanted to give you some warning. Don't hold it against me, okay?"

"I won't," Kerry responded quietly. "How's Mike?"

"Dad pulled him out of school. He's got him working in his office. I...he's been really quiet lately."

"Tell him I said hi, if you see him, okay?"

A pause. "Okay." Angie cleared her throat. "Goodbye."

Kerry thumbed the button and let the phone fall to her lap. She looked up as soft footfalls sounded from the study and Dar appeared, scrubbing her fingers through disheveled dark hair. The taller woman ambled over and perched on the back of the couch. "Trouble?" Dar gauged her expression.

"Sort of." Kerry let her head rest against the cool leather, and stroked Chino's soft fur. "That was my sister."

"Yeah?"

The green eyes took on an almost gray hue. "She was just giving me fair warning. I'm...being shunned during the hearings." Kerry was surprised at how much that hurt. "Even by her."

Dar snorted in surprise, making Chino jump. "And here I liked her."

"I don't blame her, Dar. She's...I mean, she's got to deal with them all the time. I don't." Long fingers scratched her neck comfortingly and she closed her tired eyes. "It stings, though."

The phone rang again, startling both of them, and this time Dar slipped the receiver out of Kerry's hands and answered it. "Hello?"

"Hey, Dardar."

Her father sounded exhausted, but peaceful. A wave of relief crashed over her. "Hi."

"Damn plane made it," Andrew rasped.

"So I gathered. Mom there?"

A long silence. "Yeah."

Dar nodded to herself. "You okay?" She found fingers laced with hers and she turned to see Kerry's anxious gaze on her.

Even longer silence. "I'm all right," Andrew finally muttered. "We're gonna..." He stopped speaking for a few heartbeats.

Must be the "we." Dar tensed her lips.

"Get going. I um...listen, is Kerry there?"

"Sure. She's right here." Dar gave her puzzled lover a faint shrug.

"Wouldya...just tell her I said thanks," her father muttered. "I owe her one."

Dar's brows knit. "All right. I'll tell her. Listen, if you need any-thing, you call, okay? Thanks for letting us know you got there in one piece."

"Wouldn't say that," Andrew muttered. "'Night."

Dar put the phone down slowly and smiled at her lover. "He said to say thank you."

"To me?" Kerry looked confused, then her expression cleared. "Oh."

"Oh?" Dar stretched out along the back of the loveseat, jungle cat style.

"I um...arranged for some ice cream. I figured he wouldn't like a vinaigrette pasta salad just going on what I know about his daughter."

Dar smiled. "He said he owes you one." She curled a hand over Kerry's shoulder. "Thanks. That was incredibly thoughtful of you, Ker."

Kerry glanced down, then back up, and squared her shoulders. "Hey. You guys are the only family I've got. Gotta make sure you're taken care of." She managed to hold her composure until Dar's lips tensed and she lifted a hand to touch Kerry's cheek. Then she turned and rested her head against her lover's chest. "Oh god, Dar. I never even talk to them. Why does this hurt so much?"

"'Cause you love them," was the quiet, truthful response. "And hav-ing that turned away does hurt."

They rested quietly together, with only the soft whisper of the televi-sion behind them. Then Kerry shifted slightly. "Dar?"

"Mmm?"

"I think I understand why your dad was afraid to go home." Kerry rubbed her thumb against the short, fine hairs on Dar's arm. Her eyes slowly lifted to meet the serious blue ones above her. "It's a very scary, very vulnerable feeling."

"I know." Dar leaned forward and touched foreheads with her. "But I knew my father was going to be all right."

Kerry could almost taste her, she was that close. "You did?"

"Yeah." Dar's voice dropped to a whisper. "Because my mother feels about him the way I feel about you."

"Oh." Kerry smiled as the ache in her guts eased. She closed her eyes as Dar tilted her head and they kissed.

Guess that's all right, then.

❖ ⌘ ❖ ⌘ ❖ ⌘ ❖

There was a faint rumble of thunder overhead as they left the airport, moving from the bland fluorescent glare out into a stark landscape outlined briefly in periodic lightning. Andrew shifted his overnight bag and blinked, feeling unsure and awkward, not really convinced he was here or that the whole thing was happening.

A hand slipped into his, warm and unexpected, and curled around his fingers in a strong grip. "This way," Ceci murmured as she led him towards the car.

"All right." Andrew altered his steps to match hers, slowing down and trying to concentrate on just how damn nice holding someone's hand was.

She unlocked the doors remotely, and hesitantly let go of him before walking around to the driver's side and getting in. Ceci settled into place and closed the door, then paused and turned her head. She felt like closing her eyes, then opening them, closing, then opening...just to prove to herself this was no dream. He looked back quietly, the lamplight sending glints of reflection off his pale eyes. "I'm...not really sure I can drive."

He looked down, then back up. "Slept in worse places." The voice was huskier than she remembered, but still held that faint, wry tone. The scars were vivid and cruel, but did nothing to remove the rugged nobility that was as much a part of him as the drawl, and the strength, and the character.

And the eyes hadn't changed at all. Ceci very gently touched his jaw, running her fingers along the side of his face as he stayed absolutely still, the dark lashes dropping to cover his eyes. Her hand touched the still dark hair, lightly frosted with silver and she tugged, just a tiny bit of it. "Have to get you a haircut."

The eyes opened and his soul looked out at her timidly, the fear of rejection so obvious to her it made the tears well up in her eyes yet again. His jaw tensed and she cupped it, all the things needing to be said piling up and leaving her mute.

Maybe she didn't need to say them. Maybe he knew like he had always seemed to with her. His body relaxed a bit and he exhaled, warming her arm and sending goose bumps traveling up it. "Want me t'drive?"

Memories long buried stirred. "Have you gotten any better at it?" Ceci asked, with shy humor.

"Nope," Andrew admitted.

"I guess I'd better get on with it then." She took a deep breath, then straightened and started the car, turning on the wiper blades against the newly started rain. The light obligingly turned green as she exited, and she entered the highway, resting her arm on the center console as she watched the road.

After a moment, fingers tangled with hers and the world seemed to float peacefully by, enclosing them in a bubble of timeless wonder.

❖ ⌘ ❖ ⌘ ❖ ⌘ ❖

Andrew sat quietly on the couch, only his head swiveling back and forth as he regarded the painfully neat apartment surrounding him. *Kid was right.* He let a breath out slowly, running his fingers over the oatmeal colored cloth that covered the sofa. *Place looks like a damn hospital, only the chairs aren't half as nice to sit in.*

His eyes lifted to the picture on the wall, whose form and shape he recognized as Ceci's work, one he'd never seen before. It seemed to add color to the room, but to his knowing gaze, the somber shades and bleak lines painted an entirely different scene.

Well. He wished this part were over. This was the part where they both had to pony up the truth, and maybe go past it, and maybe not. Andrew stared at the opposing wall. He'd already gotten further than he'd allowed himself to dream of and now...

Now he was in damned uncharted waters, with no damn lifejacket and fins poking up through the whitecaps.

"Here." Cecilia had come in from the kitchen and now she handed him a mug. "You look like you could use this." She sat down next to him with her own cup and cradled it in both hands, sipping at its contents in silence.

Andrew tasted the liquid. Coffee, double strength with a ton of sugar. He had to pause a bit before he swallowed, to let the tightness in his throat relax. "Nobody ever made this like you." He looked at her, watching her hands tighten on the cup she held. "Cec—"

"You know," Cecilia interrupted him softly, "part of me wants to know...what happened. Where you've been..."

He lowered his gaze.

"But there's another part of me that doesn't. That part of me just wants to sit here and look at you...and touch you...and..." She had to stop and breathe. "And somehow make myself believe you're here," her voice cracked, "and it doesn't have to hurt anymore."

Somehow, he got his cup and her cup on the table before a drop spilled, then captured her hands.

Still in silence.

What could he say?

Ceci took a moment, then bit her trembling lip. "After they came and told me..." She paused and swallowed. "I didn't know what to do. I felt like I was breaking apart into a thousand different pieces. Everything I did, everything I saw..." Her eyes closed. "It was like laying my heart on glass shards." The tears ran her face again and Andrew moved closer, sliding one arm around her for support.

She caught her breath. "I finally realized that the only way I'd survive it is to..." She looked around mutely.

"Ditch the memories?" Andrew supplied.

"No." She scrubbed away fresh tears. "Just hide them." She sighed. "Take away everything I'd known before. Just...lock out that part of me."

"Even Dar?"

The gray eyes went bleak. "Especially Dar," Ceci whispered. "Andy. I'm sorry. I know I was wrong to do that. I know how much it must have hurt." She cradled her head. "How much it hurt me knowing how you'd feel about me doing that. I knew how you felt about her." She gasped. "I just didn't have a choice. I couldn't...stand the pain...and it was the only w-way."

Andrew gently pulled her head over and tucked it against his chest, stroking the silver blond hair in silent grief. "Ceci, I'm sorry," he finally rasped. "I'da torn my guts out before I'd have done that to you."

She huddled against him. "Then why did you?" she whispered.

Andrew closed his eyes. "That thing I had to go for wasn't for what you thought it was. Wasn't for what everybody knew." He drew a breath in. "Was a place...had a squad of twenty two men stuck in it. Place I'd been to way back. Team I was with...I was the only one still kicking."

Ceci lifted her head and looked at him. His face tensed in pain. "Twenty two of 'em, Ceci," his voice held a helpless, lost note, "came to me, and I...traded them twenty-two souls for mine." He stopped for a long moment. "And I did, 'cept they caught on coming out and somebody had to hold 'em." He blinked and an errant bit of water emerged. "And I thought," the pitch dropped very low, "there weren't nothing for me to go back to."

Cecilia went still.

"So they got me."

A soft moan.

"And they tried their damndest on me, but a man's gotta care about somethin' for you t'do that and I didn't." Andy's whole face twitched. "I cursed 'em for not trying harder." He paused. "Five and some damn years. 'Bout the only thing kept me half sane was thinking of you." His voice softened. "Wishin' things were different," he whispered. "Hurtin' that we parted mad."

Cecilia gave a shuddering gasp. "Andy, I'm so sorry. I didn't mean what I said."

"Yeah. Me neither." He sighed. "Anyhow, guess I was just too damn stubborn in the end. One day stuff got loud, next thing I knew, I was on a boat headed home." There was an awkward pause. "They patched me up best they could...set me loose."

She lifted her head and looked him in the eye. "I told you I wouldn't be there if you came back."

He nodded silently.

"You believed me."

Hesitantly, he blinked. "Didn't have the guts to find out one way or t'other." He stopped and closed his eyes. "Didn't want to know if you hadn't."

"I was...just trying to get you to stay," Ceci whispered. "I would have waited my whole life for you." She buried her face in his sweatshirt. "I've missed you so much."

Andrew let his chin rest against her soft hair. "Same here."

They were quiet for a while, as the tension eased and the air cleared. "Andy?" Cecilia murmured, after a bit.

"Mmm?"

"I'm...very tired...of hurting," she said slowly. "And I can't change what happened."

"No."

"Can we just start again?" She searched his face intently. "Please?"

His head tilted slightly as he thought, intense blue eyes drinking her in with characteristic seriousness. "I do think I'd like that," he finally said, lacing his fingers in hers. "Let's do it."

So. Ceci felt numb and a little nauseous from the stress, and she had a headache that would fell Picasso at forty paces.

It felt wonderful. But she was totally exhausted and she suspected Andy probably was too. "I don't think I can remember the last time I stayed up this late," she murmured, eyeing the clock on the mantel.

Andrew regarded her soberly. "Why doncha g'wan..." He nodded towards the bedroom. "I'll be fine out here. I...um..." He stopped awkwardly. "Go on."

Maybe it was best, Ceci reflected. *They had time and it would take time to readjust to...everything. To each other. Andy was right not to push things.*

She didn't budge.

They eyed each other and suddenly, shy smiles appeared on both their faces. "You know something, Andy?"

"What?"

"Seven years is long enough to sleep alone. Come keep me company." She squeezed the hand still tangled with hers. "Or I'll be up and peeking out here all night to see if you're still around."

His lips twitched. "All right," Andy drawled softly. "Hope I don't move round too much on yer."

Cecilia stood and very gently pulled at him. "I'm so tired you could do calisthenics and it probably wouldn't bother me."

"Not hardly," he muttered, as he stood, lifted the bag Kerry had gotten him, and followed Ceci into the bedroom. He set the bag down and regarded it. "S'pose that green eyed gal remembered some jammies." He glanced around at the almost painfully neat room with its austere fabric and crisply made bed.

Ceci tilted her head. "That's not yours?"

"Didn't have time to pack." Andrew unlatched the bag, pulled the zipper open and poked inside curiously. "Lord." He took out a pair of pale blue pajama shorts with a darker blue pattern.

"What...are...oh." Ceci muffled a laugh. "They're seals." She fingered the fabric, which did, indeed, have little dark blue seals on it. "Would that be Dar's friend Kerry?"

He scowled a little. "Yeah. Got some kinda sense of humor, I'll tell ya that." He investigated further, finding a small shaving kit and other bathroom articles, a towel, several neatly folded sweatshirts, and two pairs of jeans.

And underwear. Andrew's eyebrows lifted as he removed a pair of burgundy silk boxers. "Jesus H. Christ."

Ceci clapped a hand over her mouth, as a burst of hysterical laughter threatened to escape. "Well, she's got good taste."

Andrew muttered something under his breath and pulled the pajamas out, then turned towards the bathroom, stopping when a hand touched his arm. "Yeah?"

"Since when are you shy?" Ceci tugged at the sweatshirt.

The low light in the bedroom turned his pale eyes a dim gray. He studied her for a long set of heartbeats. "Lotta marks on me. Aren't real nice to look at," he told her honestly.

"And your point would be what, exactly?" Cecilia inquired.

He was silent, then handed her the pajamas and pulled his sweatshirt off, which he folded with automatic precision and tucked it into the side pocked of the bag.

Cecilia bit the inside of her lip, but made no comment, looking with pained eyes at the burn marks and criss crossing scars that covered his chest. A jagged tear ran from the point of one shoulder down to his hip, so recently healed she could see the still visible marks of the suture scars. She handed him the pajama shirt, then ran her fingertips over his ribs.

He put the shirt on without comment, then finished undressing as she did the same, ending up face to face with her in front of the bed. They linked hands and pulled the blankets down together in comfortable silence, then crawled under them.

Ceci lay curled on her side watching the strong profile outlined in the faint light from the window, too tired even to cry anymore. There would be tomorrow for that, and the day after, and the day after. Until her mind readjusted to this wonderful new reality and the feeling of bleak emptiness she'd felt for so long became as distantly remembered as the sense of peaceful joy she now felt had been before tonight.

She closed her eyes, then opened them after a moment, to see him looking back at her. She squeezed his hand and smiled, and even in the dark, saw the movement as he smiled back. Ceci closed her eyes again and left them shut, finding herself in the unfamiliar position of looking forward to the morning.

Chapter
18

"I did not jinx you." Kerry brought the bottle of medicine into the living room, lit with the first rosy tint of dawn. "So don't you blame me." She sat down next to the grumpy, miserable figure on the couch, who was cradling her head in her hands. "It's not like I wanted to see you sick, Dar."

Dar sighed. "I know." She swallowed, trying to tame a rebellious stomach that had kept her up all night, in bouts of nauseous spasms. "God, I hate being sick."

"Well, I don't think many people enjoy it." Kerry poured a spoonful of the medication and held it up. "C'mon."

Dar gave her a pathetic look, then winced and accepted the offering, swallowing it with a grimace. "Jesus."

Kerry pushed the dark, disheveled hair out of her lover's eyes, then felt her forehead. "I don't think you have a fever. It's probably just a bug." She'd woken to find Dar huddled miserably in the bathroom and tried to find a way to make the poor thing more comfortable. "You're definitely staying home today."

"C'mon. You know I can't do that," Dar muttered.

"Dar! You most certainly can," Kerry protested. "Don't be goofy. You are not in any condition to go to work so just get over it." She rubbed the terrycloth covered back. "Curl up here with Chino, and watch cartoons, okay?"

Dar briefly considered ignoring the suggestion, then held her breath as another spasm hit her. *Well, I could always go in and throw up all over Ankow.* That might be satisfying, at least for the moment, but she knew Kerry was right. "You'll have to sit in on the Marketing meeting for me."

"Ew." Kerry made a face. "Can I call in sick too? I'd rather hang out here and watch *Space Ghost* and take care of you."

Dar looked at her.

Kerry sighed. "Okay, okay. It was just an idea."

"I appreciate the thought." The blue eyes flicked to her face and a bit of a grin appeared for a second. "Don't stay too late, huh?"

That was better. Kerry smiled. "I'll see if I can get out of there after the meeting. I don't have anything scheduled for later on." She stood up and tugged her jacket straight, then she walked into the bedroom and pulled open a drawer. She removed a soft, fluffy blue blanket and brought it back with her. "Here," she tucked the blanket around her sick friend, "keep the phone by you, okay?"

Dar exhaled, then gave up and curled up on the couch on her side, bringing her knees up to ease the cramping in her guts. "Okay." She glanced up to see Kerry gazing at her, the torn emotions very evident. "What?"

Kerry scowled unhappily. "I think I hate you being sick more than you do," she muttered. "I feel like such a turd for leaving you here."

The cool leather felt good against her skin, as Dar rested her head on the couch arm. "It's all right." She felt absurdly contented with the reaction. "Go on. You're going to hit traffic."

"Mmph." The blond woman still wasn't pleased. "Chino, you take care of mommy Dar, okay?" The puppy was curled up at Dar's feet, her pale head resting on one bare foot, and she blinked at Kerry's words. "Call me if you need anything."

"Sure," Dar agreed, biting the inside of her lip.

Reluctantly, Kerry retrieved her keys and briefcase and left, not without several aggravated backwards glances. She locked the door and headed down the steps, surprised at how much she had to force herself not to turn right around and go back. "Jesus, Kerry. Would you chill out? She's just got a stomach virus. Calm your butt down already."

She got into the Mustang and started it, then leaned on the steering wheel and gazed at the condo. Long fingers drummed on the wheel, then she sighed, and put the car into gear and backed out of her parking spot, starting towards the ferry as she punched a number into her cell phone.

"Good Morning, Dar Roberts' Office."

"Morning, María." Kerry smiled, as she realized she'd unconsciously modeled her tone after Dar's.

"Aye. *Buenos días*, Kerrisita. How are you?"

"Well," Kerry glanced in the rearview mirror, "I'm fine but Dar's not going to make it in today."

María's voice took on a concerned tone immediately. "What is wrong? She is not feeling well?"

"No, some kind of stomach bug." Kerry sighed. "She was up all night sick. Anyway, I've got to sit in a meeting for her this afternoon. Could you call Eleanor's admin and sniff out the chances of moving the meeting to this morning?" She knew María would have a better chance at that then her newly commissioned Mayte.

"*Sí, sí.*" María wrote something. "I will do that. Is there anything that Dar needs?"

A nanny? Kerry swallowed the comment. "No. She's just going to take it easy. I'm sure she'll sign on from here later." *True, knowing Dar.* "At least I hope so," she added, wondering if there was enough medicine in the house. *Should she have some Dramamine sent? What about...*

"Kerrisita?"

"Oh, sorry. Did you say something?" Kerry drove onto the ferry carefully, and put the Mustang into park for the short trip to the mainland.

"I was saying to drive carefully. There was terrible traffic this morning."

"Thanks. I'll see you in a few minutes." She hung up the phone and nibbled her fingernail. "Now what did we always take for an upset stomach? Pepto...Kaopectate...Dramamine...warm cola." She dialed another number, and waited for it to be answered. "Hi. Yes, this is Kerry Stuart. Oh, hi, Mrs. Eveans. Yes. Listen, can you have some stuff sent up to the apartment?" She spent a few minutes listing things, then hung up. "Okay. I feel a little better now." She drummed her fingers again. "Wonder if the marina store has those seasickness bands...maybe they'd help." Tones sounded over the roar of the ferry's engines.

❖ ⌘ ❖ ⌘ ❖ ⌘ ❖

Kerry pulled into the parking lot and sat for a moment, leaning on the steering wheel and collecting her composure. "Jesus, that was close," she muttered, clearing her mind of the driver bearing down on her from the wrong side of the street, whom she'd only just missed crashing into. She got out and grabbed her briefcase, then straightened her jacket with an automatic twitch and headed towards the building.

"Morning, Ms. Stuart," the guard greeted her cheerfully.

"Good morning," Kerry replied, suppressing a soft curse when she saw who was bearing down on her from across the lobby. "Then again, maybe not." She arranged a neutral look on her face as David Ankow joined her.

"Well, you are the early bird, aren't you?" he asked mildly.

"Best time of the day to get things done," Kerry answered, shifting her briefcase. "Before all the distractions show up, I mean, crop up." He wasn't sure it was an insult, Kerry knew, but he suspected. She kept an open, inquiring look on her face just in case. "Something I can do for you?"

"Just thought I'd spend the day following you around. Get a feel for what it is you do." Ankow smiled pleasantly at her. "Where's your...bitchy roommate?"

Kerry started walking towards the elevator. "Oh, probably lying on the rug chewing some cookies," she replied. "Or maybe chasing flies. She likes that." She entered the elevator, then turned and waited for him to join her, the look on his face priceless. "What's wrong?"

Ankow stepped past her and eyed her warily. "That's funny," he said. "A joke, right?"

Innocent green eyes widened as the doors closed. "Joke?" Kerry asked, puzzled. "You asked me where my dog was didn't you?" She pressed the button for the fourteenth floor. "Guess you saw her picture on my desk. She's cute, isn't she?"

"Adorable," Ankow answered, with a slight flare of his nostrils.

The rest of the ride was spent in silence, until the doors opened and they exited, and Kerry turned purposefully right and headed towards her office. Mayte was already there, following her mother's schedule, and Kerry waved. "Morning, Mayte." Her eyes and the girl's met, and Mayte's shifted fractionally to Ankow, then rolled slightly.

"Good morning, Ms. Kerry. I was going down for some *cafecito*. Would you like some?" Mayte stood up and brushed her plain, but well cut dark blue dress off. She was a tall, slim girl with dark hair and eyes, and a pretty, slightly elfin face.

"I'd love some." Kerry opened her office door. "Any for you?" she inquired, glancing at Ankow.

"No thanks," he muttered, brushing by her. "I'd like to live past forty, thanks."

Mayte stuck her tongue out at his back and made a gesture, then escaped, leaving Kerry to gather the already shredded edges of her patience and enter her office. *Knew I should have stayed home.* She sighed inwardly.

Ankow stood near the window, peering out of it at the sunlit water. Kerry ignored him, sat down at her desk, flipped her PC on, and pulled the folder off the top of her inbox. A soft buzz of the intercom alerted her and she lifted the receiver of her phone instead of allowing the speakerphone to pick up. "Hello?"

"Ah, Kerrisita." María's voice filtered through. "I have gotten them to move your meeting to ten o'clock, if that is okay."

"Perfect." Kerry was relieved.

"And I also rescheduled the conference call with the overseas group. I hope you do not mind. It was to be at four, and I thought you might have something else to do then."

Kerry suppressed a smile. "Thanks, María. I really appreciate that." She was aware of the silent, censorious presence at her back. "Anything on the boards this morning?"

"There is nothing, no."

"All right. Let me know if anything crops up. I've got a ton of stuff on my plate here." Kerry hung up the phone and opened her folder, studying the operations reports run an hour before her arrival. "Mr. Ankow, you can sit down if you like." She checked the usage tallies and took out a highlighter, marking several spikes that had run their main systems to almost capacity. "Wow."

Ankow moved over to peer over her shoulder in a really annoying way. "What is that?"

Kerry dialed a number. "Utilization reports," she answered absently, as it was picked up. "Mark?"

"Who else?"

"Did you see the U report this morning?"

"The one that made me put analyzers on all three big pipes? That one?"

"Let me know what you find. I bet I've got a mailbox full of slow-down complaints." Kerry sighed as she clicked on her email, and watched it open, then fill with line after line of exclamation points. "Oh yeah."

"Will do." Mark hung up, and Kerry went back to studying the report, then bent her head as she spotted something.

"Son of a..." She flipped through another few pages, then went to her PC, opened a session and requested information from the big database. She pushed back from her desk and jerked to a halt, almost slamming into Ankow. "Excuse me."

"What are you doing?"

"Fixing a problem. That's what I get paid to do." Kerry glanced up at him. "You can go over there and sit down, or you can stand by the window, but I need to be able to do my job."

He moved, but only far enough to sit down on the edge of her desk. "Don't like being watched, hmm?"

"I don't like being hovered over, no." Kerry pulled her fanfold report over and scanned it, then flipped to a center page and tracked a line across the bottom of it. "I knew it." She dialed Mark back. "Mark?"

"Hey. It takes an hour or so, Kerry."

"Don't bother. Check out the job request from Houston. It's buried in about three layers of subroutines."

"Huh?" The sound of rapid keystrokes came clearly through the intercom. "What the hell's that?"

Kerry sat back and folded her arms. "I don't know. But if I had to give an opinion I'd say it looked like someone was dumping load on the system to stress it." Her green eyes found Ankow's face and fastened there. "Why don't you call Brian up at CLIPC and see who made the request then pull the plug on them?"

"Son of a frigging bitch..."

"And tell CLIPC I want a filter on Houston. No big requests get through without my personal authorization."

"They're gonna have a fit."

"Let them," Kerry replied. "Make it one way, though. I don't want Maríana to have a problem transmitting the payroll files later on today."

"You got it. Give me a few minutes, and I'll have the checkpoint in place. Good catch, Kerry. I'd have had to wait half the morning for the IP analysis."

"No problem." Kerry pressed the button, then waited, her eyes on her unwelcome visitor. "When I find out who requested that, I'm going to file a formal protest," she informed him, "for deliberate and malicious endangerment of ongoing business operations. That impacted a lot of customers."

"Really? Interesting." Ankow didn't rise to the bait. He did rise, however, and stroll over to the wall, studying her certifications idly.

Kerry let out a frustrated but silent breath, then turned her attention to her inbox. "If you want to sit down, I'll just be over here cleaning up that mess." She opened a blank message and started composing a standard reply to the complaints.

It was going to be a very long morning.

❖ ⌘ ❖ ⌘ ❖ ⌘ ❖

Cecilia held herself in the dream for as long as she could. It was one she'd had countless times over the years. Memories really, she knew. Ones her mind pulled out of the corners and crevices she'd hidden them in when she had no control over things.

And the waking was the worst, because she could still, half in her dream, feel the close warmth and breathe the scent of him, which would fade as she came closer to waking, fade, and weaken until she opened her eyes.

To nothing. Just an empty spot in the bed next to her and the bleak sunlight coming in the window, silent and harsh.

Reluctantly, she let the world intrude.

But this time, this one morning, the dream refused to loose its clutches on her, and the sense of being surrounded by a strong hold remained, until her confused, sleep fogged mind forced her eyes open into a room overwhelmingly full of her dreams.

Then memory hit with a rush, and she exhaled in pure joy.

It was late. Far later than she usually slept, but considering where she woke up, she couldn't blame herself one bit. Shy they might be with each other, but after thirty some years of marriage, their bodies had merely waited for their pesky upper brains to slip off to sleep, then cuddled with each other in warm familiarity.

Strange. She'd forgotten, of all things, just how big Andrew was. He surrounded her with a living cradle of long arms and longer legs, and she found herself sleeping with her head on his shoulder and an arm wrapped snugly around him. It was a nice feeling, and one she'd always enjoyed, watching his chest move under her arm as he breathed.

He was thinner than she remembered, but there was still solid power through the broad shoulders and in the arms that were loosely wrapped around her. His face held a terrible record of pain though, outside the scars that her eyes hardly saw now, there were creases etched around his eyes and mouth that made her wince to imagine the prolonged agony that had caused them.

Andy had never been pretty. Ceci gazed at the strong, rugged face. Just full of character and strength and a powerful sense of self that had attracted her from the very moment she'd seen him.

And still did. Ceci sighed soundlessly, unsurprised when a very blue eyeball appeared and focused on her. "Hey sailor," she whispered, watching the look of startled surprise chase itself on and off her husband's face.

His eyebrows twitched, then he relaxed. "Hey there, pretty lady," he drawled in response, evidently deciding to dispense with any attempt at the half awkward bashfulness of the previous evening.

"Think you stole the covers."

Andy scowled. "It's a damn small bed."

She smiled. "You're a darn big boy." She patted his side. "And a very, very, very welcome sight to wake up to."

"Same here." He tightened his grip a little. "Do I even wanta know how many bells it is?"

"No."

"S'what I thought."

Ceci closed her eyes and let her heart float in a happy, lazy peace.

They had plenty of time.

❖ ⌘ ❖ ⌘ ❖ ⌘ ❖

Dar was curled up in an amazingly small ball for someone her size. She had her eyes closed and her head resting against the couch arm, and was thoroughly, totally, unbelievably miserable. Rather than better, the nausea and cramping had gotten worse, and she'd finally resorted to simply keeping a container next to the couch, in case the violent dry heaves produced anything further.

So far, all they'd gotten her was a mind splitting headache and a very sore body. The television played softly in the background, but she mostly concentrated on taking short, shallow breaths, and wishing she were dead.

Chino was lying on the couch next to her—unusually quiet for the generally rambunctious puppy, as though she sensed her friend wasn't feeling well. Occasionally, she'd lift her head and give Dar's ankle a lick, then put her muzzle back down and sigh.

A soft knock came at the door, and Dar groaned. Another knock, then a familiar voice. "Ms. Roberts?"

Oh God. Dar uncurled slightly, enough to give her diaphragm room to expand and sucked in a chancy breath. "C'mon in, Clemente."

The door opened and the resident services manager poked his head in. "Oh my goodness, you are not feeling well, I can see that."

Dar merely rolled an eyeball at him.

"I will just drop off these things and be on my way." Clemente hurried in with a bag and set it on the coffee table. "Let me take them out for you. Is it a stomach virus you have?"

"Yeah." Dar lifted her head a little. "What is that?"

The earnest Cuban settled on one knee and started unpacking. "*Farmacia.* We have the stomach medicine and for the nausea and some coca cola. I have some plain broth here, I will put it in the kitchen for you, yes?"

She blinked. "Uh. Sure, sure...wh...Clemente...where did all this come from?"

Clemente paused, looking puzzled. "Ms. Kerry called the market for you. Did you not know?"

Ah. Of course. Stupid me. "Right. Right...great. Just leave it. I'm sure some of it will do something." A tired smile appeared as more and more items made their way out of the box and piled up on the glass surface. "She's thorough, huh?" An affectionate thought winged its way towards her lover.

Clemente looked up. "Yes, ma'am, for sure she most certainly is that." The resident services manager set everything out, then stood and brushed off his trousers. "I hope you feel better. Give us a call if there is something else you need, yes?"

"A harpoon."

"Pardon?"

"Never mind. Thanks, Clemente." Dar watched him leave, then turned her head and studied the table. Her body chose that moment to cramp up though, and she grabbed the couch arm, leaning over and holding on until the spasm tapered off. A small, unhappy sound escaped her. "Makes up for all the times I don't get sick, Chino. The one time I do...oh boy."

Chino whined.

Dar reached out a hand and poked her new acquisitions. "Trouble with all this stuff is I gotta put it on the inside and it ain't staying there long." Then she noticed a small package. "Hmm." She lifted the seasickness bands up and eyed them speculatively. "They don't...can't hurt." She slipped the fabric bands on and settled the beads over the center of her wrists, then pulled her blanket more snugly around her and closed her eyes, hoping sleep would ease the discomfort a little.

❖ ⌘ ❖ ⌘ ❖ ⌘ ❖

"Kerry, a moment please," Eleanor called to her, as the meeting broke up and Kerry glanced at her watch.

Curses. "Sure." She tapped her pencil on her notepad and considered her strategy. *It was almost lunchtime, right?* A glance at her watch again. *Well, eleven o'clock was* someone's *lunchtime and surely if you came in at seven, as she had...*

"Ah. Thank you." Eleanor oozed up to her. "I was surprised not to see Dar here...problems?"

Kerry paused, deciding on whether or not to answer truthfully, then shrugged. "She got tied up with something. They're trying to go beta with the new network next week. You know how it is."

"Absolutely," the Marketing VP agreed without hesitation. "And I agree–she should spend all the time she needs to with that. You're much easier to deal with anyway." She gave Kerry a smile that wasn't totally snakelike. They'd come to sort of an understanding over the past few months, and Eleanor had become almost bearable. "How is the project coming?"

Kerry nodded. "Good. The structure's in place. Now's just the hard part, integration and testing."

"It'll be ready on time, you mean?" The pale gray eyes sharpened.

Kerry looked around carefully and lowered her voice. Ankow was in the corner chatting with José, and she didn't want this little bit of information traveling. "Shh, don't tell anyone, Eleanor but I think..."

"Yes?" The VP leaned closer as well.

"I think it's going to be early," she whispered. "Dar was asking me for some baseline projects she could 'borrow' as early as two weeks from now. I think she's considering migrating them to check for traffic patterns."

"Really?" Eleanor fairly dripped with greedy delight. "I can't wait to sell it. You have no idea how many people have been sniffing around, saying they'd heard we were putting up a new net and wanting the specs on it."

Kerry smiled and wiggled an eyebrow at her. "Wish we could get that guy to buy into the project." She nodded towards Ankow. "He just doesn't get it."

Eleanor regarded the tall, good looking man, then tapped one long, impeccably manicured nail against her lip. "I'm sure if he saw it from a sales perspective..." She gave Kerry a smile. "Me and José'll take him to lunch. See what we can do." She picked up her leather appointment book and slapped Kerry lightly on the side with it. Then she sauntered around the table and eased herself skillfully in to the conversation near the wall.

"You go, girl," Kerry murmured under her breath, then picked her notepad up and lifted the conference room phone. After a moment, María answered. "Hi."

"Dar has not called in yet, Kerrisita."

Kerry pursed her lips. "I could have been asking for status on the relay outage in Newark."

"*Sí*, you could," the secretary agreed, amiably.

"Thanks. Maybe I'll give her a buzz." Kerry disconnected, then tapped the receiver against her chin. She watched Eleanor and José maneuver Ankow out of the conference room, then returned the pleasant smiles of the junior marketing people left to clean up.

They liked her. Kerry smiled back at them. Everyone pretty much did, she'd realized, after they'd gotten used to her, and used to the idea of someone else working in Dar's territory, who, while being completely and unshakably loyal to her supervisor, could be approached in a far different way. And since she and Dar kept their relationship strictly out of the office, even those people uneasy at that aspect had grown comfortable in dealing with her.

"Hey, Kerry," one of the regional assistants said. "See you at the gym tonight?"

"Not tonight," she responded regretfully. "I've got an offsite meeting this afternoon, then something I've got to take care of later."

"Bummer. We'll miss you. Can't wait for the next defense class to start." The woman picked up her portfolio and tucked it under her arm. "Thanks for a great meeting. See ya."

Kerry went out with them and headed for her office, glad of the peace and quiet as she circled her desk and sat down. "Let's see." She checked her mail. "No more exclamation points. I like that." She riffled through her mostly depleted inbox. "Looking good." She checked the logon report and saw Dar's name conspicuous by its absence and made her decision. She keyed the intercom. "Mayte."

"Yes, Ms. Kerry?"

"I'm...um..."

"Going home?" her admin supplied helpfully.

"Yeah. Guess your mom told you, huh?"

"She gave me what to say to people, yes," Mayte agreed. "I have your pager and your cell. I will call you if there is anything." A soft buzz was heard. "Hold on one moment."

Kerry waited, until Mayte's voice returned. "Ms. Kerry. It is my mother. She is looking to see if you are here. She has a call. She is not sure who it is."

"All right. Put her through." Kerry frowned. "María?"

"*Sí*. Kerrisita. There is someone calling here for Dar. I think it is her father."

"Oh!" Kerry blurted. "Sure. God, put him on." A click, then she leaned forward. "Hello?"

"Morning there, kumquat."

Kerry smiled hugely and bounced in her chair, making it squeak in protest. He sounded so much better. "Hi, Dad. How's it going?"

"Not bad. Where's mah kid?"

"Ah. Well, she's not doing so great, actually. She's kinda sick," Kerry explained. "She stayed home today. Was up most of the night throwing up and stuff."

"Damn. Sorry to hear that," Andrew responded. "Well, I was just callin' to let you two know everything's all right here. That's 'bout all."

"I'm so glad to hear that and I know Dar will be too." Kerry started shutting her PC down. "Did you have everything you needed?" An impish grin formed on her face as she waited for the answer.

"Huh. Yeap. But you and I need to have a chit chat 'bout boy's unmentionables when ah get back there."

"Did I get the wrong size?" Kerry asked innocently.

"No, you did not."

She could almost see the scowl. "They aren't comfortable?"

"That is not the point, young lady."

Kerry could hear a soft, muffled laugh in the background, and she realized, with a strange sense of wonder, that it was Cecilia. *Forgot there's two halves of this.* "You didn't like the color?"

"Kerrison." Dar's father's voice dropped low, almost exactly like his daughter's.

"Sorry, Dad. I only buy the very best for people I love," she told him, softening her tone.

There was a period of silence on the other end, where she could hear a soft, mechanical sound she identified as an air conditioner cycling on and off. "You fight damn dirty, y'know that, young lady?" Andrew finally sighed. "All right. But you better be watching your back now, y'hear? I don't go by the rules much neither."

"Warning taken." Kerry smiled. "Well, I've got to go. I've got a sick friend to take care of." She paused. "Hey. How about I call you from the house? I bet Dar would love to say hi."

There was a muffled sound. "All right," Andrew agreed. "We were just scrabblin' up some breakfast."

"Breakfast, hmm?" The green eyes twinkled.

"Not one word, young lady," he rasped back. "Talk at you later."

Kerry hung up and gathered her things, then slipped out the door.

Chapter 19

Kerry pushed the door open cautiously, peeking inside before entering. She spotted her lover curled up on the couch and tiptoed into the room, after closing the door quietly behind her. Even Chino was asleep, sprawled next to Dar and twitching in some kind of bizarre Labrador dream. She put her briefcase down on the loveseat and then knelt at Dar's side and studying the sick woman's face.

Dark lashes fluttered and Dar looked up, a little disoriented.

"Hey." Kerry put a hand on her forehead. "Mmm. You're warm."

"Ungh." Dar pursed her lips and swallowed painfully. "Time?"

"Just past noon." Kerry reviewed the open boxes on the table. "Tried everything, hmm?"

A groan answered her.

"That sounds bad." She pushed a bit of dark hair out of Dar's face. "I have some good news for you."

Dar caught her hand and pulled it closer as if in comfort. "Mmm? Did you run over Ankow in the parking lot? Good girl," she mumbled. "I'll tell 'em you were here all day."

"No." Kerry chuckled, using her other hand to rub Dar's neck. "Your father called. Looks like things are working out fine up there."

Both of Dar's eyes opened and she lifted her head. "Yeah?" She forgot about being sick for a minute and pulled herself up, running a hand through her hair and blinking at Kerry. "What'd he say?"

"Just that things were good." Kerry picked up a cup of water Dar had been sucking at and offered it to her. "Here. Take a sip. You don't want to get dehydrated." She stood up. "Let me get this stuff off and we can give them a call. Okay?"

Dar got a quarter of a mouthful down, then stopped and grimaced, concentrating and trying really hard not to allow it to come right back up.

She put the cup down and gave Kerry an unhappy look, too miserable even to dredge up a smidgen of her usual attitude. "Maybe he can tell me where he's cached a gun and I can shoot myself."

Kerry made a face. "Hang in there. I'll be right back." She trotted upstairs and changed quickly, glad to exchange the restrictive linen for a pair of shorts and a T-shirt, as she unclipped her hair and let it loose around her shoulders.

Still thinking, she made her way back down the stairs and rejoined her lover, who was again huddled near the end of the couch, curled up in a ball. *Damn, Dar. You're making me hurt just to look at you.* Kerry rubbed the tense calf next to her. "Hey. Listen, you want me to give Dr. Steve a call?"

Woebegone blue eyes peeked out from over the fist Dar had curled near her chin. She thought seriously about the question for a moment, then shook her head. "All he's gonna do is give me a shot of Dramamine." She managed to straighten up a little. "Damn stuff makes me break out in hives."

"Ooo." Kerry winced, then settled back and patted her lap. "Want to come over here and put your head down? It's not medical, but at least I can keep you company."

Meekly, Dar did so, reversing her position and putting her head down on Kerry's thigh. "You cancel the marketing meeting?" she asked, as Kerry lightly massaged down her back and shoulders.

"Nope. Just moved it to the morning." Kerry could feel the cold sweat that had gathered on Dar's neck, and she wiped it away with a bit of her shirt. "Eleanor and José are entertaining Ankow. Oh, and Dar? Someone dumped a loop into the system from Houston this morning. I had a ton of complaints."

"Mmph." Dar dredged up a semblance of interest. "Let me guess. You think our friend did it?"

"Don't know." Kerry felt the tension slowly leaving Dar's body and she kept up her kneading. "Probably though. Wanted to see if he could catch us."

"How long'd it take you t'find it."

"About thirty, maybe forty five seconds." Kerry smirked, proud of herself. "You should have seen his face." She reached over and snagged the phone. "Want to give your folks a call before you snooze off?"

Dar had curled an arm around her knee and was stroking it with her thumb idly. "Okay." It was amazing, really, how just having Kerry there made her feel so much better or at least, so much more relaxed, which helped ease the spasms. "Ker?"

The blond woman paused, and leaned over. "Hmm?"

"Glad you're here."

"Me too."

Dar took a breath to continue, then bit her tongue, as her body cramped, forcing a gasp of pain from her. She doubled over and held her breath, barely conscious of the firm, steady grip that kept her from falling.

Kerry held on to Dar with one arm and dialed the phone with the other, retrieving Dr. Steve's number from the phone's memory. "Hey. Dr, Steve? Hi. It's Kerry Stuart. Yeah." She felt Dar's chest move as the pain lessened and she started breathing again. "Listen, Dar's been sick since last night. We thought it was just a bug or something, but she's in a lot of pain here, and I'm getting worried." A pause. "I don't know. Might be tough." Another pause. "Okay. That would be great. I'll clear you on the ferry. Thanks. I really appreciate it."

She hung up the phone and put it down, then rubbed her lover's back. "Easy there. Dr. Steve's going to come out here and check you out, okay?"

Dar knew she was in deep trouble, because the thought of that actually sounded good to her. "Mph." She clamped her jaw shut, not wanting to lose her mouthful of water and wished primarily that someone would hit her over the head with a very large two by four.

❖ ⌘ ❖ ⌘ ❖ ⌘ ❖

"What do you think?" Kerry hovered nervously as Dr. Steve, in a garish pink guayabera and blue Bermuda shorts knelt by the couch.

"I think you have a very sick friend," the gray haired man answered, peering into Dar's eyes with a pinpoint light. "What have you been doing there, Miss Dar?"

"Nothing." Dar closed her eye in annoyance, watching spots dance across her inner eyelid with sickening rhythm. The doctor had taken a vial of blood and probed her belly, which had gotten him a yelp of pain and an accidental kick in the side. "What the hell is wrong with me? I've never had a bug this bad before."

Dr. Steve removed a couple of small bottles and a syringe from his actual, for real, no kidding, little black bag. "Well, I'm not sure, honey, but let me give you something to relax those spasms and a little something for the nausea, okay?"

A blue eyeball popped open and regarded the syringe nervously. "Dramamine makes me itch."

"Yeah, yeah, I remember." Dr. Steve carefully drew a measure of some clear liquid from one of the bottles and picked up a swab full of alcohol. "This is something else. Now hold still." He swabbed Dar's upper arm and inserted the needle, with only a small jerk from his patient, then injected the medication.

"Ow."

"Big baby."

Kerry perched on the couch arm. "You don't know what's wrong then?" she asked, then sighed, as the phone rang. She turned and picked it up. "Hello?"

"Hey there." Andrew's growly tones tickled her ear.

"Oh, hi. Sorry we didn't call you. I had to call Dr. Steve out here for Dar," Kerry told him. "She's really sick."

"Yeah?" Dar's father's voice grew anxious. "What's he say's wrong with her?"

"He doesn't know." Kerry stroked her friend's hair. "He's giving her some shots of something."

Dr. Steve glanced up at her curiously, but kept working, removing a second bottle and syringe and preparing it. "What did you have to eat yesterday?"

Dar blinked, as the first medication started to work. "Um. Nothing much. Cuban toast and jelly for breakfast...with coffee." She thought a moment. "Mmm...chocolate chip cookies for lunch...and I didn't have dinner."

Steve looked at her. "Chocolate chip cookies for lunch?" He sighed. "Some things never change. Nothing after dinner?"

"No." Dar shook her head. "Something happened. I got caught up in it."

"You had that Kahlua milkshake at the bowling alley," Kerry supplied helpfully. "Do you think it's food poisoning?"

"Not with that menu." Steve shook his head. "I don't know. We'll run some tests on the red stuff here. This'll let her relax and sleep. That's the best thing."

"Did you hear that?" Kerry spoke into the phone.

"Yeap." Andrew cleared his throat. "Should be all right. Just not too much. She can't take it."

"Other arm." Dr. Steve injected the medicine, then sat back. "Now, you listen to me, okay?" He wagged a finger at her. "Soon as your stomach settles, get some water into you—at least two glasses."

Dar nodded mutely.

"You get any more dehydrated, and we're going to have to start using the dirty H word, okay?" Dr. Steve packed up his bag and carefully labeled the blood sample. "If I didn't know better. I'd say you'd been drinking antifreeze, Dar. It's those kind of symptoms. Is this the first time you've been sick?"

"In a long time, yeah," Dar told him. "Antifreeze? That's nuts."

"Well, you've got something in you that ain't supposed to be there." Dr. Steve stood, and glanced at Kerry. "Keep an eye on her. Make sure she drinks that water or Gatorade stuff if you've got it."

"We do." Kerry nibbled her lip. "Could it have been the drink last night? That's the only place we were at that's strange."

"Timing's about right," Steve acknowledged. "Maybe something got in there. Weirder things have happened." He ruffled Dar's hair gently. "You're going to be okay, sugarplum. Give that stuff a chance to work, and just take it easy."

Whatever he'd given her was hitting hard, Dar realized, as a sense of displacement put distance between her and the rest of the room. It wasn't entirely a pleasant feeling, but along with it came a soothing lethargy that coursed through her body, relaxing muscles tense and sore from the day's battle with her rebellious stomach.

Even better was the ebbing of the nausea and the ability to breathe normally without worrying about throwing up. She was vaguely aware of the door closing and Kerry's quiet tones, then warmth surrounded her as she was lifted up a little, while Kerry resumed her pillow duty.

Having someone in your life, she decided fuzzily, *really rocked.*

❖ ⌘ ❖ ⌘ ❖ ⌘ ❖

Kerry drifted in and out of a light sleep, the sound of the television in the background, along with the soft hiss of the surf just audible through the glass windows lulling her into a peaceful somnolence.

The golden light of sunset came in the window next to the front door, spilling across the living room where they were and painting stripes all over everything. Dar had been sleeping peacefully since Dr. Steve left, and Kerry was content to stay right where she was, with her lover half sprawled over her body.

She'd gotten one cell phone call from Mayte telling her Ankow had come sniffing around, but had been distracted by Duks, who dumped a pile of reports the size of a hippo on him with the Accounting VP's typical deadpan manner. No other crises had happened, and the Newark mess had been sorted out by the networking office, so it looked like they'd gotten away with her disappearing.

Kerry stroked the dark hair spilling over her lap. Not that she would have made a different decision, even if all hell had been breaking loose and Ankow had been sitting on her desk. She'd have gotten up and walked out, and that was just that. She put her arms around Dar and hugged her, and wondered, just for a moment, what it would be like if she couldn't do that anymore.

She had only known Dar for all of what...eight months? So much of her life had changed when she'd met her, too. Her job. Her future.

Her family.

She hadn't really thought twice about it, either. She'd just followed her heart.

A stripe of sunlight chose that moment to impudently paint itself across Dar's face, turning her tanned skin a burnished gold. Kerry wound a bit of the hair it caught into her fingers, noting the faint mahogany high-lights seldom visible.

The muscles under the sunlight moved, then tensed, and Dar's eyes opened and blinked, appearing dazed and a little confused.

"Hey." Kerry put a reassuring hand on her shoulder. "How are you feeling?"

Dar rolled over onto her back and peered straight up at Kerry, a good sign, since a cramped fetal position had been all she'd been able to manage earlier. "Better."

Kerry produced a warm smile and reached for the bottle of Gatorade she'd parked there earlier. "Good." She offered Dar the bottle, much like she would have a baby, and bit her lip to keep from laughing as Dar sleepily complied, sucking at the nozzle and folding her hands over her stomach. "See? You're not so bad when you're sick."

A couple of mouthfuls were all she could manage, then Dar closed her eyes and rested her cheek against Kerry's stomach. "Must be the quality of the care," she mumbled, feeling totally wiped out, but not too bad otherwise. "I had a dream about you."

"Oh yeah?" Kerry put the bottle down and ran her fingers idly through Dar's hair. "What about?"

Dar's body moved as she shrugged a bit. "Hard to say. You were riding a horse and reciting poetry."

"Ooo." She chuckled. "Sounds more like a nightmare. Tell you what. Why don't we get you into bed, and I'll bring you in some broth. How does that sound?" She scratched Dar's scalp, concentrating on the spot just behind her ears.

"You sure you weren't someone's mom in a past life?" her lover mumbled, a faint smile appearing. "Because you're really good at this."

Kerry considered the question seriously. "Maybe," she finally replied. "God knows, I didn't learn it at home." Surprising, really, how those bits of bitterness surfaced sometimes. She looked down to see Dar gazing back at her and put a fingertip on her lover's nose. "So I guess you get to be the object of all my maternal instincts." Their eyes met and held, and Kerry felt a tiny shiver go down her back. "Well, you and Chino, any-way."

"Right." Dar exhaled, shaking off the weird sensation of almost memory. "I'm not sure if I can handle broth, though, and I'll only go to bed if you join me there," she bargained.

"Well, you get some soup down, and I'll see what I can do."

The blue eyes closed contentedly. "Deal."

❖❖❖❖❖❖❖

Cecilia paused as she put a last container in the basket on the counter and glanced outside, glad to see the bright, sunny weather. She went to the door and slid her head around it, spending a moment just looking at the tall figure slouched in a chair nearby.

Andrew was working at fixing her can opener. He'd taken it apart already and was reassembling the mechanism with deft, confident movements. Ceci sighed, leaning her head against the wall as she realized it was going to take some getting used to having the other half of her life back. She'd have just bought a new one. "Andy?"

Sharp blue eyes looked over and blinked in acknowledgement.

"There's a nice spot up by the lake. Would you like to take a walk up there?"

"All right," he agreed, standing up and bringing her appliance back over. He pressed the button, and the battery powered item whirred. "There you go."

He'd always been like that. Ceci gave him the basket as they left the apartment, cut through the back path, and headed up a small slope just behind her building. He had an innate knowledge of how things worked and a talent for fixing them. *That had come in very useful when they'd lived on base*, she remembered, having to cope with changes in her life that had started with going from rich to definitely not rich, and progressed from there.

It hadn't been easy, not for her and not for Andy, whose ship assignments kept him away for six months at a time. He'd gone AWOL in fact, when she was pregnant, and ended up hiding out in their quarters the last month before she gave birth, just helping her live through one of the toughest times of her life.

Maybe she'd never forgiven Dar for that, Cecilia mused, as Andrew took her hand in his as they walked along. Certainly, she'd hated being pregnant and resented the restrictions she'd suddenly found herself under. But that wasn't Dar's fault, any more than it was her fault that she'd inherited the genes for height, and dark hair, and blue eyes, and the fighting nature from the daddy she'd adored since the moment she was born.

Ceci sighed. No, it hadn't been easy. Dar had been a very tough child to raise, hyperactive and wild, headstrong and by the age of twelve, already larger and stronger than the mother who was trying to rein her in. And possessing a powerful, significant intellect that made her so much more difficult to interact with than Andy was.

Not that her husband was stupid, by any means. He had a core of good, solid common sense and an orderly mind well suited to everyday problem solving. But Dar, who had always tested years ahead of her age, had developed an edgy, restless brilliance that she hadn't had the patience or discipline to cope with.

Maybe that was what frustrated her so. Dar had so much potential. She was so intelligent and could have gone into so many different fields,

that her single minded, narrow focused goal of the Navy just drove
Cecilia out of her mind. She had silently celebrated when they'd said
"No" the last time, and had cheered Dar's stubbornness for the first time,
when her daughter refused to accept anything less than following in her
father's footsteps.

Well. So she turned out to be the CIO of the largest computer ser-
vices company in the world. Guess I just had to wait long enough. Ceci
felt a smile emerge. Life was so strange sometimes. She also hadn't been
immune to a bit of unexpected parental pride, surfacing between the layers of grief, and awkwardness on seeing Dar again, all grown up in ways
she'd never anticipated.

Watching her family's jaws drop, on seeing the family member they
all considered a poor country bumpkin morph into this tall, sophisticated
woman who handled herself with poise and reserved grace, who entered
their cultured world bearing Andy's very distinctive stamp.

Yeah. She couldn't take credit for any of it, but she'd still acknowledged what she saw.

"Whatcha thinking about?" Andy asked, as they climbed up the
wooded slope.

"Just memories." Ceci led him towards a grassy area, full of sun and
overlooking the water. "Our child when she was little."

"Ungh." Andrew dropped his gaze to the ground, thoughtfully
regarding a small patch of tiny purple flowers before stepping carefully
around them. "She was a handful," he admitted. "Wild little thing. 'Member that time she jumped out that tree house and damn near broke an
arm?"

Ceci shook her head. "Oh yes. I certainly do. Thank everything you
were home or I'd never have gotten her in for those x-rays. She almost
took out three nurses as it was."

"Lord. That's the truth." Andy chuckled. "That little Kerry's got her
wrapped round her finger, though. You'd never believe it."

"She seems nice," Cecilia ventured.

"Good kid," he agreed. "Got a good heart and she's damn gone on
Dar."

"Roger Stuart's kid, isn't she?"

"Half assed bastard. Yeah."

Her pale eyebrows lifted. "Didn't know you knew him."

Andy didn't answer for a moment. "Threw her out the house when
she done told him 'bout her and Dardar."

"Mmm." Ceci pursed her lips. "He's pretty conservative. I know it
was a little hard for us too." She paused. "It was an adjustment. Must have
been quite a shock."

"Mmm." They sat down in the grass, and Andy stretched his long
legs out, leaned back against a jutting rock and looked out over the water

pensively. "More than that. He tried to put her butt in the nuthouse cause of it."

Ceci felt like she'd been hit in the chest. "What?"

Andy nodded soberly. "Yeap. Took her out of the house and locked her up." His nostrils flared a little, and he peeked at her. "Dar flew up there and busted her out."

She blinked in shock. "She did?"

Her husband pulled at his lower lip, trying to mask the look of intense pride. "Yeap."

A soft sigh. "She's definitely your daughter."

His blue eyes took on shadows. "I know you two always wrassled," he acknowledged softly. "She turned out okay though." He turned his head towards her. "Think maybe you two'd get on better now?"

Cecilia considered the statement. "Maybe," she responded with a sigh, then opened the basket and removed a wine bottle and two glasses. She uncorked the bottle and poured them each a portion. "So much has changed."

Andy took his and studied it. "Yeap."

They were quiet for a bit, just watching the flocks of birds circle the lake, some landing to feed, other wheeling over them in intricate patterns.

Finally Ceci rested her cheek against his arm. "Where do we go from here?" She felt the shift and knew that if she tilted her head back she'd see him looking at her. "Now that I can start my life going forward again, instead of just letting it drift past me."

It was curious. She could feel the minute shifts in her husband's body, as he collected his thoughts and prepared to answer the question. But she also got an undeniable sense that he was holding back a surprise, in the way that he used to unpredictably show up in her bedroom window, one hand firmly behind his back and a tiny sparkle in his eyes.

He sorted out his questions and asked the first one first. "You like it here?"

Ceci shrugged. "It was the furthest away I could get from where I was."

He just looked at her and didn't answer that for a minute. "Been living out of the VA hostels down south. Bunks and a blanket when I could get 'em. Not something you'd be wanting, I don't think."

"As long as they've got an extra blanket." She gazed peacefully at him. "That sounds great."

"Cec—"

"Listen to me." She reached up and caught his jaw, forcing eye contact. "You are my life." *Inhale. Exhale.* "I don't care if you live under a bridge. Wherever you go, I'll go."

His eyes smiled at her. "Honey, I know that," Andrew answered softly. "I wasn't gonna say you can't. I was gonna say I was damn tired of living that way and I'd got a hankering to find me a little place...out near the water. Fer just you and me."

A sense of vivid relief splashed over her and turned the colors nearby far more intense. "I'd like that very much." Ceci took in a happy breath. "In fact, with the paintings and all, I've got a little money put by. We could—" She hushed, as a large finger covered her lips. She grasped it. "It's all right, Andy. That apartment belongs to Charles. I just pay him rent for it. There's nothing holding me here, in fact—" Now she had to be quiet, because the finger had turned into an entire hand, which was larger than half her face.

"Shh." Andy removed his hand. "When Dar was up here, she had to sign some paper stuff had to do with May's trust, and—"

"Oh." Ceci felt herself flush. "Goddess...please. Don't...I'm so sorry about that."

He paused. "Huh?"

Cecilia sighed. "It was my fault. I should have checked. I should have...that stupid trust." She paused. "I'm sorry. I told her I was—"

"Ceci, what are you talking about?"

She blinked. "The trust. When the family found out I was...that I'd asked Dar to come up for the funeral, they asked me to talk to her about it."

"Yeah?"

She shrugged. "It never occurred to them or to me, honestly, that she'd have been as successful as she is." Ceci looked up to see honest hurt facing her. "I know. I know, Andrew. I fell into that trap."

He looked down at the ground.

"Richard had mentioned that Dar had recently changed all her legal papers and had named a new heir. I guess the concern was..." Cecilia stopped and took a breath. "No. I'll be honest. We—me included—were worried someone was taking advantage of her and she didn't have the sense to realize it."

Andrew sighed. "Lord."

Ceci exhaled and closed her eyes. "I don't blame her for being upset. When I realized...it was so hard, Andy. I didn't even really know what to say. What to do. I felt like a fool." She rested her head against one hand. "What a mess."

"Well," Andy put his arm around her, "that musta stung, right nuff. But I think Dar figgered out a way t'get her own back." He chewed his lip. "Put it somewhere yer family'd go nuts with."

"Mmm?" Ceci lifted her head. "What did she do? Give it to the Humane Society?" She half joked, as he slowly tugged something out of his back pocket and handed it to her. "What's this?"

"What she done."

She unfolded the paper on to her thigh and read it.

Then she read it again.

Then she looked up at her husband.

"Didn't even give me a chance t'say no." Andy smiled wistfully. "I damn near almost fell over."

"Wow."

"Yeap."

Ceci fingered the paper. "I feel pretty damn small." She had a bitter taste in her mouth. "She's so outgrown me."

Andy pulled her closer and she felt a tiny thrill as his lips pressed against her hair, despite the shame that covered her. "We all made mistakes, Cec," he murmured. "Let's just tie our shorts tight and move on." She collapsed against him. "We got all sorts of new chances now."

Yes they did, didn't they? Cecilia put her hands against her husband's chest, feeling the powerful beat of his heart under her fingers. *Dreams were possible now.* Though the only one that had ever meant anything to her was real, and breathing, and surrounding her with strong arms.

Anything was possible.

Chapter
20

The sky outside slowly turned from black to purple to gray, and the birds started piping, just barely heard through the closed window. Kerry watched their shadows through the blinds as she lay curled up in the waterbed, her arms wrapped snugly around Dar's sleeping body.

It had been a very quiet, very peaceful night. Dar had fulfilled her part of the bargain and managed to get most of a bowl of soup down and keep it there, along with a half bottle of Gatorade. Then Kerry had done her part by forgetting about all the things she had to do and crawling into bed for a very long evening of pleasant cuddling.

They'd talked for a little while, then Dar had dozed off with her head resting on Kerry's shoulder, feeling much better. Kerry wondered how much of that was the medicine, how much was her lover's own sturdy physiology, and how much was the TLC, but in the end, it didn't really matter, did it? She was content to think her care had helped, at least emotionally, and that was enough.

The hand resting on her waist moved, and she turned her head slightly, not surprised to see Dar looking back at her. "Morning."

"Mmm." Dar nodded in acknowledgment.

"How are you feeling?" Kerry inquired, smiling as the tall body next to her uncoil and stretch out to its full length, then relax. "Better?"

Dar nodded again.

"And the aftereffect of this is laryngitis?"

Dar chuckled. "No." Dar's voice was husky with sleep, but otherwise normal. "Just kick starting my brain. Still a little fuzzy around the edges." Though, to be honest, Dar mused, as she snuggled back into her warm nest of Kerry, she wasn't sure if it was the medicine, or the aftereffect of being doused in solicitous affection all night. *Boy, that felt good.* Her stomach was still a little tender, but she wasn't nauseous any more and her reactions seemed to have returned to a more normal alertness.

She stroked Kerry's side and nuzzled her, receiving a low, pleased murmur in return. "Thanks for taking care of me." Dar turned her head and peered up at her lover's chin. "You did a great job."

Kerry tilted her head down and smiled. "Glad to hear it."

A dark eyebrow waggled. "You went to bed early last night. Bet you're hungry."

"Mmm, yeah. How'd you know?"

Dar lifted her head and tapped the flat surface she'd been resting on. "That's some serious growling going on down there." She winked and gave Kerry a tickle.

"Aruum." Kerry cleared her throat, a little embarrassed. "Yeah, well, I kinda forgot lunch, too."

"Tch." Dar rolled over and glanced down off the side of the bed, where Chino was tucked in her basket. The Labrador had tried their waterbed once or twice, but decided it wasn't to her taste, so they'd gotten her a comfortable, fleece lined bed to sleep in. "Tell ya what. I'll get breakfast ready."

Kerry snorted in laughter, then hastily covered her mouth with one hand as she got a wounded look from her lover. "Sorry. You don't deserve that. You made me the best eggs I ever had once."

Dar rested her chin on her arm. "You remember that, huh?"

"I sure do." Kerry squirmed over to her. "You don't have to get breakfast though." She closed her eyes against the scarily adorable pout. "Ooo, Dardar. Not that face. Nooooo." She peeked, then rolled over and covered her face with her pillow. "Nononono—eeekk!"

Chino yelped and scrambled up to see.

"Gotcha." Dar pounced on her and tickled her belly unmercifully. "Hahaha."

"Eeeeee!" Kerry smacked her with the pillow, then wriggled out of the way, rolling herself up in the comforter. "No fair!"

Dar was up on her knees and elbows and she started slinking forward, a look of maniacal glee on her face. "Make fun of my breakfast will you."

"Yeeoo!" Kerry scrabbled to escape, but couldn't move fast enough and got caught in mid lunge, finding long arms wrapping around her and pulling her down. She gurgled and tried to twist free, but got more and more tangled in sheets, blankets, and lots and lots of Dar. "Frisfigffifng," she squealed, as a nibble tickled up her ribcage. "Darrrr!"

"Arrggghhh," Dar growled happily, making Chino bark. She rolled them both over, then yelped as she forgot where she was, and felt nothing but air under her back. "Oh shit..."

"Yeooww!" Kerry responded, as they tumbled out of the waterbed and onto the floor with a double thump. "Ow."

Dar, who had landed first and was now providing a resting spot for her lover, sneezed. "Dusty down here." She closed her eyes as Chino rambled over and licked her face.

Kerry straddled her, sat up, and folded her arms. "Oh boy. Do I ever have you where I want you now." She grinned with neatly evil intent.

Dar liberated an eyeball and turned it on her. "Uh."

"Heh."

"Okay. I surrender." Dar tried to fend off the puppy, who was now lovingly cleaning her nose. "Hey."

Kerry unbuttoned her lover's shirt and started her own licking. "Mmm. Chino, good idea." Dar jerked as she nibbled her navel. "This beats eggs for breakfast hands down."

"H-hey." Dar swallowed, her body's reaction sending colorful jolts up and down her spine. "I don't think I..." She paused as the gentle touch traveled up the slope of her belly, with the tiniest nibble on a rib. "Uh, Ker. I'm still a little...um..."

"Um what?" Kerry advanced, treating Dar's skin like an ear of corn. "Hmm?" She slid up and braced her arms, peering straight down at the pale blue eyes.

Dar gave her a wry look. "A little knocked out." She stroked the soft, fine hair on Kerry's arms. "That tussle did me in."

Kerry leaned down and kissed her forehead lightly, then rubbed noses. "Okay." She sat up and helped her lover to do the same, watching in a little concern as Dar leaned against the wall, looking a bit shaky. "You okay?"

Dar took a breath and ran her fingers through her hair. "Yeah. Combination of that stuff wearing off and not eating for two days, I think." She exhaled. "Nothing a biscuit or something won't cure."

"Woof." Chino heard "biscuit" and got excited.

"Let me guess. With butter and honey on it." Kerry got up and offered Dar a hand. "C'mon. I could use something solid myself." She pulled and put her other hand on Dar's chest to steady her as she rose. "Okay?"

"Fine." Dar nodded and followed her towards the kitchen, with the sound of two sets of bare feet and a collection of puppy pattering.

❖ ⌘ ❖ ⌘ ❖ ⌘ ❖

"Morning, María." Dar ducked inside her office and closed the door.

The secretary looked up, a little surprised. "Oh, Dar. *Buenos días.* I did not think you would be here today. Kerrisita said you felt so bad yesterday."

She grinned. "Nothing a good night sleep couldn't cure." Dar's blue eyes twinkled. "But thanks for being concerned." She continued on into her inner office and put her briefcase down, then turned on her PC and unlocked her desk drawer. "You guys hungry?"

The two Siamese fighting fish swam guardedly past each other, eyeing her suspiciously. Dar took a pinch of the fish food, opened the acrylic case, and sprinkled it inside. The fish eagerly snapped at it, and she put the cover on. She tucked the box away and folded her hands as she watched her pets eat.

She hadn't liked them at first. But as the months wore on, she'd gotten used to their colorful presence and now she liked to spend a few minutes in the morning just watching them, as the water collected the sunlight filtering in from behind her.

The door opened and María walked in, carrying several folders. "You look very nice today, *jefa*. That is new for you, I think."

Dar glanced down at the embroidered lace shirt and crisply pressed black slacks. "Um...yeah, as a matter of fact. Thanks." A surprise from Kerry materialized that morning while she showered. She had come out to find the pretty things laid out on the dresser without comment. *I don't think I'll ever get used to that*, she reflected, then sat back, oblivious to María's busy presence by her outbox, distracted by a sudden realization.

She ran through days in her mind, then exhaled. Her relationship with Kerry had just become the longest one she'd ever had.

"Dar?" María's voice sounded concerned.

"Hmm?" She blinked and drummed her fingers on the desk. "Sorry. I was just thinking of something. What's up?"

"I was saying you have the lunch meeting on Key Biscayne today and a briefing at two o'clock. Do you want me to try to move that a little? Traffic will be terrible coming back from that construction."

"Um, yeah." Dar collected herself and turned her attention to the business at hand. She'd have time later to figure out a way to mark, at least privately in her own mind, the milestone. "That'd be fine. Tell Mark I need him and his team to get me the projected traffic patterns before lunch, and schedule a conference call with the overseas group after four."

"*Sí.*"

"Oh." Dar pulled open her drawer and tugged out a manila folder with a name printed neatly on the outside in black magic marker. "Give this personally to Mariana, will you? I don't want it floating around in the interoffice mail."

"I will do that now." María took the envelope and smiled. She paused before the door closed. "Oh. Dar? I thought you would like to know this– Mr. Ankow left yesterday. He said you would hear from him later."

Hot damn. Dar grinned. "What a shame. Sorry I missed him yesterday." *Guess he didn't find what he was looking for. Shucks.* "Thanks, María." She went back to her mail, deleting whole strings of it with piratical gusto.

❖ ⌘ ❖ ⌘ ❖ ⌘ ❖

Kerry released the phone button and exhaled, her shoulder slumping as she stared at the desktop under her folded hands. It had been a great morning until that last call, too. She'd gotten a lot done, despite having to put up with a tiny, mischievous little gopher that somehow kept popping up on her screen and munching her windows.

She named it Dar and it snickered.

A rap came at her inner door and she looked up as it opened and a dark head poked inside. "Hi there." Kerry smiled a little, glad to see the relaxed look on Dar's face. "How are you feeling?"

"Not bad." Her boss sauntered into the room and perched on the desk. "Not up to Thai food, but I've been working on a bottle of juice all morning. Hasn't come back up." She cocked her head. "What's up with you?"

"What makes you think something is?" Kerry asked.

Dar put a fingertip right between Kerry's eyes, just over her brow. "You get a little wrinkle right there when something's bothering you."

The pale brows twitched. "I do?"

"Yup."

Kerry tilted her head. "Well, I just got a call from my father's lawyer." The words brought a bad taste to her mouth. "Or should I say, one of his stable of lawyers." She paused. "He um...made it official that I wasn't to approach any of the family. That I was considered a hostile witness."

Dar made a face, then patted Kerry's hand. "Sorry about that." She took in Kerry's dejected shoulders and racked her brains, thinking of some kind of treat to perk her up. "Hey. You owe me a trip to the leather store."

"What?"

"Didn't you say you'd be my date for my high school reunion?" Dar teased. "Need to get you into some leather for that, remember?"

"Errrw." Kerry bit her lip, a grin attempting to escape. "Well, yeah, I did say I'd do that, huh?"

"Yeeesss, you did."

"You...um...have some place in mind?"

"Yeeesss, I do." Dar chuckled softly, a definite wicked twinkle in her eyes.

"Uuuuhhhh. I am sooo in trouble, aren't I?" Kerry squeaked.

"Yeess, you are." The taller woman ran a light touch down her cheek. "You talked me into this, Ms. Debating Champion, and I'm gonna hold you to it." She grinned. "Besides, I bet you look great in nice, snug leather."

Kerry's mouth went dry for a second and she was suddenly short of air. She cleared her throat. "Okay. Ah, we could go right after work. Get something light for dinner. How's that?"

"Sounds great." Dar smiled. "And Ker?"

She tore her thoughts away from Dar and leather and looked up. "Mmm?"

"I'd kinda like to be there at the hearing with you, if you don't mind."

The green eyes widened and fixed on her, as Kerry sat, struck dumb for a very long moment. "But how can you just—" She stopped, as Dar merely sat, watching her. "You can't...bu—" A long breath escaped her. "God, I love you." Her eyes closed. "Of course I don't mind."

Dar ruffled her hair. "Good. I've got a couple of meetings this afternoon. I'll catch up with you on the way out, okay?"

Kerry nodded mutely.

"Clear some time on Monday or Tuesday. I've got an eval to go over with you."

Another silent nod.

"You okay?" Dar held back a laugh, at the wistful look on her lover's face.

Kerry hit her intercom button. "Mayte?"

"Yes, Ms. Kerry?" the girl's voice came back promptly.

"I'm in a confidential meeting, okay?"

A puzzled pause. "Okay. For how long?"

"I'll call you." Kerry clicked the button off, then stood up and put her arms around Dar, hugging her fiercely.

Bewildered, but pleased, Dar returned the hug, giving Kerry's back a gentle pat. She heard a soft sniffle near her ear and felt Kerry bury her face into the soft cotton shirt she was wearing. "Sorry about the lawyer, Ker. That was a lousy thing for them to do."

"Just hit home, I guess," her lover whispered. "I did this to them, Dar. I *am* a hostile witness."

There was really nothing Dar could refute that with. "You did the right thing, Kerry."

"Did I?" Kerry responded softly. "No one cares, Dar. You saw the papers. It's like, 'Oh, look. Another one who took bribes. Ho hum.'" She sighed. "I guess I want to have my cake and eat it, Dar. I want justice, and I want them to still love me anyway."

"Mmm."

"I can't have both."

"No."

Kerry leaned against her, needing the security, glad beyond measure she could look forward to Dar's presence in what promised to be a very cold place.

Justice was fine, she acknowledged sadly, *but it sure gave lousy hugs.*

❖ ⌘ ❖ ⌘ ❖ ⌘ ❖

The hands on her shoulders surprised her, but Ceci recognized the touch before she had a chance to jump. She turned her head from where she'd been gazing out the front window and regarded her husband quietly. "I really enjoyed today," she commented, unable to stop from leaning back a little against him. They'd gone into town that morning, just walking quietly around the quaint, small shops, then she'd taken him to the countryside, through the rolling hills and dew soaked fields that surrounded the area she lived in.

Just talking, a little.

Or, mostly, she talked, and Andy listened, about what she'd been doing, her art, the shows, being with her family again after so long. How they'd been more than glad to accept her back into their casually sophisticated circle, and she'd let them, returning to a world she had willingly left so many years before. It was the world she lived in now, centered around the art gallery and her small studio, where she sat alone and painted, surrounded by tubes and pallets of dreams she resisted experiencing.

Andy told her a tiny bit about what he'd been doing since his return. How he'd spent his days doing volunteer work at the VA and his nights in the local library, indulging in a lifelong passion for reading that had always surprised her.

And how he'd been out walking on the beach one night, very late, looking at the stars when he'd come upon a lone figure sitting in the sand, whose profile had shocked him with familiarity.

He hadn't intended on seeking Dar out, he'd told her. But God had up and decided the matter for him, and once he'd seen his beloved child, it had only been a matter of time before he'd been drawn back into her life.

Which, in a very real sense, had drawn him back into Ceci's, because, Andy had told her, Dar had nudged him in that direction the whole dang time.

She'd had mixed feelings about that. On the one hand, of course, she was grateful to her daughter. On the other hand, she hurt inside knowing her cold rejection of her child had been repaid with mature compassion. She suspected, deep in her heart, that the relationship between her and Dar had been fractured beyond repair and there was a part of her that regretted that.

"Yeap," Andy agreed. "Some pretty trees up here."

Cecilia turned all the way around and put her hands against his chest. "You know what I miss, though?"

His head inclined a bit in question.

"The sea."

He laced his fingers behind her head and nodded.

"That beautiful light in the mornings and the sunsets after the storms in summer," she murmured wistfully, then smiled. "Wild parrots."

That got a short, unexpected laugh. "Damn things. You never did let me chase their feathered butts outta that mango tree outside." He paused. "Not too bad a place here, though. If you'd rather stay by your folks, I kin live with it."

Ceci exhaled, surprised by the offer. Born and raised in the far South, a beach rat by nature and by inclination, she knew Andy would be totally miserable in Connecticut, away from his beloved hometown and far from his equally beloved daughter. Guilt, she knew, was making him offer, but she wouldn't have accepted even if she'd had even a tiny inclination to stick around the place. "No way." She smiled. "Take me a few days to arrange things with the gallery, pack things up here, and we can go find that little beach house of yours." She flexed her fingers, scratching him gently. "Maybe some place close to Dar's?"

He liked the idea. She could tell. His eyes brightened perceptibly and a slow, half grin appeared. "See what I can do." They gazed into each other's eyes and Andy lifted a hand to brush her cheek, the rough texture of his skin raising goose bumps on hers. "You gonna be able to stand me being 'round all the time?"

"Does that mean you're really retiring?" Ceci asked, on an uneven breath.

"Yeap. That's what it does surely mean," he replied. "They been keeping me on the books just for," he hesitated, "they made sure I had a roof, that kinda thing...least until I met up with Dar again."

Of course. She exhaled. *I had his benefits.* "You let her take care of you?" Ceci winced at the perceptible, to her, touch of jealousy in her tone.

But Andy snorted. "Let 'er? Yer joking, aren't ya? Damn kid's like a force of nature. Jest rams right over every damn thing like a runaway tank." He shook his head. "Kept things damn quiet where I was staying by, but the next thing I know, stuffs getting dropped off there, Lord knows how she found the damn address out."

"She knew you'd never take it otherwise." Ceci smiled thinly. "Or...maybe she just didn't want to risk being turned away." Her eyes dropped. "Especially by you."

"Cec..." He tweaked one of her ears, an old habit of his.

"I know." She sighed. "One step at a time." She leaned forward and closed her eyes, abandoning the bad memories up to the peace of just being there with him. They'd work things out, she was sure of it.

The phone warbled, surprising her. She picked it up without looking, still keeping her body pressed against Andrew's. "Hello?"

"Ceci?" Elli's voice sounded a touch hesitant. "Are you feeling better today, my dear?"

"I feel wonderful," she mumbled. "Why?"

A definite pause. "Well, you sounded so strange the other day. I wasn't sure...I thought perhaps you had one of your migraines," Elli told her. "I was just wondering if you wanted to pick up something for dinner, before the gallery party tonight."

Oh, rats. "I'd forgotten completely about that," Cecilia admitted. "What time is it again?"

"Cecilia." Elli sounded concerned. "What is going on? You've been acting so odd since the funeral. I'm quite concerned for you. I mentioned it to Charles just yesterday. He said he was going to stop by to see if something was the matter."

"Nothing's wrong," Ceci answered. "As a matter of fact, everything's right for a change." She looked up at Andy looking back down at her, a wry expression on his scarred face. "Andy came home."

It didn't really matter that there was now total silence at the other end of the phone. It was much more peaceful that way.

"Wh...Ceci, what did you say?" Elli spluttered. "I'm sure you just said..."

"That Andy came home. I did." She traced a line up his sweatshirt.

"Andy?"

"Mmhmm. My husband. You remember him, don't you, Elli? Tall, dark hair, beautiful blue eyes?" She gave up a little impish grin as he blushed visibly.

"He's there?" Elli sounded completely shocked.

"Right here. You want to talk to him?" She held the phone up. "Say hello to Elli."

"'Lo, Elli," Andrew drawled obligingly. Of all his wife's relatives, he'd liked Elli the best, though that hadn't been saying much. At least she'd been the least outwardly nasty to him.

"There. Heard that?" It was strange, in a way. Telling other people suddenly made it real, in a way it hadn't been before. "So. I've been a little distracted, El, I'm sorry. I did forget completely about the party tonight."

"Ceci." Elli was audibly collecting her wits. "My god. I have no idea what to say."

"Congratulations is a good start."

"Well, of course, my dear, of course. That goes without saying, but I mean...I don't understand...I thought..."

"They made a mistake," Ceci told her quietly. "What every serviceman's widow in the history of the world wanted to have happen to them, just happened to me." She looked up and searched Andy's somber face. "I'm not sure why I lucked out, but I'm not complaining."

Elli sighed. "I'm glad for you, Ceci. I truly am. It's quite remarkable. I'm sure we'd all love to know what happened. Shall I tell Mark you won't be at the party tonight, or...I mean, it is in your honor...the new exhibit and all."

"Hold on." She pressed the mute button on the phone. "I was supposed to do a party tonight."

"Mmm?" Andrew looked noncommittal.

"At the gallery. They put up a new exhibit of mine. I'm not really
fond of it, but they paid for it, so there you are."

"Don't let me stop you. G'wan," Andy told her.

"I don't want you to stop me. I want you to go with me," Ceci
replied. "Please?"

Son of a biscuit. Andy was caught between a boat and a dock and he
knew it. "Honey, teacup parties and me don't mix."

"I know," Ceci agreed. "But my whole family'll be there."

"They will, huh?"

"Mmm."

Well. Andy felt that little rebel inside him climb out. "Kin I go like
this?" He plucked his sweatshirt, a really soft, comfortable one Kerry had
sent. "Don't got much else."

Ceci smiled and let her held breath out. "I've got something else you
can wear," she whispered, then un-muted the phone. "Elli? No. Tell him
I'll be there."

"You will? Oh, all right. I'll tell him. Listen, Ceci, maybe we can
come over, say tomorrow? I know I'd love to see Andy and hear what
happened."

"We'll arrange something."

"All right. I'll see you later, dear."

She hung up the phone and put it on the counter, then looked up for
those vivid blue eyes. "Thank you."

"You sure you want me to do this?" Andy asked. "Gonna stir them up
like a bear in a honeybee nest."

Cecilia nodded firmly. "They've been telling me for seven years I
should put my past behind me and move on. I never could. Maybe part of
me knew. Certainly, a big part of me never stopped watching that front
walk, expecting you to come up it one day." She stroked his face very
gently, then brushed back the soft, salt and pepper locks. "I want them to
see what I was waiting for." She was a little surprised to find her breathing irregular as she traced the faint smile on his face.

"All right," Andy drawled, returning the touch and sending a definite
tingle down her spine. "Glad you waited." He inclined his head and found
her lips, kissing her with an almost bashful gentleness.

Ceci slid her arms around his neck and pulled herself up and closer,
craving the contact as though she were thirsting after water. His hands
slipped around her waist after a moment of surprise, then she was lifted
up into a much more comfortable position and snugged tight in a powerful
grip. "Mmm." She explored delicately, finding an unmistakable response
that started a welcome fire deep in her guts.

Ceci let her eyes drift open for a moment, finding darkened, almost periwinkle ones watching her.

They both smiled.

Chapter
21

"What…is that?"

Dar peered over Kerry's shoulder. "It's a door."

"Not that." The blond woman gave her a look. "That." She pointed.

"It's a mannequin."

Kerry pulled her partner to a halt outside the small, neon decorated shop. "Thank you, Ms. I-am-literal-as-the-day-is-long. I know that pasty white thing is a mannequin. What is it wearing?"

Dar walked forward and pressed her fingertips against the window, examining the figure in question seriously. "I'm not sure what you call it, but if it was a bull, it'd be a come hither ring."

Kerry covered her eyes. "Oh my god," she muttered. "I'm about to become educated, aren't I?"

"Not with that kind of apparatus," Dar responded mildly. "You don't have the anatomy for it." She opened the door and gave her friend a little half bow. "After you?"

"Ew." Kerry sighed and girded her mental loins. "They don't make those for girls then, huh?"

"Oh, they do." Dar put a hand on her back and nudged her forward into the neon lit space. "They just use nipple rings."

"Ni—" Kerry shut her mouth so fast she almost bit her tongue. "Ow." She crossed her arms over her chest.

The store was small and very cluttered. There were three display cases against the walls, mostly lit by pink and yellow neon light, and the ceiling was covered in hanging devices of all shapes, sizes, colors, and various degrees of hide curing. At least, Kerry hoped the ones that smelled rank were badly cured and not just badly used. She stepped forward cautiously, giving the two salespeople behind the counter a faint smile, aware of Dar's tall, confident presence at her back.

"Hey there." The girl clerk leaned against the glass, almost disgorging her considerable frontal assets out of her leather bustier. "What can I help you babes with tonight?"

Kerry sucked in a breath to answer, then realized she had no clue in the world what to say. "Uh."

"Mmm. Just browsing for now. But we're looking for something in leather," Dar answered over her shoulder.

The male clerk snickered. "Ain't everyone?" He adjusted the complex arrangement of straps and buckles that covered his somewhat unimpressive chest. "Chicks really go for this stuff."

"Oh yeah." Kerry dredged up a smile. "Why don't you check it out, Dar. I'll just...um," she waved a hand, "browse." She edged away from her wickedly smiling partner and put her hands firmly behind her back as she circled the room, peering curiously into the glass cases.

Okay. She wasn't a total innocent. She recognized the vibrators and the different brands of massage oil, the entertaining variety of rubbers, and the large, latex dildos, some of which with inexplicable appendages with tiny heads that resembled woodchucks. *What was up with that?* she wondered briefly, before dismissing it and moving on down the case.

Edible underwear.

Hmm. That had possibilities, though ice cream was just as tasty, and much more fun to put on as well as take off. Kerry stopped and pinched the bridge of her nose. "Glad I thought of that. We're out of fudge." She made a mental note to stop at the store.

Rings. Kerry blinked and cocked her head to one side. *Rings?* She leaned forward and read the tiny print on a box. "Oh." She bit her lip to keep from giggling. "Right, okay," she muttered. "It's like that *X-files* episode that mentioned autoasphixiation. Sort of the same idea." She paused. "Only lower and not quite as dangerous."

"Hey, Kerry?"

"Mmm?" Kerry turned to see her beloved bunkmate holding up something to the alleged light. "Um. What is that?"

"It's perfect. Just what you should wear," Dar assured her, with a grin. "Here." She tossed it over.

Kerry caught it, surprised at the weight. "Hey. It's leather." She sniffed it. *Okay. So it wasn't used.*

"Yes, it is."

Kerry glanced up at the decidedly mischievous tone, then examined her outfit. "Oh no." She started shaking her head. "Oh, no, no, no...no, Dar...no, no. I am not wearing a leather bikini." She held up the top, which was a creamy, cappuccino colored leather, with intricate stitching all over it.

"It's not a bikini," Dar objected. "That's a skirt."

"It's a mini skirt."

"Skirt's a skirt."

Kerry peered at the item. It was a very brief, also cappuccino colored leather bit, with a beautifully tooled leather belt. "Dar, I don't know..."

"Comes with nice boots." Dar held them up. "And some bracelets and stuff. C'mon, Ker. You'd look gorgeous in this." She turned towards the girl clerk. "Don't you think?"

The girl chewed her gum reflectively. "You work out?"

Kerry gave her a doubtful look. "Yeah."

"No sweat. It's a hot piece." She waved a hand at her. "Go for it."

Erg. Kerry was caught between a mischievous impulse and her natural modesty. She glanced around the store to give herself a moment's more time, then stopped and smirked. "Okay. On one condition."

Dar crossed her arms and lifted a dark brow. "What?"

Green eyes twinkled visibly even in the neon that tinted them almost caramel. "You wear that." She pointed.

Uh. Dar eyed the inky black leather vest doubtfully. There seemed to be more holes than leather, with strategic patches barely providing legal modesty. A fringe of leather strips depended from the shoulders and the sides were laced with the same stuff, exposing just about everything from armpit to hip.

Well. She exhaled. *Daddy had always told me, "Dardar, if 'n you got it, don't be shy about showin' it."* "Okay." She flashed a smile at the surprised and outfoxed Kerrison. "I'll take both of these and throw in those wristlets too."

"Hey." Kerry recovered and reached for her wallet. "Hold on a minute."

"Ah ah." Dar held up a hand. "Fair's fair. You get to rent the Harley, remember?"

Mmm. Right. Kerry gave in and handed the leather bikini over. Then she glanced around again and tilted her head up to examine a hanging contraption. Slowly she tilted her head one way, then the other, then she bent down and looked at it upside down. Finally, she turned to find Dar watching her with an amused look. "What is that?"

"It's a harness." Dar hefted the shopping bag and returned her credit card to her wallet. "C'mon."

"What do you use it for?" Kerry held a hand up to stop her.

Dar put an arm around her shoulders and steered her towards the door. "Have I ever told you the story of Catherine the Great and her horse?"

"Huh?" Kerry's brows knit together. "What does that have to do with a kinky sex store?"

"C'mon."

"Well?"

She sighed. "She was into animals."

"What?"

"You know, Kerry. Like all those sheep jokes?"

"What sheep jokes?"

"Or the ones about farmers and their cows?"

"Paladar Roberts, what in blazes are you talking about?"

Dar gave another sigh. "Hungry?"

"Dar."

"I've got a great idea for dinner. It's just a short walk. How about it?"

"Dar."

"She used to screw her favorite stallion."

Silence.

"Oh my god. That is so bullshit."

"No, really."

"Dar, that is so not true. Didn't you take Russian history?"

"I went to school in Dade County. They don't require history."

"Well, let me tell you, it's not true. We did a course in...wait a minute." Kerry pulled her lover to a halt. "Do you mean to tell me those hanging things were for people to use to have sex with?"

"Yes."

"Jesus, Dar. Why didn't you just say so?" Kerry shook her head. "C'mon. I'm starved."

Dar chuckled and led the way to a bayside restaurant, tucked between a marina and the abandoned shell of what had been a theatre. It was a quiet night and she had no problem obtaining a nice table by a wide window, with a great view of the water, the boats, and tiny, gray clouds chasing each other across the moon lit night sky.

They ordered from the fresh seafood menu and settled back with a bottle of light, sweet wine. Kerry twirled her glass and took a sip, then regarded her lover through the warm glow of the table's candlelight. "I don't think I've ever been here."

The shadows across Dar's face shifted. "No. I haven't either. Not for a very long time." She took a gingerly sip of the wine, hoping her still chancy stomach wouldn't object.

"Hmm." Kerry looked around. "It's nice. I'd have thought you'd like a place like this."

Dar gave a slow nod. "Yeah, yeah. I used to...I um...brought the first person I went out with here all the time." She took a sip of wine. "The last time we came here was the night we broke up."

"Oh." Kerry played with her napkin. "Sorry. We could have gone somewhere else, Dar. I didn't know."

"No, it's okay." Dar smiled, feeling the truth in that statement with a sense of incredible pleasure. "It was my choice, remember? I thought it was about time I let that part of my past go and enjoy coming back to some place I used to really like."

"Wow. Okay." Kerry was a little confused, but pleased. "Well, I like it here. It's got a great view."

Dar nodded. "Yes, it does." She gazed across the table, oblivious of the twinkling lights outside. She smiled as Kerry blushed faintly. "The last time I was here...Shari told me I was such a dysfunctional social moron, I'd never have a relationship that lasted more than six months."

"What a stupid, clueless jerk." Kerry snorted. "I mean, look. Our relationship's lasted longer than that. She obviously had no idea what she was talking about."

Dar cupped her chin in one hand and smiled. "Yes, ours has," she agreed softly. "It's a first for me and I just wanted to mark the occasion."

Kerry's jaw just dropped. She stared at her lover in stunned surprise, trying frantically to come up with some kind of response for that. "Buh." She rubbed her face with one hand. "Jesus, Dar."

"What?"

"You know what I was doing the other day?"

Puzzled, Dar shook her head. "No."

"Planning what to do on our anniversary."

"Oh." She chuckled. "Our first?"

"Our fiftieth." Green eyes met hers with quiet certainty.

Dar just looked at her.

Kerry lifted her glass and touched Dar's with it. "I was thinking maybe a tour on the Space Station." She took a sip. "They should have weekend packages by then, don'cha think?"

"Yeah." Dar's face creased into a smile. "Sounds great to me."

❖ ⌘ ❖ ⌘ ❖ ⌘ ❖

Charles Bannersley cast a critical eye over the room, reluctantly approving the starched servers who stood patiently behind the buffet and the newly buffed hardwood floors that gleamed under the soft, carefully calibrated light of the gallery.

"They did a nice job." His twin sister Carolyn eased up next to him, her ginger colored hair reflecting the light. "The exhibit looks good, too."

"Mmhmm." He nodded. "Not bad. Not bad. Press got some good shots, and Edgar Evans was making billing and cooing noises over Ceci's last piece down there. I'd say we've got a budding success on our hands."

"Speaking of. Where is she?" Carolyn asked, glancing around. "Don't tell me she isn't here yet."

Charles shrugged. "You know her. I was going to stop by there this afternoon, but I got tied up in a meeting. Elli was whining at me the other day over Ceci acting strange."

They exchanged sibling glances. "When doesn't she?" Carolyn

inquired, arching a brow. "Did you find her a date for tonight, Chucky? I'm so tired of seeing her wafting around alone like some kind of tumbleweed."

He sighed. "Hey, I do my part, Cary. She just doesn't cooperate. Apparently I can't find the right kind of guy to interest her."

His sister put an errant bit of hair behind one ear. "Have you tried the local trucker bars?" she sniped. "Maybe you're just looking in the wrong places."

They both laughed wryly. "Listen, I feel bad for the poor thing." Carolyn shook her head. "She's never going to leave that nightmare behind her until we can prod her back into some kind of social life and you know it."

"I know, I know. I'll keep try—ah, there she is." Charles turned as he spotted their younger sister entering, dressed in a plain, but classic dress, in a dark aqua color that complimented her fair hair and pale eyes. "Well, she made an effort. What do you know?"

"Mmm." Carolyn leaned towards him to watch. "Hey, she looks good. Got a little color to her cheeks for a change."

"Yeah. Too bad I didn't ask Bob to come tonight. I've been trying to get them hooked up for mo—oh my god."

Cecilia glanced behind her and held a hand out and tall figure entered, ducking slightly to clear the low doorframe. Their hands met and she drew her companion forward, turning to greet the tuxedo clad man who hurried forward.

Carolyn clutched her brother's arm. "Chuck—"

"I see." His voice was flat with shock.

"That can't be Andrew."

His nostrils twitched as he studied the man towering over his sister. Dressed in pristine Navy whites, despite the dark hair more sprinkled with grays than he remembered, and a new set of ugly scars, he surprisingly didn't look too different. "Apparently it is." His voice hardened.

"I can't believe it. After all this time? The Navy said he was dead. Where in the hell has he been?" Carolyn hissed.

"I don't know, and frankly, I don't care. But if he thinks he's just going to walk back into Ceci's life like this, he's got another thing coming." Charles twitched his jacket straight and headed towards the door.

❖ ⌘ ❖ ⌘ ❖ ⌘ ❖

"Cecilia, darling. So glad I caught you coming in."

Ceci held a hand out. "Hello, Edgar. Thanks for being here. It's nice to see you."

The art critic preened a little. "My privilege, as always. I wanted to tell you how much I love your work in acrylic in there. The seascape one, you know?"

"Yes, I know the one." Ceci smiled at him. "Would you like to meet the inspiration for that one?" She turned and held a hand out towards a diffidently waiting Andrew, who still stood just outside the door. He entered, took her hand, and came up beside her. "This is my husband, Andrew."

Edgar tilted his head back and gazed up. "A pleasure, sir. A pleasure...ah, Commander, is it?"

"That's right." Andy shifted a little inside the dress whites, a bunch looser than they had been, but all in all not too damn bad, considering. Ceci had even given him a trim, though his hair was far from its usual regulation crew cut. He took the critic's hand and returned his tentative grip with a solid one.

"Goodness. I had no idea you were married, my dear. But I'm so glad to meet someone who can inspire such wonderful art." Edgar beamed at Andrew, who gave him a dourly reserved smile in return. "Congratulations, sir. Congratulations on such a lovely and talented wife."

Andrew decided he liked the little penguin. "Thanks." A motion caught his eye and he focused his peripheral vision that way. *Well, well.* Cecilia's older brother Charles was headed in their direction, and he didn't look happy.

Charles was tall, almost as tall as Andy was, and had red hair liberally peppered with gray and thinning badly on top. He was about six or seven years Ceci's senior and had always taken great pleasure in presenting himself as the head of the family, after their father had died some fifteen years back.

He was, in Andy's estimation, a half-assed jerkwad with more breeding than sense, and they'd never gotten along. He poked Ceci gently and jerked his chin towards her brother. "Here comes a man with a bee in his britches," he muttered.

Ceci watched Charles approach and a tiny, vindictive grin briefly creased her face. "Hope it stings him right in the behind."

"Wall, I kin think of some better places but he ain't got none," Andrew drawled, as Charles reached them, his twin right behind him. "'Lo, Charles, Carolyn."

Charles stopped and inhaled, his lips twisting grimly. "Andrew. This is quite a surprise."

"Ah bet."

Ceci eased between them. "Sorry, Chucky. I didn't really have time to prepare you. Things have been happening pretty quickly." She glanced behind him. "Hi, Cary."

"Cec," her sister murmured. "Hello, Andrew." She gave her brother-in-law a guarded look.

"Ms. Roberts." A gallery aide came up looking a little agitated.

"Could you come into the display room, please? The press would like to speak with you."

Ceci hesitated. "I—"

"G'wan." Andrew gave her a little nudge. "Give me a chance to catch your kin up here."

Cecilia gave him a look, recognizing the deliberate, slight exaggeration of his usual drawl for what it was. "I'll be right back." She curled a hand briefly around his wrist and squeezed it, then followed the aide out, leaving Andrew with her brother and sister in a silent tableau.

❖ ⌘ ❖ ⌘ ❖ ⌘ ❖

A soft knock at the door brought Dar's head up and she paused in her work. "Yeah?"

Maríana stuck her head in and smiled. "Got a minute?"

Dar leaned back and rubbed her eyes. "Sure. C'mon in."

The Personnel VP entered and closed the door. She crossed the carpeted floor and seated herself in one of Dar's visitor chairs. "How's it going?"

"Not bad." Dar folded her hands. "We got most of the new boxes in place and I think we're going to start testing next week. It's going a lot smoother than I'd planned for. Nice, for a change."

"Good to hear." Mari nodded. "Listen. Duks and I and Mark and Barbara were planning on taking a ride up to the fair tonight. You and Kerry interested?"

The Youth Fair. Dar was surprised at her tickling of interest. "I don't know. Hang on." She pressed the intercom. "Hey, Kerry?"

"Yeesss?" The blond woman's voice sounded a touch smug and definitely pleased.

"You up for the Youth Fair?"

A puzzled silence. "I didn't know you were into cows, Dar. Or is this a continuance of yesterday's conversation?"

Maríana clapped a hand over her mouth and turned pink from laughter.

Dar sighed. "You haven't been to a youth fair down here, I take it." She played with a pen. "Few ducks, few chickens, few rabbits. Mostly rides and the midway."

"Oh." Kerry fell silent for a moment. "Okay. Sure. That sounds like fun. Maybe I'll win you a huge stuffed pig or something."

"I'd better drive, then, because you, me, and a stuffed pig aren't going to fit in your car," Dar advised her dryly. "Mari's doing the invite. It's us, her and Dukky, and Mark and Barb." She grinned. "You can finally challenge Mark to that slingshot competition." She waited for Kerry to stop laughing. "Okay. See you later." Dar lifted an eyebrow at Mari.

"Sounds like a plan."

"Good." Mari clasped her hands around one knee. "Actually, I didn't come here to ask that. I just finished going over the review you did for Kerry." Dar tilted her head in inquiry. "And I wanted to come over here and talk to you about it."

"Problem?"

"No. Just the opposite." Mari shook her head. "It was a very well balanced, well thought out review, that seemed objective, and professional." She paused. "Did you get someone to ghost write it? I've been reading reviews from you for five years, Dar. They don't usually look like that."

Dar doodled on her scratch pad. "No. I just wanted to be very careful. I know there's a built in prejudice there and I bent over backwards to be as fair as I possibly could." *Finding negatives,* she reflected, *had been the most difficult part.* No one was perfect, but she tended to mentally downplay Kerry's faults to an almost ludicrous point, and that wasn't fair to either of them professionally. Her biggest issue with her assistant was that Kerry tended to get totally involved in the details of a project and sometimes she lost sight of the big picture.

That was something, Dar was sure, that would correct itself with experience, as Kerry learned to watch the impact of her actions on a wider scope. But it had caused a few near misses, and she'd had to bring Kerry in the last time, and sit her down, and give her a lecture.

She wondered who that lecture had stung more.

"Well, you certainly did that. I was very impressed. Good job." Mari smiled. "Now. Do you want to give it to her, or do you want me to?"

Dar took a breath. "I'll do it." She met Mari's eyes. "But she's up for a salary action. I'd rather you handled the details of that." A faint smile twisted her lips.

Mari chuckled. "All right. Good point. But give me a guideline. What do you think she's worth?"

Blue eyes caught hers, as quiet and serious as she'd ever seen them. "The company couldn't afford what I think she's worth," Dar replied calmly. "That's why I'm asking you to work it out." She flipped her pencil over. "I'm going to talk to her about that open position we have when I give her the eval. I think with some guidance she'd do all right there."

Mari considered the statement. "We could probably post it and get someone with more experience, but Kerry's got two things going for her. One, she knows how we work, and two, she can work with you." She gave Dar a frank look. "And of the two, the second is what would concern me the most bringing in an outsider."

Dar propped her chin up on one fist. "Am I such a problem?" She asked, plaintively.

"Dar, don't even go there. You know we're friends, but you also know perfectly well that you're one of the hardest people in the entire corporation to work with." Mari smiled to take the sting out of her words. "Although you have mellowed out a whole lot in the last few months."

"I don't think I have," Dar disagreed. "It's just that Kerry's taken off so much of the bullshit from my shoulders. I don't have to be an asshole nearly as often to get things done." She pointed a finger at Mari. "But I haven't forgotten how."

"Warning taken." Mari stood and brushed her slacks off. "Have we gotten rid of our Houston pest? You know he was busting my chops to get your personnel file." She smirked. "I just loved pulling out my three hundred and seventy two page personnel directive handbook and quoting the privacy regulations to him."

"Yeah, for now." Dar leaned back and stifled a yawn. "But I've got the feeling he'll be back. He gave me the creeps. He's not going to stop until he causes major league trouble, I think." She got up and checked her watch. "I'm going to get some coffee. Interested?"

Mari nodded. "Sure. That stomach bug clear up all right for you?"

Dar shrugged as they headed towards the door. "Yeah, pretty much." She held the door for Mari and followed her out. "Glad it wasn't contagious."

Chapter
22

Andrew resisted the impulse to put his hands in his pockets and merely clasped them in front of him as he returned the veiled, hostile stares from Ceci's siblings. "Nice weather," he drawled, deliberately drawing out the words and injecting as much Southern as he possibly could into his voice and still get the words out around his tongue.

"And here I thought we were rid of you," Charles stated. "But just like a bad Rembrandt, here you are."

"Naice t'see you too, Chuckie. That a new suit?" Andrew let the hostility roll off him without any trouble, having spent far too much time in his life facing people trying to kill him.

Charles glanced around, then indicated a small door. "I've got something to say to you." He turned and walked towards the side room, fully expecting Andrew to follow. With a sigh and a small shake of his head, the navy officer did.

Charles closed the door behind them and walked across the tiny room, which featured a table, a chair and a lamp set over the table, clearing a space for examining art or other objects. "I'm not going to waste any time."

"Good t'hear." Andrew settled against the wall.

"If you think you're going to just waltz back into my sister's life, you've got another thing coming." Charles turned and folded his arms. "I'm not going to allow that."

"And jest what are you gonna to do t'stop me?" Andy inquired mildly. "Seven years and you still ain't got the sense God gave a groundhog, d'you? It ain't your choice, Chuck. Never was, never will be. It's hers, and she's done made it." He paused. "Again."

"You going to take and drag her out into the streets again?" the man taunted. "Can't you see she's better off here?"

Andy studied him. "Nope."

"You always were a selfish pig."

"If'n you think she is better off, then you've got a set of twisted ideas, cause what I see is a lonely woman half crazed needing someone t'care for her."

"She's perfectly happy here," Charles shot back. "She's got family and friends and a decent place to live for a change."

"She tell you that?"

"What?"

"She's happy?" Andy pushed off the wall and eased towards him. "Dj'a ever ask her?"

"She's my sister. I know she is," Charles answered. "That's why I took that notification they sent last year and burned it."

Andrew's dark brows snapped together and he moved his head forward, his eyes narrowing. "What?"

"Oh, sure. That notice the damn Navy sent. That you'd been found? I burned it," Charles taunted. "It came to our place and you bet I grabbed it and had my self a little party making sure my sister never saw a word of it."

Big hands flexed. "You done that." Andy's breathing slowed and deepened. "Here, I was thinking she'd done tossed it away." His voice was almost an offhand murmur.

"I wasn't going to let her fall back in that trap." Charles laughed. "She's better off out of that hell and out of your life and away from that perverted kid you forced on her."

"Charles?" Andy said slowly, "Y'all better shut up now."

"I've just started," the man shot back. "Disgusting. She shows up for a funeral with her little tart in tow, I about died of—blck." The room whirled as he was picked up and slammed onto his back on the table. "Gchk."

Hands twisted in his shirt collar and air cut off abruptly. He struggled, as he looked up into a pair of blue eyes so cold, they were almost colorless. Andrew's face had settled into stillness, save for a feral twitch running up and down either side of his nose, matching the flaring nostrils. "Now," his voice was much lower and deeper, "y'all are gonna shut up."

Charles' chest hurt and he fought to drag air into his lungs.

"Or I'm going to pull yer haid right off yer body and stuff it up your rear end." Andy leaned on him, sending pain up and down his body. "Do you understand me, boy?"

Hysterical, he nodded, and the grip relaxed, just a little. Just enough for him to suck in a tiny bit of air.

"Ah do not like you," Andrew enunciated very carefully. "Ah have never liked you, but I put up with you cause you just happened to share the same mamma and pappa as my wife." He leaned closer. "But ah will not put up with you bad mouthing mah family. You understand me, boy?" He leaned closer. "Or I will surely kill you."

Charles started shaking.

"If you ever try to get between Ceci and me again, I will rip you apart." He paused. "And if you ever speak about mah daughter like that again, I will make you a eunuch in under five seconds." Andrew lifted him up and threw him against the wall. Then he pounced across the floor and grabbed him as he rebounded and shoved him up and held him. "Are we real straight on that, Mister?"

"You're crazy," Charles croaked.

"No, sir." Andrew shook his head. "Ah am a very angry man, who knows how to kill people right well." His eyes bored into the shorter man's. "If you have any smarts at all, you will just say 'yes, sir' and shut up."

Ceci's brother stared at him for a long, hateful moment, then lowered his eyes. "Yes, sir."

Andrew held him a second more then released his grip and stepped back, standing alert and balanced on the balls of his feet as Charles slowly twitched at his clothing and gathered the shreds of his composure. "We're done now." Andy turned and walked to the door. He put his hand on the knob before turning and facing his adversary. "Asshole." He opened the door, walked through it, and closed it behind him firmly. Ceci was just coming back and she headed his way, a concerned look on her face. "Ready to see yer pictures?"

"Sure." Cecilia glanced at the door. "Everything okay?"

"Yer brother and I just clear the air a little," Andy reassured her. "C'mon."

She tucked her hand around his arm and paced lightly at his side, watching the signs of rage slowly fade. "Andy?"

"Mmm?" His eyes blinked, then met hers.

"You didn't break anything, did you?"

His lips quirked faintly. "No, ma'am, I did not."

Ceci exhaled. "All right. Come on. I think they've got those little stuffed chicken things you like on the buffet."

Andy relaxed, releasing the last of his anger out to the ether. No sense in holding it, anyway. He gazed fondly down at his wife. "You looking to spoil me, pretty lady?"

He got a much missed elfin smile for that. "You betcha." Ceci steered him towards a cluster of people around a large canvas. "See what you think of this one."

Several faces turned as they came up, staring curiously at Andrew. "Cec? Who's your friend?" one of the art gallery's directors called out, too far to read the nameplate on Andy's uniform.

"This is my husband," Cecilia answered, enjoying the surprised looks. "Andrew Roberts." She started introductions as the crowd closed in, chattering in question.

❖ ⌘ ❖ ⌘ ❖ ⌘ ❖

Kerry stood, soberly regarding her reflection in the mirror. She was dressed in her underwear and laid out neatly on the counter was her little leather outfit, draping saucily over the edge in a fall of slinky hide.

"Well." She met the sea green eyes gazing back at her. "I could pretend I was going as Pocahontas." She paused. "The blond hair's a little off, but I think I may have a feather around here somewhere."

With a sigh, she finally picked up the skirt and wrapped it around her waist, adjusting the fit with the convenient Velcro closures. "What on earth did the do before Velcro, Chino? I can't imagine it."

"Grufw." The Labrador was curled up on the bed, watching her with interest, tired out after a long afternoon's run Kerry had just finished up with.

"It's pretty, huh?" She fingered the leather belt, intricately tooled and stained in several colors, with a knotwork design. The skirt itself was a very soft rusty tan leather, so thin it draped over her hips and thighs almost like cloth. "O...kay." Kerry picked up the top next and studied it. "Hmm. A leather sports bra. This is going to be different."

After a moment's hesitation, she removed her regular bra and slipped the leather one on. She fiddled with the fastenings in back then brought the straps around to her front and adjusted them. With faint trepidation, she lifted her eyes to the reflection and chewed her lip at what she saw.

God, there was a lot of her showing. She spared a moment of intense gratitude for the months in the gym, as she twisted her body a little and watched the muscles move just under her tan. "See what she meant about needing to work out to wear this one," she murmured. "What do you think, Chino?"

"Gorgeous."

Kerry's brain almost exploded, then she realized the voice was Dar's and coming from the door. "Jesus." She covered her eyes as a laugh escaped. "I thought the dog answered me."

"Woof," Dar replied, easing the rest of the way into the room, still dressed in her workout shorts and cutoff shirt. "Mmm. I like it." She studied Kerry approvingly. "You definitely look natural in that."

"Natural?" Kerry put her hands on her hips. "Dar, it's a leather bikini. Don't tell me I look natural in a leather bikini, please, because my brain will dribble out my ears just at the thought."

"But you do," Dar objected gently. "Stand up straight."

With a sigh, Kerry did so, letting her hands drop to her thighs. In reflex, she lifted her head and chin as Dar adjusted the straps on her top, the feel of the light fingertips on her bare back striking a chord of faint familiarity. "I look like a fake Native American."

"Nah." Dar pulled her pale hair back and held it. "How 'bout we put a leather holder on this and you can put on some of that old jewelry in Aunt May's trunk. You'll look great, Ker. Honest." She peeked over Kerry's shoulder and examined the mirror's reflection, as Kerry lifted her eyes and met her gaze in it. "What's wrong?"

Kerry's lips tightened, then relaxed. "Sometimes I look in this mirror and I have no idea who that person is looking back at me is." She gave a slight shake of her head and lifted her hands a trifle, then let them drop. "I never imagined myself like this."

"Does it bother you?" Dar asked, hesitantly. "You know, Kerry. Just because I do the gym and all that, doesn't mean you have to."

"No, I like it." She gave Dar a gentle smile. "It's just that I've never felt good about myself before and it's a little strange getting used to." She tilted her head back. "You're wonderful for my ego, you know that?"

"Glad to be of service." Dar chuckled in relief.

"Speaking of egos, it's your turn to get dressed." Kerry grinned. "I'm going to finish up getting ready."

"Okay." Dar kissed her bare shoulder. "I'm going to grab a shower, then see if I can squeeze into that vest. Never mind those jeans you dug up from the closet." She gave Kerry a pat on the butt and ambled out, followed by Chino.

Kerry shook her head, and turned her attention back to the mirror. "You know something, Kerrison? For someone once voted most likely to become a republican governor, you didn't turn out so bad."

❖ ⌘ ❖ ⌘ ❖ ⌘ ❖

Dar tousled her hair semi dry, then trudged out into her bedroom wrapped in a towel. Now that it was the day of the reunion, she found herself kind of looking forward to it, in a bizarre sort of way. High school hadn't been a great time for her. Dad had been out to sea a lot and her relationship with her mother had been going downhill.

But she'd had fun, anyway, finding the most outrageous things to wear and do possible, knowing the school was just gnashing its teeth, since expelling an honors student bucking for class valedictorian just didn't cut the mustard.

It was—what?—eleventh grade when I'd stopped responding to my birth name and made everyone call me Dar? Yeah. She'd worn sunglasses inside and leather and ripped clothes, with chains hanging around her neck, ear cuffs. *Oh, and the spurs.*

And the boots.

She'd sounded like John Wayne going up in assembly that last year, to pick up not one, but four scholastic achievement awards, and she'd thoroughly enjoyed the fact that it drove every single one of the staff, and her mother, completely crazy.

Bite me. In studs, on the back of that leather jacket, too.

"What a punk." She laughed at her reflection. "And they couldn't say a goddamned word to me—not with that record and zero absences and zero tardies."

Perfect attendance. Straight A student. An excellent athlete who refused to participate in team sports. Cocky. Antisocial.

Dar sighed, meeting her own eyes in the mirror. "What an asshole I was. If I'd have met myself, I'd have kicked my butt from one end of Flagler Street to the other." With a wry chuckle, she shed her towel and slid into a pair of cotton briefs with little devils all over them. Then she picked up the pair of very faded, artfully ripped jeans Kerry had discovered in a bag shoved way in the back of the closet and stepped into them, tugging them up and pausing.

"Hmm." They were snug, but she'd expected that. She fastened the worn buttons and studied the result. *Well, nothing hung over and nothing poked out.* Better than she'd hoped for, actually. She picked up the vest and examined it, then shrugged it on and pulled the laces.

The leather was soft and pliable and readily fitted itself to her body as she finished the side laces and started up the front. There were sizable gaps in the hide, where her own skin showed, and the neckline was cut low with narrow shoulder straps, exposing quite a bit of her upper body.

"All right," she murmured, tugging the last bit into place and patting the front. "An escapee from a bad Mad Max imitation movie. Nifty."

The doorbell rang, and she blinked, then walked out into the living room and tried to imagine who on earth would be dropping by without security calling her. Clemente, probably. She unlocked the door and pulled it back, stopping in startled shock when blue eyes on a level with hers appeared.

"Oh. Hi, Dad." Dar glanced to one side. "Mother." A totally adolescent panic turned her guts to mush. "Uh..."

Andrew Roberts' eyebrows hiked up and he put a hand on one hip as he studied his offspring. "What in the hell?"

"Now, that's the daughter I remember," Cecilia murmured softly, an ironic twist to her lips. "Sorry we surprised you, Dar. We just flew in and your father wouldn't rest before he showed me where you lived."

"Ah." *Yeah. Okay. Jaw closed, brain on straight, Dar, c'mon.* "Sure, um, c'mon in." She backed up and allowed them to enter. "Mother, we have a dog."

"I heard," Cecilia replied evenly. "I'll live."

Chino bounded out of Dar's bedroom, spotted Andrew, and corkscrewed over to him in utter delight. "Stop that." Andrew scowled at the puppy then knelt as Chino wriggled against his legs in animal ecstasy. "C'mon you furball. Cut that out."

Dar found herself facing her mother, totally unprepared to do so. She felt very off balance. "Um. You want to sit down? We're just getting ready for this party we have to go to. That's why the..." She tugged at her leather laces. "I don't usually dress this way anymore."

"Ah." Cecilia kept her response to a minimum, feeling as uncomfortable as Dar looked. "What kind of party?"

"High school reunion."

"Mmm."

Andrew stood up. "You are not tellin' me you are stepping foot outside this house like that now, are you?"

"Ah. Yes, actually." Dar put her hands behind her back and tried not to breathe too deeply. "It's a come as you were thing."

Her father straightened. "Paladar, you are not goin' out there half naked."

"No. She's not," Kerry's voice interrupted–a wonderful sound to Dar's ears. "But I am." Eyes went to the stairs as the blond woman trotted down them and appeared in all her scantily leathered, booted glory. "She's kinda overdressed, as a matter of fact."

"Dear Jesus." Andrew covered his eyes.

Cecilia bit the inside of her mouth hard to keep from bursting out in hysterical laughter.

Dar slid an arm around Kerry's shoulders and rubbed her back, as the shorter woman wrapped her in a hug. Over Kerry's head, she looked up, and met her mother's eyes.

And realized they might at last have a common ground to meet on. She managed a half smile. Her mother managed one back.

Just maybe. "Want the nickel tour?" Dar said to Ceci.

"Sure."

❖ ⌘ ❖ ⌘ ❖ ⌘ ❖

"Maybe this was a bad idea, Andy." Ceci clasped her hands around one knee, as they sat together in the living room. Dar and Kerry had disappeared into the kitchen after their little impromptu tour and a lull had settled. "I don't think Dar's very comfortable with me here."

"Jest relax," her husband murmured. "She'll be all right. She just hates surprises. Shoulda called her." He looked around. "Nice place, huh?"

Cecilia let her eyes roam around the condo. "Gorgeous," she admitted. "But it's so not Dar."

"Yeap," Andy admitted. "Ah think she just fell into it and was easier just to stay."

Probably true. Ceci was drawn to a set of pictures on the entertainment center. Two were of Dar at a young age. Two were of Kerry, also older pictures, and the one in the center was of them together.

Both were looking at the camera. Dar was seated behind Kerry, and had her arms wrapped around her, with a half smile on her face. The blond woman covered Dar's hands with her own, and the film had captured just the sweetest expression on her, one that almost made Ceci smile just looking at it.

"We need to find a place to stay tonight." She tore her attention from the picture and put it on her husband. "Any suggestions?" It had been years since she'd been in the city, though it hadn't changed really much, and she'd found a thousand memories regaining their color as she left the airport and felt the tropical heat drop over her. "Someplace with sand, maybe?"

❖ ⌘ ❖ ⌘ ❖ ⌘ ❖

"Are you okay?" Kerry asked, for the third time, as she assembled some glasses and a large pitcher of fruit juice. Dar stood at the sink, staring out at the water with a completely unsettled look on her face. "Dar?"

"I wasn't expecting that." The dark head finally turned and looked at her. "I didn't want it to be like this."

Kerry cocked her head in question. "Like what?"

Dar's face twitched. "So damned...sudden."

Kerry put her glasses down, walked over and laid a hand on Dar's almost leather covered back. "Look. Take it easy." She rubbed gently. "It's not that bad, is it? Your mom's being okay, I thought."

"No. Yeah. I don't know." Dar turned and leaned against the counter, folding her arms tightly over her chest. "It's taken me all this time to get used to having him back. Seeing them together...I'm having a little trouble comprehending that right now." She lifted her hand and rubbed her eyes. "Too big an adjustment."

Yeah, it must be, Kerry thought, as she took Dar's free hand in hers. "I know it must be tough. Hang in there, Dar. Having them back is a good thing for you, I really believe that."

Dar sighed. "I know."

"But it's weird."

"Yeah." Dar made a face.

"And us being dressed like a post-apocalyptic pair of whacked out Amazons doesn't help." Kerry smiled as she got a chuckle out of her lover. "Though you have to admit seeing the look on your dad's face when I came downstairs was worth it."

"Mmm." Dar relaxed a little and rubbed her neck. "Eyah. That's true."

"Kin ah ask what you two are up to?" Andrew's voice growled from the doorway. "Starting to think you went to grow them damn fruits afore you squeezed 'em."

Kerry picked up the tray and cleared her throat. "Ah. That's my cue. Bye." She slipped quickly past Dar's father, leaving the two of them alone in the kitchen.

Andy stuck his hands into the pockets of his jeans and moved inside the room. "Think I owe you an apology, Dardar. Didn't meant to shake up your day like this."

Dar studied her father curiously. "You got a haircut."

Self consciously, he lifted a hand and scrubbed it through the trimmed silvered darkness. "Yeap."

There was something so different about him and yet familiar. "Went okay up there, I see." Her eyes smiled at him. "I'm glad." She hesitated. "I didn't expect you back so soon."

Andy took a breath. "She wanted to come home," he responded simply. "Figured we'd find a spot, near to the water. Just set down and be quiet for a bit."

"Just like that?"

"Yeap." He scratched his jaw. "You called the right range on it, Dardar. I owe you." His mouth moved into a smile. "'Cept I don't think I can pay you back for this one."

Now she realized what it was. He was whole again. Dar slowly moved forward. Oh, the scars were still there, but he'd left behind his hooded shirt and regained an equilibrium she could see plainly in the late afternoon light coming in the kitchen window. Hesitantly, she put a hand out and took his. "You don't owe me a damn thing," she whispered. "If it made you happy, that's all that mattered."

"Aw, Dardar." Andy opened his arms and hugged his daughter's sturdy form. "Ain't nothing you ever done that didn't make me happy and prouder than all get out to be your daddy."

Mmm. Dar absorbed the infrequent hug greedily and returned it. "Even dressed like this?" She joked faintly, into his nearby ear.

"Lord," he poked her through the holes, "would you just look at this?"

She nearly doubled over in laughter at the tickling. "Augh."

"Tch." Andrew released her, but put his hands on her shoulders. "Wouldja do one more thing for yer old man?"

"Anything," Dar responded warmly.

He paused. "I know a bucket of stuff's happened, Dar." He touched her cheek. "I know you got hurt." Her lashes fluttered closed. "But I'd like it if you'd give yer mama another shot at what's between the two of you."

Oh. Is that all? Dar's eyes opened. "Is that what she wants?"

He nodded.

Dar thought about the request. It would be so hard, she knew already, to work through a lifetime of friction. Just thinking about it exhausted her. Did she really have a choice though? She looked into her father's eyes. "I'll try."

That earned her another smile.

❖ ⌘ ❖ ⌘ ❖ ⌘ ❖

Kerry walked into the living room and set the tray down. "It's fruit juice." She sat down, poured a glass and offered it to Dar's mother. "Sort of a mixture."

Ceci leaned forward and took the glass. "Thank you." She leaned back with the drink and sipped it as they studied each other. "So," Ceci murmured. "I somehow didn't expect we'd be meeting again so soon."

"No," Kerry agreed. "I guess not." She scratched her nose. "This is sort of awkward."

Ceci took a swallow of the sweet juice. "That's an understatement," she admitted. "It's been a very surprising few days." She regarded Kerry's open, intelligent face curiously. "We could chat about the weather."

Kerry glanced outside. "Eighties, thirty percent chance of showers."

Ceci smiled. "Have you lived here long?"

Kerry leaned back. "Well, if you mean in Florida, about two years." She folded her arms over her bare stomach. "If you mean here, as in right here, a little over six months." She paused. "I like it. Miami, I mean. It was a little tough when I first moved down, but after a while, even the heat grows on you."

"Yes, it does." Softly clinking ice. "You're from Michigan originally?"

Kerry nodded. "My family lives there."

"Sorry I made that crack about your father the last time we met," Cecilia murmured. "Andy told me about what happened. That must have been very tough."

"In a way," Kerry admitted. "In a way it was relief, because I'd been living as part of a charade for so long and after that, I wasn't. I was free to live however I wanted to." She studied the table reflectively. "But I miss my family, sometimes. I miss knowing I'm a part of them." She glanced up. "I still love them, in spite of everything, and I always will, even if they never speak to me again."

Cecilia found those steady, penetrating green eyes boring into hers, transmitting a weight of meaning to her words it was difficult to avoid.

I think I like her. Ceci inclined her head a trifle, acknowledging the younger woman's statement. Even if she was raised a Christian Republican. "You really going to a party dressed like that?" She pointed a slim finger at Kerry's outfit.

"It's her own fault," Dar answered, reappearing from the kitchen and settling down next to Kerry on the loveseat. "She talked me into going to this reunion."

"Half nekkid?" Andrew neatly stepped around Ceci's knees and dropped onto the couch.

"Uh no, actually. I sort of wanted to..." Kerry regarded Dar's sleek form. "Anyway, we made a deal, if she went, I'd have to dress the part and go too."

"Um." Dar's mother pursed her lips. "What part exactly are you dressing for?"

Kerry glanced down at herself, then up at Dar. "You picked it. You answer."

Dar got caught napping. Her jaw opened, then closed a few times, and she sneaked a furtive glance at her mother and father, who were watching in puzzled amusement. "Ah." *Oh well.* "Actually, it was Kerry's idea."

"It was *not.*"

"She wanted to see what I looked like in leather."

"Dar!" Kerry blurted, turning an appealing shade of pink that extended all the way down to her navel.

"Jesus. Woman looks like a damn flamingo." Andrew chuckled.

"Or like one of those squid that change color," Dar remarked, eyeing her companion critically.

"Oh god." Kerry just gave up and buried her face into Dar's chest, pretending the outside world didn't exist for a little while. At least until she stopped glowing like a bad neon sign factory. "Is it time to go yet?" she muttered into the scent of skin and leather.

Dar chuckled and patted her back, then eyed her parents. "What are your plans? Dad said you were looking for a place to stay." The thought occurred to her to offer hospitality, but she wasn't sure if any of them were ready for that much close quarters so soon. However... "We've got some little cottages here on the island they use as a hotel. I could book you in one if you're interested."

The older pair exchanged glances. "That would be very nice. Thank you, Dar," Ceci finally answered. "At least until we can have a chance to look around down here a little."

"Sure." Dar was inwardly pleased with the solution. She picked up the phone and dialed the resident services number. "Hello? Yes. Hi, Clemente." A pause. "No, thanks. I'm feeling much better, really." Another pause. "Actually, I need to book one of the cottages." A much longer pause. "All right. That'll have to do then." She flashed a quick smile. "No, it's for my parents." Lengthy pause as she listened. "Not on vacation, no. They're looking for a place down here." Short pause. "Um, sure, that would be fine. Thanks, Clemente." She hung up. "All set. They'll send a cart for you."

Kerry peeked out from her hiding spot. "Everyone's really nice here."

They exchanged a few more words, then stood, and Dar watched as the reservations staff took charge of her parents' luggage and transported them down the road. "They only had the big one left," she commented.

"The one with the Cadillac sized hot tub?"

"Uh huh."

"Ooo. I'd like to be a fly on that wall."

Dar grinned. "Me too." She nudged Kerry. "C'mon. Let's get this bike revved up and get going."

"Uh, uh. I get to accessorize you first." The blond woman wagged a finger. "I saw that bag of old chains and collars."

Dar winced. "Oh boy."

Chapter 23

Kerry had almost, twice now, asked Dar to simply keep on riding instead of going into the large, buff colored building she could see looming just ahead. Riding a motorcycle was way more fun than she'd anticipated, especially when it became apparent that Dar did, indeed, know how to operate one of them. She was tucked in back of her taller friend, with arms around Dar's middle, and just having a grand old time.

"You know," she murmured into the fairly close by ear, "it would be really cool to go up A1A on the beach, all the way to West Palm on this thing." Dar's head turned slightly. "I could cope with that."

"Hmm." Dar kept one eye on the road and peeked at her. "Am I getting the message that we need to invest in a bike?" She grinned. "How about a ride down to Key West?"

"Ooo." Kerry squeezed her. "Now you're talking."

Dar chuckled and faced back around, leaning the cycle a little to turn into the parking lot of the school. There was a crowd outside the door and more people entering, and she was relieved to see most of them had entered into the spirit of the occasion and were wearing relics from bygone years. *Though.* She tilted her head. *Wearing football pants three sizes too small and a full set of spikes was of at best, dubious intelligence.* She squinted a little. *That would be Barandon Pitts*, she decided, the school quarterback her senior year. The homecoming king, boy voted most likely to do just about whatever he wanted, and senior class president had ended up going into the Navy, she remembered reading in the local press, and came out several years later to take over his father's local chain of coin laundromats.

Against the odds, she'd liked Barry. He shared her dry sense of humor and refused to take any of the high school hoopla over him seriously, getting in and winning his share of games and getting out with a comfortable slate of memories and not much else. He was smarter than they gave him credit for and wiser than an eighteen-year-old boy typically was in the way of life. Dar smiled now to see him amiably stuffing himself back into his old togs and talking to what appeared to be some cheerleaders who were reliving memories.

Kerry peered around with interest as they parked, her chin resting on Dar's shoulder and she exhaled. "This is soooo different than my school was."

"Yeah?" Dar put both booted feet on the ground.

"Private, girls only, Christian."

"Oh." The dark haired woman made a face. "Sorry."

"No. It wasn't bad, actually. It was kind of good, in a way," Kerry said. "Everyone competed a lot, but it was never mixed up in that pseudo chivalry stuff, and no one told you to be good, or bad, in anything because you were a girl. Everyone was considered equal."

"Mmm." Dar thought about that as she swung her leg over the bike's engine and stood, dusting her jeans off. "Interesting." She offered a hand to Kerry with a hint of self consciousness. "Shall we?" After some serious debate, she and Kerry had finally decided that the blond woman's outfit was just a little too...well just a little too, that was all. Kerry had switched the extremely skimpy skirt for a pair of her oldest, most faded jeans, which were very snugly fitted and tucked into the tan leather boots that she'd gotten at the store. She'd kept the leather tooled belt, though. "You okay?"

"Mmm." Kerry plucked at the soft leather jacket she'd worn while riding. "Hope it's air conditioned in there."

Dar chuckled. "It is." She straightened the silver chain around her partner's neck, holding the old fashioned, age darkened setting they'd found in Aunt May's trunk. "Matches your eyes." She flicked the ear cuffs dangling from Kerry's ears. "You look very...um..."

"Post-apocalyptic retro," Kerry decided. "But I like it. And I like that outfit on you, so let's go get stared at." She peered at some of the other people making their way towards the school. "At least ours fits." She squinted. "That's not a tube top, is it?"

Dar tilted her head, then tilted it the other way, then removed her sunglasses and rubbed her eyes. "I don't want to know," she muttered, resuming the lenses and leading the way across the heat softened tarmac. Getting stared at wasn't going to be a problem, she soon realized, as she used her darkened lenses to peer around unseen at the gawking faces. Well, that certainly wasn't any different than when she'd attended the place, that's for sure. She kept her head faced forward and mounted the low stairs up to the door. It opened and public school scent wafted out, making her nose wrinkle in memory as she passed through into the building.

The main hallway was filled with clumps of people, some in business clothes, some casual, some in outfits more appropriate to the teenagers they had once been. Dar took a breath of the air conditioned air and released it. "Looks the same," she commented peering around. Same oatmeal colored walls, same institutional tile floor with curves of oatmeal colored carpet liberally stained with toner, same rows, off to the left and down, of buff colored, paint chipped lockers.

Across the walls near the ceiling tiles were painted banners, welcoming the old students home and to the right hand side, the folding walls had been pulled back, exposing the round tables of the cafeteria.

"Haey, Dar!" Barry's voice boomed at her elbow and she turned to see the tall, heavyset man beside her. "Can't believe ya showed up."

"Hello, Barry." Dar removed her sunglasses and extended a hand. "Nice to see you again." She half turned. "This is my friend Kerry."

"Hey there, Kerry." Barry released Dar's hand and took Kerry's. "Well, ain't this a pile of pretentious preppies." He turned to Dar. "Glad to see you ain't changed any. Still the rebel, huh?" His pale hazel eyes twinkled. "At least after business hours, anyway. Saw your picture in the paper couple months back, that was a kick, lemme tell ya."

"Mmm. I can bet there's a few folks here that never expected me to grace Business Monday, that's true." Dar chuckled. "Thanks. Things are pretty good, yeah. What about you? Still running that chain?"

"Branching out." He scratched his shoulder under the pads. "Business is good. I got married, got two kids, you know." Barry looked around. "Damn, things don't change much, do they? Same groups. There's the jocks, there's the brains, and the geeks."

Dar followed his finger. "Yeah, and the outcasts." She nodded towards a group off by itself, in clothing a bit like hers, most of the men long-haired and the women with body piercing. "Is that Cathy Singer?"

"Yeah. Guess she didn't join a cult and go postal after all. I always figured her for that." The very tall, muscular woman across the floor laughed and hooked thumbs in her belt loops, exposing luridly tattooed arms that somehow matched her bright orange crew cut. Barry scratched his ear. "Unless she's out on parole again."

Dar's brow lifted. "What did they get her for?"

"Assault. When she got out the last time, she came over looking for a part time with me. I," Barry looked a little embarrassed, "I felt bad for her, y'know? But she was scaring the customers."

"Ah." Dar folded her arms. "Figures. We had a few run ins back when."

"Why?" Kerry spoke for the first time, having been busy absorbing the scene with interest. "I thought you were part of that kind of group?"

"Naw." Barry laughed. "Dar weren't part of any group, that's the trouble—she qualified for all of 'em and it drove 'em all nuts."

"I was pretty cocky and not very tactful in those days," Dar advised her lover.

"I'm sure I would have hardly recognized you," Kerry murmured, returning the polite smiles of a group of letter sweatered women in cheerleaders skirts and sneakers nearby. "Are those drinks I see in there? All this leather is making me thirsty."

Dar's nostrils flared and she bit the inside of her lip to keep from laughing. "Right. See you later, Barry." She nudged Kerry in the direction of the cafeteria, returning the wary nods of recognition from several people as they worked their way through the crowd. Dar stopped to read the brightly colored schedule on the outer cafeteria wall and exhaled.

"They're calling this the Get to Re-Know You Reception," she commented. "Then we have the Old Times Cafeteria Spaghetti Dinner and the Squeaky Shoe Gym Dance." She put a hand over her stomach. "I think my stomach flu's recurring."

"Dar." Kerry pushed her gently towards the makeshift bar, where a sweating bartender was dispensing cheap beer and jug wine. "Would you give me a tour around the place? I'd like to see where your classes were." She could sense how uncomfortable Dar was and was beginning to regret coaxing her into coming. "Barry seemed nice."

"He is." Dar ducked past two men in leisure suits, one of which she seemed to remember as a math whiz in eleventh grade. "He and I used to hang out just to make everyone wonder."

"Paladario!"

Dar physically flinched. *Oh shit.* She forced a smile on her face and turned. "Hello, Patricia."

A tall, very well endowed blond woman bore down on them, a delighted look on her tanned face. She had short, feathered hair and was wearing an old, wool band uniform. "How are you? My god, I didn't think you'd show up for this. If I'd know I would have told Sally and Carol to come too, though I think they'll be here later how've you been?" She grasped Dar's arm and squealed. "You look wonderful."

Kerry judged angles and distances, and calculated that Dar would effectively toss the woman right into the next concrete pylon, quite possibly within the next ten seconds if she didn't do something. "What a nice uniform." She smiled brightly. "Is that a cummerbund?"

"Oh." Patricia stepped back and tugged at it, necessarily releasing Dar's arm. "Why, yes. I had it dry cleaned twice and I think I got all the mildew out of it." She beamed at Kerry. "Do I know you?"

"No. Sorry. My name's Kerry." She stuck out a hand. "I'm a friend of Dar's."

"How nice." She dismissed Kerry and returned her attention to the tall, dark haired woman. "I can hardly believe it."

Fortunately, the interlude had given Dar a chance to regain her composure. "Been a long time, that's for sure." She nodded gravely. "I'm doing well, thanks. And you?"

"Oh! I have a thousand things to tell you. Just wait until the gang hears you're here, don't move, Dar, I'll be right back." Patricia bounced off, heading towards a table full of uniforms in various states of repair.

Dar and Kerry eyed each other, then Kerry firmly took her elbow and headed for the door, not stopping until they were down the left hand side hallway, in a quieter spot. "Oh, my god." Kerry took a breath. "Don't tell me that's a friend of yours."

"Ahem." Dar tugged her earlobe. "Actually, she's my cousin." She almost smiled at Kerry's dropped jaw. "On my father's side."

Green eyes peered at her, then Kerry turned around and looked at the entrance to the cafeteria. She swiveled slowly back. "Does he know?"

Dar sighed.

❖ ⌘ ❖ ⌘ ❖ ⌘ ❖

"Ah am gonna kick her butt."

Cecilia prowled around the huge cottage, all three bedrooms and two bathrooms of it, with kitchen. "Well...it's um," she put a finger out and traced the marble countertop, "not a Motel Six, that's for sure."

"Ah am gonna take that child up over mah knee and spank her till she yelps the Pledge of Allegiance in six tongues."

His wife opened a closed door and found a huge, turbidly swirling hot tub tucked behind it, raised, with ledges comfortably niched for drinks. "Hmm." She left the door open and wandered into the kitchen, peeking inside the refrigerator and finding champagne and a tray of assorted chocolates and cookies. She picked up a square of dark truffle and returned to the recalcitrant figure standing in the hallway, legs braced and arms folded.

"Ah swear, I'm—fmf." Andy bit down on the unexpected object in his mouth. His brows lifted as he chewed. "Mmm. What the hell is that?"

"Chocolate," Ceci advised him knowingly, patting him on the stomach. "C'mon, relax. It's only for one night." She looked around and shrugged a bit. "It's like being in a miniature castle." She took his hand. "With my very own prince."

"Mmph." His eyes dropped.

"Besides, you never could stand to lay a finger on that kid, and you know it. All she had to do was look at you with those big blue eyes and you folded," Ceci reminded him with a gentle poke.

Andy sighed. "Well, all right. I guess one night in here won't kill me. What is that noise?"

"Hot tub," Ceci told him succinctly. "Dar has one, outside."

"Huh." He ambled over and stuck his head in. "Jesus H. Christ. I seen swimming pools on Navy ships smaller than that." He peered over his shoulder at her. "You ever tried one?"

"Mmhmm." She wandered over to one of the closed doors and opened it, revealing a bedroom with an old fashioned four poster bed with a canopy. The room was painted in eggshell and coral, and a multi bladed fan over head passed lazily through the cool air. Two very fluffy, beige bathrobes lay folded on the dresser.

It was overwhelmingly luxurious, almost to the point where she had to laugh at it. *But you know, every life deserved a little bit of ridiculous pampering, didn't it? A day or two here and there when you could lose yourself in a marble lined fantasy, surrounded by chocolate, champagne and down mattresses.*

A tiny bubble of time to spend reveling in a restored love—a second honeymoon as it were. Of course, she and Andy had never had a first, since he'd been shipped out the day after they'd gotten married.

It was time. Ceci turned and leaned in the doorway. "Have you ever tried one?"

Andy looked up from where he was seated, with his hand stuck curiously in the warm water. "Closest I ever come to this was going out the top hatch of a hunter sub into a riptide."

Ceci walked over and sat down next to him. "That doesn't count."

"Sure was a lot colder," he agreed.

"Would you join some chocolate, champagne, and me in this one?" A hand curled over his. "We might as well take advantage of the place."

"Uh. Ah don't think that green eyed gal threw no swimsuit in that bag," Andy drawled slowly, watching her face.

His wife smiled. "That's good. Because I haven't got one either. I guess we'll just have to make do with what we don't have." She flicked a bit of warm water at him. "You up for some impromptu improvisation?"

One grizzled brow lifted. "What you mean by them three dollar words is, you and me are gonna get naked in this here bathtub, ain't it?" His tone dropped and took on a faint growl.

Ceci nodded. "Mmhm. That is indeed what I had in mind, sailor boy." She lifted a hand to his cheek and stroked it, feeling the unevenness of the scars and the light stubble of his beard. "What do you say?"

His skin tensed under her fingers as he released a partial smile. "What I say is that you are one wanton woman, Mrs. Roberts," he rasped. "But I guess we're gonna get wet." He flicked back a handful of water at her. "You got more of them chocolates?"

She stood and held a hand out. "C'mon."

They walked hand in hand into the small kitchen and collected the goodies, brought them back to the tub room, and set them on the marble surround. Ceci fiddled with the wall mounted sound system, achieving sound in a sudden jolt of volume. "Whoops."

"Yow." Andy blinked and ambled over. "They got anything that ain't the macarena?"

"I'm working on it." Ceci fiddled a moment more, then the speaker produced a much softer, lighter sound. "Better?"

"Mmph." He slipped his arms around her tentatively and she turned, laying her hands against his chest. "It'll do." He paused, and she smiled a touch, then closed her fingers and tugged the dark cotton shirt he had tucked into his jeans out.

He slid his hands around her neck and down under her collar, stopping at the top button on her white, lacy shirt, then with a small, precise motion, undid it. A touch slid down beneath the fabric and separated it. "You smell nice."

Ceci trailed fingers over his ribs and leaned close. "So do you," she whispered, getting her hands under his waistband and unbuttoning it.

"Only cause you made me use that pink soap this mornin'," Andy teased. "Making me smell all like coconuts. Good Lord." His jeans dropped loosely around him, and he undid the rest of her buttons, then slipped the pale fabric down her shoulders as she tugged at his undershorts.

"Mmm." Ceci felt the soft fabric. "I think I like you in silk."

"Don't you start." Andy ducked his head and kissed her, as their bodies slid together. They worked the rest of their clothes off and spent a moment reacquainting themselves to each other. His hands closed around her and lifted. "Need to feed you, woman."

"Look who's talking," Ceci retorted, as she was lowered into the tub, followed by a mass of ex-SEAL. The water was warm, but not hot, and pleasantly bubbly. "Here. This is a start." She picked up a piece of chocolate and offered it to him. "So. How do you like the tub?"

Andy chewed very thoughtfully as he glanced around. "I do believe I like this," he approved with a nod. "Stock some fish in it, it'd be perfect."

Ceci laughed. "Andy!"

"Heh." He stretched long legs out across the bottom of the tub and relaxed, turning to find gray eyes inches from his. "This here tub getting smaller?" His breathing caught as her hands explored below the surface, and he half turned, kissing her as he started his own touch.

Well. It certainly was one of the few things he'd never tried underwater before.

But it was as good a time as any to try.

❖⌘❖⌘❖⌘❖

It was much quieter down the hallway. Kerry glanced around as they strolled, peering at the bulletin boards, which featured announcements and posters about current school events. "It's different."

"I bet." Dar pointed. "That's the PE area. Everyone had to take it and I think the locker room was one of the true character building moments for any high school girl." She poked her head inside the alcove and tried the door. "Ah."

Kerry followed her amiably inside. The lockers were painted in virulent shades of red, white and blue, and there were encouraging paper banners plastered on the walls for various team sports. The floor was tile over concrete and the whole place smelled rather like...

Hmm. Rather like an old gym sock. "Nice atmosphere," she commented. "What teams were you on?"

"None...well, that's not true. I ran track, and did field events like high jump. But I wasn't in any team sports." Dar strolled over to a plaque and viewed it with a mixture of nostalgia and regret.

Kerry stepped up next to her and tilted her head back, reading the records hammered into the insets, made to be changed if the school records were. Her eyebrows lifted at a familiar name, in several places. She looked at Dar. "I always envied people who could actually do the broad jump." Her hand traveled over and patted Dar's thigh. "My one shining moment in high school sports was during an archery competition."

"Really?" Dar turned and cocked her head. "Didn't know you were into bows."

"I wasn't." Kerry assumed a wry look. "I shot our head mistress in the butt." She laughed at the expression on her lover's face. "I was grounded for six months, but let me tell you, was I ever famous in school." She followed the laughing Dar back out of the locker room, into the mustier scent of the hallway. "I played on all the teams, though. It was sort of expected." They walked down a long ramp, towards another section. Other guests were also roaming, and occasionally, one gave Dar a nod, or waved. "Softball, field hockey, the usual."

"No field hockey here." Dar climbed up a set of steps. "Soccer, sure. Softball, football, swimming. I did a little swimming and diving too." They exited into a long hallway, with classrooms on either side, which opened up into a center almost lab like area set up for larger groups, with audio visual screens. "This was my AP English classroom."

Kerry regarded the small chairs and old, wooden desk at the front, and tried to imagine a teenage version of her tall lover there.

It was tough. "Did you like school?"

Dar shrugged and led her down the hall, towards a set of stairs that led back to the cafeteria. "I didn't hate it, but it didn't really challenge me," she admitted. "I left here and went to work, or went home and hung around with the other brats. What was going on at the base always seemed more real to me." They ambled down the steps, moving to one side as a group of people started up them.

"Well, well," the tall redhead in their midst said, looking directly at Dar, "look who showed up."

Some people, Kerry decided, really did just have "Hi, I'm a bad attitude" tattooed on their foreheads. Following some primal instinct, she hesitated, falling a step behind Dar as her lover turned, tilting her head slightly to peer out over her sunglasses.

"Hello, Cathy." Dar's voice was neutral and brief. "Have a nice tour." She continued on down the stairs.

"Whoa, whoa. What's your rush?" The taller woman edged over, blocking their path. "Been a long time." Her friends watched in silence. Cathy's eyes roamed over Dar's body, starting at the boots. "Don't you look butch?"

Dar let her glasses slip down a little, so the redhead's eyes met her own icy ones when she reached that level. "Yeah, but I can take these clothes off. What's your excuse?"

A snicker came from the watching crowd, and Kerry suddenly felt like she was back in school herself, as the attitudes around her devolved into an adolescent tenor. She put a subtle hand on Dar's back, feeling the tension beneath her fingers, and scratched the bare skin gently.

"Smart ass."

"Yep." Dar circled around her and continued down the stairs. "Always was."

Kerry felt the eyes on her and she kept her attention on her friend's back as she followed her, closing her ears to the sarcastic comments on her body. "That was pleasant," she muttered, as they exited the stairwell and gained the relatively cheery safety of the cafeteria. "I take it you and her weren't buddies?"

Dar ducked around a pylon and edged up to the now crowded bar. "Actually, we were." She ordered a soda. "You want a beer?"

"Sure."

Dar paid for the drinks and handed Kerry hers, then pointed towards a table near the rear of the steadily filling room. "C'mon. I'm sure I'll have to suffer more of Patricia. We might as well sit down."

They took a seat and Dar tossed her glasses on the table, riffled her dark hair back and took a sip of her soda. "Cathy and I hung out together for a couple of years. She was all right. Not too many brain cells, but she was into partying and having a good time."

"And?" Kerry was secretly delighted at worming out a little more of her sometimes enigmatic lover's early years. She eyed the glass she'd been given, then wiped her beer bottle neck off and swigged directly from it.

"She got drunk and tried to kiss me and I beat the crap out of her."

Kerry spit a mouthful of beer halfway across the table, and started coughing. "Jesus, Dar." She received a penitent slap on the back. "You're kidding, right?"

"No." Dar tossed her napkin and Kerry's on the table and wiped the beer up. "I was not a nice person in high school. I was very full of myself and I had the skills and the brawn to back it all up. Not a good combination."

"Mmm." Kerry set her bottle down and cleared her throat. "Did you fight a lot?"

Dar's eyes flicked over the room, in an oddly tense movement. "I did my share." Her hands flexed.

"Dar?" Kerry deliberately closed her fingers around one of her partner's and waited for the blue eyes to flick in her direction. "You're not in high school anymore, remember? You're the Chief Information Officer of the largest IS company in the world."

Dar paused and blinked, then exhaled, and leaned back. "Yeah, I know." She gently withdrew her hand and folded her arms over her chest. "Just reliving some not so nice memories."

Kerry sighed. "Next time, we just go rent a movie, huh?" She was now definitely sorry she'd coaxed Dar into this. "Wonder what your folks are up to?"

That nudged Dar off her dark train of thought. "Oh. Walking on the beach, maybe." She released the old memories. "Exploring the island, maybe trying out that hot tub." She spotted her cousin across the room and sighed as she was identified.

"You think so? I didn't think they'd mess with that. I guess your dad could get a suit at the market, but—"

Blue eyes blinked at her. "It's indoors, Ker, they don't need suits." Dar chuckled a little. "I bet they enjoy that big bed, too."

Kerry's brows creased. "Um yeah, it looks comfortable."

"Bouncy." Dar smiled. "Hope they don't bounce off and end up on the carpet." She stopped and took in the look of wide-eyed incomprehension coming from her lover. "Kerry?"

"What do you mean, bounce?"

"What do you think I mean?" Dar laughed. "They're not going to sleep in it, Ker, they're—mmfph." A slim hand covered her mouth.

"Dar, let me explain something to you," Kerry told her seriously. "Parents don't have sex." She took her hand away. "Okay?"

Dar wasn't sure if she should giggle, or what. She rubbed her jaw and took a breath. "And you explain your presence...how? Oh right. I forgot. Private school. Let me guess. Easter Bunny brought you?"

The blond woman glanced around and noticed the band party moving towards them. She lowered her voice. "Of course I know how I got here. I figure that gave my parents a total of three times." She made a face. "And even that's stretching my imagination to its limits. I wondered about cabbage patches more than once."

Her lover buried her face in one hand and bit off a semi hysterical giggle, her thoughts of school now completely vanished. "Kerrison Stuart, you better get used to the idea that my daddy did not limit his experience to one time." She peeked out over her fingers. "We had that little father daughter chat real, real early."

Kerry regarded her doubtfully. "Like, how early?"

"When he figured out my treehouse on the base looked right inside his bedroom window." Dar flashed white teeth in a mischievous grin as Kerry covered her eyes and blushed a deep crimson, very, very evident in her outfit.

At that moment, she was rescued, relatively, as Patricia came up on one side, and Cathy came up on the other, chairs scraping as they and their respective friends sat down at the round table. The two groups regarded each other. "Just like old times." Cathy smiled.

"Hope your table manners have improved." Patricia smiled back.

"Why? Your ugly face hasn't."

Dar sighed. *It was going to be a very long night.*

Chapter
24

Kerry regarded the tray that had been delivered to her by serious helpful aproned servers. It was divided into five sections, with a sixth ostensibly for silverware. The sections contained some spaghetti, with some sort of meat, a slice of garlic bread, a salad, some green beans, and a square of carrot cake.

She had sudden insight into why Dar hated vegetables, if this was any indication of what she'd had to subsist on for twelve years, and she found herself with an insidious craving for Chinese stir fry as a result.

Or an apple.

Or something.

Anything. She glanced at Dar, who was carefully separating her strands of spaghetti from the meatlike substance, and eating them individually, alternating with bites of the carrot cake.

Kerry sighed. *Well, at least there was a carton of milk, which was sealed.* She tried not to remember she'd been drinking beer and opened the red and white box, then drank down the cold milk with a feeling of relief.

"Ker?"

"Mmm?" She looked up, slightly startled at the lull in the conversation, which had been going on around her for thirty minutes.

"You all right?"

"Uh. Yeah, sure." Kerry nibbled a bit of the carrot cake. She'd let the string of reminisces go past her, glad that Dar was at least unbending enough to trade stories with the rest of the table. It was interesting, sort of. Dar's cousin kept up a never-ending stream of questions, and she and Cathy constantly traded insults. Kerry realized that the insults weren't really serious, but more of a game and the intimidating Cathy wasn't nearly as scary as she'd like to make herself out to be.

She did, however, have her eyes all over Dar, a fact that earned her very little appreciation from Kerry, harmless though she knew it was. She turned her head and found the redhead staring at her and she lifted her chin a little, returning the stare steadily.

"So. What do you do?"

"I work with computers, like Dar does," Kerry answered evenly.

"Any money in that?"

"We do all right." She rested her chin on her fist. "It's a very fast growing industry."

"Sounds boring as shit."

"Dar, are you still working for that company. Whatever it was?" Patricia interrupted, gesturing with a fork. "You know the one."

"Yes, I am," Dar admitted. "ILS."

Cathy laughed. "Still? Man. Have they let you out of the mailroom yet?"

Kerry's eyes narrowed, but Dar merely sucked on her fork prongs reflectively. "Where is our mailroom?" She turned to her lover. "I've had mine delivered for so long, I don't know where they put it last time."

"On the first floor, near security," the blond woman supplied. "I had to drop a package off there last week."

"What are you doing now, Dar? Still in programming?" Patricia asked. "I remember when you made the report cards all print out in French our last year. I don't think Mr. McGrudber ever forgave you for that, even though you did use proper grammar." She laughed and the three girls with her laughed too. "I bet he finds you tonight."

Dar rested her forearms on the table. "Actually, he and I had a laugh about that at our last stockholder's meeting," she remarked offhandedly. "He came over to congratulate me on being promoted to CIO and just had to tell Alastair about the whole thing." She played with her paper napkin. "Alastair told him he was lucky it was only French." She paused as she absorbed the looks of surprise from around the table. "In answer to your question, Pat, I've gone a little beyond programming." She basked in the sweetness of their very visible envy. "Despite many predictions to the contrary."

"Wow." Patricia seemed at a loss for words. "That's really great. That's incredible, in fact."

"You son of a bitch." Cathy snorted. "After all that big talk about being so out there, you go and sell out and be a corporate asshole." She stood up and shoved her tray to the middle of the table, then stalked off, muttering in disgust.

Dar and Kerry exchanged glances. "Oh yes," Kerry murmured, "you turned out so stuffy and traditional." She brushed a bit of dust off Dar's bare shoulder, since the taller woman had removed her jacket and slung it over the chair.

There was an uncomfortable silence then Pat cleared her throat. "Here I thought I was doing okay being a law clerk." She laughed a little defensively. "Who knew?"

❖ ⌘ ❖ ⌘ ❖ ⌘ ❖

"Tell you what," Dar murmured into Kerry's ear as they climbed the flight of steep stairs towards the metal doors of the gym. "You share one dance with me in this place, and then..."

"Mmm?" The pink ear twitched with interest.

"Sushi and the beach?"

"Ooo." Kerry warbled in delight. "You're definitely on." She laid a hand on Dar's arm. "Listen. Sorry if this has been a bust for you."

Dar dodged a thickset man who swayed slightly as he climbed. "It hasn't been." She shrugged and looked around. "It's been sort of...not fun, but I think it's been interesting for me to see how...um..."

"Far you've come?" Green eyes twinkled at her in the dim light. "I know how I'd feel if I was at home, walking the halls of my school." A memory stirred. "I had this one teacher, Ms. Van Schuver, who taught creative writing. She told me, after giving me a barely passing grade in her class, that I'd never go outside my nice, safe box so she considered me very Republican and very boring."

Dar put a hand on her bare back and guided her into the gym. "And when is *your* high school reunion?"

"Hmm." A wash of air hit her, mixing the scents of a lot of people, alcohol, rubber, and old wood. She paused inside the door to look around, as a babble of voices in several languages and loud music added to the atmosphere.

The gym had, of course, a large clear space in the center and a stage on one side with a DJ complete with an assortment of chaser lights. On the other side, the seats had been pushed back mechanically against the wall, exposing only the lower two or three tiers for people to sit on. Tables were lined up near the back with various nibbly snacks on it and two large freestanding bars were quickly gathering customers. Kerry followed Dar to the side of the room and they stood watching quietly as a few groups broke up into twos and threes and drifted to the center of the room.

"Thirsty?" Dar finally asked.

"A little. Punch, though, please. That beer's deadly." Kerry put a hand on her stomach and watched as Dar slipped through the crowd and headed towards the bar. She leaned back against the collapsed, wooden tiers and exhaled.

It was a mixed crowd, of course. Hispanics were prevalent, with a liberal spattering of Anglos and African Americans among them. She could hear English, Spanish, Creole, and some Jamaican accents just in her vicinity, and smiled as the music changed to a Latin beat and the sports jackets started to come off.

"Hey...it's the little blond kid." Cathy appeared at her side, making Kerry jump a little. Her voice was slightly slurred and she smelt of something stronger than beer. "You're pretty cute, you know that?"

Kerry folded her arms over her chest self-consciously. "Hi." She smiled briefly. "Thanks for the compliment." She was aware of the taller woman's imposing presence and that Cathy stood within inches of her, well within her comfort zone. She eased back.

"Where's your big shot friend?" Cathy moved closer, reaching out to finger Kerry's soft leather jacket. "Must be nice to have all that money, huh?"

"Dar's just getting a drink." Kerry's heartbeat picked up. "And I have what I work for, just like everyone else does." *True.*

"Oh yeah?" Cathy pulled a flat bottle from her overalls' back pocket and took a sip from it. Its sharp scent made Kerry's nostrils twitch. "Bet you never been poor, though, have you? Not a little WASP like you." Her voice became bitter.

"No, I never have," Kerry admitted.

"Want some of this?" Cathy pushed the bottle at her. "Or are you too good to share a little drink with a poor old cracker like me?"

Kerry realized that she was surrounded by leather clad shadowy figures and a jolt of panic hit her in the gut. She forced herself not to shake as she took the bottle and sniffed it cautiously. *Well,* she felt a tinge of wry amusement, *I never thought this skill would come in handy ever again, but...* She took a long sip of the alcohol and swallowed it, then licked her lips and shrugged as she handed it back. "Mescal's better."

Cathy took the bottle back and glanced at it, then at her. "Son of a bitch."

"Ever suck a worm?" Kerry persisted. "They're not bad with a little lime on them."

The tall woman took a swallow of her own, then licked the bottle rim, watching Kerry's reaction. "Mmm. I like that taste." She moved in closer and ducked her head, her intent obvious.

Uh oh. Kerry lifted a hand and intercepted her. She pushed back slightly as she looked over Cathy's shoulder, utterly relieved to meet icy blue eyes coming towards her. "Stop." She raised her voice and put an edge in it. "You don't want to do that."

"Sure I do." Cathy reached for the hand holding her. "C'mere, cute pie. You look good enough to eat."

"I said, stop." Kerry straightened her back.

"Little tease." Cathy grabbed for her, then yelped as her hand was caught and wrenched back and her arm twisted painfully behind her back. "Let me the fuck go!"

"Or?" A low, lazy, almost purr answered her.

"I'm gonna kick your ass."

"No, you're not," Dar answered placidly. "Because we're not a couple of stupid kids."

"Let me go!" Cathy twisted savagely, but Dar's hold bested her and the dark haired woman merely went with the motion, then slammed her into the wall with a clatter of wood.

"Cathy, if I have to call the cops, you're going to regret it," Dar told her. "So knock it off." She swung her around and got between her and Kerry, then released her with a relatively gentle shove in the opposite direction.

Kerry put a hand on her lover's back, glad of Dar's calm, reasoned attitude. Her throat still stung from the harsh tequila and she took a deep breath, willing her heart to settle down.

Cathy stumbled forward, then turned, and half fell against the tiers, staring back at Dar with sullen anger. "You think you're so hot."

Dar sighed. "I'll give you some free advice. Grow up. As far as I can tell, you haven't learned a goddamned thing since we left this place the last time." She turned her head as Barry edged his big body between Cathy's friends and her.

"Hey hey hey. Nifty party, huh?"

The leather clad group faded away, and after a long, hostile stare, Cathy followed them. Dar waited for them to leave, then let out a held breath. "You okay?"

"Outside of having a graphic reminder of just why I really, really hate bad tequila, yes," Kerry responded dryly. "I'm fine." She exhaled. "Dar, does everyone in your past have a bad attitude, or is it just me?" She got a brief, guilty look from her lover.

Barry chuckled. "Girl's got a bug up her butt, always has." He tilted his head. "'Sides, Dar had herself quite a 'tude in the bad old days." He nudged Dar's arm. "C'mon over by us old, balding, fat ex-jocks, and make us feel macho, huh?"

Dar inclined her head, and they walked across the floor towards a group of men and women who were laughing around one of the bars. They waved hello, as the music changed again and took on an earthier beat.

Next time, Kerry... She accepted a cup of the frothy beer, glad of anything to get the taste of tequila out of her mouth. *Next time rent a movie.*

Go bowling.

Miniature golf?

Do laundry.

Everyone loosened up and after about thirty minutes, the music took a little break, slowing down and allowing the sweating participants to relax. The lights dimmed as well, and Kerry felt a hand touch her shoulder.

"Join me?" Dar's eyes were almost violet in the dimness.

"Sure." Kerry led the way through the crowd, until they found a small clear space, then turned and rested her hands on Dar's hips as the taller woman's arms circled her neck. She was briefly aware of a few startled looks in their immediate vicinity and the unmistakable motion as distance was put between them and their nearest neighbors.

Relax, she mentally informed the crowd. *If this was contagious, we'd have elected Liberace president.* In another forum, she might have felt self-conscious, but here, in this smelly gym, in the dark, all that really mattered was the body now closing gently with hers, leather and skin brushing against her and making everything else fade into insignificance.

She moved with the music and Dar moved with her in synch as they took small steps in a lazy circle. Idle light beams from the ceiling drifted over them, dusting Dar's shoulders in rust and ochre and catching the occasional glint off her eyes, which were fastened on Kerry's face.

They could have been completely alone, for all the impact the crowd was making on her, and Kerry relaxed into a smile as her thumbs traced the gaps in Dar's vest, feeling skin and movement and just a little sweat from the heat. She moved a little closer as Dar's thigh brushed hers and put her head down on Dar's shoulder, listening to the music of her heartbeat.

Dar felt content, something that had escaped her totally in the years she'd spent here, though the experience hadn't been all bad. She knew she was being stared at, but it really didn't matter, because she had what she wanted, found what she'd searched for, and the only thing that mattered to her was the look of love in Kerry's eyes as she gazed upward.

If the rest of them didn't like it they could just kiss her ass. She half closed her eyes and hummed along with the music, hardly conscious of what the tune even was.

❖ ⌘ ❖ ⌘ ❖ ⌘ ❖

The moon had risen when they left, and Kerry paused a moment and collected her balance as they walked down the front stairs. Her head buzzed a little and she was glad of the warm arm that slipped around her, steadying her steps. "Thanks." She returned the grip by tucking an arm snugly around Dar's waist.

"Thanks for the dance," Dar replied, with a smile. "Didn't know you could move like that."

"Ungh. Give me enough beer, and I can do all sorts of things you'd never imagine I could," Kerry admitted. "I did warn you about that." She swallowed against a mildly queasy stomach.

"Mmm." Dar glanced around the parking lot, which was still quite full. The rest of the evening had been reasonably pleasant, and she'd even gotten a few dances in with Barry and some of the others, ending the reunion on a nice note she hadn't really expected. "I had fun."

Kerry smiled and gave her a squeeze.

They walked around the corner of a large Lincoln, and right into the harsh glare of a flashbulb. "Hey." Dar stopped and threw an arm up, blinking the spots out of her eyes. "What in the hell was that for?"

"Nail on your coffin." David Ankow got off the car hood he was seated on and advanced his film, then shot a few more. "Photographic evidence, not that I needed any more, but I like to be thorough."

The shock faded, and Dar sifted through her available options, which weren't extensive. He'd nailed her, and she was smart enough to realize it.

Question was, did she care? Kerry had fallen mute and kept her mouth prudently shut, but didn't release her hold on Dar.

"Did you get my good side?" Blue eyes widened and Dar lifted a hand, glancing down at herself. "Though what pictures of me at my high school reunion prove I can't imagine."

"It's against company rules for supervisors to be in relationships with subordinates," Ankow commented mildly. "Such a tawdry little thing to nail you on." He cocked his head at Kerry. "So sweet of you to go home and take care of your bedmate, Ms. Stuart. I got excellent shots of you driving that nice little car onto that fancy ferry." He put the cap on his lens. "And now, I can leave this rancid hell hole and go home, where I have three lawyers drawing up two different suits, with three different counts of negligence, misrepresentation, and dereliction of duty against both of you." He gave them a satisfied nod. "Damn good day's work." He smiled. "Have a great day, you pair of disgusting perverts. It's going to be a great pleasure for me to see the last of you when this is all over." He turned.

"Mr. Ankow." Kerry disengaged her arm from her stunned partner and walked over to him.

He put a hand on his hip and waited, a look of smug pleasure on his face.

Kerry stopped and regarded him with concentrated seriousness. "You're ugly, you stink, and you have the brains of a sea slug," she stated. "You can take those pictures and shove them right up your ass."

Ankow was a little surprised. "You're drunk."

"You're a moron," Kerry shot right back. "I can always sober up."

"You little..." Ankow reached for her arm. "I'll—"

Without warning, Kerry lashed out a fist and caught him right in the nose with all the power she could muster.

"Son of a bitch! Don't you touch me!" A splatter of blood sprayed in the garish lamplight, and Ankow stumbled backwards.

He wiped the blood onto the back of one hand and looked up at her, his eyes narrowing. Then they slid past Kerry's shoulder, and he froze for a long moment. "You'll regret doing that," he finally said, in a very quiet voice. "Believe me." Then he turned and walked rapidly away, disappearing between two parked vans and into the darkness beyond.

They were quiet for a moment, then Dar let out a low, whistling breath. "Did that make you feel better?" she asked her lover wryly.

"Ow." Kerry examined her hand. "I forgot to mention I get feisty when you get me tanked, didn't I?"

Dar took her hand and rubbed a thumb over the skin. Then she lifted the hand up and kissed it. "I'll have to remember that."

Kerry sighed. "We're seriously screwed, aren't we?"

Dar made a faint noise.

"They're going to fire us and sue us for a ton of money, right?"

"Probably," Dar acknowledged. "Well, me, anyway. You didn't do anything. The corporate responsibility for the rule falls on the supervisor." She gazed at Kerry. "And I certainly did know what I was doing."

"Can they put us in jail?"

"No." Dar shook her head. "We're not criminals, just lovers." Her lips twitched faintly. "Though, I don't know—he might have you for assault and battery now."

"Nah. He'd never admit to a cop he let a girl punch him." Kerry smiled, then leaned against the Lincoln. She felt curiously free, in a strange way. "You know something, Dar?"

"What?"

"I don't care."

"You don't?"

"No," she answered very softly. "If all I have in the world is you, no matter what we do, or where we end up, that's okay with me." She rubbed her arm. "Worst comes to worst, we can go on the road and I'll sell my poems for food, how about that?"

Dar chuckled. "C'mon." She held a hand out. "You still in the mood for sushi?"

Kerry went willingly, allowing Dar to lead her over to the bike and settling behind her. "It's a little late for that, but boy, could I ever use some ice cream," she mumbled into the leather covered back. "A nice big double scoop sundae with lots of fudge."

"Your wish is my command." Dar started the engine and revved it. "Hang on."

"Don't worry." Kerry tightened her grip. "I'm never letting go of you."

They pulled out into the street, under a crisply starred sky with a peaceful full moon to light the way.

Chapter
25

Dar parked the bike near the condo and carefully put the cover they'd been provided with on top of it. Kerry helped her and they both stepped back and regarded the machine. "You think?"

"Oh yeah." Kerry stifled a yawn, and leaned against her. "C'mon. Chino heard us."

They walked up the stairs and Kerry keyed the lock, pulled the door open and released the excited Labrador. "Easy, Chino. Easy." She knelt and hugged the puppy, then picked her up and followed Dar into the living room.

"Hey, Dar?"

"Hmm?" The taller woman dropped her jacket over the back of the loveseat and unlaced her vest.

"I know you sort of just came into this, but if you had a choice, where would you live?"

Interesting question. Dar loosened the laces and wandered into her room, tugged the leather off and replaced it with a worn heavy cotton T-shirt. She rubbed her arms as she regarded her reflection, then glanced over at the blond in the doorway. "Honestly? A place that doesn't exist." She chuckled a little. "A nice, rustic cabin on the beach, not too close to everyone else, with a little dock."

Kerry considered that. "I'm sure there're places like that."

"Umm. With ISDN fast access lines and a shopping mall next door?" The blue eyes twinkled with wry self deprecation. "Not to mention cable TV?"

"Hmm. I get it. Microsoft rustic."

"Something like that." Dar shrugged. "A way to mix my preferences with my vocation. I think you have to trade off one for the other." She looked around. "I don't need the marble and silk, but I do love the technology. It's always intrigued me."

Kerry nodded slowly. "Yeah, me too." She paused reflectively. "It would be kind of fun to pick a new place out with you, though. I mean..." An awkward hesitation. "I don't know what I mean." She wandered forward and pulled a faded blue T-shirt from Dar's drawer. "Mind if I borrow this?"

"Since when do you ask?" Dar kidded her, then was quiet for a minute. "I wouldn't mind picking a place out with you either." They regarded each other. "Let's see what happens with this whole thing. Maybe we won't have a choice." She circled her finger in the air, then unfastened Kerry's top as the blond woman turned around.

"Are you worried about it?"

Dar eased past her and headed for the back door, with Chino dancing beside her. "Worried?" She opened the door for the puppy and watched her scamper out into the dark garden. "No. I know I'm employable, Kerry, and that's the bottom line." She glanced up. "Even if I end up getting a quarter of my salary, it's still livable, but," she shrugged, "I feel like I've put so much into the company, after all this time, it hurts a little to have to face this."

Kerry rubbed her arms, warming them in the chill of the air conditioning, and glad of Dar's shirt. "It doesn't make sense, though, Dar," she mused. "Why now? You've never had a problem with the board before, and you've got a solid history with the company. What's Ankow's agenda, I wonder?"

Puzzled, Dar waited for Chino to come back in and shut the door, then walked into the kitchen and started fiddling with the coffee maker. "I thought we knew it. He wants to take control, to oust Alastair. This is going to be damn embarrassing for him, since any disclosure of records will show he processed the overrides on our personnel records."

"No." Kerry shook her head, retrieved the coffee container, and handed it to her. "He knew something was up between us before he started all this. There's something more going on, Dar, and I can't help but notice the timing on this is awfully convenient." She moved closer and leaned on the counter, watching Dar's thoughtful face. "Something he said tonight, about us. I know he has a bad attitude about immigrants, because he made snide comments in the lunchroom."

"So he's prejudiced." She shrugged. "He's in the majority, Ker. You saw the looks we were getting tonight. We're just lucky in that most of the people close to us have accepted our relationship."

"I just have a feeling there's something more to it," Kerry objected stubbornly. "Because you know as well as I do, that lawsuit of his is bullshit, Dar. In the entire time you've been at an executive level at ILS, they've shown a healthy profit. The only thing proving we're involved with each other gets him is grounds for termination."

"Mmm."

"And it makes everyone who supported us, Alastair, Duks, Mari, look bad."

"True."

"So, it gives him the leverage to put his own people in, if it all goes his way."

"Yes, it does." Dar poured two cups of coffee and added cream and sugar, then handed one to Kerry and guided her out into the living room.

"Why?" Kerry sat down on the couch and put her feet up on the table, crossing them at the ankles. "Why this company? Why does he give a damn? I don't get it."

Dar settled back and took a sip of her coffee, thinking. Chino scrambled up on the couch and curled up next to her, putting her muzzle on Dar's thigh. "His scan came up pretty clean," she mused. "He was in the Army for eight years, discharged as a captain, nothing out of the ordinary in his records. Family lives in Oregon. Father's a lumber magnate, pretty well off. He went to school in Washington, got a degree, went to law school. Came out and worked for the father as a corporate lawyer."

"Yeah?"

"Yeah. No criminal background, good credit, Mark couldn't find a thing on him, except that he'd been an Eagle Scout, something Mark found really funny, for some reason."

"Hmm." Kerry exhaled. "That doesn't help. What does he want from us? Or from ILS?"

Dar sat absolutely still for a long moment, then she put her cup down and turned towards Kerry. "Data."

"Huh?"

"Data. It's what we do, Kerry. We carry more data for more companies and governments than any other company in the world."

"Well, sure, I know but—"

"Eighty percent of the interbank transfers. Military signal processing. The corporate network." Dar rubbed her temple. "I never thought of it this way, but if you wanted to get information on anyone and anything, we're the kind of company that could do it, easily."

"But that data doesn't belong to us, Dar."

"I know. But what would stop someone from passing all that through a filter in one of the big backbones and siphoning it off into a data storage for sifting?" The blue eyes glinted. "Someone inside the company, I mean. Someone like Mark."

Kerry thought, then she shook her head slowly. "Nothing." She tried to grasp the enormity of it. "Do you really think that's what he's after, Dar? It sounds so...so...melodramatic." She gave her lover a wry look. "Like we're in a spy novel."

"I don't know." Dar settled back and picked her cup up again.

"You're the one who thinks there's more going on. I just came up with a possibility." She got up and strolled to the sliding glass doors then opened one and stepped through it into the warm breeze.

Kerry got up and joined her, leaning on the railing as they looked out over the Atlantic. The moon lit a path through the water and turned the landscape to a silver and dark monochrome that outlined things on the shore in stark detail. "What should we do?"

The dark head shook back and forth. "I don't know. I mean, you're right, it's pretty outlandish. Maybe I can talk to Mark, see if he can dig in places we haven't looked yet." She rested her elbows on the balcony, then straightened a little and nudged Kerry.

"Hmm? What's—oh." Kerry smiled, spotting the two figures coming down the beach hand in hand. "They're so cute." She fitted her hand around Dar's biceps. "I'm so glad things are working out for them."

"Me too," Dar answered softly.

As though sensing their eyes, the two walkers angled their steps up from the water towards the condo, and Dar reached over to key the electronic lock on the garden door for them to enter.

"Hey," Kerry greeted. "It's pretty out, isn't it?"

"Yes, it is," Cecilia agreed. "How was your party?"

"Different."

"Interesting." Dar and Kerry spoke at once, then laughed. "There's some coffee inside, if you're interested," Dar added. "Did you have a nice night?"

"Very nice. Right, Andy?" Ceci nudged the tall, dark haired man next to her, who was sucking on something.

"Yeap," he agreed. "Ah found out something I would never have knowed otherwise tonight. I surely did."

"Really? What?" Kerry asked, as they walked inside and she slid the door shut.

"Knocking a bottle of that there soap into one of them hot tubs makes one hell of a lotta bubbles," Andrew drawled. "I ain't been this clean since I was in diapers."

Dar laughed in pure reflex.

"Oh my god." Kerry clapped a hand over her mouth.

"It was...spectacular," Ceci agreed ruefully. "But not nearly as spectacular as watching your father bolt outside to save a mating peacock in nothing but courage and bubbles." She gave Dar a wry look. "I hope we didn't get you in trouble."

Dar slowly slid down the wall, holding her sides from laughing, as Kerry tried not to snort up her coffee.

"Ah do not consider this that funny," Andrew remarked gruffly. "It is not my fault that bird was yellin' help."

Kerry lost it and ended up on the tile, trying to fend off a busily licking Chino.

"Try to do a good deed, and lookit what happens."

Even Ceci started laughing.

❖ ⌘ ❖ ⌘ ❖ ⌘ ❖

It was the smell of bacon that woke her up. That and coffee, and the soft sounds from the kitchen that indicated activity of a cooking nature. *Mmm.* Kerry sniffed appreciatively then she frowned, as she recognized the warm hold around her as Dar's. Both eyes opened and she glanced around. Sure enough, Dar was snuggled up behind her, one arm tucked around her stomach, peacefully asleep. "Dar?"

"Ungh?"

"Dar?"

A blue eyeball appeared partially. "Huh?"

"You haven't taught Chino to turn on the range, have you?"

That woke her up. "No." Dar lifted her head a little, then let it drop. "Must be Dad."

"Oh." Kerry yawned. "That's a relief." She stretched, then disengaged herself from Dar's hold and rolled out of bed. "Better go give him a hand. We wanted to get out early on the boat today."

"Ker?"

She stopped midway to the door and turned. "Yeah?"

"Might want to put a shirt on." Dar had her eyes closed again, but she was smiling.

Kerry looked down. "Oh." She trudged to Dar's dresser and removed a T-shirt. "Right." She tugged it on over her head and disappeared into the bathroom for a minute, then came back out with a damp face and made her way into the living room. "Dad?" She peered around the doorway and spotted him. "Morning." Chino was fastened to his kneecap, waiting hopefully.

"Yeap." Andrew stood in front of the stove, with a pair of shorts on and one of his sleeveless sweatshirts. "Been that way for a hell of a long time, young lady." He glanced at her. "You might want to be putting that thing on right side up."

Kerry peeked at herself. "Um...I like it this way." She wandered over and peered at the frying pan. "That smells great. But you didn't have to do that." She paused. "We usually do muffins or something for breakfast." She bumped him gently and got a sideways look back. "Mr. Bubbles."

"Do not start, young lady." Andy pointed a spatula at her.

Kerry grinned, then impulsively put her arms around him and gave him a hug. "Okay." She released her hold, went to the cupboard and took out some plates. "Where's Mrs. Roberts?" She had her back turned and missed the look she was getting.

"Scribbling," Andy replied. "Out by the seawall. Be back in shortly."
He studiously pushed a mass of scrambled eggs around.

"Sketching, you mean? Oh, how cool." Kerry put the plates down on
the dining room table, then came back in for cups. "I love watching Dar
draw."

Andrew paused and half turned, giving her a surprised and quizzical
look. "'Scuse me?"

Kerry took the pan he had and scooped its contents into a bowl. "I sit
next to her in meetings. She draws these amazing little animals and things
all over her pad. Bears, horses, boats, you name it. They're so cute." She
cocked her head. "You didn't know?"

Dar's father looked very thoughtful. "Nawp. I sure did not." He
turned his attention back to the stove and flipped some bacon and sau-
sages, which were sizzling there. "I sure did not. Hey, where is my kid
anyhow?"

"Present and accounted for," Dar replied, entering as she pulled her
hair back and knotted it. "You showing off your cooking?"

"Ah do not cook," her father corrected her sternly. "This is yer basic
chow."

"You know, there's nothing wrong with guys cooking," Kerry teased.
"I watch the cooking channel all the time and most of those chefs are
guys."

"You listen here, kumquat..."

"No, really. They are. Not just little wimpy guys either, okay?
They're nice, big burly guys, with deep voices, and beards and—mmffp."
Kerry chewed and swallowed the piece of sausage that had been stuffed
into her mouth. "Mmm. Spicy. I like that." She winked at him, then trotted
towards the door. "I'll go do breakfast call. C'mon, Chino."

It was very quiet after she and the Lab left. Father and daughter eyed
each other, then Dar chuckled softly. "She's something else, isn't she?"

Andy went back to removing the meat from the skillet. "Yeap." He
put a cover over the plate, turned around, and leaned against the counter
to peer at her. "And you're stuck like glue on her ain't ya?"

Dar exhaled lightly. "Looks like it." She picked up the dish and
moved into the living room with it. "We're going to have good weather, I
think." She walked over and leaned against the glass windows, watching
Kerry make her way down to the beach. "We could go out to the island.
Picnic there." Her eyes lifted, to see identical ones reflected back to her in
the window's glare. "Do some fishing?"

"Sure," her father agreed amiably. "I'll drive the boat."

Dar looked at him.

"Hey, I got my license," Andy protested. "I ain't never crashed nothing into no dock, unlike someone else I could name but will not."

Dar scowled. "I did not hit that dock."

"All right. Pulled it over. Knocked it over. Same damn thing," her father teased.

"Give me a break. I was ten," Dar reminded him. "And I wasn't supposed to be driving those double diesels. I could barely see over the console."

"Yeah, yeah. A likely story."

❖ ⌘ ❖ ⌘ ❖ ⌘ ❖

The sand crunched between Kerry's toes as she left the path, and headed towards the water. She could see Cecilia's slight figure down on the jetty and she angled her steps towards the rocks where Dar liked to sit as well. The wash of the waves masked her approach until she was almost there, then she smiled a little hesitantly as the silver blond woman looked up from her work. "Morning."

"Morning," Cecilia responded cordially.

Kerry sat down on the rocks, turning her face towards the light spray and the early morning sky. "It's pretty out here."

The older woman appeared to consider the statement seriously. "Yes, it is," she finally agreed, after some moments of quiet. "I missed it."

"It grows on you." Kerry smiled. "When I first moved here, I hardly ever went to the beach. It was so busy and you don't think of it down in Kendall." Kerry inhaled a lung full of salty air. "Then I found a few places where it was quiet and I used to go there when I needed to think." She paused. "Or when things were bothering me. Sometimes looking out at all that vastness helped, because you realize you're such a small part of what the world is, and you have so much less to worry about than surviving like the crabs."

Ceci gave a slow nod. "That's true." She cocked her head slightly "So you're a deep thinker, hmm?"

Kerry smiled. "Kind of." She waggled her hand. "Sometimes." Her eyes went to the sketch pad. "Ooo, that's nice." It was the end of the rock jetty, with a seagull in close-up, its feathers ruffled in the wind. "I feed them crackers when I come by here in the morning."

"Thanks." Ceci smiled back, resting her hands on the top of the pad. She watched Kerry close her eyes and absorb the sunlight for a moment, then cleared her throat. "Did you come down to dabble your toes in the pond, or..."

"Oh. Sorry." Green eyes appeared, a little sheepish. "Breakfast's ready." She stood up and tugged her oversized shirt down. "It's just such a nice morning."

"Mmhm." Ceci gathered her things and hopped off the rocks, then followed Kerry back up the beach. "It'll be nice to get back in the water," she ventured. "Especially on a nice, sunny day like this. The colors are very vivid if you stay close to the surface."

"Oh, yes." Kerry turned, her eyes lighting up. "I was on a really shallow reef just across from here not long ago and an entire school of yellow and purple fish rolled right over me. I felt like I was inside a rainbow." She held her hands out. "Just beams of light coming down through the water and hitting everything and then these clown fish swam by. It was incredible."

"Have you seen lobsters?"

"They're green. I was surprised." Kerry laughed. "And they're strong, too. Dar handed me a puffer fish the last time we were down. Scared the heck out of me for a minute."

"Did you learn to dive here?" The silver gray eyes watched her curiously. "I guess you did. Not much to see up in the Great Lakes."

"Dar taught me, yes." She nodded. "They do have diving up in Michigan, but for one thing, you have to wear dry suits, and for another, I'd be kind of nervous to see what's at the bottom of Lake Michigan." They both laughed. "I spent a lot of time sailing on top of it, though." They entered the back garden and headed up the stairs.

"Me too." Ceci reached for the door. "We spent summers up there." She pulled the door open. "We'll have to compare notes."

Kerry smiled. "All right. Let's do that." She entered, almost crashing into Dar who was standing right there. "Whoa!" Chino scrambled past her and crouched at Dar's feet, depositing a piece of driftwood. "Oh, look, she brought you a present."

"Thanks, Chino." Dar bent down and picked the wood up. She juggled it as they all walked into the dining room where Andrew was sprawled, examining a bit of machinery. Chairs scraped as they took their seats, then the soft clinking of dishes as they served themselves.

Then an awkward little silence fell. Kerry could see the discomfort on Dar's face and she sighed, having spent her share of meals across a less than cordial table. It wasn't, she was glad to realize, her problem this time. "Dar, do you think we can dive the shallow reef off the island? I want to try out my new camera."

"Sure." Dar gave her a pathetically grateful look as she buttered her toast. "Did you get film? I have a light you can use."

"With the sun, I hope I won't need it," Kerry replied, busying herself with her eggs.

"Should always carry a light. You kin get lost real easy down there," Andrew commented around a mouthful. "Get people thinking you're a fish."

Dar almost snorted her coffee. "Nah. Long as I've been diving, I've yet to see a phosphorescent pink and yellow fish with blue gear and a bright red tank."

Andrew looked at Kerry in aghast shock, then at his daughter. "Ye're joking."

The dark head shook back and forth. "Nope. Wait till you see the flippers. Trust me. I can spot her at forty fathoms."

"Lord."

"I was going to get those neat neon tracer lights around my BC, but Dar convinced me the weight of the power pack wasn't worth it," Kerry added, with a straight face.

Andrew covered his eyes, getting a chuckle from his wife. "Oh mah god." He peeked at Kerry. "Pink?"

"Hey." Kerry waved a fork at him. "I'm a girl. I'm allowed to wear pink if I want to." She glanced at Dar. "At least it's better than my karate gi. That got pink because I accidentally washed Chino's collar with it."

Ceci covered her mouth, as her shoulders shook.

Dar cleared her throat, then took a sip of coffee, feeling the atmosphere relax considerably. *Okay.* She let her thoughts settle. *Maybe this was doable after all. They were okay. Kerry was doing fine, and Mom's...* She got caught looking across the table, meeting gray eyes that locked with hers for a split second, then dropped.

Mmm.

I can do this. She felt a hand reach for hers under the table, and met it, tangling her fingers with Kerry.

We can do this.

❖ ⌘ ❖ ⌘ ❖ ⌘ ❖

They went to the marina in Dar's golf cart, which she only barely wrested from her father's clutches. Their gear was already stowed on board, so they had only the fresh food from the market and their beach bags to bring over the gangplank, as the sturdy boat rocked gently in the morning air.

Andrew picked up the bags and edged down into the cabin with them, as Ceci gazed around curiously at the well appointed Bertram. "Nice." Her eyes flicked briefly to Dar, who was checking the various things on the console.

"It's a little much," Dar commented absently. "We fit the back there with a fold down ladder and a hook for diving." She peered down. "You untying us?"

"Got it." Kerry had loosened the front rope and was climbing around to the second, unlashing it and jumping on board. "Go for it, Dar."

Dar started the engines and trimmed them, cocking her head to listen as she adjusted the throttles. She liked the big boat, actually. It had power to spare and enough luxury that she could appreciate the on board shower and the refrigerator after a long day of diving. She and Kerry often took advantage of the compact bed, then brought out a few candles, and ate a cold dinner by their light, under the blanket of stars overhead.

She backed slowly out, then swung the bow around and edged her way through the marina, which was starting to stir as other boat owners got the same idea from the beautiful, almost cloudless weather. A light breeze picked up and pushed her hair back and she exhaled, determined to enjoy the day as much as possible.

Chapter
26

Ceci finished her tour around the upper deck and descended into the cabin, breathing in a rich scent of polished wood and salt. She paused just inside and her eyes roamed the small, but neatly arranged space and she found herself nodding. "I like this."

"Whole lotta extra doo dads and whatnot," Andrew replied, from where he'd set down the bags and stowed them. "Half expected t'find a damn computer set up in here last time."

Ceci chuckled and wandered past him, examining the compact kitchen with interest, then poking her head in the tiny bedroom, and it's functional, if cramped bathroom. "This is adorable, Andy. I can't picture May paddling around in it, but it's nice."

"Huh." Andrew put the basket down on the counter and opened a cabinet, finding a tape player inside. "Figgers. Go out to the best natural entertainment on God's earth and y'gotta drag along one of these." He turned. "And you tell me what need there is for a damn refrigerator?"

Ceci opened it, then peeked inside the small freezer.

"Cooler's good enough for sandwiches. Damn thing's a waste of power. I surely don't know what the devil that woman was thinking of."

"There's chocolate ice cream in here," his wife mentioned. "Does that qualify as a good reason?"

Andy leaned over the counter and looked. "Huh." He gave her a squinty-eyed glare. "Ah think that is a loaded question, Mrs. Roberts." They smiled, then Andy fiddled with a piece of tie down and chewed his lower lip. "This all right with you?" His eyes encompassed the boat and its other occupants.

Cecilia paused, then nodded. "It's hard." She lowered her voice. "I know Dar's uncomfortable. I think I am too, but we have to start some-where." She looked around. "Besides. We all love doing this—we'll get through it all right, Andy."

"Right."

"You know, I really like Kerry," Ceci offered, a touch hesitantly. "She's a nice person."

"Yeap. Me too." Andy seemed uncomfortable for a moment. "Reminds me...um...don't get shocked or nothing, but she calls me dad." He glanced up at his wife, who blinked in surprise. "Family means a lot to her. Didn't see no harm in it."

"No, no of course not," Ceci murmured. "I'm sure that whole issue with her parents bothers her." She felt a curious sympathy for Kerry, almost a kinship, having gone through more or less the same gauntlet when she'd married Andrew.

Though her family had never disowned her. Not that it would have mattered—not then and not now—she'd refused all their overtures, all their proffered help, all their mock sympathy during the struggles they'd gone through over the years, preferring to work through the rough spots on her own.

A matter of pride, really.

Only after Andrew was gone and nothing mattered anymore, had she taken what was offered, letting their smug sympathy wash past her. "It's so strange, Andy. Even after what I did to Dar, I can still stand here and wonder how they could just...turn their backs on her simply for being in love with the wrong person."

"Wrong person?" Andy's eyebrows rose.

"You know what I mean." She showed a faint smile. "I don't think it's the wrong person, but from their viewpoint, it must seem like that."

"No excuse." The square jaw moved. "Yer folks didn't take a cotton to me cause I'm a Southern Baptist hick from the swamp with less education than the family dog." He pointed up the small set of stairs. "Dar ain't none of that."

"I know, Andy." Ceci put a hand on his arm. "But not everyone's as accepting as you are."

"Damn fool idiots," he muttered. "Ain't got the sense God gave a gopher, or they'd realize if'n they were lucky enough to find someone t'care about them like those two do for each other..." He paused. "Or like I do fer you. What the hell difference does them body parts make?" He was upset and it showed. "I'd like to..." He paused and sighed. "It ain't right."

Ceci chafed his fingers. "My crusader." She lifted his hand and brushed her lips against it. "I'm glad Kerry decided to call you dad."

He scowled.

"You're such a good one."

The scowl deepened.

"C'mon. Let's go up on deck." Ceci moved out from behind the counter and tugged his hand. "Where are we going, anyway?"

"Dar's island." Andy straightened and followed her. "Nice little place. Sand, few trees 'bout it." He put a hand on her back. "Had their little joiny thing out there."

Ceci stopped in mid step. "Their what?"

Her husband paused uncertainly. "Got together, few friends of theirs, and some pastor guy Kerry knew back home. He said a few things. You know, like a wedding, sort of, but not...um..." He faltered as he saw her expression. "I got pictures if you'd like t'see them?"

The slim woman's shoulders dropped a little, but she resumed her climb. "Sure. I'd like that." She felt an irrational pang of loss, at missing an event that never in her wildest dreams occurred to her would happen. "Sounds like it was nice."

They emerged into the sun, then glanced up to see Kerry standing on the flying bridge next to Dar, one arm draped casually over her and her head resting on a tanned shoulder. The wind whipped dark and pale hair back, tangling it as the boat raced out of the cut, and headed into the Atlantic.

"Yeah," Andy replied softly. "It was. Kerry said this real nice poem she had. Then Dardar sang something. I liked it."

"Is she a poet?"

"Yeap. But she don't talk much about it." Andy cleared his throat a little. "Hey. Don't you two fall asleep up thar."

Two heads turned. "We're not." Kerry smiled, detaching herself from her taller companion. "We'll be out by the reef in about ten minutes. Time to check gear, I guess." She clambered down to join them and went to the equipment lockers on either side of the stern. "We keep our stuff on board mostly."

"It ain't really pink..." Andy ambled over and looked down. "Oh mah god." He clapped a hand over his eyes. "You will scare every living thing for a nautical mile with that stuff on."

"Tch. I do not." Kerry pulled her BC and regulator out and the thin half wetsuit she used. "Fish love me. I can't get rid of them, in fact." She gave Ceci a shy look. "Did you get everything you needed? We've got some extra stuff if you didn't."

"Ah, no." Cecilia opened the next locker and tugged at the handles of a new, fairly well stuffed dive bag. "I think Andy covered just about everything. In fact, I'm pretty sure I've got enough equipment here to dive the Antarctic."

"Ah did not." Andy took the bag from her and swung it over to the deck. "You are surely exaggerating." He unfastened the grips and unzipped it, exposing a new set of diving gear. "Nothin' extra there."

Kerry knelt beside him. "What's this?"

"Multi range depth gauge."

"Um. We're diving a twenty foot deep reef, Dad."

"That is not the point, young lady."

"Uh huh." Kerry poked around. "What's this?"

"Spear gun."

"In case of dangerous clown fish?"

"You can not be too prepared in the sea," Andy stated firmly.

"Uh huh. Mrs. Roberts?" Kerry looked up. "Please. Try not to point it at anything pink, okay?"

Ceci chuckled. "Oh no. I'm not taking that thing. The last time I had my hands on a spear gun..."

"You shot a Kodiak out from under Dad," Dar's voice drifted down, a note of amusement in her tone. "Glad the hull's fiberglass on this one."

The atmosphere tangibly relaxed, as the sun rose and the ocean's spray doused them. "That's right," Ceci admitted. "And I'm really glad I was far enough away to only puncture the bottom lining and not anything more...um," Andy's eyes widened and his grizzled brows rose, "more sensitive."

Kerry laughed at the look on Andy's face. "Okay. So, we've got a gauge, we've got a spear gun. What else?" She pulled out a large yellow object. "Wh—"

"That is a light," Andy growled. "And before you go telling me it's daytime out, young lady, Ah am going to use it to hunt out some spiny critters."

"Right," Kerry agreed, with an impish smile.

"Do you not have your own stuff to check out?"

She took the hint. "Okay. I have to put the batteries in my flippers anyway."

Andy sighed. "Lord. Ah will never live this down," he grumbled. "If any of the guys saw me down there with that glow in the dark getup..."

"I'd distract them for you, honey." Ceci planted a kiss on the top of his head. "I'll tell them about your silk undies," she whispered in his ear.

A deep, aggrieved, sigh. "Might as well get me one of them pink wetsuits."

❖ ⌘ ❖ ⌘ ❖ ⌘ ❖

The boat rocked very gently on the surface as Dar leaped over the railing and landed in the shallow water with a splash. She waded through the hip deep sea and tied the boat off securely to the wooden pylon she'd brought out there so many years before.

A seagull watched her from the sandy shore and she flipped a bit of wood at him before she turned and started back, stretching her arms out into the warm sun. On board the boat, Kerry stood in her phosphorescent glory, pale head cocked to one side as she watched Dar's parents suit up.

She turned as Dar approached, and went to move the ladder over the side, but Dar waved her back, grabbed the railing, and pulled herself aboard. "Nice day."

"Boy, is it." Kerry smiled with enthusiasm. "Nice and calm, no clouds. It's going to be gorgeous down there." She hefted her newest toy, an underwater camera, then set it on the bench. "Help me get this on?"

Dar lifted her tank and BC as she got into it, then adjusted the hoses as Kerry wrapped the waist strap around her and buckled the front stays. "Whoops. Forgot the weight belt."

"I've got it." Dar picked up the web belt studded with pink weights and circled Kerry with her arms, handing her the ends in front. "There you go."

"Thanks." Kerry buckled the belt and hopped up and down a bit, shifting her shoulders to settle the weight of the tank. It was heavy, of course. Fully charged with compressed air the tank weighed close to thirty pounds and, added to the seven or eight pounds of her BC and regulator and the twelve pounds on her weight belt, it felt like she was an argonaut of old, in their metal shoes, waiting to descend into the depths.

Dar slipped on her own belt and tightened it, then crouched and got her arms into her BC and buckled it, then stood, leaning forward a little until she had all the straps fastened. Then she straightened and watched her father fussing over her mother's new gear. "Dad, this isn't a Cousteau expedition."

"Aw, put yer head in the water, Dardar." Andrew adjusted a gauge for the fourth time.

Cecilia patted her side and gave him a faintly amused look. "Andy, I really do remember how to do this." She edged away from his tinkering and sat down on the back bench and looked down. "Oh...look, a barracuda!"

"Wh—?" Andrew moved his wetsuited body over and searched the water. "Lemme check that out." He vaulted over the end of the boat and disappeared under the water with a remarkably small splash.

Dar regarded the ripples, then picked up her father's gear and set it on the wooden platform she'd had built on to the back of the boat, making it easier to enter and exit the water. She flipped the diving ladders down into the surf and gave her mother a look. "Barracuda, huh?"

Cecilia pushed her silver blond hair back. "Mmhmm."

"C'mon, Ker." Dar held back a chuckle, as she fitted her mask on and picked up her fins. "Let's get wet."

Kerry joined her at the back of the boat. "Don't you think we'd better wait for your father to check out that barracuda?" She watched Dar go to the platform and slip her fins on, then put a hand over her mask and step off into the water. "I guess not."

"There wasn't really one," Ceci volunteered, with a wry smile. "I just wanted a few minutes to put my mask on."

Kerry blinked. "Oh." She held her camera and put a hand over her own mask. "Overprotective huh?"

"Just a little." Dar's mother smiled. "In a nice kind of way."

"I know." Kerry nodded. "It's hereditary." She took a step off the boat and entered the water, the pleasantly cool shock quickly fading to a familiar, comfortable weather.

Another reason not to dive in Michigan. Even in summer it didn't come close to the eighty-five degrees she was now descending in.

Kerry released her mask and looked around, adjusting to the always odd sensation of being completely underwater quickly. The sun cut through the waves and the visibility was very good, providing her with an excellent view all around her at greens and blues, and ochres, cut through by fish and the irregular surface of the sea bottom under her. She spotted Dar floating nearby, reclining in the water with her knees half bent and her hands folded on her stomach. Periodically, a small stream of bubbles emerged from her regulator, and behind the silvered glass of her mask, Kerry could see the blue eyes roving with interest around her.

Getting used to the regulator was the hardest part. It was a soft rubber mouthpiece that fit between her teeth, providing air on demand when she inhaled through her mouth. The air was dry, and the biggest problem Kerry had with the entire affair was getting very thirsty.

Ironic. Here she was, totally immersed in water and her biggest worry was where to get a drink.

Dar motioned her over and pointed to a dark form that was moving through the water back towards the boat. Kerry adjusted her gear again, loosened in the different stress of the water, and swam towards her lover, turning her head to watch Andrew approach, take one last look around then head for the surface with liquid, undulating motions.

Wow. Kerry ended up next to Dar, and unfastened her writing slate and underwater crayon. She scribbled on the surface quickly. He's like a fish.

Dar nodded, tendrils of escaped hair bobbing. She cupped her hand and made a swimming motion, then pointed as her father reentered the water with her mother right behind him. He had his gear on now, a minimalist rig that was mostly padded straps and pockets, with a streamlined tank. It was all black, of course, as were his fins and mask, and he moved through the water in a totally natural way.

Surprisingly, Cecilia looked also very much at home, despite the fact that it must have been years since she'd done this. She adjusted her gear much the way Kerry had, then started off, peering around with interest and obvious enjoyment.

Your mom is having fun.

Dar couldn't really smile, with the regulator in place. She took the slate. It was the one part of his world she could share fully.

Ah. Kerry nodded in understanding. Then Dar moved closer, took the slate back, and tucked it into its Velcro fastening at her hip. She turned to find a tiny mouthpiece held out to her. Attached to it was a tube, which went to a slim pack she'd thought was extra padding around the back of Dar's tank. Curious, she spit out her regulator and fitted the soft rubber inside her mouth, then cautiously sucked on it, her courage rewarded with cool, sweet water. "Rgle!" She looked at Dar in delight.

Dar looked smugly pleased with herself and her new toy. She waited for Kerry to finish her drink then she rolled over in the water and swam over the reef towards a thick cluster of the colorful rocks where schools of fish swarmed.

Kerry exhaled in wonder, as the sun's rays cut through the sea and lit up the reef like something out of a dream. She lifted her camera up and took a few lazy shots, then let a bit of air out of her BC to sink closer to the living coral.

Never touch it. Dar had drilled that into her, and as she swam along a foot over the reef, she caught the motion of her lover tucking her trailing gear up so it wouldn't strike the fragile surface. She slowed her pace and watched the rock with interest, spotting a tiny bit of motion and peering closer to see the almost clear, tiny shrimp skittering over the surface. A silver shape came into view and she turned her head to see a clown fish chasing a tiny purple and orange fellow by, as a flat, omipototent grouper observed, swimming slowly past Kerry with a wary eye on her.

Ooo. A school of silver fish, tiny and nervous came right at her and she went still, letting them split around her, their tiny bodies brushing with the lightest of touches over her skin. A touch on her arm distracted her and she followed Dar's tug towards one side of the reef, looking where the taller woman pointed.

A ray. Not just a little one either, six feet wide at the least and settled into the silt, depending on camouflage to prevent its being eaten. Dar pulled her closer, and she put a hand out very tentatively when her companion did, touching the surface of the ray with nervous fingers. It was soft, almost velvety, and she could feel the flinch as the ray felt the contact.

Dar floated closer, running her hands along the animal's back and over the rounded edge of the front of its fins, surprised when the ray decided to vacate its nest for quieter waters. It lifted off the sand and moved away powerfully, taking the human that was annoying it along with it.

Kerry focused quickly and snapped off a few shots of the ray towing Dar, until it settled to the ground again and Dar released her hold, floated up and turned around with both thumbs up. A motion caught her attention again and she turned in the water to watch Dar's parents exploring the other end of the reef, with Ceci floating delicately over the rocks and Andrew circling around her with his supple, relaxed movements. Kerry noticed they'd left the spear gun behind.

They drifted closer together, then Dar suddenly ducked towards the rock, grabbed something, then headed for her father. Andrew looked up and spotted what she was holding, then back-finned, shaking a finger at her in mock warning. Kerry swam closer, then realized it was a lobster in Dar's hand. One with tiny, grasping claws she was aiming right towards Andy.

He tumbled in the water, then flipped over and tried to get behind his daughter, who rolled right with him, plopping the lobster right against his chest.

The lobster, strangely, resented this, and grabbed and flapped, making the ex-SEAL squirm in mid-water, batting at the creature with his hands until it swam off, glaring daggers at Dar with its beady little stalked eyes.

Dar had exactly ten seconds to laugh, then she had to make a hole in the water, because she had a tall, dangerous looking creature coming after her, aiming to do scurrilous things to her unprotected kneecaps. Dar took off, racing ahead of her pursuer with powerful strokes in a curving path around the reef.

Kerry stayed in the middle of the curve, resting on her back in the water and snapping shots of the action as it progressed. Andrew was faster, due to his longer length and powerful kick, but Dar was more flexible and she turned and whirled in mid-stroke so quickly he kept missing her when he lunged. Ceci found an empty spot of sea bottom to perch on and watched, shaking her head slowly as her husband and child tumbled around like a pair of demented manatees.

Kerry took a few shots of her, then swam over, settled on the silt and tucked her hands around her knees. Ceci turned her head, then lifted a hand and opened it, revealing a beautiful cone shaped shell, covered in what looked like hieroglyphs.

Kerry took a picture of it, then glanced up to see gray eyes watching her with reserved interest. She pulled out her slate. It's nice today.

Ceci nodded in agreement then took the slate. The only thing it lacks is ice tea.

Kerry grinned and held up a finger, then handed the older woman her camera and dove into the chase above her.

❖ ⌘ ❖ ⌘ ❖ ⌘ ❖

Nobody was really sure whose idea the campfire was. But the island provided enough dry, fragrant wood to make one and the sandy ground seemed safe enough to light it on. They'd taken hunks of dead coral, though, just in case and made a circle around the flames.

It was an almost surreal scene, Ceci decided. A tiny island in the middle of the coastal Atlantic, with a view on one side of nothing but black sea broken only by the faint buoy lights. On the other side, the sky-line of the city spread to either side, the lights of the beach hotels going north and the outlines of the city buildings to her south.

Above her, the stars floated, obscured by clouds drifting by, and far off against the horizon a storm was brewing, where intermittent lightning burst into view.

It was gorgeous. She leaned against an amiable palm tree and felt the warm sand between her toes, as the breeze brought a whiff of the spicy, boiling mixture in the pot they'd jury rigged over the fire, filled with fresh things captured from the nearby water.

Dar sloshed up out of the water, adding one last thing to the pot with a piratical grin. "Got one." She pulled her mask off and continued on, dropping her snorkel and mesh bag on a towel and hesitating, then taking a seat relatively near her mother. Kerry was on the boat fixing up some-thing or other and Andrew was still hunting under the waves.

Ceci eyed the 'smooth, tanned back an arm's length or so away and considered her options. The day had been pleasant, really—though they were both uncomfortable with each other, Andy and Kerry were doing their respective darndest to smooth things out. The older woman paused, then reached behind her and picked up a folded towel, glancing at it a moment before she cleared her throat gently. "Dar?"

The dark head turned, firelight glinting off pale, wary eyes which met hers, then focused on the towel she held out. "Thanks." Dar took the fabric and leaned back, opening up her posture a little. They eyed each other. "You...um," Dar shifted, "might want to think about some aloe."

"Ah, yes." Cecilia nodded ruefully. "I feel as red as those lobsters are going to be in there."

"Mmm. I think I got a little burned too," Dar admitted, stretching her long legs out in the sand and wiping them dry.

Wet, disheveled, and covered in sand, Ceci found this version of her daughter far more familiar than the one she'd been dealing with. Dar's hair was longer now, beyond shoulder length, and her body lengthened and grown into a woman's proportions that still held a distinct note of her tough, combative youth.

A gulf of time was between them. Ceci studied the strong profile, sadly at a loss for words.

Dar looked up at her suddenly. "Something wrong?"

A gust of cool wind made her shiver, and the words escaped without much thought behind them. "I keep waiting for the alarm to ring and wake me up," she murmured, regretting the statement almost as it came out of her mouth. She looked away.

Dar's own eyes dropped to the sand. *Damn, this was so hard.* She sucked in a breath. "Yeah." Her fingers found a tiny, perfect scallop in the sand. "It's a lot to adjust to."

Ceci leaned her forearms on her knees and rested her chin on them. "This must be complicating your life," she remarked wryly, rewarded with the faintest hint of a smile, that wrinkled the skin at the corner of her daughter's mouth and eyes.

Dar tilted her head in acknowledgement. "It's not an unwelcome complication," Dar replied, shifting so they almost faced each other. "I'm glad things worked out."

Worked out. What an outstandingly understated way to consider a life changing event so vast she couldn't even begin to encompass it. "Well, thank you for making that phone call." She cleared her throat. "Though I know you didn't do it for my benefit."

Pale eyes peered at her from under dark brows. "Don't assume that." The already low voice deepened. "At least credit me the ability to do the right thing when I know what it is." But the tone wasn't angry, merely wistful.

Cecilia felt off balance, yet again. She sighed. "I didn't mean you wouldn't, Dar. It just occurred to me, that, given what happened between us, I don't expect any favors from you." She sensed the restless motion and half expected Dar to get up and leave—something her daughter had always done when in a confrontation she didn't want to deal with.

But instead Dar turned further around and moved closer, her gaze now intent and strangely compelling. "Well," a faintly warm note crept in, "I've made a reputation out of doing the unexpected."

Ceci merely blinked, unsure of what to say.

"I can't change the past," her daughter stated flatly, then hesitated. "Though I would change parts of it, if I could."

The fire crackled softly, and a splash was heard off the beach. "I would too," Ceci murmured.

They looked at each other quietly.

Another splash and they turned to see Andrew emerging from the water, the fire outlining his burly wetsuit covered form. He shook himself, then trudged up the beach. "Smells damn nice round here."

"I'll second that." Kerry stepped carefully down the floating bridge Dar had built, carrying an armful of stuff and a basket. The blond woman had a white cotton overshirt on, her sun darkened skin showing vividly against it, and her hair pulled back into a knot. "Dar, can you grab this?"

"Sure." Dar scrambled to her feet and hopped onto the wooden surface. She took the basket from her lover and opened the top. "Ah. Plates."

"Well, yeah." Kerry stepped past her, with a chuckle. "Did you think we were going to just stick our hands in that pot and start chewing on whatever we pulled out?"

"Sure."

"Yeap."

Dar and her father exchanged glances.

Ceci laughed softly, pushed herself to her feet and walked over to join them around the fire. They'd set mats down a safe distance from the flames, and Kerry put her burdens on top of them and poked at the pot's contents.

"Ooo." A very spicy, very intense scent emerged. "I think I'm in love."

"Coulda tolja that...oh, ya mean with that stuff," Andrew drawled, tousling his grizzled hair dry and snapping Kerry in the butt with the fabric as he ambled past.

"Yeoow...hey!" Kerry hopped around the fire, getting off balance and stumbling right into Dar's arms. "Whoa, thanks." She caught herself. "Hey. You're all wet." Her voice caught a little at the odd sensation of the cool dampness warming as their bodies joined.

A dark brow lifted slightly.

"Tch." Kerry blushed, invisible in the dark but not to Dar's light touch on her. "Give me a hand with this stuff. Can we put the bits right in a bowl? I brought some."

"Now, don't get nervous." Dar's whisper tickled her ear, and her breathing quickened a bit.

"I'm not." Kerry knelt and pulled the round, wooden bowls out. "What makes you think I am? I don't think I am. I just want you to give me a hand divvying this stuff up, what makes you think..."

"You're babbling," Dar returned. "Relax. It's just my parents, not yours."

"Oh." Kerry clamped her jaw shut and handed Dar a set of long chef's tongs. "Right. Well, if I had to imagine my parents sitting in the sand on an island, Dar, my brain would explode. So," she cleared her throat and raised her voice, "I have some Spanish rice in that pot." She looked up to where Ceci was settling. "Yeah. There, and in that other one is some steamed broccoli." She stuck a tongue out at the face Dar was making. "It's not for you, don't worry." She looked over Dar's shoulder. "Or you either. I know better." She pointed a long handled fork at Andrew.

They sat down with their bowls of steaming saffron colored rice, covered with spicy seafood bits ranging from grouper to shrimp, with chunks of the lobsters Dar and Andy had tickled out sitting on top.

"Mmm." Ceci poured a mug of the cold, iced cider and handed it to her husband, then took one for herself. "Good stuff." The rice was fluffy and perfect, and the broccoli crisp and fresh, and a nice counterpoint to fish, her exception to a usually vegetarian diet.

Or maybe it was just the fresh air and an entire day of activity that made everything taste so wonderful.

Or something.

It really was like a dream. But the longer it went on, the more she realized it was one she was stuck with the good—like this lobster— along with the bad—like sand sticking to parts of her where sand didn't belong, and like her prickly offspring.

Too much color. Too much emotion and sensations. Making chaos of her formerly orderly existence and filling it with complications and issues. Ceci sighed in wry contentment. It felt very much like home.

Andy removed a very pink shrimp and offered it to her, and she bit down, feeling the crisp flesh give way and release a burst of spice into her mouth.

Nope. Nothing bland here.

Dar leaned back against a big piece of driftwood and settled her bowl in the crook of her arm, then reached out and gave Kerry's shirt back a light tug. They'd been running around so much all day, she'd hardly had a chance to spend any time near her lover and her body missed that.

"Mmm?" Kerry turned her head then saw the invitation in Dar's eyes. "Um..." *Eeek.* Getting all cuddly in front of the older generation still made her a bit squeamish, but... She scooted back and settled in the curve of her lover's arm, relaxing as it curled around her and gave her a squeeze. Shyly, she glanced at Ceci and Andrew, glad to see only a look of amused indulgence on their faces.

Not that she really expected any different, but you never knew. People said things and thought they meant them, but when they were hit in the face with reality that sometimes flew out the window. She speared a piece of broccoli and bit into it, as the tender skin tensed around her face and shoulders. Her body was a little sore from all the diving and swimming and she suspected she was going to pay for her fun tomorrow, but it had been a great day. She'd gotten some really fantastic pictures, everyone seemed to have fun, and she'd seen signs that Dar and her mother were cautiously approaching each other.

Kerry sighed and wiggled her toes, enjoying the warmth of the fire against the breeze coming off the water. She felt overheated and grubby and was sure she had seaweed in some highly unlikely places, but she couldn't think of anywhere else she'd rather be.

Chapter
27

Dar was curled up on the cabin's small couch, studying some small, encrusted metal bits she'd recovered from the bottom. The drone of the engines was almost soothing. If she really tried, she could put out of her mind the fact that her father was driving the big boat, after giving her a taste of what it was like to try and say no to those big, blue eyes.

A soft sound made her look up to see her mother coming into the cabin, her hair so completely in disarray it appeared she'd stuck a finger into one of the twenty amp sockets in the sidewalls. "I think your father just swamped a Sunfish."

Dar winced.

Ceci flexed her bare toes and continued across the floor. "This is a lovely setup." Her hands found a place in the pockets of the soft white cotton pants. "Very functional."

Dar spread her arms out and looked around the small cabin. "Yeah. The first time I saw it, it seemed just far too rich, but after I checked it out, most of the trimmings are there for a purpose." She stroked the wood. "This weathers well, the fabrics are designed for humidity and sealed, the kitchen gear is nothing fancy. It's a good working rig."

Her mother perched on the edge of the counter, which lifted up and doubled as storage. She folded her arms and looked around, nodding. "You could live on this thing, really."

"The thought's occurred to me," Dar admitted. "Except using a sat hook up to download mail's a bitch." Her name being called made her look up. "Yeah?"

"D—oh, there you are." Kerry scrambled down into the space. "Would you p—oh, sorry, hi. Am I interrupting?" She paused, giving Cecilia an apologetic look.

"No, no. We were just discussing the boat." She lifted a slim hand.

"Go on."

"I'm trying to describe that weird fish we saw, and your father keeps trying to tell me it was a parrot fish. I keep telling him it wasn't. Do me a favor, would you? Draw it so I can show him?"

"Didn't you get a picture of it?" Dar queried, sitting up and putting her forearms on table.

"Yes, but that's got to wait for developing." Kerry sat down next to her with a pad and pencil. "Please?"

"Oh, all right." The dark haired woman gave her an indulgent look and accepted the pencil. She propped her head up with her other hand as she moved the pad into a more comfortable position. "This was the one with the red and blue stripes and the pig nose, right?"

"Roman nose."

"Well, I always heard Romans were pigs." Dar smiled. "Okay. I remember that one. You flipped upside down to take its picture."

"That's the one." Kerry eased away and slipped into the kitchen area, giving Ceci a smile as she poured herself a cup of coffee from the thermos clamped on the counter. "Would you like some?"

"Sure, thank you," Ceci answered absently, her entire peripheral attention focused on the powerful hand moving the pencil across the paper with sure, confident scratches.

An eye formed.

A round body tapered in back, and properly three-dimensional.

A wide, sturdy tail.

Feathery fins caught in mid motion by a knowledgeable hand.

Cecilia's eyes followed the dark lines flowing easily from Dar's imagination, feeling like she'd just walked into a room and been greeted by a little gray man from Mars. Wearing a bow tie.

Speaking French.

For thirty years she'd been convinced the only thing she and her off-spring shared was a mutual antagonism and a grudging similarity in musical tastes.

And now here she sat, watching a bit of herself come alive and emerge from those long, tapered fingertips.

Dear Goddess.

A wisp of steam warmed her hand, and she started, then looked at a pair of warm green eyes over a cup of coffee. "Oh," Ceci murmured, taking the cup. "Thank you."

"You're welcome." Kerry's voice had deepened slightly. She circled the table and settled next to Dar, sipping her coffee and watching her fish emerge. "That's exactly the one."

"Uh huh. Thought so. No way was it a parrot," Dar muttered, sketching in the curious markings on the fish, in a light phosphorescence. "Did you see that little gold triangle, just above the gills?" She made a few last additions, then pushed the pad over. "Okay?"

Kerry regarded the pretty fish with a smile, then lifted her eyes and met Ceci's. "What do you think?"

A hot flush tingled Dar's skin, as she realized she'd forgotten that her mother had been standing there watching. A half dozen defensive words filled her mouth clamoring for her tongue's attention as she tensed and half turned, her tired mind scrambling to deal with the unexpected embarrassment.

Ceci pulled the pad over and studied it. "Well, I'm no expert but I think you're right. It's not a parrotfish," she remarked softly. "It is a really nice sketch, though." Her eyes slipped up to meet Dar's, finding her daughter with such a deer in the headlights expression she almost started laughing.

But no.

Instead, she looked at Kerry, whose mossy green eyes held a definite twinkle in them. *Why, that little stinker.* Ceci felt a jolt of surprise. *She did that on purpose.*

"Thanks, Dar." Kerry captured the pad and stood, then leaned over and brushed the top of her lover's head with her lips. "Be right back." She bolted out the cabin door and leaped for the ladder, scaled it, and hopped up onto the flying bridge with a chortle. "Bingo!"

Andrew looked up from his instruments and grinned rakishly at her. "Very smooth, kumquat. Fell for it, did she?"

"Hhhhook, line and ssssinker." Kerry did a little gopher dance, then showed him the pad. "See?"

Andrew glanced at the picture. "Wall, spin my tail and call me spooky. Wouldja look at that?" He tilted the small instrument light towards the pad and examined the fish. His eyebrows jerked, then knit. "Cec say anything?"

"She said it was a good sketch," Kerry replied. "And that it wasn't a parrotfish." She poked Andy in the ribs. "Did I do good?"

He ruffled her hair affectionately. "Hell, yes. C'mere, since you like this so damn much." He gave her an awkward hug and a pat on the back. "Wanna help me steer this thing?"

"Sure." Kerry peered into the pitch darkness. "Is that the buoy? Yeah. Hey, I always wanted to do something..."

"What?"

"This." Kerry shoved both the throttles forward and the bow lifted as the wind suddenly screamed past her. "Oh yeah."

"Son of a..."

❖ ⌘ ❖ ⌘ ❖ ⌘ ❖

Kerry trudged into the living room, her Tweety Bird shirt draped over one shoulder and a bottle of aloe lotion in one hand, meeting Dar coming out of her office, followed by Chino. "Hey. Can I beg a favor?"

Dar observed the nearly naked woman with two hiked brows. "Beg?" she murmured, eyes going a little round.

"Tch." Kerry butted her head against one of her friend's shoulders. "Slather me, please?" She held out the bottle. "I feel like I'm being compressed in saran wrap."

Dar took the aloe and squeezed some out, then delicately turned her subject around and spread it. "So. Did you win the bet?" she asked casually, tracing a damp, green line over the pink area across the back of Kerry's neck.

"What bet?" Kerry murmured.

"The fish," Dar drawled, her breath brushing against sensitive skin.

"What fi—? Oh." Kerry turned her head and peeked. "Um..."

"You," Dar licked her ear, "are such a little meddler."

The blond woman assumed a contrite look. "Are you mad at me?"

Dar let her stew for a few minutes, while she finished her spreading, feeling the shoulders under her fingers shift and straighten. "I should be. You caught me so off guard with that. Not a really pleasant feeling." She turned Kerry around to face her and started on the sunburned skin there, aware of the grave eyes searching her face.

"You'd have been too self conscious otherwise," Kerry almost whispered. "I just wanted her to see you have part of her in you."

Dar didn't answer, her face shifting in thought.

"I-I haven't known either of you that long but, I sort of sat down and thought about it." Kerry's nervousness came out in a torrent of words. "And what it seems to me is that you and your dad are so close. You look so much alike, and all that stuff, I thought maybe you... I mean, I thought if your mother could see there is this bit...I—" Kerry had to stop because Dar kissed her. When they parted, Kerry let out a tiny sigh. "I have this 'solve everyone else's problems' gene that just kicks in sometimes." She shrugged. "Besides, I like your mom."

Dar leaned her forehead against her partner's. "I noticed you two seemed to get along," she murmured. "Listen, Kerry. My mother and I have thirty years of whitewater rapids behind us." She kissed the sunburned skin lightly. "And there are some things that just can't be fixed."

Kerry looked at her sadly.

"At least not right away," Dar hastily amended. "Though," her brows knitted, "there does seem to be a hell of a lot less we disagree on now." She sighed. "Either she's mellowed out a lot or..."

"You've grown up," Kerry finished softly.

"Mmm," the dark haired woman acknowledged. "Maybe a little of both." She took Kerry's T-shirt, bunched up the fabric, put it over her head and settled it over her now aloe'd body carefully. "That was, by the way, an impressively sneaky move, though."

"It was, wasn't it?" Kerry essayed a tentative smile. "You're so hard to do that to. I was really kind of surprised it worked." She rubbed her fingers against Dar's bare skin, between her cutoff shirt and her soft cotton shorts. "Did your mom say anything after I left?"

"No." Dar thoughtfully paused. "But she was thinking."

"Thought so." Kerry exhaled in satisfaction. "She snitched the sketch pad before she left." One green eye winked and she patted Dar on the side, before she edged around her and headed for the kitchen.

Dar looked after her and shook her head, acknowledging her partner's pugnacious stubborn streak. Then she followed along, retrieved a glass from the cupboard and squirted some chocolate syrup into it. "Want some?"

"Nu uh." Kerry was busy at the counter, filling a handled mug with some vanilla ice cream, then adding root beer to it. "To each their own poison." She poked at the ice cream with a spoon, making the soda fizzle up. "Whew. I gotta tell you, Dar, your parents wore me out, though." She hooked her arm in the dark haired woman's and tugged her to the living room, where they settled on the couch and put their socked feet up on the coffee table. "I hope I've got that kind of energy to spare when I get a little older."

"You and me both," Dar agreed. "They're something else." She observed the foamy moustache gracing Kerry's mouth and decided to remove it. "Mmm." She licked a surprised lower lip. "Maybe I should try one of those."

"Try one of what?" Kerry had set down her glass, half turned, squirmed up Dar's body and attempted to retrieve some of her chocolate milk the hard way. "Hmm. Ooo, I like that. Yeah. And I—Jesus! Dar!" Kerry yelped, almost levitating off her lover's lap. "Your hands are *cold.*"

"Nu uh." Dar moved her touch. "Your skin is hot. Sorry, forgot the sunburn." She slid her fingers lower. "Better?"

"Oh. Yeah. Much better." She relaxed again, nuzzling the side of Dar's neck. "Thank goodness for bathing suits."

"Definitely." Dar chuckled, as she slid the cotton T-shirt up and found a tasty navel to nibble, feeling a nice shiver down her back as Kerry leaned over and tasted the top of her spine. The scent of aloe, warm skin, and a hint of coconut oil flowed around her, along with the faint rasp as Kerry's breathing deepened. Her teeth tugged playfully on the elastic of the clean cotton underwear she had on and the blond woman's body shifted towards her, obeying the pull with subtle eagerness.

The day's fatigue dropped away as she circled the lean waist with her grip and guided Kerry backwards, easing her gently down onto the couch and starting her assault in earnest.

The cold of the leather against her sunburned back momentarily distracted her, but in bare moments, tickling touches and skillful nibbles made her lose track of insignificant details like stinging skin. Her fingers slipped through Dar's hair and caressed the edges of her ears, then wandered further to the sloping muscles on either side of her neck that shifted as she touched them. She felt short of breath and tried to inhale more deeply, but the tension coiling up from her guts kept her body tensed and shifting and wanting more.

A low purring growl came from within Dar, sending a powerful jolt right to her groin, and she abandoned herself utterly to the pure, animal joy of it.

❖ ⌘ ❖ ⌘ ❖ ⌘ ❖

"Know something, Andy?"

"Mmm?" The blue eyes were closed.

"I've come to the sad realization that I'm an old fart."

One eyeball appeared. "Yeap." He yawned. "Them kids got too much spunk."

Ceci had discovered a swinging chaise in the screened in area on one side of the cottage and they were nestled together on that, rocking slowly under the lazily moving wicker fan. "Felt good to get back under the water again, though."

Her husband didn't answer for a minute, then he sniffed and cleared his throat. "Aches less under thar," he admitted. "Got a lot of hurt in these damn bones." Too many years and too many injuries, and here, at last, was the one person in the world he'd ever admit that to. At least now, though, it was mostly only bodily hurt, a hell of a lot easier to live with.

Hardly no matter, really.

"I've got some herbal rub," Ceci offered. "Can I treat you to a massage?"

"Five dollar word for back rub?" He returned a hesitant tease.

"Not really. 'Cause I was going to go way past just your back," she responded wryly, feeling the silent movement as he laughed. "Hey, Andy?"

"Yeap?"

"You know, you're going to think I'm crazy, but I've been thinking all day about how nice it was on that boat."

"Rally," came the low drawl.

"Really. Everything was handy and it was just so cute in there."

"Uh huh."

"What do you think about getting one of those, instead of a house?"

Long, peaceful moments of dead silence followed.

"You mean to tell me, you want to live on a damn boat?" Andrew finally spluttered. "Thirty some years you ain't wanted nothin' but fer me to get off the damn things and now you wanna get on board one?"

Ceci bit her lip, acknowledging the paradox. "Well, yes, actually."

"Son of a biscuit."

"C'mon, Andy. You know you've always wanted one. We could even get you one of those little captain's hats."

"Like hell."

"A blue blazer?"

"Ah have no idea where I can even get me one of these things, woman. Not like you can pick one up in K-mart." The idea had Velcroed itself to him, though.

"What. A blazer? Sure you could, honey," Ceci assured him, then laughed. "I bet someone on this island knows where to get them. C'mon, maybe they can make it special for us. You can tell them how you want it." She paused. "The boat, I mean. Not the jacket."

Fingers drummed on a cotton covered thigh. "Less you like gray bulkheads, Mrs. Roberts, you better be the decorator in this here crew."

"Does that mean yes?"

"You are serious?" he asked, honestly curious.

Ceci nestled against his shoulder and nodded. "Yes, I am," she answered quietly. "We can lease a slip over at South Beach Marina. They've got a nice area there and it's close by."

"Got it all figgered out, huh?"

"We can take off and go out to the Bahamas if we want. Dive the reefs there," his wife pointed out. "Or go down to Key West. Watch a few sunsets." The colors appealed to her. "I've been thinking about doing a set of naturescapes. Maybe I'll do an underwater."

"No more rock scenes?" Andy asked, stroking the silvered gold hair gently, thinking of the last one he'd seen, up in that little gallery that everyone'd like so much.

Waiting on the Edge of the Sea, she'd called it. A seabreak of gray slate, surrounded by sullen gray and foam seas, against a stormy sky, with a lone figure standing in the wind.

Alone.

"No. My ship's in port." A faint smile. "If I painted that today, there would be a break in the clouds, and the sun would be lighting up everything in sight." Ceci exhaled in wonder. "What a difference a week makes."

Yeah. "Wonder how big they make the engines for them things?"

Ceci looked up at him. *Uh oh.*

Forgot about the boy and his toys. "Um, honey?"

"Heh, heh. Yeah?"

"Don't forget the seatbelts in the head."

❖ ⌘ ❖ ⌘ ❖ ⌘ ❖

The phone buzzed. "Dar?"

The voice almost made her jump, so intently had she been concentrating on the network layout on her screen. "Yes?"

"I have Mr. Alastair on line *uno.*"

Shit. Dar glanced at her watch. *Bastard works fast.* "Go ahead." She listened for the click. "Morning, Alastair."

"Morning, Dar." Her boss sounded upset. "I'd catch you on the vid phone, but I'm on the way into the office."

"Really? How's the weather there in Houston?" Dar morbidly tried to delay the inevitable. "It's raining here."

"Nice." Alastair sighed. "I guess you know why I'm calling."

She toyed with the notion of denying it. "I've got a good idea, sure." She put a bit of disgust into her tone. "David Asshole got home and decided to go ahead with his lawsuit."

Alastair was silent for a moment. "I got a voice mail from him. You're about right, Dar. He's filing suit against you, personally, today for a list of things, most of which I'd just laugh at, but the last thing on the list is the fact that you made decisions intended to bring you personal profit."

"Yeah? Like what?" Dar clicked on a router and checked its configuration. "Point of fact, Alastair, since I'm a stockholder just about every decision I make is calculated to make me and all the other stockholders personal profit."

"Meaning, you hired Kerry because you two are lovers."

"I hired Kerry before we were lovers," Dar replied. "I hired Kerry before we were even friends."

"You broke company rules."

"Not then, I didn't."

"Sure you did, Dar. You hired her without benefit of the interview process and bypassed twenty other more qualified candidates."

Dar was quiet for a few heartbeats. "She was qualified."

"I'm not disputing that, I didn't then and I don't now, Dar, especially since she's turned in a sterling performance the last six months. Kerry is a good employee, a great manager, and a very good choice for the position she's in."

"But?"

Alastair sighed. "But the point is, you did break the rules then."

"And?"

"And the board came down on my ass like a ton of bricks after they had a session with your personnel file."

"When was this?" Dar's whole body tensed, but she kept her tone light. "Don't tell me they worked over the weekend."

"Yesterday."

"What's their beef? Since when do they care who sleeps with who, Alastair? You know Harby is having a public affair with that country western singer and Allan Jacobs got busted last month for soliciting underage sex on the Internet."

Alastair sighed audibly. "Their beef is, Ankow wants to make this a very public trial, exposing what happens when you let 'one of those people' be in the kind of position you are."

"He'll lose the suit."

"It doesn't matter. The exposure will be there, regardless, and it's not like we can sweep you under the carpet, Dar."

Dar folded her hands on her desk blotter, her screen forgotten. "What does he want?"

Another long sigh. "You, out. Me, resigning in a reasonable time period. The chairmanship up for a vote of the general stockholders."

She leaned forward. "And?"

"And what?"

"And, what are you going to do?" A sick feeling settled in the pit of her stomach. "You firing me?"

"I'd rather cut my own left nut off," Alastair replied crisply, dropping into an unusual earthiness. "The board is meeting Thursday night. You need to be there. What'll happen after that, I don't know, Dar." He went awkwardly silent then drew breath. "This doesn't help you, I know, but my personal position has been, and will be on Thursday, that before, during, and now I trust your judgement implicitly, and of all the decisions I've seen you make, there aren't any I regret."

Dar's eyes closed. "It does help, Alastair. He's as much after you, as me. He tried to force me into trying to oust you. I said no. That's where the lawsuit comes in."

There was a long silence, enough for her to clearly hear the sound of the AC unit in her office cycling off and on. "Alastair?"

"You turned him down, hmm?" His voice held equal measures of wryness and wistful curiosity. "Let me guess. You told him..."

"To kiss my ass, yes." Dar smiled a bit. "And regardless of what happens, I don't regret that. The man makes me sick, Alastair." She paused. "The board's spooked, huh?"

"Yes," her boss replied. "But what worries me, Dar, is that he says he has proof your relationship has subverted your judgement and that both of you have taken advantage of the company and your positions to circumvent company rules." He sounded troubled. "What's that all about?"

Dar stood, went to her window, and leaned against the glass, peering out. "Stupidity," she murmured. "I stayed home sick one day last week. Kerry rearranged her schedule and took a half-day off." She shook her head. "He followed her to the ferry."

"Well, that's not a big deal."

"No." It was embarrassing, now that she remembered it. "But we went to my high school reunion last Saturday and he got pictures of us both there."

"So?"

"With our arms around each other."

"Again, so?"

"Dressed like a pair of biker chicks."

Dead silence. "Oh my fucking god," Alastair cursed. "Tell me you're pulling my leg, Dar. I can't believe that."

"Wish I could." Dar crossed back to her desk and resumed her seat. "It was a come as you were and I don't remember if you remember how I was, but—"

"I remember."

"Well, it made quite a picture." Dar rested her chin on one hand. "I...um...screwed up there, Alastair. I'm sorry."

"Dar, you're the Chief Information Officer of the largest IS company in the world. How could you do something that stupid?"

It had been a very long time since she'd had to accept that kind of rebuke. And she really had no good answer for it, either. "It was a damn party, Alastair," she finally muttered. "I didn't really think about it."

"Jesus." Alastair sounded disgusted.

Dar sighed. "Well, now that you know the worst, I've got to go, Alastair. We're about to start bringing up the new network." She paused. "Guess I'll see you on Thursday." She felt the silence. "Unless you'd just like me to resign now and save us all the trouble and me a plane ticket."

Her boss hesitated, then made a sound halfway between a sigh and a grunt. "Are you doing anything in this picture?"

"Walking."

"It was a theme party?"

"Yes."

"Please tell me neither of you are naked."

"We aren't."

"Or drunk."

"Nope."

"Just walking?"

"That's it. We were in the parking lot. He was hanging out there waiting for us, which, now that I think about it, Alastair, is pretty damned strange, since the number of people who knew where I was that night was pretty damned limited."

"Okay," he replied, with more assurance. "At least I've got a heads up so when he pulls the damn thing out, I can laugh at it or find some way to defuse that part of the issue." He sighed. "Least I can do for you putting yourself into the line of fire for me. But for God's sake, Dar. Try to remember you're not some spike haired punk anymore?"

"All right," she answered, with admirable contriteness.

"I tried to call you last night. You didn't answer your pager."

Dar let out a held breath, but knew the reprieve was only very temporary. "We were out on the boat with some very special guests." So strange to think of, much less say. "My parents."

"B—" Alastair started, then stopped. "Wait. B...I tho..." He stopped again. "Didn't um...I thought I remem...we sent...ah..."

"They made a mistake. He was MIA and he came home." Dar smiled at the fighting fish, who blew bubbles at her.

"Why the hell didn't you tell me? Do we always have to talk only about disasters?" Alastair blurted, indignantly. "Dar, that's wonderful. I only had the pleasure of meeting your father the once, but I thought he was a wonderful guy and I was really sorry to hear something had happened to him." He paused. "That's great news."

"Thanks." An alert went off on her monitor and she switched screens. "Whoops. Backbones are coming up. I've gotta run, Alastair. If I've only got a few days left, I want to make sure this damn network falls into place first."

A soft sigh. "I'll talk to you later, Dar." The line went dead and Dar looked at the phone for a long moment, before she stood and picked up her jacket, then headed for the door.

Chapter
28

"Hey, Ker!" Colleen's voice rang across Bayside, and Kerry swerved around a clown blowing up balloons to find her. It was girl's night out, and she was more than ready for it after a long, aggravating day and Dar's grim news on top of it.

"Hey!" She greeted her friend with a hug. "We the first one's here?"

"Yep. C'mon, let's sit down and grab a drink before the crowd arrives." Colleen took her elbow and steered her to a table by the bay. She took a seat and waved at a roller skating waiter. "Your usual?"

"Make it a double." Kerry slid down and groaned. "What a bitch of a day."

The waiter took down their order and skated off. "So. Like, what's happening? Last time I saw you was at the bowling alley. Everything work out okay? I didn't want to just call and ask."

Kerry stifled a yawn. "Everything worked out great." She rolled her head to one side and smiled. "Really great. Better than I could have imagined, in fact. Dar's father went up there, they got together, and they came back here. We spent all day yesterday with them."

"Really." Colleen laughed. "That's fabulous." She leaned closer. "So. When do I get to meet this mystery lady? I think Dar's father's a hoot, I can't imagine what someone he'd marry would be like."

Kerry sighed. "Well, we might be having more free time in the near future, so I'm sure we can arrange something." Dar had tried to make light of the whole thing, but even in their brief hallway encounter, she'd picked up how upset her lover was. "Looks like that guy who was causing all that trouble may have really done it."

Colleen gave her a shocked look. "Wait. He's after both of you?"

"Me by association." Kerry accepted her large, festive looking pina colada, then selected the huge chunk of pineapple and took a bite of it.

"Dar says he's not really after her, either–he's really after the company, but he knows he has to either have her on his side, or get rid of her to do that, and she told him to kiss her ass, so..."

"Ugh." Colleen winced. "But where do you come in for all this?"

"Well." Kerry sipped at the frozen drink, blinking at the kick of the rum. "Mmm. When they say a double, they mean it. Anyway," she took another sip, "he's got this trumped up lawsuit about Dar making money off the company and taking advantage of her position. One of the things he points out is me."

"You?"

"Me." Kerry knew she should feel worse about the whole matter, but she didn't. "Me, because I got my job the way I did, and the fact that we live together, and the fact that he's got a picture of us half naked practically crawling all over each other."

Colleen just stared at her.

"It was that party on Saturday. I told you about it."

"The reunion?"

"Yeah. Dar dressed up like a punk and part of the deal was, I'd do the same, so I did. It was late, it wasn't really any big deal, we were just walking out to the Harley together, and he took a picture of it. Slimebag must have been hanging out in the parking lot half the night."

"The Harley?"

"Mmhm. Part of the costume, so to speak."

"So...you're not worried about all this?" Her friend leaned forward. "Kerry, you guys could both get fired."

"We know," Kerry replied. "We were thinking of starting up our own company. You want a job?"

Russet eyelashes just blinked and blinked at her. "You're joking, right?"

"No. Why should I be? Dar's got a few bucks set aside. She knows her stuff, I know my stuff. We've both got a lot of good networking contacts. It's not like systems design and support is rocket science, Col." Kerry sucked on her straw. "We've been talking about that for a while, as a matter of fact. Too much BS around ILS lately."

"Huh." Colleen sipped her own drink. "Wow. That's so wild."

"I know." Kerry held up her glass and nodded at the waiter. "I mean, I'm not happy about it, Col. Don't get the wrong idea. Neither is Dar. She's worked for them for fifteen years, for Christ's sake." She paused. "And I won't lie and say it doesn't hurt, I mean, I've done a good job for them and I know it."

"Kick ass, if you ask me."

Kerry smiled. "And to make it worse, that new network Dar's been busting her ass over for the last couple month's about ready. The new servers came on line today and she couldn't even enjoy it. It made me really mad. That system is killer, Col. Dar did such a fantastic job on the design and implementation. It's got everything."

"I heard my bosses talking about it." The redhead nodded. "Clyde was saying he can't wait to get switched over. It's supposed to improve our processing speed by over forty percent. He was practically drooling right there in the elevator." She exhaled. "That whole thing must sting like hell, then."

"Yeah," Kerry murmured sadly. "I feel so bad. She was so excited about the project and now she said today it'd at least be nice to see real production data running on it before they lock her out of the systems."

"Damn." Colleen bit her lip. "So, it's a done deal, or—?"

"She's got to go to Houston on Thursday. They've got a big meeting of the board there. She figures they'll do it then." Kerry played with her straw. "And I can't even be there, because I'll be on a plane for stupid Washington."

"Ow."

"She said she'd just finish up with everything there, then meet me in DC. I guess we'll figure out what to do after that," Kerry murmured. "Maybe take a few weeks off. Spend some time hiking, or do Key West, or whatever."

"Live a little?"

"Yeah." She smiled. "Depends on how they are though. They might not bother with me at all."

"Would you stay?"

"Are you nuts?" Kerry snorted. "No way. They'd make that asshole Ankow my boss, probably, and I'd have to kill him."

Colleen regarded her. "Ooo. Aren't we butch."

"Oh, please." She glanced at the table tent as their server returned. "Can I get a big basket of chips and salsa while we're waiting?"

The waiter smiled as he set down her second drink. "Sure, hon. Be right back."

"So. Tell me about this punk outfit?" Colleen sipped her drink and leaned back. "Punk as in you had safety pins in your nose, or what?"

"Punk as in a leather bikini." Kerry blushed even as she said it. "Thank *God* I convinced Dar to let me wear jeans with it. I'd have died if he'd gotten me with the little leather mini skirt it came with."

"A leather bikini?" Colleen squealed. "What's this guy's name? I want that picture. What was Dar wearing? The same thing?" Her eyes widened nearly to golf ball size. "Oh my god."

"Col, calm down before your brains start seeping out your ears." Kerry covered her eyes with one hand. "No, no. Though now that you mention it, I should have had her...well, anyway, no. I picked out a nice, lacy leather vest for her, and she wore that, with jeans and some silver chains and things I scraped up from around the house."

"Leather vest? That doesn't sound like fun."

"Well, it had a lot of openings in it. In fact, it was mostly a few scraps of leather laced together."

"Still," the redhead shrugged, "sounds kinda boring, after what you had on."

"Um, she didn't wear anything under it." Kerry lowered her voice.

"Oh." The red eyebrows knit. "Oh!" Her eyes widened. "Whoooaaa. Now I'm gonna go find that guy and pry that picture out of his hands with a set of needlenose pliers." They laughed and relaxed. "So, you spend the day out on the water yesterday? You're pink again."

Kerry nodded lazily. "Yeah. Went out in the morning, did two long, long reef dives, then went fishing, then did a couple more dives, then had a cookout on the beach at Dar's island." She dug something out of her pocket and handed it over. "Look what I found."

"Ooo." Colleen took the item and examined it. "It's a coin. Wow. Is this like, pirate treasure or something?" She watched Kerry smile and hitch one denim covered knee over the arm of her chair, consciously acknowledging just how much more self confident and comfortable with herself her friend was now. "So, how is it having in-laws?"

Kerry wrinkled up her nose. "It's so weird. I mean, I've always been so cool with Dar's father. He's a really nifty guy, and I love him to death and Dar's nuts about him. I thought her mother was going to be such a problem but in a way, she's not, because there are bits of her that are just like Dar, and I can see that." She gave her head a tiny shake. "I don't think they realize it, but they've got a lot of the same reactions and just little stuff, like the way Dar folds her arms and crosses her ankles, you know, like this." She demonstrated. "Her mom does the same thing."

"Huh." Colleen nodded. "Our family's like that. My brothers were doing their Da imitation the other day, and you know, you can just see when those huge lunks are twenty years older, it's gonna be like having six of him around." She stopped. "Oh, Sweet Mary. What am I saying?" She covered her eyes.

Kerry laughed, then waved as more of their friends appeared. "Here comes the gang. What's the plan, we just going to do dinner, or..."

"Thought maybe some dancing over at the club." Colleen nodded towards the distant sound of music. "Dar joining us?"

"She can't. She's going to be up in her eyebrows with that network tonight. I was going to stay, but she chased me out and told me to have a good time." Kerry nibbled her lower lip.

"Like she hasn't clued in yet that you'd be just as happy sitting with her and punching buttons or whatever it is she's doing?" Colleen chuckled. "C'mon, let's get wild and crazy. I'm in a Macarena mood tonight."

A chorus of groans.

"We could always do Karaoke." The redhead warned, "Remember, we had a bet on last time to see what it would take to get Kerry up there and singing."

"There is not that much alcohol in Miami," Kerry muttered under her breath, then stuffed a salsa laden chip in Colleen's reopening mouth. "Okay, let's go. The Hard Rock first, right? I'm itching for a nice big cheeseburger."

❖ ⌘ ❖ ⌘ ❖ ⌘ ❖

"Wow. This place has changed," Ceci remarked, as she edged past a roller skating half naked person coming down the sidewalk.

"Yeap," Andy agreed, as he took a breath of the salty air. "Best cheap entertainment I found yet, though." He eyed a blading woman who skimmed by, then made a small face. "Structural engineer'd have a ball with that one."

Ceci laughed. They'd spent the morning doing some research on boats and the marina, then decided to have lunch out on South Beach and take a stroll up the old boardwalk, taking in the new sights and the older ones. "I remember when this was nothing but a sleepy, weatherworn part of the beach, full of retirement hostels." She glanced over Andy's shoulder. "Is that a roller skating dog?"

"Yeap." Her husband nodded. "Usta sit over there." He pointed to a small balcony near a motel being rebuilt. "Watch that damn dog come up and down. Finally figgured out what his deal was."

"Hmm?"

"Guy owned him worked down at Penrods." Andy poked a thumb over his shoulder. "Had him a little girlfriend up twenty blocks or so at one of them little snack shops. He was taking notes."

"How do you know?" Ceci asked curiously.

"Stopped him and read one." Unrepentant blue eyes twinkled briefly. "Boy needed a dictionary and a bucket more imagination, tell ya that."

"Andy! How could you?" she scolded.

He hummed a bit.

"What did it say?"

"Heh." Andy smiled, then paused and glanced at a strip of beach visible through the buildings. He walked up the grassy slope and onto the boardwalk, then leaned on the railings and gazed at the wide, green blue expanse past the sandy shore. "That's a spot Dar likes."

Ceci regarded the wild bit of beach, near an abandoned old hotel and full of sea grapes. It was mostly hidden from the walk and, if you were down there, probably had a nice view. "Is that where she was, that first time you saw her?"

"Yeah." Andy rested his chin on one hand. "Thought my eyes were playing damn tricks on me but there weren't no mistaking that profile."

Ceci turned her head slightly and peered at him. "No," she admitted with a tiny smile. "That's very true."

"Came back a few times, usually at night, always by herself. She always seemed sad, somehow." He exhaled. "Then one night, it was real late. I'd been down off the waterfront helping out an old bud of mine and came back up here. Thar she was."

Ceci just listened, understanding how hard it must have been for him to stay away.

"That night, I was scared for her," Andy went on. "She looked t'me like she was at the end of something. Her rope, the road. I was halfway across the sand, couldn't help myself, when she just up and left." He took a breath. "Didn't come back."

"Is that why you finally contacted her?"

"Had to know if she was okay," he replied simply. "Found out later that was the night she and Kerry hooked up."

His wife nodded thoughtfully. "What did you think when you finally met Kerry?"

He cocked his head to one side, in a manner very like Dar's. "Wasn't gonna have to put up with being called granpa, fer one thing." He chuckled at her laughter. "Naw, I was glad. Damn glad to see my kid finally find someone down the road and gone for her."

"She is," Ceci agreed. "And she's a real character sometimes, too. Which reminds me, sailor boy, how much did you have to do with that very neatly staged little drawing exhibition last night?" She poked Andy in the ribs.

"Ow." He put on an innocent expression. "Ah do not know what you are referring to, ma'am. Ah was just upstairs steering the boat." Andy pushed away from the railing. "And speaking of that. Don't we got a meeting with some guy about one of them damn things?"

"Mmm," Ceci relented and took his hand as they turned and started down the boardwalk towards the marina. "She's got an interesting style, you know," she remarked casually. "Talk about a pleasant surprise."

Andy just grinned into the late sunlight.

"Hey. How about sushi after we pick out our new home?"

Wide, very round, blue eyes stared at her. "'Scuse me?"

"C'mon, Andy. There's a great place just down the beach from here. Or at least there used to be. Let's go."

"You are asking me to put raw fish into my body?"

"Everyone does it. You know it won't hurt you."

"Mrs. Roberts, if you knew as much about where them fish had been as ah do, you would not be consuming a square inch of them without it being boiled for half an hour. Then deep fried and served with potato chips," Andy warned her, glancing up as a man in nothing but a pale blue Speedo went by on a unicycle. "Good Lord."

"See? I bet he eats sushi," Ceci teased.

"Yeap. And it made his parts fall off, so's he kin ride that thing like that," the ex-SEAL stated. "Whoa. Hold on a minute." He steered Cecilia up a short flight of stairs into a nondescript building. "Lemme get one little thing here out the way."

"Sure." Ceci looked around at the plain walls. "What is it?"

"Gotta sign my divorce papers from Uncle Sam." Andy glanced at her. "Make me a private citizen fer the first time since I was sixteen years old." His eyes dropped for a moment. "Thought maybe you'd want to be there fer that."

That plain, drab office with faded bulletins on the walls, and cracked folding chairs around the edges suddenly took on a patina of wonder for her. "You thought right." She took a breath as the uniformed attendant behind a small, scarred wooden desk looked up and smiled, evidently recognizing Andy.

"Evening, sir. I've got some mail for you."

Andy walked over, pulling Ceci with him, and took the rubber band wrapped package. "Thanks." He glanced at a small door behind her. "He in?"

She nodded. "We've got the papers all ready. I think you just have to sign them." Her eyes moved to Ceci curiously. "Ma'am."

"C'mon." Andrew led the way to the door and knocked on it, then pushed it open at a grunt from inside.

The office turned out to be an oddly adapted space, evidently converted from its original use as part of an old hotel kitchen. There was a screened back door and a high ceiling and shuttered windows all painted in a dull blue. A desk was squarely near the rear of the room and seated behind it was a huge man with a bull neck and a sparse crew cut. He looked up from under lowered, pale eyebrows as they entered.

"'Lo, Andy."

"Keith."

"Who's your pretty lady friend?" The low voice was almost a growl.

Half a grin flickered on and off Andy's face. "You never did meet mah wife, Cecilia, did you?" He glanced to one side. "Ceci, this is Keith Hawkins, he sorta took care of things here for me."

The man behind the desk stood, towering over even Andy's tall height, and stuck a hand the size of a loaf of bread out at her. "No, ma'am, I never did have the pleasure. But I'm damn sure glad I have had it now." A grin shaped his craggy face. "This damn barnacle didn't mention he'd met back up with you. Just sent me a note asking for mustering out rags."

Ceci took his hand gingerly and pressed it, since shaking something that big didn't seem to be a good idea. "Nice to meet you...and thanks, for helping Andy out."

The giant took a folder from a tray on his desk and opened it, then reversed its direction and pushed it across the desk surface. "Sign."

Andy pulled a pen out of his back pocket and sat down on the corner of the desk, blue eyes flicking over the document quickly. Then he looked up at Hawkins in surprise. "Ah didn't ask fer this."

The bigger man chuckled softly. "Andy, shut the fuck up and sign it, willya?" Andy gave him a look. "Sorry for the language, ma'am."

"I've been married to a sailor for over thirty years," Ceci replied dryly. "I've heard the term before."

"I never talked like that in front of you," Andy protested indignantly.

"No, honey, but all your friends did." His wife patted him on the knee. "It's okay." She leaned over and studied the papers. "What is it?"

"You make it long enough to get retirement benefits, you need to take 'em," Hawkins replied quietly. "'Specially if you done it the way Andy did. Not spent the time behind some damn desk." Andrew carefully signed his name to the bottom. "And while you're at it, gimme a god-damned address for you so I can have the Department of the Navy, which is crawling up my butt, send you all those frigging decorations you refused to go pick up."

"Ah don't want them," Andy said fiercely.

"Too damn bad," Keith shot back. "Give 'em to your kid, if you don't like the colors."

Andrew scowled. "What in the hell would she do with the damn things?"

Ceci put a hand on his arm. "Treasure them." Their eyes locked. "This is the child who bought and made a scale model of every ship you sailed on, Andy."

"Aww." Keith grinned. "He never told me that. Ain't that cute?"

"Son of a biscuit." Andy sighed in exaggeration. "Fine, fine. Here." He scribbled down Dar's address on the paper. "Send the damn things there if you have to." Long, scarred fingers pushed the papers back across the desk. "Lemme go get my kit." He got up and ambled out the back door, leaving them in silence.

Keith sat back down and regarded her. "So. You're the missus, huh?"

"Yes." Cecilia looked around, then glanced back at him. "Bet you didn't know he had one."

"Bet you're wrong." The man snorted. "Bet I know more about you and that damn kid of his than I do my own mother." He gave a crooked smile. "Andy's private'r then hell about himself, but damn, did he mouth off about the two of you."

Ceci smiled and nodded, and they regarded each other in silence for a bit.

"He's been through Hell," Keith finally said quietly. "He lived through something woulda killed just about anybody else I ever knew."

"I know."

"Take care of him, ma'am. He's a special guy."

"I will," Cecilia answered softly.

They turned as Andy came back in, with a simple, dark blue duffel bag. "That's 'bout it," he stated, holding a hand out to Keith. "Ain't going far. Be seeing you guys 'round the docks."

Keith took his hand and shook it with a quiet respect. "Keep in touch, Andy. You know where to find us."

"Yeap." With a brisk nod Andrew turned and captured Ceci's hand, then headed for the door, walking calmly out of a chapter of his life and closing it firmly behind him. They emerged onto the sidewalk, into a wash of colorful sunlight and a blast of salsa music and started off down the street.

Ceci allowed the silence to go on for a while, as they passed trendy hotels and those in the process of becoming trendy. "How does it feel?" she finally asked, as the marina came into view. "I know they were like a family to you."

Andy walked along a few paces, visibly thinking. "Yeap," he mused, as they mounted the steps. "They were that. But I'll tell you, Cec. Having to choose all the time 'tween going and staying, that about killed me." He paused, giving her an honest look. "I know you didn't think so sometimes but climbing that gangplank again was so hard."

Ceci studied him. "Watching you walk up it just as hard for me." She held a hand out. "C'mon. Let's go buy our own this time. We can run up and down it all day long together."

A slow smile touched his face. "All right." He took her hand. "But, Cec?"

"Hmm?"

"No pink."

She pointed a finger at him, and shook it. "Just for that, pink curtains."

"C'mon now." He pulled the door open.

"Pink seats on the head."

"Cecilia Roberts."

"A pink pennant on the masthead."

"Oh mah god."

Ceci chuckled. "So, what are we going to name it?"

"Pepto Bismol, at this rate."

Chapter
29

"Damn it." Dar thumped the side of the monitor in annoyance for about the twentieth time. "C'mon, you piece of..."

"Hey, Boss. Talking nice gets you more than beating up the stuff," Mark commented, from his safe spot across the floor. They were in the operations center, surrounded by mildly humming equipment and the hiss of high-powered air conditioning units. "Honey, vinegar, you know the story."

"What?" Dar grumbled, as she initiated a command again. "What story?"

"That you can get more bees with honey than vinegar?"

"Why the hell would I want bees?" his boss muttered, engrossed in a startup script. "Ah, there you are, you bastard." She typed in a set of commands, reviewed the results, and then restarted the unit. "Boot or die."

Mark worked at his own project, keeping an eye on the tall figure hunched over the console. His mind drifted back a few years, remembering long hours spent in this very room in the company of a younger, much less polished Dar Roberts. A task made easier by the fact that the tall executive had changed into a pair of jeans and an untucked polo before she attacked the stubborn startup issues.

The pose was the same, too. Feet locked around the chair legs, one elbow propped on the desk with her head resting on it, the other hand skimming the mouse over the desktop with quick, precise motions. He could see Dar's sharp profile, too, very still except for the eyes racing over the screen, small muscles alongside them twitching in response.

A twinge of nostalgia nudged him sharply. "Y'know, Dar. I kinda miss having you in the trenches here with us." Mark had been a novice system administrator when they'd worked together, when Dar had just been made a local operations manager and took control of the data center.

It had been a shock, to say the least, but since he'd been new, he'd adapted to her style faster than the rest of the staff. "I really do."

Pale blue irises dilated almost to black turned his way as Dar cocked her head to one side. "Why?" she asked curiously. "I was no picnic to work for."

No, that was true. But one thing about working for Dar—you always knew where you stood. If you did something right, you heard about it. If you screwed up and she was pissed off, you sure as hell knew about it. You never wondered, unlike some of the people he'd worked for prior to ILS. Now, he regarded the serious, intense face across from him and shook his head. "I dunno. It was always just so comforting to have you come in and take over a problem. I knew it would go away then."

Dar smiled. "Thanks. I think."

"I've worked for supes who didn't know jack about what I did. You don't know how much it rocked to know I had someone there who not only knew what I did, but could do it better than I could." He added, "Very cool, Boss. Very cool."

Dar's face twitched into a reluctant smile. "Now, that. That's a compliment coming for you." She reviewed her console. "Ah, good." The main routers had finally booted up and they sat, ten green, lonely islands floating in a mess of dark lines that represented the network. "Now, let's see what we got here." She accessed the master system and started browsing. "Shit."

Mark winced. "Now what?"

"Who configured these?"

"Uh...why?"

"They didn't follow the EWO, for one thing, and they configured the ports ass backwards for another. So who did it?"

"Um...me."

Dar looked at him and drummed her fingers on her console keyboard.

"I just thought this configuration was better."

More drumming.

Mark grinned. "Just like old times, huh?"

A grudging smile returned. "Oh yeah. Just like." Dar typed in a command and hit enter. "Startup dialog. Here we go."

"Dar! You just dumped that whole router," Mark protested. "It took me hours to get that thing done."

"It's not done the way *I* want it," Dar replied, with a scowl. "So I guess I've gotta do it myself." She busied herself typing, glancing at a network configuration to refresh her memory on the different ports and addresses.

It felt guiltily good, she realized, to be doing the hands on again. So much of her job was subjective. Decision making, planning, arguing, pushing...so very little was simple, cut and dry work that having the opportunity to dive back into something as basic as this struck her as almost therapeutic. She checked her watch, then continued typing, glad she'd sent Kerry out to have fun.

More typing.

She was glad, right? No need for both of them to be stuck here in the cold room, doing basic routine stuff that was sure to bore anyone. Kerry deserved time on her own, with her friends, doing the stuff she liked to do.

Dar didn't mind doing that either, in fact, she enjoyed the odd night out with the girls, though she usually felt a little uncomfortable mostly due to the fact that they were by and large all employees of ILS, except for Colleen.

One would think, since she lived with Kerry, that wouldn't bother her, but it did. She believed in keeping a professional distance, and that extended to social occasions with people who were levels lower than her in the company hierarchy. That was admittedly hypocritical, and Dar readily acknowledged that, but she also knew Kerry's friends were a little uncomfortable with her for the same reason.

And of course, she wouldn't be selfish enough to ask Kerry to give up her night to keep her company. *That'd be selfish, and self centered, and mean, and...*

Dar sighed. *Damn, I wish she was here.* She finished reconfiguring a port and wrote the configuration to memory, watching the port come up and wink friendly green lights at her. *How juvenile, Dar. Why don't you ask her to get a teddy bear and spray it with her perfume, so you can carry it around and hug it when you get lonely?* her conscience prodded her sarcastically.

"Sorry, Dar. Did you say something?" Mark inquired, as he started running his own task.

"Um." She looked up. "No. Why, what did you think I said?"

"Something about bears?"

"No, no. I was just thinking about ordering...um...pizza or something. Interested?"

"Sure," Mark agreed amiably. "I'll order. Let's see..." He closed his eyes and concentrated. "Sausage, Pepperoni, beef and pork with extra cheese." One eye opened and peered hopefully at her. "Am I right?"

Dar chuckled. "Yeah."

"Wooo, you mean Kerry hasn't converted you to a veggie pizza yet?" Mark laughed. "I know she's not scarfing down that prescription for a heart attack."

"We get a half and half," Dar admitted. "I make sure to flick any errant growths over on her side of the pie." She concentrated on another part of the configuration. "Ah, there." She cut and pasted, then recycled the screen and reset the equipment. "That's better."

"Damn." Mark peered at the monitor with wry admiration. "Can I be like you when I grow up?" He picked up the phone and dialed. "Want some cheese breadsticks sticks too?"

"Sure."

"Pepsi?"

"Root beer."

"They have floats."

"Bingo."

"Right." Mark placed the order and put the phone down, then got up and manually reset a large machine. "We're going to have to replace this switch, Dar. It's been giving me fits and they can't work the kinks out of that Y2K patch."

Dar grunted and set up a test pattern. "That's the international DS3's figures."

The door opened, revealing Brent's stocky figure as he rolled an AV cart into the room. "Hey, Mark. What's up? I hear we—" His blue eyes went round, "Oh. Sorry, ma'am. Hello." He paused. "Is your machine not working? Want me to take a look at it?" Blue eyes went a little rounder as he saw Dar manipulating the big console. "Or set you up a new one?"

"Hi, Brent." Mark chuckled. "Don't get freaked out. Dar's router qualified." He smiled at the look on Brent's face. "She's reconfiguring the new network."

"Got a problem with that?" Dar growled softly.

"No, no, ma'am, of course not. I just..." Brent looked a little perplexed.

"Just what? C'mon, spit it out."

"Um...well, sure...I," the tech peered at the seated executive, "I mean, I didn't think...um..."

Dar looked right up at him, pinning him with an intense gaze. "Think what?"

He swallowed. "Well, I didn't think you...what I mean is—well, see, you're the boss."

"And?" A dark eyebrow lifted.

"And bosses do bossy things," he blurted. "Not um...techie things." He paused. "You know?"

Mark wisely kept quiet, burying his head into his monitor and typing away furiously. He knew his boss was just playing with the sometimes overly serious Brent, but hoped she didn't take it too far. Dar could be a little too intense sometimes, especially for the younger crowd who didn't know her like Mark did.

Dar finished what she was doing and folded her hands on the console. "Are you insinuating that I'm not a nerd?" Her voice took on a dangerous note.

He blinked at her.

"You think that just because they gave me a title, that I don't know what end of a cable to plug in like the rest of the people on 14?"

"B—" he squeaked, then stared at Mark in desperate appeal.

Dar got up, needing a stretch anyway, stalked over to Bent and put her hands on her denim covered hips. "Are you accusing me of techno turniphood, Brent?" She towered over him, eyeing the tech like a hungry panther.

He stuck his tongue out trying to speak then bit down on it, making his nostrils flare. A blush colored his face brick red and he looked like he was going to faint. "N-n-no, ma'am. No. I'd never do that."

She leaned forward and lowered her voice to a purr. "Good."

"Dar?" Mark peeked out from behind his console, realizing his tech was about to burst into spontaneous human combustion.

"Yes?" the same, low, sexy voice answered, rolling the word playfully.

"Unless you want to clean up the piddle, stop scaring the piss out of Brent, willya?" He glanced at the hapless tech. "Relax. Her bark is way, way worse than her bite."

Slowly, Dar turned and faced him, lowering her head a little and pinning him with an icy, merciless gaze. One eyebrow edged way up. "You have never been bitten," she reminded him. "So how would you know?"

"Uh." Mark rubbed his jaw. "I heard stories?" he ventured. "Really, really good ones?"

Dar paused, then laughed. "Yeah, right." She returned to her seat and resumed her task. "For the record, Brent. I count as a geek."

"Yes, ma'am," he replied instantly. "Maybe we can talk some EPROMS sometimes."

Mark chuckled. "Dar can talk EPROMS. Heck, Dar can burn EPROMS. Matter of fact, Dar designed this ops room," he commented. "And about fifty percent of the systems we run on, for that matter."

"Really?" Brent sounded interested. He rolled his cart in and put it away, then edged around the console desk and settled in a chair near Dar. "Hey, wait a minute. Back in the cross-patch room there's a bunch of DR's stenciled on the punch downs. Is that you?" He was obviously viewing her in a whole new light.

"Yup." Dar set up another test pattern. "This looks decent. I'm going to try and bring the rest of the subnets online."

"Wow," Brent murmured. "Hey. That means you wrote the inventory program too, huh?" His eyes brightened. "Your initials are in the code."

Dar nodded.

"You put in that subroutine that catches the boxes serial number and cross-references it against the original invoice to make sure it's billed to the right department?"

"Yes."

"Wicked." Brent sighed. "I love that subroutine." His gaze took in Dar's profile with new, intense interest. "It's my favorite one."

Dar looked up at him for a moment, then at Mark, who snickered. "Thanks." She leaned back and propped a knee up against the wood of the console, watching her program run. The phone buzzed and Mark picked it up, then stood.

"Pizza's here. That was fast," he remarked. "Be right back." The MIS chief slipped out of the door and let it close behind him, leaving the two of them alone.

There was a bit of silence. Dar remained deep in thought, memories cascading gently over her of the hours spent administering this small cog in the company. She'd been happy doing that, she realized. Probably it had been the last time she'd been able to simply go home at night and forget about her job.

Gone home and escaped to the clubs, spending her time drinking and trading bullshit stories with a group of like minded friends, dabbling in shallow attractions and losing herself in long weekends of bumming around on the beach.

Going nowhere in particular and finding herself satisfied with that as the pleasures of the moment absorbed her interest and she let a lot of things slide—ambition chief among them.

Then there'd been Shari.

And everything had changed.

Nothing was fun anymore. She'd learned to judge herself by a different set of rules and left behind the comfort zone of the ops center to push herself into the stark challenge of project management. Proving she was everything Shari said she wasn't. Driving herself to higher and higher levels until she'd broken through the glass ceiling and landed her butt in a plush office with a business card that said Vice President on it and everyone who ever said she was a loser could just chew that and swallow.

And you know what? No one had cared. No one had been left close enough to pat her on the back and say, "Good job, Dar. You did it. We're proud of you."

No one. The night she'd gotten her promotion she'd taken a bottle of champagne down to the beach and shared it with the night crabs and the hiss of the waves, feeling nothing but a sense of empty relief. So she'd decided to just allow the achievement to become its own end and convinced herself that it made her happy.

Until one damn fall day when she'd taken over a consolidation gone bad and walked into a small, boxy office to deliver a pile of bad news to some ordinary company manager she never expected to see again.

And lost her heart, her soul, and her carefully constructed self-deception all in less time than it took to think about it.

"Ma'am?"

Dar jumped a little. "Oh, sorry. Yes?"

Brent moved a little closer, the flush visible on his pale skin. "Do you mind if I ask you something?"

She shook herself, dispelling the memories and turned in her chair. "No. Go ahead, Brent." She issued him a brief smile. "I wasn't upset before. I was just tweaking you a little."

"Yeah, I figured. Um." His nostrils flared. "You and Ms. Kerry are pretty good friends, right?" He looked around and lowered his voice.

Wild, ringing alarms went off in Dar's head, so loud she was surprised Brent couldn't hear them. "Yes," she answered cautiously. "Why?" *What now?* A thousand situations ran through her head, and Ankow was at the bottom of most of them. *Did he have different information? Had Brent heard him hunting down facts? What was he up to? What trouble...*

"Uh." The man rubbed his jaw. "Well it's just..."

"What is it, Brent?" Dar asked, her interest sharpening.

"Do you...um...I know this is a weird question...but d'you know...um..."

Uh oh. "Yes?"

"Is she seeing anyone?"

Total silence. Dar sucked in a breath and clamped her jaw shut to keep the nervous giggle from emerging. She waited a beat. "Yes." She gave a grave, considered reply. "She is." *Goddamn it. Is he the last person in the whole bloody company to get the bleeping memo?*

"Oh." He looked crestfallen. "Okay. Well, I kinda thought so. I mean, she's so nice, and so pretty. But I figured it was worth asking. Thanks, ma'am. I know it's a real personal question and I do appreciate you answering it." He was still brick red.

"No problem."

"She's probably not my type anyway. Huh?" he asked in a wistful voice.

Dar stared at him. "Um...Brent..."

"It's okay." He dropped his eyes. "It's probably some real smart guy with a nice car." He exhaled and shrugged. "Kind of a stupid question."

"Um." The executive rummaged around, trying to come up with something intelligent to say. "I'm sure you're...ah... There's nothing wrong with you, Brent. She's just...um..."

"Hey, ma'am. It's okay, really. I understand. You don't have to go any further." Brent sighed. "Must be some lucky guy."

"B—" Dar was sure her brains were leaking out her ear by now. "N–"

The door opened and Mark walked in with two boxes full of pizza. "Hey. Look what I found." He opened the door further and a familiar blond figure came in behind him.

"Hi," Dar croaked gratefully.

Kerry trudged in, circled the console, put her arms around Dar's neck and kissed her head. "My transmission gave up just outside the office and I got roped into Country line dancing Karaoke charades. I'm trashed. Can we go home?" She let her cheek rest against her lover's dark hair. "Hey, Brent." Gentle green eyes regarded him wearily.

There was a tiny little silence, until Brent shuffled his feet. "Guess I had the smart and the car right," he muttered, flushing an even deeper red as he stood up and scurried out of sight behind a couple of mainframes.

"Huh?" Kerry cocked her head. "What's up with Brent?" She looked at Dar and her brows creased, then she glanced up at Mark, who shrugged in honest puzzlement.

Dar sighed. "A clue just bit him in the ass."

"Ow." Kerry peered into the gloom behind the consoles. "About what?"

Dar scratched her jaw. "Tell ya later." She patted Kerry's calf, absorbing the warmth pressing against her back as the smaller woman leaned against her. "Siddown. I've just got to finish this setup." She turned and pulled the keyboard closer as Kerry settled in the chair next to her, watching with interest.

Dar glanced at the monitor, bemused to see her reflection faintly echoing back at her from the glare, a smile shaping her lips completely without her permission. Kerry's hand casually rested on her knee under the desk, and the smile widened.

A thought suddenly crossed her mind. Would Kerry care if she was just a mid level ops manager? She turned her head slightly and studied the intelligent profile next to her. She liked the perks of their respective positions, Dar was sure, but...hadn't she said she'd be content to wander around selling poetry for food if she had to?

Was she serious?

Am I serious thinking about this? Didn't I work my tail off for years getting to where I am? Would I really want to go back to where I was then, and just settle for being good at something, content with a steady job with decent pay and benefits?

Dar regarded the diagram on the screen, its spider web of tracings indicating the elegantly designed network's far flung reach. Finished, it would change the way the company did business and toss them into the twenty-first century as one of the few corporations capable of projecting the last few year's explosion of data services into the future.

The smile in the monitor grew and became a trifle ironic. With a flourish, Dar brought the rest of the system on line and dark gray webbing came alive with the colors of the test patterns she was running. "What do you think?" she asked the avidly watching Kerry.

Mark got up and leaned over her shoulder, peering at the screen.

"Jesus. Complete redundancy." He deliberately deactivated one of the big ports, and they watched as the test traffic smoothly rerouted itself. "Holy shit."

"Wow." Kerry was running an analyzer on another console. "Would you look at that bandwidth? I couldn't bottleneck this if I tried."

They both looked up at Dar with something close to nerd awe.

Dar smiled, enjoying the moment completely. It was almost better than chocolate ice cream.

Almost.

Chapter
30

Dar tucked the edge of the towel more firmly under her arm as she poured two tall glasses of peach ice tea. Chino waited patiently at her heels, giving her leg an occasional lick. "Watch your tail, Chino," the tall woman warned, as she returned the carafe to the refrigerator and picked up the glasses. "C'mon. Let's go get mommy Kerry."

"Gruff." Chino trotted out the open glass doors and stood up on the lower step of the hot tub, looking up expectantly.

"Hey. Don't fall asleep in there," Dar warned as she shed her towel and entered the tub. Kerry was sprawled out in the warm water, her damp head resting against the tub back and her arms outstretched on the sides.

"Uh?" She opened one eye to regard Dar. "Oh, it's you."

"You were expecting..."

Kerry lifted her head and scooted up a little, reaching for her glass. "Sorry. I am so wiped. You ran my butt ragged tonight, Dar." She gave her lover a pathetic look. "Can I get Colleen to come over when we do that so we can double team you?"

"Mmm." Dar wasn't displeased at the compliment, though. They'd left the gym and Kerry's class earlier, then taken up the routines in the workout room on the island. She felt a little sore, a little tired, but in a good way. "You did great, though. I think we're going to have to move you up a belt."

"Yeah?" Kerry perked up visibly. "And here I thought I was really bombing out. Thanks, Dar." She felt happier about the bouts and pretty satisfied with herself in general after sitting through a surprisingly candid and objective review administered by her boss just that afternoon.

Criticism, she'd found, was much easier to take from someone you knew liked you, than from someone you knew didn't. Dar's variety was calm and impersonal and very direct—addressing specific, fixable items and staying away from the broad generalities that were intimidating to hear and almost impossible to change. Your attitude is an issue, for instance. She'd heard one of the girls in the breakroom repeating that bit of feedback from a superior. What exactly were you supposed to do about it?

Besides, she'd found that Dar had a delightful habit of doing all the bad stuff first. To sort of get it out of the way. Then she'd list off all the good stuff, so by the time the review was finished, she felt pretty good even if the start was kind of painful. Her's hadn't been that painful either, since she knew her own faults, and was able to discuss them with her supervisor in fairly frank honesty. "Did I thank you for my review?"

"Three times now," Dar remarked dryly, sipping her tea. "No one's ever done that before." She stretched her legs out in the swirling water and sighed, tipping her head back and regarding the stars.

Kerry felt the mood change and slid a little closer, where she could feel Dar's warmth. "Are you worried about tomorrow?"

Dar nodded.

"Me too."

Dar studied the sky, then turned her head. "Listen. I've been thinking about this." Her face was very serious. "Whatever happens tomorrow—don't feel like you have to do anything about it, okay?"

Kerry looked puzzled. "Huh?"

"You're really good at what you do, Ker. I think you should keep doing it, no matter what happens with me."

"Oh." Kerry exhaled, ruffling the surface of the water. "I don't want to stay there without you, Dar. I'd feel really bad about that, and besides, who'd say they'd let me?"

"They need you." It was the truth.

"They need you too," the blond woman shot back. "It's so unfair. Look at the job you do for them, Dar. How could they even think about removing you just for something as..." She shook her head. "It's just not fair."

Dar shrugged. "Can't say it's their fault. I made the decision, Kerry. I knew what I was doing."

Kerry stared at her. "You said you hired me for my skills. Are you saying now that's not true?"

"No."

"That is what you just said."

"No, it's not," Dar replied fiercely. "I knew I was hiring the best candidate for the job, then or now, and that, Kerrison, was never an issue."

"Then what did you mean by that?"

Dar slid down in the water. "I meant that...I knew, when I brought you on that I was attracted to you." She paused. "And I knew that wasn't going to stop after you were hired."

The turmoil subsided next to her. "Oh." Kerry's face eased into a sheepish smile. "Well, I'm guilty of that too, so there." She reflected a bit, then looked up. "Dar, I want you to know how lousy I feel about the fact that it's us that's causing this."

"It's not. It's just the excuse."

"It's a lousy excuse." Kerry scowled. "I mean, Jesus, Dar, I understand why they have the rule, okay? Because it would be easy for someone to use their position to take advantage of someone, or to insinuate that promotions or pay raises were contingent on you making that person happy in some way." She shook her head. "But that isn't the case here, and we both know it."

"I know."

"I should go talk to them." Determination squared the slightly rounded jaw line.

Dar pictured Kerry storming the boardroom, facing off against the rest of her peers, and smiled in frank reflex. "Tell you what. Let's trade. You come talk to the board and I'll go testify against your father. Deal?"

"In a frigging heartbeat," Kerry blurted. "I am so there." Then her shoulders slumped and she went very quiet. "I don't want to go there tomorrow, Dar."

"Maybe they won't ask too many questions."

"It's not the questions. It's not the panel."

Dar looked at her. "Your family?"

Kerry nodded.

"I'll be there as soon as I can, I promise." *Tell the board to shove their job, and fly back out on the next flight. Yeah. To hell with it. Maybe I could just call Alastair and tell him to...* Dar sighed. No, she really did have to be there and speak for herself, that much had been made clear regardless of what the outcome was. "I don't think it'll take long."

"Are they going to fire you?"

"I think so, yes." Strange, after all the nonsense, how much that hurt. "Actually, what they'll do is ask me to resign. At this level, you don't usually get outright fired. It looks bad and does strange things to the stock. They'll make it seem like it was a voluntary thing."

"Dar..."

"I know, it sucks. I agree, but what they're looking at is perception. Perception has nothing to do with reality, Kerry. And if Ankow goes public with his trial, then they have all that perception out there that I've gotten involved with a subordinate and maybe made decisions that were influenced by doing so."

Kerry sighed.

"It's the perception they're worried about. I know not one of them, on a personal level, gives two craps about my love life, understand?"

"No."

Now it was Dar's turn to sigh. "It's a matter of trust, Kerry. When you're in a position like I am, solely in charge of billions of stockholder dollars, and making decisions for the company on a daily basis, the inference that I might not make the right decisions scares the hell out of them and also out of the stockholders."

"That's stupid, Dar. You've been making decisions for them for years."

"Yes." Dar gave a tiny smile. "But they never suspected I had a personal side that might possibly interfere with that before." She paused. "And they'd be right. In all the years I've worked for them, I've never had something in my life I'd put before my job."

"Until now."

"Until now," Dar replied in wry agreement. "But it's not your fault, Kerry."

"Yes, it is."

"No, it's not."

"Dar, it most certainly is my fault." Pale brows knitted. "Saying it isn't is like pretending I'm this witless child who just toddled along after you when you called me." Kerry put her glass down. "An equal case could be made that I manipulated you strictly to achieve my position and that I'm milking you along, hoping I'll get your job when you leave." She folded her arms. "Maybe you're an innocent victim."

Dar simply stared at her.

"It's all just so—" Kerry turned and saw the look in her lover's eyes and reached out and cupped her cheek. "That was a facetious statement," she stated. "Or I would have taken that VP position you dangled out a couple of months back, remember?"

"I remember." The skin shifted as Dar smiled. "And even if you had, I trust you, Kerry."

It was like holding a piece of precious crystal. "Thank you." It came out in a whisper. "That means everything to me." She smiled back. "I still think you should let me go talk to them."

The phone rang and Dar forced herself to look away from Kerry's intense gaze to answer it. She lifted the portable receiver up. "Hello?"

"Hello, Dar."

Her eyebrow quirked. "Hi, Dr. Steve. What's up?"

The physician cleared his throat. "Sorry I didn't get back to you sooner, Dar, but I made the lab run all the tests three or four times, because I didn't want to give you the wrong information."

A chill went down Dar's spine that even the warm water of the Jacuzzi couldn't dispel. "Information about what?" Her alarm must have shown, because Kerry sat up and put a hand on her shoulder. "What's going on?" She felt her heart speed up.

"Remember that blood I took from you, when you were sick?"

"Yes."

"We found some toxins in there, Dar. I sent them out to a bigger lab to have them check what they were." Steve hesitated. "The results came back positive for some seriously poisonous chemicals that I won't bore you with the names of."

Dar's brows creased as she considered the information. "Steve, are you saying I was poisoned?" She paused. "Accidentally?"

There was a long silence. "Dar, the type of stuff this is, you absorbed through your skin. You didn't swallow it, or nothing like that." An awkward pause. "Had to be touching you."

"Touching me," Dar murmured, then cocked her head at Kerry. "Dr. Steve says it was some kind of poison that got me sick the other day." Kerry's eyes widened in shock. "Something I got by touching the stuff. God, it could have been anything." The phone shifted. "Steve, other than the office and the house, I was in a couple of odd places that day. What are the odds it was on something there? Like the airport, for instance?"

"Dar, this stuff," Steve hesitated, "it's not very common." He seemed uncomfortable. "I'd like you to come in tomorrow, let me take more blood and make sure you got rid of it all. You haven't been sick since then, have you?"

"No. Not at all. In fact, I feel great. We just got back from the gym and Kerry was giving me grief about running her ragged," she replied. "I was a little queasy the day after that, but even the morning after you came I was able to get some breakfast down fine."

"Good." Steve sounded relieved. "It's probably all right then, but I'd like to run some blood anyway," he insisted. "Stop by in the morning. Won't take but a minute."

"Okay." Dar exhaled. "I've got a plane to catch, but I'll swing by the office first."

"Great. See you then, Dar." Steve hung up, leaving an echoing click behind him.

Dar set the phone down and regarded her friend. "Damn." She wasn't sure how to react. "I wasn't expecting that. I thought it was just a damn bug."

"What was it?' Kerry asked. "Does he know how it got in you? I heard you say by touch. You mean it's absorbed through the skin?"

Dar nodded thoughtfully. "Well, only two people touched me that day, so that blows that theory out." She tugged on a lock of wet blond hair. "You and Dad." She looked up as a soft knock clearly sounded through the open door. Leaning over, she pressed the intercom button. "Yes?"

"Hey, Dardar."

"Hey, Dad. C'mon in."

"Dar!" Kerry gave her a look. "In case you forgot, we're naked."

"He's seen me naked," Dar protested mildly, as the door opened and ambling footsteps crossed the tile. She glanced down. "Course, I was a little smaller then." She looked up. "Hi, Dad."

"'Lo there—Jesus H. Christ!" Andrew turned his head. "Paladar Roberts. Get yer clothes on."

"Does that mean I can stay naked?" Kerry inquired innocently. "Cool."

"No, young lady, you most certainly can not."

"C'mon, Dad. They'd get all wet in here." Dar chuckled. "We're under the bubbles, look."

"No."

"Really, we are. You can only see our heads."

Andrew peeked, spotting two sets of sparkling eyes very close to the water. Dar had turned the jets up and the whirlpool provided a frothy, but effective screen otherwise. "You two little barnacles are gonna get scraped one of these fine days," he growled.

"We love you too, Dad." Kerry grinned cheekily, splashing him a little. His face was visibly sunburned, the color obscuring the worst of the scars and heightening the contrast of his pale eyes, and the tense lines had relaxed considerably in the past week. A corner of his mouth quirked, uncannily like his daughter's often did and he stuck a hand in to splash her back. "Have you been having fun?"

The quirk edged into a smile. "We've been busy, if that's what you mean," he remarked. "Found us a new home."

"Oh yeah?" Dar forgot her concerns for a moment. "Where?"

"South Beach Marina."

Twin puzzled looks peered back at him. "South B—" Dar started to say.

"Where?" Kerry asked simultaneously.

"Yer mother liked that damn boat so much, we figgered maybe we'd get us one and live on that," Andrew answered placidly, rocking back and forth on his heels. "So we did. Went down and ordered me one the other day. Be ready in about a week or two."

"You ordered a boat?" Dar blinked. "Like...as in one like ours?"

"Bigger." Her father smirked. "Some sixty damn feet long and ah had 'em put a pair of the biggest damn engines I could find in the back end of it."

Dar just gaped, totally stunned by the news. "I..." She tried to come up with something to respond with. "But..."

"Wow." Kerry leaned her chin on Dar's shoulder. "I can't wait to see it. I bet Mrs. Roberts is going to make the inside so cool." She smiled. "Can we have a boatwarming?" She managed to push the knowledge of her trip tomorrow out of her mind, replacing it with the excitement of seeing her friend's new home. "I wish it were next week already."

Dar sighed. "Me too."

Andrew cocked his head and regarded them from under grizzled eyebrows. "What's yer troubles?" He glanced at Kerry. "I know you got to go north tomorrow."

Kerry nodded, then looked up at Dar. "Dar has to go to Houston."

Dar found herself under a very familiar scrutiny and she felt years younger all of a sudden. "That guy I told you was causing me trouble?"

"Yeap."

"He did," she admitted. "I don't think I'll be working for ILS after tomorrow."

Andrew looked truly stunned. "Why?"

Dar glanced at Kerry, then shrugged. "Scandal. They've got a BS lawsuit pending, and I think they're going to ask me to resign, to keep all that from going public." She couldn't meet his eyes anymore and looked at the roiling water instead. "I...um...broke the rules with Kerry."

Her father snorted. "After all this damn time, they're gonna ask you to bail out fer *that*? C'mon now. Gimme a Christly break. They need t'get their heads out of their keesters." He paused. "Ye're not seriously gonna do it, are you?"

She gave her head a tiny shake. "I don't know."

Andrew leaned over and took her chin, forcing her eyes up. "You listen to me, Paladar. You've been givin' them people two hundred percent since you was fifteen years old. Don't you walk away from them with your tail tucked."

Kerry could, in that moment, have easily kissed him. It was exactly what she'd wanted to tell Dar, but had been reluctant to, since she was so close and so involved in the whole situation. *Besides, that kind of thing sounded better coming from her daddy.* Her instinct was to fight what she saw was an intolerably unfair situation and she was glad to see Andy was on her side. She slipped an arm across Dar's stomach under the water, and ran her fingers over the toned surface.

"I don't know if they're worth the fight," Dar objected quietly.

"Maybe they ain't, but your pride is," her father responded. "Losing's one thing–we all gotta do that sometimes. But quittin's something else." His jaw bunched. "You're my kid and I didn't raise you to run from nothin'."

Her lips tensed into a grim smile. "No, you didn't," Dar allowed. "And I never have." She closed her eyes and tilted her head in tacit agreement and felt her jaw released and patted gently.

"That's my girl."

Yeah. Dar exhaled, accepting it. So she'd go out swinging. *It would make a good story anyway, right?* "Wish I had something to throw in his face, though." She shifted a little. "Mark couldn't find a damn thing on him."

"You'll think of something, Dardar," her father predicted. "This that same guy that came after you that night?"

That night. "Yes."

"Lucky he turned you loose, munchkin. He 'bout had mah boot up his hinder quarters there."

Turned me loose... Dar straightened up and stared out at the horizon. She touched a spot on her upper arm, as she stirred her memories of that night. "He did grab me, didn't he?"

Kerry's eyes widened. "Ankow?" She sat up as well. "He touched you? That night? That little piece of slimy..."

Andy blinked. "Possessive little thing, ain't you?" he remarked.

"No, no. Dr. Steve just called. He found out some poison stuff was what got Dar sick last week. He said she got it through her skin," Kerry blurted. "I bet that son of a bitch did it. I bet he did. That slime bag. Boy, if I get my hands on him I'll—" She started to stand up.

Dar grabbed her and pulled her down as Andrew yelped and covered his eyes. "Calm down." She found herself tangled with her friend, eyes meeting at a distance of inches. "Let's not jump to conclusions." The angrily coiled body in her arms slowly relaxed as Kerry slid back under the water.

"What's she talking about?" Andy asked, still with his hands over his eyes. "What'd Steve find?"

"It's safe, you can turn around," Dar told him. "He found some kind of toxin. Didn't say what it was. Just that it was something you absorbed through your skin, and it was nasty. He wants me to drop by tomorrow so he can make sure it's all gone."

Blue eyes peeked out, then the ex-SEAL blinked. "T'morrow huh? Mind if I tag along?" His gaze had sharpened and his whole attitude shifted subtly. "I'd like to hear about this." He cleared his throat. "Might as well say hello to the old dog too."

Dar nodded absently. "Sure." Her brows creased. "You don't really think he..." She forced a laugh. "C'mon. This isn't some trashy thriller novel."

"Ah don't know." Andrew touched the skin on her arm where Ankow's hand had clutched. "But ah aim to find out." His voice had lowered and deepened into a throaty rumble that was more purr than speech.

For a moment, there was danger there. Then Andy straightened and thumped the edge of the Jacuzzi. "Came t'see if you two'd like to join us for a cup of something down yonder."

"We have to get dressed then, huh?" Kerry murmured, from her warm spot nestled against Dar.

Andy raised one brow.

"Sure," Dar agreed. "We'll join you in a few minutes." She watched him leave, hearing the faint clang of the gate as he exited the garden and headed towards the beach.

❖ ⌘ ❖ ⌘ ❖ ⌘ ❖

Dar put her sunglasses on, as she pulled off the ferry and turned right on the causeway. Her father was sprawled in the seat next to her, wearing a pair of, for him, festive dark green shorts and a sweatshirt with its sleeves pushed all the way up. "It was nice of Mother to take Kerry to the airport."

Andrew turned from his review of the streets. "She likes the little kumquat."

"So I gathered." Dar smiled wryly. "The feeling's mutual." She turned onto the beach road that held Dr. Steve's practice and headed south. She had a bag packed in the back of the Lexus and had agreed to her father's offer to take the SUV back from the airport rather than leave it there overnight.

She had shared breakfast with Kerry, out on the patio as they'd watched the sun rise together, and she'd spent an extra few minutes just hugging her lover before she'd gotten dressed and started off, wishing she were going to Washington instead of Texas.

"You know, the two of them together could be dangerous," Dar remarked, darting a sidewise glance at her father, who grunted and gave her a half nod. She turned into the parking lot of the doctor's office and parked, then got out and waited for him to join her as they walked towards the entrance. "Maybe we should have called him first. I'm not sure it's really fair to spring you on him this early in the morning."

"He'll live." Andrew pulled the door open and gestured for her to go inside. "B'sides, if he's gonna keel over, least it's in a doctor's office."

"Dad, he's the doctor."

"Got nurses, don't he?"

Dar chuckled and went to the sliding glass windows, ignoring the buzzer and tapping on them lightly. The panel slid aside, revealing a young girl in jeans and a T-shirt. "Morning, Aliene."

Dr. Steve's daughter waved. "Hi, Dar. He's in back. G'wan in, he's exp—" Aliene's jaw sagged in shock as she looked up and over Dar's shoulder. Her eyes widened for a long moment as she leaned forward. "Uncle Andy?"

"Hey there, squirt."

"Holy shit! Hey, Dad!" The girl slid the panel all the way back, scrambled right through the window and hurled herself at Dar's father with heedless abandon. Dar got out of the way and just watched with a smile on her face as Aliene enveloped the older man in a hug.

"Aliene, what in the world are you yelling? Hey, where are you?" Dr. Steve's voice came through the door. "Oh, hello Dar." Dr. Steve poked his head through the window, looking for his daughter. "What's going on...out...here?" His words just wound down as his eyes met the ice blue ones looking back at him from over his daughter's shoulder.

"'Lo, Steven," Andrew murmured, releasing Aliene with an awkward pat on the back.

Dr. Steve pulled his head in and shut the window, then came around the receptionist's desk and out the door into the waiting room. He came right up to Dar's father and stopped. "My god, it is you."

"Pretty beat up, but yeah." Andy held out a hand and it was slowly clasped and held. "Good t'see you."

The doctor shook his head in wonder. "I can't believe it," he breathed, then turned briefly to Dar, who leaned against the wall with a quiet smile on her face. "I can't believe it."

"Believe it." Dar pushed off the wall. "Listen, I've got a plane to catch. You two can spend the rest of the day swapping tales, but Dad's got to take me to the airport first."

"Pushy little thing, ain't she?" Andy drawled, sticking his hands in his pockets.

Steve just laughed softly. "My god. All right. C'mon back, the both of you. Aliene, call your mama and tell her who just walked in my door." He guided them into an exam room and turned his back, visibly collecting himself before he turned around and came at Dar with a hypodermic needle the size of New Jersey.

Dar backed up, her eyes widening in alarm. "What the hell is that for?"

"I told you I needed to take blood," the doctor scolded.

"With a harpoon? What do I look like, a fur seal?"

Andrew snickered. "Y'ere such a big baby."

"You don't like them either," Dar accused, pointing a finger at him. Then she took in the amused looks and sighed. She backed up and hoisted herself up onto the exam table with a distinct glower. "Fine." She presented her forearm and watched nervously as the doctor swabbed her arm with alcohol and iodine. "So. What is it you found?"

"Hang on." Dr. Steve pulled off the cap of the needle with his teeth and probed her skin, putting pressure on a vein expertly before he very gently inserted the sharp point. "There." He looked up at Dar. "Not so bad, hmm?"   ·

"Mmm." Dar peered at her father, who was studiously examining the tongue depressors. Then she looked back up into Dr. Steve's face, surprised to see a look of gentle compassion there. The doctor removed the needle, having gotten his blood sample, then patted her cheek and put the cap back on.

"Okay, Andy, you can turn around now." Steve chuckled. "All right. Let me tell you what the lab said." He put the needle down, opened a drawer, pulled out a file and opened it. "I can't say I've seen this before, because I haven't, Dar, but from what they tell me, it's pretty nasty stuff."

Andy circled him and peered at the paper.

"I asked the lab if it could have been on something like a chair," the doctor continued. "They didn't seem to think so, but they didn't have any really good ideas on how you came into contact with it." He paused. "Or where it came from, for that matter."

"I kin tell you that," Andrew said softly, but with utter seriousness. "That there came out of a United States Gov'ment laboratory."

They stared at him. "What?" Dr. Steve murmured.

Andrew took the file out of his hands, walked to the window, and tilted it to the light and studied it. The sun came in and splashed across his uneven, scarred features which had gone quite still and cold. Dar got up off the table and walked to him, rubbing her arm. "What is it, Dad?"

Andrew cocked his head and regarded her with steady intent. "Someone," he said with unusual clarity, "done meant you harm, Paladar."

She felt a definite chill. "Are you sure? Maybe it was just something I picked up at that alley."

"Finding this at a bowling alley is about as possible as you sprouting wings and flying to the moon," her father stated flatly. He handed the folder back to Dr. Steve. "It is kept in a small packet and held on yer fingers with a wax paper." He held up two fingers. "One hit will make you sick as a dog. Two will do worse."

Dar felt like she'd been hit with a baseball bat. "C'mon, Dad. That's too melodramatic. I'm not a character in a supermarket thriller." She tried to shrug it off. "Can't I just have had a damn bug? Or food poisoning? Granted I'm not the most liked person on earth, but I can't believe someone would try to slap poison on me."

"Dar," Dr. Steve put a hand on her shoulder, "this stuff was in you, like it or not. I don't know how it got there, but the fact is, it made you sick. If you don't think there's anything to worry about, that's great. I'm glad to hear it." He picked up the needle. "I'll make sure there's no scrap of it left, though if you've been feeling all right, I doubt it." He paused. "When we spoke, you said two people had touched you that day."

"Kerry and my father," Dar replied. "Except I was wrong. There was one other person."

"Well," Steve patted her cheek, "you think about it, okay? Watch yourself." He eyed Andrew. "And you, my old friend, better not move an inch until I get back here with a camera." He bustled out, leaving father and daughter alone.

Andrew glowered at her. "That man gonna be where you're going to?"

Dar hesitated, then grudgingly nodded. "I really don't think he'd...he's an asshole, Dad, but..."

"He been in the military?"

Dar gave another grudging nod. "Two hitches as a Ranger."

"Wall, don't that just figure." Andrew made a face. "That'll settle it. Ah am gonna go with you."

"Dad." Dar snorted. "Now, come on. This is a business trip, not an undercover game."

"Ah do not like that man and ah am going with you," her father repeated stolidly.

She put her hands on her hips. "I can take care of myself, you know," she objected. "I've been doing it for quite a while."

"This ain't your kind of fight, Paladar," he shot right back. "And besides, I have t'go." He straightened and put his hands on his hips, mimicking her stance. "I made me a promise."

"A promise? To who?" Dar asked in exasperation. "Dad, I can handle myself on a business trip for crying out loud. This is my job and my life, damn it."

A finger tapped her chest as he leaned closer and went eye to eye with her. "And you are mah only kid, and the apple of that green eyed gal's eye, and I swore to her I'd make sure you stayed outta trouble."

Dar glared at him.

Andy tweaked her nose. "C'mon, Dardar. I always wanted to get me one of them cowboy hats."

"Dad."

"Maybe I'll take you on one of them pony rides."

"I'm big enough to carry the pony." Dar gave up. "All right, fine. Waste your time and ride over there with me, if you have to. What are you going to tell Mom?"

"Um." Andrew scratched his ear. "We kinda talked about all ready."

Dar sighed.

"'Sides, she's got her own little covert mission." Andrew patted her on the shoulder. "C'mon. That there plane's waiting."

"Ah ah." Dr. Steve came back in with a digital camera. "You just hold on one minute, Andrew B. Roberts." He pointed. "I want a shot of the both of you." He waved them closer. "G'wan."

Dar shook her head, but turned and slid an arm around her father's waist, as he circled her shoulders. A pose that brought a wholly unconscious smile to her face.

Steve snapped the picture, then another for good measure. He lowered the camera. "Two of a kind."

They eyed each other, then Dar finally laughed. "Yeah." She shook her head. "He still out stubborns me, though."

"Damn straight," Andrew agreed instantly. "Had me lots more practice."

Impulsively, Dar leaned over and kissed him on the head, making him snort.

"You have been hanging around that green eyed gal some, tell you that."

Dr. Steve was busy snapping away, chortling with glee. "Want to come back and have dinner with us, Andy?"

"Can't," the ex-SEAL stated shortly. "Got me a plane to catch too. Rain check?"

Steve nodded.

"I know Ceci'd love t'see you."

Dr. Steve blinked. "She here?"

"Yeap."

The doctor shook his head. "Unbelievable." He sighed. "All right. Give me a call when you get back. It's a great excuse for a party." He watched them leave together and then walked out to find his daughter sitting on the counter. "How'd you like that?"

"Wow," Aliene replied. "That was like, way too cool."

"Mmhm," her father agreed.

Chapter
31

"Whew." Kerry glanced appreciatively around at the airport. "Boy, it's nice to go out of here instead of Miami." Her flight had been scheduled to leave from the much smaller Fort Lauderdale International Airport, some twenty minutes north of its larger, more hectic cousin. "Thank you very much, by the way, for dropping me off."

"Mmm." Cecilia held back a smile. "Actually, I was dropping us both off."

Puzzled green eyes focused on her. "Excuse me?"

"Well, the Woman's Art Museum asked me to sign off on that collection, so I can have it shipped to the South Beach place we found," Dar's mother explained.

"Oh." Kerry was surprised, but not unhappy. "Wow, that's great. Are we on the same flight?"

"Mmhmm." The silver blond head nodded. "Hope you don't mind."

"Not at all." Kerry gave her a warm smile. "I'd love the company. It's not exactly a fun trip for me." Kerry noted the bag slung casually over Cecilia's shoulder. "Is that all you're taking?"

"Yes, it is." Ceci nodded. "I see a coffee shop over there. We've got time before boarding, care to stop?"

Kerry felt a sense of relief that she'd have someone to talk to for at least the trip. "Lead on." She followed the older woman across the concourse towards the small shop, spotting cinnamon rolls also being sold. "Mmm. Cinnabons."

"My daughter's rubbing off on you, I see." Ceci smiled to remove any sting from the comment.

But Kerry laughed. "Oh, no. I didn't need any help there." She set her bag down, went up to the counter, and ordered two cups of coffee. "Want one?" She pointed at the rolls.

"Sure." Ceci took a seat and watched Kerry collect their snack and return. *What a nice kid.* She couldn't help but smile at the warm, open face. "Thanks." She found herself looking forward to spending a little time with this person who had chosen to live with her daughter, whose personality was so different from Dar's and so much like the child she'd always wished for.

Smart, social, friendly. A poet brought up in the same general class as she had been.

And her parents had spurned her.

Life just didn't make sense sometimes.

"What got you interested in computers, Kerry?" she asked lightly, sipping her coffee.

Kerry thought about that for a bit, then propped her chin up on a fist. "I think...I think mostly it was because they represented something I could totally control."

A very unexpected answer. "Really?"

The younger woman nodded. "Yeah. They're like that. Garbage in, garbage out, you know how it is. They'll do whatever you tell them to do. I think because my family was always so strict, and so confining, it maybe gave me an opportunity to have this one area of my life that I was totally in charge of." She paused. "And it was something so different. My major was in English and I took all kinds of general stuff in college, but I was fascinated by the technology, and realized in my sophomore year that all my elective courses were turning out to be programming and electronics."

Definitely unexpected. "What were you going to do with an English degree?" Ceci asked.

"Teach," Kerry replied succinctly.

"Is that what you wanted to do?"

"No." She shook her head. "It's what my father wanted me to do. Looks good for a politician, you know? One kid a lawyer, one kid a housewife, one kid a teacher. Very all American."

Cecilia blinked at her. "Well." She sipped her coffee and reflected. "My family had expectations, yes, but at least they let us pick our own poison." She sighed. "I wondered, for a while, what I'd have done in college."

"You didn't go, then?" Kerry asked surprised.

"No," Ceci replied. "We moved around a lot and I had a little girl to take care of." She was surprised at the lack of bitterness. "I just read everything I could get my hands on and besides, I'm not sure exactly how much good college does for artists."

"Maybe if you had gone, you wouldn't have gone into the art thing," Kerry suggested quietly. "What would you have picked if you had?"

What indeed? "Oh, I don't know. Anthropology, probably."

"Really?" Kerry smiled in surprise. "I took a few classes in that as part of my social sciences requirement. I had a great professor, who was a practicing anthropologist in the summers. He'd come back in the fall with all kinds of stories and pictures." She paused. "Hey. If you have a few extra minutes, maybe we could go to the Museum of Natural History in DC."

"Sounds like an idea." Ceci smiled and leaned back. She wondered if Kerry's parents had ever even bothered to talk to her about what she found interesting—this intelligent young woman who still somehow had a core of wonder inside her that Ceci could fully appreciate.

What a pair of total idiots.

She was looking forward to meeting them.

❖ ⌘ ❖ ⌘ ❖ ⌘ ❖

It turned out better than she expected. Dar adjusted the seat of the rental car she'd wrestled from the terminal and glanced at the tall figure peering alertly out the passenger window. Flying with her father had shortened the trip considerably, and she'd actually had a pretty good time playing a favorite word game with him that brought back memories of a far more innocent period in her life. "Pretty dusty, hmm?"

"Huh." Andrew relaxed, folding his arms over his chest. "So what do you have to do at this meeting?"

Hmm. Good question. "I don't know." Dar put the car into gear. "It depends on what they hit me with." She gave him a quick glance. "That's a figure of speech."

"Who's gonna be there?"

"The whole board, I guess—except the international members. They'll teleconference in, probably." Dar ran the list through her mind. "The only one I really count on as a friend is Alastair. The rest are pretty recent acquaintances." She turned onto the freeway. "Won't be much sympathy there."

"What the hell they got against you?"

Dar drove in silence for a few minutes, evaluating the last fifteen years. "I'm not the nicest person to deal with," she admitted. "I tend to ram issues I think are important through, without much regard for anyone's feelings or opinions."

Andrew watched her with quiet interest. "That what the job calls for?"

"Sometimes."

"Well then?"

"It's all right when you're on top, Dad. But if you slip, it's a hard fall with no allies to cushion it." Dar sighed. "I worked very hard to always be right, because I knew if I wasn't, there were a lot of teeth snapping at my heels." She watched the signs and turned off at the next exit. "What both-

ers me is the fact that I," she hesitated, "that they got me on something
I..."

"They caught you with yer britches down."

"Mmm." Dar had to smile. "Not literally, but yeah."

"Posterior sphincters." Andrew shook his head. "Got no more sense
than the good Lord gave a grasshopper's left...um...leg."

"Dad?" Dar gave him an affectionate look. "I know what assholes
and balls are."

"Watch yer mouth, young lady, before I turn you over mah knee and
make you sing Dixie."

Obligingly, Dar started to sing. "Oh I wish I was in the land of cotton, old times there, are not forgotten, gone away...gone away...gone
away to Dixieland..."

"Smart aleck." Her father laughed, then joined in. He had a low,
growly singing voice that sounded a bit like Dar's and wasn't unpleasant
at all to listen to. They finished the song just as Dar pulled up to the gates
and rolled the window down. She showed her ID to the guard, who gave
her a quick respectful nod and allowed them through.

Andrew peered around the huge complex as they drove in. "Holy
Jesus."

Dar chuckled and pulled into the parking area. She selected a spot
and turned the car off—now feeling butterflies in her stomach. She picked
up her security card and examined it, tracing the familiar features
reflected back at her along with the sharp black letters of her name.

Her employee number. Her hire date.

She knew a moment of profound sadness. "Guess I'd better go get
this over with." She exhaled. "C'mon. There's an area upstairs you can
wait in."

"Ah could just go in there with you," Andrew suggested, as he got
out of the car.

"Daddy." Dar leaned on the roof of the car as she removed her laptop
and shouldered it. "Thank you, but I really can handle this." She hoped.
"And whatever happens, there's one of the best steak places I've ever
eaten in down the road. Dinner's on me."

They walked into the building and Dar angled her steps towards the
security desk. The man behind the counter glanced up at her as she
approached and straightened, responding more to her sleek neatly pressed
gray suit and black silk shirt than anything else. "Morning." Dar handed
over her identification. "I need to sign in a guest."

"Yes, ma'am." The guard handed back her badge and provided a
temporary one, as Dar wrote in her name, then smiled a little as she wrote
in her father's. She signed the book with a flourish, then handed him the
clip-on identification. "Here you go."

"Ain't this special." Andy amiably clipped the badge to his shirt and followed her across the huge, echoing lobby to the elevators. The building was built with cold granite walls, and the high atrium featured a spiraling architecture that had offices and corridors overlooking the large cavernous center. "Place looks tighter than Fort Knox," he muttered, as they entered the elevator car.

"Not quite." Dar found a smile somewhere. "I caught a report the other day where they found bums sleeping inside unused offices in the upper floors." She chuckled. "Heads rolled in security." She drew a breath in as the car stopped and the doors opened, allowing them onto the executive floor. It was quiet here as usual and Dar led the way down the corridor and into the large antechamber outside Alastair's office.

Beatrice glanced up as she entered and gave her a sympathetic smile. "Hello, Dar."

"Morning." Dar held the door open. "Bea, I'd like you to meet my father." She paused. "Andrew Roberts. Dad, this is Bea. She's known me here since I was hired."

"Mr. Roberts, it's a pleasure." Bea came around her desk and offered her hand. "So nice to meet you."

"Ma'am." Andy took her hand carefully and clasped it.

"He in?" Dar tilted her head to the right. Beatrice nodded. "C'mon, Dad. Alastair remembers meeting you but it's been a while." She walked over to the door and knocked lightly, hearing the grunt on the other side. She opened the door to see her boss seated behind his desk, his chin resting on his fists.

"Dar, come on in." The older man leaned back, then blinked in surprise as his ever troublesome employee was followed by a slightly taller, older, more muscular and male version of herself. One look at the lean, angular face and Alastair had no problem guessing his identity. "Ah," he stood, "Commander Roberts, I believe." A genuine smile edged his face and he came out from behind his desk. "It's a pleasure, sir. We met once before, though you probably don't remember me."

Andrew padded forward and took the outstretched hand, shaking it, and allowing a half grin to emerge. "Ah surely do remember. Ah came by that company picnic you all were having and watched you darn near set a pair of sea grapes on fire."

Alastair laughed. "You do indeed remember correctly," he admitted. "A little too enthusiastic with the starter fluid, unfortunately."

Dar's cell phone went off and she unclipped it, stepping to one side. "Excuse me." She opened it. "Hello?"

"Dar?"

"Hey, Mark. I just got to the compound. Anything I can do for you while I still have a chance?" Dar forced the macabre humor.

"Yeah. Got a pencil?" The MIS manager's voice was full of milky satisfaction. "Listen up."

Alastair offered his unexpected guest a drink. "What brings you to Houston, Commander?" He poured glasses of honey colored ice tea and handed Andrew one.

"Mah kid." The ice blue eyes, so weirdly familiar, fastened on him. "Had to come out here and see what kind of place it was that would be thinking of kicking out someone as smart and talented as I know she is for some dumb fool reason."

Alastair blinked and took a step back, a little startled at the directness. "Oh. I see, well..." He looked at Dar, who was still busy with her phone. "You know, I agree with you on that. I've always been one of Dar's biggest supporters."

"Yeap. She did say that," Andy allowed. "And I'd like to thank you for watching out for my little girl."

"Lit—" A stunned pause. "You me—ah." Alastair cleared his throat. "I'm sorry, Commander. I've known your daughter for fifteen years and it would never in my wildest dreams occur to me to think of her as anyone's 'little girl.'"

"Sir?" The voice from the intercom.

"Yes?" Alastair answered it gratefully.

"The board is waiting. Is Ms. Roberts there?"

"Oh. Yes, yes, she's here." The CEO sighed. "We'll be right over." He straightened. "Dar? Are we ready?" He looked saw a chilling, almost predatory smile on Dar's face.

"Oh yeah," his CIO agreed. "We are definitely ready." Her phone rang again and she answered it. "Yes?"

"Dar, it is José." The Sales VP's voice was excited. "Listen to me. That new thing of yours. How soon?"

"For what?" Dar asked, as she adjusted her briefcase and prepared to follow Alastair. "José, I'm about to go into a meeting. The network's up, if that's what you're asking."

"¡Bueno! ¡Bueno!" José chortled. "It can hold up bandwidth for a T3, yes?"

Dar gave Alastair an exasperated look. "Of course it can. José, this has got to wait."

"Do not worry, Dar. I have all that I need to know. Goodbye." José hung up and Dar folded her phone and tucked it into her belt, only to have it go off again. "Jesus." She flipped it open. "Hello?"

"Hey."

Dar felt like she'd just had warm marshmallow poured over her. "Hi. Your flight go okay?"

"Mmm." Kerry's voice sounded curious. "Except I picked up a chaperone, it seems."

"Huh?"

"Your mother."

"My mo—" Dar slowly turned and looked at her father, who had his hands tucked behind his back and his most innocent novice swabbie expression on his face. "Oh, I'm beginning to see a conspiracy here. Guess who's with me."

"You're kidding." Kerry laughed. "Dar, that's just out of control."

"Well, I've gotta go into my meeting. Glad you got there safely."

"You too. Good luck." Kerry's voice was serious now. "Go with your heart, Dar. Whatever happens, I'm there with you."

Dar swallowed. "Same to you." She hung up and folded the phone, then gave Alastair a nod. "Let's go."

"You sure you don't want to turn that phone off?" Alastair gave her a wry look. "Commander, feel free to wait here, or outside."

"All right." Andy settled himself in a comfortable leather chair very near the door. "I will tell you something, though, sir. I hear any hollerin' going on directed at my kid, you are not gonna like the results." He folded his arms and glared at Alastair.

The CEO held the door to the conference room open. "Ah. Right. Well, actually, it's usually Dar doing the yelling." He escaped and let the door close, then crossed the tiny space before opening the inner door and leading the way into a chill, mostly filled room, whose eyes fastened on him. The eyes then slipped past him to stare at the tall, dark haired woman who entered behind him.

Dar brushed by her boss, went to the conference table, set her briefcase down and rested her fingers on it as she leaned and regarded them.

Ankow smiled smugly at her. The rest of them had expressions ranging from wary regard to outright disgust. Dar took a breath in and let it go and took off the gloves. "All right," her voice pitched low, "you asked me to be here for your idiotic little kangaroo court, so here I am." She straightened and spread her hands out. "Talk fast."

❖ ⌘ ❖ ⌘ ❖ ⌘ ❖

The huge courtroom was filling, half with regular people, half with press, Kerry realized as she waited her turn to pass through the metal detector. Her stomach was in knots and she felt alternately flushed and chilled as she stood anonymously among the crowd. A quick glance around confirmed no one in the vicinity knew her and she exhaled, holding her hands in front of her, clasping her subpoena.

"Haven't seen this much press in a while," Cecilia commented from her position next to Kerry.

"Must be a slow news day," Kerry joked wanly. "Listen...you know...I mean, it's really nice of you to offer, but you really don't have to put yourself through this. I'm sure it's going to be really boring."

The cool gray eyes scanned the crowd. "As an artist, I've learned even the most mundane situations can be inspiring." A smile briefly crossed her lips. "Who knows? Maybe I'll decide to do a series of character study portraits."

Kerry spotted a very familiar core of obstinacy behind that mild expression and she gave a little nod as she moved forward and handed the court clerk her paper. She waited for him to examine it, then he put a little stamp on the surface and recorded something.

"Inside, to the left." He passed her through. "Hands away from your body, please."

Kerry unclipped her pager and cell phone and handed them over, then walked through the metal detector, which remained comfortingly silent. She turned and took back her electronics, then waited while Cecilia walked through the portal, easily clearing both sides with her diminutive stature. Dar's mother was dressed in casual pale khaki cotton pants and a blue green sweater with its sleeves pushed halfway up her arms. The color contrasted nicely with her silver blond hair and lent a touch of warmth to her eyes.

Kerry liked it and wished she were dressed as comfortably. She'd decided on one of her suits she wore at work, the burgundy one Dar had picked out for her the last time they'd been shopping. She had a pale gray silk shirt on and kept ruffling her hair in back, getting used to the shorter length she'd had it cut to for summer. "There're some seats up there." She pointed, just before her eyes moved right and she spotted her family. "Ah."

Ceci followed her gaze and studied the crowd, easily recognizing Kerry's father from his television appearances. He was accompanied by an older woman dressed in a high necked, very plain gray dress, and a young man and woman, whom she deduced were Kerry's brother and sister. As Ceci watched, the older woman turned her head and met Kerry's eyes, then very deliberately looked away.

Kerry's gaze dropped.

Ceci tucked her hand into her companion's elbow and tugged. "C'mon." She guided the very quiet Kerry to a set of empty seats across the big aisle from where her family was gathered. She sat down and watched them from the corner of her eyes, seeing the younger woman and man spot Kerry and lean their heads together, whispering.

The woman, she realized, was very pregnant. Behind her sat a tall, distinguished looking man and a younger man with blond hair and gentler eyes.

Kerry kept her gaze forward, still smarting from the coldness she could feel coming from her mother and the refusal of her siblings to meet her glance.

Did they know? Kerry suspected they did know that she'd been the one who released the information to the press, proving herself a traitor on a level nothing she could ever do or say could relieve her from. At the time, she'd been angry and had felt justified. Maybe she still did, but there was a part of her that wished she hadn't done it, even though the chances of her reconciling with her parents were slim even then.

It hurt. She studied her hands, folded in her lap, her thumb playing idly with the pretty ring that circled her finger.

"That's a beautiful piece," Ceci commented softly. "May I see it?"

With a pensive smile Kerry tugged it off and handed it over, turning her head a little to watch Dar's mother examine her gift, admiring the intricate, lacy design. "Dar surprised me with it." Ceci's eyes widened a little and she turned the ring to one side, peering at the inside band.

Then the gray eyes lifted to meet hers, with a look of intense understanding in them. It was, Ceci sucked in a breath, like coming out of a dark room into the light.

She had wondered for thirty years what drove her daughter, and it had been right in front of her the entire time.

Dar had only wanted what she and Andrew had.

Goddess.

"What's wrong?" Kerry asked leaning closer. "Mrs. Roberts, are you all right?"

She sighed and handed the ring back. "Oh, yes." She gave Kerry a wry smile. "Just having a personal revelation."

"Really?" Kerry slid the ring back on, the cool metal warming to her skin immediately. "Do you have those often?"

"Not nearly often enough," Cecilia admitted quietly.

Kerry was about to pursue that line of questioning further, when the buzz around her lowered and chairs scraped. Then they all rose as the examining council walked in and then they sat down after the six people behind the elevated table got to their places.

"All right." The man in charge shuffled some papers and put a pair of half glasses on his nose. "Let's get going." He looked at the special prosecutor. "Mr. Dileko?"

"Thank you." The lawyer, a dapper Democratic political appointee stood and studied his legal pad. "I'd like to call Kerrison Stuart to the stand, please." He glanced up into the crowd expectantly. "The bailiff tells me she's here?"

Oh boy. Kerry was completely not ready to face the crowd. She gathered her shredded confidence and stood, then looked down as a hand patted hers. "Wish me luck."

"Hang in there, Kerry." Cecilia smiled. "Anyone who could tame my daughter shouldn't have any trouble with this bunch."

Kerry returned the smile gratefully, then straightened her shoulders, edged out of the row of seats, and went to the front of the room. She clenched her hand and felt her ring bite into her palm, lending her a measure of strength as she passed her family's seats and sensed their eyes on her.

Then she was on the stand and had to turn and face the room, a myriad of expressions looking back at her. She lifted her hand and repeated the words the clerk muttered, then sat down and turned her face towards the lawyer and waited.

And tried to pretend the most hostile of the looks directed at her weren't related to her by blood.

Chapter
32

"We have some serious issues to discuss with you, Ms. Roberts."
Dick Beresen folded his arms. He was a deep pockets, mostly in the back-
room kind of board member, with a deep scar running across half his face
and thin, mostly missing gray black hair.

Dar waited, her hands resting lightly on the chair back. One dark
eyebrow lifted and invited him to go on.

"We're about to close the quarter and these reports are frankly not
only disappointing, they're unacceptable." Dick stood up. "Four accounts
were total losses and three others are just barely making their numbers."

Dar remained silent, lifting the other brow.

"And then there's Allison Consulting." A murmur rose. "Care to
explain that?"

"Should I have to?" Dar asked mildly. "The operations team report
was very extensive." She folded her arms across her chest and moved
away from the table. "Their management falsified information and is facing criminal charges."

"Why wasn't it caught before we laid out two million dollars for
them?" This was from Alan Evans, a CPA whose family represented
twenty percent of the outstanding stock in ILS.

"Ask the auditors," Dar replied. "I have no explanation for that. I can
just tell you what my team reported during the integration." She shook her
head. "They were uncooperative."

"That's not what we found." Evans pulled a folder over and opened
it. "According to the interviews I had commissioned, their staff reported
that your representative was inexperienced and didn't understand their
systems and they were unfairly dismissed by yourself."

For an answer, Dar removed her laptop from its case and booted it. It
brought up her desktop and she opened a database program, then selected

a record. "The last six bids they won were forced through blackmail on the individuals making the decision. According to the police report, two of their senior management had over five hundred thousand dollars of unexplained funds in their bank accounts. Searches of the property of twenty employees turned up company equipment still in boxes piled up in their garages. And one of their clients has turned over telephone records and tapes of their chief accountant giving instructions on where to leave a cash payoff of over twenty thousand dollars or face embarrassing personal pictures being released to the local press."

She clicked the box to close it. "The integrator in question was our Operations Director, who had successfully integrated twenty accounts prior to theirs, so that leaves their last statement." She paused. "Which is half true. I fired them." She shook her head. "I don't consider it to be unfairly."

"How do you explain this then?" Evans tossed a picture towards her, an unpleasant smirk on his face. Dar glanced at it, expecting it to be the doctored one of Kerry in the bar. Instead, she found herself looking at an excellently focused shot of herself and Kerry in bed together–completely naked.

Fifteen years of troubleshooting came thankfully to her rescue. She gave her breathing several beats to relax, then glanced up at him, with the most amused, deprecating smile she could muster on her face. "Are you asking for an artistic opinion, or would you like a graphic demonstration of my technique?" She tried not to look at Alastair's shocked face, though, and she knew this was going to be uglier than she'd forecasted.

"Are you admitting that is you in that picture?" Evans leaned forward.

Dar looked at the shot, then plucked her shirt out and glanced down the opening. "Yep, that's me all right," she agreed amiably. "A perfect example of what I was talking about with Allison Consulting."

"Ms. Roberts, is that not your assistant in that picture with you?"

Grab the gonads time. Dar folded her arms. "Yes, it is."

Evans picked up the shot, then let it fall, and dropped his glasses on the table as well. "That's enough for me." He glanced across the table at a smiling David Ankow. "I don't think that suit's near enough to cover this."

"Oh, there's more." Ankow stood and stretched, very obviously enjoying himself. "Let me just read it out." He picked up his pad and walked to the head of the table, opened the leather cover, and set it on the wood surface. "Then if you gentlemen agree, we can proceed accordingly. I have security already standing by."

Dar stole a glance at Alastair, who briefly met her eyes, then let his drop, letting her know she was really on her own for this one. She felt a sinking sensation, then she lifted her head and put the regrets behind her, focusing on the here and now and gathering her thoughts and resources, ready for Ankow to start in. "I think security is a very good idea," she remarked, giving him an unexpected smile. "But you go first."

She saw the momentary doubt in his eyes and widened her grin.

No, Daddy. You didn't raise me to be no quitter.

"All right." Ankow cleared his throat. "What we're establishing with this suit is a systematic and deliberate use of company property, resources, and funds to further your personal ends and those of your live-in lover, the Operations Director of this company, Kerrison Stuart."

"Partner." Dar interrupted him.

"What?"

"Partner. Kerry is my partner." She cracked her knuckles. "You might as well get the terminology of that right, since I know you won't get the technical parts anything close to accurate."

Ankow stared at her. "Point one." He glanced at his pad. "During the integration of Associated Synergenics, the accused caused a position to be created in the Operations ORGID, which she filled with Ms. Stuart, disregarding all company policy and ignoring over thirty qualified candidates for the job."

Eyes shifted to Dar.

"Absolutely correct."

"How could you justify that?" Evans stood and pointed.

"Simply." Dar gave him a direct look. "She was the best choice." She paused. "As her subsequent job performance proves."

Evans pulled out a set of papers and read through them, with several people looking over his shoulder. He put them down and folded his arms, but didn't make any further comment.

"Next?" Dar cocked her head.

"Do we have to go through with this?" Beresen threw up his hands. "Frankly, I don't want to spend an hour listening to this crap." He stood up and pointed at Dar. "This is what you're going to do. You're going to resign and get your ass out of this building and go back to the banana farm."

Heads nodded.

"You're going to sign a paper admitting to all this, and we're going to figure out just how much it's cost us, and then you're going to cut the company a check for that and hope we don't file criminal charges."

Dar turned her back and went to the window, peering out at the parched landscape and ignoring the rising speech between the men, letting the hateful comments bounce off her back and knowing not even Alastair's face would be friendly if she turned around.

She caught her reflection in the glass and stared into her own eyes for a very long moment. It would be easy just to sign the paper and go home.

It really would be. Then she could take off with Kerry and they could go someplace nice and quiet and feed each other lobster in the sunset with nothing but surf and sun and sand to worry about.

Yeah.

She imagined calling the office and telling them.

Having María pack up her office.

Having Mark shut down her access and disable her passwords so no one got any bright ideas.

Telling Kerry.

Facing her father.

A quirk appeared at the corner of her mouth. So much for that.

She turned around. "Hey!" Her shout brought shocked silence. "Sit your asses down." Dar stalked back over and put her hands on the chair back. "Number one, I'm not resigning."

"Bu—"

"Now, hold on—"

"Shut up!" Dar snarled. "If you want me out of here, you're gonna have to fire me."

"No problem," Ankow yelled.

"And then it's *my* turn for a lawsuit," Dar barked back. "A nice, big fat one for wrongful dismissal." She leaned forward. "And one for discrimination."

There was a moment of silence. "Your perversion isn't covered under the law," Ankow finally spat. "Thank God we kept that out of the books."

"No." Dar smiled darkly. "My sexual orientation isn't covered under the anti-discrimination laws, though it is covered by the corporate bylaws, but," she started a circle around the table, "gentlemen," she emphasized the word, "my sex is."

"What the hell are you talking about?" Evans blurted.

"Check your shorts." Dar paced around the corner of the table. "Largest public IS company in the world. With a ton of US government contracts–and I am the only, single, solitary minority representative in the entire board."

"None of this has anything to do with the facts." Ankow pointed at her.

"That lawsuit has nothing to do with the facts," Dar shot back. She whirled and pointed to several members. "Since when does this slut festival care who the hell I'm sleeping with? Give me one example of one single time at any single moment that the fact that Kerry Stuart and I are lovers hurt the company." She raised her voice. "Give me one!"

Total silence.

"You big bunch of sanctimonious, useless pig farts!" Dar roared. "Between the two of us we run the fucking company. So drop the goddamn bullshit and put the cards on the table." She slammed her hand on the surface and sounded like a shot. "Fire me, and so help me God, I will take this company down." She glared at all of them "You want trouble? You have no idea what kind of trouble I can make. I know skeletons in closets so deep even the fucking Anthropological Society couldn't find them." She paced around the chair. "I know all the hiring for tit size, the payoffs to the Feds, the deliberate exclusion of minorities–you name it, I know it, I've lived in it for fifteen years and there is no," she pointed at Ankow, "no single goddamned corner of this company that I haven't been in."

"Dar," Alastair stood and held a hand out, palm down, "let's just back it down a little."

Dar gave him a murderous glare.

"Please." The CEO took a breath. "Bottom line, Dar is right."

"Figures you support her. You're probably screwing her," Ankow muttered.

"I should be so lucky," Alastair responded shortly. "The facts of the matter are, gentlemen, that none of us are saints and, operationally speaking, we are in better shape with the present management than we have been in a number of years."

"Bet the shareholders won't think so when you announce the loss this quarter," Evans snapped. "I hope they tar and feather your ass." He stood. "When that lawsuit goes public with the quarter results we'll lose the company."

"Not this quarter," Alastair replied quietly. "José just signed a four hundred million dollar contract to provide backbone services to a consortium of ISP's."

Absolute, dead shocked silence–even from Dar.

"Running, of course, on Dar's new network, which is the only one in the country capable of it." He paused. "Gentlemen, we *are* the Internet." He drew a breath. "Congratulations, Dar. That was the shortest cost of doing business assessment in the history if ILS."

Son of a bitch. Dar was speechless, the anger in her guts still boiling, but having no where to go. "Thanks," she finally muttered. She'd known she was making the right decision on the network, but being vindicated so quickly hadn't been a thought of hers. She felt mostly disgusted, and tired, not even a little bit triumphant. "Can we dump the bullshit now?"

"Oh no." Ankow met her gaze. "I'm not nearly through with you." He shook his head. "I don't care what they put on that network. I'm not going to back off exposing you for the poison you are."

"Funny you should put it like that." Dar dropped her amused attitude and went very serious. She started around the table towards him. "Speaking of poison," her eyes found his and held, for a very long moment, "makes me wonder what your game is here." She circled him, like a shark would, lazily testing the waters. "Why would a jockstrap lawyer from

Oregon latch onto an IS company and try to take control of it?"

"None of your fucking business," he snarled back. "Maybe I just want to give the stockholders some value for their money."

"Maybe you just remembered that old maxim. Knowledge is power. Only," Dar circled him again, "in the IS world we say, data is power." She paused. "Now, why would a turnip like you be interested in us?"

Everyone was watching her now.

"Maybe it's for your daddy, hmm?" Dar stopped in front of him, so they were nose to nose. "Daddy—the leader of the White Power Militia in Oregon?"

His expression changed, becoming dark and dangerous. "I have nothing to do with my father."

"Don't you?" Dar smiled, then walked around to her laptop and clicked on her mail, opening a file. She turned her laptop around to face them. "Funny. You sure look alike."

The board members leaned over to peer at the shot, one of Ankow and an older man in fatigues, with racist banners wrapped around them. Both men had fists upraised in salute. "You should read some of his manifestos–interesting stuff." She straightened. "Especially that plan of his to target specific companies and do industrial sabotage."

Ankow gave her a deadly look.

"Wonder what the stockholders would think of that?" Now, finally, Dar's smile returned. "What do you figure would piss them off more? A dyke or a Nazi?"

"You bitch."

Dar keyed in another file. "Especially a Nazi who was being paid off on the side by Roger Stuart to get his daughter fired." Now the murderous glare was hers, directed at him. "And who was stupid enough to put the details of it into a computer tied to my network."

The looks of shock echoed across the huge table. Dar felt exhausted and she rubbed the back of her neck. "Tell you what. I'm going to get a glass of milk, and you think about it." She turned and walked to the front door of the chamber, let herself out, and headed directly down the corridor towards the kitchen without a backwards glance.

Not hearing the door open and close softly behind her.

❖ ⌘ ❖ ⌘ ❖ ⌘ ❖

"Ms. Stuart, this hearing is intended to bring to light any and all information regarding the allegations against your father." The prosecutor regarded her with neutral interest. "I'll be asking you questions, but any of these gentlemen can do so as well. Do you understand?"

"Yes." Kerry folded her hands on the table and waited. The senate committee was to one side of her, making notes, and whispering amongst themselves. Then the prosecutor, or more properly the investigator, had his little table, then her father and his lawyers were seated at another little table at an angle to her.

"Fine. All right." The man looked at his notes. "You are currently living in Miami, Florida, is that correct?"

"Yes."

"How much support do you get from your father, in dollars, on a monthly basis?"

"None."

The man looked up at her. "Are you sure, Ms. Stuart?"

"Yes, quite sure, thanks," Kerry replied.

"No presents, then? No cars, boats, mink stoles?" The sarcasm was biting.

"No. I buy my own cars and boats, and I have no idea what I would I do with a mink stole in Miami." Kerry returned the volley.

"So you're saying you live on your own?"

"I live with a roommate," she corrected.

"But you pay all your own bills?"

I try to. "Yes."

Shuffling of papers. "When did you last live with your parents, Ms. Stuart?"

"Four and a half years ago."

"That was while you were attending college?"

"Yes."

"Which, I take it, your parents paid for?"

"Actually," Kerry cleared her throat, "I went on scholarship." True, though her parents had paid for everything else, including her clothes, and books. Spending money, on the other hand had come from her part-time job in the campus bookstore.

"Lucky you." The man leafed through a few sheets. "While you were living with your parents, did you have any reason to suspect your father was involved in illegal activities?"

Kerry considered that question seriously. "No," she finally answered, meeting his eyes. "I didn't."

"Really? You seem like an intelligent young woman. Are you saying you never once saw anything you thought was out of the ordinary?"

Kerry's pale eyebrow lifted slightly. "Define ordinary," she replied. "Ordinary for you is probably not ordinary for me, given who my father is and the media spotlight our lives were generally held in." She went on before he could comment. "It never crossed my mind, no, that my father was involved in any breech of the law."

"Why not?"

"Excuse me?"

"Why not, Ms. Stuart? Isn't that what politicians do, nowadays?"

The investigator circled her and leaned on the table. "Almost to be expected, don't you think?"

Kerry studied his face, which was not unpleasant to look at. Given the last few years in politics, with what had gone on and the circus the leadership of the nation had become, he was probably more right than wrong. But she shrugged. "Honestly, it's not something I spend a lot of time thinking about."

He stood up and lifted a hand towards her. "Or you weren't encouraged to think about it."

Maybe. Kerry thought back to her younger years. Politics were something her father had never, ever discussed with her, or her sister, or even Michael. On the other hand, since she'd left home, the subject had never interested her either. She shrugged. "I think I just have drastically lowered expectations." *Ooo. The guys on the council didn't like that.*

"So, you're saying it *is* something you'd expect someone like your father to do?"

"That's not what I said."

"You said you had drastically lowered expectations, did you not?"

"Well, yes, but—"

"That is what you said, wasn't it?"

"I said I don't expect politicians to have a higher standard of conduct than anyone else," Kerry clarified.

"Ah, but shouldn't they, Ms. Stuart? After all, we elect them to be our representatives, to act in our best interests, after all. Don't we?"

"Yes, but as far as I know, sir, they aren't a different species." This guy was starting to annoy her. "Most of the time people act in their best interests, not someone else's, so the fact that elected officials act like the rest of us does not, sir, surprise me."

"Interesting. And yet, you stated that you had no inkling of an idea that your father was...allegedly...accepting bribes, maintaining an entirely different family, and consorting with racists." He paused. "Were you, then, not surprised to hear the allegations when they came out?"

"Yes, I was surprised."

"Why? If politicians are like the rest of us, then why be surprised? Since you stated you don't hold them to any high standard, is that right?"

"I don't." Kerry paused. "But I do hold my father to higher standards, because he is my father, not because he is a politician. So yes, sir, I was surprised."

"Interesting double standard, Ms. Stuart. You don't find that a contradiction?" the lawyer asked shrewdly.

"Life is full of contradictions, sir," Kerry answered quietly.

He studied her, a faint smile playing across his lips. "Yes, isn't it?"

They were definitely different. Ceci watched Kerry under questioning, her body language indicating wary alertness and her answers guarded but straightforward. *Had it been Dar up there,* a smile touched her lips, *Dar would have been all over the lawyer, challenging his questions, and dominating the table with her restless energy.*

Just like Ceci herself would have been, she admitted privately. Kerry, on the other hand, preferred a more low keyed, more reasonable attitude that still used her intelligence to make her points with accuracy. *I bet she and Dar make quite a team in the office. The ultimate good cop, bad cop routine, with the natural friction that should have been caused by their radically different styles gentled and diffused by the fact that they loved each other.*

A motion beside her made her look up to see the short, brown haired man sitting with Kerry's family taking the seat next to her.

"Hi," he murmured.

Ceci's eyebrow lifted. "Hi." *Was this... Yes, Kerry had said this was her brother, Michael.* She glanced quickly at the other side of the aisle, but everyone was paying close attention to Kerry, and Michael's absence hadn't been noted. "Something you want?"

"Um." He glanced furtively around and leaned forward, resting his elbows on his knees. "You're here with Kerry Stuart, right?"

"Who's asking?" Ceci decided to play hardball with him.

His eyes lifted and met hers for a brief minute. "I'm her brother, Michael."

"Really? I understood she was told she had no family here."

He winced and looked down. "It's complicated."

"No, it's not. You just need to go find a taxidermist and rent a spine," Ceci replied. "If you've decided not to talk to her, that's one thing. But if you're letting someone else make that choice for you, it's damn sad."

They kept their voices down, but her last comment caused Michael's ears to redden and he swallowed audibly. "I just wanted to find out if she's okay," he mumbled.

"Ask her." Ceci folded her arms implacably.

They listened to the questions of the lawyer and Kerry's even answers for a minute. Then Michael peeked up at her, his long, dark lashes blinking slightly. "Are you related to Dar, by any chance?"

Ceci's eyebrows lifted. "What makes you ask?"

He didn't answer, but the corners of his mouth twitched.

"I'm her mother, yes."

Michael nodded to himself.

"Is there a problem with that?"

He gave a tiny smile. "No, ma'am."

The lawyer finished his questions and released Kerry from the table, and they watched as she circled it and headed down the aisle back towards them.

"You going to stay here or run back over there?" Ceci asked.

He stayed. Kerry spotted him as she was almost back to her seat and her eyes widened into a look of wary surprise. "Hi," she murmured softly as he stood up and faced her, then pulled her into a hug. "How are you?"

Ceci watched a smile cross Kerry's face as she returned the embrace. She winked at Kerry and got an even broader grin, complete with a wrinkled nose and the appearance of the very tip of her tongue. Her eyes slipped past the two siblings to a hostile gaze on them from across the aisle and she took the opportunity to lock eyes with the burly, gray haired man seated at the defendant's table. He jerked, as though startled, then looked away and pointedly turned his back on them.

Kerry and her brother sat down and she laced her fingers with his as they listened to the prosecutor call up Angie. "Thanks for coming over," she whispered. "I know you're in trouble for it."

"Got a spare room down there in Miami? I'll bring a sleeping bag," Michael whispered back, giving her a forlorn look. "Maybe I can get a job washing the beach sand over there?"

"Absolutely." Kerry squeezed his hand. "Oh, sorry. Michael, this is Cecilia Roberts. She's Dar's mom."

"We've, uh, met." Michael produced a hesitant smile. "Hi."

"Pleasure to meet you, Michael," Cecilia responded cordially. "Nice work up there, Kerry."

"Thanks." Kerry sighed and leaned back, tucked as she was between her brother and her new friend, she almost could make herself believe this wasn't going to be so horrible after all. She noticed several latecomers entering and turned to watch them, then heard Michael make a hissing noise. "What?"

"I can't believe they showed up."

"Who?" Kerry peered at the new watchers, a woman in her mid-forties with well coifed blond hair accompanied by two younger people, a man and a woman.

"That's them," her brother whispered. "The people Dad's supporting."

Oh Lord. "Jesus." Kerry closed her eyes.

Cecilia leaned over curiously. "What's wrong?"

Kerry sighed. "My father's other woman just came in with her kids." She gave Ceci a wry look. "Sorry—this is going to be a circus."

"Mmm." Dar's mother rubbed her earlobe. "I can't wait to see the lion act in that case."

Chapter 33

Dar slumped in the padded chair, alone in the small efficiency kitchen tucked away down the hall. Beside her, a fresh pot of coffee burbled, filling the room with its rich fragrance, and a cup sat waiting, already loaded with cream and sugar.

She should feel great, she knew. After all, she'd taken a losing situation and turned it around in her favor, winning down and dirty in a convincing way that even Ankow had no defense against.

Maybe she would feel good about it, after her head stopped aching, and she was out of this damn marble shithouse. A wry smile made its way onto her face. *Damn, José. I owe you the biggest Argentinean barbecued steak south of the Mason Dixon when I get home, you little Cuban super salesman.*

She tilted her head back against the wall and focused her eyes on the doorway, then blinked when it was filled unexpectedly with a tall, burly figure. "Hey."

Her father padded inside and turned a chair around, sat on it backwards, resting his arms on the back. "Hey, Dardar. You all right?"

"Yeah." Dar rubbed her eyes. "Just unwinding a little."

Andrew regarded the tall form sprawled across from him. "Headache?"

Dar nodded.

"Used to get me them, too. Base doctor always told me t'cut down on stress."

Dar smiled. "Yeah." She rested her head against her fist. "I was getting them every day there for a while." She was reluctant to talk about the board meeting. "One more session and we're outta here, I think."

"Mmm." Her father grunted. "You done hollerin' then?"

Dar felt a moment of surprise and she hesitated, taking in a careful breath. "You heard me?"

"Sure." Andy didn't look distressed. "Had the pictures shaking in that damn office, matter of fact."

The coffee finished and Dar reached over to pour some in her cup, then used the distraction of stirring it to give herself some time to answer. "Yeah, well," she muttered, "I wasn't really sure I wanted you to see that side of me." She sipped the hot beverage, as her father waited patiently for her to continue. "It's not very pleasant most of the time."

"Paladar, it's a damn proud thing for a father to listen to his kid stand up for herself, and everyone else like that," Andrew told her seriously. "'Specially when folks were saying some of the stuff them bastards were saying."

Dar smiled grimly. "That son of a bitch." She shook her head. "I think what made me maddest was the fact that he was going after Kerry." Her nostrils flared. "I don't know, Dad—maybe that idea of starting my own business was the right one after all. I don't know how much more of this crap I want to put up with."

"Wall, everything that lives takes a dump, Dardar. You're always gonna hafta deal with some of it."

Yeah. Dar stood up and handed him the coffee cup. "Here. Let me go get this over with, then we can get out of here. I hear a stuffed sweet potato calling my name." She put a hand on her father's shoulder and walked past him. "Hope Kerry's having a better day than I am."

Andrew turned around and propped a foot up on the chair next to him, sipping the coffee thoughtfully. "I think you're doing all right," he murmured to the empty room. "That was some of the best verbal ball kicking I heard since boot camp."

Footsteps coming down the hall made him look up, but he remained where he was as a tall, good looking man entered. The newcomer gave him a surprised look, then brushed by and grabbed a paper cup from the stack near the water cooler.

He attempted to fill it, but the spigot wasn't cooperating and after a few tries, he cursed and kicked the machine viciously, making the water slosh in its glass bottle.

"Y'know," Andrew drawled softly. "Y'd have better luck with that there thing if'n you'd turn it on."

A pair of narrow, angry eyes looked around at him. "Shut the fuck up."

"Jest trying to help." The ex-SEAL took a swallow of coffee and waggled his foot.

"Are you cleaning staff? Don't you have something you need to be doing?"

"Ahm on a coffee break." Andy held up his cup. "That there power switch is behind that white doo dad, by the by." He studied the man carefully, a quiet, almost playful smile shaping his lips, which didn't reach the cold blue eyes above them.

Ankow switched the device on, and it hummed obediently. "Thanks." He tossed over his shoulder, visibly still annoyed at the scruffy, older man sprawled comfortably on the chairs.

"Mah pleasure."

"Jerk," Ankow muttered softly under his breath, as he grabbed his cup, put it under the spigot, and turned it on sharply. The top popped off and a fountain of ice cold water hit him in the face and he yelled, releasing it and slamming a fist against the device in fury.

It toppled over, sending the glass water tank crashing to the ground and a spray of glass and liquid out, dousing him thoroughly. "Son of a bitch!"

Andy chuckled.

The drenched man turned. "It's not fucking funny, so shut your mouth, old man."

"Wall, sonny, I ain't the one standing there all wet then, am I?" Andy sipped his coffee, completely at his ease. "You oughta watch that temper now. It'll get you in trouble one of these fine days."

Ankow brushed the front of his jacket off, walked over to the seated man and stood over him with an aggressive posture. "You think so?" he asked softly.

"Yeap."

"I think it's you who's asking for trouble, old man." Ankow's eyes glinted dangerously. "Your break's over. Get lost."

Andrew put his cup down on the table and folded his arms. "Testy little feller, ain't ya?" He chuckled. "What's the matter? Some girl tweak yer shorts?"

"Oh. I am just in the mood for someone like you." Ankow snarled, lunging forward and reaching for the very welcome outlet for his temper.

Andy hooked the younger man behind the knee with his propped foot and yanked him forward and off balance. Then he coiled his other leg up and lashed out, catching Ankow in the gut with a vicious kick that sent him sprawling back onto the ground. "See thar? You just got to watch that temper, boy," he drawled, resuming his comfortable posture.

Ankow rolled with the motion and got to his feet, then grabbed a chair and lifted it over his head.

"Ya'll don't want to do that," Andrew warned.

The chair descended, hitting wood and steel as the older man slipped out of the way, ducking gracefully around his antagonist and waiting for him to go past. Then he whirled and executed a perfectly timed round-house kick that nailed Ankow in the side of the head and threw him against the wall.

He stumbled back and turned to see Andrew waiting for him, balanced over slightly bent knees. "I think I need to call security."

"Ah think you need to change yer diapers." Andy came at him, grabbed him before he could move and took him down with a powerful twist of his body. He landed on top of the younger man, pinning him down and landing a knee firmly on his genitals.

Ankow's mouth opened, but no sound came out and his eyes bugged as his adversary leaned forward and rested his weight on his chest so that they were eye to eye.

"Now," Andrew said softly, "you are going to listen to me, Mr. David Ankow, former Army Ranger, who is a sorry pissant example of a soldier."

Ankow stared at him. "Who the fuck are you?" he managed to squeak out.

Andy reached out and put a hold on his neck, making his face redden as the blood pooled. "Ah'm Dar's daddy." The eyes widened, and he smiled. "And ah do not take kindly to you messing with her." He leaned closer. "So you are gonna cease and desist bothering my little girl, or I will surely turn you into Julianne human being. Do you understand me, boy?"

"I'll sue you for this."

"Only if'n you want me tellin' the police about that little patch you stuck on my kid down south," Andrew drawled. "Which I will tell you is more than enough for me to want to toss you out that there window."

Ankow was silent.

Andrew released him, stood, stepped out of any possible range with a smooth, even motion, and waited. He would either run or fight, the ex-SEAL knew, and he was stupid enough to do the latter. "Ah think it's time for you to leave, boy."

Ankow got up in a crouch, then slowly straightened, obviously in pain. He edged out of the room without further comment and slunk down the hallway. Andy heard the door to the bathroom open and close, and only then did he relax and brush his shirt off, mentally reviewing the incident.

Well. Coulda been worse. He picked up the scattered chairs and set them right, then ambled over and studied the mess of the water cooler, turning when a low throat clearing sounded behind him.

Alastair was in the doorway. "What happened here?"

Andy tugged at an earlobe. "Feller came in, didn't like the water, I suppose," he remarked. "Picky folks you got around here."

Alastair walked gingerly into the room and surveyed the damage, then eyed Andy dubiously. "I don't suppose it was a tall guy, in a light gray suit was it?"

"Ah do believe it was," Andy allowed.

"Uh huh." The CEO sighed and gave the taller man a wry look. Very innocent blue eyes looked back at him in a very familiar way. "Commander Roberts, why is it that I get the feeling the apple on my payroll didn't fall very far from the tree?"

"Beats me," Andy rasped. "Y'all about done in there?"

"Yes," Alastair murmured. "I just want to have a little private meeting with Dar before we all leave." He turned and put a hand on the open doorjamb. "I'll call the cleaning crew up to take care of this." With a shake of his head, he left, and Andy wandered over to re-secure his cup of coffee.

Old man, huh?

A salt and pepper eyebrow quirked.

You can jest kiss mah ass.

❖ ⌘ ❖ ⌘ ❖ ⌘ ❖

Kerry shifted in her seat for the hundredth time, listening to the repetitive questions being put to her siblings. Michael had been called up and had to answer honestly to how much their parents had supported him, including the six years he'd muddled through college and the fact that they'd bought him a townhouse in Michigan and paid for his car.

It had been a little embarrassing. At least Angie was married and had her own home, bought by her well off husband, Richard. Angie looked terrible though, Kerry realized, pale and drawn even taking her pregnancy into account. She felt bad for her sister, but Angie wouldn't even meet her eyes in the audience.

Michael had gone back to sit next to her after his testimony, though, and the two dark heads were bent together in obvious collaboration.

"This has got to be killing you," Ceci murmured sympathetically.

"You have no idea." Kerry sighed, sliding her fingers through her hair and rubbing the back of her neck. "It's not like we haven't always had the press sniffing around, but to have to sit up there like that...Jesus."

Ceci patted her arm. "Hang in there, Kerry. It won't last forever. Maybe the worst is over for you. I'd think they'd move on to more fertile ground."

"Mmph." Kerry looked around, then faced Ceci. "Thank you again, by the way, for hanging around here with me." She managed a smile. "I only wish I knew what was going on with—yow!" Kerry jumped, as her cell phone vibrated, since she'd turned off the audible tones in deference to the crowd. "Jesus, I hate that."

Ceci eyed her in mild alarm, but refrained from commenting.

"Hello?" Kerry murmured into the instrument.

"Kerry?"

"Hey. I was just thinking about you," Kerry replied, hearing a tired, but not horrible tone in Dar's voice. "How's it going?"

"I was just going to ask you the same question." Her lover chuckled. "We're about finished here. I worked out a deal. Things are status quo."

Kerry blinked at the casual statement, as though Dar had arranged to have her car waxed or something. "Oh. Hey, great. We're almost done here, too, I think. At least for today. It's been," she sighed, "interesting."

"In the Chinese sense?"

"Yeah."

"Ah," Dar replied. "Well, I'm just waiting for Alastair to come back so we can wrap things up. Dad and I are going to grab dinner near here, then see if we can catch a flight up there."

"Good Lord, Dar, you guys don't have to all come up here, you know," Kerry protested mildly. "Why don't you go home and relax? I think I'll only be another day or so, at the most."

There was a distinct pause and a little silence at the other end. "All right. If that's what you want," Dar finally answered, in a subdued tone.

Be honest, or... Kerry sensed the hurt on the other end of the phone. "No, it's not what I want." She sighed. "I was just trying to be nice and self-sacrificing and unselfish and all that good stuff."

"Ah." Dar laughed softly.

"We've just got so much work to do, and I really didn't want you thinking that I considered you my personal walking and talking security blanket." Kerry kept her voice very low, but was aware of the tiny smirk on Ceci's face. "I think I'm amusing the hell out of your mother."

"I bet." Dar chuckled. "Well, I gotta go. We'll see you all later tonight, okay?"

"More than okay." Kerry balanced the situation here, with the one she knew Dar was in and decided she'd love the ability to crawl through the phone and come out the other side. Even Houston beat this. "Be safe." She closed the phone and tucked it away, then folded her arms as the lawyers all gathered up near the council table, muttering to each other. She felt a hot light on her face and only just kept from looking, as she realized she was being filmed by the reporters.

God. Her jaw moved. *I'd almost forgotten what that felt like.* "We're on *Candid Camera*," she murmured to Ceci, who had her arms resting on the chair backs in front of them and was watching things with mild interest.

"Is this where Allen Funt comes out in a clown suit?" she remarked. "You're also the subject of attention across the aisle."

"Great."

"Who's the young, blond guy?"

Kerry hesitated. "Brian. He's a family friend."

"He keeps looking at you."

"I'm supposed to be married to him and have a kid by now." Kerry managed a wry smile, then glanced down. "Or at least have one on the way." She patted her stomach.

Cecilia's pale gray eyes fixed on her, then shifted across the aisle, then moved back. "Really?"

Kerry nodded. "Actually, it's kind of a secret, but Angie's baby is his."

Dar's mother rubbed the bridge of her small, finely shaped nose. "I thought she was married to that tall man over there?"

"She is."

Ceci regarded her with a curious expression. "You ever consider contacting Jerry Springer?"

Kerry giggled unexpectedly at that, covering her mouth to keep from bursting out laughing. The light lingered on her for a minute then she felt it go off, as the camera's attention turned elsewhere. "Oh god. That was funny."

"I was serious," Ceci muttered. "You could get a novel out of this at the least."

"Ladies and gentlemen, that will be all for today. All those who were under subpoena today please return here tomorrow morning to continue the investigation. Opposing council has requested time to question some of the depositions taken today."

"Yippee," Kerry murmured. "Well, they're attacking over there. Let's see if we can get out of here while we can." She got up and brushed her jacket off, then edged down the aisle with Ceci behind her. A loud voice drew their eyes and Kerry saw one of her father's lawyers arguing with "the other woman."

"I've got a right to be here!" the woman yelled. "So get your hands off me, you pig!"

"Oh boy." Kerry turned right and plowed determinedly for the door as the cameras scuttled eagerly for the new distraction. She ignored the calls behind her, pretending it was some other Ms. Stuart people were yelling for. "How hard is it to change your name?"

"Not very," Ceci replied, ducking under a reporter's arm. "Half of humanity does it on a regular basis."

"Hmm. Good point." Kerry almost made it to the door, but a tall, burly man with a beard, a microphone, and a cameraman planted himself firmly in her way and she didn't have room to go around him. She stopped and regarded him warily.

"Ms. Stuart, that was a very interesting deposition you gave."

"Glad you thought so," Kerry replied. "I just answered what they asked."

"Our sources tell us you're estranged from your family. Is that true?" The microphone came closer and she was suddenly very aware of the round, black eye of the camera.

"Why do you want to know?" Kerry asked directly.

The reported hesitated a beat at the unexpected answer, then rallied. "This is a public hearing, Ms. Stuart, the people have a right to know the facts."

"It's not my hearing," Kerry objected. "I doubt the public much cares about my facts. Now, if you'll excuse me, I think the juicy action you want is going on over there." She pointed where her father's mistress was struggling with her father's lawyer and then hitting him over the head with her purse. Distracted, the reporter looked, then grabbed his camera-man and started wading over towards the fight.

Kerry sighed. "I said it would be a circus." They edged past a crowd of excited people, many of them pointing at her, and managed to get outside the room where even more cameras waited. A blast of flashbulbs went off and Kerry was almost blinded, stopping short so she wouldn't crash into anything or anyone. "Whoa." She threw up a hand in front of her eyes in sheer defense, then felt a tugging at her elbow and followed Ceci's lead as they dodged around two local reporters who were on the air and got a little breathing space near the top of the long, marble steps.

She could still hear the yelling inside and, briefly, part of her wondered if she shouldn't go back inside and stand by her family, despite the fact that she knew she wasn't wanted there.

She thought about that for a very long moment.

Then she turned and started down the steps. "C'mon. If we wait for them to come out, we'll never get out of here."

Cecilia murmured an agreement as she followed and they went down the steps and out through the huge wooden doors. Outside, barricades had been set up, and a small crowd milled around, seemingly trying to organize themselves.

Banners were raised, and Ceci squinted to try and read them. "I believe those are your father's supporters."

Kerry stopped and looked. America for Americans. She breathed, seeing the T-shirts and the cropped hair. The group was white, of mixed ages, and definitely growing. A bus pulled up and started unloading, with men dragging out signs and women carrying baskets. "Oh my god."

A sign went up. Framed by the Left. Supported by the Moral Right.

"How can they stand behind him, after what he did?" Kerry turned, and asked her older companion. "I don't get it."

Ceci took her arm and urged her towards the street. "Kerry, you live in a country where black men get beaten to death in the streets and sex except in the missionary position is illegal in many places. Don't try to make sense of this, all right? I've learned better." She hailed a cab, which pulled obligingly to the curb for them.

Kerry settled into the seat and moved across, allowing Cecilia room to enter. "You mean, he supports their cause, so they don't care what he does?"

"Something like that." Ceci leaned forward and gave the cab driver their hotel address. "Well, I don't know about you, Kerry, but I certainly could use a drink and some dinner."

"Yeah." Kerry nodded. "I would love a couple of beers." Kerry closed her eyes and her head dropped back against the seat. "And dinner sounds great. Dar said they're going to pick up something there, then catch the late flight out here."

"You're a beer fan?" Ceci chuckled. "And here I go, right after I say not to assume things, I do. I figured you for margaritas."

"Nu uh," Kerry shook her head, "I developed a taste for beer in college and it stuck with me." She considered. "We had a little microbrewery near the campus. I spent a lot of time there, studying and tasting." Living on campus had given her the first real opportunity to see a life other than the one her parents had planned for her. When she looked back on it, those long afternoons in the pub curled up on a nice padded bench mapping out circuits and sipping her choice of beverage were one of the nicest memories she had of school.

Mostly because she knew it would shock them, as much as demonstrating her finely honed and well developed talent of belching would. Kerry chuckled to herself, remembering Michael's face the first time he'd heard her do it.

"Well, from what I read in the lobby, the hotel's got a nice looking eat-in bar they seem pretty proud of. We could give it a try," Cecilia commented, sorting through the possible menus and deciding that, at worst, they'd have a stuffed baked potato she could order.

Or maybe some stuffed mushrooms.

"Sounds good to me," Kerry agreed. "But I gotta get out of this monkey suit. It's driving me nuts." She rolled her head to one side, idly watching the buildings go past in all their marble monstrosity. On the corner just before the hotel she spotted what looked like three of her father's supporters, with cropped heads sporting shaved, colored sigils in the back, and black leather jackets and boots. They appeared to be just standing around talking and she almost dismissed them, before she saw one of them turn, and watch the entrance to the hotel intently for a minute, then return to his conversation.

She thought about that as they pulled up.

Hmm.

Just because you're paranoid, Ker, doesn't mean someone's not out to get you.

She glanced at her watch and wondered.

❖ ⌘ ❖ ⌘ ❖ ⌘ ❖

Dar leaned against the plate glass of the window, watching the sun go down over the flat landscape. The meeting was over, and now...now all she had to do was wait for Alastair to come back in and wrap things up.

It could have been worse.

It could, of course, have also been better.

Despite what she thought of Ankow, the board could no more remove him for being a bigoted, sneaky asshole than they could remove her for being gay. It was almost annoyingly fair, but she had to admit they had nothing really significant to use to dismiss him with. Certainly, given that she'd admitted to her living with Kerry—they had less on him than what they had on Dar.

So.

An uneasy truce was the best they could manage. Ankow very reluctantly agreed to drop his stupid lawsuit and Dar agreed to keep her revelations quiet as well. It came down to consumer confidence, as always. Revealing either scandal would hurt the company and since Ankow's background had been revealed, there was no chance of him getting what he wanted to out of the bargain, so he decided to back off and find another way.

Which meant they'd still have to deal with each other. He'd still demanded that Alastair's and her positions be put up for a general vote of the stockholders and, on that, the majority of the board had agreed. None of them managed to look either of them in the eye, though.

Dar sighed and pressed her aching forehead against the cool glass. The board was uneasy about her and Kerry. She could sense that, in their words and speech, but most of them were too polite to say so to her face. It wasn't surprising, really. Most of them were older and conservative and had enough trouble with her being a woman in the first place, not even go into the fact that she was gay.

It shouldn't goddamn matter. She'd said so and Alastair had agreed, noting that it hadn't mattered to him for fifteen years, and here he was a family man, a grandfather, as conservative as you could get right down to his black socks and patent leather shoes.

The door opened and footsteps approached, scuffing across the tightly woven carpet. Dar heard a faint creak as Alastair perched on the edge of his desk and she turned, regarding him with quiet, serious blue eyes. "Not a good day, Alastair."

He tilted his head a little. "Coulda been worse, Dar. Could have been worse."

"True."

"I know you think I abandoned you in there."

Dar shrugged, and regarded the pale stripes of sunlight coming in the window. "No sense in both of us going down."

"That's not true, Dar." Alastair got up and walked to her, putting his hands in his gray flannel pockets and tipping his head back just a little to meet her eyes. "The truth is, I was out of my league. I had no idea what to say or what to do when he pulled that picture out. I was just hoping you did." He paused. "And, as usual, you handled the worst possible situation with ease and grace and you reminded me all over again why you are where you are and why I put you there."

"I doubt the board agrees with you."

The CEO shrugged. "They don't know you. I've had fifteen years to get used to you, Dar. Give them a chance. Eventually—"

"Eventually they'll forget I'm an evil gay woman with an agenda?"

"Well," her boss chuckled a bit, "they'll forget you're gay. I think it's going to be a really long time before they forget you're a woman." He watched the dark, well shaped eyebrows lift. "C'mon, Dar. We're a bunch of horny old goats in there, you don't think half the resentment floating around that room isn't because not one of us has a chance with you?"

Dar had to laugh. "Alastair, you're such a bastard sometimes."

"Sometimes," he agreed. "Listen, Dar, the fact is that you are very low profile in the company and that's hurting you, because some of these guys don't hear anything but the bad stuff about you. I'd really like you to be at the quarterly stockholders meeting and I'd love you to do the presentation this time."

"Me?"

Alastair nodded. "I've been thinking about it a lot lately and it just seems like a good idea to me. Get you out there and get you exposed to all these people who have no idea who you are, but have heard stories." He smiled. "Besides, it's a great quarter for it, Dar. The new network's up and it's paid for already. I can't think of a better scenario for you to have to present." He paused delicately. "Besides, with that vote in question, it won't hurt to let them see what they're voting on."

"Hmm." Dar felt very off balance. She hadn't expected the conversation to go this way and after the session they'd just been in, her brain was still wandering off track somewhere. "All right. I'll see what I can work up."

"Good." Her boss smiled. "Have you got plans for tonight?"

"Dinner with Dad," Dar replied. "You're welcome to join us if you want. We're heading down the road to the steakhouse."

Alastair sighed. "Dar, I'm gonna have to kill you. I have to go to my nephew's restaurant opening tonight."

"What's wrong with that?"

"It's call Tofu Gardens."

Dar cleared her throat. "I have a chocolate bar in my briefcase if that'll help." She held a hand out. "Have fun. I'll be in touch later, Alastair. We've got a lot to work out for that new contract."

"Will do." The CEO watched her leave, then sat down slowly on his leather chair and laced his fingers around one gray clad knee, as the sunset colored the room around him.

Chapter
34

"I think ah'm gonna like this." Andrew nodded approvingly as they mounted the two wooden steps onto the porch outside the large steakhouse. He opened the door and gestured for Dar to go in, then followed her into an atmosphere rich with protein, alcohol, and the inimitable dust from peanut shells. "Yep. Slab of beef and a beer and a pretty lady with me. I do like this."

"Two," Dar told the hostess, as she shook her head. They followed the young girl down a wide aisle and slid into a booth, its table complete with bowls of packet sugar and bottles of hot sauce. Dar examined one. "Nice." She put it back and rested her arm on the table, then slid sideways and leaned against the booth wall. "Glad that's over with."

"Ah bet." Andrew investigated the peanuts, cracking open the shells with powerful fingers, then offering exactly one half of the contents to his daughter. Dar had changed from her business suit into a pair of jeans and a crisply ironed cotton shirt and tied her hair back to keep it out of her eyes in the windy weather. "Things go all right up in DC?"

"Hard to say." Dar paused as the waitress arrived, a very perky young woman with tiny sparkles in her blue eye shadow. "Irish coffee, please." She glanced at her father. "Beer?"

"Yeap. One of them dark things, if you got it," Andrew confirmed. "And I'd like a rare steak and a tater and some ice cream."

The girl blinked. "All at once, sir?"

Dar chuckled. "Make it two, and no, the ice cream can come later." She nibbled on a peanut as the girl finished writing and took their unused menus back. "Mmph." She stifled a yawn and tilted her head back, idly watching the silent television above the bar. "Hey," she nudged her father's arm and pointed, "that's the hearing."

Andrew turned around to watch. "That her pa?"

"Yes." Dar nodded. "That's her mother, her sister Angie, and her brother Michael in back of them." They watched as the camera showed the investigators and then a shot of Kerry's brother on the stand, looking very ill at ease and embarrassed.

Then came a shot of a very familiar face. "Hey." Dar smiled in reflex. "Look. It's Kerry and Mom."

"Darn if it ain't." Andrew chuckled.

Dar pulled her cell phone out and speed dialed a number. "Hey."

"Hey." Kerry's voice sounded muffled against a fair amount of noise.

"I just saw you on television."

"Yikes."

"No, you look great," Dar reassured her. "You and Mom both. Though the look you were giving the cameraman could have killed a peacock at twenty paces."

"I forgot how much I hated that." Kerry grumbled. "I have no idea how they recognized me. I certainly don't look like I did five years ago." She muffled the receiver then returned. "It's getting sort of weird here, Dar. I guess those people who've been paying off my father decided to come out and support him. They're giving me the creeps."

Dar frowned. "Are they bothering you?" She noticed her father had caught her tone and was listening alertly.

"No," Kerry reassured her. "I'm sure it's just my conscience, you know what I mean?"

"Well, try to stay out of trouble until we get there."

"Does that mean we can get into trouble then?" Kerry lightened her tone. "Seriously, it's fine, Dar. I have to go back to the chambers tomorrow, but after that, I think they're going to let us go and concentrate on the clerks and police who investigated and all that."

Dar relaxed and leaned back. "Okay. Well, we're having dinner, then heading to the airport. I think the flight's due in around ten." She took a sip of her coffee and let the Irish Whiskey burn its way down. "Where are you?"

"In the hotel bar," Kerry replied. "Trying to figure out what a fuzzy navel is."

Dar grinned. "I'll show you when I get there," she offered, with a low chuckle. "'Cause you have one."

Momentary silence. "Oh, for pe—Dar!" A groan came through the line. "I'm gonna hurt you."

"Heh. It's peach schnapps and orange juice, I think," Dar supplied helpfully. "Get it? Peach, fuzzy...navel, oranges?"

"I got it. Thanks." Kerry's voice sounded mildly exasperated. "I'm going to eat my cheeseburger. No, excuse me, my 'cheddar topped grilled chopped sirloin steak over delicately sliced and toasted potatoes' now. I'll see you in a few hours."

"Eat a French fry for me." Dar grinned. "See you soon." She hung up and tucked the phone away, suddenly wishing the flight was done and over with and she was explaining fuzzy navels up close and personal.

❖⌘❖⌘❖⌘❖

"Kerry."

She stood, resting her elbows on the balcony railing and looking out at the brightly lit city, and she turned at the sound of her name. "It's pretty, with all the monuments and stuff and the lights."

Ceci came out to join her, having entered the room through the connecting door between their two rooms. "Yes, it is," she agreed. "Would you like to take a walk down to some of them? It's a nice night out."

"Anything to walk off that collection of animal protein floating in solid grease," Kerry told her, making a face. "I could have used the excess to lube my car."

Ceci laughed. "Well, I'd suggest vegetarianism, except that my mushrooms were just as greasy and I think those artichokes were older than I am."

Kerry chuckled and they exchanged looks. She noticed they were getting more comfortable with each other and she found herself liking Dar's mother very much. She had a dry, wicked sense of humor that came out around blind corners, much like her daughter's did, but was based in a totally different mindset from her vastly different experiences. "Sure," she agreed amiably. "You can explain paganism to me while we walk. I've been wondering about that since Dar mentioned it."

"Dar mentioned it?" Ceci scratched her jaw at that, as she led the way out of the hotel room and headed for the elevator. "Dare I ask in what context?"

Kerry thought about the question. "Oh. Right. We were in this Thai restaurant..."

"And that spawned a discussion of paganism," Ceci mused. "Was it those little Buddha statues?"

They exited the hotel and walked down the steps, turned to the right and headed down the street towards a well lit monument. "No. Duks and I were discussing believing in God."

"Food that bad?"

Kerry laughed. "No." She shook her head. "He's an atheist, so we were comparing belief systems. Mariana told us what her religion was, then Duks asked Dar for her viewpoint."

"Ah."

"She said that her father was a Southern Baptist and that you were a pagan and that she always knew you both believed in something." Kerry scrunched her brow. "Let me see. She said, you both believed in something, not necessarily the same something, but something, and she sort of patterned herself after that."

Ceci thought about that as they walked. "And what did you think about that?"

"What did I think? I thought holidays at your house must have been interesting," Kerry replied and chuckled. "But what really impressed me was that Dar was free to make her own choice."

"That's very true."

"It gave me a different slant on religion. I went to Christian school right up until the time I went to college and even then, it was in the same area, pretty much. So I didn't get exposed to..." Kerry hesitated.

"Heathens?" Ceci arched a brow.

"People with different value structures," she corrected gently. "I mean, we studied different cultures in school, but it's not the same thing as seeing it face to face."

"Mmm. That's true." Ceci nodded. "It was like that for me, after I married Andy and went to live on a navy base."

Kerry glanced at her, the smaller woman's profile outlined in the moonlight. "That must have been a tough transition."

"It was," Ceci murmured with a slow nod. "Andy was gone so much and we were so young."

They walked in silence for a little while. "Miami must have been a shock for you," the older woman said, as they turned into a well mani- cured park and started down a path covered in cedar chips, which crunched lightly under their feet.

"Oh yeah," Kerry agreed. "I had the opportunity to get a manage- ment position at Associated Synergenics and I'd said yes, before I'd really thought about what I was doing. My parents were livid." She sighed. "But off I went. I found an apartment in Kendall, got all settled in. Found some friends..." She paused with a faint smile.

"And?" Ceci heard the unsaid words.

"Went to South Beach and figured out I was gay." She gave a light laugh. "You know, the usual stuff. I remember the night it all became clear to me. I went out onto the beach and sat there looking at the stars, convinced I was going to Hell."

Ceci made a light hissing noise. "That's something I never under- stood about the Christian religion. Its founder is one of the few, genuine icons of love the world has ever known, yet more violence and hatred has been done in his name than just about anything else ever." She lifted her hands. "I don't understand it. I never have and that's why I could never accept its teachings."

Kerry fell silent and let those words penetrate. "I guess," she exhaled softly, "I guess my real problem with it came when I tried to reconcile the words that called me a sinner with the joy love brought me."

"Mmm." Ceci nodded as she walked, reaching out an idle hand to brush the thick marble walls as they passed. "When Dar first told us she was gay, I swear, both Andy and I really believed she was doing it just to add one more bit of rebelliousness to what was already a very shook up adolescence." She laughed softly. "I think I remember saying. 'Well, honey, it could have been worse. She could have joined a cult.'"

Kerry laughed as well. "Was it hard for D—for Mr. Roberts?"

"Andy would have loved Dar no matter what she'd decided to be or do," Ceci told her. "He did what he always did when he was faced with something he didn't really understand. He went to the library and read everything he could get his hands on about homosexuality."

"Wow."

"Mmm...and the conversation he and Dar had when he finished doing that–and he was determined to make sure she wasn't going to get herself into trouble—was one of the most hilarious things I've ever had to listen to."

Kerry covered her mouth, muffling a giggle. "Oh my god. I can picture it." She cleared her throat and pitched her voice lower. "Now you listen here, Dardar, I ain't gonna have you getting your butt into trouble, mind, so here's some of them condoms they say you should be wearing."

Ceci almost doubled over. "Oh." She laughed. "That's very good." She had to stop and lean against the wall. "And very, very close."

Kerry joined her in laughter. "Well, I wanted to be in the local gay shop in Fort Lauderdale when he went in there to by a rainbow sticker."

Cecilia laughed harder. "He didn't."

"Oh yeah. And he had one of those rainbow key chains, too," Kerry cheerfully told her. "It was such a..." She paused, becoming more serious. "It was such a wonderful relief to just have him accept us, accept me, the way he did. You have no idea how much that means to me."

Ceci took her arm and they continued walking. "I think I do," she murmured. "He's such an unsophisticated person, really. But he's good at everything he does. He was a good soldier, he's a good husband, and he's a very good father." She turned to look at Kerry's profile. "I'm glad he's become a father to you, Kerry."

Kerry didn't answer, waiting for the lump to go down in her throat. She bit her lip and swallowed, fighting the tears that stung her eyes. She kept walking, with Ceci strolling along next to her accepting the silence with quiet sympathy.

They crossed out into an open area, lit by halogen lights that turned the grassy shadows to sharp slivers of black and silver. Kerry heard a soft crunching behind her and she glanced back, surprised to see three tall forms walking slowly behind them.

Coincidence? The three had leather vests over their white T-shirts and she could just barely see the mottled darkness of tattoos across their arms. All three had shaven heads and were talking in loud...overly loud voices.

Ceci followed her gaze, then returned her eyes forward. "Into every life a few assholes must fall." She sighed, drawing a startled look from Kerry. "C'mon, Kerry. You're not one of those people who believe parents don't curse or have sex, are you?"

"Uh." She bit her lower lip and steered Ceci a little more towards the lit areas. "Well..."

The voices behind them got louder and coarser and the subject matter switched from fighting to something far less savory.

"See all them niggers over there?"

"Must be giving something out for free, lookit them gathering around for handouts."

"City's too full of fucking niggers and fags."

"They oughta nuke it." Ribald laughter. "Send fag and nigger bits up like confetti."

"Excuse me." Cecilia took three steps to her right and faced them, forcing them to stop walking. "About the only nukeable thing I see here are a couple of pieces of very white trash who need to shut their ignorant mouths."

They stared at the diminutive, silver blond woman in shock for a long instant, one shared by Kerry who never expected her older companion to turn into an activist so suddenly.

"Hey. You talkin' to me, bitch?" The first one pointed at his chest, puffing it out.

"No," Ceci replied. "I'm talking at you. Talking to you would require some intelligence on your part, and we're just not going to go there." She put her hands on her hips. "Scram. You're polluting the ozone." She gestured with a thumb over her shoulder. "Move it."

They edged around her and ambled down the path, looking behind them as though expecting her to grow a second head. "Bitch!" One shook his head. "Fucking crazy ass bitch."

Ceci watched them go. "Morons." She sighed in disgust. "What in the hell are their parents thinking? What are they teaching kids these days, anyway?"

Kerry blinked at her, then smiled. "Um..."

Ceci brushed her sleeve off then continued walking. They turned a corner in the large park, then paused, watching a larger group of people just ahead of them. One man was wrapped in a Confederate Flag and they could see flasks being passed around. "I don't think that little trick's going to work twice."

"No," Kerry agreed, turning around. "C'mon. Let's start back. This is giving me the creeps."

They headed back the way they came, turning the corner again and almost running into a half dozen men going the other direction. "Excuse me." Kerry tried to edge around them, but found her sleeve grabbed.

"Hey, cute stuff. Where are ya going? Come party with us."

"No thank you." Kerry gently tried to pull away. "I'm not much of a party person."

The man who had her arm was a tall, handsome blond, with a mostly cropped head and a necklace of silver barbed wire. "We could change that. Right guys?" His companions laughed. "Get lost, mama, we're going to show little blondie here a good time." He pulled Kerry towards him, grinning when she stopped resisting. "That's a gi—"

Kerry went with the motion and stepped in, then threw her weight upwards and slammed a knee squarely into his groin. He coughed, and she whirled, grasping his arm and pulling him over her head to land on the ground with a thump.

She backed off and stood in a balanced stance, her hands at shoulder level lightly curled into fists, and waited.

"Hey, you can't do that you little—" One of the others reached for her, and she nailed him with a roundhouse kick to the jaw, sending him sprawling.

"Yes, I can," she warned. "Now, just leave us alone."

"Like hell." A shorter man in the back stuck his head around the building. "Hey. Hey you guys. We got some boot bait over here."

"Shit," Ceci cursed. "I think it's time to leave."

"Yep." Kerry turned and pushed her forward. "Run!" She evaded the outstretched hand of the closest of them, then ducked in and kicked him in the ribs, shoving him hard against his companions as he went off balance. She used the distraction to bolt after Ceci, tucking her fists in against her side, and dashing over the grass with even, powerful strides.

A yell told her they were being followed. "Move it!" She hollered at Ceci, who was holding her own. Ahead of them, the entrance to the park loomed huge and remote, promising safely in the sparse crowds traveling across its opening. Kerry caught up to Dar's mother and put a hand on her back, pushing her forward and glancing behind her to see a crowd chasing them. A rock flew by her head and she ran faster, sensing the bodies just behind her by the sounds of breathing and footsteps.

They broke into the open, startling the wits out of several bystanders and attracting the immediate attention of a policeman on horseback trotting by. He pulled up and backed his mount, and they made for him, almost colliding with the huge animal. "Whoa there."

Kerry turned to see a crowd of men come out of the park, skidding to a halt when they spotted the policeman. She caught her breath and put a hand on Ceci's shoulder, gazing in concern at the older woman leaning against the horse. "You okay?"

Ceci nodded.

"What's going on here, ladies?" the policeman asked, his broad, bearded face wrinkled in concern. He watched the collection of sullen men fade back into the park and scowled. "Were those people giving you some trouble?"

"You could say that." Kerry sighed. "They invited us to party. We declined. They took exception."

The man shook his head and dismounted. "Damn it. I knew there was going to be trouble from those people." He dug out a book from his saddlebag and made some notes, then picked up his walkie talkie. "Simmonds to base. Looks like we've got some trouble at the FDR Memorial." He clicked off. "I'll need some information from you ladies."

"Um," Kerry backed off a step, "you know, they really didn't do anything to us, and I'd kinda rather not get involved." That earned her a very dour glare from the policeman. "I know, I know. I'm supposed to be a good citizen, but trust me, officer, you don't want to deal with the paperwork I'm going to cause."

"Listen, Ms. ..." He looked at her in question.

Kerry sighed. "Stuart." She paused. "Kerrison Stuart."

"Stuart, right. Listen Ms. St—" He stopped. "Not that Stuart?"

She nodded. "Unfortunately."

He rubbed his face. "Where are you staying?"

Kerry pointed.

"Go there and stay there, okay?"

"You got it."

"Did they know who you were?"

"I don't think so." Kerry shook her head. "And I'd rather they didn't."

He wrote something down, then nodded. "All right, Ms. Stuart, go on. Please. It's a little crazy out here tonight. Stay inside."

"I will," Kerry agreed, then took Cecilia's arm to move her towards the crossing light. "Jesus. I didn't think those classes would come in so handy."

Ceci was rattled. She took in several breaths, waiting for her heart to settle. "No kidding," she murmured. "Did Dar teach you that?"

"Yes." Kerry suddenly was extremely grateful for the long hours spent in the gym being tossed on her butt. "Are you all right?"

"Yeah." Ceci straightened her shirt out as they crossed the street and headed towards the hotel entrance. "But I don't want to have to repeat that any time soon."

"Me either," Kerry agreed, unaware of the eyes on their back. "What time is it?" She checked her watch. "Almost ten. Good." She pulled the hotel front door opened and allowed Ceci to move in ahead of her. "Let's find a movie to watch. Maybe room—yes?" She'd felt a brush against her back. "Can I help you?"

"Sorry," the cheerful looking young man apologized. "Excuse me." He pushed ahead of her and marched towards the front desk.

"No problem," Kerry murmured, twitching her shoulders, unable to escape a feeling of vague familiarity in his face, or his movements, she wasn't sure which.

Definitely, though, things were getting creepier. She checked her watch again, then shook her head and followed Ceci towards the elevator.

Chapter
35

Her message light was blinking when she entered her room and Kerry stared at it for a minute before she walked over and picked up the receiver. She dialed the front desk and listened for an answer. "Yes, I have a...oh. Yes." She listened to the message. A Mr. Selver, from the Washington Post: Call me, it's very important. "Ah, thanks," Kerry murmured politely.

But there were more. Six notes, from six different representatives of the media, all wanting to talk to her or to set up a time to talk to her. "Wow. Um. I don't really want to answer any of these."

The operator replied in a friendly manner, obviously used to people who didn't want to talk to the press. "Would you like us to screen your calls, Ms. Stuart?"

"Yes. I have a cell phone and anyone who really wants me, who I want to talk to knows the number," Kerry replied. "Oh. But if either Dar or Andrew Roberts calls, that's fine."

The sound of scribbling came clearly through the phone. "Will do, ma'am. Have a good night."

"Thanks. Oh, can you transfer me to room service?" Kerry asked, receiving an affirmative, then waiting as the call was transferred. "Hello?"

She ordered a coffee milkshake and some chips, then set the phone down and walked over to the comfortable looking couch in the corner and flopped down on it. "Jesus." She closed her eyes and rubbed them with one hand. *That had been...disgusting.* Both the attitudes of the unruly crowd and the attack on them made Kerry feel sick to her stomach.

Oh well. She looked up as a light knock came at the door. "Hey."

Ceci walked in, carrying a box of chocolates. "Want one?"

Kerry's brow creased. "Sure. Where did those come from?"

"Godiva, by way of my husband," came the wry response. "He has this very surprising indulgent streak in him that peeks out sometimes."

Kerry munched on the treat thoughtfully. "Mmm. Dar does too." She nodded. "I find stuff on my desk sometimes. A cookie, a rose...I never know what's going to be there."

Ceci sat down on the chair next to her and propped her feet up on the coffee table. "Do you reciprocate?"

The blond woman nodded. "Sure." She grinned. "I'll go out and get her a new shirt or something for her computer, like a cute mousepad, that kind of thing." She paused. "Sometimes I'll leave a little poem or something around, if I'm really in a goopy mood."

Ceci chuckled. "I used to tuck little goodies into his kit bags," she admitted. "His favorite was a little sack of Hershey's kisses."

Kerry smiled, then jumped as her cell phone buzzed. "God, I hate that." She tugged it out then opened it. "Hello?"

"Hey, Kerry. It's Mark."

"Hi." Kerry felt her mental track derail. "What's up?"

"Well, nothing good. They just blew a major node up in Virginia and half the Eastern Seaboard's ATM and interbank transfers are down."

"Ouch." Kerry winced. "That's big trouble." She reached over and unzipped her laptop case, then pulled the computer out and put it on the desk. "I'll dial in and monitor it. Do we have an ETA yet?"

A snort. "ETA? They don't even know what the problem is, much less how to fix it. CLIPC's escalating, but I think the carrier's just chasing their tail around in a circle."

"Great." Kerry got up and slid into the desk chair, booted up her laptop and plugged the modem cable into the convenient wall jack. "And tomorrow's not only Friday, it's the end of the month."

"Government payday," Mark agreed. "That's why I'm a-callin'. I was noodling around in the system when I saw the links go down. I'd guess they're about to start notifying you guys."

Kerry sighed. "Thanks, Mark."

"How's it going?"

"Yuck."

"Well, at least there was good news on the contract front today. I bet Dar almost died when she heard about it."

Kerry was busy logging in. "Heard about what?"

A knock came at the door and Ceci stood, waving Kerry back as she walked over and peeked through the eyehole. "Room service." She unlocked the door and opened it, allowing the uniformed server to enter. She was about to close the door when a large, burly man put a hand on the surface of the door and pushed it back. "Excuse me?"

"Hi. I'm looking for Kerry Stuart?"

Ceci put her body squarely in the doorway. "Why?"

"Just wanted to talk to her." The man smiled in a friendly manner. "My name's Al, Al Bainbridge. I work for the local paper."

Ceci gave him a direct look. "It's late and I don't think she's in the mood to talk right now."

"Suppose you let me ask her?"

"Suppose you move your hand before I slam the door on it?"

"It's to her advantage if she talks to me, lady." Now the man's voice took on a harder edge. "Either I get some facts from her or we'll get them some other way, and won't it be nicer if she gets to have her say first?"

"What is it, Mrs. Roberts?" Kerry came up behind her and glanced over her shoulder. "Ah. My pushy reporter friend." She put a hand on Ceci's shoulder. "I really don't have anything to say to you."

The man held a hand up. "Now, c'mon, Ms. Stuart. It's just a few questions. You're gonna have to answer them sooner or later. You made yourself too interesting a subject up there and there's lots of people digging around for info on you."

Kerry scratched her jaw. "Okay." She glanced shrewdly at him. "I'll give you a choice. Would you rather talk to me or get paid?"

"What?"

"I'm working on fixing a problem that affects all of the interbank transfers and ATM machines from New York to Virginia. I'll ask you again. Do you want to talk, or do you want me to get on with my job?"

The reporter stared at her for a long moment. "You're kidding."

"Nope." Kerry held up her corporate ID. "You choose, but make it fast, because my milkshake's melting."

He exhaled. "Tell you what. I'll beat feet tonight, but willya please agree to have breakfast with me? I'm not out to hurt you, Ms. Stuart. Honest I'm not."

Kerry thought about it. Talking to the press wasn't something she really wanted to do, but after those messages, she started to realize the scope of the interest in her. Maybe Al was right. Maybe it was better for her to at least have a chance at controlling what was released. "All right," she agreed quietly. "But I don't think it's much of a story for you."

He hid a swift smile of triumph. "Guess we'll find out tomorrow. Good night, Ms. Stuart." He gave Ceci a brief look, then turned and made his way back down the hallway.

"You sure you want to do that?" Ceci inquired, glancing behind her. "Where'd the waiter go?"

"I sent him out through your room." Kerry sighed, as she closed the door and checked her watch. "This is a mess. I wish—"

Another knock at the door. "Son of a bitch." Kerry was losing her patience. She turned, grabbed the door handle, and yanked it back, taking a breath to blast whoever it was. It came back out in an utterly relieved trickle. "Thank you." Kerry reached out and grabbed a handful of cotton and reeled in a tall, dark haired woman who came willingly and enveloped her in a powerful hug. "Ungh. I am so glad you're here."

Dar moved a little forward, very pleased at the greeting, as she let her father come in behind her. "Mother," she greeted Cecilia with wry cordiality, as Kerry burrowed into her chest, warming the skin under her shirt with a long exhale.

"Close the door," Ceci advised, as she fit herself into Andrew's arms and gave him a quick kiss. "We've had enough excitement for tonight."

Dar kicked the door shut. "What happened?"

"What didn't?" Kerry muttered, refusing to release her hold. It was nice and warm and dark where she was, it smelled great, and Dar had found just the exact right spot on her back to rub. Maybe if she stayed here long enough, everything else would just sort of go away and she'd wake up back home to nothing more out of the ordinary than a Halloween party to go to.

Ceci's lips quirked and she tugged her husband towards the interconnecting door. "I'll fill you in," she promised. "Besides, there's chocolates in there. C'mon, sailor boy."

Dar watched them leave, then turned her attention to the blond woman cradled in her arms. "Hey."

Reluctantly, Kerry opened her eyes and looked up. "Hi." She sighed, then yelped as her cell phone went off, at the same time as Dar's did. "Oh yeah. Everyfrigginggoddamned monetary transfer system in the Northeast is down."

"You've got to be kidding." Dar groaned, answering hers. "Yes?" A pause. "Thank you." She closed the phone, then tossed it on the chair. Kerry's followed. She laced her fingers behind the smaller woman's head and just looked at her, thinking about all the things she had to say, seeing her thoughtfulness reflected in Kerry's eyes.

Then she deliberately put that all out of her mind as she brushed her lips against Kerry's, then deepened the contact, getting lost in the surge of passion that lifted the nape hairs off her neck and made her knees shake just a little. They explored each other leisurely then finally parted, and Dar nibbled Kerry's nose as they gazed into each other's eyes. "What were we talking about?" she murmured.

"I have no clue." Kerry leaned forward and just breathed in Dar's distinctive scent. "I don't want to have a clue right now. I want to take all my clues, put them in a FedEx letter pack, and mail them to Queensland, Australia."

Dar wrapped her arms around Kerry and hugged her, lifting her up a bit and hearing a soft crackle as her spine realigned itself.

"Uhh." Kerry sighed blissfully. "You rock." A chuckle more felt then heard vibrated against her and Kerry smiled. They stayed like that for quite a while, then Kerry rested her chin on Dar's breastbone, peering up.

"It wouldn't take much for me to kick the plug out of that laptop and turned off the cell phone."

"I know." Dar rubbed her back. "But we'd hate ourselves in the morning."

Kerry stuck her tongue out and found it captured in neat white teeth. "Heth!"

Dar grinned and released her. "Teach you to sass me, young lady." She imitated her father's low growl. "C'mon. Let's get this worked out and trade tales." She circled Kerry with an arm and led her to the desk, stopping to select a chip and scoop up some salsa. "You and Mom get along all right?"

"Um, I think we've bonded, yes," Kerry admitted. "After you've been on a long plane flight, sat through senate investigation, and been chased by Neo-Nazis with someone..."

Dar stopped in mid motion and peered at her through a set of dark bangs that almost obscured her eyes. "What?"

Kerry came around the desk and perched on one end, folding her hands in her lap. "We went for a walk after dinner and ran into some real creeps."

"I thought I told you to stay out of trouble?" Dar straightened and put her hands on her hips.

"Walking in the FDR memorial isn't getting into trouble, Dar," the blond woman shot back. "Besides, we're both grown ups, last time I checked." She paused. "I seem to recall one of us is your mother, as a matter of fact."

Dar sat down and rested her hands on the flat surface, staring at Kerry's laptop screen without really seeing it. "Funny," she commented quietly, adjusting the computer with a small, precise motion. "She and my father were always 'us.'" She took a breath. "Something I was never a part of." She blinked at the screen and moved the mouse pointer, as a silence fell.

Kerry opened her mouth, then shut it. Then she held both hands up. "Whoa." She realized she'd just tripped and fallen into a huge bowl full of hard feelings and didn't much like the sensation. "Can we just rewind sixty seconds and redo that last minute?"

Dar looked up at her with a painfully vulnerable expression. "Okay," she agreed. "Sorry. I was just worried about you."

Kerry slid off the desk and knelt, resting a hand on Dar's knee to steady herself. "And I did promise to stay out of trouble, you're right. I just didn't think twice about taking a walk in a strange city at night and I should have."

Dar merely nodded, tiny tensions moving through her face.

"Dar, does it bother you that I like your mother?" Kerry asked gently, holding a finger up at the startled reaction. "No, no. Level with me, okay? No BS between us. Does it bother you?"

Her lover lowered her head into her hands and stared at the tabletop. Her eyes closed.

Kerry waited uneasily.

"I thought I had a handle on this," Dar finally murmured. "And then it comes around the corner and kicks me in the ass."

"Dar," Kerry moved a little closer, "just because there are things I like about your mother, doesn't mean I think what she did to you was right or that she doesn't owe you some understanding and explanations and apologies."

"I don't think she owes me anything," Dar interrupted.

"Bullshit, Dar. Of course she does." Kerry put a hand on her arm, using touch to reinforce her words. "You are her child and she abandoned you at a horrible time in your life. A parent can't just throw..." her words slowed, "throw a child away." She took a breath. "Look at me talking, the expert here."

That got through to Dar and she turned her head, her eyes warming and gentling. "Families are hell sometimes, aren't they?" She covered Kerry's hand with her own.

The green eyes searched hers. "You are my family," she whispered, blinking back the tears.

Just because you're dysfunctional, don't let that ruin something she needs, Dar, a warning voice spoke softly in her mind. "My parents are your family too, Kerry." She lifted the hand on her arm and kissed the fingers. "And I'm very, very happy about that."

Kerry rested her forehead against Dar's shoulder. "Thank you for understanding me needing that right now." She breathed a sigh of relief. "Oh, I wasn't ready for this."

Me either. "Tell you what." Dar nudged her. "Let's take this thing over to the couch and put our heads together over it."

Dar carried the laptop and Kerry brought over the snacks, and they settled on the couch in a tangle of arms and legs and cables, with chips and coffee milkshakes and enough combined brain cells to jump start a supertanker.

Kerry lay back against Dar's chest, pecking at the keyboard as the arms curled around her shifted and a long finger moved the mouse button. "Okay." She crunched on a chip. "Who are we going to yell at first?"

Dar rested her chin on Kerry's shoulder, letting her tension dissolve as she felt the shift of Kerry's breathing under her arms. "Mmm." She clipped the cell phone to the adapter that routed it through the laptop's speakers and dialed. A harried voice answered. "This is Dar Roberts."

Hesitation. "Oh, good evening, ma'am. What can I do for you? It's been a long time."

Dar smiled. "I'm in Washington," she burred, in a low, dangerous voice.

"Ah."

"And I'm out of cash."

"Oh."

Dar mentally filled in the expletive after that and felt Kerry giggle silently under her hands.

"Uh, ma'am. They're working on that."

"Define they."

"Uh..."

"Define working."

"Um. Wouldn't you like to talk to my supervisor?"

"Does he want to talk to me."

"Um, probably not, no, ma'am."

Dar laughed silently. "Nice to know I haven't lost my touch," she whispered into Kerry's ear. "All right. Have they found the problem, yet?"

"Um, no."

"Okay. What company is it?"

"That's the problem, ma'am. It's a big, shared facility, and they can't figure out whose master switch it is. Everyone's blaming everyone else."

Kerry was busy typing and she reviewed the network. "Can we...oh, damn. That's one of your new sites, never mind." She tapped on. "Damn, we don't have a reroute around that."

"Okay." Dar flipped open her palm pilot and found a number. "I'll start at the top. One ATT CEO coming right up. Call you back, Netops."

"Ooo." Kerry scooped up some salsa. "He's gonna be pissed."

"Nah," Dar disagreed, dialing a number. "He lives in Maryland and they get paid twice monthly just like we do."

Kerry stopped in mid crunch. "Oh boy." She picked up the television remote, clicked it on, muted the sound, and switched to a news station. "Uh oh."

"Hello, Alan? Dar Roberts." Dar glanced at the screen. The news anchor was gazing seriously at the camera, as a violent scene rolled behind him. Fuzzily focused bodies were clustered around a building wall, kicking and throwing things at it. The caption "ATM Terror" splashed across the screen. "We've got a problem, Alan. Either you solve it, or I'm gonna start calling people until we've got the most expensive conference call in the history of internetworking going."

Kerry watched the screen, her eyes wide.

❖ ⌘ ❖ ⌘ ❖ ⌘ ❖

Cecilia toweled her short, silvered blond hair dry and stepped back into the room, aware of a stupid smile on her face caused by the sight of the man standing in only a pair of silk boxers at the window, evaluating the surrounding terrain.

Despite his violent protests to the contrary, she'd discovered her husband had developed a fondness for the soft underwear, and she'd had an enormously good time visiting Macy's and buying him several different kinds.

No wild colors, though. Some things never changed. She walked over and slid an arm around him, leaning against his bulk and reviewing the scene outside. It was a misty day, gray and overcast, and a soft rain fell. "Nice."

"Li'l rain never hurt nobody," Andrew answered absently. "Guess I better go get me some coffee. See that stand down there?" He pointed.

"Honey, I ordered some," Ceci objected. "You're not going to go romping outside in your skivvies, are you?" She looked up and saw the expected scowl. "Let me go wake the girls up." She patted him on the butt and walked to the connecting door, then eased it open, and knocked lightly on the inside surface. She heard voices inside, so she pushed the door open and poked her head around it. "Good mo—" She stopped, startled by the appearance of the two women crouched over a laptop computer on the desk, with a large coffee pot nearby. Dar was on the phone with someone, speaking sharply, and Kerry was pecking at the keyboard, her head propped on one hand and a harried, exhausted look on her face. "Did you two get to sleep at all?"

Green eyes glanced over. "No."

"What on earth are you doing?" Ceci kept her voice down, in deference to Dar's hoarse tantrum.

"Saving the Western world." Kerry tapped in a few other things then shook her head. "Dar, we can't route this that way. It's not going to work."

Dar covered the receiver and glared at the laptop. "Fine. Then we'll pull it." She snapped in exasperation, going back to the phone. "All right, that's it, I've had it." Her voice rose to a savage growl. "I'm gonna have someone walk into CLIPC and take a wire cutter to the whole damn patch panel." A desperate voice murmured through the receiver. "Look. We're outta time," Dar broke in. "It's not my fault you guys decided to try an Y2K upgrade on a running system with no back up." She picked up her cell phone with the other hand, ignoring both Kerry and Ceci, who had edged into the room and seated herself on the bed, watching her daughter in wary fascination.

"What happened?" Ceci whispered to Kerry, who was cradling her head in both hands.

Kerry turned around in her chair and rested her elbows on her knees. "Our national carrier decided to put a patch into place last night and it trashed a major switching office." She sighed. "Affecting most of the Eastern Seaboard, and, for some bizarre reason, Dallas, Texas."

"Mmm." Ceci nodded. "What exactly does that mean in English?"

Kerry pointed towards the television, which was on CNN. A reporter was mumbling in the mostly muted newscast, showing pictures of angry people surrounding banks.

Ceci peered at them, then shook her head. "I don't get it."

"Well, most people nowadays when they go to get money, don't get it from a bank." Kerry sighed. "They get it from an ATM machine, and they have their paychecks automatically deposited, right?"

"Okay, yes, I see."

"Well, what happens when money can't move into the bank, and people can't get it out of the ATM machines?"

Ceci stared at the screen, then at Kerry. "Is that what happened?"

"Yes." She nodded. "From Boston to Miami, no one's getting paid electronically or getting cash from a machine."

"Good grief," the older woman blurted. "And that's what you two are sitting here trying to fix?"

"Yep." Kerry looked exhausted. "And I've got that breakfast to go to, then more grilling. It's not going to be a good day."

"All right. Mark, get to the punch down room," Dar said into the phone. "Tell everyone to get the hell out of your way, or I'm going to be flying down there to personally kick their asses."

Kerry winced.

"You there? Good. Take the following circuits and hot patch them." Dar read off a list of numbers and letters. "Put them in the high speed ports H1, H2, H3 and H4 on one big pipe, and H3 and H4 on the other." She took the keyboard and rapidly switched to a configuration program. "All right, hang on." Dar typed furiously, slamming the enter key in frustration as she got to the end of each line. "This better work or..."

"Easy." Kerry rubbed her knee under the desk. "Look there, wait, Dar, that's the wrong—"

"I see it." Dar closed her eyes briefly, then reopened them and corrected her error. She reset the port she'd just finished, then flipped over to Kerry's monitoring program. "C'mon...c'mon, you little b—son of a bitch."

"Dar, that's the wrong speed." Kerry took the keyboard from her and started typing, brushing the taller woman's hands away. "Yell at Mark some more while I do this."

Ceci watched as Dar's face twitched in annoyance, but was unable to react as angrily as she obviously wanted to. "Mark, are you done yet?" She growled into the phone. "Now?" A pause. "Now?" Another pause. "Kerry, go."

"Okay." Kerry finished and wrote the configuration changes, then reset the device. She counted silently under her breath up to twenty, then reconnected to it. "Done...done...wahoo." She exhaled in utter relief.

"Passing packets on those ports, Dar."

"I see it." Dar had been watching the monitoring tool in the background and now she flipped it to the foreground and watched the shifting charts, which pumped in comforting shades of green and blue. "Jesus." She leaned against the phone. "Good work, Mark. Thanks for flying up so early." The MIS chief had spent the evening scouring their local resources and trying to help Dar find a way to resolve the problem without breaching their extensive contracts with the companies involved in the crisis.

No luck. So Dar had asked him to go personally to the switching center, where he'd been consulting with the switch programmers since six a.m.

No luck. The Y2K patch had made such a mess of the firmware, even Mark's and Dar's combined programming talents had been unable to make head or tail of it, leaving the executive with a sparse list of options.

Stay down or breach their contract, and remove the services from their vendor. "I'd better call Hamilton Baird and let him know to expect some screaming." She sighed, referring to ILS's legal chief. "And he loves me so much as it is."

"Dar, you had no choice." Kerry yawned, putting her head down on one arm. "Doesn't he live in Boston?"

"Mmm." Dar tipped her head back and closed her eyes. "Yeah, he only sounds like he lives in Louisiana."

Ceci kept quiet, assuming the green things and Dar's obvious relief, were a good thing. She glanced up at the television, where talking heads were analyzing the problem, one that looked vaguely familiar. "Isn't that your boss?"

Dar looked up. Sure enough, a very serious looking Alastair was front and center, freshly scrubbed and very concerned. "They dug him out of bed early." She increased the volume. "Not the kind of publicity he wanted today, I bet."

"Mr. McLean, can you give us some idea of what is going on?"

Alastair cleared his throat. "Simply speaking? There was an attempt made to make a piece of equipment year 2000 compatible and that attempt resulted in the equipment failing."

"Your equipment, sir? Are you saying this is something ILS did?" The reporter leaned forward.

"No." Alastair shook his head gravely. "This was done at the national carrier level, although we were made aware of the fact that it was in process." He shifted. "They've been working throughout the night to correct the problem, but it's very complex."

"Mr. McLean, I don't think I need to tell you what kind of impact this is having. Is this what we can expect? Is this an early example of what the year 2000 is going to be like?" the reporter asked. "We have several representatives on the line with us who would like to discuss this with you. People who have some very serious concerns."

"Well, certainly, we can discuss the issues." Alastair looked distinctly uncomfortable. "I can't say I can answer for an entire industry, however, and an isolated incident like this shouldn't be taken as—"

"But you are the largest provider of interbanking services, are you not?"

"Yes, that's true, but—"

"Then, Mr. McLean, effectively you can speak for the industry, because you're being paid to make sure Americans aren't impacted by the changes, aren't you?"

"I can speak for ILS, yes." Alastair sighed. "And review what we are doing towards that end, while we work on getting further status on the problem at hand."

Dar smiled, flipped her phone open, and dialed her boss's cell number by memory.

Alastair looked down, then interrupted the reporter in mid-word. "Excuse me a minute, David. This might be the information I requested for you."

Then she heard the phone answer. "Good morning," Dar drawled softly into the phone. "Nice tie."

"Dar, I'm on the air and this guy's about to nail me," her boss whispered.

"I know. We're up. I moved them over to the new network."

Silence. She watched the smile spread across the face on the screen, which was half turned to hear her conversation. Alastair closed the phone without a further word, then straightened, and tightened his tie a bit, the twinkle back in his eyes. Dar turned the sound up, wondering what he was going to say.

"As I was asking, Mr. McLean, what exactly does ILS intend to do about this crisis?" the reporter asked. "Hundreds of thousands of paychecks are on the line and citizens up and down the East Coast are unable to access their own money."

"Well, David," Alastair responded. "Fortunately, we are lucky to have one of the most talented minds in the business as our CIO, and that phone call was just informing me ILS has rerouted around the problem and brought everything up on our own, brand new, internal network." If he'd had suspenders, Dar was sure, he'd have stuck his thumbs in them and smirked. As it was, he gave a good impression of doing that anyway.

The reporter was definitely taken aback. He shuffled a few papers. "That's great news," he temporized, then read something off a nearby prompter. "Yes, as a matter of fact, we just got word from Interbank that they've started restoring service." He looked down at a slip of paper handed to him. "And that would be your CIO, Dar Roberts, is that right?"

"Hey. He's talking about you?" Andrew was leaning against the wall, watching in fascination.

"He's talking about me." Dar slumped in her chair and exchanged a high five with Kerry. "We tried a dozen things with the company that ran that switch, but nothing worked. We had to end up rewiring everything and putting it on our network. We must have breached ten contracts in the process."

Cheering was heard from the screen as people were shown clustering eagerly around the cash machines.

"Sad commentary on society," Ceci murmured. "Almost Pavlovian, really."

"You know," Kerry got up and collapsed on the couch, "I don't get to see the results of my labors quite so graphically most of the time."

"No," Dar agreed, standing up and stretching her body out, wincing at a painful knot on her back. "Want me to get more coffee?"

Kerry stuck her tongue out. "Any more of that and it's going to come out my ears." She peered at the screen as she heard the senate hearings mentioned. "Oh...hot dog. Yes!" She wriggled on her back and kicked her feet out.

"Postponed?" Ceci smiled at the blond woman's unrestrained joy.

"Only until this afternoon," Dar grumbled.

"I don't care. I get to take a nap." Kerry stifled a yawn. "I'm so tired, I'd take an hour if I could get it." The phone rang, and she moaned. "No...no...go away."

Dar reached over and picked it up. "Hello?"

"Looking for Kerry Stuart," the voice came back, brisk and business-like.

"She's sleeping," Dar replied.

"Well, we've got a breakfast date."

"Not today."

"Okay, look here Ms.—"

"Roberts. Dar Roberts. I'm Kerry's boss and I'm telling you she's not available to meet this morning," Dar told him crisply, then hung up. "Who the hell was that?"

"A member of the press," her mother told her. "Kerry fascinated them, for some reason."

Dar walked to the window and peered out. "She makes good press." She leaned against the glass. "She's bright, good looking, and articulate— of course she fascinated them."

"Hey." Kerry felt the blood heat her face. "Can we not talk about me like I'm not here?"

Dar chuckled, then looked down as her cell phone rang. "Hello?"

"I love you."

Dar chuckled again. "Well, thank you Alastair, but it was a group effort."

"No, really, Dar. That was the most exquisite timing and it was much appreciated." Alastair sounded profoundly relieved. "I don't care how many contracts you busted, it was worth it to see the smug look slide right off that pig bastard's face." He cleared his throat. "Ah. I've had a request to get you on for an interview."

"Now?"

"Well, timing is everything, Dar," her boss coaxed. "The positive press is a good thing, especially right now." He left the thought hanging.

Dar sighed. "Between the press wanting to talk to me and the press wanting to talk to Kerry, we're liable to get more publicity this week than we can handle."

There was a moment's quiet. "Ah...hmm," the CEO murmured. "I forgot she was testifying this week. Her father's no friend of ours."

And if they tie it all together, it'll be tabloid heaven. "Yeah." Dar exhaled. "This could get tricky."

A drumming of fingers. "All right. Let me get Andrea in on it. I'll have her give you a call to coordinate, Dar. I don't think we can avoid the interview, and it's a good moment for it, but we have to be aware of what might fall out if the press starts sniffing around." His voice became brisk. "And if it does, it does. Our public policy is written clearly enough. Andrea can spin it positive, us being so progressive and all that."

Dar snorted.

"Yes, well, you can't turn a pig into silk lingerie overnight, my friend."

"You better warn the board," Dar responded quietly. "The very issue we talked about yesterday might be moot."

Alastair sighed. "Think positive, willya, Dar? At least we can see this coming."

"Yeah," Dar acknowledged. "Well, have Andi call me, all right?" She hung up and let the phone drop to her thigh, then she turned to face the three pairs of curious eyes on her. "Ker, I think we need to talk."

Green eyes peered at her over the couch back in apprehension. "We're about to become poster children, aren't we?"

Thunder rolled for an answer.

Chapter
36

Dar glanced at herself in the mirror, adjusting the collar of her silk shirt and brushing a speck of dust from the shoulder of her jacket. The interview had been set up faster than she'd expected, and she'd just had time to take a quick nap and get a shower before she had to get ready for it.

Kerry was on her way to the Senate chambers already, with Andrew as an escort. Dar hoped her father would behave himself and not do something irreversible.

Like slug Senator Stuart, for instance, something Dar herself dearly wished she could do. She wished the hearings were over, or at least Kerry's part in them, so they could go home and regroup and get things back into a more normal order.

Maybe we could take a few days off. Dar regarded the tired blue eyes looking back at her. *Long weekend? Maybe take a Friday, and a Monday, and drive down to the Keys, stay at one of the little places out near the beach...hey.* Dar blinked. *Yeah. Maybe for Kerry's birthday,* which was coming up. Which reminded her. Presents were in order, if she could shake Kerry off long enough to go shopping on her own.

Or figure out what to get. With a sigh, she looked at her reflection one more time, then turned as she caught her mother's image in the glass watching her. They looked at each other for a moment in awkward silence. "Thought you went with Dad," Dar finally said, turning and folding her arms over her chest self-consciously.

Cecilia looked like she wished that were the case. "He thought I should stay here, and um...help out if you needed anything."

Dar's brow arched. "He did, did he?" She sensed an ulterior motive.

"Mmm." Her mother folded her arms. "So. What do you do in a news interview?"

"I have no idea," Dar replied honestly. "I generally work behind the scenes. This'll be a first." She glanced around the room, which had been tidied by the housekeeping staff. "Guess they'll have to make do with the space in here." She straightened her sleeve cuff nervously.

Ceci regarded her, approving of the creamy silk shirt against Dar's tan, and the trim cut of the suit that outlined her athletic body. "You look very nice," she offered with hesitant sincerity, catching Dar by surprise. The blue eyes lifted and met hers uncertainly. "That must sound pretty strange coming from me, huh?"

Dar nodded. She let the silence go for a minute, then scratched her eyebrow. "I think the best you could have managed before was 'gee, that's a nice new spiked collar,'" she admitted. "Looking nice wasn't a priority of mine."

Hey, she's talking. Encouraged, Ceci perched on the arm of the couch and leaned on its back. "Oh, I don't know. Some of those vests and things were sort of cute." She smiled a little. "And I wasn't a very good example." Sweatpants and painter's overalls, to be exact. "I always did sort of want to borrow that leather jacket of yours, though."

Dar relaxed slightly. "Sleeves would have been a little long." She took a seat opposite her mother and extended her legs, crossing them at the ankles. "Thanks for sticking by Kerry yesterday, incidentally."

"It was no problem."

"I know she really appreciated it," Dar went on. "Being there with her family is tough on her."

"Mmm. I know. Almost as hard as you and I being here." Ceci managed a wry smile, which her daughter mirrored. *Now, I guess we start the tough stuff.* She took a breath. "For some of the same reasons."

Dar focused inward for a bit, then laced her fingers together. "Not really." She hadn't been ready for this talk, but here they were. She collected herself and sorted her thoughts. "I know you like Kerry. Everyone does. She's sweet, honest, smart, loyal. A dozen other things besides that."

"That's true," Ceci murmured. "She's a remarkable person."

"Most of the things I'm not," Dar continued. "I didn't give you any reason to like me." She gazed evenly at her mother. "Her parents turned their backs on her because of something she did. Not for who she was."

Ceci exhaled. "That's not entirely true." She considered her words carefully. "There were times I didn't much like you, Dar."

Even knowing, even after all this time, it stung. Dar glanced away, refusing to even swallow. "No news there," she enunciated precisely.

Ceci felt like crying, wanting to take the conversation back, and go down another path, but knowing it was too late. She took a careful breath. "But there never was a time I didn't love you." Dar went very still, her eyes widening, suddenly vulnerable. Ceci felt her way carefully.

"When...I lost Andrew, all that I could feel was pain, Dar. I couldn't take it. I wasn't strong enough." She met the quiet gaze across from her. "I'm sorry."

Dar slowly shook her head. "I wish..." She closed her eyes. "You'd have told me that before now."

Ceci felt the pain all the way down to the bottom of her soul. "Me too," she whispered.

Dar remained still, and Ceci rose slowly and moved the short distance over the thick rug, knelt in front of her daughter and put a hesitant hand on her leg. "What I did to you was wrong, Dar." She could feel the muscles under her fingers move slightly, then go still. "If I could take it back, I would."

"I wanted to help you." It was hard to talk. "I wanted to do the right thing."

"I know," Ceci acknowledged. "I drove you away." Her eyes dropped. "And you repaid that by giving me my life back."

"I did it for Daddy," Dar uttered. "Not for you."

"I know." Ceci felt a bittersweet twinge. "But you also did it because it was the right thing to do." She paused. "I felt, when I saw you, there was something you wanted to say to me, but you didn't. Now I know what that was."

Dar closed her eyes again, her way of gaining space to think in. Finally she sighed. "I had to make sure it would be all right for him. I didn't want him to get hurt any more."

"Did you think it wouldn't be?"

She shook her head. "No. But he did, and I had to be sure." The blue eyes appeared, a sparkle of anger in them. "How could you tell him you wouldn't be there?" Now there was true pain in Dar's voice, but not on her behalf.

So typical. Ceci's jaw tensed and she took a breath. "I made a mistake," she replied honestly. "And I paid for it, believe me, Dar." Her lips trembled a little. "For every minute of those seven years, knowing we parted with...angry words between us and I'd never had a chance to..." She had to stop and take several deep breaths. "I was just so desperate not to lose him."

The anger eased and gentled. "I told him that," Dar murmured. "Because if there was one thing I believed in, it was the two of you."

Ceci had no idea what to say to that. After a moment's reflection, she let out a held breath. "I wish you'd told me that before." She breathed. "I thought you just resented our being so close."

"I envied you," Dar replied, in a low, but precise voice. "I tried to find that for myself and I failed so miserably, I just finally gave up on it."

Incredible. She'd learned more about her child in the past thirty seconds than in the past thirty years. "Until it found you." Dar considered that, then nodded slightly. Ceci sighed. "I'm sorry, Dar. I didn't know. I don't think I ever really understood where you were coming from."

Dar felt the truth of that, as she looked into the eyes of someone she hardly knew.

Someone, if she was honest with herself, that she had never had much desire to know, who had mainly been viewed as either an obstacle or an annoyance to her for a very long time.

Now it was different. She wasn't sure she wanted or needed a mother back, but another friend was something she could consider having, especially one who was willing to accept Kerry and who Kerry liked. So. They'd both made a lifetime's worth of mistakes, and she could either let that poison their relationship now or put that behind her and just go forward.

Who knew? Maybe they'd even end up liking each other after a while. Stranger things had happened. Dar gave her nerves a moment to settle and forced herself to cover her mother's hand with her own. "I don't think I much understood you either." She kept her voice low. "But I'm glad we're getting a second chance at this."

It was far and away more than she expected. Ceci smiled in surprise and relief and seeing a twinkle of that reflected in the blue eyes watching her. Dar's fingers were warm and strong and she felt the gentle pressure as her daughter squeezed, then released her hand. It made her feel twenty pounds lighter, almost dizzy, and she was glad she was still holding on to Dar to steady herself. "I am too," she finally answered.

Dar exhaled in relief. She'd been half anticipating and half dreading this conversation and now that it was over, she felt little giddy. Her father would be pleased, though. He'd nudged her again gently this morning to try and spend a few minutes talking with her mom.

Hey. Dar's brows knitted. *Wait a minute.* She looked up at her mother, who cocked her head in puzzled inquiry. "Did Kerry say anything to you this morning?"

Ceci was taken aback at the question. She eased up off her knees and sat down on the couch next to Dar, lacing her fingers together. "Well, sort of, I suppose," she murmured. "She did happen to mention—why, did she say something to you?"

"No. Daddy did." Dar folded her arms and gave her mother a wry look.

"Ah." Ceci almost laughed. "Sneaky little schemers, aren't they?"

"Mmm." Dar smiled, then glanced up as a knock came at the door. "Guess it's showtime." And if nothing else, talking to her mother had taken her mind right off the impending interview, though scenes of frying pans and hot flames seemed to circle that notion.

"Right. I'll duck on out of here." Ceci rose.

"No. Stay." Dar got up and went for the door, not giving her a chance to answer.

Ceci selected a corner of the couch and curled up in it, tucking her feet up and resting her arm along the back. She watched Dar pause just before she opened the door and straighten her shoulders, pulling the jacket taut over bone and muscle and adjusting the drape over her trimly muscular form.

She opened the door. A stocky man of middling height stood there with a crowd of people and equipment behind him. "Hi," Dar drawled, glad if nothing else for the fact that her mother had neatly taken her mind completely off the interview.

"Oh, hello. Sorry, I was looking for Dar Roberts?" the man responded briskly. "I'm John McAdams, from CNN Business News?"

Dar extended a hand to him. "You've found me."

He returned her grip reflexively as he stared at her. "You're kidding, right?"

"Nope."

"But...you're not a middle aged Anglo conservative guy."

Dar glanced down at herself. "Not the last time I checked, no." She stepped back. "Would you like to come in or would you rather I find you a middle aged Anglo conservative guy to interview? I'm sure there are a few around here somewhere."

"No way." The man held up a hand and grinned broadly. "Lead on, Lady McByte. I'm all yours."

❖ ⌘ ❖ ⌘ ❖ ⌘ ❖

It was odd, Kerry mused as she stood in line to get in the door to the chambers, *to hear everyone else talking about the disaster they'd spent all night trying to fix.* The change in time and the general chaos had thrown off the crowds of supporters and there were only a few around so far, waving signs and getting organized.

They were probably still mobbing the ATM machines. She allowed herself an uncharitable thought. *Or raiding the discount beer stores.*

Now now, Kerry. She gave herself a quiet scold. *You know better than to make those generalizations. Not all white supremacists drink beer.* She peered at the milling crowd. *Some of them probably like Boones Farm.* She sighed. *Bad Kerry. Obnoxious, stuck up, WASP Kerry. Cut it out.*

"Likely lookin' bunch of pansy ass rednecks, ain't they?" Andrew drawled from behind her, his arms crossed over his chest. "They give my Southern Baptist butt a hive and a half."

Kerry bit her lip to keep from laughing, then exhaled, trying to relieve a little of the tension building up inside her. No sign of her family, of course, since they were probably inside already, but she was getting sideways looks from the people standing around her, which made her realize she was being recognized from the previous day.

People were giving Andrew little glances too, and she half turned, giving her companion a little smile. He really was a distinctive looking person, she realized, with his height and muscular body and the sense of presence he carried himself with. And of course, the patchwork of scars across his face, which she didn't really even see anymore. At least the two worst were gone, replaced by the slightly rough covering of synthetic skin that restored his face to something approaching normality. She'd understood his need to remain hidden before, but she had a feeling that now, since the one opinion that really mattered to him was secured, he'd have discarded the hood even without the surgery.

And the eyes. Dar's pale, electric blue, set off by the tan skin creased in wrinkles on either side of them. Right now they were roaming everywhere, drinking in the crowd, the guards, the protestors—alive with interest and curiosity.

She was glad he was here. It made her feel utterly safe to be standing next to him. "Hope this doesn't last long." Kerry sighed. "I think I'd rather be getting dental work." She walked forward at the guard's request and edged through the detector, then turned and waited for Andrew to follow.

"Ahm gonna set that off," the tall man drawled to the guard as he ambled through, sure enough making the machine react. He stopped on the other side of it, watching the nervous reactions. "Don't get yer britches in a square knot. I got me two plates here." He tapped his upper thigh. "And a couple odd shells tucked up inside me somewhere."

The guard approached cautiously and ran a hand held device over him, getting readings near his leg, and stomach. "Um..."

"Ain't nothing up mah sleeve." Andy lifted his shirt and displayed a scarred, but still muscular abdomen. "Here." He pulled his identification wallet from the back pocket of his jeans and flipped out a card. The guard took it and examined it, then handed it back respectfully.

"Go ahead, sir." He lifted his wand in a little salute as Andrew moved past him and joined Kerry at the door to the chambers.

"Jest goes to show you, stay in the damn Navy long enough, something'll salute you," he muttered, half under his breath.

Kerry grinned and tucked her hand inside his elbow as they walked inside. "You didn't make the airport one go off," she commented curiously. "And those catch my car keys, for heaven's sake."

"Looking fer different things," Andy replied cryptically. He paused as they reached the threshold of the inner chamber and looked around, since the people in front of them were deciding where to sit. A cluster of people were around the defense area and heads turned as they entered.

"C'mon." Kerry wanted to sit down and be out of the spotlight.

"That yer folks?"

She nodded as they walked down the center aisle, chose seats, and watched the room fill up around them. Michael, she noted, wasn't there and neither was Angie this time. Just her mother, father, and the lawyers. She felt a little nervous at that, since it appeared she was being singled out. Kerry folded her hands in her lap and regarded them, her fingers twisting her joining ring idly.

I wish this were over. She silently sounded the words. *I wish it was over, and I was out of here, and we were home.* Her stomach was tied up in knots, having rejected breakfast, and her head hurt from not sleeping.

A hand touched her arm and she looked up. "Kinda loud in here."

Andy gazed at her. "You all right, kumquat?"

Kerry sighed, "I'm tired, I'm cranky, and I don't want to be here." She hesitated. "And I'm a little scared of why they want me back to testify."

The room quieted then, as the session got under way. First, there were some meetings, then they talked about procedure.

Then they called her up. Kerry stood and took a deep breath, then carefully made her way out of their row and towards the table, getting a comforting pat on the leg from Andy as she went past him. She took her seat and folded her hands as her father's lawyer came over to face her.

It was a very lonely feeling. She knew the man, and had for years, but it was as though he considered her nothing but some trash off the street, given his expression. Not to mention her parent's faces. Cameras flashed, and her peripheral vision caught the round, black single eyes of the television crews.

"Ms. Stuart," the man hardly looked up from his papers, "you work for a company called ILS, is that correct?"

"Yes."

"For how long?"

"Almost a year."

He scribbled a note. "When was the last time you spoke with your parents, Ms. Stuart?"

Kerry felt the heightened interest almost beating against her skin. "Thanksgiving of last year," she answered quietly and heared a faint murmur rise.

"Why is that?" The man looked up.

"Why do you want to know?"

"Excuse me?"

Kerry shifted. "I asked, why do you want to know? What does something personal between my parents and myself have to do with anything here?"

He tapped his pen on his pad. "Because, Ms. Stuart, there was some very damaging and potentially libelous material released to the press last year, coincidentally," he put a sting on it, "a day after the last time you spoke to your parents." He paused. "So I ask you again, Ms. Stuart. Why?"

Oh shit. Kerry caught Andrew sitting forward, gazing at her in concern. *I am in such deep trouble.* She sucked in a breath though and collected her thoughts. *Don't let them rattle you,* Dar's voice intoned in her mind. *Think.*

"We had a disagreement about the direction my life was taking," Kerry answered carefully. "It happens all the time, in families." She paused. "Or so I'm told."

He nodded. "A disagreement so severe, it caused you to break off contact with your family entirely?"

"No." She shook her head. "I speak with my brother and sister and our extended family."

He made another mark. "Several years back, your uncle was fired by ILS."

"That's true," Kerry agreed.

"And yet, you chose to go work for them." He paused and looked at her. "Why?"

That, at least, was an easy question. "I'm an information services professional. They're one of the largest IS companies in the world and they offered me a promotion, with a thirty percent pay hike." Kerry cocked her head. "It wasn't exactly rocket science." Several of the senators behind her laughed.

"Even though your father was actively campaigning against them and was working to have them thrown out of government contracts in Michigan?"

"Because he held a grudge due to Uncle Al. Yes," Kerry answered back, a trifle sharply. "I investigated the files regarding that when I became an employee of ILS and I was satisfied that the company acted fairly." She folded her hands.

"As a matter of fact, your current...supervisor...fired him. Is that right, Ms. Stuart?"

Uh oh, take two. "Given the information we had on him, sir, I would have fired him," Kerry answered quietly. "But yes, in answer to your question, it was Ms. Roberts who did it."

The lawyer nodded. "Exactly." He leafed through a few sheets of paper. "It was the first step, in fact, in a plan to discredit your father." He looked up. "And you played right into it."

Kerry blinked. "What?"

He leaned on the table. "We know where that libelous information came from, Ms. Stuart."

She didn't answer him, her pulse racing against her skin.

"It's been a careful, underhanded campaign to discredit your father and turn you against him and it's resulted in this hearing, where these gentlemen are forced to question your father's very morals." The man turned, making sure the cameras had a good shot at him. "I put it to you, gentlemen. The company who stood to lose by the senator's investigations, who duped his daughter into working for them, who had the ability, and the resources to manufacture this information...it's so obvious."

Kerry could hear the murmurs of agreement. "You have no idea what you're talking about," she pronounced carefully. "ILS didn't manufacture anything."

"They could have, though. What about that problem this morning?" One of the senators behind her leaned back. "Damn computers are too powerful nowadays."

The lawyer circled her. "Don't you see, Ms. Stuart? You've been tricked by your boss. It's obvious that she made this stuff," he slapped the dossiers on the desk, "up and sent it out, to stop Senator Stuart from canceling those contracts."

Kerry took a deep breath. "No, she didn't. And ILS had nothing to do with this."

"You can't be sure of that, Ms. Stuart." The man now gave her a pitying look. "Or should I say, you've got a vested interest in denying it, since she seduced you in the process."

A shocked silence occurred, then low whispers. Kerry's nervousness faded and was replaced by anger. "Oh, I most certainly can be sure of that."

"You're not denying the seduction then? We know you two live together."

The whispers were getting ugly and Kerry could feel the hostile eyes now on her. "That information was not manufactured by anyone and Dar Roberts did not release it."

The man crossed to her and leaned on the table. "Oh really? And how do you know that?"

Crunch time. Kerry met his eyes. "Because I did."

Dead silence.

"I validated the source, I confirmed the contents, and I released that information to the press and to the FBI." Kerry spoke into all that frozen quiet. "And, sir, it's the bribes, and the malfeasance, and the buying of votes, and the moral decrepitude that's at issue here. Not me, or my relationship with my family, or who in the hell I sleep with." Her last sentence was spoken in a rapid crescendo.

He stared at her in total disgust.

Kerry just sat there, breathing hard.

"That will be all for now, Ms. Stuart," one of the senators said, carefully adjusting a pile of papers in his hands. "I motion for a brief adjournment."

Somewhere, she found the strength to stand up with quiet dignity and face the explosion of flashbulbs. She stared through them to find her way back through the muttering crowd to a safe haven outlined by a tall, angry looking form who put an arm around her and visited the surrounding crowd with a lethal glare.

She sat down, shaking.

Andrew sat next to her and hissed out a long, aggravated breath. "That boy is going to have his pecker pulled out his damn nostrils fore I'm done with him."

Kerry swallowed, not daring to look up, knowing everyone was looking at her. Then a warm hand dropped onto her other shoulder and a graceful body lifted itself over the row of chairs and settled into the one next to her, feeling and smelling and sounding like Dar. She peeked over and saw a wry, compassionate gaze looking back. "Can I go home now?" she managed to whisper.

Dar pulled her closer, ignoring the press, having gotten to the chambers just in time to hear Kerry's admission. "Don't worry about it, Ker. You did what you had to. Whatever happens, you and I will deal with it." She exchanged looks with her father. "Take it easy. I've got you."

Kerry closed her eyes, momentarily safe in her warm haven. *Surely, it couldn't get any worse, right?*

She sighed.

Chapter
37

They pushed their way out of the hastily recessed chambers, surrounded by people who were grabbing and shoving and plucking at Kerry's sleeve. "Ms. Stuart. Ms. Stuart, a moment with you please!"

Kerry kept her head down and kept walking, relying on Dar's guidance to keep her from slamming into the press crews and other impediments. A hand grabbed her arm and she looked up to see her microphone shoved in her face. "I'm sorry." She took a breath. "I think I've said enough for now."

"Wait!"

"Ms. Stuart!"

"Is it true?"

"Excuse us." Dar put an arm around Kerry and put a hand out, shoving hard and making some space in the crush of bodies. Andrew came up on the other side and tucked Ceci between them, slipping an arm behind Dar's and clasping her above the elbow.

"You all right?" Ceci murmured, patting Kerry's arm.

"No," Kerry whispered.

"Take it easy. We'll get out of here." Ceci glanced up at the two determined, serious faces above her head. She and Dar had gone down to the crowded building after Dar had finished her interview, doing a more than creditable job so far as Ceci could tell and fending off the repeated passes from the reporter with a wry good grace. They'd gotten to the stairs just as Kerry was speaking and stopped in the very doorway just as she'd admitted to releasing the information.

Gutsy kid. Ceci had followed Dar closely through the chaos, almost swallowed up by Andy's welcoming grip as she reached the seats.

She'd been out of life for so long, Ceci suspected this was the Goddess' little revenge.

They forced their way out the door and finally felt fresh air against them, and Kerry sucked in a huge lung full of it, trying to ignore the shouting of the protestors not far away. The cameras had followed and reporters were yammering, but her senses were on overload and she shut them down in self-defense, covering her ears with her hands and shivering.

"Down there," Dar directed. "We'll get a cab and get the hell out of here."

"I'm not going back in there," Kerry muttered. "I don't care what they say. That's it."

They headed down the stairs, past the crowd, and Dar flicked her eyes over them, seeing the angry faces and surging motion. "Look! There they are! That's the one!"

"Shit." Dar turned her shoulders just in time to deflect a large rock. "Let's move."

"Son of a biscuit," Andrew growled. "Dardar, switch spots with me."

Another rock pelted the dark haired woman and she gritted her teeth. "Just keep moving."

Epithets rolled over them. Nasty, dark words full of hate, and anger, and more rocks with them. The police struggled to keep the crowd back, but several men broke through, grabbed a barricade and moved towards them with wild intent.

Andrew cursed and ducked around Dar. "Stay with yer momma," he growled, giving them all a shove towards the cab as he jumped to intercept the two men. "And where d'you think ye're goin', dog face?" He grabbed the barricade coming towards him and wrenched it from the man's hands, then he tossed it away and towards an empty spot on the stairs. The man closest to him—a tall, thin youngster with cropped hair and ugly ears—reached for him, but a policeman caught him up from behind, and hauled him towards the line of barricades.

"You stupid bastard!" the boy yelled at Andrew. "I'll kick your ass!"

His companion jumped on Andrew and rapidly realized what a bad mistake that was when the ex-SEAL got a grab on his neck and his crotch and flipped him over his head, landing him on the hard marble stairs. Three more men broke through the ranks and ran towards them with sticks.

Andy grinned and bounced on the balls of his feet, feeling a rush of blood through him that left a pleasant tingle behind, prickling a lust for fighting that had never quite faded. "C'mon, y'little pollywogs," he yelled, flexing his hands.

A cab pulled cautiously to the curb as Dar signaled, yanked the door open, and hustled her mother and Kerry inside.

"Where ya goin'?" the cabbie yelled.

"Anywhere but here," Dar replied, looking around quickly and spotting several reporters heading their way. "Jesus. I shoulda left that damn system down this morning." She turned to see her father holding his ground, then she sighed. "Be right back."

She bolted up the stairs and grabbed Andrew's arm. "C'mon, Dad."

"Aw." Andrew threw a last punch, then ducked an outstretched arm and followed Dar back to the cab. They beat the reporters by a few steps and got the doors closed just in time—the cab pulling quickly away from the curb as a stumbling cameraman slammed against its bumper.

For a moment, there was silence. Then Kerry slowly released a long held breath and leaned against Dar, who wrapped her up tightly and pulled her close.

"Hope there's a back entrance to that there hotel," Andrew remarked. "Haven't seen this much hoohaa since that Pamela Lee Anderson showed up at a damn liberty near Mexico." He half turned and regarded his wife, who was rubbing her ear. "You all right, Cec?"

Cecilia mentally caught her breath. "I think so." She looked at Dar, who was pressed against the cab door with Kerry huddled against her. "You?"

Dar nodded, as her lover burrowed further into her sweater. "I'm fine." She put a hand against Kerry's head as she heard her take a shaky breath. "All right. Let's just get back to the hotel and regroup, then I'll figure out what to do." She half expected a protest from Kerry, but the blond woman didn't say a word. *Okay.* Dar mentally sorted things out. *What Kerry had just done had derailed two possible problems that had been niggling at her.*

One was the fact that she and Dar lived together, which had been rolled right over.

Two was the fact that the information on her father had come from within ILS, which had also been rolled right over, obscured by the blond woman's startling confession.

ILS's position then was simple, that its employee's personal lives was none of their concern. *One problem out of the way.*

As for Kerry bursting out of the closet with a howitzer... Well, from the company's standpoint they were on the high ground, able to placidly say their employee's sexuality was also none of their concern, and the equal treatment of such was assured under the corporate bylaws. Made them look damn progressive, which ILS in most cases certainly wasn't.

Okay. So she didn't have to worry about the company. On the other hand, she did have to worry about the desperately upset woman in her arms, who was emotionally devastated and rapidly unraveling before Dar's eyes. With a sigh, she pulled her cell phone out and dialed a number. Alastair answered on the second ring.

"Well, hello there Dar." Her boss's voice was wry. "Just saw your interview. Fantastic job. I got a call from ABC and CBS right afterward, asking for in-depth stuff."

"Alastair—"

"And, I just saw the hearings."

Dar was silent, wondering what he'd say.

A pause. "She's a damn brave kid." Alastair's voice was warm. "Give her my regards, willya?"

Dar smiled quietly. "I will."

"Think they'll call you up there? Just so I know the worst?" Alastair sounded peacefully resigned. "I've called a teleconference for tonight with the board."

"Not if they're smart," Dar replied.

"All right. Keep me advised, Dar. I want to know what's happening."

Dar chuckled wryly. "I'll keep the company's nose as clean as I can, Alastair."

"Couldn't give a damn about the company, Dar."

She stared at the phone for a moment.

"Ah...surprised you, huh?" The CEO laughed. "That's a first. Later, Dar." He hung up, leaving her to close her phone bemusedly and tuck it away. Kerry finally loosened her grip and tilted her head, gazing up at her with sad eyes.

"Hey." Dar leaned forward a little to touch her forehead against her lover's. "Bet you could use some ice cream." She got a very tiny tired, hurting smile back, then Kerry exhaled and put her head back down. Dar stroked the pale hair comfortingly, glancing up to see her mother watching her. For an awkward moment they stared at each other, then Ceci tightened her lips into a brief smile and turned her attention to her husband, who was scowling at the surrounding, busy streets.

They got to the hotel and the cabbie drove into the parking garage, going down a level and arriving at a lower entrance that was pretty well deserted. Gratefully, they paid him and got out, slipped inside and grabbed an elevator. "Hold on." Andrew held a hand up. "Let's take that one there." He pointed. "S'got a fireman's control."

"We don't have a key," Dar remarked, her arm still around the very quiet and withdrawn Kerry.

"Pshaw." Her father pushed her inside and waited for the others to enter, then he pulled a small gadget from his pocket and used it to jimmy the fireman's lock as the doors closed.

The elevator made a soft, whooshing noise as it climbed the floors. Kerry's eyes went from face to face as they waited. "I'm sorry you all had to go through that," she finally said. "I wish..." She fell silent.

"S'allright, kumquat," Andrew drawled.

"What did you call her?" Ceci consciously tried to lighten the atmosphere. "Good grief, Andy. How could you compare poor Kerry to a small, bitter orange?"

The doors opened and they peeked out, then edged into the empty corridor and made their way quickly to the Dar and Kerry's room. They got inside just as they heard the elevators open and voices come their way. Andy closed the door hastily, then held a finger to his lips.

Kerry couldn't have cared less if the entire Mormon Tabernacle Choir was outside. She trudged over and landed on the bed, spreading her arms out and closing her eyes in weary relief.

Sweet Jesus, what have I just done?

After they'd named her a hostile witness, she'd felt sure her parents knew she'd been the one to release that information. What other reason would there be to estrange her? Surely it couldn't just be Dar.

But no. They hadn't known. One look at her father's face had told her that. Utter shock. Utter betrayal. He'd though that revealing Dar as the source of the information would have driven a wedge between them, never realizing what he'd force her to say.

No, Daddy. It wasn't Dar. She'd have deleted the entire file, left up to her.

I did it.

Me.

Your little girl.

Kerry heard Andy and Ceci move into their own room, mentioning something about ordering room service over there, then it got quiet and the bed next to her dipped and moved, bringing a warm body to settle against her. She opened her eyes to see Dar propped up on her side, a tired look on her face. "I fucked up." Dar lifted an eyebrow at the use of the epithet. She never said that, unless it was the worst of the worst of things and her partner knew it.

"No, you didn't," her lover disagreed. "They did."

Kerry exhaled. "He didn't know." Her eyes went to Dar's. "He didn't know it was me, Dar."

"I know."

"Now they have a good reason to hate me."

Dar leaned forward and took her hand. "Listen to me a minute." Her voice was very serious. "Stop blaming yourself, Kerry. I mean it."

Kerry looked at her.

"You're not the one who did the wrong thing."

"I released that information."

"*You* are not the one who did the wrong thing," Dar repeated. "You are not the one who accepted those bribes and you are not the one who let industry pay you off to look the other way while wildlife was slaughtered and you are *not* the one who used government funds to maintain a mistress and two illegitimate children."

"I could have just kept quiet like everyone else does," Kerry murmured. "If I had, maybe someday I could have eventually sat down and talked to them about us."

Dar sighed and rubbed her fingers. "Kerry, even if nothing had happened, do you really think they'd have accepted me? Accepted us?"

Kerry shook her head slightly. "I don't know. I'll never know." She sighed, seeing Dar's perplexed look. "I can't help it, Dar. They're my parents and I love them." She regarded the ceiling. "How could I have done that to them?"

Dar nibbled her thumbnail, trying to figure out what to say. She was tired, her stomach was in knots, she'd had a very, very rough day, and it was only the afternoon. Sensitive discussions were never her forte at any time, and frankly, there was no good answer to Kerry's question, was there? "Well," she finally responded, "I can only tell you what I would have done." She paused. "I think if I'd have gone through what you'd just gone through, with the hospital and all, I'd have been furious." Another pause. "Hell, I was furious."

Kerry turned her head and studied her friend's face.

"Sometimes you do things when you're really angry, that seem right at the time," Dar went on. "I know I have. And then when you look back, later on, you second guess yourself and think about all the other things you could have done or said."

"Mmm," Kerry agreed glumly. "Hindsight."

"Yeah." Dar nodded. "But the other thing I've realized over the years is, that there's no point in beating yourself up over what you've done. It's done."

"Move on." Kerry extended the thought. "Recover and deal with it."

"Yeah."

"So. How, exactly, do I deal with knowing I ruined my parent's lives and am going to be on every tabloid cover in America next week?"

Dar squirmed a little closer. "First, just like you have to accept responsibility for what you did, you've gotta realize that they have to do the same thing." Dar put a hand on Kerry's shoulder. "Your father did those things, Ker. He knew if anyone found out, this could happen. He accepted the risk."

Kerry sighed. "It hurts."

"I know."

But her brain was starting to work again, Kerry realized. She could feel it, the shock was fading and her mental processes were settling back down into a more normal pattern. "So what about the tabloids?" she joked faintly.

"Well, I was figuring." Dar laid an arm over Kerry's stomach and smiled as the blond woman rested a hand on her shoulder. "When you and I are ancient, those things'll make one hell of scrapbook to pull out and show people."

Kerry's face pulled into a real smile at the image. "My fifteen minutes of fame, you mean?"

"Something like that, yeah." Dar returned the smile. "I'll throw in a tape of my interview, and we got it locked down."

Kerry moved a bit of dark hair out of Dar's eyes. "Oh. How did that go? Is it on? Let's turn CNN on. I want to see you." Then she stopped. "Hmm. Maybe not. I think I know what the lead story's going to be." She rubbed her temples. "You don't have any aspirin, do you? My head's killing me."

"Sure." Dar rolled off the bed, went to her briefcase, and tugged a bottle out. "Feel like eating something?"

Kerry shook her head.

Dar came back with the pills and some water and sat back down on the bed. "That can't be helping your headache," she commented, as the blond woman curled onto her side and took the glass, swallowed several of the tablets, and washed them down.

"Probably not, but I think I'd lose whatever I tried to get down." Kerry put the glass on the bedside table and put her head down on her arm. "Maybe later."

Dar stretched out next to her, letting her body relax against the bed's mattress. She studied the tense back next to her and gave it a tentative scratch. Kerry's shoulder blades moved, and Dar heard a soft grunt as she expanded the motion, making little circles with her fingertips.

I'm a big girl. Kerry closed her eyes as the touch continued. *I don't need to be coddled like a little kid.* One eye opened and peered around the empty room. "Hey, Dar?"

"Yeah?"

Kerry rolled over onto her back and turned her head. "Think we have time for a nap?"

A nap. Boy. That sounded good. Dar spread an arm out, smiling in invitation. "Sure. C'mere." She gathered Kerry in and fitted her body around the smaller woman's, until they were a warm tangle in the center of the bed. It was quiet for a bit and then Kerry sighed.

"Dar?"

The dark haired woman had her eyes closed and kept them that way. "Mmm?"

"Would you have done it?"

Dar considered that seriously. "I don't know. I can be pretty vindictive, Kerry." She shrugged. "Maybe it would depend on whether or not I was PMSing."

"Dar, you don't PMS. I had to listen to an hour long discussion on that in the lunchroom last week."

"Sure I do, Kerry."

"No, you don't."

"Yes, I do. It's just that no one can tell the difference," the placid response came back. "Think about it. What's typical dropping eggs behavior? It turns you into a raving, overbearing alpha bitch with a thing for chocolate."

Kerry had to laugh. She buried her face into Dar's shoulder and muffled her snickering.

"This differs from my normal state exactly how?"

More snickering.

Dar smiled at the popcorn ceiling, glad she'd succeeded in making Kerry laugh a little. The chuckles wound down, and a warm hand slipped under her shirt and rubbed the skin gently.

"Thanks," Kerry murmured. "I needed that." She exhaled and closed her eyes, hearing Dar's jaw crack as she yawned. Everything else would just have to wait for a while.

❖ ⌘ ❖ ⌘ ❖ ⌘ ❖

The soft burr of her cell phone nudged Dar out of a really good dream, one that involved fudge and cherries and a very messy boat deck. She pried an eye open and glared at the instrument, then reluctantly disengaged one arm and answered it. "Yeah?"

A breath. "Um...is that...is...Dar?"

"You had a fifty percent chance and you won. What can I do for you?" Dar closed her eye.

"Dar, it's Angie. Can I speak to my sister, please?"

Dar jolted awake. "Sorry. I didn't... You don't sound like..." She gently shook Kerry. "Are you okay?"

"I'm in the hospital. Please, can I talk to her?"

"Ker." Dar shook harder, feeling the gathering resistance as Kerry dragged herself out of a very deep sleep. "Kerry, c'mon. It's your sister on the phone."

"Mmm?" Kerry sucked in a breath, and rubbed her eyes. "Wh—" She lifted her head and peered upward. "Who? Angie?"

"Yeah. Here." Dar handed her the phone. "She said she's in the hospital."

"Oh." Kerry pressed the phone to her ear. "Angie?"

"Hey." Her sister's voice sounded exhausted. "Listen. The baby's coming and I'm having a really tough time."

"My god. What's going on? Are you okay?" Kerry pulled herself up, her pounding heart sending blood to her head in a painful wave. "Where are you?"

"I saw you on TV," Angie replied. "I...they brought me here yesterday, Kerry. It's been hell all night. It just hurts...and hurts. I don't know what's going to happen, and I wanted...I wanted to talk to you, so you...so I could tell you. I didn't want anything to happen, and then I..."

"Angie, it's okay," Kerry murmured. "Don't worry about anything. What's important is how you're doing."

There was a brief silence. "Ow." Angie finally sighed. "I'm so tired of hurting." A rustle of linen. "I saw you on TV, Sis."

"You did, huh?"

"Yeah." Angela took a breath. "I'm sorry I didn't come over when Mike did yesterday."

"It's okay."

"No, it's not okay," Angie replied. "You have to stand up and be counted sometime, Kerry."

"Angie, don't worry about being counted. Just worry about yourself and your baby," Kerry told her. "Where are you? Can I come over and see you? Is Richard there?"

"No," Angie whispered. "He's out of town."

"What about Brian?"

There was a long silence and then her sister sighed. "He's chosen not to be involved."

Kerry's eyes closed. "Oh, Angie."

"Yeah, well. Better this way for the kids," Angela replied. "Maybe I'll at least get points for a cute baby, right?"

"I'm sorry, Sis." Arms closed around Kerry in a secure hold. "Listen, hang in there. I'm going to come over and see you."

"Be careful," Angie whispered.

"I will. Take it easy, Sis. I love you."

Angie hissed in pain. "I love you, too."

Kerry hung up and then scrubbed her face with a hand. "I feel like I've been run over by a bus, Dar." She sighed. "Can we find a way over to the hospital without dragging half the DC press corps with us?"

Dar kissed her head. "We'll find a way." She looked up as the room's phone rang and then answered it. "Yes?"

"I'm sorry, ma'am, but this is the hotel operator, and I have a Mr. James Herkins who is very insistent on wanting to talk to Ms. Stuart."

"It's the prosecutor." Dar held her hand over the receiver. "You want to talk to him?"

"Now he wants to talk to me?" Kerry answered with a touch of sarcasm. "Not really but I guess I'd better." She took the phone. "Thank you. Put him through. Sorry if this is being such a pain for you."

"Oh." The operator seemed surprised. "Well, thanks for saying that. Most people don't." She clicked off and then a male voice came through.

"Ms. Stuart?"

"Yes," Kerry answered.

"I'd like to set up a meeting. We need to talk."

"Now that I have something to say that you want to hear?" Kerry shot back, getting a mildly raised eyebrow from her listening partner.

There was a pause. "Ms. Stuart, I had no reason to think you were the cornerstone of the situation. My information on you was that you were just another one of Roger's kids." Herkins hesitated. "It's not like you came forward and said otherwise."

Well, that was true. Kerry had to admit.

"And I don't think you want to go through another day like today. Am I wrong?"

Also true. "All right. But it can't be today. I have something I have to take care of," Kerry told him. "Besides, I've pretty much said all I have to say."

"Except why."

"Excuse me?"

"Why, Ms. Stuart. You solved a big problem for me today by saying how—there was always a question as to how that information got released. The question that's coming to everyone's mind right now is why. Why would one of Roger Stuart's kids—seemingly a nice, intelligent, successful young woman—deliberately release information so damaging?"

Kerry was silent for a moment. "I was just asking myself that same question. I guess I just felt it was the right thing to do at the time."

"Still think that?" Herkins asked shrewdly.

Kerry let a breath out. "Morally? Yes. He did things that were not right and not legal."

"Well," the prosecutor's voice sounded satisfied, "I'd agree with you there, Ms. Stuart, and you sent a very powerful message today, whether you realized it or not. How about you and I meet for breakfast and we can talk? Maybe I can work things out so you can finish up here and go home."

Home. "I'd like that," she admitted. "Honestly, I really don't have anything else to add to the case one way or the other. I didn't know—or even suspect—until I was looking at it in black and white on my screen."

"I believe you, Ms. Stuart," he replied. "He fooled a lot of people." He paused. "Tomorrow morning then? I'll pick you up in the back. We'll go over to a little place near the hearing chambers. Okay?"

"All right," Kerry agreed. "Are the hearings over for today?"

A soft snort. "They requested a delay. Apparently you rocked their apple cart pretty thoroughly."

"Okay."

"Ms. Stuart, don't be surprised if they contact you. It's up to you if you want to talk to them, but I think you realize they're not your friends."

"I understand," Kerry answered. "I'll see you tomorrow. Eight all right?"

"Perfect. Have a good night, Ms. Stuart."

Kerry hung up the phone and stared at it. "He's supposed to be the good guy." She looked up at Dar. "So why do I feel like such a traitor?"

"Because you have a conscience," Dar responded promptly. "And a good heart."

Kerry sighed. "I want this to be over, Dar." She rubbed her neck tiredly. "I want to be back in my office, listening to José complain and having something stupid and disastrous to work on waiting for me." Her shoulders slumped. "I want to have a cup of *café con leche* and one of those cheese pastelitos, and know when the sun sets that there's a climbing wall waiting for me."

Dar rested her head on her arm. "Are you telling me you're happy with your life?" The question slipped out without her realizing it and was more serious than she'd intended.

"Yes." Kerry's eyes were unfocused, as she stared across the nondescript hotel room. "Maybe I didn't realize until this moment just how happy I am." She blinked. "True hearts are such a rare gift, Dar."

Dar wasn't sure where this was coming from. "Yes, they are," she answered cautiously.

Kerry turned and put a hand on Dar's chest, right over hers. "How in the hell did I rate one?"

Dar had no idea of what to answer to that and was saved from having to improvise by a light knock on the connecting door. "Yeah?" She kept her eyes locked with Kerry's, searching the shadowed green depths as the door opened inward and her father's head emerged.

"Thought I heard voices." Andrew cocked his head at the two of them. "You two all right?"

Kerry exhaled, then turned her head. "We're fine, Dad. But my sister's in the hospital having trouble with the baby. I need to go see her."

"All right, kumquat. We'll put on the hip waders and slog through all the pony paddies wherever you want to." Andrew pulled his head back inside to relay the request.

"Dar?" Kerry turned back to regard her lover seriously. "You need to have children."

"Wh—?" Dar's eyes went round and huge.

"You just do." Kerry got up and went to the sink, rinsing her face with the cold, metallic water.

Chapter
38

"Alastair, it's gone past where we can control this." Evans was upset and his voice showed it. "We have the company's reputation at stake here."

Alastair fiddled with a pencil, tossing it back and forth between his fingers. "I really don't see a problem, John—"

"Oh, c'mon," Berensen augered in with a disgusted sigh. "For Christ's sake, Alastair. We're in the middle of a political nightmare here. She admitted to releasing that information. What more do you want?"

"Well, it's not against company policy to tell the truth," the CEO reminded them mildly. "Despite what you might have heard." He looked up as Bea stuck her head in and they exchanged rueful looks. "Besides, we got some great press yesterday, didn't we?"

"Yeah, until they all figure out the connection and realize those two," a vicious pause, "ladies are shacking up together. Then what, Alastair? You want to put your puss on television and explain why we've got a couple of—"

"John," McLean warned in a low voice, "our company policy is one of non-discrimination on paper, and we all know that, so—"

"Alastair, no one's gonna give royal crap what our policy is. This'll be front page news. You better do something about it right now."

Alastair got up, walked around his chair, and paced in a small circle. "Like what?"

"Fire Stuart!"

"For?" the CEO shot back. "Honesty? Integrity? Good job performance? What would you like me to fire her for, John?"

The air crackled with tension. Alastair leaned forward towards the teleconferencing session, where the two board members were displayed,

having stayed after his general session that had completed not much earlier. It hadn't been either smooth or cordial, and the CEO had a feeling he
might be on the losing end of at least one of these battles. "Well?" he
asked again.

"For using company resources to get that information on her father
and use it for personal reasons," Evans stated in triumph.

"We don't know she did that," Alastair told him. "We don't know she
used company resources, and given what the poor kid just had to go
through, it's hard to see where she got any personal gain from it."

"Oh, c'mon, Alastair!"

"I'm just protecting company assets, John," the CEO reminded him
placidly. "That is what you pay me for."

Berenson slapped his hand on his desk, audible through the connection. "McLean, enough of this stupidity. Look, I know you've got a thing
for Roberts, but for Christ's sake, is it worth your job?"

Alastair stared at the screen for a long moment. "Well you know, let
me get back to you on that one." With a quick motion, he slapped the dis-
connect key and cut off further discussion. With a disgusted sigh, he sat
down at his desk and propped his chin up on his fist as Bea entered again
and brought him a mug. "Don't think I need any more coffee, thanks."

"It's bourbon," Bea answered with a wry smile. "I just put it in a coffee cup to cut down on the gossip." She set the cup down and perched on
a corner of his desk. "Tough situation, huh? I saw the footage."

Alastair rolled his eyes.

"You knew this might happen if you promoted Paladar."

"Yeah, I knew," the CEO agreed, with a rueful smile. "But you know,
Bea, I still think it was the right choice. Look at all Dar's accomplished
since then." He exhaled wearily. "I just hope the little bugger hasn't
achieved more trouble than I can handle this time." He glanced at the
media feed, which had Kerry's image displayed prominently, running on
the corner of his computer desktop. "Gonna be a close one."

❖ ⌘ ❖ ⌘ ❖ ⌘ ❖

Having a father who spent the balance of his life in clandestine operations was, Dar discovered, a damn useful thing when in the public spotlight. Andrew guided them out of the hotel and around the corner into a
small alley, then out onto the street where they captured a taxi with little
trouble.

They were surprised to find a crowd outside the hospital, but it
wasn't anything having to do with the hearings. The hospital was home to
a family planning facility that performed abortions and the group was protesting outside, picketing the entrance and chanting.

Dar was ambivalent about the subject. The slightly frantic, almost overdone aggressiveness of the protesters set her on edge, but on the other hand she firmly believed a person had to take responsibility for their actions, and that included having sex and the potential result of it. *You play,* Dar reasoned, *you pay, and once the child was started, you owed it the right to come into the world.*

They sat in a small waiting room outside the hospital's obstetrics wing, while Kerry approached the nurses' station in search of her sister. Dar paced quietly in one corner, reading the meaningless notices on the cork board while her mother claimed a chair, and her father poked around the few vending machines nearby.

"Dar?" Ceci cocked her head, after she watched her daughter for a few minutes. "Is that list of pregnancy symptoms so fascinating?"

Dar nearly jumped out of her skin. She turned and gave her mother a dire look. "No." She paused. "Why?"

Ceci's brow knit. "Just asking. You've been reading it for a couple of minutes and I know you read faster than that."

Dar paced over and sat down. "I wasn't reading it." She tucked her hands under her arms.

"Okay," Ceci murmured. "I...um...don't think it's anything you have to worry about. Unless you two are um..." She found herself the recipient of an outraged, blue eyed gaze. "Guess not. Hmm?"

"Oh yeah, I'd make a wonderful parent," Dar muttered. "No, Chino's family enough for us."

Ceci cleared her throat and pulled a small sketch pad from her shoulder bag, set it on her knee and removed a pencil. "Well, her college costs should be minimal." She flipped the pad open to an empty sheet and paused, then started to work.

❖ ⌘ ❖ ⌘ ❖ ⌘ ❖

"My sister is here. I think she's in labor?" Kerry asked the nurse, who was busy writing something behind the desk.

"Well, if she's here, she sure ain't got a broken leg," the woman answered. "Hang on a minute." The nurse struggled with a terminal keyboard. "Stupid thing. Jesus, I hate these stupid computers."

Kerry scratched her jaw. "Make a deal with you."

The nurse looked up. "Excuse me?"

"Tell me where my sister is and I'll fix your computer."

Long, dark lashes flickered. "You're one of those nerdy people?"

Kerry nodded.

"Sure. Have at it. What's your sister's name?" The nurse moved out of the way and let Kerry get at the terminal.

"Angela." Kerry unplugged the terminal and gave it a whack, then turned the keyboard over and rapped it smartly on the desk. Crumbs the size of a postage stamp were dislodged and she brushed them away as she flipped the keyboard back over and restarted the machine. "She's been in labor a while, she said."

"She's in that third bay down there." The nurse watched Kerry in fascination. "She's having a bit of a rough time. Hey, that worked." She took the keyboard back and typed in something. "Wow. That was really cool. Is that what you do? Are you one of those field services people?"

"Mmm. I don't usually do hands on, but yeah, something like that." Kerry leaned on the counter. "Is it okay for me to go see Angie?"

"Sure, sure. Um, we're kinda outside visiting hours, so if anyone says anything..."

"Don't worry." Kerry smiled. "I just want to see her for a minute."

The nurse paused, then looked at Kerry for the first time. "Stay a while. It really helps the mothers sometimes and she hasn't had anyone in with her at all. I felt kind of bad for her." She held a hand out. "Call me if she needs anything. My name is Stacy."

"Kerry." She took the hand and grasped it. "Thanks. No one else has been here to visit?"

"No." Stacy shook her head. "The doctor said he's going to give her a little while longer, then he might have to look at other options after that."

Kerry nodded. "Okay, thanks." She left the desk and walked quietly down the hall, passing two darkened bays before she reached the third. The room was partially lit, lamps making a friendlier atmosphere than harsh fluorescent would. "Angie?"

Her sister turned her head, sweat dampened hair plastered across her forehead. "Oh...hey." A tremulous smile crossed her face. "Nice to see someone I know." She held a hand out and Kerry walked over and took it. "God, it's so good to have you here, Kerry."

"Hey." Kerry put her arms around her and pulled her into an awkward hug. "Wish you'd called me sooner. It's not right for you to be here by yourself, Angie."

Angie curled half onto her side and kept hold of Kerry's hands. "You were busy."

"I'd have rather been here," Kerry admitted.

"I bet." Angela blinked wearily and put her head down on the pillow. "You looked great on TV, though. The cameras kept showing you in the gallery before they called you up there." She inhaled and winced, her face tensing in pain for several very long seconds. Then she relaxed. "Who was that guy you were with? He's scary looking."

Kerry leaned on the bed rails. "That's Andy. Andrew Roberts, Dar's father." She adjusted the sheets. "He's the sweetest, most wonderful man I know."

"Yeah?"

"Yeah." Kerry smiled quietly to herself.

"He knows about you guys, I guess."

"Absolutely," Kerry told her. "He's so cool about it, and you wouldn't think he would be, because he's from the military and all—but it's like...Dar's his daughter and it wouldn't matter what she was or what she did. He just loves her."

Angie shifted uncomfortably and sighed. "That's different."

"Mmm."

"Um, I saw Dar on TV today too," Angie commented. "She looks great. I didn't understand one word in six of what she was talking about, but boy, she impressed that reporter."

Kerry smiled. "I haven't seen the interview yet. It was happening the same time as I was in that hellhole." She exhaled. "But after last night, I guess they wanted to talk to her." She caught Angie's puzzled look. "The ATM thing yesterday?"

"Ew. That was you guys?"

"Sort of. It was the guys we used for the network, but Dar fixed it." Kerry rubbed her eyes. "We were up all night though. I'm so wiped."

"You look as tired as I feel," Angie admitted, grimacing as a contraction took hold again. "Augh. God, I'm getting tired of this."

Kerry took hold of her hand. "Anything I can get you? Water or something?"

Angela shook her head. "It's just nice to have someone to talk to." Her lips curled into a smile. "Are you here alone?"

"No. You up to a few more visitors? I'd like you to meet Dar's mother and father. I don't know when I'll have the chance to introduce you again. "

Angela shifted and pulled herself up a little, pushing her hair back. "I must look like a mess. Was that who was with you yesterday? Her mom?"

Kerry nodded. "Don't worry. They're not really formal people." She ducked out.

"Yeah, sure," Angie whispered to herself, listening to the footsteps come back down the hall. A moment later her room door was filled, and a slight, silver blond woman entered followed by the tall, scarred man she'd seen on television. Then Kerry came back in with Dar right behind her, the dark haired woman glancing nervously around the room like something was going to bite. "Um...hi."

Kerry slipped in front. "Okay. Angie, this is Andy and Cecilia Roberts. Dar's mom and dad, and of course, you already know Dar."

Ceci came over and smiled at her. "Nice to meet you, Angela." She laid her hands on the railing. "Having a rough time of it?"

"Ungh." Angie glanced shyly at her. "The doctor thinks it's a nice, big baby, and that's what's causing the problems."

"Ah, yes." Ceci nodded seriously. "Been there, done that." She smiled at Angie's puzzled look, then turned and glanced first at Dar, then back at the woman in the bed. "Eight pounds, thirteen ounces." Then she indicated her slight form and raised an eyebrow.

"Ooo." Angie made a face. "I think you just made my toe hairs curl up."

"Hey!" Dar affected an insulted look. "I wasn't that big."

Angela and Ceci looked at her, then snorted. Andy chuckled and patted his offspring on the back.

"You were a bouncing baby girl, all right, squirt," he told her.

"Emphasis on the bouncing," Ceci remarked dryly. They all chuckled and the tension relaxed.

"So. Do you have any tricks I should know?" Angie asked. "My first wasn't this bad but she was a preemie." She held her hands apart a little. "All of five pounds. This one's gone full term and more."

"Well, there's a famous Eastern technique that involves transcendental meditation and the out of body thing, but I found drugs to be the best trick," Ceci replied. "Have they tried to dilate you?"

Kerry leaned against the foot of the bed content to listen to the conversation and watch Dar and Andy edge curiously around the room, investigating the machinery. They both had a way of cocking their heads a little when they were figuring out something and seeing them do it together was pretty funny.

Seeing Angie smiling was pretty nice too. Her sister was trading animated baby stories with Ceci, which Kerry was keeping tabs on to tease her partner with later. Dar had been, unsurprisingly, a very active baby who had gotten into some wild situations.

"And there she was, sitting on top of the car hood with the garden hose," Ceci was saying, "terrorizing the squirrels."

Dar sighed, then returned her attention to a blinking readout.

"Did you really?" Kerry murmured, bumping her with a hip.

"I don't remember a thing," Dar muttered back. "She could say I picked my butt up and flew across the front yard and I'd never know if it was true."

"Sure you would," Kerry disagreed. "There'd be a National Enquirer article archived somewhere."

Dar rolled her eyes. "I'm sure I wasn't half as homicidally destructive as my mother describes." She picked up a device. "What's this?"

"It's to suck fluid out of the baby's nose," Kerry advised her, as the taller woman dropped the instrument as though it was hot. "Dar, relax, would you?"

"I hate hospitals."

"You're just visiting, so calm down."

"Yeah? So what was that about me having kids?" Dar whispered.

"Shh." Kerry had to muffle a grin. "I just meant that I think you've got really good genes, and they deserve to stay in the pool." She paused. "If you know what I mean. Besides, your dad would make a great grandpa."

"Oh." Dar peeked at her father. "Well, maybe you have a point there." She smiled quietly to herself.

Kerry blinked. "I do?"

Angie laughed. "Oh my god. If my kid ever did that I think I'd just die on the spot."

"Wall," Andrew stuck his hands in his pockets, "ah seem to remember a morning where I had to be standing in the CO's office, having to explain to him how an M1 tank happened to get cross the repair yard and take out half the mess hall."

"Oh no." Dar winced. "Not that story."

"Is it true?" Kerry whispered. "Never mind. It must be. You're blushing."

"Well, given the food in there, I can't say I blamed her," Ceci remarked, drawing a laugh even from Dar. "If I remember correctly, we had to have Marriott cater the base for two weeks, and everyone came over and gave Dar candy."

"Heh, heh." Andrew nodded. "Fergot about that part."

"Mmm. I didn't." Dar licked her lips.

Angie laughed again, relaxing back against her pillows. Then she gasped suddenly and her hands went to her belly. "Oh my gosh."

"Water break?" Ceci asked immediately.

"Yes." Angie hissed, grabbing for the railing as a contraction hit. "Whoa. I think I just jump started something." All the unproductive pushing of the previous hours faded, as her body seized up. "Oh...my...God..."

Kerry swallowed, her hands tensing on the rails. "Um...is there...what can we do?"

Cecilia glanced up. "First off, get those two out of here before they end up on the floor. Second, stop and tell the nurse."

"Wh—?" Kerry turned her head and saw the widened, rounded pairs of blue eyes. "Oh boy. Right. Okay." She grabbed Dar's and Andy's arms and tugged them towards the door. "C'mon, guys. Let's go boil water."

They emerged into the hallway and headed towards the desk, their footsteps echoing in the quiet space. "I wonder if it'll be a boy or a girl?" Kerry mused, as they turned the corner.

And came face to face with her parents.

There was a deadly silence.

"That young lady in there needs some help." Andy deliberately turned his head towards the nurse.

The woman took one look at the tableau in front of her and immediately trotted towards Angie's room purposefully.

"You have no place here." Roger Stuart spoke in a low voice. "So take yourself, and whoever you have with you, and get out."

Kerry let out a breath, hoping she wouldn't throw up. "My sister asked me to come. It's her choice. Not yours." She forced herself to meet her father's eyes and felt the disgust there hit her with almost physical force.

"You're not part of this family. I thought I made that clear."

Kerry sensed Dar and Andy moving closer. "You're not a part of my family," she responded bravely, "but Angie and Michael are. Excuse me." She turned her head and walked deliberately around them, towards the waiting room.

"Not if they know what's good for them," Roger said after her, not turning around. "Don't be here when we come out." He took his wife's arm and walked down the corridor.

Kerry stopped just inside the waiting room door, her knees shaking so badly she almost fell. Dar seemed to realize it and got an arm around her, as Andrew came round front of her and patted her cheek.

"Kerry?"

She swallowed a few times, then looked up at him. "I'm okay," she whispered. "I just wasn't expecting that." She tucked her trembling hands under her arms. "I can't even blame him for feeling like he does." Kerry dropped her eyes to the highly polished tile floor, the reality of what she'd done hitting solidly home.

Andrew scowled, then looked up at his daughter gazing at him with a helpless, beseeching expression over Kerry's shoulder.

He knew that please-fix it-look, all right. "C'mere, kumquat." He put his arms around the blond woman. "Don't you be chewing on your-self, hear? If I'd done what that man did, I'd hope mah kid would have the guts and the honor you had in letting everyone know about it."

Kerry absorbed the words and the emotion behind them, in this little pocket of grace she found herself in. Andy's fingers scratched the back of her head lightly as she slipped her arms around his large and solid form. She wasn't sure he was right, but it helped. "Thanks." She released him and hoisted herself up on her toes and gave him a kiss on the cheek.

Andy blushed. "That's enough a'that." He pointed to the chairs. "Sit yer butt down. I'm gonna go find me some coffee." He escaped out the door, leaving Dar and Kerry to link hands and cross the room. They sat down and exhaled in perfect unison.

They looked at each other.

"You'll be okay," Dar told her reassuringly.

Kerry nodded. "Yeah, I think I will." She glanced towards the empty doorway and smiled, just a little.

❖ ⌘ ❖ ⌘ ❖ ⌘ ❖

"Ooo." Angie winced, biting down on her lip. "Now you're in a hurry?" She held her breath until the spasm was over, then panted. "Kids."

"Tell me about it." Cecilia straightened the covers and helped the younger woman into a more comfortable position. "I was in labor for twenty-two hours."

"Oh my god." Angela breathed. "I can't imagine anything enjoyable I'd like to do for twenty-two hours."

"Well," Cecilia mused, then chuckled to herself.

Angie blinked at her, blushing as she caught the reference. "Um...thanks for distracting me, by the way. I know I hardly know you...but I..." She glanced up as the nurse hurried in, giving her a tense, professional smile.

"I see things are moving. Let me get the doctor." The nurse moved into an alcove and picked up a phone.

"Don't worry about it. I was glad to help." Ceci turned her head at the footsteps, seeing the two older figures fill the doorway.

Interesting. Chinese version. "Hello," she greeted Kerry's parents, noting the angry, flustered glare she got in return.

They ignored her. "I thought I told you no contact." Roger Stuart addressed the woman in the bed.

Angie curled up in a ball, her face tensing with pain. "I just—"

"Easy." Ceci patted her arm.

"How could you, Angela?" Kerry's mother said, visibly upset. "After all she's done to us."

"I just wanted someone to talk to," Angie got out, as her contraction relaxed. "She's my sister—"

"No, she isn't," Roger responded sharply. "And if you need someone to talk to, I'll hire you a secretary. You can talk all you want." His eyes went to Ceci. "Do you work here?"

"Unfortunately no." The anger settle into the pit of Cecilia's stomach. "If I did, I could call security and have you thrown out." She plastered a searing polite look on her face and held a hand out. "I don't believe we've met. I'm Cecilia Roberts."

They stared at her.

"Kerry's mother-in-law?" Her eyebrows lifted in sarcastic emphasis.

❖ ⌘ ❖ ⌘ ❖ ⌘ ❖

Ceci entered the room and ran her slim fingers through her silvered hair. "Well. That was certainly a treat." She glanced at Kerry. "Your sister's settling down to some real pushing."

"Sorry," Kerry apologized. "I should have warned you my parents were here."

"How?" Ceci asked, reasonably. "Send up a flare?" She turned her head, then gave Dar an inquiring look.

"Coffee."

"Ah." The older woman took a seat and laced her fingers around one knee. "I hope there's a second waiting room, or this could be a very long evening." She gave Kerry a wry look. "My telling your parents I was your mother-in-law was not a popular choice."

Dar swiftly stifled a laugh.

"I'm really, really sorry," Kerry told Ceci.

"I'm not." Dar's mother smiled. "No offense, Kerry, but I've never liked your father's views and meeting him in person doesn't do anything to enhance them. It was a pleasure making him attempt to swallow his tongue."

She was still mad.

Not that she was a perfect parent. Oh no. In a group of a hundred of those, she'd come in last. But for the sake of the goddess, even she'd have the sense not to come in an yell at a woman trying very hard to give blessed birth.

Well, all right then, if the Stuarts were included, she'd come in ninety-eighth out of a hundred.

Moving up in the parental world. Who'd have thought it?

"Poor Angie," Kerry murmured. "That looked like really hard work."

"Oh yes," Ceci muttered. "Ranks right up there with your retail jobs like expelling a watermelon out of your urethra." She got up and went to the door, in search of her husband.

"Dar?" Kerry whispered.

"Mmm?"

"I think you should hire your mother."

Blink blink. "Wh...for what?"

"The marketing department."

Dar thought about that. "They'd all jump out the windows of the fourteenth floor, Kerry."

"Mmm." Kerry scratched her nose and nodded. "Yeah, but can't you picture her and Eleanor in a meeting together?"

Dar nibbled her lower lip. "Hmm."

They heard Roger Stuart's angry voice approaching and Dar dropped her hands to her lap. "That's it." She stood up, ready to meet him as he entered. "I've had about enough of his—"

"You!" Stuart had reached the doorway and pointed at her. "This is all your fault, you disgusting piece of filth. I want you and the rest of your rabble out of here before I call my security and have you thrown out."

"Who are you calling filth, you adulterous, swindling asshole?" Dar bristled, moving towards him. "Take your judgmental bullshit and shove it right up your—"

"Dar—"

"Roger—"

A deep rumble suddenly slammed through the room, stopping the shouting and motion for a frozen moment.

Then the shock wave hit and the lights went out and the world started to crumble around them.

Chapter 39

It was very dark. Dar forced her eyes open anyway, coughing sharply as a lung full of concrete dust invaded her chest. All around her, creaks and groans, crashing, and the sound of screaming could be heard.

She was on the ground, half covered in chunks of plaster and wall, shocked and dazed, and momentarily unable to think past rubbing the dirt out of her eyes in an attempt to use the tiny gleam of emergency lighting edging through a gap in the collapsed room.

Shit. Her scattered mind tried to focus as she rolled over and pushed herself up, blinking her stinging eyes. *Kerry. It was too quiet.*

"K—" She ended up coughing, as she felt around anxiously, the shadows very slowly resolving into gray, dim shapes in an eerie silence that set her heart pounding erratically. "Hey...hey..." She pawed through the debris with shaking hands, pulling down chunks of wall tangled in strips of wallpaper until she spotted a very still, dusty form half buried under some carpet and what was left of a chair.

Her world stopped.

She scrambled over the rubble and stared at the silent figure, a fear clamping a hold on her chest as she faced the possibility that the worst had happened.

"K-Kerry?" She barely heard her own whisper. "H-hey?"

There wasn't a twitch of response and in the dimness she couldn't see any movement at all.

Dar closed her eyes for a long moment, too scared to even breathe. *This couldn't be happening, could it?* Maybe it was all a dream and she'd wake up in her bedroom with Kerry poking her in the ribs.

Maybe?

Please?

You can't take her from me. Dar's eyelids drifted open, blinking them a few times to let the tears wash the dust out. Then she gathered her courage and leaned forward to put a hand on the still shoulder, her heart beating so fast it made her shake. *Not yet. No...*

A soft groan responded to her touch and Dar almost collapsed in sheer relief. "Hey...Kerry?" She clawed the debris aside and very gently brushed the crumbled plaster off her lover. "Sweetheart?" Her voice was shaky.

Kerry drew a rasping breath. "Ow," she answered weakly. "Dar?"

It was too dark for Kerry to see the tears and she was glad for that. "Yeah. What's wrong? What hurts?"

Kerry started to turn over, then gasped, and curled into a more fetal position. "My shoulder...oh God..."

Dar examined her anxiously, noting the odd angle under the cotton shirt Kerry wore. "Um...I think it's..." She bent closer, straining her eyes. "Maybe it's dislocated. I can't tell." She put a careful hand on the blond woman's hip. "How's everything else?"

Kerry was silent for a moment. "Okay, I think." She took in a ragged breath. "What happened?"

"I don't know." Dar looked around her for the first time. The waiting room had mostly collapsed, leaving them in a small, irregularly shaped pocket near one side. There was no sign of anyone else and the doorway Kerry's parents had been standing in was a large mass of silent rubble. "Something exploded, I think."

Kerry was facing away from the door. "Wh—?" She stopped. "What happened to everyone else?" She kept looking at a twisted piece of metal in front of her face, so close she could smell the rust on it. Dar hesitated, the light touch on her leg moving a bit and becoming warmer as her lover spread her fingers out over the denim material. "Dar?"

"I don't know that either," came the careful response. "It's just the two of us here. I don't see anything...anyone else."

There was a moment of utter quiet. "Dear God, I'm glad you're all right," Kerry whispered. "I don't know what I'd do if I were here...alone." She eased slowly over onto her back, so she could see Dar, then halted as the faint light reflected off a tear streaked face.

"Careful." Dar swallowed, putting a supporting hand under her back, as Kerry's face tensed in pain.

"Augh." It was like a red hot spike drove into her shoulder and Kerry almost screamed. She bit down on her lip instead, until she could taste blood. "Ow."

"Okay. Listen," Dar told her hesitantly. "If you want...I could try putting it back, then—"

"No!" Another jolt. "Don't touch it...ow...gods..." Kerry didn't know what to do. Every movement hurt and the pain was getting very intense.

"Kerry, listen—"

"Nooo." She tried to roll away from Dar, scrabbling in the debris as hands tried to hold her still.

"Kerry. Kerry. Please. Just stop moving." Dar's voice sounded a touch frantic.

"I can't." She was taking short, shallow breaths. "I can't stand it, Dar."

"Okay." Dar carefully slid her calf in behind Kerry's back to support her. "Easy. Just try to relax. If you get tense, it's worse."

Kerry just moaned, but she listened and tried to do what her lover asked. "Okay," she finally whispered, her cheek pressing against the shattered rock.

"Okay. Now listen." Dar shifted and braced one foot on the other side of Kerry's body. "Honey, we have to get out of here, because it's raining rocks, okay?"

"Yeah."

"Okay. You can't do that hurting the way you are."

"Dar, I can't. Please don't touch my arm."

"Kerry."

The concrete around them shifted ominously, sending a shower of small chunks down on top of them. Dar huddled over her injured friend, letting them hit her instead. "We don't have much time."

Kerry drew in a shaky breath and curled her fingers around Dar's ankle. "Okay," she whispered, the pain almost choking her.

Dar stroked her hair in a helpless attempt at comforting. "Hold on tight," she warned, hoping she knew what the hell she was doing. The grip on her leg tightened. "Okay, I'm doing it." She wiped the back of her hand over her forehead, then very carefully touched Kerry's arm, trying not to hear the stifled whimper. "Easy, baby...easy."

Dar managed to get her left hand under Kerry's bicep and laid her right hand on top of the grossly misplaced shoulder. She made a picture in her mind of what she was going to do, then took a deep breath. "Scream if you need to."

Kerry knew that meant it was coming and she held her breath, biting the inside of her lip as she felt Dar shift, and the pain exploded through her, wrenching a guttural cry from deep inside her. It grew and grew as Dar pulled the injured arm towards her, a feeling so intense she reeled on the edge of unconsciousness for a long agonizing moment.

Then it was over.

Dar felt the bones slip into place with a sodden click, as Kerry's entire body relaxed and she started to cry. "I'm sorry." She sat down in the rubble and Kerry crawled into her lap and she cuddled her in careful arms. "I'm sorry, Kerry." She stroked her shaking partner with small, helpless motions.

The pain slowly subsided, changing from a raging agony to a tense throbbing, but she could breathe now, at least, and move her fingers without screaming. "It's...okay," she mumbled softly. "Oh my god."

Dar just sat there, with her eyes closed, absorbing the living, breathing body cradled in her arms. The shattered room around her meant nothing. The creaking walls, the sound of falling plaster, the stink, the far off yelling...none of that mattered to her at all.

Not when she'd faced losing Kerry.

That had touched something very deep and she still shook inside from it.

Finally, Kerry was able to ease herself back and look around in the dim wreckage. "Thanks." She rubbed her aching eyes. "That really helped. I'm sorry I gave you such a hard time."

Dar gazed at her and touched the dirty, tear streaked skin of Kerry's cheek. "It's okay."

Kerry tensed her lips into a faint smile then she slowly turned her head and surveyed the wreckage. Her eyes fell on the rubble filled doorway and she stared at it. Then she looked up at Dar in dawning horror. "D—" A long finger fell against her lips, silencing her.

"We don't know," Dar whispered. "Let's get out of here and we'll see what happened."

Kerry's bewildered gaze moved back to the door. "They were just there, Dar." Her voice cracked. "And...what about...I have to find Angie...and...your mother and—"

"Shh." Dar helped her stand up. "One thing at a time." She stumbled over to where one collapsed wall revealed a storage closet, its contents spilling out. "There's some sheets here. If I can find a knife...or...maybe I can rip them. I can make a sling for you." She plucked at the linen. "Or maybe I can use a pillowcase...that's smaller—"

"Dar," Kerry supported her injured arm with her good one and made her way slowly over the debris, "why don't you just use one of those?" She indicated a canvas item dangling from a box, its straps hanging limply.

"Oh." Dar retrieved the sling and climbed down. "Sorry." She helped Kerry get it over her head and adjusted the buckles. "I'm not really thinking straight."

Relieved by the support, Kerry tucked her fingers into Dar's and led her back over to the one possible exit, a plate glass window now half crushed, its panes darkened. They both jerked as the ceiling settled and chunks of plaster rained down. "Okay." Kerry's voice wavered. "Now what?"

Dar faced the thick glass. "Guess we find out if all those years of martial arts were worth a damn."

"Dar, you can't—" Too late. Kerry felt the air move as her lover took a step back, then launched herself forward, turning and slamming the glass with a picture perfect kick. The surface buckled and with a surprising groan toppled outward, sending debris raining everywhere. "Wow."

Outside the skewed sill the corridor wall had collapsed, leaving a tiny, triangular space near the floor, full of plaster chunks, that led into a further darkness.

"Guess we crawl." Kerry sighed. "C'mon." She sensed no motion behind her, so she turned. "Dar?"

Her lover was very still, one hand resting on the now empty frame, her eyes fixed on the tiny space left open to them.

"You okay?" Kerry came closer, peering up at her in the very dim light. "C'mon. Let's get this over with. I want to see where everyone is."

Dar's jaw muscles twitched. "I can't." Her voice was hoarse.

"Wh—?" Kerry turned and looked at the opening, then back at her partner, seeing the sweat rolling down Dar's face. "Oh my god. You're claustrophobic?" The confirmation was clear by the expression. "Dar, it's the only way out."

A visible shiver shook the taller woman.

Kerry fought the panic that nibbled at her. "Dar." She took her lover's hand, which was icy cold. "I'll go first...okay? And you just come with me."

"You go." Dar's voice cracked. "Get out of here."

Kerry lifted a hand and touched her cheek, gaining eye contact. "No." She shook her head. "I'm not going without you. We both get out of here, or neither of us will."

She had no choice. "I'll try." Dar allowed Kerry to very gently guide her to the window and paused. "Wait."

The dimly seen pale eyes turned her way in question.

"Let me go first."

She stepped over the sill and into a personal little Hell.

It would be belly crawling. Dar slowly got down on her knees and peered into the dark tunnel. *I can't do this.* Already her hands were shaking and her stomach was in knots. Just the thought of going forward made her want to get up and run in the other direction.

She felt Kerry's hand close on her calf. "Ready when you are," the blond woman's steady voice prodded her and she reluctantly dropped down onto her hands, somehow forcing herself to move closer to that tiny, narrowing tunnel.

She couldn't.

But she had to, for Kerry's sake.

Just think about that, Dar. That's what matters. Close your damn eyes, and just do it for her.

Kerry tensed her lips and watched Dar lower herself to the ground and start to crawl forward. She edged along after her, using an elbow and both knees, keeping her injured hand resting on Dar's leg. She had no idea what it felt like to be claustrophobic, but she did know she'd never seen her lover so obviously coming apart. "Take it slow, okay? I'm short a paw."

Dar had to smile a tiny bit at that. She kept her eyes firmly shut and kept moving, the first bit of the tunnel wide enough to admit her shoulders without touching. *Okay.* She could hear the rumble as the building settled again and a bit of rock fell on her back. It also felt warmer. She move a hand forward and sensed something close to her head, but opening her eyes only found shadows. She moved aside anyway. "Watch your head up here."

"Okay." Kerry's muffled voice came back at her. "You doing all right?"

"Yeah."

Her voice didn't sound all right. Kerry inched forward, then yelped, as she put her hand on a nail.

"What?" Dar tried to turn around and realized she couldn't. Her whole body shivered.

"It's okay. Just a nail." Kerry winced. "Go on." The dust got in her nose and she stifled a sneeze.

Now the walls were getting closer. Dar could feel the brushing against her arms and the top of her head and she ducked in reflex, becoming more and more uncomfortable.

A few more feet and she banged her head against a piece of debris and halted, now really feeling the tunnel pressing in on her. Cautiously, she felt ahead of her position, finding the space moving to the left, and getting lower and tighter. She also couldn't feel any air coming down the tunnel and she hesitated, considering telling Kerry to just back up, that they couldn't go any further.

Then she let her head drop and laid down on her belly, drawing in a breath full of concrete dust and fear. "Gets close up here," she muttered hoarsely, preparing to crawl. Kerry's presence suddenly came closer and she felt a hug around her leg, then a gentle pressure that sounded suspiciously like a kiss. "What was that?"

"Me saying thank you."

"Uh huh."

"C'mon, Dar. You're always inviting people to kiss your ass. Who else but me would have the guts to actually do it?"

Dar bit her lip as her frame shook with an unexpected laugh. Then she faced the tunnel and crept forward, squirming through the tiny space, trying not to think of anything but the moment she'd be out of the damn place.

It got tighter and tighter and Dar had to force herself forward each small bit, battling her own mind as much as the uncomfortable space. She crawled determinedly around a crooked bend then halted, as her head banged into a piece of collapsed wallboard and the collision caused a heavy board to drop down over her shoulders and pin her in place.

She couldn't move. Her hands pushed against the ground ineffectively and the board settled lower, shoving her face into the sharp rocks.

"Dar?" Kerry's concerned tone floated forward.

Dar felt panic rising and she was almost helpless to stop it. She struggled, her breathing coming in short sharp gasps as she tried to dislodge the board.

"Hey...hey...take it easy. Let me..." Kerry's hands moved up her. "Oh...god. Okay, I can...damn it, this piece of... Dar, stop fighting it. Let me try to help."

It was almost impossible to do. All her instincts were urging her to move. Twitching, she managed to hold herself still as Kerry worked at the obstacle, hampered by her injured arm.

"I think I can." Kerry's voice was strained. "Ow...oh, wait, I think I've got it." She tensed her muscles and pulled backwards, feeling the wooden plank shift. "Ah. Hold on a minute there, Dar. I've almost—" The motion surprised her, and she jerked, then felt the walls around her start to move. "Oh...sh—" She managed to throw her body forward over Dar's just as the tunnel collapsed around them, pinning them together and blocking any chance at retreat.

It was her worst nightmare come true and Dar found herself frozen, unable to move as her mind recognized what had just happened. They were trapped, with only a tiny bit of air.

They were going to die.

She could feel Kerry's warm breath on her back, where the blond woman was pinned as they lay in a momentary, numb silence.

Dar swallowed, already aware of the stuffiness of the air around her. Her panic surprisingly receded and she turned her head to one side. "Ker?"

"Mmm?"

"Doesn't look good."

"I know. I'm sorry, Dar. I thought I was helping." Kerry pressed her face against Dar's back, breathing in her familiar scent. "Are we out of options?"

"I think so."

They were quiet for a few breaths. "I'm glad we're together," Kerry finally whispered.

Dar blinked in the darkness. "Me too."

"I always thought I'd be scared..." Kerry fell silent as they listened to a soft rattle of debris falling and shifting, far away. "I guess this is where we're supposed to say all sorts of profound things to each other."

"I guess," Dar replied. *Thirty years.* She reviewed them in silence.

And only the last one meant a damn thing. "I'm sorry we never got to go to Key West."

Kerry felt sleepy. "Maybe in our next life," she murmured, "we've had such a short time in this one."

It's always too short. Dar felt a tide of frustration well up inside her. "Yeah."

"I love you, Dar." Kerry pressed her lips against the warm back.

She couldn't answer for a minute, around the lump in her throat. "I love you, too," she finally rasped. "You know you've been the best thing in my life, right?"

A sniffle. "Ditto." Kerry sighed. "I wasn't ready for this to happen," she murmured softly. "I just found what I wanted, Dar. I don't want to give it up yet."

"Me either." Dar felt a deep sense of anger rising. She tensed her muscles and tried to straighten her body out as her feet gained a purchase on the fallen debris behind them. She could feel the heavy pressure of the wood over her shoulders and her spirit rebelled against its captivity. "I know it's pointless, but..." She coiled her legs up and set her back against the wood.

"Wh-what are you doing, Dar?"

"Trying." There wasn't any reason or thought behind it. She took a breath, then pushed, straining her muscles against the obstruction. It didn't budge even slightly, but she tried harder, reaching inside and calling up slumbering reserves of strength she rarely ever had tapped.

She closed her eyes and an echo of memory flowed through her, the stale air made her head buzz, and smelled a sharp, harsh scent and just decided she needed to be out of where she was.

Kerry needed to be out of where she was. No way was she going to let Kerry die. No way.

No.

Way.

A hot surge of energy hit her in the gut and she uncoiled, a yell of rage erupting from her chest as her body straightened, to the sound of crashing and a roar and a blast of hot, stinking air. Dar reeled on the edge of unconsciousness, dimly aware of hands grabbing her and voices hammering at her ears that were curiously familiar.

Kerry felt things move around her and she tried to keep hold of Dar as plaster and drywall collapsed on top of them both. She knew a moment of total panic, then the debris behind her gave way and she tumbled out of the tunnel and into a clear space. Ceiling tiles dropped on top of her head and she rolled, trying to get into the clear. Then her motion was stopped by something solid and she flailed an arm out, making contact with unexpected fabric and warmth.

"Kerry!" Never had a voice been more welcome. Kerry blinked her eyes open through the plaster dust and made them focus on Andrew's dusty, scarred face. The tall man knelt at her side and pulled the drywall off her. She clutched at his arm, pulled him over awkwardly and hugged him. "Easy there." He gently freed her of the plaster and ended up on the floor with Kerry in his lap. "Lord, ah am glad to all hell to see the two of you."

"Same here." Kerry managed a smile, as she carefully sat up, cradling her arm and looking around. Dar was sprawled full length in the dirt, with her mother kneeling over her, and she could smell smoke nearby. "I'm glad you're both all right." Her eyes went to the far corridor, blocked by the collapsed ceiling.

Dar lay on the floor, trying to catch her breath. The voices came much closer and she felt fingers touch her forehead, for a moment throwing her back into childhood, when a fall from the tree outside their base quarters had dazed her. It had been the same touch and she opened her eyes to see her mother crouched over her, an anxious look on her face.

"Dar?" Ceci said.

"Hi, Mom," Dar murmured. "Watch that last step. It sucks."

Ceci went still for a second, then her face creased into a wry smile, as she shared the memory. "What luck. You're already at a hospital." She looked over to where Andrew was tugging Kerry free of the last of the debris. "I'm glad we found you. There's a fire in the next section. We have to get out of here."

That explained the heat. Dar caught her breath and looked around. What had been the nurses' station was now just a mass of rubble and the ceiling had fallen down in the corridor, blocking the way forward. Kerry scrambled to her feet and, as Dar watched, she walked over and laid a hand on the blockage. The emergency lighting was a little stronger here and displayed the liberal bloodstains on Kerry's cotton shirt, from the scratches and scrapes covering her skin. Dar looked down, finding herself in the same condition.

"Dar?" her mother prompted her gently. "Are you okay?"

Dar didn't think so. Too much was happening too fast. But she gathered her wits and nodded. "We had kind of a tough time getting through that mess."

Ceci patted her shoulder. "C'mon. Let's see if we can find a way out of here."

They both stood and walked over to Kerry and Andy. Dar suffered a hair ruffling from her father, as Kerry thumped against her in a heartfelt embrace. She put her arms around the smaller woman and exhaled, trying to put the very recent past behind her for the moment.

"Thank you," Kerry uttered. "I don't know how you did that, but thank you."

Did what? Dar deferred the question until later. "We have to get moving." She indicated a half passable exit to the right.

Kerry lifted her head, then moved away from Dar to the piles of debris blocking the way towards where Angie's room was. "How can we get through here?"

They gathered behind her. Dar put a hand on the fractured wall. "Kerry...it..." She fell silent. The heat was increasing. "I don't think..."

"Dar," Kerry picked up a chunk of concrete and tossed it aside, "my family's behind here."

"Kerry," Andrew went to her side, "ah think whatever it was that blew up, was right up under that wing there."

Kerry looked at him. "I have to know for sure." She pulled another bit off and threw it behind her. "I'm not going to live my life—now that I have one again, thank you, Dar—wondering if there was something I could have done to help them."

A thin haze of smoke had started to drift in and the heat was getting uncomfortable, but Dar merely sighed and set to work, tugging on the stubborn concrete in an attempt to clear the wreckage. She glanced at her parents. "Why don't you guys go on?"

"Why don't you grow wings and fly?" Ceci retorted. "We'd better hurry. It's going to get nasty in here."

They started to work as an eerie roar became subliminally audible, along with the echo of far off screams.

Chapter 40

What are you doing, Kerry? She pushed the sweat-dampened hair off her forehead and stifled a cough. *Do you really think you can get through all this? Then what?* She glanced to her right, where Dar and Andrew worked together to move a huge piece of wall. Father and daughter took opposite sides of the section and lifted, noses wrinkling up in effort in almost mirror image. They got the piece off and went back for more, while Ceci helped her move the smaller chunks. *You're risking their lives, and they probably don't even understand why you're doing it.*

Her hand touched something that wasn't rock and she gasped, drawing back from what was identifiably a human arm.

It had been cold.

"Dardar, g'wan over there by Kerry. I'll check this out," Andrew ordered, in a quiet, businesslike voice. He knelt in front of Kerry, blocking her view of the body with his own as he gently moved aside the plaster, exposing the features. For a moment he was silent, his head bowed as though saying a prayer. Then he turned his head. "It's that nurse."

Kerry closed her eyes and let out a breath, then released her grip on Dar's arm.

"Dar, gimme a hand here."

It was the last thing she wanted to do. Dar swallowed, but forced her body to move and knelt down at her father's side as he cleared the rest of the debris away. The nurse had been running, apparently. She was face down and there was a lot of blood where a sharp edge had punctured her back just below her skull. Andrew took hold of one arm. "Take 'er there." He motioned to the other arm. "Pull when I tell ya."

Dar flexed her hands, then reached out hesitantly and did as he asked, unpleasantly shocked at how cold and rubbery the flesh felt.

"Dar?"

She looked quickly up at her father.

"First time I had t'do this, I chucked up so bad I nearly coughed up my kneecaps out my nostrils."

Dar nodded and took a breath. "Thanks." She took a firmer hold and helped him drag the body clear and over to one side. Andrew gave her a pat on the back as they walked back over.

"Gonna be okay?"

"Yeah."

They went back to working their way through, glancing over their shoulders as the smoke started to thicken. Kerry pulled up one large chunk, then a second, then stifled a cough. She watched Andy and Dar wrestle a large half girder out of the way, then reached out as they came back, catching Dar on her sleeve. "Listen. It's getting pretty bad in here. Maybe we'd...better get going that other way."

Andrew glanced over his shoulder, then shook his grizzled head. "Don't think that's an option, kumquat. Let's just keep diggin'."

Kerry gave him a confused look, then she turned and peered down the other corridor, only then seeing the flames through the small glass window in the door. They were trapped and it was her fault. *Oh my god.*

Oh. My. God.

Oh, God please. If I am being punished for something, don't bring them into it. Kerry suddenly felt a warmth against her cheek and she looked up, right into Dar's eyes.

"Hey." Dar had a smudge of soot over her eye and it gave her a rakish look. "No time for second guessing. C'mon. Let's get this done."

"Dar...I..."

"Don't think about it." Dar gave a warning shake of her head. "C'mon."

Kerry exhaled and nodded, then followed Dar over to the dent they'd made in the debris.

They worked in silence, broken only by coughing as the air grew thicker with smoke and an eerie roaring sound coming from the other side of the dividing wall. Andrew paused for a moment, then tugged his shirt off and removed a pocketknife from his back pocket that he flipped open with a negligent flick of his wrist. Then he sliced off the sleeves, handing one each to Ceci and Kerry, in a curious chivalry that made Dar smile. She pulled up the collar of her own knit shirt and covered her mouth and nose, then kept working.

They made good progress for a several minutes, then Andy cursed, as a bit of wall he was pulling on refused to budge. "Damn it all to hell. This thing's one big piece."

A blast of heat hit them and they ducked, as the wall opposite them collapsed into flame, spitting chunks of burning debris near where they were standing. The smoke rolled upward and they stared at it, all of them frozen for a long moment.

Dar felt the adrenaline hit her in the gut and she blinked, deliberately turning her back on the fire and studying the wall. There was a large, tilting section they'd ignored, because it was leaning in their direction and not in their way.

"All right." Andrew sounded grimly resigned. "You two get in that there space, hear? Maybe we can pull some of this stuff up on over us, and it'll pass by."

"No." Dar's brain kicked in, as she remembered what it was she did for a living. Just another problem to solve. "Help me get those cables hanging there. We'll tie it around this section here." Dar scrambled up and grabbed the cables and wrapped them around the leaning section. The rest of them helped her, tying the huge metal ropes together. "Now..."

The fire jumped across to the nurses' station, its heat blanching them.

Dar tugged at the edge of the leaning section. "If we can just get this to fall over..."

"Lord." Andrew leaped up and caught the edge, lending his weight to the effort, but the section didn't budge. Kerry and Ceci pulled also, straining against the stubborn concrete.

"The one damn thing in this place that stayed put," Ceci muttered.

"Hang on." Dar leaped up and pulled her body up and over the edge of the wall, getting between the section and the one blocking them. She placed her feet against one surface and her back against the other and pushed, using her powerful legs and hands braced against her knees. "Get out of the way," she gasped, as the rock shifted under her back.

Andrew pulled himself up and over the edge of the concrete, and added his strength to his daughter's. "This thing lets go, we're gonna have to jump."

"Yep." Dar grimaced, as the heat made her close her eyes. "Ready? One...two..."

"Six." They both pushed at once, and the wall creaked, then started to fall, sending them tumbling off as it tipped over, hesitating at its apex, before surrendering to gravity and falling, pulling the huge section blocking their way with it.

"There's a way through," Kerry yelled, in utter relief. "C'mon!" She had Dar by the sleeve and pulled, as Andy dove into the gap with Ceci clinging to his back. A burning piece of insulation fell and Kerry yelped as it hit her shoulders. Dar pulled her forward, though, and it fell off as the flames licked at the ceiling they were just standing under. She squeezed through the narrow opening, scraping her arms and legs on the shattered bits of internal wall structure that poked through the debris. It was darker where they were going and she blinked, trying to see ahead of her.

Then a roar sounded behind her and a hot wave slammed against her body, burning the hair on her arms as she yelled a warning.

Then she felt a tremendous lurch, and something fell on top of her, and it got a lot darker.

❖ ⌘ ❖ ⌘ ❖ ⌘ ❖

Things were moving. Kerry jolted back into awareness to the sounds of things falling and a dull roaring sound. She heard yells and realized she was being carried in a cradle of strong arms that gripped her around the shoulders and under her knees.

It was still very dark, but it was cooler and she tried to collect her scattered senses as the pace quickened and a puff of cooler, fresher air washed over her.

She heard a rapid pounding noise and puzzled over that until she realized it was a heartbeat against her ear. She forced her eyes open, to see a familiar profile outlined in the low, reddish light. *Of course.* It was Dar's heartbeat, sounding rapid and strained.

Well, you know, Kerry, her mind muzzily considered the problem, *you aren't the lightweight you used to be and it probably would speed things up if she wasn't carrying your butt.* "Dar?"

The blue eyes looked down at her. "Hey." Dar was clearly out of breath, but she kept moving, following a dimly seen back just in front of them.

"I can walk. Let me down." Kerry hoped that was true. She had no real recollection of what happened after they'd started going through the wall.

"You sure?" Dar ducked under a piece of protruding wall framing and almost tripped, keeping her balance with her load by some miracle of luck.

"Yes. C'mon, before you pass out," Kerry insisted.

"Okay."

She was let down onto her feet and she straightened tentatively, finding everything relatively in one piece, save her still aching shoulder and now a tender, burning forearm. Dar put a hand on her back and guided her after her father and mother.

"What happened?"

Dar didn't answer for a moment. "That blowout knocked you against a piece of the wall. Just had to get you out of there, that's all."

"You okay?"

Dar nodded. "Yeah, c'mon. Dad thinks he sees an open area up there."

Kerry looked around. They were in the corridor that led towards

Angie's room, but it was almost unrecognizably full of debris. "Any sign of my parents?"

"No." Dar pulled up short as Andy stopped ahead of her and turned towards them. "Problem, Dad?"

"Shh." Andrew put a finger up to his lips. "You hear something?"

Lots of things. Dar was exhausted from the emotional and sensory overload of the past few hours. "Like what?"

Kerry put her uninjured arm around her partner and listened. "I don't hear anything but the fire."

Andrew cocked his head to one side and closed his eyes.

They were all silent for a moment. Faintly, there was a scream, then a sodden crash off to the left. Then... "Wait...is that..." Kerry could hear something vaguely rhythmic. "Is someone pounding?"

Andrew nodded. "S'what I thought I heard." They walked along the shattered wall and slowly, the sound got louder, then stopped.

Then started again, this time with an unmistakable frustration and urgency behind it.

"Lord." Andrew sighed, hefting a sledge hammer that seemed to have magically appeared in his hand. "Stand out the way, let's see if we kin make a dent in this."

"Where did you get that?" Ceci murmured, putting a hand on his arm. "Andy..."

"Damnfool construction guys musta sealed it up behind the drywall." The ex-SEAL lifted the hammer and swung it against the surface before them—a section of wall that had fallen down and covered a corner of the corridor. "Must be a damn room back there."

Dar exhaled, then started pulling chunks of fallen concrete away, clearing a path for her father to edge down. There was only room for two, so Kerry stayed back out of the way with Ceci, who had tied her husband's shirt sleeve over her eyes to keep her hair back. "Are you okay?" she asked the older woman.

"I've had better days," Ceci admitted, leaning against a bent wall support. She looked exhausted. "Most strenuous thing I've had to do in a couple years is walk down to the drugstore."

Kerry gave her a wan look. "Don't feel bad. I spend four to five nights a week in the gym and I feel like I've been run over by an rhino."

"Well, seeing as how you got blown ten feet through a plaster wall back there, you're entitled." Ceci patted her good arm. "I'm glad you're okay."

Ten feet? Plaster wall? Kerry blinked. "I guess that's why I have such a headache," she murmured, watching Dar's back tense as her lover lifted a huge chunk of something or other out of the way. "I'm sorry about all this."

"Why? Did you plant a bomb?" Ceci inquired.

"No." Kerry smiled. "Of course not, but..."

"Then why apologize?" The smaller woman gazed at her with surprising compassion. "Kerry, we all do enough things in our lives to feel sorry for. Don't take on someone else's karma on top of that."

Kerry could barely see Ceci's face in the dim light, but she could feel the sad smile directed at her. She was about to answer, when a crash drew her eyes towards the wall. "Oh. Looks like they've about..." She edged forward, helping Dar to move a last two by four.

Only a wooden door was now between them and the hammering and Andy took a swing at it, the heavy sledge shattering the surface just over the warped knob. Splinters flew, and she ducked, then the frame sprung free from the wall and it tilted towards them. Kerry took hold of its edge one handed and wrenched the wood back, then stumbled as the panel burst outwards and two figures half fell out, almost on top of them.

They halted and stared at each other.

Kerry felt a roiling uneasiness almost mitigated by a sense of profound relief as she recognized her father's face, covered in plaster and soot though it was. A tremendous weight came off her shoulders and she took hold of the crumbled wall, as her knees threatened to collapse on her. "I'm glad we found you."

"Get out of my way." Those pale eyes just looked through her, as her father walked right past, brushing by them and stumbling down the hallway without another word. Kerry's mother glanced uncomfortably at them, the front of her shirt covered in blood spots.

"Thank you." She addressed herself to Andrew, though her gaze slipped briefly to Kerry's face, then she dropped her eyes to the ground and followed her husband.

Kerry's shoulders slumped, as she studied the concrete chunks at her feet.

Dar brushed her hands off, went over to her, circled her with both arms and patted the back of her head gently as she gave her a hug. "C'mon." She motioned with her head.

"Ah do believe," Andrew spat carefully and precisely at the floor, "that there fella just ran out of his allotment of being nice to from this old seadog." He shouldered his hammer and put an arm around Ceci. "Ah am gonna go find him and shove this damn hammer right up his—"

"Andy." She patted him on the belly. "Let's just get out of here, okay?"

They headed down the hallway, dodging the obstacles in their path and climbing over the buckled floor that seemed to bisect the building, tilting the outer section at a dangerous angle, as though the entire corner was in the process off falling off.

Kerry scrambled over the last barrier and went to the doorway of her sister's room and stopped in the doorway, stunned.

There was nothing left of the room. It was just a jumble of plaster and iron, so dense and tangled it was obvious that nothing could have remained alive inside it.

"No," she whispered, as Dar and her parents came up beside her and peered in. "She must have gotten out, right, Dar?"

In the midst of labor? Dar rested her hands on Kerry's shoulders. "We'll find her," she reassured her lover.

Kerry nodded once, then stared at the wreckage. A silent knowledge came over her and she turned, putting her head against Dar's chest in silent appeal. "But she didn't get out, did she?" she uttered softly.

"Dear God." An angry voice spoke from behind them. They turned to see Roger Stuart, one hand resting on the shattered doorway. "One more thing for you to carry on your conscience, you little... I hope you rot in Hell!" He advanced towards Kerry, oblivious of the others. "I should—"

"Stop." Dar's voice was sharp and sudden, as she stiffened to her full height.

"You shut up you—"

"One...more...step." Amazing how forceful that low voice could get. "One...more...word...and I'll wrap that girder around your head." A rage ran through Dar, bringing welcome energy, and she let it. "Leave her alone."

"You ruined her," the man snarled. "You twisted her mind, you perverted little—"

"Hey." Andrew stepped between them, putting his hands on his hips. "You watch yer mouth with my daughter."

"Your..." The senator shook his head. "You must be real proud of her, mister."

Dar stirred.

"Damn straight," Andy replied mildly.

Roger Stuart stared at them, then at the room. He pointed at Kerry. "If something happened to your sister, it's your fault. You'd better hope it didn't." Then he turned and left, his hand firmly around his wife's arm.

Kerry leaned against the door frame and lifted a shaking hand to her face. "He's right," she whispered. "They'd have been home in Michigan."

Andrew tugged on a bit of Kerry's hair. "Kumquat, ye're wrong about that. We don't got the time to be stewing in ourselves here. Takes energy we're gonna need for better things."

It was just too much. Kerry gazed at the wreckage of her sister's room, then gave in and just buried herself in Dar's arms, too tired to even cry.

"I think we all need to sit down and rest a minute," Ceci said firmly. "The fire's not in this area yet, and we're all about to drop. Let's go over there and just regroup." Tired nods agreed and they settled in the corner of the wreckage, Dar with Kerry cradled in her arms, listening to the chaos in the darkness around them.

❖ ⌘ ❖ ⌘ ❖ ⌘ ❖

"That's it, McLean." Ankow entered and closed the door behind him. "You've run out of bullshit. Now do it. You can't deny what this is going to look like when it hits the papers tomorrow morning."

A pool of light from the desk lamp spilled over Alastair's desk, lighting the folded hands on its surface but throwing the CEO's face into shadow. "I really don't think—"

"No." Ankow slapped the desk. "The board agrees with me and you know it. We can't afford this, no matter what smokescreen you want to put up around your favorite little bitch. Stuart's kid released the information. Where do you think she got it from? You think it was just coincidence she got hold of it after she started working for ILS?"

Alastair sighed. "We have no evidence—"

"Yes, we do." Ankow dumped a folder onto his desk. "There it is. In all its glory, the entire information request with every little, disgusting detail." He opened the folder top and pointed. "Run under Dar Roberts' personal login."

Alastair shrugged. "Well, the press doesn't have that."

"They will," Ankow hissed. "Trust me, because I'll be the one handing it to them."

Alastair's face went very still. "You'd do that, would you?" he asked quietly.

"I'll do whatever I have to do to win my point," Ankow rasped. "Now cut the cord, damn you. Get rid of both of them."

Alastair got up and walked to his large window, gazing out across the star laden sky over Texas. For a long time, he studied the shadows, splashes of moonlight picking up glints of steel and stone as a few clouds raced past. Finally he turned and looked at Ankow, who sat with arms folded in triumph on the edge of his large, oak desk. "That's what you want, hmm?"

Ankow smiled. "That's what I want. That's what you're going to give me."

The CEO exhaled, then walked back over and put his hands on the back of his chair, facing the much younger man. "Well, you know, given that, there really is only one thing I can say," he mused, in a soft voice.

"You're right," Ankow agreed. "So say it." He smirked. "I want to hear it."

Alastair leaned his weight on the back of the chair and looked right into David Ankow's eyes. "All righty then, here you are. Kiss my ass."

There was a moment's stunned pause. "What?" Ankow hissed.

"Kiss my ass," Alastair repeated. "In Texan, that means get your butt out of my office before I throw you out of it."

Slowly, Ankow got up, staring at his adversary as though the man had grown horns. "Do you understand what you're saying, you moron?"

"Absolutely," Alastair told him, with a gentle smile.

"I'll go have the damned board remove you, you—" Ankow snapped.

"Probably," the CEO agreed. "Have fun, you little pea brained no character excuse for a gutless nosepicker."

Ankow's jaw dropped. "What?"

"OUT!" Alastair snapped, his voice now rising sternly. "Before I get my Winchester out of the closet and make you into a wall hanging."

"You've lost your mind." The rattled board member turned and went through the door and slammed it behind him.

With a sigh, Alastair pulled his chair out and sat down in it, smoothing his hands over the clean surface. After a moment's reflection, he nodded, and a soft chuckle forced its way out into the silence. "You know something, Dar?" He spoke to the emptiness. "If I'da known how good that felt, I'da done it more often. You shoulda told me."

A soft buzz startled him and he looked at his phone, where the internal line was ringing. "That was fast." He pushed it. "Yes?"

"Mr. McLean?" a voice asked, hesitantly. "This is the switchboard. I have a young lady here who is desperately trying to get in touch with you."

"With me?" The CEO gazed puzzled at the phone "All right. Put her through." A click was heard. "Go ahead. This is Alastair McLean. What can I do for you?"

"Oh." There was noise in the background, as though from an airport or—Alastair heard an echo—a hospital. "Hello...um...sorry...is this the boss of ILS?"

For the next ten minutes, perhaps. Alastair glanced at his watch. "Yes, it is."

"My name is Angela Stuart," the voice went on, with a hiss and a ragged break. "Sorry. I just had a baby."

Alastair blinked. "I...um...congratulations. Stuart? Are you—"

"Kerry's my sister. Listen. Something really awful happened. I was in the hospital here in Washington and I think something blew up."

He looked quickly at the news feed, which now featured helicopters and an overhead view of a burning building. *Teach me not to leave the sound on.* "Oh, well, I'm sorry to hear that but..."

"Dar and Kerry were visiting me. I don't know what happened to them."

A lifetime of handling crises came to Alastair's rescue. After the initial shock, he took a breath and released it. "Thank you, Ms. Stuart, for telling me. I'll see what I can find out about it."

"O-okay. Thanks. Sorry." Angela coughed. "I—"

"Goodbye." The CEO released the call and spent a moment gathering his wits. Then he punched the phone button again, dialing with hasty purpose.

Chapter
41

Andrew looked around as they rested, reviewing the battered hall-way. A few minutes was all they could take—he could already see smoke clustering at the ceiling a little ways back.

What a damn mess. He glanced at Ceci, who was seated at his side resting her head on his shoulder. "How you holding up, pretty lady?"

"Well," she replied thoughtfully. "On the one hand, here I am, in a burning building, covered in the goddess only knows what, scraped and dented like a 1960 Ford truck, and wishing like anything for a big bottle of mineral water."

"Huh." Andy examined a nasty looking scrape on his arm, then brushed a bit of ceiling tile off his wife's shoulder.

"On the other hand, you're here with me," Ceci went on, exhaling lightly. "So I think I'm doing just fine. How about you?"

Andrew cleared his throat. "That's a damn frilly thing to say in front of these kids, ain't it?"

Ceci glanced at where Dar was seated, with Kerry curled up in her arms. "They'll survive." She watched her daughter in bemusement, remembering all too clearly a teen's angry insistence on pristine person space. When was the last time she'd hugged Dar? Grade school, probably. Those last few years of innocence—well, relatively—before puberty had kicked in and ended any shreds of closeness they'd clung on to.

Kerry seemed the touchy feely kind though, and apparently Dar had adjusted to that, not grudging the fair-haired woman the comfort her phys-ical presence provided. Certainly, Kerry soaked up the affection, as Dar kept up a light rubbing on her back, collecting herself visibly with a few deep breaths.

Adjusted? Ceci covertly noted the look of weary contentment on Dar's face as she rested her cheek against Kerry's pale head. *Maybe I should have tried a few more hugs to start with.* Kerry definitely was showing her an unexpected side to her daughter—that was for sure. A warm, gently affectionate, playful facet she frankly hadn't thought Dar possessed.

Ah well. Hindsight was a very frustrating thing, especially for a parent. You just really never knew if you were doing the right thing, the wrong thing, or whatever, and by the time you figured it all out, it was too late. "Guess we'd better get going," she murmured, with an apologetic look in Kerry's direction. "You doing any better?"

Kerry nodded. "Just needed to catch my breath, I think," she murmured, then she tilted her head up and gazed at her quiet protector. "Thank you."

Dar's head cocked to one side. "For being a backrest? No problem."

"That too." Kerry folded her fingers around Dar's longer ones and brushed her lips over their knuckles. "I always seem to be getting you into trouble."

"Keeps life interesting," Dar assured her with a faint smile, as she hauled herself to her feet and tugged Kerry up with her. "C'mon." She kept an arm around her lover's shoulders as they made their way down the hall, climbing over obstacles together in silence.

They'd gotten most of the way down towards the end of the building, when Andrew paused and put his hand against the wall, looking around carefully. "Damn."

"What is it?" Ceci asked.

"Ain't no way down from here. Stairs were up behind that part." He pointed at a pile of wreckage. "Looks like that whole damn section fell in on top of itself."

Dar watched the smoke fill the end of the corridor back the way they came from. "Well, let's get to an outside room then. Must be people trying to get folks out of this damn place." She took the lead, scrambled over an overturned mobile bed and turned the last corner, then stopped short.

The end of the hallway was full of huddled, frightened people, who stared at them with wild eyes. Kerry's parents were there, against one wall, the senator caught in mid-word.

"A disgrace." His eyes fell on them and he paused. "No one to help, no one who knows anything. You can bet something will be done about it after this."

"If we get out of here," a woman sitting on the floor with a young boy cradled in her arms responded. "No one even knows what happened. It was like a bomb went off."

"Don't be ridiculous," the senator snapped. "Probably some inferior imported gas heater blew up. This place is known for cutting corners."

"With this amount of damage?" Dar snorted. "It'd have to be a water heater the size of the Titanic." She started around the area, examining any possible way out. "It probably was a bomb." She gave the senator a dark look. "Someone probably got tired of your hate policies."

"Shut up."

"Kiss my ass."

"Dar." Kerry looked from face to face, closing her eyes when she didn't see the one face she was looking for. The end of the building was open and had large windows and there were perhaps a dozen people there, some injured, some patients, and some, about a half dozen, children.

Then she realized the room was full of colorful furniture and toys, and guessed they were in the pediatrics area. Two of the children were in wheelchairs and they looked scared. Kerry smiled at the closest one and tried not to think of her sister.

Surely, Angie had gotten out. Maybe she'd been on her way to the delivery room. Maybe she was on the other side of the damage and already outside.

Maybe Kerry was already an aunt again.

Maybe it was a little boy. She stopped, and fought the tears down. *I am not going to give up on you, Angie. I know you made it.*

"Does anyone actually know what happened?" Dar finally asked, as Andrew went to the window and peered out.

"Hell if I know," one man answered, holding a dirty piece of cloth to a cut on his face. A little girl clung to him, evidently his daughter. The child was pale and wearing a hospital jumper and she looked frightened and uncomfortable. "One minute we were watching the television, the next...the whole place blew apart."

Dar glanced behind her. "We should block off that hallway."

"Are you crazy?" A woman seated against the wall objected. "That's the only way they have of getting to us. We're in a cul de sac."

"It's also the only way the fire has to get to us," Dar replied. "And it's gonna get here before help does."

A murmur of fear greeted her words. Against the far wall, Kerry's parents simply turned their heads and ignored her existence. Over near the entrance, a small kitchenette had been mostly spared and readily plundered. There was a five gallon bottle of water sitting on the counter half empty and Kerry went for it, aware of being desperately thirsty all of a sudden.

A dull explosion threw her against the wall and she grabbed on, as debris fell all around her. After a few tense moments, though, the creaking stopped and they all coughed in the film of plaster dust fogging the room. Part of the drop ceiling collapsed, throwing broken tiles everywhere, and the already stuffy air seemed to thicken around them.

Then with a halfhearted flicker, the faint emergency lighting went out, and they were in darkness, broken only by the city lights coming in from the windows that ringed them.

Kerry stopped with her hand on the counter. Meager though it had been, the light had served to at least give them some idea of what was happening. Now anything could come out of the dark. She jumped as she felt a touch on her back and gasped.

"Easy." Dar's voice tickled her ears. "Let me get that for you." The dark haired woman rummaged in the scattering of debris near the lopsided refrigerator and retrieved a cup, then lifted the bottle carefully and poured some water into it.

Kerry gulped the liquid gratefully, draining the cup, then stared at it in the gloomy half light. "Could you..."

"Sure." Dar poured her another cupful, then she took a deep breath. "I don't think blocking the hall is gonna help."

"Prob'ly not," Andrew, standing next to her invisibly, agreed. "Think we need to get that there winder open." He glanced at the dimly seen profiles against the glass. "Dar, let's you an me go check that out. Cec, keep by here, all right?"

"All right." Cecilia leaned against the counter next to Kerry and exhaled, as she turned her head. "Mind if I steal a sip of that?"

Kerry offered her the cup. "Least I could do after getting you into this."

"Kerry?" Ceci gave her a sideways look, taking a sip of the water. "If you don't cut out the blame game, I'm going to be forced to get maternal on you and that could get ugly."

Kerry blinked at her, then smiled against her will. "Sorry. I babble when I'm nervous." She rubbed her eyes tiredly. "My brain's running on empty right now." She was achingly aware of her parents watching from across the room.

"I can tell. You know what Dar does when she's antsy?"

"Pulls things apart," Kerry responded, with a wan grin. "Paper clips especially. She shapes them into little figurines."

Ceci chuckled. "I'm glad some things didn't change. I used to keep a collection of the damn things."

Kerry studied her for a moment. "I bet you still have them," she stated unexpectedly. "Don't you?"

The older woman pursed her lips, then glanced down at the counter they were leaning on. "You caught me. Yes, I do," she agreed softly. "Along with a couple pairs of tiny shoes and a first grader's efforts at spelling."

Kerry absorbed that, her gaze unconsciously drifting over to her parents. "I had to do all of my own saving." Her voice was low and quiet. After a moment of pensive silence, she turned her head towards Ceci. "Mrs. Roberts, you can get maternal on me any time you want."

Incredible. Cecilia drew a breath in. *Someone who thinks I'm parenting material. I must be getting ancient as the hills for that to happen.* "Well then," she answered reflectively, "you'd better stop calling me Mrs.

Roberts." In the gloom, she could just barely see Kerry smile.

Incredible.

The children were starting to cry, frightened to an even higher state by the darkness. Dar and Andy made their way across the crowded floor, pressing up against the glass windows as they reached them and looked down.

"Jesus." Dar's eyes widened, at the huge collection of lights, emergency equipment, and people swarming about below. "Guess they are working on getting people out." She watched as a fireman tugged a wrapped form out a window two stories beneath them. They were on the seventh floor, almost near the top of the building, and from what she could see whatever had happened had ripped out almost half of the side of the structure.

Andy pushed his hands against the glass. "Ain't gonna be easy." He shook his head. "Thing's made not to break. But them folks down there ain't gonna know we're here less we tell 'em." He lifted his sledge hammer and paused, looking for a place to start. "Damn lousy time fer you to lose that cell phone of yours."

"Mmph," Dar muttered, annoyed at herself for that very fact. "Came off my belt." Kerry had left hers charging in the room and she wasn't really sure what kind of reception she could expect inside the chaotic wreckage anyway. She cleared a space for her father to work, then realized there were some living obstacles there in the half light. "You'd better move back," Dar told the watching Stuarts coldly.

"Go to Hell," Roger Stuart answered, then jerked as he was suddenly face to face with a sledge hammer head and a pair of icy cold eyes behind it.

"You will move your carcass out of mah way, sir," Andrew rasped. "Because I have about run out of my patience with you." He poked the senator with the hammer handle. "Now take this little lady of yours and go back of there fore I throw you head over buttocks."

"Do you know who the hell I am?" the senator growled.

"A right jackass. Now move." Andrew poked him again.

"Listen here, you stupid hick." Stuart stood up, then stopped speaking as he was lifted and pushed against the wall, the hammer handle cutting off his wind. "Jesus," he rasped.

"That would be Commander Hick to you, useless excuse fer a gov'ment paycheck." Andy released him, then gave him a shove, sending him sprawling into a pile of roof tiling. "Waste of mah good tax dollars, that's for damn sure."

"Just wait until we get out of here," Kerry's father threatened. "I'll slap lawsuits on the lot of you."

Andrew turned his attention back to the window. "Jackass." Kerry's mother hurried to her husband's side and knelt by him, brushing the pieces of plaster off his stained and burned jacket. "Those who can, do, those who can't become lawyers. Those who ain't got no use at all, run fer gov'ment."

Dar almost laughed at the look on the senator's face, but she was too tired. Instead, she forced her attention on the glass. "Dad," she ran a hand over the surface, "try here, near the frame."

"Not in the middle?" Andrew drawled, cocking his head at her in question.

"No. I think its designed to flex there. It'll be more rigid, and have a higher tendency to shatter here, at the edge."

Andy gave her a look. "All right." He lifted the hammer and faced the glass, concentrating on it carefully. "Make sure everybody's staying back. This stuff's gonna fly."

Dar took a quick look around, ignoring the glares. "Everyone cover up. We're going to break this window." People scrambled to get out of the way and the frightened children were gathered into the corner. "Okay. Go ahead." She held her arm over her eyes and stepped back, stifling a cough as the air seemed to thicken again with smoke.

It would be such a relief to breathe fresh air. Just the thought of it made her dizzy.

Andrew took aim, then swung the hammer back, and launched it forward, getting his entire body into the swing as it hit the edge of the window. With a spectacular crash, it shattered into millions of tiny bits, exploding in both directions.

Andy threw himself backwards to avoid the flying glass, then felt himself picked up and slammed against the frame as the air pressure sucked the heated air out of the building, bringing a hot, roaring explosion down the hall and heading right for them.

❖ ⌘ ❖ ⌘ ❖ ⌘ ❖

"Get down!" Kerry yelled, pulling herself and Cecilia painfully to the floor as a superheated rush of fire and air exploded over her head and out the window, its crashing roar slamming against them like a physical force. Then the flames licked at the ceiling. She got to her feet and bolted forward regardless of the falling chunks of burning material.

Three people had been caught in it. She tried not to look at them and panic as she dove over a smoldering chair in the smoky darkness and was caught up abruptly by a pair of hands. "Let me..." Then she realized it was Dar.

"C'mon!" Dar yelled. "Everyone get over to the window!"

The heat was increasing quickly and now it was anything but silent as the chaos outside filtered in. The children screamed and the survivors scrambled over to the opening, clinging to the frame as smoke poured out of it.

"You almost got us killed!" Roger Stuart raged.

Dar ignored him as she peered back into the smoke, shading her eyes. Outside, the firemen had spotted them and were working to get the huge basket cranked up to their level, shouts of alarm and encouragement echoing up to them. Andrew pushed the last of the glass out of the way, one hand protectively curled around his wife, and Kerry helped a young woman over the fallen furniture.

The two wheelchairs. Dar grabbed Stuart by the arm. "Give me a hand with those kids." She pointed, realizing only then she could have made a better choice of assistants.

Well. No time. Stuart stared at her, half his face lit in fire, half in shadows, and for a long moment Dar thought he was going to refuse. Then he wrenched his arm free and shoved her away from him.

"Go there," he ordered Cynthia, pushing his way past a fallen book-case and towards the frightened children, who were unable to maneuver their chairs through the debris. It was very hot as they got to them, and Dar felt like she was breathing the fire itself as she touched the chair, then jerked her hands back at the heat. "Hang on." She unbuckled the petrified little boy and picked him up in her arms, ducking as a burning part of the ceiling fell, and almost stumbled as the flaming chunks hit her shoulder.

She shook them off and plowed forward, the child shivering so violently his teeth chattered in her ear. "Take it easy. We're gonna be fine," she told him, as small hands clutched desperately at her. The fire bucket was just reaching their level when she staggered to the edge of the window and the two firemen inside yelled orders almost impossible to hear over the roar of the fire and the noise of the crowd outside.

One had a hose, and he yelled something, then he opened a valve, and a jet of water exploded past them, hitting the fire behind them and making it hiss in protest. Someone screamed next to Dar and she realized it was Kerry's mother. She looked back, but nothing was visible through the smoke, then she searched the survivors huddled nearby and didn't see the senator among them. "Shit." She started to put the child down, intent on going back when her mother caught her arm. "Can you watch him for a minute?"

"Where are you going?" Ceci asked.

"See if I can..." Dar watched a ball of black smoke billow forward, stopping her speech.

Then a coughing, soot covered form stumbled out of the darkness, soaked from the hose's spray but carrying the other crippled child.

Dar felt Kerry lean against her, and she glanced towards her partner, whose soot covered face was almost unrecognizable in its weary tension. Her eyes, with an indescribable expression in them, were on her father, as the man came up to them, staggering under his load as a gust of wind from the circling helicopters washed in.

A spotlight hit them from above, and Dar shaded her eyes, blinking back spots as the firemen came closer to the building. They threw ropes over and Andrew caught one, tugged it back and tied it off around the steel window frame. "We got kids here!" he yelled. "We'll hand 'em over to you."

"Tie that to yourself!" the fireman hollered. "Don't want you falling out the window while we're doing this."

Andrew nodded, hastily fastening the heavy rope around his waist and tying it with an efficient knot. "All right. C'mere, squirt." He held out a hand to the nearest of the children and caught the boy around the waist and hoisted him out over the open space between the edge of the window and the bucket. The fireman grabbed him and lifted him in, then handed him to another fireman who had climbed up the long ladder zig zagging behind them.

The crowd clustered closer, nervously edging away from the fire at their backs, momentarily dampened by the fireman's efforts. They started to push and Dar braced her legs to keep her balance. "Stay back. Let's get the kids out first."

"She's right," Roger Stuart yelled. "Pushing won't help. Stay where you are."

An explosion sent the floor shuddering under their feet and people screamed, trying to keep their balance. One man panicked and jumped for the basket, his feet slipping on the wet floor and making him miss his hold, leaving him hanging from one arm. Andrew leaned out, grabbed the back of his pants, and yanked him up with a single, powerful heave into the basket head first.

The fireman pulled him in, then looked over. "Better hurry up. We can't hold this."

Two more people pushed to the front, clawing blindly at Andrew's arm. "Get back." The ex-SEAL pushed them gently. "C'mon now. Let the kids out. Dar, gimme that little boy."

"I've got him." Dar had tied the end of the second rope around her and now she leaned out and handed the child carefully to the fireman hanging on the front of the basket. "Careful. He can't walk."

"You be careful, ma'am," the fireman warned, as he passed the child back.

Kerry got between the panicked survivors and Andrew. "Okay. Just take it easy. We're all going to get out of here," she yelled to be heard over the noise. "There aren't that many of us...and look, the fire's not getting any closer for now." She pointed with her good hand. "Don't start rushing the window. You'll fall out and then you'll really get hurt."

They passed three more children out, then Roger edged forward, ignoring Andrew's offered hands and getting to the very edge of the opening before handing out the little girl he was carrying. "Watch the braces," he warned the fireman, then stepped back. "All right, women next."

Two women made it out, then a rumble filled the building and part of the ceiling collapsed behind them, sending a wash of heat out the window. The remaining glass crackled and popped, and Dar shielded her face and turned her back to it. "We'd better hurry."

Kerry's mother went next, with Andrew taking one arm and her husband taking the other. "You next, Cec." Andrew turned, to see a stubborn look crossing his wife's face. "Now, c'mon." He grabbed her bodily, lifted her, and passed her slight weight to the fireman over her half spoken protests. "Careful with that one. She bites."

The fireman let a brief grin cross his tired face. "Yes, sir."

"You be careful, damn it!" Ceci yelled back, then her voice dropped. "Please?" Their eyes locked and Andrew smiled at her, giving her a reassuring wink that didn't seem to work.

Kerry started to untie the rope around Dar. "Guess we're next."

"Go on." Dar gently removed her hands and nudged her towards the opening. "I'll be right there."

Andrew held a hand out and she took it, pausing to glance at her father as she stepped into the glare and backwash of the endlessly hovering helicopters. The fireman reached out just as a gust of wind knocked her off balance and she wavered, then felt a steadying hand on her back as the rescuers took a secure hold on her and lifted her over the gap. Once in the bucket she turned immediately and met three sets of eyes watching her.

The hand, she realized, had been her father's.

She felt a guiding touch and started carefully down the ladder, keeping her eyes always on that dark, smoke filled gap.

"You next." Dar exhaled, motioning to the senator, the last one left besides Andy and herself. She thought he was going to argue with her for a second, then he merely stepped forward and accepted the fireman's arm clasp as they sprayed again into the opening. Smoke billowed out continuously and now, at last, Dar moved towards the window.

She and her father exchanged glances. "G'wan," Andrew said quietly.

Dar quirked her eyebrow. "You first."

Andrew's eyebrows lifted. "Paladar, get yer butt into that bucket before I whup it."

Dar shook her head. "Not this time. You're about to keel over. So move it." She folded her arms and met his eyes with an inflexibly stubborn look. "C'mon, c'mon. We don't have all day."

Andrew untied his rope and chuckled, shaking his head as he moved to the opening and paused, then jumped across on his own, disregarding the fireman's helping hand. Then he turned and took hold of Dar's arm as she crossed, out of the smoke and heat at last.

"Okay. Pull her back!" The fireman spoke into a walkie talkie. "Let's get the hell—oh, shit!"

The low rumble warned them. "Get down! Get down!" The fireman slammed them both into the bottom of the bucket and threw himself over them as a ball of superheated air and flame came roiling out of the hole in the glass, melting it and sending shards of concrete flying towards them.

The bucket reeled wildly, then swung away from the building, swaying as the engineers fought to keep it upright. The hapless survivors clung to the ladder desperately, until it finally steadied.

"Son of a bitch." The fireman exhaled, hauling himself off the two rescuees in the bottom of the bucket. "Oh. Sorry, ma'am."

Dar slowly straightened and gazed over the lip of the bucket to where the fire now shot out of the wall, raging up the side of the half collapsed building. Then she looked at her father, who gazed thoughtfully back. "I've heard people say being on the edge is a big rush."

"Mmm." Andrew rocked his head.

"They're full of shit." Dar sat down in the bottom of the bucket, where she could see nothing but plastic and the clouds overhead.

Andy patted her knee comfortingly, then leaned an arm on the bucket edge. "We need to get climbing?"

"Hell no." The firefighter sat wearily on the edge of the contraption. "We get a ride down. It'll just take a few minutes." He glanced at them. "You two deserve it. You saved those people's asses. We were about to back off and let the building blow out." He held a hand out. "Josh Beard."

Andy took it. "Andy Roberts. And this little sprout's my daughter Dar."

Josh looked quizzically at the six foot plus woman sprawled at his feet and grinned. "You musta used a decent fertilizer."

It struck Dar as funny and she laughed softly, too exhausted to otherwise move.

"Hey. Was that really Senator Stuart and his wife?"

"Yeap." Andrew nodded. "How'd you know?"

"Oh, they're turning the place upside down looking for him. You kidding? When they pulled his kid out and she said he was still—"

Dar grabbed his leg in a vise grip. "What? Are you saying his daughter Angela got out?"

"Ouch." He winced. "Yeah. About to pop. She was on the west side of the building and they got her out first thing." He took off his helmet and scrubbed his hand through short, curly hair. "Probably a momma by now."

Dar felt a wave of relief flow through her and she let her head drop back against the plastic. "Thank God." Then she pulled herself to her feet and peered over the basket edge, towards the slowly approaching ground.

Chapter
42

Kerry found herself on the ground and for a long moment, she simply stood there, letting the chaos around her pass her by as she absorbed the steadiness of the earth under her feet and took in breaths of air untainted with smoke and dust. Then she turned and tilted her head back, reassuring herself of the slow progress of the bucket on its way down before she turned and paid attention to the paramedic who was talking to her. "I'm sorry. What did you ask me?"

"I said, would you come over here, ma'am, and let us take a look at you?" the woman repeated, taking her elbow.

Ceci appeared at her side. "She had a dislocated shoulder," she told the paramedic, as Kerry obediently allowed the paramedic to lead her over to what appeared to be a triage area, where she sat down on a bench.

"Doesn't look dislocated." The woman gently removed the dirty singed sling Kerry still wore. "Someone put it back in for you?"

Kerry nodded. "Yes." She took a breath. "It really hurt."

"I bet it did." She carefully manipulated Kerry's arm. "How's it feel now?"

"Sore." She sighed. "But then, just about everything's sore. It's kind of hard to judge." She winced as the medic touched her forearm. "I think I got burned there."

"Mmm. Yes, you did." The medic looked around. "How about you lie down on that gurney over there and let me get someone to take a look at this, okay?" She took Kerry by the arm, led her over, and then helped her settle down on the rolling cot, pulling the sheet up to her waist and positioning her arm carefully on her stomach. "You just stay right there."

"Okay." Kerry let out a breath, glad to be still. She turned her head towards Ceci and blinked. "Are they down yet?"

The gray eyes lifted then returned. "Almost." Ceci seated herself on the grass next to the gurney and leaned against a stone disposal. "I see the press has found your father."

Kerry turned her head that way and watched. "He did okay up there." Her voice took on a note of tired wonder.

"He proved his paternity," Ceci remarked dryly.

Kerry gave her a puzzled look.

"That was a compliment."

"Oh." She rubbed her face, blinking her stinging eyes, then looked up as a man in green surgical scrubs knelt next to her. "Hello."

He glanced at her. "Hi there." Professional hands carefully lifted her forearm and examined it. "Well, that's a nasty burn, but I think you got lucky."

"Lucky," Kerry murmured.

"Let me look at your head now." Gentle fingers probed. "That's a pretty bad bump."

"Bump?" Kerry thought about that. "I don't remember that."

"Probably when you went through the drywall," Ceci supplied, glancing at the basket finally making its landing. "You were out for about fifteen minutes."

"I was?"

"Ummhmm."

"I think we need to take you in and take some x-rays. Just stay quiet here and we'll transport you in a little while, okay?" The doctor spread a faintly spicy smelling salve over the burn on her arm and covered it with a light layer of gauze. "Have you been coughing? Does your throat hurt?"

"No. Not really." Kerry cleared her throat experimentally. "Kind of raw, though."

"Okay. We'll check you for smoke inhalation. Just lie back and relax."

That sounded like a good idea. Now that it was over. Well, sort of. All the little scrapes and cuts and bangs were surfacing and she felt like she'd been run through a trash compactor.

There were so many things to think about and she didn't want to think about any of them. "Doctor?"

"Mmm?" He looked up from cleaning a cut on Kerry's collarbone.

"Kerry!" Dar's voice cut in, and she dropped to one knee, smiling. "Hey. I've got great news."

Kerry's eyes fastened on her face trustingly. "What is it?" She could see the honest happiness on her lover's face and it brought a smile to her own. "Did you find Angie?"

"Not exactly." Dar twined their fingers. "She's already at the other hospital. You're an aunt."

Every bit of pain just vanished for a simple, golden moment. "Yes!" She exulted. "Oh god. Yes. I knew it. I knew she was all right, Dar." She was halfway between laughing and crying. "Thank you. How'd you find out?"

"Everyone knows," Dar replied. "She was one of the first ones out. She told everyone who she was and the place went berserk."

"Oh."

"That explains all the press," Ceci remarked. "Otherwise a fire hardly would have drawn Dan Rather."

"Fire?" The doctor finished his work. "Ma'am, that was no fire. It was an explosion." He patted Kerry's uninjured shoulder. "I'll be back."

There was a moment of silence, as they looked at each other. Then Andrew came up and took a seat next to his wife. "Some dumb bastards blew the place up?"

"Who?" Kerry asked. "Who would want to blow up a hospital?"

The ex-SEAL shook his head. "They dunno yet." He sighed. "Got them a coffee tent over there. You all want some?" He pushed to his feet and Ceci joined him. "We'll bring some back."

"You want anything else?" Ceci asked, as her fingers brushed Dar's hair lightly.

Dar sighed, swallowing her first, instinctive answer. "Coffee's fine. Thanks." Then her parents were gone and she and Kerry were relatively alone, the surrounding chaos effectively isolating them.

Kerry breathed in the damp air. "What time is it?"

"I have no idea." Dar leaned her arms on the gurney and ran her thumb over Kerry's fingers. "I'm glad about your sister."

Kerry lifted her other hand and ran it through Dar's dark and very tangled hair. "Me too." Dar looked up, her face covered in soot and scrapes, and her eyes bloodshot. "Crappy day, huh?"

The neatly shaped lips tensed into a smile. "You and I are here at the end of it. That's good enough for me," Dar admitted. "But yeah. I think I've had better twenty-four hour periods in my time."

Kerry cupped her cheek and Dar's eyes fluttered closed in reaction. "I love you."

Dar opened her eyes and gazed at her. "I love you, too."

"I'm really glad nothing happened to you, Dar," Kerry went on. "Because I don't think...I would have wanted to make it out of there if it had."

Dar's jaw clenched, moving the muscles under the skin. "Yeah," she muttered hoarsely. "You gave me a scare in there a few times." She leaned into Kerry's touch, glad it was over, and not really caring what happened next.

Footsteps approached and Dar looked up, expecting to see her parents or the doctor, and surprised when it was a young woman in khaki pants and a blue shirt who knelt at her side. "Ms. Roberts?"

She blinked. "Yes."

"Whew. Glad I found you." The woman held up a very familiar look-ing identification badge. "Mr. Baird asked me to see if I could locate you. He's got a motorvan available to take you over to the hospital...or wher-ever you need to go."

"Hamilton's here?" Dar looked towards the coffee tent for her par-ents and only then realized what logo was blazoned on the flap. "Commu-nity support team?"

"Yes, ma'am. Here to help, and also because we got word you and Ms. Stuart were maybe trapped in there. You've got a lot of people really, really wired up, Ms. Roberts."

"I bet." Dar almost laughed. "All right. Let me just find my parents and...where in the hell is he?"

She pointed towards a sleek, streamlined Winnebago idling on a side street. "You might want to hurry. I think the press is looking for you."

Dar sighed, pushing herself to her feet. "You okay to walk?" She assisted Kerry in standing. "They've got a nice, cushy couch you can lie down on in there. That's the thing they use to take the board members to the Super Bowl."

"Does it have wet towels?"

Dar waved her parents over and pointed towards the van. "C'mon. A little piece of my world just plopped itself down very conveniently." She took her cup of coffee and they started off, just as a clamor of voices lifted behind them.

❖ ⌘ ❖ ⌘ ❖ ⌘ ❖

The motorvan was quiet, cool, and full of leather furniture. Dar con-sidered that ample exchange for the fact that it was also full of Hamilton Baird. The tall, well-built lawyer settled a smile on her the minute she cleared the door, as he sat with not one single silver hair out of place.

Their relationship could best be described as cordial, mutual antago-nism. Dar sighed inwardly. Hamilton was without doubt, a supremely tal-ented lawyer, but they mixed like oil and water and he was one of the few people in the company who was neither intimidated nor impressed by her.

Of course, Hamilton also was one of the few people in the company who had a nastier reputation and was more disliked by just about every-one than Dar was, which was quite an achievement to his credit.

Right now, however, she didn't care if he were Satan personified, so long as he didn't get between her and the thick, comfy looking leather chair near the teakwood bar. "Good morning, Hamilton."

"And a fine morning it is, too, Dar." The lawyer's rich, Louisiana tinged speech curled around the air conditioned atmosphere. "Now that ah can call Allie and tell him to stop messin' in his silk shorts."

"He wears cotton briefs." Dar sat down and extended her legs.

"These are my parents, Cecilia and Andrew Roberts, and Kerrison Stuart, our Ops Director." She tilted her head. "This is Hamilton Baird, ILS's chief council."

"And bottle washer. You forgot that part, Dar." The lawyer chuckled. "Ah would make a nasty comment about what you look like, but ah figure you deserve a little slack just considering." He inclined his head toward Kerry. "Ms. Stuart, it's a pleasure to meet you finally. After hearing so much about you from so many people."

Kerry had sat down next to Dar and was simply being quiet. "Nice to meet you too, Mr. Baird."

Andy and Ceci had settled on the long couch that just barely fit against the far wall of the van and were sucking on sodas.

"Ah take it we need to run by the hospital?" Baird picked up the phone as he asked and dialed. "Hello, Allie. I was trolling through the streets of DC, and what d'you know? I found our missing CIO lookin' like the ass end of a trash heap." He held out the phone. "Not even so much as a 'thank you, Hamilton.' Lord, what did his mother teach him?"

Dar took the phone and cradled it to her ear. "Hi."

A long, long exhale. "Jesus H. Christ, Paladar."

"Was that a statement, an accusation, or a question?" Dar closed her eyes, obscurely pleased with the reaction. "It's not my fault, Alastair." She paused. "Thanks for sending the troops in, though."

"Are you all right?"

"Pretty much."

"What about Kerry?"

"She's banged up a little, but she'll be fine." Dar glanced at her and winked. Kerry smiled back. She heard a clicking noise through the phone amidst a chunk of silence. "Alastair?"

"Hang on, hang on." A few last clicks. "There. I just sent out a bulletin. Thank God it's good news."

"A bulletin?" Dar's brows creased. "For what?"

"Well, that you two are all right, of course, Dar. What did you think?"

"To who?"

"Users All."

Dar stared at the phone for a minute. "Well, that was a waste of network bandwidth." She snorted. "I'm sure there are a hundred thousand people who didn't want to know that bit of news."

Now it was Alastair's turn to be quiet for a moment. "You know something, Dar?"

"What?"

"For someone so bright, you're a real idiot sometimes."

Dar had no answer for that one.

"That's all this company's been focused on for the last twelve hours.

Not one goddamned bit of work got accomplished and probably fifty percent of the net bandwidth corporate wide was taken up by everyone tuning into streaming video feeds from CNN."

"Oh."

"Yeah, oh," Alastair responded. "You think I'd be sitting here at four a.m. in the goddamned morning, after spending the night pacing the halls for just anyone?"

"No...I..." Dar felt very off balance. "I'm sorry, Alastair. It's just been a very long day."

"I know it has," her boss told her gently. "Kerry's sister called me and told me you two were in there. I can't tell you how that made me feel."

Dar blinked, then rubbed her eyes. "Thanks."

"Go get some rest. You sound like hell."

"It was like that in there."

"Hell?"

"Yeah," Dar replied. "We got out right before the place we were in blew out."

Alastair rattled some keys. "Wait, I thought I saw... Sweet Jesus, that was you," his voice sounded shocked, "hanging out of that damn window!"

"Yeah."

"Handing those kids out!"

"Yeah." Dar sighed. "Dad and I were the last ones to get off that floor."

"After the senator? The press made a huge deal about that."

"Yeah."

"That must have been comfortable for you all."

"It sucked."

"Mmm. Well, put Ham on for a minute, willya Dar? And you go get some sleep. That's an order."

"I will. Goodnight, Alastair." Dar hesitated. "Um...thanks for being concerned." She handed the phone back to Hamilton and slid down, letting her head rest against the chair back. She felt a warm touch on her arm and she turned her head, to see Kerry gazing at her. "Apparently we're the news at eleven."

"Ah." Kerry stifled a yawn. "I don't want to be news. I just want to be clean and asleep."

"Right there with you," Dar muttered. "Hope it doesn't take long at the hospital."

There was a moment's silence then Kerry cleared her throat. "Listen. I'm feeling a lot better. They put some stuff on my arm and the doctor said everything else pretty much looked okay. Could we just go back to the hotel?"

Dar rolled her head to one side and peered at her. "You sure? That's a nasty bump on your head. Might be better to have it x-rayed."

"I can go back tomorrow," Kerry argued. "You know it's going to be packed there with all these people. I want to go tomorrow early anyway, to see Angie, but right now," she hesitated, "I'd kinda like to just go to bed."

A quiet room. A shower. A bed, clean clothes, and Kerry. Dar didn't even stop to think or argue. "All right," she murmured. "That sounds great to me." She glanced over to where her mother was already dozing in her father's arms and nodded. "The hotel it is."

❖ ⌘ ❖ ⌘ ❖ ⌘ ❖

Alastair leaned back in his seat and blew out a long, relieved breath. "Damn, that was good news." He glanced at his monitor, where responses were coming in acknowledging his announcement.

A denim clad admin seated across from him nodded. "Yes, sir, did you want to have an official statement made up? With the heavy presence, I'm guessing the press will be calling shortly."

The CEO put his hands behind his head and grinned. "Yeap. I sure do want a statement. In fact, I want a couple of them. Got a sharp pencil?" he asked. "Let's start with the one about how relieved we are about our two very, very valued employees."

The man grinned. "Gotcha, sir."

"Then, I want one about how it doesn't surprise me that one of...ahem...*my* employees turns out to be a hero."

The admin stopped scribbling and glanced up. "Y'know, sir, this is going to be great press for us," he said, earnestly. "Between this and the great stuff over the ATM crisis, our stock's gonna go through the roof."

Alastair chuckled softly. "You betcha, son. You betcha."

❖ ⌘ ❖ ⌘ ❖ ⌘ ❖

They managed to get to their rooms without major incident, though Dar spotted several packs of reporters roaming in the main lobby. She slid her card into the door with a sense of utter relief and watched the green light blink, then pushed the handle down and shoved the surface inward.

It was dark and quiet inside, lit with only one light, and the bed was turned down invitingly. The message light was blinking, but neither of them had any intention of answering it. Kerry trudged into the bathroom and turned the light on, then leaned against the doorframe wearily. "I'm going to need some help here."

Dar had gone to their bags and was kneeling next to hers. She peered over her shoulder. "I figured." She held up two pairs of pajamas.

"Mmm." Kerry nodded. "Wish I had some hot tea to go with it. My throat's raw."

"Mine too," Dar admitted. "How about you start the water, and I'll have some sent up?"

"Deal." Kerry turned the shower on and let it run over her good hand to test the temperature. It took a while to warm up, long enough for Dar to finish her task and enter the bathroom. "Almost ready."

"Mmhm. Here. Let me get that off for you." Dar carefully removed the sling, then studied her gauze wrapped arm. "You want plastic over that?"

"I guess." Kerry swayed on her feet. "I don't think I...oh, okay. Yeah. That'll work." Dar unbuttoned Kerry's shirt and slid it off and down both arms, taking care not to pull her injured one. "Ew." She gazed down at her body, covered in dirt and smoke residue. "I look like I live in a garbage can."

"Nah." Dar unhooked her bra and removed it, exposing startlingly white skin against the rest of Kerry. "Remind me to send a nice note to..." she glanced at the tag, "Hanes."

"Tch." Kerry fumbled with her belt. "I don't think they had this in mind when they designed that model."

Dar stripped her own shirt off and glanced down. "Hmm."

Kerry glanced up. "Oh, shit, Dar." She forgot about her trousers and focused her attention on the raw, vertical shallow slashes across Dar's belly. "Where did you? Oh, wow. That must hurt."

"Um." Dar reached around and unhooked her bra, wincing as the fabric slid down and caught on a jagged cut just below her collarbone. "I think I was crawling over that glass I broke down that first tunnel."

"Jesus." Kerry wet a washcloth and gently cleaned around the injuries. "Dar, you should put something on these. They're going to get infected."

"Later." Dar unbuckled Kerry's belt, undid her jeans, tugged them down, and pulled them off over her already sneakerless feet. "Glad we were wearing denim." She patted one thigh, then slid a finger under the waistband of Kerry's cotton underwear.

I should be way too tired to feel anything. Kerry closed her eyes briefly, as the familiar tingle worked its way up her body from its center in her groin. *That must say something about us.*

"Kerry?"

"Mmm?" She blinked her eyes opened to see Dar's concerned look. "Oh, sorry. Just reflecting...here, let me..." She managed, one handed, to undo Dar's jeans and watched them slip down. "Ooo, are those new?"

"Yes." Dar dredged up a weary grin. "C'mon. I have grunge in places even the biology books couldn't find." She pulled off her bright red briefs and helped Kerry step into the tub shower, letting the warm water wash over the both of them.

Twin sighs of appreciation emerged. Dar took the soap and a wash-cloth and set to work cleaning Kerry's skin, rubbing very gently over the scrapes and bruises that liberally covered her upper body. "Does your neck hurt?"

"Yeah." Kerry rocked her head back and forth a little. "And I've got a headache that would drop a manatee at two fathoms." She took a little soap in her good hand and started to work on Dar's tall frame.

They were quiet for a few minutes as they rinsed off, then Dar got some shampoo and carefully worked it into Kerry's thick blond hair, avoiding the lump on the left-hand side.

It felt so wonderful. Kerry moved a step forward and just leaned against Dar, nuzzling her chest as the water washed the soap away, taking the dirt and sweat with it. She stayed there while Dar scrubbed her own hair, then stepped with her outside the shower and let Dar towel her dry.

The room air felt cold against her skin as they left the bathroom and she stopped long enough for Dar to ease her T-shirt over her head, the soft fabric smelling of sunlight and cedar from her chest of drawers at home. Then Dar led her over to the bed, pulled the covers back, and guided her down onto the soft surface. "Easy."

"Ungh." Kerry slid under the sheets and put her head down, glad beyond reason to be still and quiet and comfortable. She closed her eyes and listened to the soft sounds of the room, hearing a faint knock, then Dar's low voice as she answered it. The door closed and there was a soft clink as a tray was set down, then the sounds of liquid pouring and a spoon being stirred.

The bed next to her moved and dipped and she opened her eyes to see Dar seated next to her, damp hair slicked back, with a mug of steaming tea in her hands. "You're pretty darn good at this."

"Good at what?" Dar got an arm behind her and supported her as she took the mug.

"TLC." Kerry sipped at the tea, which had a wonderful mint scent and a nice, sweet taste. It slipped down her throat and warmed her and she sighed in relief. "Here. Have a sip."

Dar obeyed, then leaned back, letting out a long, exhausted breath. The bombardment of people and emotions was over at last and she sat still for a moment, collecting herself with a weary effort.

But she found herself not wanting to think at all. She just wanted to lie here, with her arms around Kerry and block out the last twelve hours, setting it aside until her mind could deal with it.

Right now, that wasn't an option. Dar shivered a little, not entirely from the chill air. She cradled Kerry in her arms and closed her eyes.

Hoping like hell she wouldn't dream.

Kerry put her nearly empty cup down and snuggled down into Dar's

embrace, letting out a sigh and tugging the covers up a little around them
both.

    It was over.

    She was safe.

    For right now that was enough.

Chapter

43

Waking up this time felt like she was ascending from a deep dive, Dar groggily thought, as she slowly drifted up from a well of sleep that had been mercifully dreamless indeed. Half of her wanted to just sink back down into the pleasant warmth of the bed, but the other half was crankily aware of her body's stiffness and it was poking her towards consciousness and movement.

So she reluctantly opened one eyelid and surveyed the room, noting the dim, gray light coming from the window. Rain. An even better reason to stay in bed. She rotated the eyeball towards the bedside clock and blinked at the red numbers displaying back at her.

Oh.

No wonder I feel stiff. I've been in the same damn position for twelve hours. Dar peered down at Kerry, who was curled half on her side, with both hands tangled in Dar's shirt and her head tucked into her shoulder. The blond woman hadn't moved much either, but her breathing was steady and regular and her skin tone had returned to its normal healthy state rather than the drawn grayness of the night before.

Dar remained still for a little while, just watching Kerry sleep and feeling the warmth of her friend's breathing through the thin cotton of her shirt. Then the discomfort forced her to straighten out, stifling a groan as her back protested the motion fiercely.

Even the slight sound was enough to get a response from Kerry, however, who murmured and opened her eyes, reaching instinctively out as Dar shifted. "Hey."

"It's okay. I'm just stretching," Dar reassured her, seeing the sleep fogged and slightly dazed eyes peering anxiously back at her. "How are you feeling?" She cleared the very disheveled hair out of Kerry's eyes and watched her blink a few times in confusion. "Ker?"

"Yeah, yeah." Kerry's brow creased slightly. "Mmph." She cleared her throat slightly and tentatively shifted. "Not too bad," she murmured, in a surprised tone. "What time is it?"

"Five."

"Jesus." Kerry swallowed. "No wonder my mouth feels like cotton wadding." She drew in a breath and rolled over onto her back, stretching out cautiously under the covers. Other than her sore shoulder, everything seemed to be pretty much okay, and she wiggled her toes, feeling a hundred times better than before she'd gone to sleep.

Except for one thing. "I'm starving," she informed the popcorn ceiling. "Are you starving?" She laid her hand over her very empty feeling stomach.

"I dunno. Let me get enough kinks out to stand up, then I'll let you know." Dar groaned, as she slowly extended her legs and arched her back. "Son of a..." She felt like one huge cramp. "Ow."

Kerry patted her thigh. "Easy there, tiger," she murmured. "I can't believe we slept so late. I wonder what's going on."

Dar slid out from under the covers and got to her feet, rubbing the back of her neck and walking gingerly. "I'll turn on the news." She limped over to the connecting door between their room and her parents and stuck her head inside, smiling at the dark, quiet room with its sleeping occupants. She drew back out and shut the door carefully. "Still snoozing." She yawned and scratched her belly, then hit the remote for the television and trudged towards the bathroom. "I think I am hungry, now that you mention it." Walking around loosened things up a little, though her back was still protesting.

"Good."

Dar listened to Kerry rustle around for a minute, then she used the restroom, ran water in the sink, and splashed handfuls of it over her face. It was cold and faintly metallic smelling, but it worked to wake her up. She patted her skin dry and regarded her reflection, smoothing her dampened hair back off her face. "Mmm." One finger touched a bruise covering half her cheekbone. "Last time I had one like that, I was still in high school."

She met the eyes in the mirror for a moment, then turned the light out and reentered the room to find Kerry sitting up in bed, cradling her arm. "Oh, wait." She grabbed the sling and held it up. "Need this?" She walked over at Kerry's nod and adjusted the canvas support around her, then sat down on the bed and glanced at the menu Kerry had open in front of her.

"Ooo." She made a grab for the folder, spotting something interesting.

"Ah ah." Kerry tugged it back one handed. "Dinner first, then dessert." She scanned the choices, then picked up the phone and dialed room service. "Hello...ah, yes, it is." A pause. "Thank you. Um...I'd like to order something for dinner?" She scowled at the television, which was on a shopping channel. "Put on CNN, will you?"

Dar keyed the remote, but left the sound down.

"Yes, thanks. Um, two of the clam chowder." She put the phone against her chest. "How do ribs sound?"

Dar tickled hers lightly. "Fine."

"Stop that." Kerry hissed. "Two orders of the ribs. No, the full rack." A pause. "Do you have anything bigger? A what? No. No. That's okay. I'll pass on the cow." She rolled her eyes. "Baked potatoes sound great and the salads, yeah." Another pause. "A large pot of coffee, and um," she flipped the page, "two of the Death by Chocolate Killer Mountain Brownies with vanilla ice cream and fudge sauce."

Dar scratched an ear. "When you put it like that, it sounds so excessive," she muttered.

"It is." Kerry smiled. "Yes, thanks, that's great." She hung up the phone. "About thirty minutes." She reached over and turned the sound up, as a familiar scene appeared.

"The explosion, believed to be centered in the middle of the seventh floor, set off a chain reaction when it touched off the gas supply inside the hospital," the announcer said gravely. "Two hundred people are believed dead, and today the FBI has started investigating, citing a tip they received that this horrible tragedy might not have been an accident."

"Two hundred people." Kerry breathed. "Oh my god, Dar."

"Senator Roger Stuart, in Washington for Senate hearings on his conduct was an eyewitness. Seen here, as he assisted in evacuating victims from the floor worst hit, he stated that so far as he could tell, there was no warning, just a huge explosion that shook the entire building."

Kerry stared at the screen, seeing her father's battered face and burned clothing through a faint haze of memory. The camera showed the firefighters perched outside the broken window, and what was, unmistakably, her father's outline as he handed out one of the children. Through a billow of smoke she could also see Andrew's distinctive form, but it seemed like a dream to her, not something that she'd lived through only half a day prior.

Dar blinked at the screen, which showed further film and a close up of the window as a thick puff of black, oily looking smoke poured out. "Damn." She watched a dimly seen figure holding onto one of the women, as they climbed into the firefighter's basket and it occurred to her suddenly that she was watching herself. "Is that..."

"You," Kerry murmured. "Yeah it is."

The film cut to Dar clambering over the edge of the basket herself, then all of them ducking as an explosion shook the screen, sending a fireball out inches from the erratically weaving platform.

"Oh my god. You just..." Kerry's eyes widened. "Dar." She turned her head.

"Yeah." Dar put a reassuring arm around her. "It was kinda close. I made Dad go before me. I wanted to make absolutely sure he was okay."

Kerry leaned her head against Dar's shoulder. "I'm glad I didn't realize how close you came. I'd have had nightmares, I know it."

"I thought I was going to have nightmares but I didn't." Dar sighed. "I think I just want to forget the whole thing." She looked down at her hands, which were covered with tiny cuts and scrapes and really stung. "It's sort of a blur already."

Kerry thought about that. "I remember you being very brave," she commented softly. "I remember you saving my butt a few times along with some other people's."

"I just wanted to get you out of there," Dar replied. "I didn't really care about those other people."

"That's not true. You cared about your parents," Kerry objected.

"Well, yeah."

"You cared about those kids."

Dar didn't answer.

"Dar, why is it so hard for you to accept your own heroism?" Kerry asked.

She didn't get an answer for a while, then Dar shrugged one shoulder. "I don't know."

Kerry tucked a hand inside her elbow and studied Dar's face, its battered profile still and somber. "This really rocked you, didn't it?"

Dar nodded.

"You want to talk about it?"

Dar drew in a breath. "Not yet." She gave Kerry a brief, honest look. "But I will...and you'll be the first one to hear it."

Kerry smiled at her. "Fair enough." She leaned over and kissed Dar's arm. "How are you feeling?"

Now she got a bit of a wryly raised eyebrow.

"Like a truck ran over me," Dar answered honestly. "I think I pulled a few things. My back's really hurting."

"Maybe they can slide a few x-rays on you when they get my shoulder tonight," Kerry stated pointedly. "I'm not surprised your back hurts. You carried my butt for fifteen minutes. Good grief, Dar. I'm surprised you didn't get a hernia on top of it."

That even got a smile. "Didn't even occur to me. I wasn't in a reasonable frame of mind, I don't think."

The television caught their attention. "The Senate committee investigating Senator Stuart has informed CNN that they have postponed further hearings for a short period—perhaps until after the holidays to allow the senator to recover from his ordeal."

"Oh my god. Did he just say we can go home?" Kerry blurted.

"Yeah. I think so." Dar now smiled again in frank relief. "Maybe you don't have to come back."

"In related news, International Logistics Services confirmed that two of the survivors from the explosion were ILS CIO, Dar Roberts, and Director of Operations, Kerrison Stuart, who is Senator Roger Stuart's daughter. Both were reportedly there visiting Ms. Stuart's sister, who was in labor at the time."

"Ew." Kerry scrunched her face up. "I don't like being a sound bite."

"According to Chief Executive Officer, Alastair McLean, both employees were among the group rescued from the seventh floor, and he identified Ms. Roberts as the person CNN has been showing in this spectacular piece of footage all afternoon."

"Ew." Dar covered her eyes. "Alastair, did we need the publicity that badly?"

"Mr. McLean stated that he was not surprised at the heroism shown by Ms. Roberts, a fifteen year employee of ILS, and that he was glad to rush ILS resources to the scene to assist the injured." The announcer cleared his throat. "CNN featured Ms. Roberts in a Businessline interview only this morning, regarding the ATM outage the previous day."

Dar watched a clip of her interview and sighed. "I look like an idiot."

"You do not." Kerry gave her a look. "You look gorgeous and that guy is all but drooling on you, Dar."

Dar made a face.

"You're such a nerd." Kerry kidded her gently. "I think you look great on TV."

Dar fiddled with her pager, then turned it on and dropped it onto the table. She stared at it for a few seconds, then jumped as it started to vibrate. They both watched in fascination as the device skittered all over the table, then hopped off to the carpet, where it continued to vibrate. "Wow." Dar waited a few minutes until it finally stopped, then she picked it up and reviewed the pages. "Twenty five. It maxed out the memory." She thumbed through them. "Guess I should probably give Mark a call...maybe have him call María..."

"Why don't you call her?" Kerry got up and walked over to the window, which was covered in raindrops. "You know she'd love to hear from you directly, Dar. She really likes you." She turned and leaned against the glass.

"Yeah." Dar rose and went to the desk, sat down behind it and took a breath, then booted up her laptop. "You should give Colleen a call." She picked up Kerry's cell phone and turned it on, then dialed Mark's number, which she had to fish in her still slightly foggy memory for. It rang twice, then was answered. "Hi."

There was a brief silence. "Dar?"

"Yep."

"Son of a goddamn bitch. I am so glad to hear your voice."

It brought a surprising tightness to her throat. "Thanks. Everything all right there?"

"Here? Yeah! Ah, everything's great. Perfect." Mark blurted. "Well, I mean, like the usual stuff is going on, you know. Canada's down, and we lost the overseas routers this afternoon, so that's a mess, but...um..."

"I get the picture. Glad things are pretty much as usual," Dar replied.

"Hey guys! I got Dar on the phone," Mark yelled, muffling the receiver with one hand. "Man, it's fantastic to talk to you. I've got that whole clip digitized and in Quicktime. The server's been going wild serving it."

Dar covered her eyes. "Great. If you blow an array with that, I'm going to kick your ass."

Mark laughed in delight. "Now that sounds like my boss. How's Kerry?"

"She's fine. She's got a dislocated shoulder and few bumps, but she's okay." Dar couldn't seem to get rid of the lump in her throat. "Is...um...is María still there, or did she leave already?"

"She's here. I'll transfer you. Listen, I really mean it, Dar, I'm glad you're both okay." Mark put her on hold a minute, then the call clicked through.

"Hello?"

"Hi, María."

A gasp. "*¡Madre de Dios!*" María sounded like she was crying. "Dar, I am so glad to hear you. I was so frightened that something bad had happened to you and to Kerrisita."

"No. We're both okay, María. Thanks for worrying though." Dar cleared her throat and blinked, shocked to find tears stinging her own eyes. A touch fell on her shoulder and she glanced up at Kerry, then just handed her the phone, covering her face with her other hand.

"Hey, María," Kerry said into the cell, rubbing Dar's arm with her other hand.

"Oh, Kerrisita!" The secretary sounded overwhelmed. "I thank God everything is all right with you. I have been praying every minute."

"Thanks, María. It's great to know people were concerned about us," Kerry told her. "The great news is, it looks like we're coming back. And let me tell you, I can't wait to get home."

"Are you all right? Is Dar all right?"

"We're fine," Kerry assured her. "A little scratched and dented, but that's it. But I think God was watching over us, so we did just fine." She scratched Dar on the back of her neck and watched as her lover rubbed her face, then straightened, her composure restored. "You don't know how wonderful it is to know how you all were watching out for us too."

"Kerrisita, I know God watches over you and I will be glad when you both are back here, safely and soundly." María exhaled. "Now I can go home and my family will be happy tonight. Mayte was so concerned also."

"Thanks." Kerry smiled. "Tell her I say hello and that she's going to have to help me with typing for a little while."

Dar held hand up and took the phone back. "Thanks, María. Pass along my regards to everyone, will you? We'll see you Monday morning."

"*Sí*, Dar. I will do that. You take good care, yes?"

"I'll do my best. Good night. Have a good weekend." Dar hung up and sat there, staring at the phone for a moment before folding it and putting it down.

Kerry perched on the edge of the desk, running the fingers of her good hand through Dar's hair as her partner gazed at the floor, her head bowed. "You know, I'll never forget the first time María caught me red handed in fussing over you," she remarked, conversationally. "It was after one of those awful marketing meetings, where you'd stormed out and then gone out onto the balcony to cool off."

"Mmph," Dar grunted softly, nodding her head a little.

"I'd gone downstairs for some ice tea and, I don't know, I was just frustrated and pissed off, I think. I went into the shop next to the cafeteria and got you a pint of Haagen Daz and a little stuffed bear before I thought about what I was doing and went back upstairs with it, snuck into your office, and just as I was done setting it on your desk, María walked in."

Dar chuckled softly. "I remember that day."

"I think I could have explained the ice cream." Kerry also chuckled. "I had no idea what to say about the bear," she admitted. "But María just acted like she didn't even see it."

"It was a cute bear," Dar murmured. "And my favorite ice cream."

"When I came out of the office, though, she stopped me and told me how glad she was that I was really part of the team," Kerry went on. "Then she said 'thank you, Kerrisita, for being so considerate of our *jefa*, because she is one of a kind.'"

Dar turned her head and looked up at her.

"And that's so true." Kerry leaned over and kissed her on the forehead. "You're very special."

The pale blue eyes took on a look of gentle adoration that snared Kerry in utterly. "Thanks. I feel the same way about you." She laced her fingers into Kerry's and kissed the back of her hand. They both smiled.

"My turn." Kerry picked up the phone and clumsily keyed in Colleen's number, then pressed the send, just as a knock sounded at the door. "You know, I realized we have a problem," she muttered, as she waited for the line to ring through.

"Hmm?" Dar had gotten up and headed for the door.

"Ice cream's gonna melt."

Dar paused, with her hand on the knob, and turned her head. "Like hell it is."

Chapter
44

"Ms. Stuart, could you move over just a little?"

Kerry obligingly shifted slightly, peering up at the x-ray machine and trying to relax. It was hard, though, since the table was cold and her skin was warm and the machine was making weird little chuckling noises that made her jump.

"Okay, now hold still," the voice called, and she heard a buzzing noise. "Thanks. One more." Another buzz. "Okay." The technician came over and helped her sit up. "There. That's all for me. Now they said you needed to go," she consulted a chart, "to CAT scan next."

"Mmm, yippee." Kerry sighed. "Do I have to? I don't even have a headache now."

"Not for me to decide," the tech told her cheerfully. "I'm just a stop on the way. We can't force you to do anything you don't want to do, but if the doctor thought it was a good idea, it probably is."

"I guess." Kerry fastened her short, hospital issued little tunic thing up, which tied in front and was a vast, vast improvement over the old backless gown number. At least they'd let her keep her jeans on, since her lower body seemed to have taken good care of itself, and her sneakers which kept the cold floor from chilling her toes. "I wonder where my friend is?"

"Let me guess." The tech ticked off her fingers. "Tall, dark hair, built like a brick we won't say what, and with an attitude from hell?"

"Uh."

"Clear blue eyes?"

"That'd be her," Kerry admitted. "Did she give you trouble? She doesn't mean it. She just really hates hospitals and after what happened yesterday, I'm not surprised she didn't want to be messed with." She paused. "I kinda made her get checked out. She's probably really pissed off at me."

"She's more pissed off at the tech who was with her. He made a crack about her working for the WWF."

"World Wildlife Foundation?" Kerry gazed at her, totally bewildered. "What brought that up?"

The tech scratched her chin. "World Wrestling Federation," she muttered. "You know, the..."

"Oh." Kerry muffled a chuckle. "Yeah, I bet she was pissed. She hates that stuff. I can see why he asked, though."

"Mmhm." The tech cleared her throat. "Think she's available?"

Kerry smiled. "Nope." Then she walked out and ran her fingers through her hair to free its ends from her gown as she made her way down the hall towards the prominently labeled CAT scan area. She knew she should have waited for the wheelchair to come take her, but she was anxious to get the tests behind her and go visit Angie.

Then get out of there before she ran into her parents and get back to the hotel, where they had nothing more strenuous planned than an outing with a pay per view movie and a bucket of popcorn. Then tomorrow—a plane trip and by sundown she'd be home.

Home.

"Kerrison."

Shit. Kerry almost didn't stop. Almost didn't turn. But she knew, in her heart, that sometime, someday she'd have to face her father, and maybe—who knew?—maybe she could head off whatever it is he wanted right now. She stopped and turned, but didn't answer. Her father was dressed almost casually for him—pressed slacks and a sweater over his shirt and tie, and this close, she was struck by how much older he looked to her.

"Step inside there." He pointed to a small room, used for consultation. "I'd like a word with you."

Kerry felt her heartbeat double, but she walked inside the chamber, going deliberately behind the desk to put some distance between them. She sat down in the almost comfortable chair there and waited, in guarded silence.

Her father entered and closed the door, then leaned on the desk with both hands and gazed at her.

Kerry forced her own eyes to remain steady, refusing to allow his posture to intimidate her. "If you're thinking about telling me not to see Angie, don't bother." She kept her voice low and controlled, like Dar had taught her. "That's not your choice."

"No, I can see you're far too under her control."

"Who? Dar?" Kerry could have laughed, thinking of her bullying her stubborn lover into getting examined. "You have no idea what you're talking about."

Roger Stuart shook his head. "It's you who's being blind, Kerrison. Can't you see the path she's led you down?"

Kerry studied him for a moment. "Why does it always have to be someone else's fault?"

"What?"

"Why can't you just accept that this is my choice? Dar didn't do anything to me." Kerry straightened. "If that's all you wanted to say, I've got more important things to do."

"How could it be your choice?" her father protested. "You were fine, up until the minute you met that horrible person and then you changed."

"I was never fine."

"What are you talking about?"

Kerry exhaled, too tired, still, to be frightened of him. "I was never fine. I was headed towards a life I had no interest in." She looked up. "Every time I tried to change that, I got punished."

Roger stared at her in bewilderment. "What the hell is that all about? Change what? You had everything any child could have wished for, you ungrateful piece of—"

"Like I said." Kerry stood up. "I've got better things to do than this." She paused. "You never did listen to me before. I don't know why I bothered now."

"Just you hold on a minute—" Her father lifted a hand towards her.

"Don't you even think about it." Kerry's temper flared unexpectedly. "I'm not the little dishrag you tossed around in Michigan. You touch me and I'll hurt you."

Roger drew back. "Is that how you speak to your father?"

"You're not my father," Kerry spat back. "You made that crystal clear."

Slowly, Roger nodded. "All right," he murmured. "So I did."

They stared at each other. "You know, I risked my life and the lives of some of the people I love most in the world to make sure you got out of that building," Kerry said. "So if you think I owe you anything for having brought me up, I don't."

"You owe me an explanation," her father replied. "Why? Why did you abandon and betray your family?"

"Why?" Kerry sat down on the edge of the desk. "Because I was angry." She exhaled. "Because you hit me and held me against my will and you would have had me drugged senseless all because I told you the truth." He opened his mouth, but Kerry held a hand up. "Because it was very satisfying to expose such a hypocrite after I'd spent my whole life trying to live up to your ideals."

Her father wasn't stupid. Kerry could see the thoughts going on right behind those gray eyes. "And here I thought I was working to give you a decent life."

"Your idea."

"Of course, my idea," Roger snapped back. "I raised you, put you through school, gave you every advantage, so you can sit there and call *me* a hypocrite?" He shook his head. "Last year, I made the mistake of believing if you could just be talked to...explained how taking the path you were on was so wrong, you'd just wake up, and realize the truth. I was wrong. There is something very evil in you."

"You're the one who won't realize the truth." Kerry felt nauseous. "You're so sure you're right, you won't even consider how I feel, will you? How I felt when you banished my friends and told me what I could think, or look like. What my limits were."

"It's my right to bring you up properly."

"Or being told my chief value to the family was as breeding stock, because I'm better looking than Angie."

"That's ridiculous. Your mother merely complimented how nice the two of you were together."

Kerry could feel tears rising, but she ignored them. "Or what it was like to be told not to do too good at school so I wouldn't make Michael look bad."

"We were trying to help him excel." Roger looked annoyed. "Surely you wanted to help your brother."

"How it felt when you had my dog poisoned."

Her father stared at her.

"Kerrison."

"How it felt when your bodyguard raped me and you made me apologize to him."

"We're back to that story, are we?"

"Maybe I should have just had my gynecologist call you."

He went silent for a long, tense moment, just watching her.

"I didn't think of it then. I should have," Kerry whispered. "But I was too ashamed to tell her my father didn't believe I was raped."

For a moment, she thought she might have reached him, might have shaken that bullheaded wall of belief. Then his eyes narrowed thoughtfully.

"Is that what this is all about then? This is your reaction to...that? You went off and found this woman?"

A wave of disgust rolled over Kerry. "You're so clueless." She got up. "No." She was curiously relieved though, having said what she had to say. "My falling in love with Dar had nothing to do with Kyle or Brian, or you, for that matter. It was just between the two of us."

"You understand you're going to Hell, if you don't put a stop to this, don't you?"

"I spent twenty-six years in Hell," Kerry answered. "Dar was my ladder out of that and it's been wonderful living in the sunlight." She walked around the desk and put her hand on the door latch. "I spent all that time trying everything I could to make you proud of me and it was never enough. Now the only one I have to worry about making proud is myself." She turned the latch and opened the door, keeping eye contact with him. "And I am."

The door closed behind her and she leaned against the wall for a long, sick moment. Then she pushed off and walked unsteadily towards the first doorway she saw, ducked inside a small waiting room and sat down quickly, trying to control her rebelling stomach.

A nurse found her there. "Oh, there you are, Ms. Stuart. We thought we'd lost you."

Kerry took a deep breath and straightened up. "No...I um," she put a hand over her stomach, "was feeling a little queasy, that's all. Thought I'd better sit down for a minute." She stood up. "Sorry."

"That's okay. I'll walk you down to the CAT scan room. Unless you'd rather have a wheelchair? You look sort of pale." The nurse put hand on her arm, her tone concerned.

"I'm okay." Kerry managed a smile. "Lead on."

"Great." The nurse kept hold of her and eased out of the waiting room. "Listen. Your friend is giving us a little trouble. Maybe you could talk to her and calm her down?"

Like a light switch flipping, Kerry gladly turned her thoughts from one problem to another. "Why? What's wrong?"

"Well, they want to scan her back. The doctor's a little concerned about something he saw on the x-ray, but she's refusing," the nurse explained. "Of course, we can't force her."

"Mmm. They strap you down for that, don't they?"

"Yes, to keep you from moving, for the pictures, but..."

Kerry sighed. "I'll see what I can do." In the state she knew Dar was in, she had her doubts. "Maybe we can compromise?"

Something her father lived with in public life, but would never succumb to in his private one.

❖ ⌘ ❖ ⌘ ❖ ⌘ ❖

"Hi, Angie."

The woman in the bed looked up and her eyes widened. "Ker!"

Kerry slipped around the door frame and entered, tugging her dour and grumpy companion with her. "Boy, it's great to see you." She released Dar's hand, went over to her sister, hugged as much of her one armed as she could reach.

"Same here. Hello, Dar." Angie glanced shyly at her. "I'm glad you're okay."

Dar rested both hands on the bed rail. "Thanks. It's good to see you made out all right as well." She gave her partner's sister a smile, just glad to be finished with a brief sojourn into one of her worst nightmares. Five minutes, she'd finally granted the technicians, and no straps. Five long minutes only made marginally bearable by Kerry's grip on her hand and an iron self control that still hadn't been enough to keep the twitching from starting, as they hastily pulled her out of the machine and got out of her way as she bolted off the table.

She hoped they got what they needed, because there wasn't any second chances at that. She'd calmed herself by talking to Kerry as the blond woman took her turn on the platform, lying quietly as they took pictures of her head and shoulder.

And she felt kind of stupid, really. After all, it's not like the machine hurt, not nearly as much as her back did, at any rate.

"What's wrong with your arm?" Angie asked Kerry. "I'm glad you came now. They're about to bring the baby up."

"Well, I dislocated my shoulder," Kerry explained. "They just took x-rays."

"Ow." Angie made a face. "The labor is mostly a blur—they'd started to take me out and down to delivery, when the explosion happened. We were actually inside the elevator, and I thought I was going to give birth right there I was so scared. But somehow, the power stayed on and we just kept going down and right out the emergency entrance in the back. It was horrible. Everyone was screaming and no one knew what to do. And I was so scared, knowing you guys were all up there."

"It was kinda rough, yeah," Kerry replied quietly. "But we managed to dig ourselves out and get to where they could get us down."

Angie held Kerry's good hand and she rubbed the fingers with her thumb. "You got the folks out."

Kerry and Dar exchanged glances. "Yes, we did," Dar said.

"Mom told me." Angie searched her sister's face. "She's pretty shook up."

"Yeah, well. I had a run in just now with him," Kerry told her. "Maybe that'll be the last one."

"You didn't tell me that," Dar interjected, her brows creasing. "When?"

"You were a little preoccupied." Kerry gave her a faint smile. "It was before I met you in the imaging room."

Dar scowled. "That was more important than the stupid machine."

They turned at a rattle in the door and found a nurse there, holding a neatly wrapped bundle. "Here you go, little man. Say hi to mama."

"A boy?" Kerry asked.

"Yes." Angie took the bundle and cradled it, showing off her new baby. "Isn't he sweet?" The tiny, prune faced infant burped. "I called Richard. He's thrilled." She and Kerry exchanged wry glances. "I tried to call Brian, but there was no answer at his place. I'll try him again in a little while." She glanced at the baby. "Want to hold him before he latches on to the milk bar?"

"Sure." Kerry carefully took the baby and cradled him with her good arm. "Oh, he's adorable." She grinned. "What a cute nose."

Angie smiled. "I think so." She glanced up at Dar. "Were they taking a scan of you, Dar? Is everything okay?"

"Mostly," the dark haired woman answered grudgingly.

"Nothing a little bed rest and chocolate won't cure," Kerry amended. "Poor Dar unfortunately had to drag me around for a while and tore two muscles in her back."

"That's not when it happened."

"Uh huh. Anyway," Kerry shifted the baby and smiled, "the doctor prescribed a couple of days of rest and some painkillers. About the same thing he suggested for me."

"You guys should go off somewhere on a vacation," Angie advised. "Otherwise you'll get all tied up in that stuff you do."

Hmm. Kerry chewed the inside of her lip, then impulsively handed off her wriggling bundle to Dar. "Here. Say hello."

"A...bu—" Dar brought her hands up and took the baby in an instinctive gesture, then stood there staring nervously at him. "Yeah, he's cute. Here." She tried to hand him back, but Kerry made a show of straightening her sling. "Kerry..."

"Just hang on there for a minute." The green eyes blinked innocently at her.

Dar sighed, then brought the baby closer and examined him curiously. Babies weren't her thing, generally, though she had nothing against them. This one was a fairly good size and was kicking inside his covers, probably hungry, she figured. He had a wrinkled face, with tiny, pouty lips and a bitty nose, and his head was covered in a little white hat.

He gurgled. Dar raised an eyebrow, then tentatively touched a clutching hand with one fingertip. The baby grabbed at her with surprising strength, causing the other eyebrow to raise.

Kerry watched in amused fascination. "What did you name him, Angie?"

Her sister sighed. "I haven't yet."

Both Dar and Kerry looked at her in surprise.

"I know, I know. Nine months, you'd figure I'd have a name already." Angie laughed wearily. "To tell the truth, I was really expecting another girl, so I had a bunch of names picked out that wouldn't really suit him." She paused. "What would you name a little boy, if you had one, Dar?"

"Andrew," both women answered together, then chuckled.

"Yeah, you got me there." Dar unbent a little and relaxed, playing idly with the baby's hand. "Dad would pretend not to like that, but he would."

"Your parents seem really nice." Angie smiled. "Your mom really helped me out last night. I hope I get a chance to thank her." She held out her hands as Dar returned her baby to her and she cradled him. "You hungry, little man?" The baby yawned, and smacked his lips. "I guess so, huh?"

"Well, we don't want to hold up dinner." Kerry smiled and rubbed her sister's arm. "We just wanted to stop by and say hello. We're leaving to go home tomorrow."

"Are you?" Angie looked surprised. "Is it over?"

"For now," Dar replied. "Hopefully for good."

Angie glanced at Kerry, whose lips tensed. "I know that was really tough for you to do, Ker. But I'm really proud of you for doing it." The dark haired woman gazed at her newborn son for a moment, then looked back up at her sister. "I'm sorry I went along with them at the hearing. You didn't deserve that."

Kerry's eyes dropped. "Maybe not," she murmured. "But I'm glad everyone got out of that hospital okay. I don't think I could have lived with myself otherwise."

"Kerry, it wasn't your fault." Angie frowned.

"I know." Her sister exhaled wearily. "I know. But it doesn't stop me from feeling the way I do, Angie, because if this whole hearing thing hadn't happened, you'd have been home." She looked up. "I can't escape knowing that."

Dar put a hand on Kerry's shoulder in mute comfort.

"Not to mention how I would have felt if anything happened to you." Kerry turned and met Dar's eyes.

"Well, it didn't," Dar said, simply. "We're all okay, and you've got a cute new nephew."

"Right," Angie agreed quickly. "Everything turned out fine."

Kerry regarded them both for a moment, then smiled. "Yeah," she admitted. "I guess maybe sometimes old fashioned prayer does still work."

Chapter
45

"Don't much see why a new momma needs flow'rs," Andrew muttered to himself. "Think they'd need something more practical, like a truckload of Pampers." He glanced around as he walked, searching for a logical place for them to have put an ex-pregnant woman. Ceci had paused downstairs, intent on picking out a bouquet, and he'd decided to do a little scouting far from the scent of daisies.

He ambled along, ducking his head into the various rooms. "Closet. Head. Papers. Whoops." He jerked his head back out of a waiting room, after spotting a dour figure inside. "He ain't in no mood to be chit chatting, I don't think."

Andy got four or five steps further on when he heard a voice from behind him.

"Commander Roberts?"

"Lord." The ex-SEAL gave the bulletin board a plaintive look. "And just what did I do today to deserve this?" But he turned and went to the doorway, putting one hand on the sill and peering inside. Roger Stuart was now standing, his tie slightly askew, looking back warily at him. "Yeap?"

The two men studied each other, from worlds so vastly different, Andrew doubted they had a single common frame of reference. Stuart was perhaps ten years Andy's senior, educated, sophisticated...

And stupider than the day was long about his damn kid. "D'jou want to cuss me out some more? 'Cause if you did, I've got lots better things fer me to do then listen to you vent hot air."

"No." The other man lifted a hand. "My people looked you up."

Andrew grunted.

"You have quite an amazing record, Commander."

"I just did what Uncle Sam paid me t'do, Senator," the ex-SEAL answered quietly.

Stuart sat down and rested his hands on his knees, not meeting Andrew's eyes. "Well, you did the right thing yesterday. Good job."

One of Andy's dark eyebrows lifted. He moved into the room and took a seat next to the older man. "Wall, you did too," he allowed, graciously. "Ah think everbody done pretty well in that there mess."

There was an awkward silence, but Andrew didn't see any reason to break it.

"I wanted, also, to thank you for stopping and giving us a hand to get out of that room," Roger finally said, clearly embarrassed.

A good SEAL learned to recognize an opportunity and exploit it.

Andrew had, surely, been a very good SEAL, having lived long enough to retire as one. "Hell, don't be thanking me, Senator," he stated. "Kerry wasn't leaving till she found you." He absorbed the quick look from wary gray eyes. "And my kid wasn't going anywhere without her, so..." He shrugged. "Ah just moved rocks."

"Yes, well." Roger made the words sound distasteful. "I'm sure she felt she had an obligation."

Andrew let out a breath. "Makes me feel real comfortable knowing someone like you's up making laws, when you don't even know squat about your own kid."

"Commander—" Roger replied stiffly.

"Don't you commander me, ya twenty watt bulb." Andrew snorted. "What in the hell's wrong with you, anyhow? You been wearing a necktie so damn long it cut off the flow of blood to yer brain or something?"

"All right. That's enough, mister. Or I'll—"

"Or you all will do what?" Andrew snorted. "Slap me around like you done to her? You will not like the results, ah can tell you that."

"I didn't—"

Andrew stood up. "Senator, you will not sit there and tell me you did not take hold of Kerry and put her up somewhere," he told the other man sternly. "Because even if she were the storytelling kind, which she ain't, mah kid surely is not and she told the same tale." He paused. "And Dar would not lie to me."

Roger Stuart also stood, paced to the wall and slapped it in frustration. "Goddamn it, I was just trying to make her see reason." He turned and put his hands on his hips. "It's my right as a father to bring my children up as I see fit and I don't care what anyone, including you, thinks of that."

"By locking her up?" Andrew asked, incredulously.

"By putting her somewhere people could talk to her and give her guidance and whatever help she needed to get...to get over this...this," the senator swallowed bile, "perversion."

Andy's eyebrows contracted and he put both hands on his hips. "'Cause she's in love with my daughter? Is that what you call that?" His voice dropped warningly.

A visible shudder went through the older man's body. "How in the hell can you just sit there and say that and not throw up?" he asked. "You're married. You're in the military. You're not some whacked out whiney assed liberal."

Andy sat down and crossed one ankle over his knee. "Wall," he scratched an ear, "ah can tell you, Senator, ah ain't never had feelings for any other male type individuals."

Stuart snorted.

"But being as ah spent thirty some years in the Navy, it ain't exactly a foreign notion to me," he continued dryly. "I got to tell you that 'don't ask, don't tell' notion you all came up with weren't a bad idea. 'Cause if they all told, you all'd roll right up outta Capital Hill and bounce yer asses into the Potomac."

Stuart just stared at him.

"Look." Andrew sighed. "Mah family came from Alabama. Mah daddy was one of the hatingist bastards ah ever did meet and ah got two brothers who got sent to prison fer beating half to death a young feller who didn't do nothing but be born a different color than they were."

The senator shifted uncomfortably. "Well, certainly that was the wrong thing to do but—"

"No buts, Senator. It ain't right to teach a child to hate. No matter what the cause."

The gray eyes were pinned on him intently.

"Ah grew up hearing how what we was made us better than what everybody else was, and believe you me, when ah chose to marry outside what we were, it was not a pretty sight." Andrew paused, reflecting quietly. "What her folks done and what mah folks done, hurt both of us." He shook his head.

"I don't," Roger hesitated. "It's not the same thing."

"Ain't it?" Andrew asked.

"The Bible says it isn't," he replied stiffly.

"That there book was written by folks just as mixed up as you and me, Senator." Cool, blue eyes regarded him. "At any rate, ah looked at what damage all that hating had done to us and I figgured out with myself, that if ah ever had kids, ah would not do to them what mah folks did to me." He took a breath. "Ah told myself, that no matter what them kids turned out like, if they was mean, or ugly, or stupid as a rock, I'd still hold 'em, and love 'em, and bring 'em up as best as I was able to."

Stony silence.

"Wall, sir, I got lucky in the ugly and dumb departments." Andrew lifted his head proudly. "Cause mah kid ain't neither of those things." He nodded slightly. "She's real smart, and real pretty, and she was damn lucky enough to find somebody out there in the world who'll love her the same way I love her mama."

"That's disgusting."

"It is not," Andrew shot back. "It is not, Senator, and if you'd spend just an hour with the two of them and not think that, you'd know it too."

"Never." Stuart shook his head in disgust and waved a hand.

"Your loss." Andrew shrugged and stood up. "'Cause your daughter is a damn fine human being, Senator, and I am glad the Lord let me live long enough to know her." He was getting mad and that wasn't a good thing. Punching elected officials only got a man into more trouble than it was worth.

Stuart snorted. "Until she can find a way to betray you. Have fun."

Andrew turned and pointed. "Don't you blame her fer that." He shook his head. "Be a man, fer once, and take the responsibility fer what you get yerself into. Kerry didn't force you into none of that, Senator, and it's a sign of her goodness that she's able to see past her love fer you and do the right thing."

And then he escaped into the hallway just in time to meet his wife getting off the elevator with a large arrangement. "Good Lord." Andrew took it from her. "Thought you were getting flowers."

"I thought fruit and snacks would be more useful," Ceci told him amiably. "Where have you been? Making trouble?"

Andrew glanced at her innocently from between two stalks of celery. "Hardly had time to do that," he blinked, "much."

"Oh boy," Ceci muttered.

❖ ⌘ ❖ ⌘ ❖ ⌘ ❖

"Oh my god." Kerry trudged into the hotel room and over to the bed, fell face first down on top of it, then yelped, and rolled onto her side. "Oh, that was stupid."

"Yes, it was." Dar chuckled and eased down next to her, with an expressive sigh. "Damn, I'm tired," she remarked. "I'm glad we went, though."

Kerry smiled slightly. "My sister and brother really like your folks," she commented. "And Dad was so cute with the baby. He's such a mush-ball."

Dar rolled over onto her belly and rested her chin on her arm. "Yeah, he was, wasn't he? I can remember him playing with me when I was really little. I wasn't sure which one of us had more fun."

A little silence fell. "Wow." Kerry sighed. "Long day."

"Mmm," Dar agreed. "Oh, we're booked on the one p.m. flight back to Miami tomorrow. All four of us." She started to roll over onto her side, then paused as her injured muscles cramped. "Oh, yeowch."

"Yeah." Kerry shifted her sling. "Hey, Dar?" Her brows contracted.

"You know, the press is going to go nuts over this thing for a while. Maybe it's better if we lie low for a few days."

"Hmm?" A thoughtful eyebrow lifted. "Yeah, maybe." Dar reached around and probed her back gently. "You know, come to think of it, sitting in an office chair is gonna be damn uncomfortable for a while." She considered the problem and the germ of an idea that had occurred to her in Angie's hospital room suddenly sprouted.

Kerry wiggled her fingers. "So's typing," she reminded her boss. "We could work from home, though."

"We could," Dar agreed. "But we're not going to."

"We're not?"

Dar cautiously eased off the bed and trudged over to the laptop on the desk, sat down at it and rattled the keys for approximately five minutes straight while Kerry lay and watched her. "There," she hit a final key, then sat back, "we're on vacation."

Kerry's ears perked up visibly. "We are?"

Dar nodded and allowed a tired smile to cross her face. "I promised you a trip to Key West."

"Dar, we can't both just go on vacation like this." The blond woman smiled. "Not that I don't want to."

"We can," Dar disagreed. "We are. I just told Alastair and Maríana. If they don't like it, too damn bad." She got up, went to the bed, sat down, and reached a hand out. "You, me, and Chino in a bungalow on the beach for a week. It's a done deal."

Kerry clasped her fingers with her own. "Sounds wonderful but...you had those meetings this week, Dar...and the new network. I know how important that is to you."

"It's not." Dar's voice was quiet and soft. "It doesn't mean a thing to me, not anymore."

Kerry fell silent. It occurred to her that Dar was being completely truthful at the moment, as she studied the pale blue eyes, shadowed with the strain of the last few days. *Maybe some time off wasn't a bad idea.* "Okay," she agreed. *What was the worst they could do? Fire them?* Well, she'd never been fired before. It would be a new experience in that case. "I'd really like to spend time with you. We haven't ever really been able to for more than a day or so without work or some other disaster happening."

Dar looked pleased. "Good." Her face creased into an unexpected smile. "I'd really like that, too. It's been a while since I took some time off."

"Skiing, wasn't it?" Kerry prodded her memory. "You getting up and personal with nature, if I'm not mistaken."

"You remembered that?"

"Mmm. I thought it was really interesting. Most people would have lied and said they skied the black diamond slopes," Kerry replied. "Not you. I remember being impressed at how secure you were with yourself."

Dar slowly let herself lie down and stretched her legs out on the bed. "I never thought of it like that," she admitted. "I was just praying you weren't going to ask me when, precisely, that skiing trip was."

Kerry cocked her head. "When was it?" she asked, predictably.

"My senior year in high school."

The blond woman's hand dropped to the bed and she stared. "Are you telling me you haven't had a vacation since high school?"

Dar nodded sheepishly. "The last time Maríana checked I had enough rolled over time built up to take off an entire year."

"B—" Kerry rubbed her face. "But what about that place in North Carolina? You spent time there."

"Weekends." Dar shrugged.

"Good Lord, Paladar A. Roberts." Kerry shook her head. "Damn right we're taking next week off. I may kidnap you and keep you down there for a month."

Dar grinned happily. "Promise?"

This was a new Dar. Kerry smiled back at her and interlaced their fingers. "Promise." It would be nice, actually, and she could take the time to let her arm heal, before she had to come back and deal with the usual stuff...

Yeah.

Kerry slowly rolled over and got up. "Key West, huh?" She exhaled and started unbuttoning her shirt one handed. "I think I'm going to like this." Fingers took over from hers and she used that hand to explore the soft, warm skin now inches away. Dar had bruises all over her and little scrapes, tiny dark lines against her tan that rubbed rough against Kerry's fingertips. "You smell nice," she commented idly, reflecting that being her height wasn't a bad thing when it got you the view it got her when Dar was naked.

"Thank you," the taller woman rumbled. "It's that scrub stuff you got from the Internet. I kinda like it."

"Mmm." Kerry got her nose closer, then took an experimental lick. "Smells different on you than on me." She nibbled further.

Dar chuckled unexpectedly. "We're dif...ah...that tickles."

"Really?" Kerry repeated the experiment, feeling Dar's ribcage contract sharply under her other hand as she laughed again. "Hmm..."

"Kerry." Dar unhooked the sling holding up her arm and carefully lowered it. "Easy." She slid the device off, then removed the blond woman's long sleeve cotton shirt. "What have we here?" She plucked something off Kerry's bra strap and held it up before her eyes. "Two timing on me, hmm?"

Kerry focused her vision on the tiny item. "Just like in the movies.

You find a blond hair on my underthings too short to be mine." She sighed. "My cover's blown. I'm having an affair with our dog."

They started giggling, the long days tension dissolving in absurdity.

"Lemme guess. It's the tail, right?" Dar replied.

"Nah, that six inch long to—"

"Hey, girls?"

The inner door started to swing open and Kerry's eyes almost turned the size of baseballs. "Oh shit!"

Dar kicked her brain into gear and quickly wrapped her arms around Kerry, neatly covering both of them as her father poked his head in. "Hi, Dad."

"Hey list—" Andrew's face turned an odd shade of coral. "Good Lord, ah beg your pardon."

"No problem, Dad," Dar reassured him, bolstered by years of board-room experience in poker faces. "I was just helping Kerry get undressed."

Andrew scratched his jaw. "Done a right professional job at it, looks like."

Kerry laughed, her breath tickling Dar right between the breasts.

"I always try to do things right." Dar managed to keep a straight face. "Did you need something?"

Andrew found something interesting on the opposite wall to exam-ine. "We were gonna order us up some ice cream. Thought you might be interested."

"Sure." Dar smiled. "Great nightcap."

"With lots of syrup." Kerry's muffled voice rose up from the depths.

"All right," Andrew agreed seriously.

"And cherries." Another half heard request.

"You can have mine," Dar remarked dryly. "Make sure there's nuts, though."

"Now. Ah'd have thought them would be—oh. You mean the eat'n kind," her father drawled back. "All right."

"Dad!" Kerry squealed, turning her head and peeking at him.

Andrew gave her a rakish grin and disappeared.

"I can't believe he said that," Kerry spluttered.

"Why?" Dar released her and continued removing her clothing. "He knows the difference between boys and girls, Ker. And despite rumors to the contrary he knows I don't have anf...ffof." She peered at her friend over a hand clamped firmly across her mouth.

"Thank you so much for the biology lesson," Kerry muttered. "I'm just not really used to parents making comments like that. Mine never did." She paused. "It would have been like the statue of George Washing-ton cracking an X-rated joke."

Dar nibbled Kerry's palm, exploring the soft skin, which shifted and was removed. "You know what they always said about George, right?" she

teased, then inclined her head and found Kerry's lips about to make a protest. Then she circled Kerry with her arms again and drew her closer as
they kissed, reveling in the solid reality she'd almost lost the day before.
One hand slid up and cupped Kerry's neck, her fingers tangling in the pale
hair as she allowed the intensity to build, blocking out everything but the
emotion of the moment.

They paused to breathe and swayed together, moving to inaudible
music they both heard, eyes locked, souls bound.

Finally Kerry smiled. "Guess I'd better get my jammies on before
the ice cream gets here," she commented, still almost lost in Dar's gaze.

"Yeah," Dar agreed amiably, not moving an inch.

A silence fell again for a while.

"We're going to really embarrass Dad if he comes back in here."

"Yeah." Dar sighed. "I'll have to start teaching him all the 'how
many lesbians does it take to change a light bulb' jokes." But she finally
shifted, and unhooked Kerry's bra, then retrieved both of their sleeping
outfits from the suitcase.

Kerry settled on the bed in her Tweety shirt and cradled her arm.
"So," she watched Dar as she folded everything and put it away, "how
many does it take?"

"What?"

"Lesbians. To change a light bulb?"

"Well." Dar came over to the bed and laying on her side carefully,
stretching long, mostly bare legs out. "There's the two with the wood—"

"Wood?"

"They have to build the ladder first."

"Why?"

"Power tools. Anyway, the two with the wood, then four to plan the
strategy—"

"Four?"

"Yeah. A representative sample—one butch, one fem, and two that
self identify as androgynous."

Kerry giggled.

"Then you need six more to research where to buy the bulb—"

"Six?"

"Gotta make sure those dyke dollars go to supportive stores, hon,"
Dar drawled. "And we can't forget the dozen academics to analyze the
process, and determine if changing a bulb could be considered the subject
of a 'Changing Role Relationships in the American Workplace' seminar."

Kerry giggled harder. "And that's how you'd change a bulb?" she
asked, skeptically.

"Nah." Dar shook her head, as she heard sounds in the next room.
"I'd hire someone else to do it." She leaned over and stole another kiss. "I
hate stereotypes."

Chapter
46

"You about packed?" Kerry came out to find Dar busy at her laptop. "Dar?"

"Mmm?" Dar looked up. "Oh, yeah, almost." She nodded.

A knock rattled on the door in a familiar rhythm. "That's Dad." Dar chuckled, going over and opening the door, and stepping back to allow her parents to enter. "Just about ready to leave?"

Andy carried both their bags and now he ambled over and took possession of Dar and Kerry's as well.

"Hey!" Dar put her hands on her hips. "I'm capable of carrying a couple of bags."

"Don't bother." Her mother waved her off. "I've tried that. He's just in a feisty mood today or something."

Dar shook her head and finished packing up her computer. "Fine, fine. Let's just get the hell out of here. I hear a conch fritter calling my name."

"Wait." Kerry smiled, pulling out her camera. "I want a picture." She waved them together. "C'mon." She waited for Andrew to shed his burden, then join his wife and daughter in front of the window. Light poured in the other side of the room, and Kerry smiled as she focused her shot, shifting the lens slightly to frame her subjects. Andrew had taken the center and put an arm around the women on either side of him. Ceci, of course, was almost dwarfed by his height, but she leaned against him with a warm sense of familiarity. Dar had amiably wrapped her arm around her father's back and looked at the camera with her usual air of wry self deprecation. "Perfect." She snapped the shot, then lowered the camera. "Thanks." She grinned at Ceci.

"Just you wait until you see what I have I mind for revenge," the older woman warned, smiling back. They gathered their things, slipped out the door, and managed to achieve the freight elevator without much trouble. They got to the bottom floor and were about the leave, when Dar heard her name called. "Damn." She turned. "Yes, Hamilton?"

The tall, urbane lawyer caught them up, and ushered them into a small antechamber, out of sight of the press. "Where do you all think you are going?"

"Home," Dar replied. "Why?"

"Not yet you can't," Hamilton told her blithely. "This afternoon you have to be here so the mayor, bless his heart, can give you both a pair of shiny little old medals." He waggled two fingers at Dar and Andy. "Now Dar, don't give me a hard time with this, it's great PR for the company and ah've got two choice interviews set up, not long ones, with some very top news personalities."

"Son of a bitch," Dar reacted.

"Now, now. Flattery will get you nowhere, Paladar," Hamilton informed her. "Just sit your butt down and make us look good, and it'll be over sooner than you think." He patted her shoulder. "Ah've been work-ing real hard to get us some very positive press and have painted you as just below an archangel, so don't mess my garden up, hear?"

"Hamilton, I am going to kill you," Dar told him, seriously. "I have tickets on the one p.m. flight out of here."

"Phone call will take care of that for you, so just you relax." The lawyer chuckled. "C'mon now. How often do you get to get up on TV and get a medal pinned on you?" He glanced at his watch. "Let's duck into the Batmobile. We've got an hour or two before the first TV spot. Wait here. I'll find a good way out." He ducked out the door, leaving them staring at each other.

"I am not going to stand here for—" Dar started in, her voice rising, as Kerry put a hand on her arm.

"Dar," Andrew spoke very quietly, making his daughter fall silent, "ah have a box of medals for killing folks. Ah think I'd like just one for saving 'em."

You could have heard a pin drop easily in the silence that followed, Kerry mused, *just like that old cliché.*

"Okay," Dar replied in a subdued voice. She walked over to a bench near the door and sat down to wait, letting her briefcase rest on the floor. Ceci walked over and sat down next to her, but didn't speak. Kerry just stood next to Andrew, cradling her arm, unable to come up with a thing to say.

❖ ⌘ ❖ ⌘ ❖ ⌘ ❖

Dar squinted, shading her eyes as the bright lights invaded what Hamilton had insisted on dubbing the Batmobile. Technicians bustled around, moving cables and arranging cameras, and the interviewer was off to one side, going over some notes with two assistants. It was cramped inside the bus, but it was private, and the news people appreciated the closed environment and ready access to phones, power, and a fax machine.

Kerry was curled up in one of the leather chairs nearby just watching and Dar's parents had taken over the long couch, also reviewing the chaos with interested eyes as though it had been arranged for their benefit.

Hamilton had wanted Dar to dress up, but she had put her foot down, refusing to force her still tired and aching body into a wool skirt and blazer, not to mention heels. She stubbornly insisted on her faded jeans and sneakers and had grudgingly agreed to wear her gunmetal gray jacket over her plain white T-shirt as her only concession.

A makeup person approached, carrying a case. Dar glared at her until she slowed down, pausing hesitantly outside her reach and giving her an overly bright smile. "Hi." The woman was of middling height and athletic build, with wavy blond hair not very different from Kerry's.

Dar strategically lifted an eyebrow. "Got a problem?"

"Well, I thought you might like some powder...or...something...eye shadow?"

"No thanks," Dar replied. "I'm allergic."

"Oh." The makeup woman smiled easily. "It's hypoallergenic. It's safe, really. I mean, you don't need any blush or anything, maybe just a little color...fluff your hair?"

Dar's nostrils twitched and she rotated an eyeball over to where Kerry was biting her knuckle to keep from laughing. "Can you make my hair look like hers?" She indicated her lover's wavy locks.

"Um, no. I don't think so." The woman eyed Kerry apologetically.

"Then forget it." Dar settled back, sipping her root beer. "I'm just fine as is, thanks." She glanced up as the interviewer came over and settled down in the chair next to her.

Cheryl Abramson was tall, almost as tall as Dar herself, and slender, with exotic, high cheekbones and rich chestnut hair. She had a tiny spattering of freckles and intense hazel eyes, which she turned on Dar along with a dazzling smile. She wore a meticulously tailored navy blue suit, with a pale blue silk shirt, and the effect was clean and sophisticated and quite attractive.

"Ms. Roberts? Let's go over a few things before we start." Abramson spoke in a low, melodious voice. "I have most of the details I need on you, but I want to just check a few things."

Dar leaned on the chair arm and sucked at her straw. "Sure." She deliberately injected a touch of the South into her speech. "What would you like to know?" The other woman glanced up at her and unconsciously straightened, a hand going up to touch her hair in an instinctive gesture

Dar well understood. *Interesting.*

"Well, we've got your professional details—ILS provided them to us. You've been with them for fifteen years?" Her voice lifted in question and she peered over her papers at Dar's youthful appearance.

"That's right." Dar didn't see any reason to relieve her confusion.

"Okay." Abramson went back to her checklist. "You've been the CIO of the company for...six months? And before that you were the VP of Operations for three years, is that right?"

"Yep," Dar agreed readily.

"Right. You normally work in Miami, correct?"

Dar nodded.

"And you were in Washington for..." She looked up in question.

Why indeed? Kerry and Dar had discussed what they were going to tell the press, who had been sniffing interestedly around Kerry as well, and now Dar stretched her legs out, crossing them at the ankles before she answered. "My co-worker, and friend, Ms. Stuart, was called to testify in her father's hearings. I was just here for moral support." *Strict, absolute truth.*

Abramson glanced at Kerry who had slumped in her chair, curling a leg over one arm of it and dozing off. "I see." She scribbled a note. "You're headed back to Miami now, I take it, after the ceremony?"

Dar nodded.

"Okay." Cheryl scribbled more notes. "Let me make sure I've got this down. You arrived. You were involved in the ATM shutdown, you were interviewed by one of my colleagues, you went to the hospital to visit Ms. Stuart's sister, the explosion happened, you dug out some survivors, you directed the escape and rescue of the people you found, then you got out...are those the high points of your week?" Her tone was dryly humorous.

"Essentially." Dar chuckled, finding herself liking the woman. "We were hoping for a short investigation, a few days sightseeing, and maybe a tour of the White House, but you take what you can get." Her face relaxed into an easy grin.

Cheryl looked up and met her eyes, then went back to her writing, the edges of her own lips twitching a little. "Do you have any idea who did it?"

"No," Dar answered. "I leave that to the police."

"Do you think the senator was the target?"

Dar shook her head. "Again, that's not something I want to speculate on."

"Okay." Abramson nodded at the cameraman. "We're ready. Do you have a good angle?" She shifted in her chair and motioned the makeup woman over, checking herself in the hastily provided hand held mirror. The makeup woman took out a rotary brush and carefully fluffed the anchorwoman's bangs, then backed off to study her work. "You want highlighter?"

Cheryl peered at her reflection, then took a sideways glance at Dar, who ran her fingers through her dark locks, settling them in sort of an order, before she folded her hands over her stomach in a waiting attitude. "No. I'll be fine." She nudged the makeup woman out of the way and carefully arranged herself, posing with her pad in Interviewer Position A. "Ready?"

Dar cocked her head. "Whenever you are."

❖ ⌘ ❖ ⌘ ❖ ⌘ ❖

"Well, Dar, I have to admit, you do one hell of an interview," Hamilton complimented. "You were made for the camera. Now, just one more little jaunt up on to that stage out there and you can get on your little plane and make tracks for the Sunshine State."

"Great." Dar exhaled, wishing she had half a bottle of aspirin at her fingertips. "Dad, you ready?"

"Dar, do you think you could put on a collared shirt? You look like a beach bum," Hamilton complained.

"No." Blue eyes pierced him. "One more comment like that and I'll pick up the damn thing in my sports bra."

The lawyer tapped a long finger against his teeth. "Hmm. Be good, Hamilton, be good."

Andrew walked over and laid a hand on his daughter's shoulder. "Ah think she looks just fine," he said. "Leave her be."

"Or?" Hamilton inquired archly. "I have to know what the consequences are of giving up my favorite entertainment."

Andrew blinked at him. "Or I will take hold of them parts that makes you a man and pull them up out your eardrums," he rasped seriously.

Dar watched Hamilton's face with interest, knowing the level of unflappability the corporate legal chief possessed. Certainly, she'd never been able to put a dent in it. Hamilton eyed the taller, burlier Andrew, then shifted his eyes to Dar.

"You know, Dar. I always knew I'd find something to redeem you in my eyes. I just never expected it to be that you had a proper Southern daddy." He inclined his head towards Andy. "My pardon, sir. I'll leave her be." He wandered over to the bar and poured himself a drink, chuckling under his breath.

Dar paced across to the window of the bus, leaned her arms on the wall and tried to stretch her tense back out. The long interview with charming Cheryl had made her stiffen up and she just wanted to get the ceremony over and leave. Kerry was curled up in a corner of the couch, the painkillers she'd been taking for her shoulder making her very sleepy, and Ceci had settled her coat over the blond woman's shoulders and was seated next to her, sketching.

Dar stared out at the gathering crowd, watching the various technicians preparing the platform, putting cameras in place, and setting up microphones. She felt a warm hand on her back and turned to see her father peering over her shoulder.

"You all right, Dardar?"

Dar rubbed her eyes and exhaled. "Got any aspirin?"

"Yeap." Andrew fished in the small pouch he wore around his waist and removed a bottle. "Gave me this stuff at the hospital, after I got back. Take care of any kind of headache you can come up with, I'll tell you that."

Dar accepted the tablets gratefully, walked over to the bar and poured a glass of water, then swallowed the small pills. "Thanks." She glanced enviously at Kerry's dozing form. "How much longer?"

"An hour, Dar." Hamilton shrugged into his impeccably cut jacket. "I'm going to go romance the press. I'll send a runner over when they're ready." He ducked out the door and closed it behind him, leaving them in relative peace and quiet. Ceci got up and moved to a different seat, tucking one leg under her as she resettled her pad. She caught Dar's eye, then motioned towards the couch, smiling when her daughter didn't argue and took the place she'd been sitting in and trying to relax.

Kerry must have sensed her presence, Dar mused, because the blond woman stirred, reached out a hand and touched Dar, then reversed her position and curled up with her head in Dar's lap and one arm tucked around her lover's thigh.

"Aww." Andrew chuckled.

Dar draped an arm over Kerry's body and stretched her legs out, then let her head rest on the back of the couch. The pills seemed to be working, she idly mused, as the cramping in her back eased and the throbbing ache in her head subsided. She closed her eyes and breathed a sigh of relief.

The bus was silent for a few minutes then Dar's mother peeked over her sketch pad and shook her head. "Out like a light." Ceci laughed softly. "What did you give her?"

Andrew juggled the small bottle, then tossed it to her. "Don't know, but they put me out, so I figgured they'd work on her too."

Cecilia reviewed the label. "Muscle relaxant and painkiller." She looked up at her husband. "Hope they wear off before the ceremony or you'll be up there by yourself, sailor boy."

Andrew ambled over and sat down next to her, laced his fingers together and cocked his head at her drawing. "Kid was stiffer than a board. I figured a catnap was a good idea. What is that?"

Ceci tilted the pad. "It's that platform outside."

Andy grunted. "It's empty."

His wife smiled. "It won't be for long."

❖ ⌘ ❖ ⌘ ❖ ⌘ ❖

The wind had died down, and the late afternoon sun had come out in full force, warmly lighting the platform now decorated with red, white, and blue bunting. Staff had set chairs in place as well, and dignitaries were gathered, networking together and sharing cups of distilled water while the television crews warmed up their equipment.

At last, it was time and everyone took their seats. Kerry tucked her feet under her in the somewhat uncomfortable chair in the front row of the audience and fastened her eyes on the two figures at one end of the platform's plusher chairs.

Andrew was seated with military erectness, even though he was dressed in dark blue denims and one of his hooded sweatshirts instead of a uniform. His hands were folded in his lap and he faced forward, but his eyes flicked everywhere, watching the crowd, the dignitaries, and the security officers.

Dar looked... Kerry sighed. *Her beloved friend looked like she'd just woken up, a fair statement since she practically had, and her eyes had a faintly dazed look about them as she peered around idly.* "I think Dar's toast."

"Mmm," Ceci agreed wryly. "I told Andy he shouldn't have given her two of those pills. He takes them, but he forgets he's twice her size." She sighed. "Poor kid."

"Well," Kerry analyzed, "at least she's not nervous." She casually turned her head and reviewed the crowd, unsurprised, but disappointed not to see her family there.

The television crew gave a signal and the mayor stepped up to the microphone and cleared his throat self-importantly. "Ladies and gentlemen, thank you for joining me here on the Mall for a celebration of gratitude to people, ordinary people, who risked their lives to save the lives of their fellow men."

The crowd applauded wildly.

He thanked the police next, and the firefighters, and gave out a plaque to the fire company who had rescued them from the building. Kerry smiled at that, glad to see they'd gotten some recognition. Then the mayor made a long, somewhat boring speech about how terrorists only succeeded when they inspired terror.

"Duh," Ceci and Kerry managed to say at the same time.

And that the city would never bow to that kind of pressure, being the capital of the land of the brave, and all that patriotic stuff. Kerry, having heard political speeches all her life, tuned most of it out. She knew the mayor was up for re-election this year and most of the speech was directed more towards raising his polls than celebrating heroes.

At last, it was over, and he cleared his throat, carefully arranging two velvet cases resting on the podium.

Ceci nudged Kerry, spotting a familiar figure making his way towards the mayor. "Hey."

Kerry was very surprised to see her father there. "What on earth is he doing?"

Roger Stuart arrived next to the mayor and straightened his jacket with a smooth motion. The mayor turned and gave him a welcoming smile.

"Senator Stuart has asked, since his was one of the lives affected by the rescue, that he be allowed to present the medals. I am honored to turn the podium over to him."

"What?" Kerry blurted, almost falling off her chair.

"Shh. Take it easy," Ceci whispered, as her husband and daughter exchanged identical, startled looks.

Roger Stuart placed his hands on either side of the podium and acknowledged the applause. "Thank you." He had a low, powerful voice. "It has been a hard, anxious week for us all."

Applause.

"But through it, strangers and friends, family and adversaries, have come together to save lives, and push past the normal, everyday disagreements to work together in what was, without doubt, a horrible tragedy."

"I can't believe he's doing this," Kerry muttered.

"When my wife and I were trapped inside that building, we thought our lives were at an end. Instead, through the courage of the two people we're here to honor today, our lives were saved, along with those of seven helpless children and many others."

"I think Dar's going to lose her lunch," Ceci commented. "I seem to remember that particular look on her face."

"Oh yeah," Kerry agreed. "Hope she waits till she's up there to do that." Her voice took on an edge of anger. "I can't believe he's cheapening this just for his own publicity."

"Kerry," Cecilia watched her husband and daughter stand when Stuart called their names, "maybe this is the only way he has of saying thank you, without having to say it."

Andrew and Dar walked quietly across the platform, their steps slightly hollow on the wooden boards. Dar was a half step behind her father and she stood, her hands braced behind her back in a very military, but very unconscious pose as the gleaming, golden medal was lifted up and settled over Andrew's close cropped head.

"Good job." Roger Stuart held a hand out, his eyes meeting Andy's. "Thank you, Commander."

"You're welcome, Senator," Andrew replied in a quiet voice. Then he stepped back and glanced to his right, where Dar was waiting.

Stuart was very lucky, Dar considered, that the drugs still in her system put a slightly hazy barrier between herself and her instinct to kick him in the groin. Right there on national TV.

"Ms. Roberts?" Stuart opened the second case and removed the medal. Dar forced herself forward, aware of the camera eyes leering at her greedily, and stood absolutely still as his hands came close to her, lifting above either side of her face to settle the ribbon over her neck.

For a bare instant, their eyes met.

"Good job," the senator stated flatly. Then his gaze wavered. "Thank you, Dar."

She was too shocked to even raise an eyebrow.

"And thank you for being such a good friend to my daughter, as well," the senator finished, as though it were the most natural thing in the world, there on television, and in front of a thousand watchers, as his words echoed softly over the grass.

Into the tense silence, Dar said, "You're welcome."

The crowd applauded and stood and cheered. Roger Stuart nodded briskly, lifting a hand and waving it as he turned and walked off the platform.

Andrew retreated in the other direction, holding Dar by the elbow as they headed towards the steps leading down, to a crowd already clustering and press calling questions. "Son of a biscuit," he uttered under his breath.

Dar merely exhaled.

Chapter
47

The boardroom was quiet as Alastair froze the image on the screen of Dar gracefully ducking her head to receive her medal. He turned in his chair and folded his hands, gazing amiably down the table at the six men seated around it. "Well now, gentlemen. I believe the next item on the agenda was a request from Mr. Ankow regarding dismissing our Ms. Roberts there."

Ankow gave him a disgusted look. "Don't think that bullshit changes anything, McLean."

"Doesn't it?" Alastair asked mildly, gazing down the table and judging the temper of its occupants. Instead of the hot anger of the previous days, there was now more bemusement looking back at him. "Well, I don't know, David. I might find it a little hard to explain to the press, much less the stockholders, why I'd do something as stupid as let go someone who is as obviously valuable as Ms. Roberts. You want to give it a try?"

"That doesn't change what she is. Or what's going on between her and that Stuart woman." Ankow stood and pointed.

"David, siddown," Evans muttered.

"What?"

"Siddown," the financial magnate said more forcefully. "Much as I hate to admit this," he looked at Alastair, "and I do hate it, I want you to know that, Alastair. I think the fact that you let this go on is reprehensible."

The CEO shrugged one shoulder.

"But to do something now would be stock market suicide," Evans continued. "And I think we all know that."

Alastair nodded gravely. "Very true. The press office tells me they've gotten a ton of requests for interviews with Dar and everyone wants details. Now, I can happily go on the record about her achievements here at the company." He paused. "And they've been very extensive."

Ankow slapped the table in disgust.

"Well, honestly, David. They have," Alastair protested. "I'm not making it all up, y'know. It's in her files. Read them for yourself."

"We have. It's the reason we're all sitting here, instead of out with the stockholders demanding a vote on ousting you," Evans told the CEO with startling honesty. "You think I want to look like an asshole when I have to explain why I want a top ranked employee with a commendation list the length of my arm tossed out? Just because she's gay?"

"Just?" Ankow taunted. "I can see the backpedaling now, Evans. You're a gutless coward."

"No, just a realistic one." The financier turned on him. "I don't need the boycotts and the bad press. Maybe someone like you, who already has a White Knight skeleton in his closet doesn't care about that, but I do."

Ankow's eyes narrowed. "Bastard."

"And having it made public you were working for Stuart's father...well, there's no way we can make that look good, David," Alastair mentioned. "I can see public sympathy being with Kerry, after all, she's just stood up to the man, then we find out he was undermining her at work, as well as having had her thrown in the hospital. It's just bad press."

"Yeah? How's the press going to respond to knowing ILS found that information out about Stuart's father?" Ankow countered, but his confidence was slipping and it showed.

Another shrug. "Well, really, it was our duty to disclose the information if it came to our knowledge," Alastair remarked. "If you want to look at it that way. We provided a public service."

"Oh, bullshit."

"Y'know," Yves Gallreus, heretofore completely silent, now spoke up, "it occurs to me we come out of this quite golden, Alastair. Now that the hearing has been pushed back, our reputation for fairness, for good works, for innovation. It is very striking."

"Yes, it is," Alastair agreed gravely, with a tiny twinkle in his eye.

"You really believe that?" Ankow stood up again.

"But of course." Yves shrugged. "It is always you are thinking about sex here in America. Quite extraordinary, you know? But look, we have provided a good service in the ATM crisis, our new network is much praised, and our employee is accepting medals for bravery on the television. I am not surprised if our stock does not double before the end of the week. So please, why are we sitting here?"

They all looked at him. The Frenchman lifted both hands, assuming a mild expression.

"So you don't care that this dyke is running your company?"

Ankow's face was red. "Or that she's sleeping with her assistant?"

"Not at all," Yves replied. "Just so long as she provides me with stock splits, why should I give a care to her sexual exploits? Is she perhaps to make a movie of them, to sell at the next stockholder meeting? It would certainly make it more exciting, no?" He glanced down the table. "Alastair, I am so sorry I missed the last meeting. It seems I would have been much amused by it."

"So am I, Yves." Alastair appreciated the Continental viewpoint very much. "Well, gentlemen, I think we're finished here, unless someone else has further points to raise. Do we want to take a vote on the last motion?"

Silence answered him. "Very well then." Alastair folded his hands with a satisfied look. "David, you've demanded we put the question to the general stockholders at the next meeting whether to retain Dar's services."

"That's right."

"I'd be glad to have it printed on the schedule, but you're going to have to get up and explain to the stockholders why, I'm afraid," Alastair said cheerfully. "Since Dar will be presenting first."

Ankow stared at him hatefully. Everyone else got up to leave and Yves even chuckled at the comment, shaking a finger at the CEO playfully. After a moment of relishing his victory, Alastair got up as well and walked past Ankow towards the door.

"You won this time." Ankow stood up, circled him, and held the door shut as the rest left. "But not next time."

The CEO paused and regarded him. "Y'know, David, I'd be careful if I were you."

The younger man snorted. "Not to overstep my bounds going after her?" he asked, tauntingly.

"No." Alastair smiled. "Be careful she doesn't turn and come after you." He removed the hand holding the door shut, opened it, and walked past Ankow and into the outer hallway without a further backward glance.

❖ ⌘ ❖ ⌘ ❖ ⌘ ❖

Kerry's eyes drifted open, taking in the clear, blue sky she could see beyond the edge of the porch roof. It was a beautifully warm, sunny day, with a nice cool breeze coming off the ocean, brushing over the two somnolent figures cuddled together in the rope hammock.

She was perfectly content to remain right where she was, curled up with Dar in the late afternoon light, with a belly full of lobster salad and garlic rolls and a banana milkshake comfortably digesting. It was Wednesday and they were halfway through their vacation. Chino had been having a blast as well and was now sprawled near the hammock, her nose covered in sand.

Kerry sighed happily, as she snuggled a little more closely to the soundly sleeping Dar. The taller woman's arms were wrapped around her and she could smell the nutty scent of sun tan lotion with its hint of coconut still clinging to Dar's skin. They were both wearing soft, loose fitting cotton shorts and T-shirts, having gotten back just before lunch from a long morning's dive off a catamaran diving boat. They had a bike ride planned for just before dinner, then Dar had suggested they merely meander down the main street in Key West and pick out some place to eat that they hadn't tried yet.

Sounded good to her. Kerry wiggled her toes. She had never, ever, in her life felt this relaxed and she mentally thanked Dar yet again for suggesting the time off. They'd spent their days so far sunning, diving, taking long lazy naps like this one, and getting their heads into a completely different space that had nothing to do with work or the bustle of their usual lives.

She'd gotten some killer pictures, including one of Dar sitting on the bottom of the clear, green tinted ocean, nose to nose with a curious dolphin. That one she was going to have enlarged and framed. It would look fantastic on the wall next to the dining room table and she had two smaller ones of colorful fish she could put on either side. Dar was dubious about the one of her, but Kerry knew it was going to turn out great, especially since she was wearing just a light tank kit and you could see most of her body, including those real, long legs stretched out on the white sand, with her flippers crossed at the ankles.

Mmm. Kerry could picture it, the sleek form in its black swimsuit, with the sheer fabric that just barely let her see the skin underneath.

Gorgeous. She only hoped Dar let her get the thing framed and hung before she realized just how sexy she looked in it. Kerry chortled softly to herself.

The place they were staying in was a small, sort of exclusive resort with little cottages and she found she liked that better than the tiered hotels a little further down the shore. They had privacy, for one thing. The cottage was surrounded by sea grapes and palms and had two doors, one opening to a path leading towards the resort's tiny restaurant and shop, the other leading directly out onto a smooth white beach and the sea.

Inside, the cottage was comfortable, more weathered than fancy, with wooden walls and furniture, and colorful, roughly textured fabrics. There was a small refrigerator, and a two burner gas stove, and best of all, a gorgeous back porch with a two person swing, a chair, and the huge rope hammock they were both currently nestled in.

Heaven. Kerry stretched, feeling the tingle of a faint bit of sunburn on her skin.

Of course, the office was in chaos. She and Dar had decided on a compromise and every night after dinner they sat down and picked up mail, trading the more frantic bits with each other as their respective staffs scrambled to try and handle things while they were gone. And to be fair, they carried their pagers, carefully reviewing the various text messages and deciding which ones were really urgent and which would be good to let junior people handle.

Everyone was learning, and that wasn't a bad thing at all. Kerry briefly wondered if they couldn't just make this arrangement permanent, what with teleconferencing and all, then admitted to herself that their positions really did need a little more hands on than this, at least to be done right.

On the other hand... Kerry eyed a bit of color moving past. She hadn't been able to try parasailing yet, in deference to her healing shoulder, and she really, really wanted to. Maybe she could ask Dar to continue their exile just a little while longer.

"No." A low, sexy rumble tickled her ear.

Kerry peeked upward and grinned. "If we stay here long enough, I'll be able to." She waggled her fingers. "It feels a lot better. Honest."

Dar's half open eyes regarded her. "Hmm...maybe," she replied thoughtfully. "If we went double I could sorta hang onto you."

"Ooo." Kerry's eyes lit up. "Yeah!" She squirmed around and ended up half sprawled over Dar's body. "I like that idea."

"Really?" Dar tickled her sides and watched her squirm some more. "Okay. Let's give it a try tomorrow. Worst they can say is no." She yawned and closed her eyes again, taking a breath of the salty air with a sense of decadent pleasure. "Mmm. I could so get used to this."

Kerry stifled her own yawn. "Me too." She gave Dar's shirt an idle nibble. "How about we chuck ILS and open up an E-commerce consulting firm down here? Something we can run from a pair of cell phones and a laptop."

"Okay."

Kerry paused, then lifted her head and peered at her half dozing partner. "You're not serious."

Dar nodded.

"Really?"

A blue eye appeared. "In a frigging heartbeat." It closed again.

"Hmm." Kerry put her head back down. Dar had visibly unwound in the past couple of days, erasing, to Kerry's eyes, years off her age. Even her speech had slowed down a little, taking on just a touch of her father's distinctive drawl, and Kerry suspected her lover was going to have a tougher time than she was getting back into work mode come next Monday morning. "You like being a beach bum, don't you?"

Dar opened her eyes and studied the wood ceiling as it swayed over head. "I guess," she replied. "Yeah. Maybe I do, I mean..." She shifted a little. "I don't mind working hard, but yeah, I'd like to do it in cutoffs and sneakers sometimes."

"Well, you are the CIO and top honcho in Miami. Change the dress code," Kerry replied practically. Then she paused and winced. "Oh. Wait. No. José in shorts." She buried her face in Dar's shirt. "Never mind."

Dar laughed. "I know, I know." Her lips pursed slightly. "Besides, I'm pretty sure you don't feel the same way. I think you like the snazzy office and it fits your style."

Kerry glanced up, startled.

"That was a compliment," Dar assured her.

"Mmm. You make me seem so preppy." Kerry's nose wrinkled. "But yeah, you're right. I like dressing up. It makes dressing down on the weekends so much nicer."

"Well," Dar considered the issue, "how about I let you take over ILS and I can run a consulting firm out of the condo in my jammies and we can get a place like this to bum around in on the weekend?"

Kerry's brow contracted, as she tried to figure out if Dar was joking, or serious, or halfway between both of those things. Maybe it was just the general chaos they'd been through, which wasn't over, either.

Maybe Dar was only joking.

Kerry watched the pale eyes open and gaze dreamily up at a blackbird perched on the edge of the roof. "Is that what you really want to do?" she asked quietly. "Leave the company?"

Dar took a long time to answer, as though she were looking at the question from a number of different angles. "I've done a lot there," she commented.

"Yes, you have. But there's a lot more to do," Kerry replied. "You're changing the way the entire company does business, Dar, and you're doing a hell of a job at it."

"Thank you." She paused. "Part of me wants to finish that." She looked at Kerry. "But part of me wants to stay right here. The part of me that got the shit scared out of it in the building."

Kerry stayed quiet.

"I don't want to put so much energy into my job anymore, Kerry," Dar admitted. "I want to spend more time doing things like this. Enjoying the act of living. Enjoying being with you." She shook her head. "It can go so fast."

Kerry let out a little breath. "Well, if that's what you want to do. Do it."

"But that's not what you want to do." Dar touched her nose. "I don't know. Maybe we can compromise or something."

"Maybe." She smiled. "We'll work it out, Dar. But you know, a weekend place down here isn't a bad start."

Dar smiled back. "No? Hmm. Well, it's further north, but I know of a little spot you might be interested in. It'd take a lot of work though. The place is pretty run down."

Kerry lifted her head right up. "I get to see you use power tools?" She watched the grin form. "Ooo, I'm not gonna pass that up. It'll be fun. I'd like to kinda start from scratch. See what we could make of a place."

"We'll go take a look, then," Dar promised, then glanced at the sun. "Hmm. I think we've got a date with a couple of bikes, don't we?" She stretched her body out, yawning again. "And something spicy for dinner?"

"Sounds good to me," Kerry agreed, sitting up and carefully getting out of the hammock, the wood floor warm under her bare feet. She walked over to the railing and leaned on it, then turned as Dar joined her and walked hand in hand with her partner inside the cottage.

❖ ⌘ ❖ ⌘ ❖ ⌘ ❖

They watched the sunset from the beach, the sky painted in so many shades of color Kerry lost count of them. She lifted her camera and took another shot, then lowered her hands, to wait a few minutes before her next exposure. Chino had tired herself out racing up and down the sand and was now curled at Kerry's feet in a damp ball.

"That's going to be a nice series," Dar commented, leaning back against a piece of driftwood.

"Sure is." Kerry lifted her longneck beer bottle and took a swallow. She was seated between Dar's legs and now she leaned back against her, as Dar wound an arm around her waist. They were both barefoot and half covered in the grainy sand of the beach, and Kerry sighed as she finished off her beer.

Her third, as a matter of fact, since today was the first day she'd been able to drink, having stopped taking the pain medication for her shoulder. Her head buzzed gently and she could feel the faint displacement as the alcohol hit her system. "Think I better stop."

Dar peered over her shoulder, then nibbled her ear. "Getting light-headed?"

"Mmm." Kerry closed her eyes. "Yeah and I don't feel like staggering back to the cottage." Dar's arms tightened around her. "It's so beautiful here."

"You're not looking at anything." Dar chuckled.

"Here." Kerry put her hand over Dar's and squeezed. "Right here, where I am."

"Oh."

"I'm really glad you thought of this, Dar. I'm having such a good time. Are you?" Kerry murmured.

Dar gazed out at the sunset, which washed them in golds and reds. "Oh yeah," she agreed, with a smile. "Best vacation I've ever had."

"Like that's saying much." Kerry laughed. She opened her eyes and lazily lifted her camera, focused on the newly painted sky and snapped a frame. Then she shifted and turned around, rolled onto her back, and aimed the lens at her companion.

Oh. Kerry found that sharp profile softened and gilded in the crimson light, its dark frame of hair wind whipped, leaving a lock half obscuring one glistening eye. She closed her finger over the shutter and squeezed it with infinite care to protect the image gazing back at her with a gentle, loving expression. It was Dar's soul showing, and Kerry captured it, knowing she had in her hands something very special. She lowered the camera and put the lens cap on.

"Needed to waste the last exposure?" Dar inquired, with an arched eyebrow.

Kerry moved the hair out of her eyes. "No." She traced a lighter streak. "Stay here long enough, you'll be as blond as I am."

Dar snorted. "I'll have solid gray hair before that." She fingered the sun-streaked mahogany bit. "Speaking of which...see any in there yet?"

With a feeling of vague familiarity, Kerry patted her lap, then bent over Dar's head and ran her fingers through the dark strands. "There better be. I found two in mine the other day." She riffled a thick patch over Dar's ear, near her temples, then checked the other side. "Damn it, Dar. Did you use hair color?"

The blue eyes looked up with a hurt expression. "It's not my fault," she protested. "And no. I most certainly did not use anything of the kind."

"Lucky genes." Kerry leaned over and kissed her on the forehead. "You ready for Cajun shrimp?"

Chino heard her voice, got up, and shook herself vigorously, scattering sand all over them. "Oh, thanks, Chino."

"Rowf." Chino came over and licked her face. They got up and shook out the large towel they'd been sitting on, then walked up the beach towards the town, with Chino trotting at their heels.

❖ ⌘ ❖ ⌘ ❖ ⌘ ❖

"I don't think that's going to work," Dar said into her cell phone, her eyes on her laptop screen as she leaned back and propped her feet up on the small table. "We're going to have to route around that section. It doesn't have the bandwidth to keep up with the new net."

"But that is where they are located, Dar. What are we supposed to tell them? To move?" José asked testily.

"No," Dar replied in a mild tone. "Build a new drop point into the contract and tell them we'll foot the front end cost of the installation, with the understanding that they'll have to pay it out over the course of the five year pact."

A momentary quiet. "All right. I can do that," José answered slowly. "That's a workable idea."

"Great," Dar replied. "Anything else for me?"

"Uh." José shuffled some papers on his end. "No. There is nothing else. Eleanor?"

"I have something." Eleanor's cultured, but New York accented voice came over the line.

"Yes?" Dar stroked Chino's head and ruffled her soft ears.

"What are they drugging you with?" the Marketing VP asked. "I really wanna know."

Dar laughed, drawing Kerry's attention. The blond woman had been outside on the porch and now she came indoors, wandered over and cocked her head in question. "Eleanor wants to know what you're drugging me with."

Kerry leaned close to the phone. "Watermelon wine coolers," she called through the receiver, having discovered Dar's fondness for the odd drink, "and barbecued shrimp."

"You guys should try it sometime," Dar added, stifling a yawn. "Maybe we can have the next executive strategic retreat down here."

"Maybe you should stay there," José groused, but with a note of humor in his voice. "We get more things done this way, when we're not screaming at each other."

Dar pursed her lips and acknowledged privately that the sentiment wasn't wholly unjustified. "Maybe I'll bring some back with me," she bantered back. "We can replace the bottled water with this watermelon juice."

Both VP's and Dar chuckled.

"Hell, I'll chip in for an entire watermelon patch if it keeps you like this," Eleanor remarked. "You're turning human."

"Amazing what a little sun will do," Dar replied drolly. "Or maybe it's not having to see the inside of those walls for a week."

"Whatever." The Marketing VP snorted. "Well, we've got work to do, so we'll let you get back to communing with fish, or whatever it is you're doing."

Dar accepted a tortilla chip loaded with spicy salsa and munched it nosily. "Okay," she managed around the mouthful. "Later." She hung up and finished chewing, then swallowed the mouthful. "Mmm." She circled Kerry's leg with one arm. "Wanna commune with some fish with me, my little Yankee?"

"Only if the fish is broiled and on a plate." Kerry leaned over and kissed her, removing some chip crumbs in the process. "Keeping up with you on a jet ski all afternoon worked up an appetite." She went back for another kiss, this one lasting longer. "But a little night diving might be fun."

"Oh yeah?" Dar slid a warm hand over her hip. "With or without water?" She took advantage of Kerry's position and nibbled her exposed ribcage, nipping a fold of skin lightly between her teeth.

"Eek." Kerry captured her jaw and pulled, finding a better place for her lips. "How about both?" she suggested. "That way I can have that brownie dessert again and not feel like such a piglet."

Dar chuckled. "You're on."

"Not a long trip out though. We've got an early start planned for tomorrow," Kerry reminded her.

Ah yes. Their all day long excursion. "Did you make sure we can take Chino?" Dar asked. "Some dive boats allow dogs, some don't."

"Yes, we can. They asked what breed she was and when I told them a Labrador, they asked me if I wanted to reserve a dive kit for her," Kerry smugly informed her. "I thought they were joking, but they're not. They've got these bubble helmets for dogs, so I said sure."

Dar's jaw dropped a little. "We're taking the dog diving?" She glanced at Chino, who wagged her tail. "Cool." She scratched the animal's ears. "You gonna like that, girl? Play with the fishies?"

"Growf." Chino stood up on her hind legs and licked Dar's arm.

"Take that as a yes." Dar got to her feet and pulled Kerry closer, fitting their bodies together in a sensual slide of sun-warmed skin. "How about an appetizer before dinner, then?" She stole another kiss.

Kerry smiled, tangled her fingers in Dar's shirt, and tugged her gently towards the large, comfortable bed.

The taller woman came willingly, grasping the zipper on Kerry's fleecy, sleeveless cutoff shirt and pulling it down slowly to expose sun tinted skin. She ran a finger down the center of Kerry's breastbone, and her lover inhaled sharply in reaction.

Kerry moved closer and nuzzled a button open, exploring with the tip of her tongue and tasting Dar's skin, the soft, fine hairs tickling her senses. "I like the new oil you're using." A tang of banana and coconut filled her nose as she breathed in and she nudged another button open.

"Mmm. If you're going to do that, I'll skip the oil and just smear bananas all over me," Dar teased, as she undid the zipper at the bottom of Kerry's shirt and peeled it back over her shoulders, slid her hands down her lover's back and down under the waistband of her cotton shorts.

"Sticky." Kerry nibbled playfully around the curve of one breast. "But definitely nicer than coconut bits." She undid the other two buttons impatiently and ran her hands over Dar's body. "That could get..."

"Gritty," Dar agreed, sliding slowly out of Kerry's reach as she knelt and pulled the smaller woman's shorts down with her, allowing Kerry to step out of them, then easing upright again as she ran her fingers along the backs of Kerry's thighs.

"Umpf." Kerry uttered a small sound, as she loosed the brass button holding Dar's faded denim shorts closed. Her body pressed forward in simple reaction, rubbing skin on skin, as Dar brushed her hair aside and nipped lightly at the skin just under her ear, then suckled her earlobe, warming the side of Kerry's face with her heightened breathing.

She moved the shorts down Dar's hips, and her lover stepped out of them, then settled both hands snugly around Kerry's waist. "Ah ah," she scolded softly, "no lifting."

A soft growl vibrated in her right ear, almost a purring sound, and she chuckled in response, as Dar shifted her hold lower and half turned, simply falling backwards onto the bed and pulling Kerry along with her. "All right. Gravity works," she rumbled, as Kerry slid up the length of her body and settled above her, pinning her arms down with a seductive smile.

"I gotcha."

"Yep," Dar agreed, thoroughly enjoying the view. "Now what'cha gonna do with me?"

Kerry kissed her. "Well. I'm gonna start here," she bit the skin over Dar's jugular playfully, then continued down her throat to her collarbone, "and see where I end up."

"Ooo. I'm in trouble," Dar teased, moving her lower arms and running her fingers up and down Kerry's sides.

"You bet you are," Kerry agreed, as she threw herself into her task.

Chapter
48

"Morning, María." Dar poked her head through the office door, feeling a little strange after being gone for over a week.

The secretary looked up, then beamed at her. "*Buenos días*, Dar. It is so good to see you again." She stood up and came around her desk as Dar entered, then paused, obviously stopping herself in some action and folded her hands in front of her. "I am glad you are back."

Dar came over to her and managed to feel only slightly awkward as she gave María a hug. "Thanks." She received an enthusiastic response, as the smaller woman hugged her back, then she released her and ran her fingers through noticeably sun-lightened hair. "It's good to be back. But I had a great time."

"I can see that you did." María smiled warmly. "You are so tan. You had nice weather, I know."

Dar stuck her hands in her pockets and nodded. "We sure did. So what's going on here this morning?" she asked casually. "I think I processed through most of the things in my inbox over the weekend. Wasn't anything major in there."

"It is quiet, yes," María agreed. "Mark is saying that with the new network, there is much less problems." She looked proudly at Dar. "This is your fault, yes?"

Dar chuckled. "My fault. Eyah. I guess you could say that."

"There is many calls from the newspapers and twice they came here, but the security would not let them come in," María advised her. "You are famous, I think. My husband taped all the times you were on the television. We showed them to my family when they were over for dinner this weekend."

"My parents did too," Dar admitted, with a smile. "I finally saw it last night. Thought the first one went pretty well, but I wasn't fond of the second." She glanced around. "I'd better get to work. I think I've got three conference calls scheduled this morning."

"*Sí*. You do." María nodded. "Is Kerrisita here?" She leaned closer. "You know what day tomorrow is, yes?"

Blue eyes twinkled. "Of course." Dar grinned. "Kerry's living in fear. She thinks I'm going to have a male stripper delivered to her office."

"Tch." María looked shocked. "You are not, surely?"

"No," Dar reassured her. "She's trying to play down her birthday, though. How did she put it? She's gotten enough bad press in the last few weeks?"

María grinned at her. Dar grinned back and then she ambled into her office, pausing as she cleared the door to appreciate the sunlit view of the ocean. "Nice." She circled her desk and said hello to her fish, who blew bubbles at her, then swam in expectant circles as she got the food jar out and gave them a sprinkle. "Hey, guys. Didja miss me?"

The fish waved feathery fins at her as she sat down in her comfortable leather chair and leaned back. Glad of the tall chair's sturdy support. The diving had been great, but she'd overdone it the last two days and her back was feeling very cranky with her.

Maybe the tandem parasailing wasn't the best idea I'd ever come up with. Dar leaned her chin on her hand as she waited for her PC to boot. *But damn, Kerry'd had such a blast.* The phone buzzed and she slapped lazily at it. "Yes?"

"Dar, I have Mr. Alastair on *número uno*," María told her.

"Sure." Dar hit the other button. "Morning, Alastair."

"Morning Dar. You up for a teleconference?" Alastair's voice was cheerful. "Didn't see you logged on, so..."

"Yeah, hang on." Dar logged into the system and started up the network meeting software. "Go ahead."

A moment later, the black window cleared, and she was looking at Alastair's round, freshly scrubbed face. He wore his usual starched white shirt and sober navy blue tie, with its company tie clasp. His eyes shifted to his monitor, slightly off to one side. "Boy. You got some sun, huh?"

Dar leaned back in her chair and rested her elbows on the arms of it. "Sun, sand, water. I didn't go to Key West to snow ski, Alastair."

The CEO chuckled. "No, I suppose not. Well, you look great. Really relaxed." He watched Dar nod. "Good."

"Uh oh," Dar drawled.

"Now, Dar. What makes you think I've got bad news?" The blue gray eyes twinkled. "C'mon. You've had a nice, relaxing week, no stress, no frantic phone calls. No urgent emails."

A dark brow lifted.

"All right. We're planning a recap and strategy session tomorrow for the stockholder's meeting. Remember you're our main presenter this quarter." Her boss relented. "I had a very interesting pow-wow with several of the senior board members on Friday. Seems they're now finding you sort of intriguing."

Dar rolled her eyes.

"You didn't tell me your father was so highly decorated either, Dar, or that your mother was a critically well known artist. Erlich was sniffing around, saying how it was great timing to put your bio in this year's company yearbook, so he dug out the files on you and your parents. Quite the family you are."

Dar sighed.

"Nothing to be ashamed of," Alastair told her mildly. "It's just great press."

Dar leaned forward. "So what about the part where I'm gay?"

Her boss shrugged. "Do you want to make it an issue? I never pictured you as a crusader for gay rights, Dar." He studied her. "In fact, I don't think you ever personally mentioned it to me. I mean sure, we heard rumors, and there was that whole mess with Elena Nechovia, but..."

Dar shrugged.

"Of course, you never mentioned anything personal about yourself. I mean, you could have actually had three heads and sixteen children by a Tibetan yak, and I'd never have known." Alastair now sounded a bit peeved.

"I have an 'if you ask, I'll tell' policy," Dar remarked dryly. "You never asked." She glanced up as María entered with a small tray and set a gently steaming cup on the desk along with a plate of pastries. She winked at María and gave her a tiny wave, as the secretary waggled her fingers back and left. Dar picked up the cup and sipped from it. "I'll pencil in the meeting. What time is it?"

"Four-thirty our time," her boss stated. "Good. I'm looking forward to it. Maríana has been giving the press what details they wanted about you, by the way."

Dar looked distinctly alarmed.

Alastair grinned and waggled his fingers. "Bye."

"Hold it, hold it." Dar held a hand up. "Listen. I'm going to go ahead with that project of mine today. Is that still fine with you?"

Alastair considered thoughtfully. "Well, we discussed it at the board meeting. I don't see any problem with it, no." He paused. "Is it on my worklist?"

Dar nodded.

"Hang on." Alastair pecked at his keyboard for a minute. "Wh—oh, that. No, no, no. No, no. What, are you kidding? No, no...ah." He rested his chin in his hand and read the screen intently, then flicked a gaze towards the camera. "Did you write this?"

"Partly."

"Nice job," her boss complimented. "All right, go ahead with it, but let's not make a press announcement until the stockholder's meeting. It would be a little on the sensational side right at the moment."

Dar nodded. "Will do."

❖ ⌘ ❖ ⌘ ❖ ⌘ ❖

"Ms. Kerry, here are the reports you asked for. Is there anything else I can get you?" Mayte put the folders down and gazed at her boss.

Kerry tugged one over and opened it. "No. That'll do for now. I've got to make the decisions on who's going to migrate to the new network first, and every single account manager is giving me a sob story over why they should be put on the top of the list." She glanced over her shoulder towards the window, with its late afternoon shading. "Thank goodness it's been quiet here today. Haven't heard a peep out of anyone in an hour."

Mayte scratched her ear. "Um, yeah. I was going to get some hot tea. You want some?"

"Sure."

Mayte eased out of the office, leaving her in the quiet of the big room. Kerry leaned back and stifled a yawn, reflecting on the fact that though she had a fantastic time on vacation, it was nice to be back here. She slid down in her leather chair and carefully turned the cuffs on her silk shirt up another fold, gazing down at her stockinged feet under her desk. She looked up as a little gopher popped up on her screen and chittered at her. "Hey!" She chased after it with her mouse pointer, but it scuttled behind a window, and peeked out at her, poking its tongue out. "How in the hell does she do that?"

The little gopher program was one of Dar's and she frequently amused herself by changing it around and sending it over to pester Kerry. The animal was cute, with a snub face, and little black button nose, and the neatest thing was, every time he was different.

Today, GopherDar was wearing a tiny surfer outfit, complete with flip flops and wraparound sunglasses, and he proceeded to dance a hula across the bottom of her screen while she giggled in pure reaction. "You are sooo twisted." She popped up a netmessage screen and typed exactly that in and sent it over to her boss' computer.

Her phone rang and she hit the button, half expecting it to be Dar, but saw it was an outside line. "Operations, Kerry Stuart speaking."

"Hey girl!" Colleen's voice rang through the speaker. "How is it, being back there after a week in paradise?"

"After four days in Hell?" Kerry inquired wryly. "It's nice. I'm tired as heck, since I've been busting my butt all day trying to catch up to everything, but I'm starting to make a dent in the piles. What's up with you?"

"Busy making copies of videotapes for everybody you know," Colleen answered smugly. "You rocked in those hearings, Ker. We were all so proud of you."

Kerry blinked in surprise. "Really?" The office had been conspicuously quiet on the subject. In fact, she'd gotten the idea all day she was being slightly avoided. People had stopped talking when she came into view and she suspected she'd been the topic of some very juicy gossip for the whole week. "I just answered what he asked. They were pissing me off though."

"No kidding," Colleen said. "So, listen. What are your plans for tomorrow? You up for a little party?"

Kerry sighed. "Not really, Col, no," she answered honestly. "It's just been such a weird few weeks. I'd kinda like to keep a low profile for a while on a personal level. Dar and I were just going to go out to dinner or something like that."

"Awwww." Colleen drew the word out. "Keeerrryyy. C'mon. That's not fair. We haven't seen you for weeks and weeks. We weren't going to cater the Queen Mary, just a few of us."

True. Kerry rubbed her eyes. "Yeah. Um, I know, Col. I know." *Would it hurt?* "How about Wednesday? I have to take it really easy at the gym because of my shoulder. Maybe we could all go out afterward?"

"Mmmph." Colleen sounded mildly mollified. "Yeah, that'd be okay. How about Dave and Busters? We can have dinner and play some pool."

Hmm. Kerry perked up. "Yeah, you know, that sounds like fun." *Mindless electronic entertainment, good food, a few beers...* "Good plan. Hey, you feel like coming over tonight? I've got a ton of pictures to show you."

"You bet." Now Colleen sounded pleased. "Y'know, Ker, we were really, really worried about you."

Kerry smiled a little. "Thanks. It was an awful time up there." She shifted and leaned against the desk. "If Dar hadn't been there with me, I don't know what I would have done. She was so there for me." She chuckled. "Not to mention her folks. You know Mrs. Roberts introduced herself to my parents as my mother-in-law?"

"Ohmigod."

"Yeah. She's such a trip," Kerry agreed.

"What was that all about with your father giving Dar and her dad those medals?" came the curious question. "Was that like, for real?"

Kerry shook her head, even though Colleen couldn't see it. "I wish I could say yeah. That was his way of getting as close to an apology as he's capable of. But honestly? I think he just did it for the good press."

"Mmm."

"It was great for him. Here he is, national spotlight, handing out medals. That's why they had to postpone those hearings. His public approval rating went through the roof. They saw him in that window and they think he's wonderful." Kerry's voice held a bitter tone and she knew it. "If they only knew. Andy had to practically kick him in the ass to get him to help out."

"Wow," Colleen murmured. "Hey, tell me all about it tonight. I'll pick up a six pack of Corona. Okay?"

"You're on." Kerry smiled as she hung up, swiveling as her inner door opened. "Hey, look. It's GopherMom." She snapped a rubber band at her boss. "You are so out there sometimes."

Dar sauntered over, hitched up her skirt, and perched on the edge of Kerry's desk. "Just proving I can still put out a little code if I have to," she drawled. "How was your day? I haven't seen you since nine. I've been pretty buried myself."

Kerry lifted a hand and indicated her full outbox. "I'm about half caught up. I was digging through all the facilities requests today, sorting them, trying to find an equitable way to move people to your new net. Fielding questions from every single account manager we've got practically." She patted Dar's nearby knee. "You caused me so much work, Boss."

The outer office door opened and Mayte came in with a steaming cup. "Oh," she paused, when she saw Dar, "I'm sorry. I can..."

"Nah." Dar waved her in. "I was just getting a status report."

The slim girl smiled, then deposited the cup on Kerry's desk. It was a dark, fragrant brew, and Kerry sniffed it appreciatively before she took a sip. "Oh wow. This is nice. Blackberry?"

"*Sí.*" Mayte blushed a little. "I saw you liked that." She lifted her eyes and met Dar's, then cleared her throat. "I am going to drop off the mail, then go home. Unless you need something else?"

"Nope. Go on." Kerry leaned back, both hands cradled around the mug. "I'm going to finish up here, then head home myself." Her assistant left, closing the door softly behind her, and she sighed.

"Tired?" Dar asked.

"A little." Kerry flexed her arm. "My shoulder's aching. I don't want to take those muscle relaxants until I get home though. They put me out like a light." She studied Dar. "And it's been a little weird here today. I kinda get a creepy feeling people are avoiding me."

"I think you're imagining things."

"No, I'm not. When I walk through the halls, people used to say hi, make small talk." Kerry gazed at her desktop. "I don't know. Maybe they're wondering what kind of person would do what I did." Then she shrugged it off. "Anyway...or maybe I'm just overly sensitive." She glanced up at Dar. "Col's coming over. I wanted to show her my pictures and the stuff we brought back and give her the present I got her." Dar nodded. "She and the gang coerced me into going to D and B's on Wednesday. You up for that?"

Dar straightened her back a little and winced. "Not skeeball, but yeah, that sounds okay." She cupped both hands around one knee. "I had a visit from Gerry Easton today."

"Really?"

"Mmm. Yeah. He had a very interesting proposal," Dar said. "He's gotten approval to contract us to provide high level consulting services to the Navy." She shifted. "To review all their processes, systems, and procedures and recommend, procure, and implement technological improvements."

Kerry's eyes widened. "Wow. That must be huge."

Dar slowly nodded. "His one condition was," she chuckled, "I head it up."

"Big surprise there," her lover remarked. "Wow. What do you think about that?"

"I think," Dar got up and walked over to the window, pressed her fingertips against it and looked out, "I think I'm very, very intrigued." She turned. "Means I'll have to travel a bit but most of the analysis can be done from here." A bright, interested look came into her eyes.

"Do you get to go out to the ships and stuff?" Kerry asked, folding her arms. "Like to the aircraft carriers and those things?"

Dar nodded.

"Ooo, that does sound interesting. Can I help?"

Dar gave another nod. "You bet. I wrote up the prospectus and sent it up to Alastair. He approved it in nothing flat."

"Wow." Kerry exhaled. "I'm glad. I know you were looking for another project to do. This sounds right up your alley." Her speaker buzzed. "Operations, Stuart."

"Kerry? This is Eleanor," the Marketing VP announced crisply. "I have a conference call on with all the regional managers regarding the new network and I can't find Dar. Can you please come down and join us, so I can get a coherent explanation of the new system?"

Kerry rubbed her neck and sighed, giving Dar a plaintive look.

Her boss shrugged and held up both hands. "You'd do it better than I would anyway," she whispered.

"Yeah, yeah." She shifted a little. "Okay, Eleanor. I'll be right there. Where are you, anyway?"

"The big presentation room. Can you come down now?" The VP sounded impatient.

The big presentation room? Kerry's brows knit together. *What on earth was the woman doing in that huge place all be herself?* "Uh, sure." She at looked Dar in confusion. "Was the conferencing bridge broken in the executive center?"

"It was booked." Eleanor drummed her fingers impatiently. "Anything else?"

"No. I'll be right down." Kerry released the call. "I can just picture it. That cavernous room. She probably just likes to hear her voice in there."

"Probably," Dar agreed amiably. "Well, I better let you go. I'm going to finish up some stuff in my office. Catch you when you're done?" She patted Kerry's arm.

"Sure." Kerry stood and shrugged into her jacket, lifting the collar of her silk shirt above the lapel. "This shouldn't take long. 'More pipes, bigger pipes, faster service, better network,' right?"

"Right," Dar agreed, clapping her on the back. "Go get 'em, tiger."

Kerry gave her a bemused look, then turned and went to the door, opened it, and slipped out into a quiet hallway.

❖ ⌘ ❖ ⌘ ❖ ⌘ ❖

Kerry leaned against the back wall of the elevator, watching the floors change slowly. *That new project of Dar's really sounds neat*, her mind mused. *I'm glad.* A smile crept over her face, as she realized just how glad she was that something had come along to keep her boss' interest, since she really had no desire to see Dar leave the company any time soon.

Part of that was very selfish, she acknowledged. She liked having the security of Dar's presence down the hall and the benefit of her experience and knowledge. Not that Dar would refuse to answer her questions even if she weren't part of the company, but still.

Yeah. She was glad.

The doors opened on the tenth floor, and she walked out, turned right, and went down the long hallway. "Boy, it's quiet," she commented, hearing the faintest of echoes. The late afternoon sunlight painted the occasional stripe from the offices she passed, but only a muted buzz of the phone system broke the silence as she continued through the marketing area towards the big presentation room.

She was pretty sure the company'd be glad Dar was sticking around too. After what she'd achieved so far this year, the moaning and whining had subsided to less than nothing, and even José and Eleanor seemed a lot happier. Sales were up, the new network was the talk of the industry. Heck, they should throw Dar a freaking party.

Kerry paused before the conference room door and straightened her jacket, then ran her fingers through her hair. Eleanor tended to have teleconferencing running, and who the hell knew who she had on the big screen? She put her hand on the door latch and pushed down, then pulled the door open and walked inside.

"SURPRISE!" A roar greeted her.

Kerry stopped dead in her tracks, shocked beyond speech. The entire of the huge room was filled with colorful banners, balloons, confetti, and lots, and lots of people.

Hundreds of them, it seemed.

Cheering and coming towards her, with flashbulbs going off and laughter. To one side, a huge table was set up, with a cake, and bowls of chips, on the other side were chafing dishes of something hot or other. Kerry managed to get her jaw closed and she blinked, as Mariana reached her and patted her arm. "Oh my god."

"You all right?" The Personnel VP laughed. "Happy birthday!"

On cue, everyone started singing with the usual success that a group of unrelated non-singers had.

At least it gave her a minute to start breathing again, Kerry realized, as a belated flush darkened her skin and her mind finally acknowledged exactly what had happened.

They'd given her a surprise party.

Wow. Kerry sucked in air, and looked around in amazement, finally finding a pair of twinkling blue eyes near the back of the room, just watching her. "Wow," she managed to say. "I'm...uh..."

"Freaked," Mark supplied helpfully. "Man, what a facial expression." He held up his digital camera. "Happy birthday, Kerry."

Kerry rubbed her face. "Oh my god." She laughed helplessly, as they closed in on her, and hands touched her arm and patted her back. "Wow. I have no idea what to say here." Laughter. "I've never had a surprise party before. Thank you, guys. This is amazing." A smile spread across her face. "Totally amazing."

Then she spotted Colleen lurking in the back and she put her hands on her hips. "Hey. Waitaminute." She pointed at her friend. "Didn't I just talk to you?"

Colleen held up her cell phone and grinned, then pointed. "I brought the Corona." She came over. "Sorry, Ker. I know you wanted to be low key but..."

"Well," Kerry looked around and laughed helplessly, "so much for that. At least I didn't have to plan it all."

"Nope," Colleen agreed, clapping her on the shoulder. "Vacation did you good, Ker. You look great. Look at that tan, wouldja?"

Kerry ran her fingers through her hair a touch self-consciously. "Yeah. I scared myself in the mirror this morning." She joked. "It was great though. We had a fantastic week."

"About time," her friend told her firmly. "G'wan and enjoy the party." Colleen gave her a little bump.

A buzz of voices surrounded her and Kerry just shook her head, moving further into the room and murmuring thank yous to people who came up to wish her a happy birthday. She wandered over near the cake and glanced at it, then laughed uncontrollably. "Oh my god. Who did that?"

The frosting was ocean blue and green and someone had, somehow, crafted an entire darn tropical reef, complete with little fish and what looked like a lobster. It was gorgeous. "I can't eat this," she yelped. "Look at that angel fish. It's almost real."

A soft throat clearing caught her ear and she turned to see Dar standing behind her, reviewing the cake diffidently. "My mother is gonna be really ticked off if you don't at least try it."

"Your..." Kerry glanced at the cake, then back at Dar. "Oh my gosh, I can't believe it."

Dar chuckled.

"Can't believe what? That she has a mother?" Eleanor gave Dar a sweet smile. "We couldn't either."

"No, no. I've met her mother. But..." Kerry laughed and just shook her head. "Thanks, guys. This is incredible." She stole a tortilla, scooped up some salsa, and munched on it as everyone mingled and grabbed food and drinks. "And you," she muttered in a very low voice to Dar, "are so busted."

"Ah, ah. Not me." Dar shook her head solemnly. "I found out about it when I got back to Miami. I had nothing to do with this."

Kerry pointed mutely at the cake and lifted her brows.

Dar shrugged. "Apparently they found out this was going on and Mom offered."

"Ahem. Excuse me folks." Maríana had taken control of the mike at the nearby podium. She tapped the mike for effect, making a squeal as her nails hit the screen grid. "Whoops."

"Hey Mari, maybe we can find a geek somewhere around here to help you with that."

The Personnel VP shaded her eyes with one hand and made a production of scanning the audience intently. "Don't see any here."

A round of laughter echoed.

"Anyway," Maríana cleared her throat, "as a representative of company management I just wanted to wish Kerry a happy birthday." Cheers. "And to welcome her back after her vacation."

"Thanks," Kerry said from where she'd just cornered a Corona and taken a sip of it. "This is really nice and I'm amazed at the effort you guys put into it."

Cheers.

"Ahem." Mari regained control of the audience. "As long as we're all hanging around here, I might as well take the opportunity to give Kerry her official birthday present from ILS." She held up a small, thin item wrapped in gold paper, with a blue bow, and tiny, embossed company logos all over it.

Everyone quieted and turned to watch as Kerry, visibly blushing again, put her drink down and walked forward to take it gingerly from Mari's hands. "Um...thanks. I didn't expect anything from the company."

"Well, sometimes we just have these things lying around. So..." Mari shrugged and leaned on the podium. "Go on and open it."

Dar moved silently up behind Kerry and stood there watching, her hands folded in front of her.

"Well," Kerry peered around, obviously embarrassed, "I mean, okay, sure." She cleared her throat and carefully removed the ribbon. "Oh, isn't that cute?" She admired the embossed logos, then tucked the ribbon under her arm and continued opening the wrapping.

It was a very flat, heavy something, whatever it was, and she found her curiosity piqued, trying to imagine what it was. *A base for her PC? A paperweight for her desk? A bookend?* She peeled the tape off and eased the wrapping back, very aware of the expectant silence around her. A hint of brassy metal appeared and she opened the other side of the paper, then flipped it over and exposed the front.

She blinked three times.

Vice President of Operations, Kerrison Stuart.

"Urk." Kerry uttered a tiny noise, then her knees unlocked and she almost went crashing to the ground in pure surprise. A powerful hand gripped her arm and held her up, and she just swayed, glad of Dar's close presence. "Oh boy," she whispered, "I wasn't expecting this."

José cleared his throat and stepped forward, sticking a hand out to her. "Congratulations, Kerry. I am glad you will be on the team with us."

Kerry returned his grip, as a rush of blood returned to her head after her heart seemingly stopped for a minute. "Thank you." *Holy bleep.* She and Dar had discussed the possibility, sure. When Dar had given her that damn evaluation, and she'd agreed that it looked like she felt comfortable with it but...

After what she'd gone through in Washington, she'd figured that was on indefinite hold.

"Yes, congratulations, Kerry, for a purely selfish reason, of course." Eleanor also shook her hand. "You have no idea how much more pleasant you've made my work here." She gave Dar a smile over Kerry's shoulder. "Not to mention you freed up the uber-nerd here to finish our new network."

"Um, thanks, I think," Kerry murmured.

Duks was next, studiously patting her shoulder. "Do not worry that you have big shoes to fill, Kerry."

"I wasn't." Kerry chuckled. "Thanks. I'm glad I'll get a chance to work more with you guys."

"Congratulations." Maríana now smiled at her. "It was well deserved."

"Hey Kerry." Mark snapped yet another picture. "This is gonna look great on the front page of the department newsletter."

Kerry winced. "C'mon. I must be as red as a lobster."

"We'll just tell 'em it's sunburn," the MIS Chief replied cheerfully. "Hold the plaque up, huh?"

Dar settled back against the wall, enjoying her partner's position in the very center of the spotlight. Kerry's smile just kept getting bigger and bigger, and Dar felt a distinct sense of pleasure as she listened to the crowd's comments and watched them cluster around the new VP, chattering and congratulating.

Yeah. It was a pretty damn good day after all. She snagged a Frito and scooped up some chili dip.

Chapter
49

Kerry was curled up in the passenger seat of the Lexus, watching both Dar's profile and the city lights flash by as they headed over the causeway towards home. Dar kept smirking to herself, a little tensing motion of her lips, and Kerry suspected she was remembering the high points of her party.

That was okay. Kerry was too. It had lasted longer than she'd thought it would. "Hey, Dar?"

"Hmm?" Dar glanced at her, then returned her eyes to the road.

"Did you really not know anything about the party?"

Dar's nose twitched. "Well," she chuckled softly, "I got this phone call two weeks back asking me what your favorite foods were. Figuring there wasn't a *Kerrison Stuart Cooks!* videotape in the works, I pinned the caller to the wall and tortured the details out of them."

Kerry muffled a laugh. "That explains the Snowballs. I was wondering about that, because I'm damn sure I never told anyone but you that I liked them." There had also been chafing dishes full of Thai foods and a conspicuous presence of chocolate scattered around. "God, I'm stuffed."

"Did you have fun?"

"Yeah. It was really nice. I was surprised at how many people were there." Kerry mused. "I can't believe they brought gifts and stuff."

Dar turned into the ferry terminal and pulled onto the boat. "Why? Kerry, people really like you, for one thing, and for another, they're damn grateful they have you to deal with and not me."

"Dar, that's not true," Kerry protested, but her partner didn't look distressed at her statement.

"Would they hate to lose me? Sure," Dar agreed readily. "Everybody knows the company is better off with me doing what I do. But they'd rather work with you. Which is fine, Kerry. That's exactly what I intended when I made you my assistant. In fact, I commented to Mari at the time that it might reduce her personnel complaints."

"Just so I could generate other kinds of personnel complaints," Kerry remarked wryly.

"No one complains about you." Dar shook her head.

"Well, not many people complain about you anymore, either," Kerry shot back. "So there."

Dar was quiet for a moment, deep in thought. "Yeah," she finally said, sounding surprised. "You're right. They haven't been."

Kerry settled back in her seat, satisfied. She was quiet for a minute, then looked at Dar. "I don't have any other surprises waiting for me, do I?"

"At home?" Dar smiled. "No...well..." She chuckled. "I don't know. Maybe a box or two." She squeezed Kerry's knee. "I saved mine for tomorrow, but I think my folks might have dropped by something."

Kerry wrinkled up her nose in a smile. "This is so cool," she admitted. "At home, after about...age eight or so, I guess, we got gift certificates to various department stores, which my mother took and used to get things she thought we needed."

"That's no fun."

"No," Kerry agreed. "I used to save up my allowance and go out and get myself one thing, a toy or whatever, that I wanted." She considered. "I remember the year I got myself an Erector Set. My mother was so pissed off at me. She took it away and gave it to Mike, who turned around and gave it back to me, of course. I kept it under my bed and played with it when she was out shopping."

"An Erector Set? What problem did she have with that?" Dar asked in a puzzled tone.

"It was a boy toy."

"Your mother needs an injection of the late twentieth century." Dar snorted. "I don't want to tell you how many expansion sets I had for mine."

Kerry smiled. "Did you make anything significant?"

Dar pulled into her parking spot and turned the Lexus off. "A mechanical system to turn off and on the lights, the stereo, and adjust the sound in my room." She got out and popped the back hatch to retrieve Kerry's gifts. "And a car that got my sneakers from my closet."

Kerry giggled so hard she had to lean against the Lexus' door.

"I did one that unloaded my mother's acrylic paint tubes and moved them into the garage, but that didn't last long."

Kerry slid down to the ground, holding her sides.

"Then there was the dog," Dar went on. "I gave up trying to get its tail to wag, though. The little motors just wouldn't start and stop when I wanted them to." She lifted the box out of the back, then paused, as her abused muscles protested. "Ow."

"God, sorry." Kerry hauled herself up off the ground and hurried over to help. "Sorry, sorry. I keep forgetting your back."

"Me too," Dar admitted, wincing.

"Well, the most extensive thing I made with mine was an amusement park," Kerry told her, as they edged up the stairs with their burden. "A Ferris wheel and a merry go round. I even found little plastic horses for the carousel." She keyed in her code, then grabbed the knob and pulled the door open. "Whoa, whoa. Easy, Chino."

"Rooo!" The Labrador hurtled out, nearly knocking her owners over.

"Easy, easy." Dar laughed, as she maneuvered past the excited dog and got into the condo. They put the presents down on the dining room table, and Dar continued on into the kitchen. "I'm going to put some coffee up. Turn the TV on, willya?"

"Sure." Kerry trotted to the TV and did just that, then sat down on the loveseat to pet Chino. "Hey, honey. How are you?"

"Agurff." Chino mouthed Kerry's hand enthusiastically.

"Here." Dar returned from the kitchen, with a handful of mail. "Looks like you got some cards." She handed over five or six envelopes, then dropped down onto the couch to leaf through the remainder. Idly, she reached a hand out to scratch Kerry's back, and the blond woman leaned back, settling into the curve of her arm.

"Dar?"

"Yes?" Dar opened a letter one handed, scanning its contents. "Oh. More stock options. Great."

"Thanks."

"For what?" Puzzled blue eyes gazed at her. "Getting you your mail?"

"Just thanks." Kerry gave her a one armed hug, then stayed curled up where she was to open her cards. "Oh look. Baby pictures." She showed one of Angie and the new baby. "He's a lot less wrinkled now, huh?" She turned the picture over and drew in a surprised breath. "Oh, Dar. Look."

"Hmm?" Dar inclined her head to read the black penned inscription. "She named him Andrew?" Her voice rose.

"Yeah." Kerry laughed in delighted. "Wow. That is so cool." She put the picture down and opened the next one, a funny card from Michael. "He's so strange sometimes." She lifted out a golden red leaf. "He sent this because we don't have season changes."

Dar snickered.

"What else? Oh, this must be from Aunt Penny." Kerry smiled, seeing the creamy white, heavy paper. She opened the top and pulled out a card. "I sent her a picture of us, by the way." She opened the card. "Oh, hey, she's going to be here in Miami and she wants to come see us."

"Huh." Dar cocked her head. "Interesting handwriting."

"She wants to meet you." Kerry gave her a gentle elbow.

"Uh oh." Dar stifled a yawn.

"Nah. She's really nice. You'll like her." Kerry tucked the card away, then opened the last envelope, pulled the sedate, gold foil card out and opened it.

"I'm sure she is," Dar answered absently. "You want to take her out on the boat?"

There was no answer.

"Ker?" Dar peered at her partner.

Kerry swallowed and tilted the card in shaking fingers so that Dar could see it. "It's...it's from my parents."

Dar blinked. It was a simple card, with only "Happy Birthday" in ornate script in the center, and "mom and dad" written in. "Huh. How d'you like that?" She smiled and gave Kerry a hug. "Does that make you feel better?"

Kerry just stared at the card, turning it over in her fingers and shaking her head. "I don't know what I feel," she answered softly. "Bewildered. Amazed." She paused. "Relieved, maybe." Kerry thought about that. "Yeah, relieved."

Dar felt her partner's body relax and she did as well. "I'm glad." She nuzzled Kerry's hair.

"Me too," Kerry replied, feeling a weight lift off her shoulders. She tipped her head back and caught Dar's lips. "Now I can start to leave that behind. Who knows? Maybe one day we can all sit down and talk." She regarded Dar's face thoughtfully. "Maybe meeting your folks and seeing how accepting they were helped."

Dar's eyebrow lifted. "Could be." She glanced at the television screen as she caught a familiar scene. "Hey." She nudged Kerry, who turned the volume up.

"And this late breaking news bulletin. The FBI announced, just a few moments ago that it had concluded its investigation into the explosion at District Memorial Hospital. Here's the announcement as it happened."

"Oh. That's the FBI guy Dad spoke to in the back there," Kerry whispered, pointing.

"Hmm." Dar nodded.

An older FBI agent stepped up to the podium and cleared his throat. Behind him, an easel was set up with a diagram of the hospital on it. "Our investigators have searched thoroughly, and what they have determined was this." He picked up a pointer. "The explosion started at this point, in the hospital kitchen. We've determined that the natural gas storage tanks ignited, and sent a firestorm through the pipes up the utility stack here."

"Huh." Dar blinked.

"Then, because these pipes run concurrently with the oxygen pipes, when the gas pipes overheated and blew, the oxygen lines went also. That sent off multiple explosions here." He pointed. "Here, and here." Another tap. "Ending up igniting the gas storage areas right around the operating theatres."

"Wow." Kerry drew in a breath. "So it wasn't a bomb."

"The FBI is satisfied that, pending further investigation into what ignited the gas tank in the kitchen, that it appears to us that no criminal act has taken place here, beside the design flaw that allows the two types of gas pipes to exist in the same space."

"How do you like that?" Dar murmured.

"Yeah." Kerry exhaled. "I'm glad."

"Mmm." Dar studied the screen pensively, unable to disagree.

❖ ⌘ ❖ ⌘ ❖ ⌘ ❖

Buzz.

Dar opened a sleep fogged blue eye and peered at the clock in outrage. "Who in the hell is calling here at three a.m.?"

Buzz.

Slap. "Hello?" Dar growled sleepily.

"Hey there, Dardar."

The other eye opened, then both blinked. "Daddy. It's a damn lucky thing this is you."

Her father chuckled. "Wake yer butt up and c'mon down here to the docks. We just got our new quarters."

Dar closed both eyes. "Wouldn't it be better to see them in daylight?" she inquired hopefully, as Kerry stirred, then crawled up and rested her chin on Dar's breastbone.

"Aw. C'mon now. First time we got something brand spanking new," Andrew rasped. "Get your butt down here."

"Can we come as we are or do we have to get dressed?" Kerry warbled.

There was a momentary pause. "'Sperience tells me I should tell you to put yer clothes on," Andrew finally decided. "'Sides, it's a little chilly down here."

"Okay. We'll be right there." Dar yawned and rubbed her eyes as the line disconnected. "Wait a minute. How could they have *just* gotten that at three a.m.?"

Kerry had rolled over and carefully levered herself out of the waterbed and padded naked across the floor towards the bathroom. "Light."

Dar closed her eyes.

"They had to pick it up in Palm Beach, remember?" Kerry reminded her, as she splashed water over her face. "Probably took their time coming down the coast."

"Mmm. Wonder if they had a waterbed put in," Dar joked faintly.

"They loved ours."

Kerry jerked upright, green eyes popping wide open as she stared at herself in the mirror. Slowly she turned, leaned in the doorway, and glared at the light splashed naked form tangled in the sheets. "What?"

"Well," Dar crossed her ankles, "it was either down here, or up in your room. That single in the guest room's a little too short for Daddy."

Kerry covered her eyes with one hand. "Ohh. Back, back, back." She groaned, trudging towards the dresser. "I tell you what, honey. I'm going to flush that image right out of my cache. Okay?"

"Okay," Dar agreed amiably.

"Don't you dare hit reload."

"Okay." The taller woman rolled up out of bed and stretched, producing a satisfying pop as her shoulders seated themselves. She pulled a shirt and a pair of shorts from her drawer and tugged them on as Kerry settled for one of her longer shirts. "C'mon, Chino, let's go see grandpa's new toy."

They walked down the front stairs and, moments later, Dar was steering the golf cart down the completely empty, moonlit road towards the marina. "Pretty night," she commented.

"Mmm." Kerry ducked to one side and peered up at the cloudless sky, speckled with stars faded from the city lights nearby. "Yeah, it is." The tires crunched on the gravel, sounding loud in the darkness, and she pulled her head back in and settled in her padded seat. Chino sat in the back and had her head resting on the brace between them, sniffing with interest.

They rounded the turn and proceeded into the marina, the sound of the waves merged with the soft clinking of ships' riggings. "Good grief," Kerry murmured. "That thing is huge."

"Yeah. Don't all guys love to hear that?" Dar muttered back, as she muffled a chuckle. "Well, it is their house now, so..."

The Bertram was tucked up in a guest slip on the edge of the Marina, shiny fiberglass glistening in the moonlight. All of sixty feet long, it featured a flying bridge like Dar's and a long foredeck she gauged would be excellent for her mother to set up an easel on. "Nice."

She parked the cart and they got out, then they walked up to the back of the vessel as her parents came out to meet them. "Morning." Dar lifted a hand towards them.

"Hello, you two." Cecilia gave her husband an exasperated look. "I tried to make him wait. Honestly."

Kerry chuckled as she hopped on board. "That's okay. Wow. This is nice." She peeked up at the bridge console, which glowed with green LED's.

"Mmm. Yeah, it is," Ceci agreed cheerfully. "Happy birthday, by the way." She hesitantly offered Kerry a hug, which was accepted with enthusiasm. "Were you surprised at your party?"

"Was she." Dar laughed, as Kerry received another hug from her father. "She was shocked speechless."

"Now that, ah would have paid to see," Andrew drawled. "Ah, ah. None of that, young lady, or I'll be grabbing that tongue and keeping it."

"That cake was gorgeous. Thank you so much." Kerry turned sea green eyes on Ceci. "I was very, very surprised at everything. Did you know what Dar pulled on me?"

"About your promotion? Yes, we knew," the silver blond woman answered. "I wish we could have been there, but Andy was very anxious to take possession of this little boat."

The ex-sailor in question was bouncing on the balls of his feet. "Y'all want a nickel tour?" he asked, hopefully. "And ah got to tell you, I have spent a good bit more on the gov'ment's behalf than what this here boat costs, hell, my naval training cost more. But sitting down in that man's office and writing him out a check for this thing was about the weirdest thing I have ever done."

"He was impressed," Ceci commented, "and May would have definitely approved." She smiled. "C'mon. I put some coffee up to inaugurate the machine."

They moved into the cabin, which was laid out not too differently from Dar's. There was a living room area in front, with a comfortable looking couch and a table with clamp downs and a set of built-in bookshelves. Across from that was an area with cabinets and a drafting table, custom made for her mother, Dar suspected.

Behind the living area was a compact galley, with a built in microwave and stove, and a fair sized refrigerator, and next to it a cozy table and wraparound booth to eat in.

Stairs descended behind that to the bedroom, with its built in drawers and recessed lighting, its bed larger than the one in their boat, and longer by several inches. Next to it was the head, which had a nice sized shower in it. There were storage areas built into all the bulkheads, and the living space was all lined in warm, rich honey toned wood with recessed brass hardware. "This is so nice." Kerry breathed. The colors were blue and maroon, with the odd exception of the toilet seat, which was an interesting shade of pink.

Dar decided not to ask about that. "Definitely comfortable." She clapped her father on the back. "Better than an eighteen inch wide bunk, huh?"

"Lord." Andrew laughed. "I hate to see some of my buddy's faces when they see this thing. They're gonna keel right over." But he looked very pleased with his new home. "I do like this, though. I really do."

Ceci leaned against him and exhaled. "Me too." She gave his arm a squeeze, then moved over to the galley and poured cups of steaming, nutty smelling coffee. "Oh, I almost forgot." She set the tray on the table, and nudged them towards it. "I have something for the two of you. Just a little picture I finished a few days ago."

"Heh." Andrew doctored his coffee and sucked down a mouthful from the navy blue mug. Dar and Kerry joined him, while Dar peered past his shoulder curiously as her mother pulled something out of a veneered closet nearby.

"Kerry got a birthday card from her folks," she informed her parents.

"Yeah?" Andrew was surprised. "Hell, I guess he does have a conscience after all that."

"I'm glad to hear it," Ceci said quietly, as she brought forward a canvas, then turned it for them to see and propped it up against the table. "I thought your living room could use a little color."

Dar and Kerry gazed at the painting, then at each other, then back at the painting. "Wow," Kerry murmured. "It's gorgeous."

Dar blinked. "It's..." She leaned closer. "How did you do that?"

"I'm an artist," Ceci remarked dryly. "It's what I do." But she seemed pleased with the reaction.

The painting was a jungle scene, deep greens and blues of the grass surrounding its two subjects, a large black panther, reclining regally on the mossy ground, its paws outstretched. Between them sat a russet and gold fox, peering coyly out at the watchers, its fluffy tail neatly tucked around its small feet. A cheerful red apple rested nearby.

It was the eyes that got them. Ceci had somehow captured, in the panther's clear blue gaze, her daughter's wild spirit, and the fox's pale green eyes reflected Kerry's sweet intelligence.

A chord rang, deep and somewhat wistful in Dar's memory as she studied the images, a whisper of a past she didn't remember, the ghost of a gentle clasp on her shoulder that almost made her turn around.

"It's amazing." Kerry's laugh bubbled up. "Thank you so much."

Dar smiled. "Thanks, Mom."

"You're welcome," Ceci remarked briskly. "Now, since I have the three of you together and where is that dog?"

Chino, curled up near the door where Dar had ordered her to stay, looked up. "Gruff."

"Excellent. I need a picture of you all." Ceci shooed them all together. "C'mon now. It'll take a second."

"Dressed like this?" Dar questioned, plucking her shirt. "For what?'

"Shh." Her mother waited for Chino to get into the picture, then snapped it. "You think only you computer people can manipulate images? I can dress you however I want once I paint the picture."

"Picture?"

"Paint?" Kerry chimed in. "You're doing one of us?"

"Gruff!"

Andrew chuckled. "You wanna go for a ride? I had them tuck a few extra ponies in this here thing and we got enough chow on board for a sunrise gig."

Oh boy. Work would be hell after that. "Sure." Dar grinned. "Let her rip, Dad."

"Dar."

"Uh."

"Heh."

Tropical High
by Melissa Good

Continuing from where *Eye of the Storm* leaves off, this 4th story in the Tropical Storm series has Dar Roberts and Kerry Stuart's lives seeming to get more complex rather than moving toward the simpler lifestyle they both dream of. Dar gets involved in an investigation of the military and Kerry takes on new challenges at work. Old memories are ignited and Dar questions some of her youthful choices as her past causes present problems for Kerry. Of course, Dar and Kerry make it through the latest set of challenges with their usual good sense and indomitable strength.

Other titles to look for in the
coming months from
Yellow Rose Books

Prairie Fire
By LJ Maas

Lost Paradise: Book Two - Daredevil Hearts
By Francine Quesnel

Many Roads To Travel
By Karen King and Nann Dunne

Second Chances
By Lynne Norris

Innocent Hearts
By Radclyffe

Strength of the Heart
By Carrie Carr

Northern Peace and Perils
By Francine Quesnel

Faith
By Angela Chapman

Printed in the United States
4375

WORLD MAP

Greenland

United States

Canada

United States

Northern Mariana Islands

United States

The Bahamas

Mexico

Cuba
Jamaica

A

Belize
Guatemala
Honduras
El Salvador
Nicaragua
Costa Rica
Panama

Venezuela

Guyana
Suriname
French Guiana

Marshall Islands

Federated States of Micronesia

Nauru

Solomon Islands

Tuvalu
Vanuatu
Fiji

Kiribati

Samoa

Tonga

Colombia

Ecuador

Peru

Brazil

Bolivia

Paraguay

New Zealand

Chile

Argentina

Uruguay

A

Cuba

Haiti   Dominican Republic

Puerto Rico

Saint Kitts and Nevis

Antigua and Barbuda

Guadeloupe

Dominica

Martinique

Saint Lucia

Barbados

Saint Vincent and the Grenadines

Grenada

Trinidad and Tobago

Colombia

Venezuela